Table of Contents

One

It is chastening to consider how easily fate can change our lives and by what apparently trivial means — a careless remark, a chance meeting, an apple plucked from the tree, a mould grown in a dish, an idea so green as to be little more than a bud.

In the case of Jack Daventry, who called himself the Captain, it was an expression of private tenderness seen on the face of a woman he neither knew' nor cared for; in Miss Ariadne Bradbury's case it was a moment of idle gossip heard while she was watching the start of a funeral procession; for Suki Brown it was a jugful of hot water.

The summer of 1755 had been exceptionally warm and on that particular July morning the air in Bath was as soft as a peach. The escarpment of Beechen Height was lush with foliage, the river Avon peacefully blue under a clear sky, and sunlight was reflected so strongly from the new honey-coloured facade of South Parade and the new clean paving stones before it that it looked overbright and theatrical, like a stage set rising dramatically above the untamed, plebeian grasses of the Ham.

Behind the facade, in the apartments Sir George Bradbury had hired for the season, daily life continued with predictable hubbub, for his was a family that required incessant drama to establish its position and importance. The chair ordered to bear Sir George to the baths had arrived late, and been roared at. So breakfast had been delayed and the two young misses had taken such exception to the postponement of their meal that Cook had been forced to prepare a platter of coddled eggs to placate them; and Lady Bradbury had been prostrated with the vapours from the moment she was dressed, because that was the best way she knew to distance herself from the tantrums of her impossible offspring.

But Suki Brown was immune to all of it. As a wet nurse, her duties were simply to feed the Bradbury infant and keep him clean and comfortable. At that moment she was sitting in the chimney corner suckling her own infant, Jack, which was strictly against the rules, her feet in the warmth of the grate and her neck in the warmth of the sunlight streaming through the kitchen window, languorous with sensuous pleasure and the pride of ownership.

The baby was nearly three months old but Suki was still amazed by how perfect he was — with those tiny fingers, that soft skin, the extraordinary darkness of those limpid eyes — still stunned by the overpowering love he'd roused in her from the first moment she saw him.

'If you'd have told me, afore he come, how much I'd love him,' she said to Cook, 'I'd never have believed you.'

'You know now, though, don't you gel?' Cook said. 'You fed the other poor little mite, have you?'

'Still asleep,' Suki said. 'He don' make demands. Not like you, eh, my 'andsome?' Jack had lost hold of her nipple and was wobbling his head around furiously, trying to find it again. There 'tis! There 'tis! Don' go gettin' out of humour!'

At that moment, the master's bell clanged against the wall, ringing so violently that young Bamaby, who was the under-valet and general factotum and much in awe of the man, ran out of the laundry room as if he'd been shot.

'Oh lor'!' he said. 'Now I'm for it. He wants his hot water.' 'Aren't you ready, you great lummock?' Cook asked.

'No I ain't,' Bamaby said, looking round him wildly. There was hot water aplenty bubbling on the stove, but the towel wasn't warmed, the shaving soap hadn't been prepared and he'd been in the laundry room frantically sharpening the master's cut-throat

razor when the bell rang. Nobody offered to help him. Cook and the kitchen maids were too hard at work preparing the dinner which had to be ready for three o'clock that afternoon, Mr Jessup, the butler, was out on an errand, Hepzie, the lady's maid, was with the young misses, and Mrs Sparepenny, the housekeeper, had been upstairs with the mistress for nearly an hour. Nobody, that is, except for Suki, the kind-heart.

'I could take it,' she'd offered. 'I'll get this baby settled an' then I'll go up for you. T'other's still sound asleep. He'll wait another minute an' no harm done. I don't mind.'

'You'm a good gel, Suki,' Cook said. Thank'ee kindly.'

There was no false modesty about Suki Brown. Yes, she thought, so I am. And she smiled as she carried the heavy jug up the servants' stairs and through the open door into the constipated mustiness of the master bedroom.

Sir George Bradbury was standing by the window gazing down at the neat new paving stones below him, and absent-mindedly gouging his teeth with an ivory toothpick. He's a hideous old thing and no mistake, Suki thought, as she set the jug down on the washstand. Such a belly on him under that damask dressing gown, such flabby purple jowls, such nasty little piggy eyes. And he smell like a chamber pot, so he do.

'Here's the hot water for 'ee, sir,' she said. 'Barnaby'll be up directly.'

'Air the bed... um... um...' he said vaguely, still busy with the toothpick.

The bed linen was heavy and evil-smelling, and there was a fat brown flea squatting on the top pillow. It jumped and was gone the minute she looked at it. All that work with the turpentine and camphor when we got here, she thought, and they'm back already. It had been a bad summer for bugs and fleas. As she smoothed out the creases in the bottom sheet, her skin began to prickle. At first she thought it was the flea walking along her arm, but then she realized that it was the knowledge that she was being watched. She glanced up, straight into the full force of her master's lecherous and calculating stare.

'A fine wench,' he said, as much to himself as to her. 'New are yer?'

'No sir,' she said politely, and she hurried to strip the bed and get away from him as quickly as she could. Unfortunately her speed made her breasts swing provocatively as she leaned forward to plump up the pillows, and the sight of that soft, pliant flesh was enough to lift Sir George from the costive stupor that usually weighed him down after a too hearty breakfast. Not a big lift, to be sure, nor a particularly strong one, but sufficient to lead to pleasure, given the rub. And she was a fine wench, there was no doubt about that. A pretty bosom, clear skin, good teeth, big dark eyes. There'd be time for a little dalliance before the shaving tray arrived.

'Lie back on the bed, me dear,' he said mildly, unbuttoning his gown.

'I got to be in the kitchen directly, sir,' Suld said, hoping to discourage him. 'They'm awaiting me. Barnaby'll be here presently.'

He was surprised at such effrontery from a servant, but continued in his usual mild manner. 'Oblige me,' he said, smiling his amorous intentions at her. But she set the last pillow to rights and made to walk out of the room. What is the matter with the wench? he thought, blocking her way. Is she half-witted? 'Adjust your petticoat,' he suggested and he edged her towards the bed with his belly and put down one podgy hand to lift her skirt.

There was no hope of avoiding his intentions now. 'No!' Suki said firmly, twisting her body away from that hand. 'No I won't!' She would have to push past him and make a bolt for the servants' door. But his knee was already solidly in her way and now he had his hands on her shoulders and was pressing her down towards the mattress.

A wench with spirit, Sir George thought. Well, if she wants a struggle, I'm just the one to give it to her. Despite his flabby appearance, he was a powerful man and knew how to use his weight to advantage. Her opposition excited him. This was going to be really pleasurable after all.

'I aren't willin', sir,' Suki said, trying to wrench her shoulders out of his grasp. ''Tain't right.'

'Want a fight, do you, me dear?' the sweaty face said happily, as it loomed towards her. She swung her head frantically away from the bad cabbage of his breath and her cheek was caught in a kiss at once brutal and wet.

'Aren't willin',' she said again, clawing his hands away from her shoulders. She was panting with anger that he should press on with his assault when she was doing everything she could to get him to stop. But even her anger was against her. It brought a flush to her cheeks, and the sight of heated flesh made him more lustful and determined than ever.

He was blotting out the world with the pressure of his body. The embroidery on his nightgown was right in front of her eyes, and somewhere below it, he was pinching her breasts and forcing her legs apart with that gross knee. She was frantic with revulsion and terror and anger. Where was the bedpost? If only she could hold on to something solid, she might be able to kick him away. But her sightless hands were clutching at air.

He raised his body away from her for just a second to hoist up his nightgown, and in that eye-blink of time she caught sight of a weapon. It was the great brass enema syringe that always stood ready for use on the bedside table. She seized it at once and brought it down on his skull with a crack like an axe splitting wood.

For a second there was an absolute silence, then Sir George sank to his knees beside the bed, groaning and clutching his head, and Suki ran like a rabbit, hurtling down the back stairs so precipitately that she missed more stairs than she trod and it was a wonder she didn't fall headlong.

Barnaby, ascending carefully with a warm towel over his shoulder and a tray full of shaving tackle carried in both hands, got an elbow in the ribs as he was hurled against the wall, but before he could think of a suitable rebuke or even catch his breath, Suki had already tumbled into the kitchen and, in any case, the master was making such a dreadful noise above his head that he knew he must attend to him at once. Agog for sensation, he ran to see what had happened.

The master bedroom was empty, but it was easy enough to see where the master had gone. The enema syringe lay on its side on the carpet beside a glossy little puddle of blood, and a trail of red gouts led away from it across the room and out of the door.

Sir George was stamping up and down on the landing, dabbing at his temple with a bloody handkerchief, and roaring down the well of the stairs, 'Hermione! Hermione! 'Od's bowels, are they all gone deaf? Hermione, have I to bleed to death up here with no one to attend me?' His turban was over one ear, and below the stained kerchief, his face was as pale as putty.

Behind him, the door to Lady Bradbury's bedroom opened just enough to reveal the housekeeper's disapproving face.

'What's amiss?' she asked Barnaby.

But for the second time that morning, Barnaby didn't have time to reply. There was a commotion down at her feet, as the mistress' horrid little lapdog, Benjy, scrabbled out of the room. He was more than half blind and grossly overweight, but his sense of smell was still acute and there was enough of the hunter left somewhere inside his bloated carcase for the scent of fresh blood to excite him. Before either of them could stop him, he had slavered his way across the polished floor and sunk his teeth into his master's stamping calf.

Then all hell was let loose, as the dog growled, and Barnaby shouted, and two of the kitchen maids, who'd come up to see what was happening, peered through the servants' door squealing with excitement, and Sir George bellowed and swore and tried to kick the cur from his leg.

But Benjy remembered the training of his youth and hung on grimly to complete his kill.

'Someone pinch his nose!' Bamaby instructed, but the maids shrank back behind the door as Sir George continued to kick and curse with the dog still firmly embedded. Flecks of blood and foam spattered the banisters and the noise was deafening. Reluctantly, Barnaby fell into the melee and covered the dog's nostrils

with a daring hand — his left, of course, so as to leave his working hand free from certain injury. Rather to everyone's surprise, Benjy let go and fell heavily to the floor, where he was kicked viciously into the wall for his presumption.

''Od's bones!' the master yelled. 'Is the whole world gone stark, staring, raving mad?' And he kicked the squealing animal down half a flight of stairs and lost his blood-soaked bandage in the process.

At that the maids bolted back to the kitchen before they were kicked too, and Barnaby and Mrs Sparepenny took action quickly before anything else could happen. Between them, they supported their reeling employer into his wife's boudoir, and set about bandaging his head properly, with the towel, dodging his wrath and enduring his complaints as best as they could.

Lady Bradbury' was not at all pleased to have her vapours so rudely and totally interrupted, and just at the very moment when she was enjoying them.

She had taken great pains to arrange herself artistically across the sofa, and was gratified by the fashionable image that was now reflecting back at her from her long mirror. Her new silk day-gown matched the striped sofa to perfection, and her lace cap was quite excellent. It set everything off so well and was still safe and comfortable even when one was obliged to swoon. Her temples had been rubbed with lavender water and a warm compress applied to both her ankles, so that the day had really begun to feel quite agreeable. And now her great oaf of a husband was blundering about her room, bleeding and swearing and reducing her costly elegance to an undignified shambles.

'Oblige me, my dear,' she said mildly, maintaining her composure despite the commotion. Pray endeavour not to bleed upon the chair.'

'''Od's teeth!' he roared back at her. 'I wall bleed where I please, madam. I paid good money for this apartment, I would have you know. I will bleed where I please.'

'To be sure, my love,' she agreed, staying calm deliberately, because she knew how much it annoyed him. 'But 'twill anger you tomorrow, when the stains are dried and the landlord is pressing. I make this observation for your own good, my love.'

''Od's teeth!' he said again. 'That damned dog of yours has torn me to shreds. I shall take the rabies I shouldn't wonder. See my pate, madam. I am cut to the brains! To the very brains! 'Od's bowels, I cannot think what the world is coming to, I really cannot! Have the goodness to assist me, madam.'

Lady Bradbury rose elegantly from her prostration, wearing the face of a martyr. 'I'm sure I don't know what I ever did to deserve such torment,' she complained mildly and to nobody in particular, 'but there it is. I can see I am not to be allowed to be unwell this morning or I shall never hear the last of it. Tell Jessup we need a surgeon,' she said to Mrs Sparepenny. 'Mr McKinnon, if he is not at the baths, otherwise Wrencher. Send up hot water and clean linen and a good handful of lint. And you,' turning to Barnaby, 'see what is become of my poor dear Benjy. I would not have the poor creature miscarry for anything in the world.'

Her servants went about their errands and Sir George discovered to his discomfiture that he was suddenly alone with a wife who was very far from mild.

'And what were you doing, pray,' she asked acidly, looking down her long sharp nose at his wounds, 'to receive such a blow?'

'Your damned dog,' he tried, shifting uncomfortably in his chair. 'Seized me by the leg. Look 'ee here. Wants destroying, pernicious, snappy creature.'

But Lady Bradbury wouldn't be deflected. 'Oh no, my love,' she said, sweet as vinegar, and smiling her sour smile directly down upon him. 'I think not. You were roaring a full five minutes before my Benjy ever came near you, and I'm certain sure he did not bite your head. A nip to the leg is understandable, but the head I do not believe.'

Sir George decided to brazen it out. 'It's come to something,' he said, 'when a man can't give a pretty girl a kiss without being cut to the quick.'

'Fought back eh?'

'Went lunatic, damme.'

'Which one was it?' his wife said. 'Just tell me her name, my love, and she shall be dismissed instantly.'

'How should I know which one it was?' her husband said tetchily. 'Little thing with dark eyes. Brought up the water, I believe. How was I to know she was lunatic? You should be more careful whom you hire.'

'Tis of no consequence,' Lady Bradbury said, and her smile was terrible. 'Now that I know the cause of the trouble, you may be sure I shall deal with it immediately.'

The cause of the trouble was sitting beside the kitchen range with most of the other servants gathered round her and Bessie, the youngest scullery maid, crouched at her feet, chafing her hands. It seemed foolish when she'd been so strong and determined during the attack that she should be trembling now that it was all over. But she'd given a good account of herself above stairs and now she was giving an equally good account below them. 'I hit him straight round the lugs,' she told her admiring audience. 'You should of seen his face!'

'He's bleedin' prodigious,' one of the kitchen maids confirmed as she cracked six eggs into a bowl. 'Great gobbets a' blood everywhere.'

'Which you shouldn't have been there to see,' Cook reproved.

'Serve him right,' the second maid said, beating the eggs with more than necessary vigour. 'That's what I say. He's a lecherous old varmint! I'm glad you done it.'

Hepzie, the lady's maid, was filling a ewer with hot water ready for the young misses. She paused to wipe the sweat from her eyes. 'There'll be trouble,' she warned. 'You'd have done better to have give in to him. It wouldn't have took long an' you could have been made for life. Now you'll be dismissed, sure as God made little apples. Once the missus finds out, you'll be out that door afore you can say knife. I seen it all afore, many and many's the time.' She had never really approved of Sula's rapid rise to favour, even though the girl was pleasant enough and good company in the kitchen. She had a sneaking feeling that her baby was a bastard, for all the talk of an absent husband, and to be wet nurse to a family as rich as Sir George's when you were little better than a whore was too much like undeserved good fortune. 'You should have took what was. coming to you an' made the best of it.'

'Why should I?' Suki asked.

'Because that's the way the world goes.'

The idea that had stirred in Suld's mind under the revulsion of her master's attack, stirred again, took hold and began to expand. 'Well then, it shouldn't. He don't own me.'

'Course he does,' Bessie said, reasonably. 'He's the master.'

'Not body an' soul,' Suld argued. 'He hires my titties for his babba, that's all. The rest of my body's mine. An' if I don't give permission, no one got no right to use it.'

'Such nonsense!' Hepzie said. 'What of that husband a yours? He got the right to it, for a start. 'Tis his by law.'

Suki coloured. That was a different matter altogether. He could have her whenever he wanted because she loved him too much to deny him anything. 'The law don't come into it,' she said. 'Not between man an' wife.'

'You're such a goose, Suki Brown,' Hepzie mocked. 'Course it comes into it. Marriage is a matter of law from start to finish.'

'Then it shouldn't be,' Suki said stoutly. 'That's my opinion of it. If the law can step in atween man and wife then the law's wrong.' But she was out of her depth in this conversation so she swung the subject back to Sir George. 'As to the master, I'm as good as him any day of the week. 'Tis only money makes him the master and me the maid. How if 'twere lost. What then?'

'I can tell you what now, which is more to the point,' Hepzie said, tartly. 'They'll send you a-packing when they know what you've done. You'll be laughing the other side of your face then, you mark my words.'

'No they won't,' Suld said, defiantly. 'Not when I got that babby of their'n to feed. Anyways, no man takes me when I aren't wallin', and that's all there is to that.'

There was a swish of skirts, a snort of disapproval and the housekeeper was in the room.

'What's this?' she said sharply. 'Is the work all done, is that it, that you think you may sit by the fire and gossip? I wonder at you, Cook!

13

Hepzibah, that water is waited for in milady's room. The surgeon will be here presently. Look lively if you please.'

There was a rush to show her how diligent they could be and Hepzie flounced out of the room with the ewer.

'You fed that other babby yet, gel?' Cook whispered.

In the trials of the moment, Suki had forgotten all about him. 'No, I'aven't,' she whispered.

'Best see to 'un then or she'll have something to say about *that* an' all. I'll make up a dish of groats an' bring it to 'ee presently.'

Poor little thing, Suki thought, smitten with sympathy for him. He must be hungry by this time. He haven't been fed since early morning. And she went off at once to attend to him.

The nursery was just along the corridor, set apart from the kitchen and the servants' stairs by the butler's parlour, the wine store and the pantry. When both babies were asleep — as they were at the moment — it was very quiet. William Bradbury lay in his fine cradle under his embroidered quilt, firmly swaddled and motionless, his eyes tightly shut. Her own pretty Jack was in his cushioned box making sucking noises as he turned his head from side to side.

'No more for you, my lad,' she said to him happily. 'You've had more than enough.' And she pulled back the quilt to wake her other infant.

The baby was as white as wax and cold to the touch. 'Come along my 'andsome,' she said to him, cheerfully, as she lifted him from the cradle into the warmth of her arms. 'We can't have you cold. Not on a fine warm morning like this. Open your little eyes.' But even as she spoke she knew that he would never open his eyes again. He was limp in her arms, his pale head lolling.

'Oh my dear life!' she said. 'You aren't dead! You can't be dead.'

But he was. There was no doubt about it. The shock of it made her tremble so violently that she had to sit down on her little nursing chair for fear of falling. She couldn't understand it. How could he possibly be dead? He'd been sleeping peacefully not ten minutes ago, when she put Jack in his cradle, before... She was overwhelmed with pity for him. Poor little thing, she thought, to die before he even knew he was alive.

For a few seconds she sat in her nursing chair with the dead child on her lap, still trembling and too upset to know what to do. Then her mind began to function with a speed and clarity she'd never experienced before, slotting facts into line, one after the other, so that she saw all the consequences of this death — and all at once.

She would lose her nice comfortable post in the household, and all the good food that was making milk in abundance for young Jack and keeping her so healthy. The Bradburys would be furious and accuse her of neglecting their child and God alone knows what might come of *that*. On her first day with the family, Lady Hermione had impressed upon her that she was to feed her 'noble charge' at regular intervals but she rarely had. He was always asleep and didn't seem to mind whether he was fed or not, whereas Jack woke at a touch and roared far too loudly to be asked to wait a minute. Now they would claim she'd been disobedient and make trouble out of it. Especially after whacking the master.

Even if they didn't, she'd lost her job. She would have to go home and five with her family again, which would mean raising her lovely infant in all the dirt and squalor she thought she'd left behind. Worse, she would have to appear before the justice and be shamed as an unmarried mother, to stand there in open court and be bullied to 'name the father'. The humiliation of it. And all so that the parish could force him to marry her or to pay for the upkeep of the child, neither of which were possible, as he'd explained to her right at the start. The thought of being publicly shamed was more than she could bear. It would be terrible even if she had the knowledge and the will to tell them what they wanted. But she didn't. She didn't know her lover's surname or where he lived or even where he was at that moment. In fact, she hadn't seen him since before their baby'd been born. He was Captain Jack, that was all. He rode in and out of Bath as he pleased, never gave her any other name, as free and easy as the air he breathed. How could she 'name the father in circumstances like that?

There was nothing for it. She had got to stay where she was. It was imperative. But how? Struggling with her thoughts, she looked down at the poor little dead baby. His face was oddly peaceful, which was curious, because until then he'd always seemed to be scowling, even in his sleep. Now he looked innocent and angelic — like her Jack. It was the first time she'd seen any similarity between them, although they were both of an age with round faces and snub noses and the same dusting of fine pale hair.

And suddenly, she knew what to do. It was simple and obvious. She would swap babies.

She turned the dead baby over on to his stomach, took off his cap and his embroidered coat and unbuttoned his long gown. Then she pulled one of Jack's patched gowns from the clothes horse, where it was hanging to air, dressed him in it quickly and carried him across to Jack's box, holding him against her shoulder so as to avoid the sight of his little dead face.

Jack was sound asleep, his long eyelashes casting blue shadows on his cheeks. She set the dead child alongside him and took him out of the box very, very gently so as not to wake him. By now she was alarmed by the sinfulness of what she was doing and her heart was beating painfully. But it had to be done. She was driven by desperation, feeling she had no other choice, her senses still in uproar from Sir George's attack and her own crazy ideas, her mind spinning with panic. She couldn't let them dismiss her. Not now. Not after what had happened in that bedroom. Not when she'd made a stand.

It took longer to dress her Jack in the Bradbury clothes because her fingers were clumsy with panic and she had to work delicately so as not to wake him. But at last it was done and he was settled in the cradle and tucked under the quilt, still sleeping.

She found she was panting and afraid and very near tears. She picked up Jack's discarded gown and put it in the dirty clothes basket, working automatically. And at that moment, Cook pushed the door open with her foot and came in with the promised dish of groats.

'Land sakes!' she said, alarmed by Suki's stricken face. 'What's the matter with 'ee, child? You aren't still a-grieving over that old varmint, surely to goodness?'

It was as if she'd given Suki leave to cry. The tears spilled from her eyes in such a flood she couldn't speak. Choking and sobbing, she waved her hand weakly at the dead baby and fell back against the table for support. Now her heart was beating in her throat for she was sure she was going to be found out. But no. Cook accepted the dead child as Jack without a second look.

'Now you sit right down, you poor dear gel!' she said. 'What a terrible thing to happen! An' after all that business with the master too. 'Tis cruel, so 'tis. But you must be brave about it my dear, same as all of us.

There aren't a woman in this town what en't lost a babby some time or other. Tis the common lot of womankind, so 'tis. You'm young yet. Grief will pass, believe me. There'll be others. Have a good weep, but don't'ee cry too much my dear, or you'll spoil your milk. Have you fed the other one?'

Suki nodded.

'You'm a good gel, Suki Brown,' Cook said. 'Now you sit there and see if you can't eat those groats. You got to keep up your strength no matter what. I'll go an' find Mr Jessup. He'll know what's to be done.' She patted Suki's shoulder and turned to leave.

Mr Jessup was already on his way down the corridor. He'd completed his errand and was returning to his parlour when he was alerted by the sound of weeping. As the Bradburys' butler, it was his job to know everything that was going on in the household and crying of that sort was too extreme to be ignored. He took command as soon as he entered the room, examined both babies without recognizing either, told Suki to stay where she was and Cook to get on with preparing the dinner. Then he went off to inform the mistress.

'He'll see to everything for 'ee,' Cook comforted before she left. 'Don' 'ee fret.'

Suld sat where she was, dried her flowing eyes and began to eat the groats, for she was hungry despite fear and panic and the enormity of her deception. Cook was right. Whatever she might be feeling, there was a baby to feed and she had to keep her strength up.

Things had happened so quickly that morning that, shameful though they were, there was a sort of graceless inevitability about them that stunned her sense of guilt. Reason told her that she'd done a terrible thing and that she would be punished for it sooner or later, either on earth when the missus found out or in heaven when she had to give an account of herself to her Maker. But to her senses it felt more like a victory than a sin — secret and ignominious but a victory nevertheless. A step away from squalor, poverty, lack of food. A step to protect her darling. A vindication after the humiliation of being expected to serve the master's lust. In any case, now that Mr Jessup had taken over, it was beyond her control. I've burnt my boats, she thought. The deed is done and there's no going back on it now.

Two

'Oh dear!' Lady Bradbury said, drawing her eyebrows together in the slight scowl of annoyance that was all she would allow herself in front of the servants. That is most inconvenient. You are sure she was the one, Mrs Sparepenny?'

'Quite sure, milady,' the housekeeper said with conviction. 'She makes no secret of it.'

'You were well to tell me,' Lady Bradbury' approved. But she was thinking what an unconscionable nuisance it was. Now she would be put to all the bother of finding another wet nurse, and just when the baby was coming along so well. There were times when the fates seemed to conspire against her. For this to happen today of all days, when three of her most important friends were due for cards at two o'clock and the renowned Lady Fosdyke and her husband were coming to dine, was annoying in the extreme. She'd taken such pains over the menu, insisting on a salamagundi and pigeon pie and mutton with lemon pickle and a cornucopia of comfits. And now this. It was too bad.

However she saw no reason why she should change her plans simply because her husband had allowed his lust to get the better of him. She would go to the Pump Room as she intended, while he was having his wound dressed and his bowels relieved, and then she would make up her mind what was to be done.

But even that limited comfort was denied her, for at that moment Mr Jessup arrived at her door, coughing in that odd, apologetic way of his — krrm krrm krrm — to inform her that Suki's baby was dead.

Hermione's concern was instant and medical. 'Was it a fever, Jessup?'

'No ma'am. Found dead so I believe.'

'An infection then?'

'I would think not, ma'am. There were no signs.'

'Is William well?'

Mr Jessup assured her that he looked very fit indeed, but that didn't satisfy his mother. 'Have the cradle carried up here directly,' she commanded. 'The surgeon shall see him the instant he has attended my husband.'

Suki was still eating her groats when Barnaby and one of the grooms strode into the nursery. She was horribly alarmed when they picked up the cradle, baby and all, and carried it through the door.

'Where you goin' with my babba?' she cried, springing to her feet to defend him. 'Put him down this instant.'

'He's to be took upstairs,' Barnaby explained. 'To the boudoir. Missus' orders.'

The anguish of being parted from her darling so abruptly and unexpectedly was so extreme that Suki felt as if her guts were being squashed in a vice. 'You can't take him away from me,' she cried, her face distraught. 'How shall I know when he needs feedin'?'

'Don' ask me,' Barnaby said. 'He's to be parted from the dead'un, that's all we been told.' And with that they were through the door and jogging the cradle along the corridor.

This was a consequence Suki hadn't foreseen. Surely she don't mean to take him away from me altogether, she grieved, trotting along behind them. She couldn't intend that. Not when I'm feedin' him. 'Twould be too cruel. But Lady Bradbury wasn't in the boudoir and couldn't be asked what she intended. There was only Mr Jessup, standing by the window, dour in his black coat and breeches, thin mouth downturned, black eyes stern, sharp nose pointing straight at her.

'Go back to the kitchen, Suki Brown,' he said. 'You'll be called for when your sendees are required. The surgeon will be here presently to examine the other child. That will be all.'

So Suki had to trail bleakly down the senants' stairs again and wait in the kitchen, feeling more anxious than she'd ever felt in her life. It was a long wait, even though Bessie kept them all amused with a running commentary on everything that was happening above stairs.

'Here's Mr Wrencher come,' she said, peering out of the area window. 'I can tell by his boots. That won't please the master. The missus is in the hall. Hear her? And that dratted dog a-yappin' on the stairs. Who's he going to bite next? Now here's the master on the landing. You can tell that tread anywhere. Oh, we shall 'ave screamin' presently.'

Voices were raised. The master roared and swore. Jessup was rung for and returned to the kitchen with demands for more hot water — and more — and more.

'What's he doin' with it all?' Cook wanted to know. 'Throwin' it on the floor? That'll improve the carpet. I hope he won't want us up there cleanin'. We got enough to do with all this food to prepare without mopping up spilt water.'

She was none too pleased when the surgeon put his head round the kitchen door and said he was to examine the baby.

'Not in my kitchen you aren't,' she told him. 'And you'd best look sharp about it. We got work to do.'

As a mere sawbones, Mr Wrencher knew his place in any domestic hierarchy and deferred to her at once. He followed Suki meekly along the corridor to the nursery and, when she'd stripped the baby naked, examined the chill little body front and back without a word. When he was gone Suki was no wiser than she'd been when he arrived. And nobody had told her how her own baby was, nor called her up to the boudoir to feed him.

'What'll happen, do you think?' she asked Cook.

'You'll be dismissed,' Hepzie said. 'I told you so.'

'Cut up the lettuce,' Cook suggested. 'An' don't cross bridges till you come to 'em.'

So Suki chopped the lettuces to shreds and went on worrying. Upstairs in the boudoir Mr Wrencher had examined the live baby and was making his report to Lady Bradbury.

There is no infection for your child to take, ma'am,' he said. ''Twas a death, no more. A frequent occurrence among such women. The stock is poor, d'ye see.'

'Then she may continue to feed my William?'

'Indubitably. She is a buxom wench and full of health and now will have but one child to think on.'

'Yes,' Lady Bradbury said, 'to be sure.' And dismissed him with a wave of her white hand. 'Send your account to Sir George.'

It was good news but it didn't solve the problem of whether or not the girl should be dismissed. If anything, it made it worse. But she couldn't put her mind to it at the moment — not with this dinner to attend to.

She walked across the room and looked down, almost idly, into the cradle. Like so many women of her class she had avoided too much contact with her infants when they were young and vulnerable. There was nothing to be served in growing fond of a baby only to have it die on you before it reached a twelvemonth. She had handed over all her babies to wet nurses as soon as they were born, checked their progress once or twice a week but otherwise ignored them until they were five years old and less likely to succumb to fatal illness. It was much the best way and saved a deal of unnecessary heartache, as she'd proved when six of her infants died. However a peep at this baby, now he was in the room, would be harmless enough.

The peep became a long appreciative gaze because she was so well pleased by what she saw. A fine fat child, she thought, admiring his rounded cheeks. He puts on weight apace so he does, and he's uncommon handsome. I'd no idea he looked so strong. The girl has done a good job with *him,* whatever else may be said about her. He sleeps peacefully enough so he shall stay here until my guests arrive. I will show him to Arabella and see what she has to advise. Now I had best attend to that foolish husband of mine.

The foolish husband was sitting in his easy chair, washed, shaved, dressed and stitched and declaring himself too exhausted to move. He could feel his brain positively straining to comprehend the things that had happened to him that morning — like that damned dog and the extraordinary behaviour of that crazy servant and all that to-do over a dead baby, when dead babies were two a penny. Just thinking about it gave him a headache, although, he had to admit, that could have been caused by the stinging pain in the skull where that fool Wrencher had stitched him so clumsily and the punching blow to his gut that the enema always delivered. Whatever the cause, it left him feeling as he always did in the face of his own incomprehension, defeated and inadequate and full of undirected ill-humour.

'You are due at the Harrington Rooms, I believe,' Hermione reminded him, as she rustled into the room. 'Your friends will be waiting.'

'Let 'em wait,' he growled. 'I've a mind not to go.'

'And who will make a four at cards if you do not, pray answer me that? They will question your valour methinks.'

The thought of having his courage brought to question was most unpleasant. Whatever else, a man should always be valiant and he knew he was the most valiant of men. He had earned his money the hard way, on the stinking traders that plied between Bristol and the Slave Coast, and the hot, disease-ridden sugar plantation that he had gradually acquired and developed from the forests of Nevis. If he was rich and idle now and renowned for being a man with plenty of 'bottom', it was no more than he deserved. He couldn't help feeling aggrieved that he hadn't been rewarded by a rather fatter portion of happiness and contentment too. Still, the thought of being among his friends cheered him. As a man among men, he would be admired as he should be, and he could deal with all these stupid situations by reshaping them until they were comfortable.

'You are right,' he agreed. 'I should be gone. My wig will cover my injured pate. Is the chair come?'

Within half an hour he was in the centre of a group of admiring cronies, telling the tale and this time entirely to his advantage. 'A fine wench!' he bragged. 'Built for passion, be gad. Such an eye! Such a bosom! Couldn't resist the temptation, and that's the truth of it.' And he looked at his old friend Sir Arnold Willoughby for approval.

'You're a lucky dog, George,' Sir Arnold said with envy.

'In the whole of Bath,' young John Smithers said, 'there en't a single filly he couldn't get astride if he had a mind, eh Arnold?'

'I remember a plump little creature in Harrogate once,' Sir George said, happily feeding his fantasy. 'Every afternoon for nigh on a month. Such passion! We loved like turtle doves, I tell 'ee.'

Lord Fosdyke picked up the cards and changed the subject, far too abruptly to suit Sir George, but at least to a topic he approved of. 'Heard the news about Pitt?' he enquired, and when faces turned towards him, 'Took a house in the new Circus so they say. Number Six.'

'A sick man,' Sir George told them. 'It don't surprise me at all. Worn down by ingratitude, and that's the truth. All these years fighting for the right to deal with the Frenchies and opposed at every turn, damme.' As a Member of Parliament and a major sugar trader, he had supported William Pitt through thick and thin. 'The man is right in what he says. Always has been. When trade is at stake we must defend it or perish.'

Their talk turned most happily to the need to destroy the French fleet and capture the sugar islands of Martinique and Guadeloupe for their own purposes. Then Lord Fosdyke informed them, with salacious leer and 'apropos of the West Indies' that Lady Bradstone was having an affair with her Jamaican coachman. They were instantly caught up in the joy of gossip and a-babble with such wonderfully prurient questions that Sir George forgot about his wounds and the indignity of being refused, and became quite himself again.

Lady Bradbury was having an equally pleasant time with *her* cronies. Her new gown had impressed her friends and turned Lady Fosdyke pea-green with envy. And despite her lack of concentration, she had won a considerable amount on the very first table, and that had annoyed the formidable lady too. In fact, if it hadn't been for the worrying business of that stupid wet nurse, she could have enjoyed her afternoon very much. But knowing that she would have to make a decision sooner or later upset her balance. From time to time, she brooded over the cards and forgot to smile, even to Lady Arabella Willoughby, who was her dearest friend.

'You are vexed, my dear?' Arabella enquired, in her soothing way, inclining her powdered head towards her friend.

Hermione decided to confide. 'I cannot think what I ever did to be so cruelly plagued,' she said, sighing.

'Sir George up to his old tricks, eh?' Lady Fosdyke said, happily. 'Clubs are trumps I do believe.'

'Too much red wine and ginseng,' Hermione said, 'even for the strongest constitution, however much he may try to pretend to the contrary.'

'But what has occurred, my dear?' Lady Fosdyke insisted, her grey eyes avid for scandal.

'He made amorous advances to our wet nurse, this very morning,' Hermione said, quite enjoying the scandalous nature of the tale she was about to tell, 'and got beat about the head for his pains.' She began to chuckle at the memory of it. 'With a brass clyster, of all things. Wrencher had to be called to insert three stitches in his pate.'

The ladies hooted with delight. 'A wench of fire!' Lady Fosdyke said with great approval, as the laughter subsided.

'Sir George would hardly agree with you,' Hermione said. 'He did nothing but roar for her dismissal.'

'The girl is a good nurse, I believe,' Arabella said, her brow puckered with thought, 'and good nurses are not easily come by, as we all know only too well. I do see the difficulty, my dear. Jack and two queens.'

'The worst of it is,' Hermione said, 'that her own baby was found dead this very mom.'

'All to the better,' Lady Fosdyke told her brusquely. 'Now she'll have but the one to feed.'

'They don't feed their *own* babies, surely?' Mrs Smithers asked, in her timid way. 'Ours take precedence. Or am I in error? I thought that was the arrangement.'

'If you can get 'em to stick to it,' Lady Fosdyke told her. 'They're artful baggages, the lot of 'em. Your call.'

'But should this one continue in our employ?' Hermione worried.

'Suppose my dear, that you contrive for us to see the child and the nurse together,' Arabella suggested. 'Perchance we may be able to advise you.'

So Suki was rung for and sent to collect the baby which she did most joyfully and within a minute. By this time she was so nervous she was afraid to look at Lady Bradbury and her heart was pounding so alarmingly she felt sure that all four ladies would notice it. She kept the baby cuddled to her chest as long as she could to hide the state she was in.

But the ladies — out of sympathy for her loss — pretended not to see her and waited patiently until she was ready to hand the child to his mother. Then they passed him from hand to hand and unwound his swaddling so that they could see how fat his legs were.

Lady Willoughby was most impressed with him. 'He is coming along splendidly,' she said to Hermione. 'Why if I hadn't seen him with my own eyes I would have said he was another baby altogether. Such lovely fat limbs. And fine eyes. Just like yours, my dear, and turning brown already. You must be very proud of him.'

Lady Fosdyke prodded him with her forefinger to test his quality — which was the method she employed with all livestock — and pronounced him a fine specimen. Unfortunately, being prodded annoyed him and he roared so loudly that he had to be handed back to Suki to be pacified.

'You must feed him, my dear,' Arabella said. So Suki settled in a chair in the corner of the room where it was shady, unlaced her bodice and let him suck.

'I can see no problem,' Arabella said to her hostess. 'My advice would be to leave well alone and to continue as you are for the next three years or so, until the child is weaned. He plainly thrives, the nurse is healthy. Tis all to your advantage.'

Three years! Suki thought. It was a parlously short time. But about right for a wet nurse, as she knew very well. They mean me to leave him when he's weaned. Well, I won't, and that's all there is to that. I shall think of a way round it. I en't to be parted from my little Jack. Not now. Only I can't call you my little Jack now, can I my 'andsome. You'll have to get used to a new name. And so shall I. But we shan't be parted. Not ever. For I couldn't abide it.

However, for the moment the matter of her dismissal seemed to have been forgotten and the ladies were playing cards again and ignoring her.

'You may take him back to the nursery,' Hermione said, when the baby had been fed to his usual capacity. Time for another hand I believe, Lady Fosdvke, before the gentlemen arrive to interrupt us.'

Suki made a thankful escape, clutching her milky darling to her breast. She had set her feet on a fearful path but her first steps had been taken without mishap. It would all work out. She would *make* it work out.

Hermione waited until Suki was out of earshot. There were other things she wanted to discuss with her friends, and it would not do for a servant to hear them. 'Well now,' she said. 'You have seen the wench, and the child. What should I do about the other matter, d'ye think?'

The ladies were universally of the same opinion. She should contrive to keep the girl out of Sir George's way but she shouldn't dismiss her. 'You would be a fool to entertain the idea,' Lady Fosdyke said trenchantly. 'A good nurse is rare as gold, and that girl is a good nurse. Why I've never seen a baby thrive like that one. Skin and grief he was, my dear, and none of us could deny it, and now look at him. You keep her. You won't get another as good.'

'I suppose you are right,' Hermione said, 'but what if my husband should light on her again? I cannot help feeling that I might be sacrificing the poor girl's honour for the sake of my child.'

'And what better reason?' Lady Fosdyke said, looking down her nose at Hermione's doubt. That is precisely what servants are for.'

So the matter was settled and as Hermione took her husband's arm to lead their guests in to dinner, she dismissed it from her mind. The trial of her dinner party was more than enough to occupy her at that moment. As they entered the dining room, she noted details, taut with anxiety. The cutlery was correctly set, and the fruit in the centre of the table looked well enough, although she could have wished for more roses to set off the redcurrants. Hot water in the urn ready to wash the cutlery' between courses? Yes. Finger bowls? Yes. That old cat Fosdyke was noting everything too. She would. Lady Carstairs was deep in conversation with Sir Arnold. How wearying political affairs were to be sure. It made one's ears ache to listen to such nonsense, but at least it kept one's guests occupied. Sighing, she watched until her two daughters brought up the rear of the procession and took the last two places at the table, then she signalled to Cook to bring up the salamagundi.

The fish was not as fresh as it should have been and the bank of lettuce leaves and cresses was already beginning to wilt. I shall have words to say about that in the morning, she thought. She was saved by Lady Carstairs who said it was delicious and ate a considerable quantity of it, which was most unladylike, but at least silenced criticism. How difficult these parties were. It was so easy to be out of fashion and mocked behind one's back. Her husband seemed to have recovered himself completely and was loud with gossip at the other end of the table. It is all very well for him, she thought. All he has to do is to make conversation. He don't have to withstand the failure, if failure 'tis to be.

Actually he was enjoying himself retelling the story of Lady Bradstone and her coachman to the attentive ears of Lady Carstairs. 'No morals at all, some of these women,' he said unctuously. 'Don't know what the world is coming to, upon my life.'

'Fie on you Sir George!' the lady said, twinkling with delight to be told such a tale. 'It ain't a fit thing for a lady's ears! How can you be so bold?'

The second course was a great deal better than the first, the lemon pickle sharp, the mutton prettily garnished, the little peas shining with butter. Hermione kept a wary eye on her guests and noted with subdued relief that the men were all gobbling with happy gusto and that even Lady Fosdyke was nibbling, tight-lipped, of course, but with a grudging enjoyment. She could hear Sir George still booming away at the other end of the table. Perhaps the occasion would go well after all.

And then, just as she was beginning to think she could relax, the abbey bells started to chime, the brazen sound so loud that it stopped all possibility of conversation at once and reduced Sir George to instant fury. Although he certainly knew it was the height of bad manners to do such a thing, he rose from the table, rushed to the window, and jerked it open, so that the sash cords threaded and the room re-echoed with the rolling sound. 'My love!' she tried to protest, but nobody could hear her.

His head out of the window, Sir George was roaring to somebody in the parade below. 'Who is it this time, eh? Must we have the bells rung for every dammed arrival? I never heard such nonsense. A man can't eat his dinner in peace, damme, without some jumped-up jackanapes having bells rung.'

They couldn't hear the answer, but Sir George caught the drift of it, and it made him angrier than ever, to the delight of his guests, and Hermione's consternation. She tried to send eye signals to the ladies, that they should continue their dinner and ignore the commotion, but only Arabella chose to understand her. Benjy was barking so much he was beginning to foam at the mouth, and Lady Fosdyke was looking insufferably smug. It was too bad! The meal was ruined and she would be mocked to scorn for the rest of their stay. What a disgrace! She would never live it down! She controlled her feeling as a lady of breeding was expected to do, but inwardly she was very near to tears.

Sir George was stamping with rage at the open window, his fists clenched against the sill. 'There he is!' he shouted into the din, and he turned and waved his guests towards the window, his face purple. Soon the entire dinner party was leaning out alongside him, their ears ringing, enjoying the spectacle within and without.

A chair had drawn up immediately below them, and two liveried servants were easing the occupant and his luggage out of the narrow door. 'A jumped-up jackanapes!' Sir Arnold said. 'You were right,

George. Just take a look at that waistcoat, be gad. Hardly a creature of taste!'

The gentleman was certainly most unfashionably dressed, in an antiquated travelling cloak, a very old bob wig and a waistcoat so plain as to be positively servile. The rich faces at the window enjoyed his awkwardness, and priced his attire to their own comfortable self-enhancement. But their faces changed expression when the butt of their mockery gave them a courteous bow and walked in through the front door of their establishment as though it were his own. The chair was trotted away and the two servants followed their master into the house and the bells stopped clanging at last.

''Od's bowels!' Sir George swore into the silence. 'What is the world comin' to? The man is a common tradesman. Are we to have common tradesmen living in the same houses as we do? I never heard the like.'

'I daresay he has taken the top floor, my love,' Hermione said. ''Tis merely a matter of money after all, as you have had occasion to remark so many times.'

They could hear the servants clattering up the back stairs, and calling instructions to one another. 'Easy as she goes! Mind that turn!'

'It has come to something pretty parlous,' Sir George said, 'when a man can't take a simple meal with his friends without being interrupted by tradesmen masquerading as gentry.'

'Well said, George,' Sir Arnold approved. 'Ruined the joint so he has, dammit.' And he gazed happily at his empty plate, and the congealing remains on Sir George's. Hermione decided that it was time for the next course to be served. At least syllabub couldn't get cold, and sometimes it had been known to put her husband into quite a pleasant humour.

But it didn't work any magic that afternoon, for just as Sir George was spooning the first mouthful into his now smiling face, a cacophony of shrill strings and strained voices broke up their conversation yet again. The waits had arrived and were playing on the landing.

'This,' said Sir George with an air of finality, 'is not to be endured.' And he got up at once and stomped out of the room to put paid to the annoyance, with his enraptured guests following the bad tempered flip-flap of his coat tails and Benjy barking and growling dangerously close to his feet.

The waits had very bad breath and very shabby clothes, but they put up a spirited defence of their trade, and kicked Benjy away from their heels and swore they wouldn't be bullied by any man, not even the Duke of Cumberland, and that was saying something! At this point the new arrival stuck his ancient wig over the bannisters and called encouragement. 'Bravely said, lads! I'll pay 'ee well, so help me!'

'Fetch my cane!' Sir George roared. 'If reason won't prevail, dammit, we'll try what a beating will do.' He'd quite forgotten his injuries. What were a few stitches when he had the chance to administer a good beating?

Despite Hermione's protestations, some fool found a cane, which was passed from hand to eager hand until it reached Sir George's towering temper. The landing was packed with people, the dinner party, the waits, the new arrival and a motley variety of servants and promenaders who had come in through the open front door to see what all the fuss was about and, sensing that the matter was about to become violent, stayed rooted to the staircase avidly ready for bloodshed.

Sir George laid about him with a will but fortunately with very little sense of direction. Some of his blows hit the waits, most fell upon the wall or the outstretched arms of his guests. Within seconds all pretence at gentility had gone and they were all enjoying themselves in a wild melee of blows and screams and resounding abuse. Sir Arnold trod right through a violin, one of the waits struck Lady Fosdyke on the backside with his bow, and Benjy bit as many people as he could in the general confusion. Finally Lady Bradbury fell to the floor in a graceful swoon and had to be carried through the mob into the safety of the drawing room, and the waits took advantage of the diversion to fight their way down the seething staircase and escape at last into the happy audience in the parade.

By now, Sir George was so out of breath he couldn't speak, and Lady Bradbury refused to open her eyes, so Lady Carstairs took command. She ordered brandy to be brought for the menfolk and aqua vitae for the ladies, and set about reviving the whole company, declaring that this was just the sort of thing one had to expect when common tradesmen were allowed to mix with quality folk. Under her spirited ministrations the dinner party recovered, and soon they were all congratulating themselves on the courageous way in which they had resisted those unpleasant upstarts, who, as they could now see so clearly, were simply asking for a beating.

'Now we will leave the gentlemen to finish their brandy in peace,' Lady Carstairs suggested, sending the slightest signal to her hostess.

Hermione took her cue, gratefully. 'You must take tea with me before you depart,' she said. 'I do insist. After all the trials and tribulations of this abominable afternoon we need a cup to cheer us and sustain us.'

So the men remained in the dining room with the brandy decanter, and the ladies retired to the drawing room where Hepzie arrived with the kettle, and set the tea caddy reverently before her mistress so that the ceremony of tea making could begin. Presiding over the tea always soothed Lady Bradbury. There was something so agreeably powerful about it, unlocking one's own caddy, mixing one's own blend, rewarding one's guests each in turn and rank order, and yet at the same time it was an undeniably feminine occupation, allowing one to display the lace at one's wrists with a whole repertoire of elegant gestures, and to sit at the centre of the company with one's gown seen to advantage, while all the other ladies in the room sat at an angle to the best light and did not display half so well. As she fitted her key into the little brass lock of the caddy, she smiled for the first time since dinner began.

'An uncommon entertaining dinner,' Lady Carstairs said, accepting the first cup. 'Better than a seat at the theatre, my dear. I ain't seen my old feller laugh as much in years. Sir George has "bottom", I'll say that for him.'

Even Lady Fosdyke was smiling as she sipped from her little porcelain cup. 'There is no problem that cannot be resolved with a little tea,' she said.

Hermione gave her formidable guest a superior smile. How very little she knew about life, and how very few problems she'd had to face if that were her opinion. And she remembered Jessup and his errand and the problem that had barked at her own heels since the seventeenth year of her life.

Three

For the first time in her short healthy life, Suki Brown anguished through an entire night without sleeping. While the needs of the day had been carrying her along, she'd been able to pretend that everything would work out for the best, but alone in her truckle bed with the household snoring and grunting around her, the enormity of what she'd done weighed her to wakefulness. The hours dragged by, leaden with guilt, as she turned the same brute facts round and round in her mind, like a dog in a treadmill, struggling against their unyielding constraint, unable to move beyond the monstrous sin of the position she was in.

A lie was a lie, no matter how necessary, and it was bound to cause trouble. Lies always did. What if she were found out? What if someone were to recognize the baby? What if they knew already and were simply biding their time before they spoke out and shamed her? In the darkness, retribution loomed like a ghoul.

Because his mother was in such a state, William-who-had-been-Jack was restless too, waking to suckle and then refusing to be put back in his cradle. Suki tried rocking him and coaxing him but he wailed so miserably every time she put him down that she was afraid he would wake the household. Eventually she gave up the struggle. She wrapped him in a towel to soak up as much of his piddle as she could, tucked him into her own bed beside her and let him sleep and suck as he pleased. When the morning light finally seeped its reluctance through her subterranean window, she was so tired she could barely open her eyes.

She yawned into the kitchen with the baby on her shoulder. Despite energetic rubbing, her eyelids felt as though they were glued together and she was desperate for beer and vittles.

'You had a bad night, 'ave yer gel?' Cook said sympathetically. 'Beer's in the jug, me dear. Help yourself. Is the babba fed?'

'On an' on an' on,' Suki said wearily. 'All night.'

'Eat hearty!' Cook instructed, cracking eggs into a basin. 'Then you got to go an' see Mr Jessup.'

Sula's mind was still addled from her long vigil. 'What for?' she asked.

'Why the funeral, poor soul. The funeral.'

Suki hadn't even considered a funeral, but of course there would have to be one and she would have to attend it, since the dead baby was supposed to be hers. What was worse, she would have to leave her darling behind in the house, because they would never allow her to take him to the graveyard. The thought made her quail. What if he woke and cried for her when she wasn't there. 'Vittles first,' she said, helping herself to a chunk of cold mutton. Troubles were always worse on an empty stomach. I'll get Bessie to watch out for him. If he wakes she can sneak him out of the house and carry him up to me. I'll make amends to her, help her rake the ashes of a morning or scrub the kitchen table or some such. I can't leave the poor little mite to cry. On which sensible decision she carved herself a good thick slice of bread from the loaf and set about her breakfast.

The butler was totting up the household accounts in his private sitting room when she came knocking, but he paused, quill in hand, and looked up to attend to her.

'Arrangements are made,' he informed her, when he'd beckoned her into the room. ''Twill be a' Thursday at the Magdalen Chapel after morning service. Are there — krmm, krmm — persons whom you wish to be invited? Your — krmm, krmm — husband, for instance?'

'He's at sea,' Suki said, glad that she could tell the old lie so easily. 'On a slaver.' It was a neat excuse, for service on a slaver accounted for his long absence and reduced the need for further questioning. As it did now.

'Your family perhaps?' Mr Jessup continued. 'We could send a message.'

She'd forgotten about her family. They would have to be told and quickly before one of them arrived in Bath to give the game away. But they certainly couldn't be invited to the funeral.

'No. Thank 'ee kindly,' she said. 'They'm all a deal too far away.'

'As you prefer,' the butler said. 'My lady wishes me to inform you that you are to rest and recover for the next few days and that you are to report to me night and morning as to the progress of your charge. Mind 'tis done.'

So there were only two mourners to follow the tiny white coffin to the Magdalen Chapel on that misty Thursday morning, Sula and the undertaker's assistant who'd been sent to push the little cart. He was a lank, greasy individual with a concave chest, the eyes of a startled hare and nothing to say for himself. But he stood on one leg with his greasy boot braced against the wheel of the cart and waited patiently as Suki made her final arrangements, speaking to Bessie, quietly and seriously, through the area window.

'The minute he cries, Bessie,' she instructed. 'Don't let him roar. He en't to roar. You promise me.'

The promise was given, earnestly and with much nodding.

'An' you'll mind they don't see you. You'll choose a good moment.'

Oh, she would, she would. 'You'd best go, Sula. He's awaitin'.'

Above their heads, Ariadne was saying much the same thing, as she and Hepzie watched from the dining room. 'What is she about to keep the fellow waiting so?' she asked in her tart way, looking down at Suki's nodding mop cap. 'You'd think she would want it over and done with, surely. I know I would if 'twere me.'

Hepzie snorted and looked knowing. 'Ah, but then 'twas a punishment for *her* sins,' she said. 'Which don't apply to you now, do it miss? No indeed. A different matter altogether.'

Her smug smile annoyed Ariadne. 'You are too harsh, girl,' she rebuked her. 'No matter what sins she may have committed, she don't deserve to bury her child.'

'Harsh I may be, miss,' Hepzie retorted, 'but then that all depend on the nature of the sin, don't it.'

'Which you are agog to tell me,' Ariadne drawled, 'so you'd best be about it before your eyes pop out of your skull.'

Hepzie enlightened her with great satisfaction. '*She* was the one what beat your father about the pate,' she reported.

Ariadne's casual interest sharpened into admiration. 'Did she so?' she said, looking down at the wet nurse. Now that puts an entirely different complexion on the matter. A wench with spirit.

Hepzie was continuing the tale. 'She say he don't own her,' she confided, 'if you ever heard the like. By her reckoning, her body's her own an' she ought to be allowed to do what she likes with it. The very idea! Can you imagine how things would be if we all thought *that* way?

33

There'd be no more great marriages arranged for a start. No alliances. How would the royal family make out then? And what if wives expected to have dominion over their husbands instead of t'other way about? Where would *that* lead? 'Tis all a great nonsense an' she's got no business saving such things, an' that's my opinion on it. She's only hired for her titties when all's said an' done. She's only kept here on account of the babby. Any other chit would have been sent packing long since. Well, she'll come to no good in the end, you mark my words.'

'I daresay,' Ariadne said, but her voice was vague because her thoughts were in such a turmoil. What an idea to conjure with. What if a woman's body really were her own? 'Twould mean a daughter could refuse her father's choice and pick a husband for herself, could love where she would — love where she would — what a thought *that* was!

'I shall take a promenade, methinks,' she announced, turning to her maid and assuming her commanding expression. 'Fetch me my new pelisse and my Leghorn bonnet. A turn in the air would revive my spirits. The mist begins to clear, I do believe, and they seem to be off at last.'

From the long windows of the withdrawing room, Lady Hermione was watching the departure too, with Jessup standing dutifully beside her. But her attention was perfunctory because she had another and more important matter to attend to. Her family were all otherwise occupied and out of earshot, Sir George at the baths, Melissa at her toilette, Ariadne entertained by the cortege. It was the opportunity for Jessup to make his report at last.

'You saw the young person, I assume?' she asked. She spoke lightly as if the question were of little concern, but her eyes were sharp as needles.

Mr Jessup inclined his head. 'I did, ma'am.'

'When did he arrive?'

'Yesterday morning, ma'am. On the London coach.'

The lady rested her jewelled hand on the curtain. 'Is he well?'

'He seems so, ma'am. I would say he is — krmm krmm — in good heart.'

The lady's face showed no reaction. 'You made it clear to him that his arrival is inopportune, did you not? You told him he must take lodgings in some other town until we quit this place, as he did last summer.'

'I did, ma'am.'

'You made it clear that he will receive no part of his remuneration until I learn that he is safely away?'

'He seemed eager to comply, ma'am. There are debts outstanding I believe.'

'I'm uncommon glad to hear it,' Hermione said, allowing herself a slight nod of satisfaction. 'Indebtedness is a great aid to obedience in the young. Ah! They are off at last.'

Below them the little procession was indeed on the move, the cart trundling across the empty pavements of the parade, wheels rattling. Suld walked beside it, her head bowed and her arms tucked inside her shawl for comfort, for the mist swirled about her shoulders and she was chill with anxiety.

They crossed the wide meadows of the Ham, where the mist lay like swathes of white gauze, and half-hidden sheep cropped the grasses, rhythmically and endlessly, twitching their cacky flanks. As the apprentice pushed his little burden through the meadow, they stood back nervously, lifting their heads to bleat in their flat, melancholy way. The sound made Suki shudder. If only this baby hadn't died. If only she hadn't swapped them round and told that lie. If only it wasn't such a long climb to the church. Jack would be sure to wake, poor lamb. And she couldn't even call him Jack now, because he had to be William. Oh how difficult everything was! If only she hadn't told that lie. The dark escarpment of Beechen Height rose above her, primitive and brooding, shaggy with beeches and pines, heavy as a judgement seat.

'Can't you walk a little faster?' she complained to the apprentice boy as they set off along the hollow way. 'We shall be all day gettin' there at this rate.'

But he merely turned his hare eyes towards her, looked baffled and didn't answer. So she had to continue at his cart-laden pace, chaffing all the way.

The Magdalen Chapel, and the lepers' house beside it, had originally been built of the same cream-coloured stone as the bright new lodging houses in South Parade, but nobody would have guessed it, for time, rain and mist had smudged them with soot and lichen until it was hard to see where stone ended and the surrounding pines began. But at least they stood above the mist, where it was marginally warmer and at least the priest was waiting to receive her.

Paupers' children and the infants of the poor were buried here along the edge of the churchyard, their tiny graves huddled together to take up as little space as possible, for, as Sir George had observed in his heartless way, such deaths were a daily occurrence, especially in high summer, and of very little significance. Three children had been committed to that very earth the previous week and the mounds over their bodies had barely grown grass. Was it any wonder the priest scrambled through the service so inattentively?

The body of William Montmorency Bradbury, son and heir to the Bradbury estates, was laid to rest in six careless minutes, under the name of Jack Brown, baby of no consequence. Suki wept freely as she scattered earth upon the coffin because she felt so sorry for the poor little thing. To die before he knew he was alive and be buried so thoughtlessly. But then she heard another baby crying and recognized her own, and there was Bessie toiling up the hollow way with William-who-had-been-Jack protesting in her arms.

'Give him to me quick!' Suld said, running to take him. 'Oh my poor lamb! Did I keep 'ee waitin'?' And she unlaced her bodice and let him suck where she stood.

Bessie had walked up the hill so quickly she was quite out of breath. 'I best get back,' she puffed. 'They don' know I'm gone.'

'I'm uncommon grateful to 'ee,' Suki said, gazing down at her infant. 'I meant what I said about the fires, don' forget.'

But Bessie was already tumbling downhill, holding up her skirts so that she could run more easily. It wasn't in her timid nature to take risks and the sooner she was back the better.

Suki strolled out of the churchyard, carrying the baby very carefully so as not to disturb him. The world was suddenly an easier, happier place now that they were together again. The funeral was over. The mist had cleared. The sun was warm. The sky a lovely summer blue above her head. She pulled the gate ajar and sidled through into the meadow, where she sat with her back against the trunk of an old beech tree and her feet cushioned on mosses and gave herself over to the delights of suckling and to the gradual return of her natural optimism. Problems could be solved, no matter how difficult.

Below her, between the horseshoe curves of the river, the city of Bath lay in its cradled hollow. The great abbey looked so small from this distance that it was as though she could pick it up and hold it in the palm of her hand, and around it, the little houses of the old town huddled together in topsy-turvy proximity, blackened and stumpy and decidedly old-fashioned. But there was no doubt at all that Mr Wood's fine new houses were absolutely splendid, so tall and straight and well designed, their stone walls the colour of pale honey in the milky sunlight. The long lines of the parades looked very fine, and so did the symmetry of the new Queen's Square, and further up the hillside, she could see workmen preparing the ground for the very latest splendour, the new Circus, which Cook said would be the wonder of the age.

There'd be work in this city for years to come and plenty of rich pickings. And in the meantime, all she had to do was to keep her job with the Bradburys, feed this pretty baby and watch him grow. Sooner or later his dadda would come back to Bath again and he'd know what was to be done. Dearest Jack. He was so clever and so handsome. Oh she couldn't wait to see him again!

Her mind drifted back to the pleasures of the previous summer when he'd courted her so ardently and pleasured her with such passion. They'd always met in the Spring Gardens among the trees and flowers and the gravel walks, like lovers in a play, and she'd always been so happy to see him. Oh, so happy. It made her heart lift just to remember it. She hadn't thought to ask him anything, not where he lived, or where he'd come from, or where he was going, not even his full name. Once, she remembered, she'd asked him what he'd been christened, but he'd flown into such a terrible rage she'd dropped the subject immediately. So Captain Jack had had to suffice. Not that she minded. It sounded so romantic, and it was just the right name for him, with his fine dark eyes and that sun-browned skin and that swaggering military bearing. But knowing so little about him wasn't going to help her now, when she needed to find him. And she *did* need to find him. She realized that. He was the only person she could confide in. The one person who would know what was to be done.

'He must be back soon,' she said to the baby. 'He should have been here long since.' But if he *had* been in town he'd have come and found us. He knows where we are, when all's said an' done, for wasn't he the one who'd told her to find work with the Bradburys should she ever need another job, although he hadn't known then what work it would turn out to be.

The long wait suddenly seemed intolerable. There was nothing to be gained by being patient — even if she could. No, what was needed was a thorough search. She would visit all their old haunts, starting this morning, and ask after him. Somebody was bound to know if he was back. He had friends all over town. I'll send him a message or write him a billet and *then* he'll come to us. Bound to. She looked down at the baby, happy with her decision. 'He'll want to see you, won't he my 'andsome,' she said. 'You might be William now, but your dadda's your dadda for all that.' And she was touched when the baby stopped sucking to smile at her.

At that moment, she became aware of a movement on the road below her, and lifted her head to see what it was. There was a cart rattling along the Twerton Road and it was pulled by a bay mare that she recognized at once. Farmer Lambton's. What a piece of luck! Now she could get a lift to the city, instead of trudging all the way home with the baby on her back. Better still, she could send a message to her mother to alert her to what had happened so that she wouldn't come blundering into town and say the wrong thing.

She stood up at once and called down the hill as loudly as she could, her voice echoing across the empty fields. 'Farmer Lambton! Farmer Lambton! You going in to Bath?'

The farmer looked up, recognized her and reined in the mare to wait for her, sitting very still in the cart, patient and stolid as always. He never seems to change, Suki thought, as she scrambled down the steep hillside towards him. Her father and mother had worked on his farm ever since she could remember, and now her brothers were working there too. When they'd all been little, they'd played in his yard and helped his wife to feed the chickens and gather up the eggs, and he'd always been the same even then, a tall, thick-set, quiet presence, as slow and dependable as the soil itself, and, now she came to think about it, very much the same colour.

'Thank 'ee kindly,' she said, as she reached the side of the cart.

Farmer Lambton hauled her up on to the seat beside him, and clicked the mare into motion again, without comment and without greeting. The cart was full of strawberries and raspberries, packed close together in long straw punnets, buttressed by thick bundles of leaves. Their scent filled the air with sweetness. But they'd travelled more than a hundred yards before he spoke, and then it was with the laconic brevity she'd come to expect.

'Looks like you,' he said, nodding at the baby. 'Has your eyes.'

The words gave Suki such a surprise that she could feel her jaw falling. Until that moment she hadn't given a thought to the baby's appearance. He looked like a baby, that was all, with a dear little round face and an upper lip like a pink M and a snub nose and big dark eyes. If he really *did* look like her, the lie would be out, and no mistake. She leaned over him, examining his face intently. No, she thought, he en't like me. My eyes are blue and his are a-goin' to be brown like his father. But then another thought struck her. She could hardly send an explanation home to her mother now that Farmer Lambton had recognized this baby as hers. He would know she was lying and that would cause no end of trouble.

By this time, they'd reached the south gate, and she could see that the day's activities had well and truly begun. There were scores of sedan chairs about, on offer and in use, and the carriages were out too, being galloped along the narrow alleys at such precipitate speed that it was a wonder their wealthy occupants weren't tipped into the road. So naturally the beggars were on the streets too, clustered at every corner, displaying their deformities and demanding charity with their usual hideous boldness. There were three huddled inside the south gate itself, giving off their particular noxious air, a powerful combination of advanced decay and stale shit. It drowned out the smell of the strawberries and alarmed Sula so much that she covered the baby's nose with her hand for fear of him taking infection.

Fanner Lambton coaxed his bay mare through the heave and clamour of the throng, talking to her gently. 'Walk on my beauty. That's the way.' It was a necessary encouragement, for the noise was ear-numbing. All along Stall Street, sellers shrieked their wares, for pies sweating in the basket, and fish already stinking in the warmth of the sun, for eggs and bread and vegetables coated with the dust of traffic. At every turn there was an argument, ostlers raking their poor horses with vicious curry combs in a vain attempt to improve their tattered coats and increase trade, bearers vitriolic in their competition for custom, ballad-sellers dangling their wares so close to the eyes of the passers-by that it was impossible to see beyond their grubby song sheets, quacks offering to cure anyone of any illness they could imagine, by one short draught from a poisonous-looking bottle that was thrust into every hand. And above it all the bells of the abbey clanged yet another welcome to yet another newly arrived, newly rich nonentity. After the peace of the churchyard it made Suld's head spin.

At the corner of Cheap Street, two gangly young men were posting a notice for the theatre, flicking paste to right and left like spittle. 'Tonight at seven,' it said. 'The comedy of *The Fair Clorinda*. We promise you an unforgettable spectacle which you will miss at your peril.'

'Mrs Lambton has a mind to go to the theatre,' the farmer observed as they turned the corner. 'Would she like to see this comedy, think 'ee?'

'She'd be bound to,' Suki told him, 'if 'tis the same company as were here last summer, they're uncommon entertaining. We went to every play.' And she remembered how much the Captain loved the theatre and how at home he was there, calling out to the players from his seat in the stalls, with his friends around him. That's where I'll start, she thought. 'Tis on my way. 'Twouldn't take but a minute.

No sooner thought than acted upon. 'Could you set me down here, Mr Lambton, if you please,' she said. 'I can take a short cut through Orchard Street, an' save a bit of time.'

He reined in the mare. 'I will tell your family I saw you,' he said. 'Have you any message for me to bear home to them?'

She was already on the pavement, tying her shawl to keep the baby firmly on her back. 'None save my love,' she said. 'Which, pray tell 'em, I send aplenty. I will visit as soon as I can.' And sped away.

Orchard Street was empty except for a skinny cat slinking apprehensively towards the alley. But the stage door had been left open and, as there was no porter to guard it, there was nothing to stop her from stepping into the hall. Once inside, she realized that the actors were all too busy to notice her, but she took a seat in the stalls and decided to wait anyway. They were bound to take a rest sooner or later.

Three of them were swearing a canopied throne into position in the centre of the narrow stage, and two more, stripped to shirt and petticoats, were rehearsing a love scene, with a good deal of extravagant gesture and intermittent abuse. The actor was a handsome fellow even with his hair plastered to his skull with sweat, but the actress was fat and forty, and in the filtered daylight Suki could see that her face was pitted with scars, her teeth broken and discoloured. Beside the wings, an unswaddled baby slept in a pile of dusty costumes and beside it an absorbed toddler was peeing into an upturned helmet. Two other scruffy children played tag between the busy legs and trailing finery of their elders. There was a lilt to the activity here, a sense of enjoyment even amidst the effort on that crowded platform. Suki felt at home among them, and hopeful. Surely these people would help her if they could.

'Fairest Clorinda!' the actor intoned, singing the words and striking a noble pose. 'Queen of all Queens, from Africa's... S'blood, Charlie, I can't say this!'

'Teeming shore,' a voice prompted from the wings. 'Yes you can. Africa's teeming shore.'

The actor sighed. 'Do breathe in another direction, darling,' he said to his leading lady, 'or I may suffocate.'

'Rain kisses on my burning lips,' the actress intoned, not in the least put out by such rudeness. 'With fire of passion set my heart aflame!'

'This canopy is too low,' one of the scene shifters observed. 'Twill hide the helmet, sure as fate.'

'Try the helmet, Claude,' said the voice in the wings. Suki looked up at once, remembering what the toddler had been doing as she entered the hall. But the leading actor was already lowering the helmet on to his head, and showering his face and shoulders in the process. 'Beelzebub and all the bleeding devils!' he roared, as the company applauded and shrieked delight all round him.

'I must say, Mr Clements,' the leading lady remarked mildly, 'there will be scant cause to comment upon such a small matter as my breath, when our patrons find themselves downwind of your pate.'

I'd better not laugh, Suki thought, although the temptation was very strong indeed. She looked away quickly from the uproar on stage, turning her head towards the only other person who was sitting in the stalls. And found herself gazing straight into the big bold eyes of Miss Ariadne Bradbury.

For a split second they stared at one another, both equally surprised. Then Suki recovered, and changed her expression rapidly to one of innocent and acceptable enquiry. But in that second she'd noticed a great many interesting things; that Miss Ariadne was embarrassed and annoyed to be seen in such a place; that she was wearing her new Leghorn bonnet; and that she wasn't laughing at the predicament of the unfortunate Claude, but was watching him out of the corner of her eye with concern and cow-eyed affection. Then she too recovered and assumed a different expression, lifting her head and pouting with the drawling indifference that Suki had seen so often and so irritatingly at South Parade.

'La! Suki Brown!' she said, pretending to yawn. 'Who sent you here to spy upon me so? Mamma, of course! You need not tell me.'

Suki looked down, and said nothing. How annoying and embarrassing this was! Why couldn't the silly girl just go away and pretend they hadn't seen one another. Now she would have to escort her home and forego the chance to ask about the Captain. And just when the rehearsal had come to a halt and an opportunity was about to present itself.

Miss Ariadne was speaking again. 'Tis too bad,' she complained. 'Am I not to be allowed to take a simple stroll to buy two little tickets for this evening's performance without being harried from pillar to post like some common criminal? 'Tis a pitiful thing not to be trusted by one's own mamma.' She had forced tears from her eyes and was pouting pathetically.

Suki felt prevailed upon to say something to explain her presence. 'The streets of Bath arn't no fit place for an unaccompanied young lady,' she tried, secretly uncomfortable because she sounded smug. But Ariadne seemed to approve.

'How foolish!' she said, half smiling. 'Why 'tis hardly more than two steps across the street. Were you sent after to protect me or to spy upon me?'

'You got a careful mother, Miss Ariadne,' Suki said, because it was the only answer she could think of.

Claude had taken himself off for a wash. 'Very well,' Ariadne decided graciously. 'We will walk home together. Then I shall be chaperoned and my foolish mamma will have no possible reason to complain. Come along.' And she straightened her pelisse, relieved the strings of her bonnet, and set off for the door. It was infuriating but there was nothing Suki could do but obey her.

They followed the curve of Orchard Street, crossed the new neat cobblestones of Pierrepont Street and strolled on to the pavements in front of South Parade. Apart from a two-horse chaise that had just arrived at the far end of the terrace and the gentleman in the brown bob wig who was negotiating the price of a very damp chair at the other, the place was deserted. Now Suki had another anxiety to confront. If Lady Bradbury were to glance out of her window, she could hardly fail to notice them and, if she saw the baby, there would be serious trouble. For the second time that morning she found herself wishing speed on her companion.

Most of the first-floor windows were wide open and she could see heavy wigs and powdered heads bobbing between the curtains, like huge untidy flowers. If only everybody wasn't so quizzy here in Bath. If only Miss Ariadne would walk a little quicker. Three more steps and they could be through the door and home and dry.

'Dear child!' Lady Bradbury's voice said, acidly sweet and directly above their heads. *'There* you are. I was growing concerned about you. You must come up at once, *must ycm not*, and tell me where you have been gadding.'

Ariadne assumed her dutiful daughter expression and smiled obediently up at her mother. 'Yes, Mamma!' she said, demurely.

Co in! Suki thought, silently urging her young mistress forward. Make haste. Before she sees *me* too.

But it was too late. Hermione had leaned out of the window to get a better view. 'Whom do you have with you, sweet child?' she asked, and her voice was as sharp as her face. 'How now? I do believe 'tis one of the servants. Ah! I see! I will send for *you* presently, Suki.'

Suki grimaced as she followed Ariadne into the house, and wondered how long 'presently' was likely to be.

She was soon to discover. She'd barely settled William back in his cradle before Jessup arrived in the nursery to summon her to the boudoir.

'Adjust your cap,' he commanded. 'Milady is seriously displeased.'

Suki shifted her cap — marginally — and jutted her chin. If I'm for it, she thought, I must take it, but I shall give as good as I get.

Four

Sir George and Lady Bradbury were engaged to dine with the formidable Lady Fosdyke at three that afternoon, so naturally Lady Bradbury had commanded *the friseur* to attend her at noon. She was aware that a good head cannot be rushed and hers had to be the best at the table on such a prestigious occasion. No matter how many household problems she might have to contend with, it was imperative that her social life should continue smoothly and in its customary style.

So she sat before her dressing-table mirror, *en deshabille* in her shift and her frilled dressing gown, and watched intently as the hairdresser transformed her front hair into the required confection, curling it with hot tongs, padding each curl with black wool, stiffening each ascending layer with strong pins and a larding of pomade, made according to her own particular specification of the best hog's fat, heavily perfumed. His working sketch lay on the table before her, so that she could check it at every stage, holding it firmly in place with a dictatorial finger, ready to correct the least deviation. Appearances were *so* critical. Her jewels were chosen, her rouge pot primed, her patch box full of new velvet patches, her servant, Hepzibah, ready to dress her and standing obediently at her elbow as was proper, her dinner gown laid out upon the bed with a new pair of neat-skin slippers set side by side beneath the hem, their toes pointing right and left, like a fashionable lady in a faint. It was her third new gown of the season and quite the most elaborate and anyone with half an eye could see how expensive it was. For, as she knew so well, the value of ones gown was *so* important.

But so was controlling one's family and servants. And nobody had a more exquisite knowledge as to how that could be accomplished than Lady Bradbury. When Suki was brought into the room, she made her wait for a stern and deliberate five minutes until the final layer of wool-stuffed hair had been pinned to her head and her satisfaction.

It was a wasted effort, for Suki was determined not to be impressed by her mistress's hair nor subdued by her behaviour. She'd seen the lady play exactly the same game with most of the other servants, so she recognized that she was being put in her place but, after a morning buffeted by strong emotions, the manoeuvre seemed petty and unnecessary.

She'd been caught in a blameworthy act, thanks to that idiotic Ariadne and her foolish dawdling, and now she would have to endure being scolded for it. But that was all. So she set her chin, stood where Jessup had left her and watched and waited, aware that Hepzie was looking smug, that the *friseur* was nervous, that Benjy was asleep and snoring, and that the room was overheated and full of objectionable smells — singed hair and hog's fat, milady's scent and the *friseurs* sweat, orris powder and stale piddle and the stableyard stink of that steaming dog.

Watching her from the corner of her eye, Hermione was affronted by her boldness and annoyed by her red cheeks and bright eyes. A servant had no right to look so well, and it was downright unseemly for her to be brazen after the way she'd been comporting herself recently. She should have been ashamed or downcast, at the very least. My instincts about her were right, she thought. She has a deal too much spirit for a common girl. She will need to be watched. Or more fully employed. She ain't to be trusted.

Her coiffure having been completed, she signalled to the *friseur* that he should pack his tongs and leave, and to Hepzibah that she was ready for her shoes. Then she looked sternly at her wet nurse through the mirror, took a fierce breath and opened her attack.

'I trust you have an explanation for your behaviour this morning,' she said, and lifted her head, her expression a query.

Having prepared herself to stand silent under a scolding, Sula was momentarily at a loss to know how to answer, but she murmured, 'Yes, ma'am,' and hoped it would suffice.

'Very well then, out with it,' Hermione ordered. And when Suki still hesitated. 'Oh, come along, come along. You haul my infant about the streets as though he were a sack of coal, or some dirty tinker's child, you expose him to every rheum and vapour in the town and I know not what gross infection besides. You must have something to say about it.'

Suki steadied herself for a plausible lie, since the truth was impossible. She could hardly say he'd been brought up to the graveyard so that she could feed him. The lady would never understand *that*. The kitchen was hot, ma'am,' she explained. 'I thought to cool him.'

Hermione snorted. 'Thought!' she said. 'The impertinence! You ain't paid to think, gel, you're paid to do as you're told. The child is to be treated with more care. Should he need a cooling breeze, which I consider exceedingly unlikely, but should he need such a thing, he may take it for five minutes and no more beside the river and well away from the common herd. Hepzibah, gently, gently! Have I not suffered enough at your hands this morning? Pray make some small endeavour not to force my foot so vilely.' Hepzie muttered an apology and did her best to force her mistress's foot less vilely, and Suki waited. Hermione closed her eyes and wore her martyr's face for several seconds until both shoes had been squeezed on to her feet, then she sighed, propped her fashionable head on her hand and watched as the *friseur* left the room, bowing nervously. 'Yes, yes,' she said as he opened his mouth to address her. 'You may send your account to my husband. That will be all. You may leave me.'

Then there was a pause while Hepzie lifted the lady's dress from the bed and Hermione stood to be enrobed.

'Am I to leave too, ma'am?' Suki asked hopefully.

Hermione held out her arms, to be eased into the sleeves. 'No,' she said. 'You are not.'

So Suki had to wait while the gown was arranged and the lady held her breath to be laced into the tightness of her long boned bodice, and the hem was settled, and the wrist ruffles fluffed, and the final image in her cheval mirror assessed and approved. But as soon as Hepzie had been dismissed and was safely out of hearing on the other side of the door, die interrogation began again, and now milady's face and tone were sharp.

'I have neither the time nor the patience for prevarication,' she said, 'so YOU will oblige me by telling me the truth. I know everything that goes on in this house either before my face or behind my back. Nothing can be hidden from me, you may depend upon it.'

Despite her self-control, Suki's heart contracted with alarm. What she talking about? Is this to do with thumpin' the master? What *do* she know? 'The truth, ma,am?' she repeated, trying to keep her voice steady.

'The truth, gel,' Lady Hermione insisted. 'Don't play the innocent. I can read your countenance as clear as daylight. You know well enough what I mean.'

'No indeed, ma'am.'

'No indeed!' her mistress mocked. 'Oh come now. What was Miss Ariadne doing out and about this morning, all by herself? You followed her did, you not?'

So 'tis Miss Ariadne who'm at fault, Suki thought. It en't me. And she relaxed at once. 'Yes, ma'am,' she said easily. That weren't a lie, for she *had* followed the young lady, in a manner of speaking, into the theatre. An' if telling her mother got her into trouble, well then serve her right. If it hadn't ha' been for her I could've asked about the Captain.

As Suki had suspected, maternal concern for anything as troublesome and insignificant as a baby was beyond Hermione's experience, but spying she could understand. The two women looked at one another for a significant second. 'Well?' Hermione asked.

'She went to the theatre, ma'am,' Suki told her.

Hermione's voice was cool. 'Did she so? Why was that, think 'ee?'

'To sit in the stalls, ma'am, an' watch the actors.'

Lady Bradbury raised an eyebrow. 'Which one?'

''Tis hard to be sure,' Suki told her, pretending to be discreet. 'But I should say 'tis one they call Mr Clements. That's the one she was a-watchin' most of the time.'

'Closely, would you say?'

It was a moment of sweet revenge. 'She couldn't take her eyes away.'

Lady Bradbury considered this, her face sharper than ever. 'Hm,' she said thoughtfully. 'Did the actor return her *oeillades?*'

'No, milady,' Suki reassured her. 'He were more interested in what were going on in the play. And a helmet he were trying on. That concerned him quite a lot.'

'Did he look at her at all?' Hermione said, pursuing her thoughts.

'Now an' then,' Suki told her, understanding the point of the question, and remembering the way the Captain used to look at her. 'Not in no partic'lar way though.'

'I'm glad to hear it,' Hermione said. If that was the case, then something might yet be done to rescue the poor child from the worst excesses of her folly. 'She tells me she means to take her sister to the play tonight. 'Tis all mere foolishness you understand but one must be careful of her reputation. You shall attend her and watch her closely till the play is done. Jessup shall order chairs to bring them home in safety and you shall guard them in the theatre. Never leave Miss Ariadne for a second, you understand. Mischief is speedy, as well as I know. It takes but a second's folly to ruin a reputation.'

This was so unexpected and so annoying that Suki couldn't control her expression. She'd expected to be scolded for taking William out into the street, but to be asked to play the nursemaid to a silly young woman was a consequence she hadn't foreseen. How could she look for the Captain if she had to tag along after *her* all the time? 'How of William?' she asked. 'He'm bound to need feedin' in the evening. He always do, some time or another. Would it not be...?'

'You may leave him a bowl of pap,' Hermione interrupted, adding carelessly, 'Twill do him no harm. 'Tis a fine strong baby.'

Suki couldn't argue, for the matter was plainly settled, but she was aggrieved to be given such heartless instructions. All that fuss about taking him out on to the street, she thought, an' she's prepared to let him feed on bread and sugar-water.

'The very idea!' she exploded to Cook when she was safely back in the kitchen telling the tale. 'As if I'd leave my — any babba of mine with a dish of pap. He'd get the bellyache as sure as fate. There's no sense to her at all, an' that's a fact.'

'What will you do?' Cook asked. 'Take 'im and risk another scoldin'?'

'Bessie can watch out for him,' Suld said. The same as she done this morning. If he wakes, she can trot across to the theatre and fetch me. Can't you, Bessie? Tis only a step. I can be here and back in a jiffy. I aren't leaving him with a dish of pap. The very idea!' And she'd go out and look for the Captain that very afternoon, the minute they were all out of the house, just to show them. She was warm with annoyance.

'You watch they don' catch you creepin' back, that's all,' Cook warned.

'She should've asked me,' Hepzie said, hard-faced with jealousy. ''Tis folly to send you. What do *you* know of the ways of the world?'

'Enough,' Suki said, paying her back for being so smug in the boudoir, 'or she wouldn't have asked me to do it. You'm to attend her when she rings, by the bye. She told me to tell you.'

Hepzie's narrow eyes were sharp with anger. 'You watch your tongue, Suki Brown,' she warned, leaning across the kitchen table so as to bring her face closer to her rival. ''T'aint your business to tell me what to do. You're only the nursemaid here...'

'Enough of that,' Cook said, barging her away from the table. Just you remember where she've been this morning, poor soul, an' what she'm a-suffered. I'll have some Christian charity in my kitchen today, *if* you don' mind. I hopes that's understood.' And when Hepzie scowled and didn't answer, she went on, 'Now we best shift our shanks or we shall have the master back, roaring for breakfast and nothing ready. There's your bell, Hepzibah. Jump to it.'

Hepzibah was very annoyed to be stopped in mid-rant and sent out of the kitchen so unceremoniously, so she stomped up the back stairs in a bad mood. But as soon as she entered the boudoir she cheered up at once, for there lying across the bed, where milady's dinner gown had been but a minute before, was a dimity day gown. It was out of fashion and a trifle sweat-stained but extremely pretty, with pink rosebuds embroidered all over the swirling skirt and three lace cuffs frothing at each elbow — and it had to have been put there for a purpose. She licked her lips, composed her expression and awaited orders.

They were a surprisingly long time coming. First milady had to powder her face and apply her patches. Then gloves and fan had to be inspected and fault found, most unnecessarily, with both of them. Then her necklace had to be fastened and her ruby drops hung in her ears. But then and at last and very casually, the real topic was broached.

'One must be so careful,' the lady said, admiring her reflection, 'must one not. A moment's inattention, the slightest lack of care and irreparable damage is done. 'Tis uncommon hard.'

Hepzie made murmuring noises to show that she agreed and tried not to look at the day gown.

'There are so few people who can be trusted these days,' the lady went on. 'We live in dishonest times, I fear.'

Another murmur.

'I have set Suki Brown to watch over my errant daughter,' the lady confided languidly, 'but *quis custodiet custodes.* Who is to watch the watcher?'

It was all that needed to be said. Hepzibah offered her services at once, her pale eyes bolting out of her head with eagerness. Five minutes and some detailed instructions later, she had the promise of the day gown if her sendees were satisfactory and was set upon her career as a household spy.

'Now you may clear the room,' Hermione told her, graciously, 'while I visit my daughters.'

And with one final glance at her reflection, she swept off to Ariadne's bedroom to ensure that they were both dressed and ready for their afternoon's entertainment.

But she'd barely taken three paces along the landing before Jessup came up the stairs with a letter on his silver tray. It was for Sir George, from his brother. She recognized the hand at once. Good news or bad, it was singularly inopportune on such an important afternoon.

'Ah, Jessup,' she said. 'Is the master home?'

Not yet apparently. 'I have this billet for him.'

'If it could be contrived,' she advised, ''twould be better to delay delivery of it until he is dressed for dinner.' If 'twere given too soon he would answer the wretched thing and make them late, which would be unpardonable. 'Barnaby is ready to attend him, I trust?'

He was. And the chairs were ordered. Were there any other matters that — krmm krmm — required attention?

She was at her daughters' door. 'Not for the moment,' she said. 'Sufficient unto the day are the difficulties thereof.' And swept through the door, her silk gown rustling its expense before her.

Ariadne was sitting by the window, elegant in her saffron gown, nibbling at a sugar plum and looking down idly at the pavement. She paid no attention to her mother's entry at all, one scolding being quite enough for one day, but turned her head aside so that the line of her throat could be seen to advantage and her mother could be left in no doubt that any conversation, of whatever kind, was completely out of the question. Hermione couldn't help admiring her style. For all her disobedience, she had charm and spirit, a fine straight nose, a pretty neck, an admirable head, which was uncommon well-dressed that afternoon, a truly fashionable mouth, small and pursed as a rosebud, all the right attributes for catching a noble husband, providing she don't throw it all away in a moment of folly, like...

But Melissa was a different character altogether. She lay sprawled across the bed with a novel open before her and her chin propped on her hands, reading. Reading for heaven's sake, when she should be spending her time making herself attractive. She looked so plain and preoccupied that it made Hermione's heart quail. She is so exactly like her father, she thought, looking down at her daughter, the same plump face and the same dull little eyes and skin the colour of putty. How will she ever catch a husband, even in the prettiest gown and the most becoming bonnet? Sir George should be inviting eligible suitors to the family table instead of all those babbling political friends of his, talking and eating at the same time, and married into the bargain.

'Dear me, Melissa,' she reproved. 'You will crush your pretty gown, my dear, if you lie about in such a fashion and then the gentlemen will think you a blue-stocking, an opinion which you would never desire, nor court, I'm sure. Do sit up. I beg you.'

Melissa sat up slowly, her eyes still following the print. 'It ain't crushed, Mamma,' she said.

'Here's Eliza!' Ariadne called in exaggerated excitement. She threw up the window and leaned out to call down to her friend. 'La, Eliza! Ain't you the fine one. I declare we shall all be in the shade with you around this afternoon! I'm pea-green with envy, my dear.'

Hermione tugged Melissa's skirt back into some semblance of order, smoothing out the worst of the creases. 'Now mind your appearance, the pair of you,' she warned. 'Appearances are *so* important.'

'Oh, Mamma!' Melissa sighed, picking up her straw hat. 'We ain't green!'

Ariadne was already in her new Leghorn bonnet and tripping gaily out of the room — without a backward glance. Then they were both clattering down the stairs, lilting out on to the parade, giggling into their friend's carriage. So there was only Sir George's tardiness for Hermione to worry about. Which is no new thing, she thought to herself, sighing, as she returned to her boudoir, for the creature has no conception of time. An hour will pass and mean nothing to him.

Sir George had spent the last hour at the baths and had enjoyed every minute of it, wading in the warm sulphurous waters, agreeably titillated by the proximity of a plentiful supply of rounded breasts and flushed faces. There had been more pretty flesh to admire in the great King's Bath that morning than there had been infirmity to avoid, and that was a situation that invariably improved his health, so he'd stayed in the water as long as he could, and had emerged from it much invigorated.

And then, to gild the lily, whom should he see as he climbed damply into the nearest sedan chair, but his two bosom friends, Sir Arnold Willoughby and Mr Smithers, beautifully dressed in their embroidered coats and fine breeches, and leaning towards one another in an absorbed and obviously interesting conversation.

'Well, here's an unexpected pleasure, gentlemen,' he called. 'What's the news?'

'Some farmer fellow from Virginia has up and attacked the Frenchies, so he has,' Sir Arnold told him, strolling across to the chair. 'In the papers this morning. Look'ee, here. Feller by the name of Washington. Captured a fort. What was the name of the damned place, John?'

'Fort Duquesne,' Smithers provided. 'Good news, what, Georgie?'

Sir George glanced at the paper in his friend's excited hand. 'And not before time,' he said with booming satisfaction. 'If I've said this once in the House I've said it a hundred times. There'll be no increase of trade until the damned Frenchies have taken a trouncing. I trust this Washington will give'em the hiding of their lives. Diplomacy is all very well, dammit, but it don't get the traders through.'

'And that's not all,' Smithers said. lie was flushed with the excitement of it all. 'I had a billet from Alexander, by the first post this morning. You are like to get one too, if it ain't arrived already. No? Well then, the Company of Merchants are to hold an extraordinary meeting in London next Monday. We are urged to attend.'

'Then matters are serious,' Sir George said with great satisfaction. 'With any luck we might just declare war. I'm on my way home for breakfast, be gad. Shall you join me?'

'Thank'ee, but no,' Sir Arnold declined. 'We've breakfasted long since, don'tcher know. Besides we're engaged to dine with Lady Fosdyke in an hour or so, an' 'twould be a parlous thing to be late in *that* quarter. Never be forgiven, what!'

So they agreed to defer their conversation until dinner and Sir George went home in high spirits to read his letter.

'Tell Cook to serve breakfast,' he said to Jessup, removing his damp dressing gown as he strode into the hall. 'Where's my billet, what? Come has it? That's the style. Good news brings good appetite.'

So despite his mistress's instructions Jessup had to hand the letter over there and then in the hall.

As Sir George broke the seal, he was still smiling happily. But the news this billet contained was not from London and Mr Alexander. It was from his brother in Bristol and as shocking as a douche of cold water. One of his traders had beaten the French and come safely home to port, but the second had been boarded ten leagues out and all its cargo taken. Most of the crew had been killed or captured or had jumped ship and, although the master had survived and managed to steer his tattered vessel back to port, their local factor had written to say that he now feared 'some difficulty at the Barbadian end' and would await instructions.

''Od's bowels,' Sir George said. 'Here's a kettle of fish.' It was a parlous blow. A third of their annual trade. To say nothing of the ship and the crew. He knew it was the sort of setback any sugar trader had to expect in piratical times but the shock of it gripped his bowels in a vice. A third of their trade completely lost and just when they were banking upon it. ''Od's bowels!'

But, as always, bad news brought out the best in him. As he stuffed the note into the pocket of his breeches, he was already thinking of ways to counter the loss, estimating costs, wondering how much capital he could raise, his mind money-sharp. We shall need to commission another ship at once, he thought, or we shall miss our next cargo on the Guinea Coast. Poor old Frederick. He'll be at his wit's end. I must go to him at once. The thought of his brother's distress renewed his anger. Damned Frenchies, he raged, to do this to the poor feller. And he stomped upstairs, still in his damp clothes, to tell Lady Bradbury.

'See this,' he shouted, pulling the letter from his pocket and waving it at her. 'Damned Frenchies! They want stringing up by the thumbs and setting in the stocks. They want shooting out of the water, 'od rot 'em. They should be hung drawn and quartered, so they should. All the whole confounded lot of 'em, lock, stock and barrel. There'll be no peace till we go to war. Ain't I always said so? 'Od's bowels, it makes me mad! They needn't think they own the ocean. What are they, eh? Tell me that. Just a parcel of plaguey foreigners, dammit. A parcel of plaguey foreigners. We should give 'em a damned good hiding. That's what *they* need. Damned good hiding. I'm off to Bristol.'

The lady had been reading a book in a desultory way but she set it aside at once, realizing that the letter had been given too soon and that the news had been bad. 'Indeed?' she said coolly. 'In that apparel?'

He looked down at his damp chemise and his slippery slippered feet. 'Ah, to be sure,' he agreed. 'Jessup shall have the carriage brought up while I dress.'

'Chairs are ordered for half past two,' she reminded him, 'since we are engaged to dine with the Fosdykes at three.'

In his sudden anger, he'd forgotten. 'You must make my excuses,' he said.

'Do you think that wise, my love?' Hermione observed mildly. 'I say this for your own good, you understand, and mindful of the fact that the noble lord is the chairman of the consortium.'

Sir George dismissed that with a wave of his podgy hand. 'Fossy won't mind,' he said. 'Business, don'tcher know. Read that.'

'Lord Fosdyke might well be agreeable to it,' Hermione agreed, taking the letter languidly. That I do not doubt. Lord Fosdyke is an agreeable man. His wife, I need hardly remind you, is a horse of another colour.'

That was true and uncomfortable. 'Dammit!' Sir George said. 'It's come to something when a man ain't allowed to bring a little comfort to his own brother. We've lost a third of our trade, dammit. We shall have to find another ship — and not just any ship, mark you, a ship of the proper tonnage' — hire another crew, a reliable master — and they're not easy to come by — and all by the end of the month if we ain't to miss the Guinea trade. There's others'll take it if we default.'

Hermione was reading the letter. 'This is most unfortunate,' she observed. 'I trust you will not allow it to affect Ariadne's dowry.'

Sir George's mind was still in full problem-solving flow, so he was baffled and looked it. 'Ariadne's dowry?' he said. 'We ain't talking of dowries, woman. This is a matter of business.'

Hermione gave him her stern look. 'Then perhaps we should,' she said. 'In my opinion — and 'tis merely my opinion and therefore of little consequence — 'tis high time our eldest was married.'

'What nonsense!' Ariadne's father said, his mind still busy with balance sheets. 'She's a child.'

'She is seventeen,' her mother corrected, which is a dangerous age for a young gel. An age ripe for mischief.'

'If that is the case,' Sir George said, 'you must take her in hand. Women's work, don'tcher know.'

'Depend upon it,' Hermione told him, 'I shall do all that lies within my power to dissuade her from folly. But you are aware, are you not my love, how grudgingly she obeys. 'Tis an obstinate wretch and uncommon hard to persuade. She is firm in her opinion that her health will suffer if she is not allowed her every whim. No, no, 'tis time she was married and tamed. She's a deal too headstrong. And I have to say this, mv love, a marriage is a matter that *you* must arrange.'

'Well, well,' Sir George temporized. 'I'll think on it. Later. This other matter takes precedence.'

He was rewarded with unexpected praise. 'How wise you are, my love,' his wife said, rising from her chaise longue to pat his arm. The equal of Solomon himself. A man of action and bottom and uncommon good sense. I find myself particularly blessed in your good sense, as I told Lady Fosdyke only the other afternoon. She is peculiarly appreciative of your good sense, which is why you are *so* wise in your present decision to dine with her today.' And when he tried to speak. 'No, no. Say nothing. I would not dream of dissuading you. Now pray do dress, my love. I would not have you take cold for the world. I will order the carriage to be ready when we return and Barnaby shall pack such linen as is necessary for your journey. You may leave all to me.'

He could feel his mind numbing as he strained to understand. He knew that he was being outmanoeuvred and that his ability to prevent her was being drained away by her speed and decisiveness. He gulped, blinked, tried to make a stand. 'Lady Fosdyke's dinner is quite out of the — ' he began.

But before he could even get his tongue round the word 'question', she had finished the statement for him.

'...ordinary. How very true! What a mind you have! No, no, you need not explain. If you are to finance a replacement for your lost trader you will need capital. That is quite understood. And who better to provide it than Lord Fosdyke, your oldest and most trusted friend? I do understand. You are uncommon wise in these matters and not to be gainsaid. If you wish to attend the dinner I shall do nothing to dissuade you. You may depend upon it. I will see to everything on the instant. Leave all to me.'

Which, warmed by her compliments, stunned into acquiescence by the speed of her strategy, and in such confusion that he even forgot about breakfast, he did.

Five

Having decided to start her search the minute the Bradburys were out of the house, Suki was taut with impatience to see the back of them. She and Bessie stood on the bench below the kitchen window and watched every movement so as to speed their departure, but it didn't do any good.

The trouble was that three chairs had arrived on the pavement simultaneously, and when Sir George and Lady Bradbury emerged from the house in full fig and ready to be assisted into their transport, Lady Bradbury took exception to such abundance and declared that the third chair was not required and had better be off. That provoked a spitting argument between the bearers, none of whom would admit to the indignity of being the third chair. Jessup ran frantically in and out of the house, coughing his embarrassed cough — krrum, kr-krrum — and the mistress ordered one chair after another to be 'on its way' without any of the bearers taking the least bit of notice, and so much time passed without movement it was as if they'd all been glued to the road. Finally the master threw a handful of coins on to the pavement and roared, and that seemed to settle the matter, for after a scramble only two chairs remained.

Bessie and Suki watched as two pairs of elegant silk stockings climbed inelegantly aboard, Jessup was sent running yet again for 'my dear darling Benjy' and returned with a snarling bundle under one arm and a new yellow stain all dowm one white stocking, and at last they were gone.

Cook gave a cheer. 'About time too,' she said. 'I never knew such a long-winded lot. Still they'm gone now, me dears, an' that's the main thing. The cats are away, the mice can play. I'm off out.'

She wasn't the only one, for the two senior servants had the same idea. Mr Jessup was gone so quickly he practically followed his master down the road, his yellow-stained legs scissoring past the area window, swishing with urgency. And the very next moment, Mrs Sparepenny swept from her parlour in her best bonnet and her smart pelisse to announce that she too was off 'to the Pump Room to take the waters'.

'The rest of you may visit as you please,' she said to her assembled staff, frowning her displeasure as Bessie and Suki scrambled down from the bench, 'now you've stopped gawping. You may visit, as I say, providin' you are discreet about it and providin' you make certain sure to be back in this kitchen in time to prepare the supper. A cold collation, Cook, if you please. Suki will watch the house, being she can't walk abroad with a baby to keep within doors.' And with that she left them.

Oh will I? Suki thought, her face mutinous. That's all *you* know, Mistress Sparepenny. I arn't stayin' here twiddlin' my thumbs all precious afternoon. Not me. But at that point her thoughts froze into her head because she was so shocked at what she was seeing. Cook was undressing, actually removing her clothes, right there in front of them all. Lawks a' mercy! She an't takin' that skirt right off, surely to goodness. But she was. Within seconds, she stood before them stripped to her chemise, with the wicker frame of her two side panniers protruding on either side of her petticoats like two great bird cages.

'Now,' she said happily, 'to the vittles.' And she grinned at Suki's widened eyes. 'You watch gal, an' you'll see the full beauty of the new fashion. I'm off to me sister's to see what I can do to help the poor soul.' And walking to the larder she produced two iron meat hooks and attached them to the top rung of her false hips. 'Ham to the right and mutton to the left,' she announced suspending the remains of the two joints on the hooks, 'and no one a penny the wiser when I leaves the house.' She winked at her fellow servants. Take what you will, me dears, providin' 'tis hid.' And as Suki was still looking surprised, ''Tis only an extension of vails, me dear, when all's said an' done. If we may stand with our hands out for money when the guests take departure, then I'm certain sure we mav take the leftovers when they deigns to leave the house. 'Twould only go to wrack an' ruin, an' we don't want that.'

The other servants needed no encouragement. The kitchen was already a blur of activity, as dishes were clattered down upon the table, skirts whisked, feet trampled and kicked, and rough hands scrabbled for the best pickings. Broken pies disappeared into pockets, chunks of bread and oily pats of butter were secreted in a basket full of soiled linen, Hepzibah hacked lumps of sugar from the loaf and hid them in her skirt pockets, Barnaby grabbed up the last of the comfits and stuffed them into the pocket of his waistcoat with such force that he split the seam, even eggs were being seized, wrapped in a kerchief and tucked into a pleated bodice, whether they cracked or no. Within seconds the table had been cleared of all the choicest leavings and Cook was sailing from the room, her skirt replaced and her panniers swinging heavily on either side of her.

'Take what you will, me dear,' she said to Suki as she passed. 'You too, Bessie.'

'There arn't a deal left,' Suki told her. But her purloining mentor was already out of the door.

The kitchen was so quiet they could hear the coals shifting in the grate. Now, Suki thought, once Bessie's taken herself off wherever she's a-goin', I can get out an' find the Captain. Come on gal, shift your shanks.

But Bessie didn't seem to be in any great hurry to leave. She was eating the last crumbs of the pie, gathering them from the plate with a damp finger and licking them up as though they were a great delicacy. She'll have to be urged, Suki thought. I'll move that plate for a start.

'What you goin' to do, Bessie?' she asked, lifting the offending dish.

Bessie was vague. 'Dunno. But you can go out if you like. You got fam'ly hereabouts, ain'tcher? What I means to say is, there's no need for you to stay indoors. I'll look after the house.'

It was such an unexpected offer that Suki was shamed by it. 'Will you?' she said. 'That's uncommon land.'

'I don' mind,' Bessie told her. 'I ain't got no fam'ly to visit. Not here, least ways. Well, not anywhere really. Never 'ave 'ad. Not that I knows of.'

Suki was already lifting her bonnet from its hook by the door but at that she paused and turned to look at Bessie's round honest face, moved from shame to sympathy. 'None at all?' she asked.

'Not that I knows of,' Bessie repeated. She didn't sound particularly concerned about it. 'I'm a norpheen. Lived on the streets afore I got took on by milady when they come up to London. Lucky to get the place, really.'

The news came as no surprise to Suki. Despite her round face, Bessie looked like an orphan. She had the sort of scraggy hair you would expect on a child uncared for, her wrists were thin as twigs, she was a deal too small for her age, and always hungry. Poor little thing, she thought, and here I am trying to get rid of her. And she changed her mind at once and rushed to make amends.

'Look'ee here,' she said. 'I'm off to town to find my...' She'd nearly said 'husband' but checked herself just in time. What a nuisance lying is! '...brother. You can come with me if you like. I can take the babba on my back. He'm sound asleep. House don't need lookin' after.'

So the two young women set off together, with William sleeping and secure in Suki's shawl.

''Twon't take no more'n a minute,' Suki promised, happily, as they stepped out into the parade. 'He'm bound to be somewhere hereabouts.'

But that afternoon Bath was not the easiest place for a search. The narrow thoroughfares were quarrelsome with chairs and carriages and it was oppressively hot, the air full of dust and the pavements brown stained and sticky as though they'd been smeared with treacle. They struggled through the traffic in Pierrepoint Street and pushed their way into the great square before the abbey, where Suki peered in through the long windows of the Pump Room in case the Captain was taking the waters. But there were so many people squashed inside that all she could see were rows of fat rumps and scores of red faces with their mouths open, and she was afraid that if she stood there staring too long, she might come face to face with Mrs Sparepenny.

So she and Bessie pressed on into the complications of the high street, which was a very uncomfortable place indeed, for here the citizens were out in force, come to haggle over the stale loaves and dusty pies still on offer, and they had no intention of allowing anyone else to beat them to a bargain, however tawdry. The two young women were pushed against rough arms and rigid backs, buffeted by baskets, struck by canes, hemmed in by bad breath and sour sweat at every turn, until Bessie declared that she was bruised all over and Suki grew fearful for her baby's safety.

But at last they reached the first coffee house that Suki could remember and elbowed their way in. It was full of gallants all drinking coffee in the most stylish way they could contrive and making the loudest conversation. None of them took any notice of Suki at all and it took several minutes before she could attract the attention of a waiter. He was in a rush and very short with her. No, he didn't know the Captain and he certainly wasn't open to carrying any messages.

'Do I look like a fee'd post?' he said haughtily, adding, 'An' if you don't mean to sample the merchandise you got no reason to occupy no space, so I'll wish you good afternoon — if you'd be so obliging.'

'Never mind,' Suki said stoutly when she and Bessie were out on the pavement again. 'There'm plenty of other places. Can't expect to strike lucky first time.'

'Is he a seafaring man an' all?' Bessie asked.

Suki wasn't paying attention. 'What?'

'Your brother,' Bessie said patiently. 'You called him the Capting. I mean your husband's at sea, ain't he? I mean, are they on the same ship?'

'Oh,' Suki understood. 'No. They're on different ships. My brother's...' What could she say her brother was? This lying was terribly complicated. '...on a trader. Come on, let's go in here.'

But although she tried every coffee house in the area and was either ignored or scowled upon because she didn't buy the wares, nobody could help her. Some of the waiters admitted that they knew Captain Jack, but none of them knew where he was. The nearest she got to any information was the grudging admission by one coffee housekeeper that he hadn't seen the young gentleman since last season and wished he could, bein' he was owed a great deal of money. She trailed back to the abbey, footsore and thirsty and heavily disappointed.

The abbey clock was striking half past four. They'd been out of the house for two hours and ten minutes and every one of them wasted. Now William was awake and making grumbling noises to show that he was ready to be fed. If she didn't attend to him there and then he would begin to cry and she couldn't bear that, after dragging the poor little thing all over town.

'Are we a-goin' home?' Bessie said hopefully. ''Tis horrible dark. I think there's a storm brewin' up. Wouldn't surprise me. Didn't we oughter go home? I mean, we don't want to be out in a storm.'

Yes, Suki thought, we should. She'm right. Heavy clouds were already massing behind the tall frontage of the abbey and the air was prickly. But she couldn't stop now. Not when she hadn't found out where he was. 'Twould be admitting defeat. And she wouldn't be beat. 'I'll feed him first,' she decided. 'Then we'll see. We'll go to the Orange Grove. 'Twill be quieter there.'

Which it was, for although there were still plenty of people about, taking the air between the orange trees or standing in carefully posed elegance to converse with their friends, many more had cast a weather eye at the clouds and were heading home.

The two girls found a quiet spot beneath an orange tree and the baby was fed. As always, suckling eased Suki back to contentment and renewed her optimism.

'What appetite you got, my 'andsome,' she said, admiring the little thing. 'No wonder you'm a-growin'.' And the baby paused to smile at her, patting her breast with one chubby hand.

'You *do* love 'im, don'tcher,' Bessie said, watching them enviously.

Suki answered without thinking. 'Well course I do. He's my babba.' And then remembered.

'Not really though,' Bessie corrected, her round face solemn. 'I mean ter say, he's Lady Bradbury's really, ain't 'e?'

Suki explained at once, her heart tugged fearful by how easy it was to make a mistake. 'I feeds him, so that makes 'im as good as mine. Don't it, my little lovely.'

The baby smiled again but Bessie went on worrying about the problem. 'You'll have ter give 'im back when's he's weaned though, won't yer.'

'I'll face that when I comes to it,' Suki said shortly. But even the thought of having to give him back was stabbing her with anguish again. Oh, she'd *got* to find the Captain. She'd simply got to. She couldn't cope with this on her own. But where could he be?

'I wish I could have a baby,' Bessie confided. 'Be married an' everything. Little place ter live. I s'pose you'll settle down somewhere nice when your husband comes home. Place a' yer own. Must be lovely.'

This is getting worse and worse, Suki thought, and looked around wildly for a way of changing the subject. 'What's that dirty old beggar doing over there?' she said, feigning outrage. 'We don't want beggars in the orange grove. 'Tain't seemly.'

He was squatting under the next tree and having tipped his takings into his hat, he'd pushed up the dirty bandage that was usually wrapped round his eyes and was examining the coins, biting the ones he wasn't sure about.

Bessie was horrified. 'Artful of thing!' she exclaimed. 'I seen him by the abbey, many's the time. I thought he was blind. With all them bandages an' all. I felt sorry for him, poor blind beggar I thought, an' now look at him, he can see as well as you an' me.'

'Beggars are up to all sorts of tricks,' Suki said. 'I can remember one used to sit outside the Dog an' Ducat picking his sores open with a skewer.' She remembered the man and the place so clearly and the Captain saying, 'Tis a fine place for gaming. You could win a fortune there,' and she wondering what it would be like inside. The memory swung her spirits high again. A gaming house. Why hadn't she thought of it before? He was parlously fond of gambling. They'd be bound to know where he was in a place like that. 'I've thought of somewhere else to look,' she said to Bessie.

'Tis gettin' monstrous dark,' Bessie said nervously. By now, the clouds were the colour of black grapes and pressing down heavily upon them. 'We don't want our babby to get drenched.' No, we don't, Suki thought, but I got to find his daddy. 'Come on,' she urged, lacing her bodice. 'One more port of call. That's all. I really know where to find him this time.'

Bessie wasn't convinced. 'Is it far?'

It was on the southernmost edge of town, down by the south gate, where the beggars slept. 'No distance at all,' Suki lied. 'If we look sharp, we can be there an' back before the rain so much as starts.'

The walk took nearly ten minutes and brought them to the most insalubrious part of the town where the air was foul and the noise deafening, for the narrow street was teeming with people, most of them shouting at the tops of their voices, and heaped with rubbish, from broken carts and baskets to dead cats and piles of horse shit. But at least the old tavern was easy to find because it was the biggest building in the street. Unfortunately, and rather unexpectedly, there was a doorman standing guard at the entrance and the doorman didn't know who the Captain was and had no intention of letting Suki in to find him.

'Tain't no place for the likes of you,' he said. 'Get you off home before the storm starts. Anyways, you can't take a babby into a place like this.'

Suki stood her ground. 'Why not?'

''Twouldn't be seemly.'

'My friend'll look after him,' Suki said, unwinding her shawl and signalling to Bessie that she was to take him. 'I won't cause the least bit of bother. Just let me see if he'm there, that's all I ask. You could allow that, surely to goodness. I could be in and out again in a two shakes of a lamb's tail. They won't even see me.'

'Be the devil to pay if they do,' the doorman said. 'I'd go straight on 'ome, if I was you. You don't want your eyes scratched out, now do you? Pretty lady like you.' His face was wrinkled with concern for her safety and anxiety for his job. But there were three gallants picking their way through the filth towards him and he had to attend to them too. If I may take your canes gentlemen, if you please.'

'I got to give him some money,' Suki persisted, as the men were ushered in. He'd understand money. Doormen always did. 'He's sent for it, d'you see. That's all 'tis. Twon't take a minute. I could be in and out like greased lightning.'

He was harassed and uncertain but in the end he gave in to her badgering. What else could he do? He'd been hired to handle drunken men not headstrong women, and this one was so determined and so prettily aggressive, with those red cheeks and that thick dark hair. 'Two shakes then,' he agreed. 'An' make sure that's all 'tis.'

She was gone before he'd finished speaking.

It was dark inside the tavern, for the curtains were drawn and few candles lit, so it took a second or so for her eyes to adjust to the lack of light, but even before she could see properly, she realized that this was no mere gaming house, that the doorman had been right and that she'd made a very serious mistake to push her way in. The room was suffocatingly hot and smelled strongly of sweat and sex. She recognized at once that there was a threat here, and danger, and then her eyes cleared and she knew — although she'd never been in such a place in her life — that she had stumbled into a whorehouse and that the sooner she got out again the better.

Luckily, nobody seemed to have noticed her entrance. They were all too absorbed in what was going on. In one corner of the room, two slatternly women were playing instruments — one a lute, the other a drum — and standing on a wooden tray in the centre of the table. And a third woman was dancing, gyrating slowly and vaguely in time to the wailing tune, and gradually unwinding herself from her clothes as she turned. Her leather stays, dirt black in the candle light, had been slung across a chair, and her grubby stockings lay like discarded snake skins at her feet. Now she was lifting her petticoats slowly and tantalizingly, swaying a plump white leg at her clients, and revealing the occasional temptation of a pitted thigh.

All around the table men watched with lecherous anticipation, their eyes moist and their mouths agape, while the other whores plied them with drink and picked their easy pockets, and allowed them to take what liberties they'd paid for. A skinny servant scuttled in the shadows gathering up empty glasses and being goosed for her pains, and the madame sat in the midst of the company, memorising the money as it changed hands. A hard, calculating, dangerous woman, Suki thought, appreciating the doorman's warning, and she looked round quickly to check that her exit was clear. There was no point in searching for the Captain in a place like this. He would never make one in such horrible company. And neither would his friends.

But she was wrong. She'd barely taken two steps towards the door when she caught sight of a face she recognized, the shrewd dark face of a man with a deal of black stubble on his chin and a velvet patch over his left eye. She couldn't put a name to him, but he was certainly one of the Captain's friends and sitting with two or three others she thought she recognized too. Was there time to ask him? Did she dare? The madame was watching a man in an embroidered jacket. If she was quick about it, she might just...

'Beg pardon,' she said, stepping towards the group and speaking in the lowest voice she could manage. 'But do any of you know where Captain Jack is? I got a message for him.'

The eye nearest her focused with some difficulty and she realized that the man was rather drunk. 'Who'sat, Charlie?' he asked his.friends. 'What she say?'

'One of the Captain's wenches,' the man called Charlie explained. 'Ain't you my luscious lovely?' His voice was slurred with drink and he was leeringly amorous, lurching at her, hands outstretched to grab, his breath rank with garlic and wine. She dodged his hands but humoured him because he might be useful. 'That's right,' she agreed. 'You seen 'im have you?'

'Ain't seen *that* worthy for nigh on six months,' the third man told her. 'In Lonnon *I* reckon. Take another lover, my charmer. Plenty here be happy to oblige you.'

Suld looked at their grimy linen and their ugly, seamed faces and shuddered inwardly, but kept smiling nevertheless. 'Arn't he comin' to Bath this season?' she asked.

'Don' look like it,' Charlie said. 'Come an' sit with us, my pretty. We'm a sight better than the Captain. Love you an' leave you, 'e would.'

'Can't do that,' Suld said, avoiding him again. What parlous rough hands he do have! 'I'm with my mistress.'

'Wish I was,' Charlie grinned, nudging his companion in the ribs.

'Should you see him, sir, would you tell him Suki was asking for him. Say I need to speak with him. Tell him 'tis important.'

'Anythin' else?' the man asked sarcastically.

'Tell him he'm a father. Tell him he got a son.' And she suddenly remembered the name of the man with the eye-patch. 'You will, won't you, Mr Cutpurse?'

Quin Cutpurse was instantly sober and annoyed to be addressed by his name. 'Get rid of her, Charlie,' he ordered. 'Afore there's trouble.'

Charlie's tone changed too. 'Hop it!' he ordered. 'You heard what he said.'

She persisted. 'You'll tell him then, won't you, Charlie?'

He took her by the shoulders and swung her body towards the door. 'He'll be here for the fair,' lie said, speaking low and close to her ear. 'Promised me, as a sworn brother, so he did. But that's all I'm a-telling you. Now go, if you know what's good for you.'

It was too late. As she ran towards the door, eager to escape, her way was blocked by the newest arrivals, three staggeringly drunken young men who, being still dazzled by daylight, reached out for the nearest female flesh to hand. For the second time that afternoon she found herself being mauled by clumsy fingers and, although she struggled away, her denial took her straight into difficulty. Being thwarted, the gallants protested loudly and at that the harlots took notice and protested too, and the madame rose to her feet, saw a stranger in their midst, and was instantly foul-mouthed with fury.

'Who sent that bawdy basket here to queer our pitch?' she roared. 'You stay in yer own scalding house, if you please! Artie! Artie! Throw this dirty piss-kitchen out the winder!'

'I was only looking for my brother,' Suki tried to explain, but it was no use. An enormous blackamoor filled the doorway. He wore a formidable cutlass and looked as if he could break bones by just leaning on them, so when he took her shoulder in his huge hand she went meekly where she was guided, and without another word, praying that he would simply lead her to the door and let her go without damage.

'We don't want none of you skains-mates in this house!' the dancer called after her, and her patrons cheered her, sliding their unsteady fingers up her skirts.

Out in the street, Bessie was sitting by the wall dangling the baby in her lap. The storm had broken at last and large drops of rain were falling, making dark coin-sized circles on her skirt and bodice. She looked up in horror as the blackamoor threw Suki forward out of the door and, seeing her, Suki suddenly felt weak to tears. She'd been manhandled and shouted at, and she still didn't know where the Captain was, only that he'd be at the fair, if that man was to be believed, and that was more than a week away. And now her darling was getting wet and she and Bessie would be scolded for being late back and heaven knows what Lady Bradbury would say if she knew she had taken the baby out into town again.

'We'll have to run,' she said, as she took him. 'We'll go round the side roads. They'm not so crowded.' And she settled the child into her shawl, tied it firmly and set off at once.

'Did you find him?' Bessie asked, trotting along behind her.

'Not in there,' Suki said. ''Twas a fearsome place. A whorehouse. I wish I'd never gone in.'

Bessie's eyes were as round as the rain spots on her bodice. 'My lor!'

Suki quickened her pace, pushing past a woman with a broken barrow who was scavenging among the rubbish heaped against the walls. The thunder rolled and grumbled above their heads and there was such a racket in the street that at first she wasn't aware that someone was calling her, 'Mistress! Mistress! Wait for me!' But after a while, as the voice grew more insistent and people seemed to be looking her way, she turned to see what was going on.

It was the skivvy from the brothel and she was running to catch up with them, waving and calling. 'Mistress! Do wait!'

Bessie looked a question at her, but Suki didn't stop to think. They were so late already they might as well be hung for a sheep as a lamb. So they waited.

'Not meaning to butt in or nothink,' the child said as she reached them, 'but you was arskin' fer the Captain, wasn't yer?' And she rubbed her nose with the back of one chapped hand and looked at them hopefully.

'Yes,' Suki said at once. Could she know anything? Was it possible? 'You don't know where he is, do you?'

'Used ter come in a lot onst,' the urchin said. 'En't seen 'im this year though. I should try Mrs Roper's, if I was you. That's where he stayed last time. Nowhere Lane. On the comer by the King's Arms. I thought you'd like to know.'

Suki didn't stop to consider the implications of the fact that a servant in a brothel knew where to find her Captain. It was enough that she had been given an address. After all this effort, she knew where to find him. At last! 'Thank'ee kindly,' she said to the child and searched in her pocket for a coin to reward her with. All her money was gone except for a farthing, and that seemed very little for such wealth. But the skivvy took it with delight.

'Ta ever so,' she said. 'That's handsome.' Then she wiped her nose again, straightened her cap and was gone.

'Well, fancy that!' Bessie said.

'Yes,' Suki said, smiling with the delight of it. 'Nowr we must run or we shall certain be late.' But being late didn't matter any more. The thunder didn't matter any more. There was no harm in the rain. No harm in anything. Hope shone through the rainclouds like a six-pointed star. He could be in Bath any day, she might find him at the theatre, or see him at the fair, or Quin Cutpurse might tell him, or that man Charlie, and failing all else she had his address.

Six

The three horsemen were waiting, sitting out the storm, as still as statues at the top of a rise above the Bristol Road. From time to time, lightning silhouetted their watchfulness against a lurid skyline; the wind whipped their cloaks until they cracked like sails; the incessant rain stung their faces, obscured their vision, made their horses twitch sodden flanks, but they sat on, menacing and patient, watching the road — waiting for their quarry. Quin Cutpurse, Charlie Moss and Captain Jack.

'Here's another,' Charlie called into the wind.

A bedraggled carriage toiled round the bend in the road, hauled by two horses, both blowing and mud-spattered and struggling to keep their balance in the mud. The driver sat huddled into his cape, his whip heavy with water and, as they laboured on, another roll of thunder made the lead horse flinch and stumble. To the watchers' delight, the carriage gave a lurch to the right, tipped a little, seemed about to fall, steadied and stopped.

'Likely?' Charlie yelled into the wind.

Quin grunted. 'Possible,' he allowed, brushing the rain from his one sharp eye. 'Hold your horse.'

The carriage door swung open and a stout man pounced out, plainly in a temper. They could hear him shouting, even above the noise of the storm. ''Od's bowels! Now what?' Then the coachman climbed down too and the pair of them trudged through the mud to inspect one of the nearside wheels.

'Sitting ducks,' Charlie shouted, gathering the reins ready for a charge down the hill. 'Are we game, Jack?'

But Quin held up his hand. 'Wait,' he ordered, as the two dark figures stooped towards the coach. The stout man was removing his hat and cloak. He rolled them into a bundle and tossed them into the coach. 'On his own,' Quin observed, 'or he'd not have done that. On his own and not a rich man.'

'How can you tell dammit?' Charlie complained.

The stout man was stooping again, wedging his shoulder against the wheel, gathering his strength ready to push. 'Wears fustian,' Quin said, still watching closely. 'Look at his coat. And those breeches. A merchant. In a poor way of trade if I'm any judge. Have you ever seen a rich man put his shoulder to the wheel? No. There'll be poor pickings in that quarter.'

'Devil take it, Quin,' Charlie warned, 'if we let this slip, 'twill be the third tonight. Ain't we to strike at all?'

Quin shrugged. 'Not with this one. The game ain't worth the candle.'

'I'm for hot punch and dry clothes back at the Pelican,' the Captain announced, turning his horse's head. 'We drown here and to no purpose. I told you 'twould never sene. Only a fool would travel in weather as wild as this.' And he was gone before either of his companions could argue to prevent him.

Down on the road the stout man looked up as the last horse disappeared behind the trees. 'Our company's gone,' he observed.

The coachman grinned with relief. 'Aye, Sir George sir, so I sees. Thanks be! For a minute back there I thought we was for it.'

Sir George pushed his coat aside to reveal the pistol tucked into his breeches. 'Never travel without it,' he said, winking at the coachman, 'and I'm an uncommon good shot, let me tell 'ee. Uncommon good. Now then Johnno, one more heave and we shall be clear. Put your back into it. I need to be in Bristol before midnight. 'Tain't the sort of weather to be out of doors.'

The Pelican Inn was cramped, old-fashioned and set much too far back from the road to attract the custom of the regular stagecoaches, so it was an ideal hiding hole for Quin Cutpurse and his dubious associates. The Captain had a low opinion of it, for the rooms were dark and riddled with fleas and the mattresses stuffed with straw and scratchily uncomfortable, but having been ordered out of town, he had a poor choice of accommodation and had taken it on Quin's suggestion and for lack of anything better. At least the food was passable, the drink swiftly served and there was a barmaid to admire him whenever he glanced in her direction. He'd learned young that an amorous look was the easiest way to sweeten service. The canary punch he'd ordered as he strode into the snug was standing by the fire waiting for him when he came down the stairs, dried and dressed in his usual fine clothes.

He threw himself down on the settle alongside the fire, draped one leg over the arm with the sole of his boot towards the flames, and signalled to the barmaid that she should pour the first three tankards. He and his friends had the room to themselves, except for a gentleman in an old-fashioned brown bob wig and a very antiquated coat who was sitting quietly in the far corner drinking ale and doing his accounts in a small notebook — plainly not a man of any consequence.

'You'll not prise me out again tonight, Quin Cutpurse,' he said after a long draught of the hot liquid, 'not if you plead till you're blue in the face. I intend to stay here and drink punch till I'm as dry as hay in sunshine.' And he held up his tankard to be refilled.

'Amen to that,' Charlie agreed, as the steam rose from his boots and breeches.

'Never mind hay,' Quin teased them, 'you're men of straw, damme if you ain't. No bottom, either the one of you.'

Captain Jack gave him a lazy smile, accepting his insult for the compliment they both knew it was, for if his companions understood nothing else about him, two things were certain, he was undeniably courageous and uncommon handsome. More than six feet tall, his face bold to the point of insolence, with dark almond-shaped eyes under determined brows, an aristocratic nose, a fine head of thick dark hair and the easy elegance of the long-limbed, he caught attention wherever he went — and dressed to catch it. Now, in his black breeches and his claret coat, with the white ruffles of his shirt framing his long hands and the embroidery on his cream silk waistcoat rich in the firelight, he looked like a member of the ton out for an evening to sample the low life. But his suavity was deceptive. His past was burdened with too much pain for him to care to remember it, and since he had no prospects and no hope of inheritance, there was no future for him to look forward to, so he lived in the present, dancing from moment to moment, motivated by profit and pleasure and with no thought for consequences.

'I'll tell 'ee what, Quin,' he said. 'Your milord was a man of linsey woolsey.'

'How so?' Quin asked, preparing himself to enjoy the joke.

'He dursn't travel in the rain for fear of shrinking.'

'Now that's true, Jack,' Charlie chortled. 'Uncommon true, an' he's an arrant knave to boot.'

'I'd boot him if he were here,' Jack said, happily. 'For here's two hours of my time gone to waste on his account and not a penny made and if that don't deserve a good kicking, tell me what does.'

'He'll be on the road by first light,' Quin predicted easily. 'We shall pick him off then, I guarantee.'

'And then on to Bristol,' Charlie said, returning to his drink. 'Ain't that right, Quin?'

'Bristol it is,' Quin agreed. 'What about you Jack? Shall you come with us?'

Jack considered the invitation, as the coals shifted and the man in the bob wig wrote scratchily.

'I shall follow you, as soon as I may,' he said. 'I've a mind to see a play.'

'And a deal else besides eh, you rogue?' Charlie teased.

'I'm not a man to turn down a good offer,' Jack agreed.

That nudged Quin's memory.

'Saw a wench of yours this afternoon,' he said, pressing tobacco into his clay pipe.

Jack wasn't interested. He smiled languidly, 'Like enough.'

'Don't you want to know which one?'

'Not particularly. All cats are grey in the dark.'

'Not this feline,' Quin Cutpurse told him. ''Twas a handsome wench. A pearl. Red cheeks. Dark eyes. Fine pair of titties on her, as I recall.' He recalled, happily, his cheeks flushed by the memory. 'Name of Suki, so she said. A fiery spirit. She'd been searching for you high an' low. Most persistent. On account of you've fathered a child.'

The Captain feigned disinterest. But he ran his hand through his hair and was comforted by how thick and luxurious it felt under his fingers. 'I daresay I've fathered several,' he said casually. 'What o' that? I ain't to be tied. They know that from the outset. I make no bones about it. I'm a free spirit.'

'An eagle,' Charlie admired, having heard him say as much on many occasions.

'Aye. An eagle,' Jack agreed, taking off into his familiar fantasy, 'soaring where no man may touch me, free as the air, a creature of the wild, untrammelled, flying where I will, living as I may.' It was an image that he particularly enjoyed, expressing power, freedom, boundless energy. 'An eagle. If you take my freedom from me, Charlie, I am nothing, tied and bound, a beast of burden, less than a carthorse, an ass, a dog cringing, a skinned cat, dead meat from Smithfield.'

'There's a price for freedom,' Quin pointed out, drawing on his pipe. 'Have you thought o' that when you're a-soaring?'

'What price?' the Captain asked, piqued to be brought down to earth again so soon. 'Freedom is free to my way of thinking.' 'Even an eagle must eat.'

That was acknowledged. 'I have my annuity. When I can persuade the lady to pay it.' The delay this time had been irksome, given the number of creditors pressing.

'Ain't it come yet, Jack?' Charlie asked, half sympathetic, half mocking.

'Promised by Sunday at the latest,' Jack assured them both, 'and if it don't come then I shall return to Bath to collect it in person, damme if I don't.' It was a fine-sounding boast but, even under the gathering fog of the punch, he knew it was beyond his power and the knowledge irritated him, so that he shifted in his seat. 'I've a mind to write and tell her I need more this time. Damme, if I'm a father I've greater expenses to meet.'

'A capital idea!' Charlie encouraged. 'Sting the old skinflint for even penny you can, say I! What's a rich patron for, if she ain't to be skinned?'

Encouragement gave Jack pause. Perhaps he was being foolish. He could hear folly in the words as well as daring. 'I've a mind to,' he repeated, struggling in the tumble of emotions that strong drink always stirred and consequently speaking more boldly this time. 'Why not? She owes me a deal more than she ever condescends to give.' He should have been settled long since with a place in society, not left an annuitant, out on the edge, with no claim to fame or fortune. Alcohol fumes were drifting him into self-pity, which irritated him too because he despised self-pity. He wondered briefly what it would be like to have a family name, to be married with a wife to tend to him whenever he required and children to honour him and a fine house to call his own. 'She don't treat me as I deserve, damme. My grandfather was a Duke.'

'Were he to acknowledge your existence,' Quin said shrewdly, having heard all this before, ''twould be an advantage to you. As it is...'

'Write your billet,' Charlie urged, eager for mischief and more spending money. 'Nothing ventured, nothing gained. I'll fetch pen and paper.'

So the materials were provided and the letter written, in terms a great deal more forceful than they would have been had they all been sober.

Madam,

I have the honour to inform you that being of an age, I intend to marry and to further the family name. (That will rile her, Charlie, depend on it.) In consequence whereof I send to inform you that my present allowance will no longer serve to answer the needs of such an household as I must needs initiate. My affianced bride is well bom (she could be, Quin — 'tain't polite to make such a grimace) and will require an establishment of some note, as befits the wife of a man whose grandfather, I scarce need to remind you, was a Duke and a man of high esteem.

Yours, in happy expectation of an honourable response,

Jack

It was sealed with a dollop of wax and a crash of thunder and laid upon the table with an enhancing sense of achievement.

'There's a carter calls in the morning,' Charlie said, still happily plotting. 'He can carry it. The landlord will see to it if you pay him sufficient.'

'The storm don't abate,' Quin said, from the window. He pulled the curtain aside to peer at the sky. 'I'm for my bed. We've an early start come morning.'

As Jack turned to wish him goodnight, another thought penetrated the thickening fumes of the punch. 'I trust you kept your counsel, this afternoon,' he said. 'You didn't tell the wench where I was.'

'Do you take us for fools?' Charlie grinned. 'I hope we know the score in that quarter. Women are the very devil.' What with excitement and fatigue and having drunk his last tankard rather too quickly, his speech was decidedly slurred. But his sentiments were clear as the purest water.

They gave Captain Jack a moment of equally unblemished pleasure. No matter how ignominiously he was treated elsewhere, how grudgingly his allowance was paid, how often he was sent away as if he were of no consequence, how cruelly his creditors pursued, what black and necessary lies he had to tell, what flea-ridden rooms he was forced to endure, he was part of the brotherhood of the road, the great, trustworthy, honest fraternity of men, who stood together in times of trouble, drank together, fought together, looked out for one another, protected one another from the encumbering wiles of women.

''Predated,' he said. 'Uncommon land of 'ee.'

Seven

By the time Sir George arrived at his brother's house in Bristol that evening, the storm was spent but it was pitch dark and still spitting with rain and, what with arriving much later than he'd intended and having to endure a most uncomfortable journey, he was in an ill temper.

The inside of the carriage was miming with moisture and deucedly uncomfortable, and the horses strained up the hill, blowing with effort as their hooves slipped on the greasy cobbles and steam rose pungently from their wet flanks. Sir George stuck his head out of the window to tell his coachman to urge them on but, after one glance, being a better judge of horses than women, he decided against it. The poor brutes had done all they could to keep their balance. In fact, if it hadn't been such a deucedly inclement night, he would have got out and walked to ease their burden.

Frederick was standing just inside his doorway, holding up a double-headed candlestick, and peering into the darkness, his face peaked with anxiety. He was more than five years younger than Sir George but so slight and stooped and careworn that he looked considerably older.

'Oh, my dear, dear brother!' he said as Sir George strode into the hall, his travelling cloak wrapped about him. 'How glad I am to see you. Come in, come in. You mustn't take cold, my dear feller. Such a night! Did you hear the thunder? I was quite afraid of the consequences. I thought you would be unable to travel, upon my soul.'

Sir George drew himself up to his full height. 'You forget,' he said, 'I have endured three hurricanes.' He had a sudden searing memory of the last one, of the noise and the darkness and the sky screaming, of being stuck to the ground by the force of the wind, unable to shout and barely able to breathe, as the sugar cane was scattered as though it were straw, and his field hands were tossed backwards into the air, their limbs spreadeagled and their faces crazed with shock and terror. Now that *was* a storm. 'This is nothing, believe me. A bagatelle.'

Frederick was impressed but his anxiety continued. 'We've been watching out for you since seven of the clock,' he said. 'This is a sorry business. What is to be done, think'ee?'

'First, I will take a little brandy and hot water,' Sir George said with the air of a man to whom all problems are capable of solution. Enhanced by the memory of his own courage and freed from the smelly constraint of that carriage, he felt better already.

'Yes, yes of course, to be sure,' Frederick agreed, signalling to his housekeeper. 'I've a fire upstairs. Oh what a night! Come in, come in!' And he stooped towards the stairs.

Sir George looked at his younger sibling with sympathy. He was such a poor creature. Frail from childhood. 'All will be well,' he promised. 'You may depend upon it.'

But Frederick had never truly felt that he could depend on anything, even though he'd spent his entire sixty-two years in a vain endeavour to pretend that he could. As a child he had been withdrawn and anxious, as a youth mild-mannered and unobtrusive, so, not surprisingly, he had grown into a man with a marked propensity for unquestioning obedience and a strong sense of family obligation. When his father told him it was his duty to marry and consolidate the family fortunes, he didn't argue even though he had no hope whatever of a happy union. He simply did as he was told. Within two months, he had married his 'suitable' bride and within two years he had fathered two extremely noisy babies, both, fortunately, male. When his brother told him he needed a trusted lieutenant to run the business from the Bristol end, he undertook that too, a great deal more willingly.

Married life had not been at all to his taste, but he'd endured it stoically. The noisy babies grew into noisier boys, who filled his days with rattling toys and asinine babble, and his suitable bride became a garrulous wife, who filled his nights with self-centred gossip, pecking away at his patience like a woodpecker in a nightcap. He answered her as well as he could when a pause in her high-pitched monologue indicated a reply and suffered his headaches without complaint. But it was only outside the house — down at the quayside among men and merchants, with his quick brain making accountancy simple and his dry wit endearing him to the company, or out in the manufactory, wiiere molten cane was poured into cones to become sugarloaf, rum was bottled and syrup and molasses oozed into barrels — that he was himself and happy, providing there were no setbacks or sudden catastrophes. As there were now.

'What is to be done?' he said again, as he led his portly brother up the stairs. 'Such a tragedy! We're ruined, Georgie. Ruined. A third of our trade lost and gone and heaven knows what damage to the trader.' He was so agitated that his wig was askew and he wasn't aware of it. There w'as no order or comfort in his life at all. Even the sight of his well-appointed parlour — with its embroidered fire screens, its well-polished sconces, its two fine windows elegantly curtained against the storm — did nothing to calm him. 'There's no justice in the world. To lose all, Georgie, after all our labour. Oh, there's no justice in the world at all. No justice.'

'Come now, brother,' Sir George teased, as he settled into one of the two chairs drawn up beside the fire. 'You're a widower, ain'tcher. The fates were kind to you in that regard. Envy of the town, so you were, when your lady passed to glory.'

That had to be admitted, although with the familiar residue of shame, for it had all happened so quickly and he'd been so glad of it — a swift fever, a decent period of mourning, his two troublesome boys packed off to boarding school, the sheer relief of his return to bachelorhood. But it was no comfort to him now.

'What is to be done?' he repeated. He was limp with distress, flopping into his own chair and turning his face to the fire. 'We must forego the slave trade now that our slaver is gone, must we not?'

Sir George took command. It was time to put the poor feller out of his misery. On his hideous journey he'd rehearsed all the difficulties Frederick might raise and thought of an answer to almost every' one. Now, as the brandy and water was borne quietly into the room and set carefully before them, he outlined his plan.

'Quite the reverse, brother,' he said. 'We must buy another trader, as soon as we can find one to suit.'

Frederick's eyebrows disappeared into his wig. 'I doubt the wisdom of such an action,' he said worriedly. 'What if 'twere an omen? A sign to desist? Perhaps we should consider it so. 'Tis an uncertain trade at the best of times. Negroes are uncommon poor cattle. Think how many of 'em die.'

'We must take the hazard, brother,' Sir George said, drawing his pipe from his pocket and helping himself to some of his brother's excellent tobacco. 'That's the fact of the matter here. Beggars can't be choosers. If we limit our trade to sugar, we shall cut our profits by a good two-thirds and all hope of growth what's more.'

That was true and had to be admitted. 'But think of the cost of a new ship,' Frederick went on. 'We are fully stretched at this time of year, as I need hardly point out. Would the expense not prove a difficulty?'

'Not an insurmountable one,' his brother said, easily. 'There will be monies from the assurance company.'

Frederick wasn't cheered. 'If you can persuade 'em to pay.'

'Oh, I'll persuade 'em,' Sir George said with cheerful certainty. 'I've uncommon powers of persuasion. The premium was high enough, in all conscience, and certainly high enough to preclude argument.'

'But 'twill take time. 'Tain't a matter to be rushed.'

'Agreed, but meantime there is the cargo to sell which you will doubtless have examined.'

Frederick had, and even in his present pessimistic humour, allowed that it was fair. 'But that will take time too. 'Twill be a month at least before 'tis through the manufactory and we cannot assume that the price of sugar will remain stable.'

'It might rise.'

'A fall is the more likely.'

'Well, rise or fall,' Sir George said, tetchily, 'twill earn a return eventually.'

'But not in time, brother, not in time. That is my point precisely. Even if we find a ship to suit, which is doubtful, 'twill be a month or more before 'tis fit to sail, which takes us to November, and we must allow two months or more at sea, which takes us into February or March, and if we're to catch the trade winds the ship must sail again before May. 'Twill cut too fine. Much too fine, if you want my opinion of it.' He sighed heavily. 'I doubt it can be done.'

'We shall do it,' Sir George said, heavily determined.

'I do not see how,' Frederick said, 'without capital.'

'We will raise a loan.'

Frederick's face wrinkled with increased concern. 'Think of the risk.'

'Hermione will stand guarantor,' George said. 'Her name's good for a thousand or two.'

'We shall need a deal more than that,' Frederick said. The ship alone will cost at least four thousand, at today's prices. Then there's the matter of supplies and a new crew, to say nothing of a new master.' The complications seemed so extreme his mouth was bowed with woriy.

His excessive pessimism was beginning to irritate Sir George. 'Then we will take Mr Smith into the company.'

Frederick's eyebrows disappeared into his wig. 'Is that wise?' Ebenezer Smith was a minor banker with ambitions and had been eager to join the company for several years. 'I've never liked the man, as you well know.'

'He's mercenary, I'll grant you that. And slippery. And pernickety. But he's got ready money, which is what we need.'

'He ain't to be trusted,' Frederick warned him. 'I ain't forgot the matter of the trust fund last year. If he's to join us I hope you will set limits. Two years at the very most.'

'Leave all to me,' Sir George said. 'I will undertake to raise the capital, if you will hire the crew and buy in supplies and suchlike. Courage, man. We ain't beat yet. Between us we shall work wonders. Look on the bright side.'

But Frederick sagged into his chair and wouldn't brighten.

''Tis in my nature to foresee difficulties,' he confessed.

'And in mine to forestall 'em,' his brother said. 'I shall have a ship by noon a' Saturday, or my name ain't George Bradbury. We will start first thing tomorrow morning.'

They set off on their search extremely early, after a sustaining breakfast had been silently served to them and Frederick had given his housekeeper the most careful instructions as to their exact requirements for dinner.

'Meals are the lynchpin of the day,' he explained to his brother as they left the house and walked down the hill towards the buzz and pulse of the harbour and the forest of masts that filled Broad Quay. 'If we are nourished by good food, our quest will not appear so arduous.'

But well-fed or not, it was a lengthy process, for Sir George had a merchantman's approach to buying and selling and examined every ship on offer from figurehead to bowsprit, hull timbers, deck timbers, masts, sails, rudder, rigging and all, working on the cynical assumption that he was sure to be cheated if he were not excessively cautious; while Frederick, methodical as always, kept a pencil behind his ear and wrote a precis in his pocket notebook of everything that was discussed.

The first ship, which they found at the head of Broad Quay, was trim enough but too small to carry the size of cargo they needed to make a profit. The second was a three-masted frigate called the *Yorick*. She was in excellent order and capacious, with an impressive array of canvas, but the asking price of £3,700, was beyond their range.

'I've a mind to put a reserve on her, notwithstanding,' Sir George said, as he and his brother took a stroll to consider. 'She could be just the vessel for the consortium and they could withstand the cost. What think 'ee?'

Frederick muttered and was unconvinced. 'We've expense enough, in all conscience. Tell him we'll consider and let him know our minds in a day or two. That should suffice. There are other ships to see.'

But the third on offer was a scruffy, ill-kempt hulk and not seaworthy, although its owner did his best to persuade them that all could be 'made good' with the application of 'a little tar'.

'Does he take us for fools?' Frederick said, as they clomped across the cobbles.

'The feller's either a rogue or a villain,' Sir George growled. 'It don't compare with the *Yorick* and that you *will* allow.'

By this time the sun was up and the day's business well under way, the quayside lively with merchants come to oversee their own cargoes and to survey the prospects of their competitors, and the road busy with innumerable horse-drawn sleds, laden with rum barrels and rolls of cotton.

The Bradbury brothers were hailed on every side as they made their way through the bustle. The noise was as loud as a manufactory, as barrels were rolled on to the quayside, carts racketed over the cobbles, men swore and spat, factors yelled instructions, and innumerable dogs, who'd come to sniff out a possible meal, yelped and howled as they were kicked away from the action.

Above the river, the green slopes of Brandon Hill rose invitingly, their fine new houses clean and quiet above the cacophony of the quay.

'Twill soon be dinner time, I think,' Frederick suggested, gazing up at his own house, longingly.

But Sir George was eager to go on. According to an advertisement on the quayside, there was another likely ship down on the Frome, a three-masted brig, called the *Bonny Beaufoy*, newly back from the Indies. 'We've sufficient time to inspect her before we dine. Well take a ferryboat. Twill be easier than pushing through the streets.'

'You may be right, brother,' Frederick tried to remonstrate, 'but would it not be more politic... The backs can be uncommon noisesome in summer...'

He was wasting his breath, for Sir George had already found a ferryman. There was nothing for it but to take his place in the stem of the boat and make shift to protect himself from the stench by covering his nose and mouth with his linen kerchief.

It was exceptionally bad that morning, for it was neap tide and the waters of the Frome were low. As they passed the long rows of rickety shacks that backed on to the river, they could see and smell that the wooden privies that protruded from every ramshackle gallery were so high above the waterline that they hadn't been washed out for a very long time. Frederick burrowed his nose deep into the scented folds of his kerchief but it was no use. Within seconds he was retching.

'Have the goodness to make better speed,' he begged the ferryman.

'We're here sir, an't please you,' the feriyman said. 'That's the *Bonny Beaufoy*, over there.'

It was a rather smaller ship than they'd expected and directly downwind of the shanties.

'Should we not defer our examination until a more propitious time,' Frederick said hopefully. 'It grows late. We shall be expected for dinner.' And when George made a grimace at him. 'I must be mindful of my constitution. I ain't as young as I was.'

'You may be as old as you like,' Sir George teased him, paying the ferryman, 'I ain't turning back now. Not when we've come so far. She's a sturdy vessel.'

'She ain't got the capacity, if you want my opinion of it.'

And so it proved, although, after an interminable inspection, it passed muster in every other respect. A price of £2,400 was suggested and bartered down to £2,150. Then the Bradburys announced that they would 'think on it' and retired to the first hostelry beyond the stench, so that Frederick could calm his stomach with a glass of Hollands.

He was still unsure about the purchase. 'If we take a full complement of negroes,' he warned, 'there will be inadequate space for supplies.'

That is a problem capable of resolution,' Sir George said. 'Ten per cent will die on the crossing. They are poor cattle. You said so yourself. So we will cut supplies by twelve per cent, instruct the master to adjust their rations according and wait for nature to do the rest.'

'How if more survive?'

Then they'll survive lean. We can fatten 'em up for market when they get to the other side.' And when his brother grimaced. They're only savages, dammit. They don't feel pain like civilized men. Would a farmer waste good hay on sick stock? They'd be off to the slaughterhouse within the hour, or to the knacker's yard, depend on it.'

'Tis a risky stratagem, in all conscience.'

'Not a bit of it,' Sir George said, forcefully. 'With a good master 'twill present no problems at all.'

'Well, well,' Frederick said, returning to his gin, 'you may be right. Howsomever, there is still the capital to raise and that *will* present problems I fear.'

''Tis as good as done,' Sir George bragged.

In fact it took him until late on Saturday afternoon to persuade the Merstham Assurance Company to agree that a settlement would be proper and possible and might even be payable within the month, and well into the evening to coax the bankers to provide the sum he needed for the initial deposit. And there was still the matter of the crew's wages, and the initial cargo of guns and cloth and so forth, which could run them into total costs of over £27,000. There was nothing for it but to approach Mr Smith.

The two men met by the nails on Sunday morning and it was an even more difficult meeting than Sir George had anticipated, for the banker moved into the attack with his opening words.

'I hear commiserations are in order, sir,' he said. 'You lost a slaver to the Frenchies, I'm told.'

Sir George countered boldness with boldness. 'Plague on 'em, so I did sir. But there's another bought and commissioned.'

'I'm glad to hear it,' the banker said, his expression sour.

No class at all, Sir George thought, looking at the man's sharp face, his cheap black suit, his brown wig tied with a bombazine ribbon, besides being untrustworthy. 'As a matter of fact, sir, we are looking to expand. Might take on another partner, don'tcher know. We're testin' the water.'

The offer had been made, as they both realised.

'Well, as to that, I've a deal on hand at the moment,' the banker said.

The conversation embarked on its familiar carousel, both men pretending scant interest, both sharply aware of the potential hazards and the potential profits.

'I've had a mind to enter the slave trade for some months,' Mr Smith said after five minutes, 'as you and your brother are aware. Were I to do so now, however, I should need some particular inducements, given the parlous state of seas around the sugar islands vis-a-vis French intervention and suchlike.'

'We are men of business, sir,' Sir George assured him. 'We can come to some arrangement.'

What they came to, after more than an hour's bargaining, was an agreement that Mr Smith was to become a member of the company for the next two years, was to fund one-third of the enterprise in exchange for one-third of the profits, and was, in addition, to be allowed to sail on the *Bonny Beaufoy* as its purser with full control of all monies while he was on board and to be given his choice of three slaves at the time of their purchase.

Sir George demurred at that, for if the purser were to be offered three slaves the master would expect the same number. 'Two is customary,' he pointed out, 'and would be more appropriate.'

Mr Smith persisted, narrowing his eyes and tightening his lips. 'I would expect three.'

'Then, sir, we must make some alteration of your percentage profit in lieu. Bait the hook with money and the fish will leap.'

Mr Smith considered. Having won on all points so far, he could afford to back down. Sir George, sensing a possible victor, pressed on. 'All expenditure is known aboard ship,' he said. 'A balance has to be maintained, as I'm sure you can appreciate.' And waited.

'Two slaves and the profits to remain as agreed,' the banker decided at last.

So the bargain was struck on the nail and the two men shook hands, both having saved sufficient face to claim themselves the victory.

Then there was nothing more for Sir George to do except meet the vendor, this time outside the Exchange in Corn Street and this time with money in his pocket. It was another hard bargain but at last the price was agreed, the capital provided and paid on the self-same nail, and the matter was settled.

*

When the Bradburys sat down to dinner that Sunday afternoon, Frederick fresh from church, George smug from the Exchange, they were the new owners of the *Bonny Beanfoy*. They had an unwanted purser, which didn't please Frederick, and they'd signed away a third of their profits, but providing they could find fittings and victuals and a new crew and a competent master in good time, there was no reason why they should miss the trade on the Slave Coast that autumn.

'We've earned our dinner, damme,' Sir George said, tucking his napkin into his stock.

It was an excellent meal, cooked to perfection, served in silence and eaten at leisure. For the first time in more weeks than he could remember, Sir George cleared his plate without suffering from indigestion.

''Od's teeth, brother,' he said appreciatively, undoing another button on his waistcoat. 'You keep an excellent table. Excellent, damme.'

Frederick glanced at the waistcoat with approval. 'Obliged to ee,' he said, accepting the compliment, gracefully.

'Our cook is a dab hand at pastries,' Sir George said, picking his teeth, 'but she ain't a patch on your Mrs Thurston, that she ain't.'

'I will see that she gets your message,' his brother promised.

Sir George glanced towards the window where a knot garden sloped towards the river in a succession of neat terraces, each herb bush trimmed and graded into proportions that would please the eye. At the river's edge a line of conifers stood to attention like troops on parade, all exactly the same height and exactly the same thickness. There was even symmetry on the river, where two traders were returning to port, side by side, eased and controlled by their little pilot boats, the long line of oars catching the sunlight. It was soothing and reassuring, for everywhere he looked, both inside and outside the house, a perfect balance had been achieved. The dining room was a triumph of design and good taste. Six fine paintings, two to each wall, and the pair opposite the windows exactly the same height and shape as the central panes; two candelabra to each side table, three to the sideboard, and four set at regular intervals down the polished length of the dining table itself; two high-backed chairs beside the fire, even two fire screens beside the chairs, for although there were no ladies in the house to avail themselves of protection, their presence was necessary to balance the view of the fireplace. It was an admirable, peaceful room, the apotheosis of classical taste, organized proof that by the power of reason man could achieve supremacy over the disorganized world of nature. A fitting place for men who could turn the disaster of loss into the potential of gain and all within three short days.

'You're a lucky dog, Frederick,' Sir George said, 'to have a home like this. Best house in the city, damme if it ain't. Shan't want to leave tomorrow and that's the truth.'

'You are welcome to stay,' Frederick told him.

Sir George sighed. 'Can't be done. I've to be in London by Monday.'

'Ah, yes,' Frederick said remembering. The consortium.'

'That and to find a husband for Ariadne.'

'Oh dear!'

'Hermione insists upon it,' Sir George sighed again. 'I'd leave well alone myself but you know what women are.'

'Put in this world to plague us,' Frederick said sympathetically. 'They ain't capable of reason, that's the truth of it. Different breed altogether. Given to passion and gossip and suchlike extravagances. What can you expect? I never knew any trouble in my life, but there wasn't a woman at the bottom of it. Different breed altogether. A man's better without'em. That's the truth of the matter.'

'True!' his brother agreed with feeling. 'I tell you what, Frederick, marriage ain't a fitting matter for a man of honour.'

Eight

That Saturday evening the noise in the Bradbury apartment made Suki's head spin. In the three months she'd spent with the family she'd never known them so shrill, not even out on their country estate in Appleton where they'd gone when the babies were a week old and where the two young misses had spent most of their time screaming at one another from opposite ends of the long gallery. Now they were both shouting at once: Ariadne because she was ready to leave for the theatre and Melissa was still dressing; Melissa because she was 'sick and tired of being nagged so'. And, as if their bad temper was infectious, everyone else was screeching too: Mrs Sparepenny calling for Hepzibah, Cook berating poor Barnaby for breaking the eggs, the scullery maids screaming and kicking one another, and to make matters worse, a new family was being moved into the top-floor apartment — the gentleman in the bob wig having departed — and their porters didn't seem to be capable of carrying so much as a hand case without roaring. Benjy was beside himself with so much noise and so many legs to bite. Was it any wonder poor little William couldn't settle? And she did so need him to settle.

Only Lady Bradbury was quiet and that was because she was too furious to trust herself to speak. She sat on her striped chaise longue, splendid in full evening dress, with the Captain's letter in her hand, trembling with repressed rage. How dare he write to her so? The impudence! Just as she was dressed and ready to leave for the Assembly Rooms and her last evening with her dear friend,

Arabella, who was leaving for Harrogate in the morning. It was insupportable. 'My present allowance will no longer serve,' The unprincipled boldness of it! The effrontery! As if he had a right to an allowance. Had he no sense of his true position?

Jessup was clearing his throat. 'Will there be any answer, ma'am? The carter is waiting.'

Oh yes, there would be an answer. She couldn't wait to write it. ''Twill be to hand in five minutes,' she promised, as she walked to the escritoire. 'You shall take it tomorrow when you deliver his allowance. Pray tell the carter we have no further need of his services.' As he left the room, she took up her pen and set her face.

After so many years of private affliction it was a pleasure to write from the heart.

My dear Jack,

I have provided you with lodgings and vitals for twenty years to my most certain reckoning. Now, in all conscience, since you will be one and twenty come Michaelmas, I have to tell you, sir, you are of an age to make shift for yourself. Your importunities grow tedious. Consequently, this will be the last allowance I shall send YOU. Whether or not you marry is entirely your own affair. Howsomever, if you consider yourself old enough for wedlock, you must, in all conscience, accept that you are old enough to make shift for yourself.

My advice to you is to take ship to a far country and there seek your own fortune as best you may. There are ships aplenty in Bristol and crews always in demand.

She paused, laid her pen aside and considered. Writing had softened her rage, not a great deal, but enough to allow her old sense of responsibility towards him to reassert itself. Perhaps she should assist him a little, not with any more money, nor the promise of more, for he must understand that her purse was closed from now on, but at least with the opportunity of some advancement.

By good chance, I happen to know that Mr Frederick Bradbury of Brandon Hill requires a new ships master at this present, one who is capable of handling slaves and not averse to hard work at sea. It would be laborious but would in consequence pay handsomely.

This from the hand of her who, despite all, wishes you well.

Lady Hermione Bradbury

Then having sealed it and left it on the escritoire for Jessup to collect, she swept out to silence her daughters.

'If you mean to attend this play with any possibility of a seat from which to see it,' she said acidly to Ariadne, 'you should have departed ten minutes since.'

'Exactly so,' Ariadne agreed. She was obviously and impressively ready, resplendent in her new blue watered silk, with her curls powdered to match, and so thoroughly drenched in *eau de chipre*, that it made

Hermione's eyes sting to be standing beside her. 'You see, Melissa, Mamma agrees with me. She thinks you a slowcoach too.'

Melissa flounced from her chair, declaring 'twas not to be endured. 'I could have been ready hours since had you not been peck, peck, peck upon me all the time.'

I will be the model of all patience, Hermione vowed, as her daughters bristled at one another. I will show good breeding. I will *not* be moved to anger no matter how foolishly they may behave. And she spoke at once while Ariadne was drawing breath to renew her attack. Is Suki not ready to attend you?' she asked, deflecting attention to the servants. Always a wise move in times of domestic difficulty. 'Go you directly, Hepzibah, and fetch her.' William was asleep at last, and Suki was easing him into his cradle when Hepzie arrived with her summons. 'Hush,' she begged. 'Speak soft or we shall have him crying again and I shall never get out.'

'I'd ha' thought you'd have had enough of the theatre for one week,' Hepzie said, in her sneering way. 'Tis three nights in a row.'

Suki tidied her cap. Three nights and three chances to find the Captain. Oh, let him be in the audience tonight! He must be there tonight. 'How well you count,' she mocked. And strode towards the stairs, swift-footed with hope.

Because it was Saturday, the theatre was full to capacity. As Suki followed her two young misses into the throng, she felt as though she was stepping into an overcrowded aviary, the noise was so shrill and there was so much flapping and pirouetting, so many feathered fans and plumed head-dresses, for the playgoers were providing their own prologue, as they greeted their friends, and fluttered to display their rich gowns and splendid coats, gorgeous as birds of paradise, in crimson and rose pink, grass green and saffron yellow, white and silver, sky-blue and gold. Bright eyes gleamed with self-conscious coquetry; jewelled throats were lifted to catch the candlelight; there was a tangle of trailing ribbons and frizzy hair, a sea-froth of frills, a convolution of gold braid, and on every side, excited voices soaring to be heard. And as in every aviary, the combination of scent and stench was dizzying, rank sweat and farts like rotting cabbages, ointments and unguents, powder and paint and rancid pomades, peppery snuff and the fumes of tobacco, and floating above them, like clogging oils on very dirty water, a medley of heavy perfumes, musk and amber, *eau de luce* and bergamot and Ariadne's *eau de chipre*, which she was distributing to right and left with flirtatious waves of her swan's down fan.

She embarked upon her own promenade at once, because several of her acquaintances had come to the play that night which gave her the chance to greet them all like old friends, and criticise them afterwards.

'La, Charlotte,' she called, swooping to embrace a dark-haired girl in a crimson gown. Behind their kissing heads, Suki saw a row of embroidered waistcoats, a hedgerow of green leaves and improbable flowers. But she couldn't see the Captain anywhere. If only they'd all sit down, she thought, I could get a better view. Oh he *must* be here. He must. There's a claret-coloured coat. Can that be him?

Ariadne was beside her again, demanding attention, declaring that her dress was incomplete and had no style or grace at all.

'Everybody has a nosegay tonight!' she complained. 'I'm sure I shall be put to shame if I don't have a nosegay. Everybody sees us. They will think us poor country fools without a nosegay. How vexing it is, to be sure! There ain't another lady in the hall without a nosegay. Run at once and buy one, set with roses, pinks and forget-me-nots, if you please, or 'twon't serve at all. You have the ticket to gain re-admittance, have you not? Bestir yourself, gel!'

'Two!' Melissa said. 'I must have one too, Ariadne. Set with orange flowers, if you please, to match my gown.' She was dressed in bright yellow lawn, garishly hand-painted, and looked fatter and even more sallow than usual. 'Bestir yourself, gel!'

So Suki had to drag herself away from her search and run their stupid errand.

Outside the theatre, the narrow street was still crowded with chairs and playgoers, beggars and onlookers. Even the fortuneteller, Old Sheena, was there, enthroned in an elaborate chair with a table set before her, covered in a red velvet cloth trailing tom threads and holding her crystal ball and cards. It took Suki quite a while to jostle through the throng to the nearest flower-seller, and even longer to find two appropriate posies. When she returned, the audience were beginning to take their seats and Ariadne and her complacent sister had disappeared.

Artful baggage, Suki thought angrily. All that nonsense about a nosegay was just to get me out of the way. I should have known better than to leave her for a minute. Now what shall I do?

There were so many people still milling about in front of her eyes that it was impossible to see anything more than a confused blur of colour and movement. Perhaps she ought to try and he her way into the galleries for a better vantage point. She glanced up to see if there was a space anywhere and there, sitting on one of the front benches of the first gallery, were Farmer Lambton and his wife. They were delighted to see her, and called down to her at once.

'What brings you to the playhouse?' Mrs Lambton asked. 'You'aven't never left your babba and come out on your own?' Her face was drawn and even a flowing sack-dress couldn't disguise the bulge of her belly.

Suki explained her mission, and how she'd been gulled by her crafty young mistress, scanning the crowd around her as she spoke, for now she had two faces to find.

Farmer Lambton considered the situation, smoking his pipe slowly as he deliberated. 'If she's fallen for a player, then she won't leave the playhouse,' he said. 'That's one comfort. I should look close to the stage, if I were you. She will want to be in his eye.'

It was sound advice. As the audience continued to take their places, Suki suddenly saw her mistress sitting in the front row of the stalls, leaning forward towards the curtain, as though she would draw her beloved through it with her eyes.

'You have seen her,' Farmer Lambton understood.

'In the front row where I can't sit anywhere near her,' Suki told him.

'Then you'd best sit here with us,' he suggested, smiling his nice warm smile at her through the tobacco smoke. 'There's room for a littl'un.'

Once she'd pushed through the crowd to deliver the posies, she thanked him kindly, thinking how marvellously dependable he was. He never changed, not even for a visit to the play. There he was in his plain brown broadcloth, calm and ordinary and as solid as a rock among all the painted popinjays around him. But Mrs Lambton looked downright unhealthy. 'You keepin' well, ma'am?' she asked politely.

'Mustn't grumble,' Mrs Lambton said patiently. 'Breedin' ewe arn't a spring lamb.'

'Last weeks are enough to weary a saint,' Suki agreed. 'Never mind, ma'am. 'Twill soon be here.'

Mrs Lambton smiled. 'I suppose you couldn't keep me company when the time comes?' she asked. 'Your mother's promised to be midwife again, but if you could be there too 'twould be... Your babba's doing well I hear.'

The hesitation in her voice kindled a rush of aching pity in Suki Brown. Poor lady, she thought. She've carried all those babies and lost them all, miscarried or still-born or dead within the year, no wonder she wants a bit of help. 'Of course I will,' she said at once, 'and glad to.' But she had to add 'if I'm anywhere nearabouts', for there was no knowing where she would be by the end of the year and they both knew it.

Fortunately there was no time to say anything else for at that moment the trumpets sounded and the overture began to play. The audience hushed and settled and presently the plush curtains looped open, and Clorinda, Queen of Africa made her last and lop-sided entrance in her bright pink barge. It rode so high above the rolling waves that the rope that pulled it could be clearly seen and the oars sticking out of their three large portholes rotated wildly and uselessly more than a foot above the cardboard water. Criticism was instant and vociferous.

It was a ridiculous play. Pistols were fired and passion declared; two handsome heroes fought a duel with such ferocity that the front row was spattered with saliva; a savage appeared with a soot-black face and white hands, and delivered a very long speech so haltingly that the audience ran out of patience and pelted him with orange peel. But Ariadne was still enraptured by it and sat with her gloves to her mouth, living every word her hero uttered, glowing with admiration and the heat of the crowded hall.

To Suki, uselessly scanning the audience for sight of the Captain, it was simply a booming irritation and it got worse as her hopes fell. He wasn't there. She had to admit it. He wasn't there and now there would be no more plays to visit and no more hope of finding him until the St Lawrence Fair and that wasn't for another five days. How could she keep patient for five whole days? And how could she get out to the fair, even then? There was bound to be plenty of work to do on a day like that. And what if he wasn't there either? Oh, he had to be. Of all places he was bound to be at the fair. That man Charlie had been sure of it and Jack had given her his word. 'I will see you next summer,' he'd said, sitting on that fine horse of his, looking down at her. Oh such a long time ago. And now she'd got to watch that stupid actor in his silly helmet for the rest of this stupid evening and she was bored enough already. Why couldn't milady have found somebody else to chaperone her lovelorn daughter?

A growl of applause and gratified laughter woke her with a start at the end of the second act. She was warm with sleep and for a second she couldn't remember where she was. But then the smell of the theatre filled her nostrils, and she realized she must have fallen asleep with boredom. She looked down into the stalls and saw that Ariadne was promenading again and that two of the actors were walking through the crush distributing leaflets. Neither of them was that Mr Clements, which was just as well, but Ariadne had seized a leaflet at once and was reading it avidly.

'What is it?' Mrs Lambton asked as one of the little papers was thrust into her hand.

'Tis notice of the play we're to perform at the fair,' the actor told her. 'I trust we shall see you there, ma'am.'

Mrs Lambton waited until he'd moved along the row before she spoke. 'I doubt it,' she said to Suki. 'Twould be wearisome, I fear, out in the sun and on my feet all day. I've parlous little energy and that's the truth of it.'

But Suki was watching Ariadne and barely heard her. This will take her to the fair, she was thinking, and if she goes I must be there to chaperone her. What good fortune.

After that, the rest of the play was endurable, and the song and dance and the one-act comedy that rounded off the evening were really quite entertaining. She found she was able to applaud at the end of it all with some enthusiasm. Hooray for the play at the fair!

'Now,' Ariadne said, as the three of them were leaving, 'we will go to the stagedoor and congratulate the players.' She was holding her head high with determination.

'Your Mamma has chairs ready an' waiting at the theatre door,' Suki told her firmly. 'An' Jessup in attendance. She won't take it kindly if you am t there too.'

'Oh!' Ariadne said pettishly. 'Tis too tiresome. It truly is. 'Tis come to something when a person may not even visit the stage-door without reproof.'

There's a fortune-teller at the top of the street,' Suki said, aiming the remark at Melissa.

'*Is* there?' Melissa asked, instantly interested. 'Would we have time to consult with her, think'ee, before the chairs arrive?'

'If we hurry,' Suki said pressing her advantage, and hoping she would be proved right and that Old Sheena would still be there.

'You don't want to consult a fortune-teller,' Ariadne said scornfully. 'How childish!'

'I do,' her sister said. 'Why shouldn't *I* have *my* way once in a while? Why should you be the only one to do as you please? Tain't fair.'

'I have delicate health,' Ariadne told her with a superior smirk. 'Do you wish to make me ill?'

'I don't give a fig for your health,' Melissa said. 'I could have delicate health too if I wanted to. 'Tis simple enough, in all conscience, for I've seen you do it, many and many's the time.'

'Have a care, sister,' Ariadne warned her, 'lest you make my fingers itch. If you press me too far I may have to chastise.'

'Pooh!' Melissa said, and before her sister could act or remonstrate, she ran off towards the entrance. Despite herself Ariadne had to follow, and she was scowlingly annoyed about it. But they were all saved by Old Sheena, who had now taken up a prominent position on the steps that led down to the fields, and was doing a brisk trade in soulful warnings and romantic predictions.

She was in excellent form. 'Well now, my pretty,' she crooned, taking Melissa's plump hand in her mysterious grip. 'I see a lover in this hand. You en't met 'im yet, an't that right, but the time approaches. The time is nearer than you think. Tis a hand of great happiness. Wealth a-plenty. Love in abundance.'

'When?' Melissa breathed, entranced.

'Well, as to that,' the gypsy said, searching the three faces bent towards her, ''tis uncommon hard to be exact in such a case. Looks to me like the springtime, the start of the year, when love is fresh and tender. Could be the next springtime. Maybe the one after. But sooner than you think.'

'And what do you see in my hand, pray?' Ariadne demanded, removing her glove and thrusting her hand arrogantly beneath the gypsy's nose.

'That will depend, my lady,' Old Sheena said, and her tone was a rebuke, 'on how I'm used and how I'm paid. Vision is a curious thing. Speak fair to see true.' She stared her latest client full in the face and, to Suki's delight, Ariadne dropped her gaze and fished about inside her pocket for the necessary coins.

Old Sheena secreted the silver in her sleeve and gave her attention to a hand now rather less imperious, tilting the palm carelessly towards the nearest torch. Her oiled skin was mahogany brown in the moonlight, the line of forehead, cheek and jaw edged with silvery blue. She looked outlandish and sounded shiveringly mysterious, her silk shawls rustling like leaves and the bells at the wrists jangling softly as she moved. The crowd edged forward to hear the lady's fortune, and Suki noticed that for all her air of superior unconcern, Ariadne's neck was rigid with alarm.

'Look into your soul,' the gypsy said. ''Tis a rash black soul an' full of passion. Strife I can see most clearly in this hand. See how the lines of life and love entangle. A Gordian knot as clear as ever I see, an' all entangled at the time of youth. Woe to your rash black soul! Fie on your passionate heart! You bring a sorrow to your father's house, and bitter grief to them as loves you true. Remember the fifth commandment, my lady!'

'A priest could tell as much,' Ariadne said scornfully, trying to withdraw her hand, 'if he had a mind to give as much offence.' But Sheena was in her stride and wouldn't let go or be deterred. Her litany had mesmerized the crowd, the flow of fortune wasn't to be stopped. 'Your heart is given to a fair young man,' she said. 'Anguish will be your portion if you yield. Bitter regret and sorrow mar this love. Discord and rancour where you seek for passion, torment and trial where you hope for peace.' The crowd was swaying to the rhythm of the words, and Ariadne was burning with embarrassment.

'I'm sure the chairs are come,' she said to Melissa. But there was no sign of Jessup and all the chairs scrambling outside the theatre seemed to be for other people. She gave a shudder and turned to the attack.

'Can you find nothing good to say at all?' she demanded. ''Tis a poor fortune with nothing good in't.'

'Well, as to that,' Sheena said, reverting to her business-like voice, ''twould depend, so 'twould. Takes a powerful amount of spirit to see far.'

Her beleaguered client paid at once for better fortune, and the crowd nudged even closer, hungry for her humiliation. Both were confused. Sheena looked away from the hand she still held firmly locked, and turned her concentration upon Ariadne's face.

'Get you to the fair on the feast of St Lawrence,' she advised. 'There your happiness will make or mar. Enough! I have done!'

Ariadne was very cross. 'We will walk home,' she said to Melissa, tucking her discarded hand into her sister's plump elbow, and setting off at once. 'Chairs are a folly.' She had no intention of standing in the street to be mocked. Suki, who had been wondering whether she could spare a coin to have her own fortune told, was caught unprepared and had to run after them, pushing against the crowds and tripping on the uneven cobbles.

'We *must* go to the fair, Addy,' Melissa said as they bustled home. 'I have the strangest feeling about it. Do promise we shall go!'

'Mere superstition!' Ariadne said. 'I hope you don't allow yourself to be moved by such nonsense, Melissa. If we go 'twill be for the entertainment, not the fortune.'

'Then we'll go?'

Her sister's answer was drawlingly casual. 'Twould do us some benefit to amuse ourselves in the fresh air, I daresay. Good sport is *so* hard to find in a city devoted to the sick.'

'Here are the chairs, Miss Melissa,' Suki said. Miss Ariadne was wearing her arrogant expression, so the sooner she got them both home, the better. 'Your mamma will be waiting to hear your opinion of the play.'

She also required a detailed account of Ariadne's behaviour in the theatre and, when it had been given, allowed herself to ask a direct question, in the most casual manner she could contrive. 'Was there any communication between them, would you say?' 'No, ma'am,' Suki assured her. Nothing of that nature at all, he bein' on stage and she in the audience.'Twas admiration on her part, no more. All from a distance.'

'The chairs arrived in good time, I trust.'

'Yes, ma'am,' Suki assured again. 'They came straight home.' But not before you'd allowed'em to consult a fortune-teller, Hermione thought, which I notice you don't see fit to mention. 'Twas as well I required

Hepribah to keep watch in the street when the play was done, or I'd not have known *that*.

However, given her own good sense and forethought, her foolish daughter might yet escape without ill effect. The wet nurse's presence had served to remind her of her position, and even if the wretched girl was too artful to give a full report, Hepzibah could keep watch on them both. I shall instruct her to be extra vigilant in the next few days, reward her with that gown perchance, and see what she has to report. Like most servants she was short of wit and venial. She would work w'ell given a bribe or two. Meanwhile something had to be said to Suki.

'You have done well,' she said, pulling out her purse and considering how small a coin wrould serve as reward. 'Continue your watch for a day or two. William is well, I trust. Good. Be so kind as to tell Mrs Sparepenny that we will attend morning sendee tomorrow. Then you may retire.'

And about time too, Suki thought as she took the proffered groat. It had been a long day.

Nine

The next morning the household woke to find that the weather had completely changed. A fog had curled up from the surface of the river, yellowing as it gradually absorbed the smoke from the city's chimneys. Now it hid the surrounding hills and lay in the hollow of the town like a deflated cloud, cold and sulphurous and dank. The two Miss Bradburys took one look at it, and decided it would be politic to stay in bed for another hour or two. Unfortunately their mother swept into their room to rouse them, and she would not permit any such idleness.

'I agree with you my dears,' she said. The climate in this town is a positive disgrace but that is no reason why we should not attend morning service. We have a position to maintain.'

Hepzie couldn't see why she had to maintain the position too. 'Cook ain't been asked to go, I notice,' she said tartly.

Cook was in a bad humour because Bamaby had forgotten to bring in the kindling overnight and now it was damp and the fire wouldn't take. 'I ain't a family servant,' she said. 'That's for why. Hired by the day I am, an' only to cook, not to sit about in that draughty old abbey an' be spat on by that old Bishop.'

Mrs Sparepenny was giving orders, right and left: Barnaby was to wash his hands and comb his hair; Suki and Bessie were to be sure to wear their best bonnets; the baby was to attend the service.

'They've never took un to the abbey before,' Suki complained as she wrapped him in her shawl, tight and snug like a little rosy sausage. 'All in this nasty weather. He'll catch his death of cold, poor lamb.' She didn't want to go to church either, not in her present sinful state. She was telling lies every single day — she couldn't avoid it — and the more she told the more complicated they became, and church was where they preached about the wages of sin and the hellfire that was sure to follow, which was something she didn't want to hear or think about. 'I don't see why we can't stay here in the warm.'

''Tis all a poppy-show,' Cook told her. 'They'm a-taking him to impress their precious friends, I shouldn't wonder.'

Which was how it turned out. For as soon as they were inside the abbey, the baby had to be handled and dandled by everybody within reach, by that awful Lady Fosdyke and Mrs Smithers and her sister and her two aunts and sundry other simperingly interested persons, and was passed back and forth across the pews until he was so perplexed and tearful he could only be comforted by being fed.

The Bradbury family sat in the seventh pew that morning, which was just far enough from the pulpit to be beyond the range of the Bishop's infamous spittle, which was a mercy, but right in the middle of all the noise and babble of the occasion. If only they wouldn't shout so, Suki thought. They'm like a flock of starlings. People never used to shout in church at Twerton. Twas quiet there and reverent, the way it should be. Anyway they wouldn't have dared, not with Farmer Lambton's eye on'em to keep'em in order. The clergy here got no authority at all. 'Tis like being at the play, with everybody so loud and busy. Even the pew ends were busy, with all that carving swirling around, and so was the glass in the great window above the altar, and so was the altar itself. Busy, busy, busy, shout, shout, shout. An' he'll be on about sin any minute now, bound to be.

Loud hymns and prayers booming, then much feet-scraping and blethered comment as the congregation resumed their seats, and the Bishop rose with a fart to deliver his sermon, which he began by clearing his throat like a thunder clap.

But he didn't lecture about sin. Instead he announced that he wished to draw their attention to what he called 'the serious matter of Christian obedience'. 'I take as my text this morning,' he said, showering spittle before him, 'St Paul's epistle to the Colossians: "Wives, submit yourselves unto your own husbands; children, obey your parents in all things; servants, obey in all things your masters according to the flesh."'

Well that's a mercy, Suki thought. At least we arn't having the eighth commandment for I couldn't have borne that. She composed her expression to listen to him, the way she usually did in church, with half an ear and less than half her mind. You didn't have to listen hard in church because they always said the same thing and everybody agreed with it. But that morning halflistening was more difficult than she expected, and after a while she realized that she was actually paying attention and that almost everything he was saying was provoking her.

Questions rose to the surface of her mind to explode like bubbles in a stew-pot. Why? What if...? Why should wives be expected to obey their husbands? Why shouldn't they be equals the way lovers were? When she and the Captain had been together, they'd neither the one of them given the slightest thought to obeying or being obeyed. What they'd done was simply for delight, sweet and simple and full of pleasure. Obeying didn't come into it. As to children obeying their parents, what if a parent told his child to do something they knew wasn't right, something unlawful? Should the child be obedient then? Surely not. 'Twouldn't be right.

But it was when he began to talk about the duty servants owed to their masters that the bubbles reached boiling point, exploding into her mind in a red-hot certainty, and she knew that, bishop or not, he was wrong. For if his teaching was to be followed, a servant had to lie down for her master simply because he was lustful and commanded her to do it, 'according to the flesh', and there was no way she would agree to that. Not now. 'Twas plainly a bad thing and, as a man of morals, he ought to see it. But then, as she looked around at all the masculine heads that were solemnly nodding agreement, another idea came pushing into her mind. The Bishop is a man for all he's a bishop, and husbands are men, and fathers and masters are men, and lawyers and politicians — and it occurred to her that the people who were expected to obey were mostly women and children and usually poor. And she knew there was no justice in this man's teaching and felt quite lightheaded with the boldness of what she was thinking.

At that point, the choirboys began the psalm, bouncing its cadences straight up into the high fan vaulting, where the stone erupted into vast ribbed trumpets, and the sound echoed and reechoed, and made such battering patterns inside her head that they shattered her thoughts to confusion. How much longer is this service going on? she wondered. 'Tis giving me a headache. And she looked round to grimace at Bessie and noticed that the butler wasn't with them.

'Where's Mr Jessup?' she mouthed.

'Gone on some errand for the missus,' Bessie whispered, leaning towards her to be heard. 'Bristol way, I think.'

'In this weather!' Suki whispered back. 'Rather him than me.' And she shuddered to think of travelling any distance in all that fog. There'd only be one thing that'ud take me out in such weather, she thought, an' that would be to see the Captain. And how she yearned to see him again, with that bold handsome face and that easy way of walking and talking, and those beautiful brown eyes and that gentle mouth. Oh, I wonder where he is and what he'm a-doing.

*

He was standing in the sunshine in the garden of the Pelican Inn with Lady Bradbury's opened letter in his hand and Jessup waiting stem-faced the required six paces away — the man was always nauseatingly correct — and he was struggling to keep his expression calm and his emotions under control. Whatever else, he wasn't going to allow a servant to see how he was feeling, and especially a superior servant with a sneering mouth and cynical eyes.

He and his friends had had another disappointment on Friday morning, when their much-desired traveller had failed to appear for the second time. They'd had to make do with a merchant and his wife who'd had so little of value about them that they were barely worth the effort. Quin had ridden off to Bristol in a temper immediately afterwards, taking Charlie with him, swearing they'd been peached and vowing to find out who was to blame. But Jack had stayed on at the inn, where he'd run up huge bills for food and drink while he waited for his allowance to release him. And now this cruel letter had arrived and he was cast adrift, suddenly and without warning, with one last payment between himself and penury. He was profoundly upset, aching with anguish at her unexpected rejection, torn with fury at his own drunken bravado in provoking it, stunned by his impending poverty, in a black rage at the unfairness of it and, worst of all, with the old familiar rush of panic at being abandoned and lost.

A slight breeze rustled the corn in the field beside him, and Jessup shifted his feet and gave his nervous cough. Krrm, krrm. Was there any message?

'No, no; Jack said, pleased that he was managing to keep his voice steady. 'You may tell Mrs Roper I shan't be requiring her rooms for a month or two.' That was well said, and in exactly the right tone, as if it were of no consequence. A man has his pride. 'As a matter of fact, I've accepted a position which will take me abroad. Thought I'd see the world, don'tcher know.'

Jessup smiled his faint half-smile. 'Yes, sir.'

What a knowing rogue he is, Jack thought, itching to hit him, what an unprincipled, arrogant, upstart, time-serving, penny-pinching, dung-crawling, arse-licking villain. Oh, if I could give you a trouncing, I'd wipe that smile off your face, Mr Sneering Jessup. You'd not condescend on me again in a hurry, I can tell you. But the butler was smiling again, looking straight at him in his superior way, as if to say, there ain't a thing I don't know about you, and there ain't a thing you can do about it.

Rage rose in the Captain as black as bile. 'Twas not to be endured. If I meet with you on a dark road one night, he promised, I'll not rate your chances at a groat. Or a farthing. He turned on his heel to walk into the inn. 'That will be all,' he said, giving a lordly wave of dismissal. And more than enough.

He had to get away and quickly. This place stifled him. Pay the bill, gather his few belongings, stride to the stable to check that his horse was properly groomed and ready to ride, then up and off, out on the open road where speed and distance could restore him to himself and calm this awful sense of panic.

But it was several miles before he could accommodate his thoughts to the monstrous unkindness of that letter. 'You are old enough to make shift for yourself.' How dare she treat him so! After all he'd had to endure at her hands. 'Twas more than human flesh and blood could stand.

The horse cantered steadily, the rhythm of its stride soothing to his senses and his pride. He had a good seat and rode well and he knew it and the knowledge was a comfort to him. A good horseman on a good horse, for Beau was a very good horse indeed, mettlesome and as high-spirited as he was himself, with a sensitive mouth and a handsome mane and inordinate strength.

'We make a fine pair,' he said to the animal, patting his neck. We won't be beat.' And Beau pricked his ears and snorted by way of answer.

But how would he fare once his allowance was spent? He'd not have a farthing to his name come that day. He would have to find some way to fudge. Panic stirred again. I shall do it, he told himself, deliberately summoning good sense to his aid. But what would he do? He rehearsed the possibilities. Join Quin Cutpurse perhaps. The man was an unconscionable rogue but he was a good judge of a situation and one of the bravest villains in England. Except that in his trade the risks were uncommon high and the more risks you ran the nearer you came to the gallows, which was *not* a consummation to be wished. Go on the stage? He'd spent a season with a travelling company, playing the hero and the fool and the villain, and he could do it again should the worst come to the worst. Except that the pay was poor and the work uncertain. Join a travelling fair, then? Except that they were mostly gypsies and uncommon clanny. Didn't welcome strangers. Or go to sea, the way milady counselled? He had an uncomfortable feeling that she'd suggested it as a challenge and didn't expect him to rise to it. Well, if 'twas the case, she was mistaken in her unkindness. He could rise to any challenge, no matter how hard. She needn't think him craven. He'd as much bottom as any man in England. Twould be a hard life but 'twould put him beyond reach of his creditors and wenches who thought to foist paternity upon him, which would be no bad thing. He was on his way to Bristol in any case, so 'twould make sense to look into it. He knew very little about the slave trade, except that it was full of dangers and employed some very tough seamen. But one thing was certain — if you survived the voyage and came home to port, you came home a rich man. He'd heard that much, sitting in the Llandoger Trow with Quin and Charlie.

At that moment, he reached a turn in the road and there before him lay the city of Bristol, elegant in the afternoon sun, the spire of St Mary Ratcliff bold against the skyline, the long curve of the River Avon gleaming like polished pewter, Queen's Square honey-rich in the green of its central garden, the streets of the old town busy with carts, chairs, carriages and a bustle of men and business, the floating harbour forested with masts, and beside it, the three half-timbered gables of the Llandoger Trow clear-patterned as patchwork, even from that distance. The sight of it made up his mind. He would go straight there and put his ears to work. If there was a job on Mr Bradbury's slaver and it was worth the taking, he would know of it by nightfall.

The Llandoger Trow faced the harbour and was renowned for its ale and was well known as a meeting place for seamen who were looking for employment. It was a well-kept house, consisting of one large low-ceilinged room, with doors and windows giving out to the quayside and the street. It had a well-sanded floor, two long bars, lined with brass-handled beer pumps, and an abundance of wooden chairs and settles, invariably occupied. The walls were papered with bills of advertisement, the air blue-clouded with the smoke of tobacco, the gossip peppered with the latest news of ships — arriving, sailing or at sea — and their owners - rogues, cheats or men 'as honest as you're like to get in this trade'. Jack hadn't been inside the place for more than thirty seconds before somebody mentioned Mr Bradbury.

He took up his pipe and his pint, pushed his way through the throng to the nearest settle and prepared to eavesdrop.

The speaker was a grizzled sailor with a mahogany-coloured face, a gold ring in his left ear and a tar-covered plait hanging down the back of his blue smock. 'The Frenchies are at the root of it, you may lay to that, Mr Tomson sir.'

'How d'you make that out then, Mr Reuben?' his companion said, removing his pipe from his mouth and examining the bowl. He was a striking-looking man, short of stature but broad-shouldered and barrel-chested, with strong scarred hands and a heavy face, red-cheeked, leather-skinned, dark-eyed and resplendent with black hair. It sprang in large oily curls from either side of the red bandanna he wore about his head, curved into eyebrows like arched black wings and grew luxuriantly about his mouth, which was moist and red, in a heavy moustache and a thick black beard combed into ringlets. But unlike the others around him who were wearing the seaman's uniform of coarse canvas breeches and blue smock, this man was dressed like a master in a blue jacket with fine brass buttons. 'Construe!'

'Well, like I said, Mr Tomson sir, they'm in a rush. You onny got to go down the quay to where she lies to see that. I heared tell they got to get her rigged an' provisioned an' ready to sail in three weeks, which is on account of they got to catch the Trades, an' they got to catch the Trades on account of they lost a ship to the Frenchies. Took six leagues out of Barbados she was, so I heared tell, and narry a man jack of 'em saved. Old Coster, 'e reckons we could ask any sum we cared to name an' Mr Bradbury would be glad fer to pay it.'

'Old Coster's a fool,' Mr Tomson said, returning his pipe to his mouth, slotting the stem neatly into the space left by two missing teeth. 'And you'm another if you believe his jaw.'

'She'm a good ship, Mr Tomson sir,' another sailor ventured.

Mr Tomson nodded. 'I've no argument with that.'

'Mr Bradbury's a good master.'

'Nor that neither, on account of I've worked for 'un before an' I daresay I shall again.'

'Then why not this time?' a third man asked. 'We'd join with 'ee, Mr Tomson sir, you knows that.'

'If I were part owner an' could take part share of the profits, 'twould be a fine prospect,' Mr Tomson said. 'Or if 'twere merely a matter of captaining the ship, I might think on it — think, mind 'ee, no more'n that — but 'tis a deal more'n that on this trip, as well you know. Tis a matter of slaves on this trip an' all that suchlike signifies, which is to say, plagues an' agues an' the bloody flux an' so forth — stinks an' filth an' foul air an' so forth — burials at sea an' so forth — loss of pay an' so forth, which I ain't too sharp to take on, all things considered, no more than you should be if you'm men of sense. She'm a good ship, you'm right about that. If I could just sail her an' so forth and find another to manage all the business of the slaves, 'twould be a different matter, a different matter altogether. As it is...'

At that point half a dozen Dutch sailors came rolling into the inn demanding beer in their odd guttural lingo and the noise of their arrival drowned out what Mr Tomson was saying. But Jack had heard enough. It was a godsend and he had to take it. He could guard slaves as well as the next man. They'd be no danger if he kept 'em chained, and looking after 'em would be no worse than looking after any other cattle, like sheep or pigs, a matter of feeding and bedding down and keeping in control. He'd got enough bottom for *that*. Taut with hope and excitement and a sudden renewal of panic, he stepped forward, doffed his hat and made an elaborate bow to Mr Tomson.

'I give you good day, sir.'

The seaman looked at him quizzically. 'And you, sir.'

Press on. Quickly. 'I believe I have the honour of addressing Mr Tomson, master mariner?'

Another shrewd look. 'Aye, sir. You do. What of it?'

Panic swirled in Jack's chest. The offer had to be made now while he still had the bottom for it. 'Mr Daventry, sir, slave master.'

'Well now here's a thing, my lubbers,' Mr Tomson said raising his eyebrows at his mates. 'I ne'er beared tell of a such a trade as slave master afore.'

'No, sir,' Jack agreed. 'There ain't a many of 'em, being as most masters are content to handle the ship *and* the slaves. Howsomever some...'

'Which you been overhearin',' Mr Tomson said. 'So you'm proposin' I hands my slaves over to you on this here trip we was a-talking of, is that the humour of it?'

'Which I could handle for you.'

'I take it you got some experience in the trade,' Mr Tomson prompted.

'Two voyages,' Jack lied. 'One as assistant and one as a slave master.'

'What ship?'

Jack fished a name out of the air. 'The *Pelican*.'

Mr Tomson looked dismissive. 'Never heared of her,' he said. 'She arn't out of Bristol. That I *do* know.'

'No, sir.'

'Where then?'

Fear of being found out was making Jack's mouth dry. He swallowed and pressed on. 'Liverpool,' he said. Was that far enough away? Would he believe it? Better sink her before he asks any more questions. 'I'd have sailed with her a third time except that she was sunk by the Frenchies.' And he looked at Mr Reuben as if he was expecting confirmation of his story.

'Plaguey Frenchies,' Mr Reuben obliged. 'What did I tell 'ee, Mr Tomson? They're the root of our troubles, if you want my opinion of it.'

Mr Tomson ignored him. 'How would 'ee propose to split the purse, my lubber? Tell me that.'

Half and half, Jack thought, but reconsidered at once. 'Three ways,' he suggested. 'Two for you and one for me.'

'Um,' Mr Tomson said, fondling the ringlets of his beard. 'An' you to take all responsibility for the cargo whatsomever, as to losses an' provisions an' so forth?'

It looked as though a bargain was being offered. 'Yes,' Jack said. Too eagerly.

'Buyin' an' sellin' and so forth?'

'Yes.'

'Then tis a bargain, Mr Daventry,' Mr Tomson said, smiling hugely, and he spat on the palm of his hand and held it out for Jack to shake. 'Meet me on Brandon Hill at eight of the clock tomorrow morning.'

Which, having made sure that he was up in good time, Mr Daventry duly did.

Frederick Bradbury interviewed all would-be ship's masters in the comforting order of his ground-floor office. Surrounded by ledgers and with pen and ink before him, he felt he made more of an impression on the seafaring men than he would have done aboard ship. It gratified him to see how impressed they were by his urbanity and learning. So he was a little put out by the young man who arrived with Mr Tomson on that humid Monday morning. For a start it was highly unusual to be offered a slave master and anything unusual disquieted him. And then there was the young man's appearance. All the other applicants had been rough and ready men, wearing the canvas breeches and bluejackets favoured by seamen with aspirations, but this fellow dressed like quality and seemed entirely at home in the house, scanning the books with a reader's eye and standing easily before the desk as though he were about to sit down and write.

'I should point out that this position is one of considerable responsibility,' he warned.

'No doubt of it, Mr Bradbury sir,' Mr Tomson replied, 'and 'twill be reflected in the remuneration, doubtless.'

'Naturally, providing you catch the trades and make a good profit on the cargo.'

'Which is understood, sir.'

'You've seen the ship, I daresay?'

He had and thought it a good one.

'And you sir,' Frederick said, turning to Jack. 'I assume you have the necessary experience for this venture. I must tell you I have no room for greenhorns on any ship of mine.'

'No fear of that, sir,' Mr Tomson assured.

'Let him speak for himself,' Frederick said, watching the young man's bold face. ''Tis a dangerous trade. How should you fare were you to be attacked by pirates, which God forfend? Or boarded by 'em, which God forfend further. 'Tis a common hazard in the Indies and one that deters all but the stout-hearted. Best to be thought on.'

'It don't deter me, sir,' Jack said. 'I've a good pair of pistols and know how to use 'em.'

'I'm glad on it,' Frederick said and allowed himself to be impressed by the lad's bearing. 'You have references I daresay?'

It was the last hurdle and time for daring. 'Not from my last ship sir, no,' Jack admitted, on account of'twas sunk by the French, but there is a lady who is known to you sir, and would vouch for me should you wish it.'

That was a surprise. 'Indeed? Who might that be?'

'Lady Bradbury,' Jack said, looking him boldly in the eye. 'Wife to Sir George Bradbury. I have done her family some service in the past. I think 'tis safe to say she knows my character.'

The revelation surprised both his hearers. This accounts for his bearing, Frederick thought, and his easy way of speaking, and he looked at the young man with renewed interest. 'Yes,' he said. 'That seems satisfactory.' Then there was a pause while he considered. 'The purse is fifty guineas,' he offered at last, 'if 'tis agreeable.'

Jack made a rapid calculation and spoke up quickly before Mr Tomson could agree to it. 'Fifty-one would be preferable, sir.'

And to Mr Tomson's second surprise, fifty-one was agreed to. 'I shall have detailed instructions for you later, Mr Daventry,' Frederick said as they left, 'as to cargo, wastage, rations and suchlike. My usual letter of instruction will be prepared for you, Mr Tomson, as you will need to gather a crew with all speed. Howsomever, I daresay I may leave such matters in your capable hands. I give 'ee good day.'

Upon which cheerful note, he went upstairs to report his good news to his brother, who was finishing a leisurely breakfast in the sunny dining room.

'We've a good ship's master,' he said triumphantly when the tale was told, 'a man well known to us — and a better I could not have found anywhere in Bristol — to say nothing of this new young man to handle the slave side of things. Known to your wife, so he says. Done some service to the family.'

'Which family?' Sir George asked.

'Hers I believe.'

Sir George lost interest. 'Ah, the famous family!'

'He will serve our turn, famous family or no.' Frederick laughed. 'He's young and eager and like to be quick, which is what we need, you must allow, since time and tide wait for no man. I shall give him the fullest instructions to make assurance doubly sure. But I have to say I have hopes of him. Yes indeed.'

'Well now that's settled, I'd best be off,' Sir George said, wiping the crumbs from his belly. 'I've a husband to find for that idiot daughter of mine or my particular scion of the famous family will have something to say that I shan't wish to hear. We've done uncommon good work brother. Did I not tell 'ee how 'twould be?'

That evening Frederick took himself off to his office and detailed his instructions for his new slave master.

Sir,

On arrival at the Gambia, make speed to purchase a full complement of slaves, which is to say 250 in all. Be sure to choose those who are the deepest black and have woolly hair. Avoid those with straight hair and light skins for they are like to be mulattos or quadroons that will not sell easily. Avoid Wolofs for they are idle. Take no more than forty to fifty women and those young and preferably without children. They will suffice to satisfy the crew.

Above all be sure to choose men who are well formed and strong and none older than twenty-five years for these have the most labour in them.

Lay in stocks of leg irons and shackles to secure all the men and those women who give trouble. Mr Holdcastle whose establishment is next door to my sugar house will help you in this regard. Buy three branding irons with the double B upon them and plenty of tallow to use beforehand. Be sure to carry a plentiful supply of whips and one cat-o'-nine-tails for correction and let them hang in full view that they may act as a deterrent to wrongdoing.

Be sure to carry ample supplies of water, lest you be plagued by the bloody flux or suchlike. Carry a good stock of vinegar for sweetening the decks and washing out such mouths as require it. Lay in a sufficiency of yams, meal and wood so soon as the cargo is spent. As slave master, it is your responsibility to keep the ship clean and to avoid riotous behaviour.

You may take one slave for yourself at the time of purchase, as may the cooper and the ship's surgeon. Mr Tomson and Mr Smith, the purser, are allotted two slaves each as is the custom on a ship of this size.

In all other respects be ruled bt Mr Tomson.

I wish you a safe and prosperous voyage.

Yr obedient servant,

Frederick Bradbury

Jack had to read this missive twice before he could make proper sense of it and it sounded more ominous at the second reading with its talk of 'the bloody flux' and 'riotous behaviour'. Were riots likely? he wondered, touching his pistols for comfort. Were there other diseases this man hadn't mentioned? Was that why he said 'and suchlike'? He could see that this was going to be a much more difficult undertaking than he'd imagined. But he had taken on the job and if that meant buying in supplies of shackles and whips and branding irons — and ultimately using them — so be it.

Ten

Lady Bradbury and her daughters were at breakfast, pink from the baths and still languidly *en deshabille* when Sir George came roaring back to South Parade.

'How now, wife!' he boomed, striding into the room. 'Still at table. Shame on 'ee for a slug-a-bed. You should take a leaf from *my* book, damme. I've been up and about since six.' He sat down heavily in the carver chair and helped himself to two thick slices of boiled ham.

'How was Bristol, my love?' Hermione asked, speaking with deliberate gentleness to remind him of the correct way to deport himself.

'Bristol is no more,' he told her happily. It was extraordinary how confident he felt. He'd just taken on the biggest debt of his life and run the most formidable risks, yet he felt as though he'd won a great victory. 'Bristol is settled. Signed, sealed and delivered.' He beamed upon them. 'We're catching the twelve o'clock stage to London.'

Melissa went on spooning coddled eggs into her mouth, her face vacant, but Ariadne was instantly and irritably alerted. She couldn't go to London. Not now. Not before the fair.

Hermione inclined her head, gracefully. 'We?' she questioned.

'The family,' he said waving towards his daughters. 'All of us. Capital idea, what!' He was so full of himself and his success that he didn't notice that Ariadne was bristling.

'Not the baby,' Hermione said firmly. 'Not to London. London is no fit place for a baby, especially in summer.'

'London, my love,' Sir George corrected, 'is chock-a-block full of babies. Mr Coram's Foundling Hospital is bursting with 'em. Can't take any more. Arnold was telling me. They have to cast lots to get in. Little coloured balls.'

His wife cut him short. 'Foundlings may do as they please,' she said. 'What foundlings do is all one to me. William ain't to go to London. Unless you require him to take an infection.'

Sir George ignored her sarcasm. 'Farm him out, then,' he said easily. 'You can do that can't you?'

'Not before noon.'

'Leave him with the wet nurse. Let her attend to it. Be a fine time for our gels to be in the capital, be gad. Right in the thick of it all. What think 'ee, Ariadne? You'd like to go to London would you not?'

Ariadne had been sitting bolt upright, taut with aggravation. But she tried to make an acceptable reply. 'I agree with Mamma, sir,' she said. ''Taint a fit place in summer. We must think of the infections. Besides, how can we travel today? You have only to look at the weather and consider the hazards.'

'Tosh!' her father rebuked her. 'What kind of talk is this? Hazards? A shower ain't a hazard, miss. A hazard is what happens in Nevis when your sugar crop gets blown to smithereens and your field niggers are tossed into the air. That's a hazard. Now bestir yourself and get ready for your journey and let's have no more silly talk.'

But battle had been joined. 'I have commitments, Papa. I am engaged to dine with Charlotte this very afternoon.'

'Then cancel it.'

Ariadne was stiff-necked with annoyance but she kept her composure. 'Twould not look well, Papa. After all, as you have so often had occasion to remark, we have a position to maintain.'

'I have a position to maintain,' her father corrected. 'You have nothing to maintain except what comes to you through me, which you'd do well to remember.' Her manner was annoying him. After his great success in Bristol he expected to be praised and pampered by his womenfolk, not opposed. 'Bestir yourself and prepare to travel. For, mark this, Ariadne, travel you will and this very afternoon.'

Ariadne couldn't restrain her temper a moment longer. 'I won't,' she cried. 'You can't make me.'

'You will,' her father roared at her, 'or I'll take a stick to 'ee, so I will.'

To be threatened was frightening but she fought on, colour flooding her throat and blotching her cheeks. 'How heartless you are, Papa! Am I never to see my friends? Am I to have no life at all?'

''Od's bones!' her father shouted. 'Am I to arrange my life to suit your acquaintances? Am I to stay in Bath so that you may go gallivanting about the town? Is that it? Am I to be told my business by a chit of a girl?'

'No, Papa. You may go where you please.'

Her desperate boldness sounded like impertinence. 'I will not be spoken to in such a manner.'

'I was not...' Ariadne tried.

But he was in full roar. 'Hold your tongue, miss! Speak when you're spoken to!'

Hermione tried to calm the situation. 'Could we not follow you a little later, my love, when our arrangements have been made?'

'No you could not,' her husband said. ''Od's bones woman, I've to meet with the consortium tomorrow. The country could be at war for ought we know.'

'I merely made a suggestion, my love,' Hermione smoothed. 'Of course if you wish it, we will do what we can to accommodate you.'

'Quite right,' Sir George said. 'So we will travel on the twelve o'clock stage, as I said, and dine at Oxford.'

He was gratified when Hermione gave another of her graceful inclinations of the head and murmured agreement.

But Ariadne was adamant. 'Mamma may give in to you if she chooses,' she said, her voice tight with fury, 'but depend upon it, I will not leave Bath! Not this afternoon. Not tomorrow. Not ever! I have arrangements and I mean to stick to 'em. Tis a matter of honour.'

'Leave the table!' Sir George commanded. 'I will not be addressed in this fashion, d'ye hear. Honour! Whatever next? You will do as you're told.'

'I will not!' Ariadne yelled again, leaping to her feet with such passion that she overturned her chair. Her face was burning now and her eyes wild. She shook off Hermione's restraining hand, like a horse twitching away flies. 'Do you wish to send me into a decline?' she shrieked.

'You may decline wherever and whenever you please,' her father said, 'but you ain't disobeying my orders. You'll do as you're told, miss, or you'll take the consequences. Now I'm off to the ticket office to buy four tickets to London, which we shall use this afternoon, depend upon it.' And he strode out on to the landing, bellowing for Jessup. ''Od's bowels. There's never a servant when you want one. Jessup! Where are you?'

Ariadne looked at her mother for support. 'Mamma?'

None was offered. 'If you will take my advice, child,' Hermione said coolly, 'you will try to regain control of yourself or you will overstrain your constitution.'

'Oh!' Ariadne cried. 'How cruel you all are! You treat me despicably. I can't bear it!' And she flung herself face downwards on the carpet and abandoned herself to a luxury of hysterics, drumming her feet, beating her fists and screaming at the top of her voice. Even Melissa stopped eating to look at her.

Hermione was caught between disbelief — the girl was given to play-acting — and a sudden fear that this display might prove to be the first indication of a brainstorm. Whatever it was, the child would have to be quietened before her father came back into the room, or his rage would be roused even further, which would be exceedingly unpleasant. But it was too late, he had already returned, with Jessup stooping after him.

She decided at once that play-acting or not, her daughter's behaviour should be perceived as evidence of illness, if only to prevent a scandal below stairs. She sank elegantly to her knees beside her daughter's waist — where there was less chance of being kicked or punched — and looked up imploringly at the two men who were now gazing down at her. 'La! Poor creature! She has taken a fit,' she explained. ''Tis a weakness in her constitution. Jessup, pray run for Mr McKinnon!'

Her husband would have none of it. 'Weakness my foot!' he said. 'If that's a fit, ma'am, then I'm a...' he cast about wildly for a suitable comparison, and could only find, 'a boiled egg, ma'am. She's a thwart disobedient wretch, that's what she is, and now she must take the consequences. Let her suffer for it. That's what I say. Stay where you are, Jessup!' And as Ariadne continued to roar and roll, he swung a foot at her pummelling fists. 'Have I to take a stick to 'ee, miss?'

Hermione caught his ankle before the kick could land. 'Mercy upon us!' she cried. 'The child is sick. Do you wish to make her worse? Run for McKinnon, Jessup. Why do you stand there?'

Jessup didn't know whether to stand or stay. He stood in the doorway coughing with embarrassment, while Ariadne wept and flung herself from side to side and Melissa gazed at her with open mouth and her mother tried in vain to lift from her exhibition. Her screams were deafening, and the more her father roared, the louder they became.

''Od's bowels and bones,' Sir George bellowed above the din. 'I'm off to the coffee house, be gad. This ain't to be endured. There's no peace in this house!' And he stormed from the room, pausing at the door to shout at his wife that *he* was going to London, come hell or high water, and that she could do as she pleased.

So Jessup ran for the doctor, and Melissa returned to her food and Ariadne allowed herself to be coaxed into a chair.

Mr McKinnon was back with Jessup as fast as his little short legs would carry him, for he knew from experience that if one of the Bradbury ladies were ill, the result would be both dramatic and lucrative. He was full of professional sympathy for the terrible suffering of the young Miss Ariadne, and having diagnosed a rising of the mother, with the possibility of brain fever, applied two leeches to her arm at once to reduce the danger of hysteria, which they did with impressive speed, since Ariadne had no intention of being bled white even to get her own way. Then he turned his soothing attention to Lady Bradbury, explaining that her daughter had sustained a shock to the system, and needed to be most careful of her health.

'My husband wishes us to travel to London this very afternoon,' Hermione confided, when Hepzie had assisted her to recline upon the chaise longue and warm compresses had been applied to her temples. 'Would that be wise?'

Mr McKinnon was horrified. 'My dear lady!' he said. 'Neither of you should move from Bath on any account whatsoever. You must stay here for at least four days to let the mother sink to its proper sphere and to alleviate the shock to your constitution.' Hermione, who was feeling agreeably weaker by the minute, was happy to let him rearrange their lives. She promised that she and Ariadne would take the waters twice a day from then on, and avoid all noxious airs, and call for him again — and immediately — should either of them take a turn for the worse.

'We cannot be too careful, ma'am, in cases of this land,' the doctor said. 'I will do myself the honour of waiting upon you at the Cross Bath tomorrow morning.'

Hermione waved her agreement — weakly — but as soon as he was out of the house, she sent for Suki Brown and returned to her usual brisk manner.

'Miss Ariadne is unwell,' she said. 'She will need most careful nursing and someone to keep a close eye on all her movements. *All* her movements, you understand.'

Having heard the gossip below stairs, Suki understood entirely. ''Tis possible,' Hermione allowed, 'that she may wish to take the air to clear her senses a little. I cannot know her mind, you understand, but we must be prepared for any eventuality.'

'You wish me to accompany her, ma'am?' Suki said.

'To follow her, perchance,' Hermione said vaguely. 'At a suitable distance. 'Twould be less distressing for her to be unaware of your presence, unless 'twere needful, were she to be taken ill again. I could be worrying about her unnecessarily, but mothers have these concerns. We cannot avoid them.' She sighed and closed her eyes. 'Tis a precaution, no more. I am sure you understand.' And when Suld nodded and seemed to appreciate what was required of her, Tray tell Hepzibah to attend me. That will be all.'

'Sit by the window,' Cook advised, when she'd heard all about it. 'If I'm any judge she'll be off in two shakes of a lamb's tail. Babba's been fed, haven't he?'

Sure enough, the lamb shook its tail ten minutes later, just after Hepzie came back into the kitchen.

'Follow on her heels,' Cook advised. 'She'm a-going at a good old lick.'

Which Suki did, walking close to the buildings so that she could slip into a doorway should the young lady look back. But Ariadne was too concerned with her own affairs and walking with such urgency that Suki could hear the swish of her skirts from twenty paces.

She's off to the theatre, Suki guessed, as her quarry reached the end of the parade. But she was wrong. Ariadne crossed the road and sped off towards the abbey and the centre of town. Where *was* she going? Was it a lover's meeting? And if it was, how had she arranged it? The chase was becoming quite exciting, as chases invariably do. When her mistress's embroidered gown disappeared into the throng before the abbey, she quickened her pace until she was almost behind her, agog to see where she would run to next.

Through the abbey green, where two dandies were having an elaborate argument, past the Pump Room, where a line of chairs were still waiting damply for the last of the bathers, across the abbey yard, through a dark alley into Cheap Street and then westwards, dodging the carts and carriages that jostled towards the west gate and the Bristol road, and on into one side street after another, half walking, half trotting. Then without any warning, she turned a corner and disappeared.

Suki was cross and frustrated, but being a sensible girl she set herself to solve the problem. There were no carriages or chairs in the street, so she couldn't have been carried away, and the only place she could have gone on foot was into one of the little shops that lined one side of the street, and of all the shops presenting their curved windows to custom, the two most likely were the apothecary's and the milliners.

She walked carelessly past the apothecary's. No. Only two gentlemen and a lapdog. Approached the milliner's. And there, caught in a pretty tableau framed by the window, were Ariadne and the shopkeeper, head to head beside the counter.

Where can I hide? Suki thought, looking about her. Quick before she sees me. There was a narrow alley between the houses almost opposite the shop. It was dank and smelly but it would serve. If she stood in the shadow, she could watch without being seen.

The milliner was taking something from a wooden hatbox on one of the shelves. Something small enough to be held in her palm. She was a short, stooped woman, and walked very slowly in an odd rocking movement as though she were deliberately tipping herself forward at every step. It took her a long time to rock back to her customer, and then the two of them stood nose to shoulder in a long conversation, during which the milliner held up the object from the hatbox, which turned out to be a letter of some kind. She seemed to be beating time with it, the creamy paper fluttering like a huge pale moth against the darkness of the panelled walls.

Something's going on, Suki thought. There ain't a bit of doubt about that. And in her eagerness to find out what it was, she stepped out of the shadow. And at that moment, Ariadne looked up, stared straight through the window and saw her.

She was out of the shop door and calling to her before Suki had time to think what to do.

'La, Suki Brown!' she said. 'Has Mamma sent you to carry my packages? I thought 'twas so. Well, come in and collect them then. Don't stand about. They're almost ready.'

So Suki had to follow her into the shop. There was no sign of any packages except for a length of ribbon that the milliner was wrapping, and once the door was closed, Ariadne changed her tone. 'Walk to the counter,' she instructed, 'and stand to my left. Turn towards the window. So. A little more. Now tell me, whom do you see at the corner of the street?'

It was Hepzibah, looking very smart in a new sprigged cotton dress, and walking up and down as though she was waiting for somebody.

'The dress is one of Mamma's,' Ariadne explained. ''Twas what caught my eye when I first looked into the street. Sent to spy on you I shouldn't wonder, in the same way as you were sent to spy on me, and by the same person.' Her voice was exactly like her mother's, calm to the point of insouciance. 'Tush gel, there's no call to blush. 'Tis the way of the world. Spies are legion.'

Suki didn't know what to say. To be caught in the act was embarrassing enough without discovering that she was being spied upon in her turn.

'Have no fear,' Ariadne said, smiling at her discomfiture. 'We will outwit them both.' She leaned across the counter to the milliner. 'Have this delivered,' she said, taking a billet from her pocket and sliding it across the counter. 'Now we will leave by the back, which I daresay you wall open for us.' She picked up her parcel and laid a shilling on top of the letter.

The milliner picked it up without looking at it. 'Without question, mademoiselle,' she agreed. 'If you will be so good as to step this way.'

So Suki and her quarry escaped together, through a small parlour, past a dark scullery, very much at odds with the delicacy of the shop, and out into a jagged courtyard, enclosed on all four sides, where the night soil was heaped in an open box, the flags were piddle strewn and the stone walls were slimy with damp lichen. They gathered up their skirts and picked their way through the mire with great care so as to protect their shoes, until they came to a low doorway, where two stone flags gave them a clean patch of ground on which to stand.

'Now,' Ariadne said imperiously, we must decide how to proceed. I must tell 'ee 'tis all your fault.'

Suki's eyes widened but she didn't answer for fear of giving offence. How could it be her fault? She hadn't asked to be a spy.

''Twas your idea that set me on,' Ariadne said. 'Hepzibah told me about it.' And as Sula was still gazing at her, wide-eyed and saying nothing, she explained. That women should own their own bodies, that we shouldn't belong to our fathers, that we should chose our own lovers, marry where we will. The minute I heard it I knew 'twas true. So I have put it to the proof.'

Suki was so astonished she didn't know how to answer. She realized that she had found an ally, that this unlikely young woman had understood as she did, that they were linked and changed by their understanding, but it was such a surprise that it was a minute or two before she could take it in. The idea blossomed between them in that dank smelly place, fresh and green and full of hopeful buds, and the minutes held them still, hidden, out of time, and charged with emotions — recognition and admiration, excitement and daring and an invigorating sense of danger. They were no longer mistress and servant but two passionate young women, both of them in love, caught up in the wonder of their extraordinary idea and speaking the truth to one another.

'I have found the man I wish to marry,' Ariadne said. 'We have exchanged letters and soon we shall exchange vows. What think 'ee to that?'

'Mr Clements,' Suki said.

'Mr Clements,' Ariadne agreed, speaking the name with lingering affection. 'Oh, Suki, he is such a proper man and so handsome. I love him with all my heart. Mamma suspects as much, I fear, which is why she has commissioned you to watch me, is it not?'

Suki nodded.

'What did she pay you?'

'A groat.'

Ariadne laughed with delight. 'A groat? When she gives that flouncy Hepzibah a gown. La, she is even more foolish than I thought.' She laughed again, showing her white teeth. 'And will be the more easily fooled. We must decide what she is to be told, when you make your report.'

'There'll be little to tell,' Suki said, laughing too. What sport to outwit milady and serve her right for being so stingy. That you went to the milliner's and bought a yard of ribbon to trim your bonnet.'

'And came straight home to trim it,' Ariadne agreed. Capital.'

They could hear the rumble of traffic beyond the wall. 'Time to be gone,' Ariadne said and creaked the door open. They were out in another side street that Suki didn't recognize. It was comfortably full of shoppers and there was no sign of Hepzie. Ariadne led the way, walking briskly.

'You chose *your* lover, did you not?' she asked as they turned the corner.

'Yes. I did.'

Ariadne's interest was intense and hopeful. 'And have much joy of him I daresay?'

'Aye, I did.'

The use of the past tense roused Ariadne's sympathy. 'Did?'

'I haven't seen him since the baby was born,' Suki admitted. 'I'm a-waitin' for him. He should be here any day. I'm hopin' he'll be at the fair.'

'You don't have somewhere to live together?' Ariadne asked. 'No, no. I remember. He is at sea, is he not?'

Suki hesitated. Admitting to a love affair was one thing, unravelling a lie another. But before she could decide how to answer, Ariadne was speaking again. 'Mr Clements will be at the fair,' she confided. 'I'm to meet him there. Oh the joy of it! I shall see him again in three days. Three days, Suki. Think of it. You shall accompany me there and we will find our lovers together. Oh this is admirable. Admirable.'

They were back in the abbey yard and would soon be home.

'I'd best walk behind you,' Suki said. There were too many people to see them here and no proper sonant would walk alongside her mistress.

'Yes.'

'I'm sorry I was set to spy on you.'

'Pray do not consider it,' Ariadne said magnanimously. 'We shall use it to our mutual advantage. The first thing we must do is to ensure that we both go to the fair. I shall get Mr McKinnon to advise it, don't you think so?'

'Look pale,' Suki advised her, 'and cast your eyes down. Gentlemen like that.'

'Aye, I've noticed,' Ariadne said. 'Poor fools! What a game it all is!'

But she played the game the following morning and played it well, splashing her face with cold water to achieve the necessary pallor and wearing her prettiest dressing gown. She had bathed and taken the waters and swallowed a pill large enough to choke a horse. Now all she had to do was to charm the doctor.

'I declare I feel better every hour, my dear Mr McKinnon,' she sighed. The julep you prescribed was most cooling. I trust you will prescribe it again. Do you not think I improve?'

'Of course, dear lady,' the physician said, flattered that his medicines were so acceptable. That is the way of all good cures. A little better every day. Have I not always said so?'

Hermione was still red-faced from the heat of the baths and the colour made her expression look more disagreeable than usual. 'I trust we shall soon see her well enough to travel, Mr McKinnon,' she said. 'Her father is most anxious that we should join him in London at the earliest possible moment. Delay is all very well for the lower orders, but *we* are descended from the Dukes of Daventry. *Noblesse oblige*, you know.'

Mr McKinnon could see his hopes of a fat fee receding. He looked round anxiously at his patient, who was drooping prettily in her seat against the wall. 'Well, of course, dear lady,' he said, 'I appreciate the urgency of this case, but then again it would not do to spoil the ship for a ha'p'orth of tar, so to speak. Miss Ariadne is improving, as we are all glad to observe, but I feel we should complete the treatment. Young constitutions are so remarkably tender. I'm sure you would wish to effect a lasting cure.'

'Even one more day, Mamma, would make such a difference,'

Ariadne urged, assuming a pathetic expression. 'Until Friday, perhaps.'

'Indeed yes,' Mr McKinnon agreed, buying another day. 'Perhaps we could postpone a decision until tomorrow.'

'We will see,' Hermione temporized. Another day would make very little difference and she still had to arrange to farm out the baby. I shall send for the wet nurse as soon as this wretched man has gone.

Suki wasn't surprised to be summoned. It would be about the fair, bound to be, and she'd thought out what she was going to say.

She wasn't prepared for milady's announcement.

'I've to travel to London in a day or two,' Hermione said, 'and must decide what is to be done with William.'

'Yes, ma'am. Shall I pack his things?'

'I suppose so,' Hermione said vaguely. 'Wherever he goes, he will need clothes and cradle and so forth.'

The words sounded ominous. Wherever he goes? 'Ain't he to travel with you, ma'am?'

'Indeed not,' Hermione said. 'He's to be farmed out to the country, which is why I sent for you. Do you know of any suitable place hereabouts? Some good woman who lives on a farm perchance. Someone who can be trusted, naturally, for he will stay with her a good while.'

The shock of being told she was to share this precious child of hers sent Suki into a panic. Stay with her, she thought. Not while I'm alive to stop it he won't. If he'm to stay with anybody it's to be with me. There was such a tumult in her chest it felt as though it was boiling. What could she suggest? She *couldn't* let them farm him out to some other woman, poor little mite. He had to stay with her where he was happy. Then she suddenly remembered Farmer Lambton and knew what to say. 'He could come home with me,' she said. 'I live on a farm.'

That was a surprise. 'Do you so?'

'Yes, ma'am. Born and bred on a farm.'

'In the farmhouse?'

Lie. It was the only way. 'Yes, ma'am.'

'But you cannot read and write, can you? I shall need a letter every week to tell me of his progress.'

Lie again. 'I can read well enough ma'am, and write too. I could send you letters.' Please, please agree to it. I can't have another woman looking after my darling. 'I should have to go with him in any case, shouldn't I ma'am. To feed him.'

That was true. 'Twould be another three years or so before he was weaned and whatever else she might think about this girl she was a good wet nurse. 'I will consider it,' she said. ''Tis an arrangement that might serve. Meantime there is the matter of Ariadne and whether or not she is strong enough to travel. The doctor thinks she will be sufficiently recovered in a day or two. Do you agree? You have watched her, have you not?'

'She'm gettin' better by degrees,' Suki reported, 'so far as I can tell, ma'am, and I *have* watched over her, as you instructed. A few more days an' we shall see her quite herself again.'

'A few more days is too long,' Hermione said. 'Her father left particular instructions that we were all to follow him to London at the very first opportunity.'

Suki looked sympathetic and decided to risk a suggestion. 'What we need ma'am, if I may make so bold,' she offered, 'is a test of her constitution. An outing of some kind to show whether she is strong enough to undertake the journey.'

'A ride in the hills perchance?' Hermione wondered. 'Something a sight more strenuous, I should say,' Suki added, as though the idea had just occurred to her. 'There's a fair coming to Barton Fields on Thursday.'

'Yes,' Hermione said tartly. 'I know that. Melissa tells me they plan to attend, which I can hardly countenance. I do not consider a fair to be a suitable amusement for my daughters. They are such vulgar places and uncommon noisy.'

'Howsomever,' Suki said, smoothly, 'if Miss Ariadne has the strength to withstand a fair, she can't never pretend she am't fit to travel, now can she?'

The logic of it was impeccable, as Hermione was quick to appreciate. The girl might be devious — giving Hepzibah the slip was evidence of that — but she had a native wit and plenty of common sense. There were risks in agreeing to her plan, but on the other hand...

'Should I allow this,' she said, 'which I ain't saying I shall, you would accompany her, would you not, and keep a most careful eye upon her?'

'Of course, ma'am,' Suki said, and she managed to look meek and obedient.

Eleven

Sir George Bradbury had ambivalent feelings towards his capital city, although, of course, he never admitted them to anybody and only to himself on particularly honest occasions. A man has his pride. They existed nevertheless and their existence turned every visit into a test of his endurance.

He admired the place, naturally. Who would not? The new squares on the west side of the city, where he and Hermione had chosen to live, were uncommon fine, classically proportioned, pavements swept clean, roads free of traffic, central gardens trim and well kept, comfortably away from the stench of the old city, and inhabited by people of undoubted wealth and some quality, many of them sugar merchants like himself. There were pleasure gardens and theatres and coffee houses aplenty; there were clubs to provide the relief of an exclusively masculine environment; there were whores available in all the main thoroughfares whenever he felt the need of them; and above all there was a sense that this was the place where important matters were decided, the centre of power and money, the home of royalty and the ton.

Living in the city presented no difficulty to Hermione at all. She took to society as to the manner born, which was no surprise as she *was* to the manner born. But Sir George felt awkward there, a Johnny-come-lately, nouveau riche, one of the lesser gentry, even on occasions a rough colonial, tolerated but never quite accepted. He could only cope with his first twenty-four hours in the place by getting rolling drunk beforehand. And on this occasion he had the added anxiety of his commission to find a husband for that dratted child. Marriage broking was all very well for people like Hermione with the right sort of contacts and no awareness that she was putting herself at a disadvantage among her friends, but for him it was a source of grumbling unease. He knew it would have to be done, or she would scald him alive, but it would be uncommon hard and would need a deal of liquor to screw up the courage for it.

The first meeting of the Committee of Merchant Traders was consequently an ebulliently drunken occasion. It was held in the library of Lord Fosdyke's splendid house in Cavendish Square, where all sixteen members of the committee could sprawl in comfort around his elegant library table. There was a plentiful supply of London Particular, brandy, Hollands and such like, all ready to hand, and it began well. Stirring news had arrived that the young farmer from Virginia had been harrying the French again. A local skirmish apparently and an easy victory as Lord Fosdyke told them with much head-nodding satisfaction. So naturally they had to open proceedings by drinking a toast to the gentleman.

'Here's a health to George Washington!' Sir Arnold Willoughby proposed, raising his glass. 'A good man, be gad. Long may he trounce 'em.' The French had lost him a vast amount of capital over the last few years, paying nine ounces of gold per slave when his company could only afford to offer eight. If it hadn't been for the government grant, he might have gone bankrupt.

'I'm told he's something of a landowner, what?' Lord Fosdyke said.

'He was,' Sir Arnold confirmed. 'Owned a deal of land around Fort Duquesne apparently, before the Frenchies drove him out.'

The young Colonel Washington's campaign was instantly understandable.

'Ah well,' John Smithers said, 'if *that's* the case, no wonder he harries 'em.'

'They bit off more than they could chew with that young man,' Ponsonby-Smith said happily. That's the truth of it. Pesky Frenchies. High time we built a few forts in the region ourselves, if you ask my opinion, or 'twill be French territory from the St Lawrence to the Mississippi. We should have learnt that when General Braddock was killed.'

'I was speaking to Mr Pitt on Friday about that very matter,' Lord Fosdyke told them, with the careless ease of a man who could claim the formidable politician among his friends. 'He tells me 'tis in hand and 'twill be called Fort Necessity.'

'A capital name,' Sir Arnold approved. 'I trust the Frenchies will see the virtue in it!'

'Mr Pitt is the only man in the Commons who understands how to defeat the French,' Ponsonby-Smith told them, helping himself to more brandy. 'Diplomacy ain't worth the candle, these days. We should wage war upon 'em with all the ships at our disposal. He said so only last week. 'Twas in the *Gazette*. "When trade is at stake, we must defend it or perish", he said. I recall the very words.'

'A naval war,' Sir Arnold agreed. 'That's what we need. A war to smash her fleet and capture her bases. Long overdue if you want my opinion of it. We've lost enough ships to'em. They took one of Georgie's this very summer, ain't that right Georgie?'

Sir George acknowledged the truth of it, although his mind was still caught up in the memory of his most recent sighting of the renowned Mr Pitt, standing at the dispatch box in the House, great tall fellow, with a commanding air about him, uncommon lean for a man of property he'd always thought, but there was no doubt about his presence or his authority, nose like a hawk, eyes flashing. He'd been giving somebody a trouncing and the poor fellow was fairly cringing. What a gentleman to call one's friend! 'Good chap Pitt!' he said.

'We shall declare war come the finish,' Ponsonby-Smith said. 'I'm dammed if I can see why we go on dallying.'

There was a murmur of agreement from the other members of the committee.

'That being the case, gentlemen,' Lord Fosdyke said, smiling in his sardonic way, 'shall we proceed to business and see what may be done to hasten the event?'

At their last meeting there had been some talk of fitting out two or three privateers and sending them into the Atlantic to harass the French and search for boot. To equip three privateers was a costly business, and hazardous, for although the capture of a French ship could make them all rich, there was always the unspoken possibility that their expensive warships might actually be sunk or captured instead. However, Sir Arnold had offered one of his traders and had sought out several estimates for the necessary conversion. But that evening he'd barely pulled the papers from his pocket before one of their three new members — who turned out to be a scion of the de Thespia family and consequently a man of some influence — spoke up to suggest that the time for timidity was over and that they should be aiming at six ships 'at the very least' and thinking to double their commitment.

His enthusiasm encouraged Sir George to speak out too. 'I saw a likely vessel in Bristol,' he told his colleagues, 'when I was buying a replacement for the ship the Frenchies took.'

Interest was instant and intense.

'What was her burden?' de Thespia asked.

'Three hundred and sixty tons.'

De Thespia translated that into the number of guns she would carry. 'Twenty-four nine and six pounders,' he said. 'We shall need a crew of two hundred and fifty, I should say, and a surgeon.'

John Smither's eyes were shining with excitement at the thought of the extra booty they would earn if they doubled their fleet. He could already see their newly anned vessels setting out, flags flying, to capture all the splendid French prizes that were out in the Atlantic waiting for them. 'The more guns the better,' he urged.

'Twill cut speed,' de Thespia pointed out. 'How long would she take to cross?'

'Six weeks with a fair wind,' Sir George told him, 'and a good commander.'

'My vote's for fire power,' Lord Fosdyke said, dipping his long white nose into his port. 'Damme, we ain't racin' the beggars! Blow 'em out of the sea. That's what I say. Damned Frenchies! What's the news on the three we have in hand?'

Sir Arnold handed out his estimates, one from Mr Tasker and the other — much cheaper — from a newcomer to the trade, one Mr Williams. There you are, gentlemen,' he said, passing the documents to right and left, 'with a warranty to have 'em seaworthy and ready to cruise by mid-July.'

'Tasker's for twenty guns and a crew of two hundred, I see,' de Thespia mused. 'A man to trust, Mr Tasker. I've made use of him myself from time to time.' He waved the estimate at his new colleagues, delicately as though it were a perfumed handkerchief. 'I would be inclined to accept his offer.'

On which recommendation the matter was decided, and so, twenty minutes later, was the number of ships they would commission. Then they turned their attention to the other and rather more important matter of how and when they would start to lobby their colleagues in the House. For as Lord Fosdyke said, 'If we want a war, we can't leave it all to Mr

Pitt. We must press for it.' So the pressure was planned. The number of sugar planters and slave traders in the House was comfortably high, between a third and a half of all members, and one or two of them — like Mr Beckford and Mr Lascelles — were men of considerable influence in the City, so they were confident that they could win with a large enough margin if they could prevail upon the House to put it to the vote.

'Most satisfactory,' Sir Arnold said as he left the house with Sir George and John Smithers at the end of the meeting. 'I'm off to the club. I quite fancy a game of hazard. Shall you join me?'

So the three friends set off to continue their evening together. They were so deep in drunkenness that a few more glasses wouldn't make any difference.

'Soon be at war, begad,' Sir George said, as they settled into their favourite chairs, and he treated them all to a bowl of hot sack, as the sort of manly drink appropriate to the moment. 'Stirring times, what!'

Patriotism and the excitement of the risks they'd decided to take gave them all a prodigious thirst, which took several hours to satisfy. They progressed to cognac and drank the health of the gallants who had 'risked life and limb' to smuggle it into the country for them: they played faro until Sir Arnold was seriously out of pocket; and at two o'clock in the morning they staggered from the club, arm in arm and singing raucously, to find chairs to carry them back to Cavendish Square.

'I tell you what,' Sir George said, focusing his voice and his eyes with difficulty. 'That Dr Johnson's a rum sort of chap but he's right about one thing. Any man who can trier — try — tire of London must be deaf, dumb, blind, out of his senses altogether.' He'd quite forgotten his earlier mistrust of the place. Now he saw it as an invigoration, better than any medicine. Why, just looking at the crowds still thronging Piccadilly at that hour of the morning would tell you that. He'd never seen any other place so full of life. In the Indies most people were lethargic with heat, in Bath they hobbled about on sticks spitting and coughing, on his estate they moved at the pace of a plough, but here it was all speed and colour and purpose, changing minute by minute before his eyes. 'Better than medichine, London is. Besht place in the world.'

'Get in,' John Smithers advised, holding upon the door of his friend's chair, 'and sit down before you fall over.'

It was sibilantly quiet in Cavendish Square. Moonlight silvered the balanced facades and made the fine glass of their elegant windows glint and gleam. The neatly mounded beds of the central garden were striped with shifting shadows as though they were growing strange horizontal blooms, the pavements shone white as though they'd been new scoured, and through the gap between the terraces, the three carousers could see the wooded slopes of Hampstead Heath, where the highwaymen lurked for their prey, and the chequered fields and night-black copses that spread in every direction around the village of St Mary le Bone and the fine new pleasure garden there.

As he stumbled into the hall of his house, Sir George was awash with drunken happiness. But then Barnaby emerged from the kitchen, his face still folded with sleep and his hair standing on end, and held out a tray with a letter on it. The sight of that small square of paper sobered Sir George so rapidly that he turned pale and would have fallen had he not reached out to support himself on the arm of the chair.

Sir Arnold leapt to assist him. 'What is it, me dear fellow? What's amiss?'

'Hermione, I'll lay money,' Sir George said, lowering his bulk into the chair. 'Wants me to find a husband for Ariadne, be gad. I'd clean forgot. This is to remind me.'

'Ignore it,' Sir Arnold advised. 'Time enough for that sort of caper in the morning.'

'Ignore Hermione?' Sir George blinked at him. 'You ain't seen her in a bad humour! I should never hear the end of it. No, no. It has to be done, deuce take it.'

'Take heart, Georgie,' John Smithers urged. 'There's husbands the length and breadth of London.'

That didn't cheer his friend in the slightest. 'And all of 'em married,' he said gloomily.

Barnaby was yawning so widely it was a wonder he didn't dislocate his jaw. The grandfather clock struck half past two. Sir George closed his eyes and began to snore.

'We'll put it about in the Mall tomorrow,' Sir Arnold decided. 'That's the best way. Too late for it now, be gad.' He was so drunk and so fatigued he could barely keep his balance. 'Assist your master to bed.'

'Mush obliged,' Sir George said, trying to open his eyes as Bamaby hauled him to his feet. 'Nasty' business, marriage. Shouldn't be allowed. Against all reason, damme if it ain't.'

Drunk though he was, Arnold Willoughby had actually made a sensible suggestion. The late morning promenade between the trees in the Mall was the best place for the exchange of gossip and one of the best for the opening gambit when seeking a marriage partner for a member of one's family, for that was where all established and would-be members of society took their daily constitutional in the hour between breakfast and their visit to the Exchange, dressed in their very best and sharp-eyed to criticise and compete. The King took his exercise in the privacy of Bird Cage Walk but the ton filled every other space in the park. Many a prestigious social wedding had sprung from a fortunate encounter along that *breezy* walk.

Within an hour of their arrival the next morning, the three friends had dropped their hint into every possible ear, from the great ladies Holland and Home to a second cousin twice removed of Mr Tuite the planter. The dowry had been suggested, amended, and generally agreed upon, except by Sir George who considered it a deal too high. But at least, as he told his two friends over dinner that afternoon, he had the satisfaction of knowing he had done what he could. 'Can't say fairer than that, damme.'

'We're to dine with old Fosdyke tomorrow,' Sir Arnold said. 'You should hear something by then. Meantime we've the City at our disposal. They say the gardens are uncommon fine this year.' He'd bought three tickets for the Ranelagh Gardens that evening and was eager to sample the delights.

So as there was no longer anything to prevent them, and it was already late in the afternoon, the three friends commandeered a cab to take them to Chelsea.

The Gardens were even better than they expected, for they had chosen the night of a masque so all the guests and most of the entertainers were sporting visors in various styles and complications. Sir George bought himself a boar's head with a fine set of bristles, Sir Arnold became a red fox, and John Smithers decided on a blackamoor's visage, which made his blue eyes look even bolder than usual. Then the three of them set off through the alleys, hoping for a conquest and horsing about with excitement.

The entire area had been strung with garlands of flowers that looped and swung from tree to tree, and there were tents in every space, large ones for tea and coffee, lesser ones for gaming, smaller still for assignations. Bands played at every corner, here a group got up as huntsmen, blowing French horns, here another playing tabors and pipes and dressed as peasants in cream smocks, with their legs cross-gartered with red leather and with wild flowers in their hats. There was a troop of harlequins and scaramouches leaping and cavorting on the mount, and down on the canal, a gondola rowed up and down, dressed overall with flags and streamers, and with yet another band aboard, playing discordantly but with great brio.

Sir Arnold estimated that there must have been over two thousand people there and there was certainly plenty of trade. All round the outside of the amphitheatre the shops were busy selling the latest goods: Dresden china, tea caddies, head-scratchers and suchlike necessaries. And the amphitheatre itself had been transformed. It was so brightly lit that Sir George declared it was like broad daylight inside, there were so many candles in the chandeliers, and it was aromatic with greenery. The bower in the centre was full of fir trees, from twenty to thirty feet high, each standing in its own wooden tub, and beneath the firs were orange trees, with small golden lamps glowing prettily inside every orange, and beneath the orange trees were mounds of multi-coloured auriculas in tiny earthemvare pots. There were firs between the arches too and in the balconies above them. When the dancing began it was like being at a ball in the middle of a wood.

After an hour John Smithers slipped away with a lady masked as an angel, which Sir George said was uncommon unfitting. But angel or no she didn't serve him well for he was back within a quarter of an hour looking doleful and declaring that 'Whores ain't what they were'. Sir George renewed an acquaintance with one of his old flames, who sent him an invitation by the gentlest flicker of her fan, but he didn't venture more than a dance, there being a husband in the offing. Only Sir Arnold struck luck and he was still missing at midnight when the gardens closed.

'Lucky dog!' John Smithers complained. 'I thought 'twould be you, Georgie, upon me life, not the old fox.'

Sir George was disappointed not to have made an assignation but at least he had a face-saving excuse for it. 'I've got to keep my wits about me,' he explained. 'Ready for tomorrow. Marriage broking takes a cool head, don'tcher know.'

It actually turned out a deal easier than he expected, although it wasn't until dinner was over, the port had been passed, the pipes lit, the chamber pot taken from the sideboard and used until it was awash, and all the gentlemen were thoroughly comfortable, that they set their minds to the matter of his proposed son-in-law, and by then he was dyspeptic with anxiety.

Between them they'd come up with three possibilities. One was a rich widower in his sixties, who'd just lost his third wife in childbirth and was, according to Lord Fosdyke's account of his circumstances, desperate for company. The second was a cloth merchant, who was an acquaintance of Mr Tuite's and had a house in Golden Square, 'old fashioned but well furnished', and an estate in Herefordshire, and was looking for a healthy young wife to provide him with a son and heir. The third was the youngest son of the Duke of Errymouth, one Humphrey de Thespia, who was a cousin of the formidable de Thespia who was now heading the Committee of Merchant Traders. Apparently he was young and feckless and had been told to marry and settle down if he wished his father to redeem his current debts. 'Has the makings of a fine chap,' his cousin told them, 'with a good wife behind him, don'tcher know.'

Sir George thanked them all kindly and said he was much obliged to them, which on this occasion was the exact truth. 'I will acquaint my wife with what you say,' he told them.

'Is she not in London?' Lord Fosdyke asked.

The memory of their row flooded Sir George's mind with embarrassment. 'No, no,' he said, trying to sound nonchalant. 'Stayed in Bath for the fair, don teller know. I've a mind to go down there tomorrow and visit it myself.' He could break his good news to Hermione at the same time. I quite like a fair, damme. 'Tis all good clean harmless fun.'

Twelve

The day of the fair was hot and sticky, but that didn't deter Ariadne in the least. She hauled her sister out of bed at birdsong, and the two of them were off to the baths long before anyone else, and back, breakfasted and dressed with a speed that left their mother deeply suspicious.

The more Hermione thought about this visit to the fair — and she'd thought about it obsessively during the last two days — the more she feared she'd made an error in agreeing to it.

'Keep the closest eye upon Miss Ariadne,' she said, giving last-minute instructions to Suki. Take Bessie with you and make sure she stays beside you every minute of the day. We must be prepared for any eventuality. Should there be the slightest folly of any sort whatsoever, I trust you take my meaning, Bessie is to be dispatched to the house directly to report to me.' She sighed dramatically, that being the only way she could express her disapproval in front of a servant. 'How I shall survive this day I really do not know! The vulgarity of it! 'Tis a mercy that none of my family are here to see it! 'Twould lacerate their sensibilities! How people can demean themselves to attend such functions is beyond my comprehension.' She sighed again. That will be all.'

'What you goin' to do with the babby?' Bessie asked, as she and Suki put on their bonnets.

'Take him with me,' Suki said.

Bessie was surprised. 'Does milady know? I mean I thought you was s'posed to keep him indoors. That's what she said, didn't she? He ain't to leave the house except for little walks.' Her round face was wrinkled with anxiety at Suki's disobedience.

Suki lifted the baby from his cradle and wrapped him in her shawl ready to be carried on her back. 'What the eye don't see, the heart don't grieve over,' she said, knotting the shawl at her waist. 'He can't stay here an' starve all day, can he? The idea! Very well then. He'm a-coming with me.'

So the four young women set out on their adventure, Ariadne and Melissa in their prettiest gowns and their new Leghorn bonnets, Bessie with a basket 'in case there's anything to carry home', Suki with the baby, and all of them in high good humour.

The streets were thronged with people, all strolling westward towards the enticing clamour of the fair and all perfectly happy to demean themselves no matter who they were — persons of quality, beggars and bailiffs, merchants and their wives, farmers and farm labourers, men on horseback, ladies in chairs. Westgate Street was so crowded it was almost impossible to keep upright in the crush, and Suki was alarmed for the safety of the baby, and told Bessie to hold on to her shoulders and stay as close behind her as she could. But at last they'd squeezed through the narrow opening of the old west gate and were out in the lane, scrambling towards Barton Fields, where dogs barked and drums beat, three bands were playing against one another and the hucksters were shrieking their wares.

The Barton was a well-cropped meadow that rose above the west wall of the city. According to popular belief, it had been given to the citizens of the town in perpetuity and was never to be built upon. Whatever its origins, it was a good site for a fair, being flat and circular, with only the very gentlest of inclines, like a green plate tilted towards the river. It was surrounded by hedgerows and low trees, where lovers could court in relative privacy, and it had a commanding prospect of the enclosing hills above it and the buff stone city below.

Not that any of its visitors took time to enjoy the view that day, for the place was crammed with other delights. Here were bulls being baited and cocks set to fight one another, pigs racing, thrashed by sticks and squealing as they ran, and a dancing bear, red-eyed and foaming at the mouth; here were tumblers and jugglers, actors and mimes, all doing impossible things as though they were easy. Clowns swaggered their placards through the crowds, their wild wigs blue and saffron and rose madder, their faces starkly white around black-rimmed eyes. There were tents for beer and tents for tea and cakes; here they sold frumenty, there gingerbread men; there were football players and fortunetellers and every imaginable game of chance; and down by the ale tent a line of drunken men did their best to break their jaws and dislocate their necks by pulling hideous faces through the aperture of a horse collar.

Melissa was entranced by it and set off at once to sample everything edible and to find the dazzling hero of the gypsy's predictions. Her sister made straight for the actor's tent, where she edged inch by inch towards the front of the crowd and the sight of her beloved. Sula was momentarily jealous of her, because she knew where her lover was and could find him at once, but then she turned her attention to her own affairs and became sensibly practical.

'We can leave her there safe enough for the time bein',' she said to Bessie, 'and we've no need to keep an eye on Miss Melissa, for all she'm like to do is eat. You can see the sights if you like. I'm off to find the Captain.'

'Which one?' Bessie asked.

'What?'

'Which Capting? Your brother or your husband?'

'Both,' Suki said. 'With any luck.' She'd forgotten the lies she'd told poor Bessie but there wasn't time to explain them away, even if she could. Somewhere in this excited crowd her darling could be striding towards her at that very moment. Only last year they'd strolled from tent to tent and stall to stall together, she hanging on his arm like his own true love, he gazing into her eyes and telling her how dearly he loved her. She'd visit all the places they'd been to last time and she wouldn't stop until she'd found him. Oh, he *had* to be here. That man Charlie had promised he would be and she'd waited so long to see him again. Where should she begin? There were so many possibilities.

She tried the cockpit, knowing how much he loved to gamble, but he wasn't there, which was just as well for the smell of chicken's blood and excited sweat was thick as a fog and made poor William sneeze so much that she had to unwind him from her shawl and carry him in her arms to comfort him. She tried the pig race, where scores of men were laying bets and threatening to cut the throats of the losers, but he wasn't there either. She looked in the beer tent and the tea tent but there was no sign of him in either place. By that time she was trembling with hope and excitement.

Come now, she told herself, this won't do. You arn't a-goin' about things in the right way, rushing from place to place. She set about her search more systematically, walking steadily round the edge of the fair and gradually working her way into the centre, looking for him in every direction while she was on the move and threading through every crowd she joined until she was sure she'd checked in every corner of it. She passed the actors' tent, and noticed that Ariadne was still standing in the same place, squashed against the edge of the stage and watching her lover with adoring concentration. She glanced in at the frumenty booth, and saw Melissa there eating a large bowl of gritty-looking gruel liberally sprinkled with currants like rabbit droppings. She walked by the star-studded tent where Old Sheena was murmuring fortunes, and presently she came to the prize fighters' canvas stage, which was right in the middle of a huge tent that stood right in the middle of the fair. It had already attracted a large crowd, because the first fight was about to begin and the betting was fierce. Oh yes! That's where she'd find him.

The first two combatants were already in the ring — an Englishman with a battered face, brown hands and a body as white as buttermilk and an African in a red turban and white canvas breeches, with skin like burnished copper and a formidable scar across his chest. They certainly looked the part and were just the sort of sparring partners that the Captain would love to watch.

He'd spent an hour in this very tent last year and won a great deal of money. So she paid her penny and joined the crowd, which was so dense that it was almost impossible to move in it. But she *knew* he was there. She could feel it. It was just the very place to find him.

At that moment, the bell clanged for the first round and the fighters picked up their weapons and took their stand. They were to fight with broadswords, which looked dangerous and heavy, and at first both of them were wary, circling one another for the first advantage as the crowd pressed forward for a better view. The first attack clashed sword against sword with a showier of sparks and at that there was a roar of delight and every face turned avidly towards the action. Now it was easier for Suki to scan the crowd but, to her intense disappointment, the Captain wasn't there, although she saw several pick-pockets she recognized and two of Farmer Lambton's labourers and both the kitchen maids. As she was wondering where she could search next, and how she was going to get out of the tent, there was another throaty roar and turning she saw the African stagger on to the ropes with blood spurting from a long pink cut just below his left nipple. The horror of such a wound transfixed her to the spot but the punters around her were frantic with excitement, cheering and throwing shillings and crowns on to the canvas to show their appreciation, and the Englishman's seconds were clambering into the ring to gather them up as quickly as they could. Nobody paid any attention to the injured man who stood trembling against the ropes as his second did what he could to staunch the blood with a towel.

I can't abide this, Suki thought, gazing at him in an anguish of pity. Surely it weren't like this last year. They'd fought with bare knuckles then, hadn't they? Not like this. Not with people getting cut open. The sight and smell of it was making her feel faint. I must get out, she thought, now, afore it gets any worse. All this veiling'll upset my William as sure as fate. But the baby didn't seem to be upset at all. He was watching wide-eyed from the shelter of her arms and before she could begin to struggle out of the throng, the bell was rung for the second round, and at that the crowd surged forward again until they were even more tightly wedged together than they'd been before. She was squashed between a fat man and his equally fat wife and there wasn't an inch of room for manoeuvre.

'Oh, please,' she begged, tugging at the man's sleeve. 'Let me through.' But he wasn't listening to her, for in this round the two men were attacking one another with swords and daggers and the fight was quicker and even more vicious. Within seconds the African had taken another nasty wound, this time a slash across his knuckles, but he fought back immediately with a violent swashing blow that knocked the sword clean out of his opponent's hand and cut off all the buttons on one side of his breeches. The excitement was ear-splitting and this time coins were thrown for the African's benefit. And Suki still couldn't extricate herself.

The coins were gathered up and the fight continued into its third round, with both men blood-spattered and breathing heavily and watching one another with red-eyed concentration. The smell of blood and sweat pervaded the tent, for the audience was heated with happy anticipation of an even better injury. They didn't have long to wait. Thirty seconds into the round the African took a blow that slashed his face open from the left eye right down his cheek to his chin. It hit his jaw with such force that Suki could hear the sword grating against his teeth and the wound opened until it was as wide as a thumb with blood pumping from it in long red streams, covering his chest, his arms and his breeches and forming a gleaming pool on the canvas. To whistles and catcalls, a barber-surgeon jumped into the ring to stitch up the wound, and, to Suki's horrified admiration, the African stood where he was to endure it, shivering but without making a sound. The audience cheered themselves hoarse and threw more coins for the Englishman. But their movement towards the stage gave Suki an inch of space, at last, and the chance to escape. Panting, she struggled through the mass of bodies and squeezed out into the open air, where she was immediately and violently sick, with William yelling in protest because she was holding him so tightly against her chest for fear of letting him fall.

I should never have gone to such a place, she thought, as she caught her breath and wiped her mouth. It was the most abhorrent thing she'd ever seen and her heart was still juddering with the horror of it. Misery and disappointment pulled her down until her shoulders sagged and her eyes filled with tears. She felt exhausted and defeated. I've searched and searched, she thought miserably, an' I've seen a man cut open, an' I'm no nearer to finding him than I was at the start. What if he ain't a-coming back here? What if he don't mean to find me? What if he don't love me no more?

Now that she'd relaxed her hold, William was whimpering and nuzzling to be fed. She found a quiet spot beside one of the chestnut trees, settled with her back against the trunk, lay the baby across her knees and unlaced her bodice. She was working automatically because she was too tired and miserable to respond to him as she usually did. In fact, as she was honest enough to admit, she was feeling resentful, irritated that he was making demands on her at the very moment when she was least able to respond to them. But he had to be fed. It wasn't his fault that she couldn't find his father, poor little thing. So she let him suck and was gradually soothed by the sensuous pleasure that suckling always aroused, and as if he was recognizing the change in her, he stopped sucking and lifted his head to smile at her. She was touched to tears. Even in the midst of her search, when she was too harassed to attend to him properly and she stunk of sick, and she'd held him so tightly she'd made him cry, he loved her. In his own uncomplicated, total way, he loved her. She was instantly flooded with returning love for him, for his soft skin, his downy hair, his lovely milky smell and the total trust of that smile. No matter what anybody might do or say, no matter whether she found his father that day, next day, next week, or whenever it was going to be, she would never allow anybody to part her from this baby.

The sun was a great deal lower in the sky and throwing long blue shadows across the Barton, and she noticed that some of the stall holders were beginning to pack up and count their takings. The performing dog lay on his side like a dead thing in the doorway of his tent, the clowns had taken off their placards and their shoes and were drinking beer outside the beer tent, their white paint streaked and dishevelled, and the gypsies were gathered in the frumenty booth, sucking clay pipes and filling the rank air with eruptions of evil-smelling grey smoke. She wondered where Miss Melissa had got to — and didn't much care — and whether Miss Ariadne was still watching the play which, amazingly, was still going on. The trumpets were braving at that very moment.

She've been inches away from her lover all afternoon, she thought, an' I've searched and searched for mine an' I still don't know where he is. You can love as strong as you like, but if he don't return your love, you got no power in the matter at all, an' if he arn't in town an' you've searched every place you can think of, what else can you do? But then, optimism and confidence returning, she corrected herself. Every place bar one. There was still his lodgings with that Mrs Roper. If anyone ought to know where he is, she should. 'We'll go there the minute you'm full an' satisfied,' she said to William. The fair had lost its relish. She'd seen quite enough for one afternoon and Bessie could keep an eye on two young misses for a few more minutes.

But as she laced up her bodice, she saw Bessie herself, hurrying towards her through the crowds, her round face anxious.

'Miss Melissa's bein' sick,' she reported.

Suki had no sympathy for her. 'Serve her right for bein' a pig,' she said.

'She's ever so bad.'

'Where have you left her?'

'She's lying down in the tea tent. She's ever so bad, sort of greeny yellow.'

'You'd best take her home if that's the case,' Suki said. 'I'll look after the other one.' Her visit to Mrs Roper's would have to wait.

Twas a nuisance but there was nothing to be done about it. 'Find a chair if she ain't up to walking.'

139

William was sound asleep across her lap, so she tied him in her shawl, slung him on her back and set off for the theatre tent. Ariadne was still there, her bosom jammed against the edge of the stage, and still watching her lover with the intensity of infatuation. The crowd was thicker than it had been for the first performance and extremely vocal, roaring advice and obscenities. Mr Clements was being torn from his lady love, again, and signifying anguish and a broken heart, as usual. But his leading lady was drooping in the heat, her make-up striped with sweat and her wig askew, and as Suki arrived and began to skirt the crowd to get closer to Ariadne, she looked up to see what was going on and missed her cue.

'We part my fair, never to meet again,' Mr Clements repeated with nudging emphasis.

To everyone's surprise he was answered by a member of the audience, in a rapt, adoring, bell-clear, familiar voice.

'Love cannot part us, junctured as we are.

We shall be always bound and always true.

Give me your hand, your lips...'

He turned from his leading lady, smiling devilishly, and bent into the audience, seized Ariadne about the waist and lifted her up, up, until her slippered feet were touching the stage. Then as the crowd howled their approval, he pulled her towards him, and caressing her nipples with his thumbs, kissed her long and deeply and with such professional expertise that her cheeks blazed and her stomach shook visibly.

'My love, my fair, never to part again,' he declaimed and bowed to the audience, doffing his cap and sweeping it until its feathers trailed the boards.

And Ariadne opened her eyes from her rapture, and found herself looking straight into the apoplectic anger of her father's purple face.

Thirteen

'I turn my back for ten seconds, and what do I find?' Sir George roared. 'Melissa rolling around the fields like a gypsy, covered in filth and eating unspeakable rubbish, and your precious Ariadne disporting herself like a common whore. Have you no control upon your daughters, madam?'

'Allow me to correct you, my love,' Hermione said acidly from the sofa. 'You were not away for ten seconds. You were away for the best part of a week. Accuracy would assist us in our deliberations, I do believe.'

'Hold your tongue, ma'am!' her husband roared. 'Time is of no consequence here. We are considering behaviour.'

Melissa was sitting at the far end of the drawing room, her head and shoulders drooped over her stays, uncomfortable with guilt and nausea, her eyes half shut. Her usually pasty face was tinged with green and a strong smell of vomit rose from her skirts. Ariadne stood upright before her father, holding her head high in defiance. Two red patches burned shame in her pale cheeks but her eyes were steady and her mouth tight with self-control.

The drawing room door was firmly closed but outside on the landing and at the top of the stairs the servants were gathered to eavesdrop and to be entertained. As soon as the master had stormed back into the house with his two daughters trailing miserably behind him, Suki and Bessie, who had followed him home at a discrete distance in case he saw the baby, had run to the kitchen to spread the news. Now they were listening with the rest, for although Suki was impatient to be off to Nowhere Lane, it was plain that there were going to be repercussions and she needed to know what was going to happen next.

Hermione raised a handkerchief to her eyes, flicking the ends of it like a flag in the breeze to signal her displeasure and her intentions. If this abuse doesn't stop at once, the gesture said, I shall prostrate myself with the vapours.

But the situation was so serious her trick didn't work. 'What were you thinking of, pray,' Sir George demanded, pushing his angry face down towards her, 'to allow such folly? I found your precious daughter Melissa spewing — out in the open, right in the public eye mark you — while as to Ariadne... 'Od's teeth, it makes my blood boil to think of what she was doing! Have we bred our daughters to fornicate with tinkers and make public exhibitions of themselves in the market place?'

'He was not a tinker, my love,' Hermione corrected again, still trying to make light of the whole unpleasant affair. 'He was an actor, I believe, and a fair is hardly the same thing as a market place.'

'If you've nothing sensible to say,' Sir George shouted, 'then pray hold your peace. Here I've been working day and night to make a match for this... creature... and this is how she repays me.'

Hermione was caught between desire to know what manner of husband he had found and annoyance at the way in which he was addressing her. For the moment curiosity won out. 'And whom did you find, pray?' she asked, her tone implying that it would be a poor catch whoever it was.

'A city merchant for one,' Sir George told her, with heavy satisfaction, 'and old Mr Matthews who's as rich as Croesus, which even you will allow, and if he don't suit, the younger son of the Duke of Errymouth. She could scarcely rise to greater heights than a man of that calibre. And all gone to waste, if your negligence has allowed her to ruin her reputation.'

'Permit me to contradict you,' Hermione said. 'Her reputation ain't ruined. 'Twas a moment of youthful folly, no more...'

'Do you contradict me, ma'am?' her husband roared, puce with anger. 'Do you? Do you? Hold your tongue, woman.'

Hermione tried to freeze him with the most venomous look she could contrive. 'You forget, sir,' she said, 'to whom you speak. My father, the Duke of Daventry, would never have addressed a lady thus. He would have considered it a mark of low breeding.'

'Your father was an artful scheming rogue, ma'am,' Sir George retorted furiously. 'Made a bad bargain with me, so he did, silly young fool that I was. I wouldn't be caught so easily today, ma'am.'

'So now I am to be called a bad bargain,' Hermione said icily, 'as though I were a roll of cloth or sugar loaf. How cruel! How uncommon cruel!'

'I'm a better judge of sugar than any man in this town!' Sir George roared, 'and without me, ma'am, you would be nothing. I don't notice your precious father ever allowing us to visit: I don't see his card in the hall, ma'am, or his horse in the stable. Cut you off, ma'am, so he did, and cast you out. And I'm the fool that has to endure your foolishness for the rest of my life. It makes my blood boil so it does.'

Hermione turned her head away from his onslaught and closed her face and her eyes. The listening servants were delighted by their master's indiscretions. 'I always said her family got shot of her,' Hepzie whispered to Bessie. They could hear Sir George pacing angrily.

'You ain't got a family!' he continued. 'That's the whole truth of it. Only those two empty-headed scraps of folly and wickedness.'

'And a son,' Hermione said quietly. 'You forget I gave you a son.'

'No, ma'am, I do not forget,' Sir George growled. ''Twas the one and only good thing you ever did in your life. The one and only.' He resumed his pacing, trying to remember the original target of his fury, for somehow or other he seemed to have been side-tracked. 'A fine baby,' he said, 'and too young to be present at such an iniquitous assembly. We must be thankful for small mercies.'

He had reached the far end of the room, where he stood contemplating the long bar of sunlight that sloped in through the end window to brighten the carpet. The sight didn't cheer him or clarify his muddled thoughts. He turned to scowl at his sickly daughter.

'No!' she said suddenly. The need to sting him was too intense not to be gratified. 'No, Papa, you are wrong. William *was* at the fair. Mamma sent Suki with us to keep guard, and Suld took him along.'

''Od's bones and bowels and brains!' Sir George shouted, swearing his longest oath in an extremity of fury and incomprehension. 'Are you all gone stark staring raving mad? My son out in the blazing sun all day long! My son! Have you no sense at all, Hermione? I despair for your sanity. I do indeed. Why ain't he been farmed out eh? Tell me that.'

'The matter is in hand,' Hermione said. 'He is to go to a place nearby as soon as we leave here.'

'He'll go now,' her husband interrupted. 'This very minute. Before there's any more harm done.' He growled across the room towards the bell push and rang and roared for Jessup.

The listening servants melted into empty rooms around the landing before the butler could make stately his way up the stairs but as he closed the drawing room door behind him, they re-emerged, eager to hear his instructions. They were curt and to the point. The family would be leaving Bath on the early-morning stage the very next day. He and Mrs Sparepenny and the rest of the servants were to be packed and ready by six o'clock. Bamaby was to take the baby to his new quarters at once. 'At once. You understand that.' Everybody else would be paid off at the end of the evening. Vails would be at five minutes to six.

'Oh, and lay out clean linen for me, will you,' the master ended. 'I shall be visiting the Assembly Rooms directly.' Temper was over. Decisions had been made.

The instructions put Suki into a turmoil for she hadn't given any thought as to how she would persuade Farmer Lambton to take her into his household and she certainly wasn't ready to leave at a moment's notice, certainly not until she'd been to Mrs Roper's. As she sped off towards the nursery to pack the baby's clothes she was scheming hard.

Cook was beaming. 'Vails at last,' she said to the kitchen maids. 'An' not afore time. Don't forget to wear a clean apron and hold your hands right out. The wider the palm the more the coin. Milady's pretty open-handed but you never know where you are with that Sir George when he m a-rushin' into things. Give me a pair of old maids any time. Now what?'

The bells were jumping like wild things — for Milady's room, the two young misses' room, even the drawing room. Mrs Spare-penny swept into the kitchen to despatch servants to answer: Hepzie to Milady, Bessie to the young misses, Suki to the drawing room. 'The baby is asleep, is he not?'

The three girls ran up the back stairs together, complaining.

''Twill be Bedlam till they leave,' Hepzie grumbled. ''Twas just the same the last time. An' who's in the drawing room? That's what I should like to know.'

It was Ariadne, pacing the carpet in exactly the same way as her father had done a few minutes before. 'Oh,' she said, when Suki entered. 'I'm so glad it's you. I was afraid they might have sent you off already. He's watching me like a hawk. Take this letter and give it to the milliner. She will know where to send it. And there's money for her. Don't tell anyone else.'

Suki took the letter like the conspirator she was. 'Course not.'

'Did you find your husband?'

They were talking freely again, looking at one another with understanding and fellow feeling. 'Not yet,' Suki admitted. 'I'm still looking.'

'Papa's found some wretched suitor for me. Have you heard? Three actually. He says tis time I was a married woman and off his hands. Little does he know, foolish creature.'

'What will you do if they come a-courting?'

'Refuse 'em,' Ariadne said firmly. 'I won't marry where I don't love and there's an end on it.' There were footsteps on the landing so she drew herself up, looked away and assumed her imperious tone. That will be all.'

It was Barnaby, knocking timidly, sent to say that the dog-cart was outside the door and was Suki ready.

'You can carry baby's things down, as soon as they'm packed,' Suki told him as they went back below stairs. 'He'm sound asleep. I got two errands to run afore we go. They won't take two shakes.'

He was horrified to be told such a thing. 'You can't run errands,' he protested. 'We're to go straight to this farm of yours — I got instructions.'

'Who's to stop us?' Suki said, annoyed by his caution. 'Just don't say nothin', that's all. 'Twon't take more than a minute.'

'It'ud better not,' he grumbled, 'or we shall get soaked. It's a-comin' on to rain.'

The first spots fell on them as they set off to the milliner's and by the time that rocking lady had been given her letter and her silver sixpence, it was raining in earnest, sharp, stinging rods of water that fell diagonally upon them from a very grey sky.

'We should ha' done this yesterday,' Barnaby complained, turning up his collar, 'when it was dry. I'll bet it's miles to this farm of yours. Now where d'you want to go?'

She told him, turning her back to the weather so as to shield the baby from the worst of it.

''Tis a horrible place,' he warned. 'You won't like it, I can tell you.'

It was an old-fashioned, ill-kempt alley, heaped with decomposing garbage and too narrow to take the horse and cart. Most of its houses were so grimed with age that they looked black and they were all in such a bad state of repair that they sagged into one another like drunkards on the point of collapse. Mrs Roper's was five stories high and badly out of alignment. It leant sideways against its next door neighbour, its front door ajar beneath a lintel at least five degrees out of true, its squiffy windows tilted like tired eyes. There was a half-starved mongrel sniffing through the night soil piled against the wall, but apart from that the place looked empty. Suki left Barnaby sitting in the cart at the end of the road, wrapped her cape tightly around the baby to protect him from the rain, and dodged in.

She found herself in a narrow hallway, from which led six cracked doors and a rickety staircase. The floorboards had been stained with beer and soot in the old style and scattered with rushes, but the walls were uncoloured plaster and slimy to the touch. As she stood, shivering a little in the dank enclosed air, she heard footsteps on the stairs above her and a man's voice talking quietly but importantly.

'The mistress was most particular about that, Mrs Roper,' the voice was saying. 'Most particular. If the young gentleman returns to this address, his position is to be made clear to him. There will be no further remuneration.'

'Of course, sir,' a gruff female voice replied. 'That's perfectly comprehended. There's no call to mention it again, I'm sure. As I understand the matter, sir, the person has made other arrangements.' She sounded a little put out, but that didn't mollify her companion.

'Most particular,' he repeated. 'Matters have to be made crystal clear.' And he cleared his throat. 'Kernim. Krrm. Krrm.'

The cough froze Suki where she stood. It sounded just like Jessup. But it couldn't be Jessup. What would he be doing in a dirty little lodging house like this? She glanced up the stairs at the feet descending upon her, two split boots kicking a linsey woolsey petticoat, and a pair of fine buckled shoes below two white stockings, one of them streaked with an unmistakeable yellow stain. It *was* Jessup. She'd know those splayed feet

146

anywhere. Heaven'a mercy! He mustn't see *me* or I shall really be for it. But where could she hide? Without stopping to think, she eased open the nearest door and edged herself behind it, holding her sleeping baby close against her chest.

She was in a broom cupboard, among grimy bristles, dusty feathers, wax polish and sacks of soot. There was very little air and very little room, but at least she was hidden, and William was still asleep, and she wasn't in somebody's bedroom, which, as she now realized, she very easily could have been. The footsteps crunched above her head, continued into the hall and trampled out of the house. The gruff female was saying goodbye.

Then there was a pause while Suki tried not to breathe in too much dust, and the dog began to bark in the alley. There was no sound of footsteps or voices. How much longer shall I stay here? Suki wondered. Has she gone? It wouldn't do to emerge from her hiding place and find the lady standing in the doorway. How would she ever explain that? There was more dust than air in the cupboard and standing crouched among the brooms was beginning to make her back ache.

Then, to her relief, the gruff voice spoke again. 'Past seven o'clock, Mr Thomas,' it called, and somebody growled some sort of answer and then the footsteps scuffled up the stairs again. She waited until they were almost out of earshot and then crept out of the cupboard.

'Who's there?' the voice called down the well of the stairs.

'Only me,' Suki said, looking up at the boots and the folds of brown petticoat.

'Stay where you are, miss,' the voice commanded. 'I'll be down to 'ee direct.' And down direct she was, looking extremely fierce, a small brown wrinkled woman, with a narrow mouth and eyes as black as jet. A chatelaine of heavy keys and a man's leather purse hung from her belt, and her cap and collar were rigid with starch. Not a lady to trifle with, Suki thought, with a sinking heart, and wondered how on earth she could open the conversation.

Mrs Roper didn't help her at all. 'Yes?' she said, folding her hands across her apron and glaring.

'If you please, ma'am,' Suki said, hoping excessive politeness would placate the lady. 'I got a message for the Captain.'

'Oh yes,' Mrs Roper said, and her tone implied the gravest and most superior doubt.

Press on. 'Is he here, ma'am?'

'He is not. Nor like to be.'

Suki was half expecting this but to hear it was a crushing disappointment, even so. 'He was s'posed to be in Bath this summer, ma'am,' she said. 'I been expecting him.'

The landlady was even more caustic. 'Oh yes,' she said and this time her voice conveyed disbelief and disapproval in equal measure.

It was demoralising to have to beg, especially from a woman as unhelpful as this one, but it had to be done. 'Can you tell me where he is?'

Mrs Roper gave her a calculating stare. 'What's that to you?' she said. 'Those as need to know, know well enough and don't need to ask. Be off with you!'

'I got a message for him,' Suki insisted, standing her ground.

'And who sent this precious message? If I may make so bold as to ask.'

'A gentleman,' Suki tried.

'Has he got a name?'

This was getting worse and worse. 'He haven't give me leave to reveal it.'

'Sounds a load of arrant nonsense to me,' Mrs Roper said, folding her arms across her chest. 'Out with it then, gel. I haven't got all day. What's your message?'

'If you please, ma'am,' Suki said. 'I got to deliver it personal. To the Captain. The gentleman was most particular. He said he'd have my ears if I gave it to anyone else.'

'Have your ears, eh?' Mrs Roper said, picking the phrase out of the conversation and considering it, with a smile of recognition. 'I might ha' knowed it. He wouldn't have a velvet patch over his left eye, by any chance, this precious gentleman of youm? An' a pair of silver pistols at his belt? An' debts as long as your arm?'

'Well,' Suki hesitated delicately. The lie was offering a little hope. If she was careful she might get away with it. 'He might. But then again he might not. I am t supposed to say. I just got to deliver the message.'

'Gentleman my eye!' Mrs Roper said, and at last she unfolded her arms. 'Arrant nonsense, that's all 'tis. And just what you'd expect from a rogue like that Quin Cutpurse. Yes, miss, I know who's sent you. You needn't look so surprised.'

'If I tell you the message is from Quin Cutpurse,' Suld tried, will you tell me where to find the Captain so's I can deliver it?'

'No I will not!' Mrs Roper said. The very idea! If that sneaky varmint wants to find the Captain, let him do it for himself. He'll have to wait a parlous long time. Your Captain's at sea and has been these many days. You take my advice gel, and keep well out of it. Leave them two varmints to fools and whores and suchlike, where they belong.' And she turned away, bringing the conversation to an end. There was nothing for Suki to do but drop a quick curtsey and leave the house, her thoughts bubbling with frustration. Could he really be at sea? Or was the horrible old thing just saying it to bring the conversation to an end? What an awful thing 'twould be if her thoughtless lie turned out to be the truth after all. But he wouldn't go to sea, surely to goodness. Not the Captain. He was a horseman and a swordsman, a gallant, not a sailor.

It was still raining, the street was empty and the cart gone. Barnaby must have seen Mr Jessup and driven off to hide somewhere. And that was another thing. What was Mr Jessup doing in such a place? She tried to remember what he and Mrs Roper had been talking about. A remuneration, wasn't it? And 'strict instructions from the mistress'. Was he working for more than one family then? Or did he mean Lady Bradbury? That hardly seemed likely. What would Lady Bradbury be doing sending her butler to a woman like Mrs Roper?

She set off along the road, protecting William with her cloak, trying to puzzle it out, and as she strode along she fancied she heard someone calling after her, and looking back she saw that a skivvy was running down the street towards her, a small skinny child who looked vaguely familiar. She wore somebody else's faded gown, badly cut down and horribly stained with soot and sweat, and as she came trotting up alongside, Suki saw that there was a brown cold sore at the comer of her mouth and that her hands were red and chapped.

'Why,' she said, 'you're the gel from the theatre. What you doing here?'

'Got the push,' the child told her. 'On account of they said I should've stopped that baby piddlin' in the helmet. Never even seen it but they wouldn't believe me. I wasn't supposed to run off after you neither. They was ever so cross. So anyway I come here. You got to eat, ain'tcher. You was arsking fer the Capting.'

The relief of finding an ally made Suki's cheeks flush. 'Do you know where he is? She said he'd gone to sea.'

'So he has, miss. Days ago. All in the dead of night. Two gentlemen come a-callin'. Pebbles at the windy for to wake him, an' 'e was up and away. Dressed as 'e went, so 'e did, all on that great horse of his. You never saw anyone ride a horse like the Captain.' Her eyes were shining with the remembered excitement of it.

'And he didn't come back?' Suki prompted.

'No, miss. An' then Mrs Roper had a letter and she said he'd gone to sea, so I s'pose he must have. Anyway she waited a day or two an' 'e never come back, so she said to clean his room, an' she took all his things an' sold'em off, on account of all the debtors come a-knockin'. All except for this. I found it under his pillow. So I took it to keep it, for fear someone 'ud thieve it.'

It was an expensive silk kerchief with a coat of arms embroidered in one of the corners — blue stars on a field of gold in two of the quarterings, a silver helm and three red martlets in the third and fourth, all of it surmounted by a yellow crown and supported by a wild boar, spread-eagled in ungainly motion, but looking uncommon fierce.

'Good heavens!' Suki said. 'How did the Captain come by such a thing? You sure 'twas his?'

'Certain sure!' the child said, nodding her head. 'I seen it in his hands at the theatre, 'onest.'

'Tis a rare thing,' Suki said, passing the silk through her fingers. She wondered why he'd left it behind. It must belong to him, for if it didn't, he must either have stolen it, which was unthinkable, or borrowed it from a friend, and if he'd done that he'd have returned it or taken it with him. No, it *must* be his, and if it *is,* then he must be a member of a noble family. The thought didn't surprise her, for she'd always known there was something special about the Captain, something that marked him out from the rest. Maybe the gentlemen had brought him a message from his family. Some business he alone could understand. Maybe he'd been sent on a journey on their behalf. Or even a sea voyage. The romance of such an idea was most appealing.

'Should I keep it, do'ee think?' the skivvy asked, fearful of the long silence of Sula's thoughts.

'No,' Suki said. 'You'd best give it to me. I'm his wife. I'll look after it for him.'

There was somebody whistling from the end of the street. Someone calling, 'Come on!'

'I got to go,' Suki said. She pulled a silver sixpence from her pocket and pressed it into the child's chapped hand. 'Thank 'ee kindly,' she said. 'I'm uncommon grateful to 'ee.' And holding William safely against her chest she ran to the cart. She still didn't know exactly where the Captain was, nor when he'd be coming back, but at least she knew where he'd stayed and where he'd gone. If he *was* at sea, he'd come home again in the end. She hadn't lost him entirely.

Barnaby was full of importance. 'You'll never guess who I've just seen,' he said as she climbed up into the cart. 'Good job I did too. I got the cart out of sight in the nick a' time. Another minute an' he'd've seen me, and *then* what would have happened? We'd've been for it I can tell you. You'll never guess...'

'Mr Jessup,' she said. 'Take the Bristol road.'

He was put out to have his tale cut short and annoyed that she knew. 'What's he a-doin' of in a place like this?' he asked, clucking the mare into movement.

She said the first thing that came into her head, hoping to shut him up. 'Visiting his granny.'

That astounded him. 'Was he?' he said, eyes rounded. 'I never did! Fancy Mr Jessup having a granny. You'd never imagine that now, would you? What's she like? Did you see her? She must be *ever* so old.'

Suki let him run on and didn't listen to him. It wouldn't take long to drive to Twerton, even in the half light, and she needed to marshall her thoughts before she arrived, to work out how to persuade Farmer Lambton to accept her into his household, how to explain that there was only one baby — which would be parlously difficult if they recognized him — how, above all, to avoid going back to her parents' chaotic hovel.

Fourteen

Lambton Farmhouse had been built by Constant Lambton's greatgrandfather, who, being a shrewd countryman, had chosen its location with great care, placing it where it had a commanding view over his fields, apart from the rest of the farm buildings but standing in a slight hollow to protect it from the prevailing wands and to give shelter to the pigs and chickens that lived in the yard. It was built of local stone which had weathered over the years until it was as mottled and settled as the earth that surrounded it. It was as familiar to Suki Brown as her own hard-working hands. Even now, in the shadowing light of that August evening, with its walls darkened by the candlelight that shone warm and golden through both kitchen windows, she recognized every stone and lintel of the place.

This was the yard she'd played in as a child, where she'd scattered corn for the fowls and mocked them as they'd run 'kroo kroo kroo' to peck it up, where she'd scratched the old sow's back with a long stick, leaning over the low wall of the sty and dreaming idly of love to come; this the house she'd walked to every Saturday evening, neat and respectable, to collect her father's wages; those the wheat and barley fields that had been the swishing centre of her childish universe and that she'd thought she'd left for good when she headed off to Bath more than a year ago. And now here she was, back again, with a four-month-old baby in her arms, no wedding ring on her finger and her heart in her mouth. For it was one thing to have offered the farm to Lady Bradbury as a lodging for the baby and quite another to arrive there as a supplicant to ask for it.

Barnaby pulled the mare to a halt and jumped down from the cart to carry her carpet bag into the porch. 'I'll be off then,' he said, straightening his back, 'now you're here safe an' sound. You got your purse an' the address an' everything.'

She thanked him, vaguely, her mind on the problems ahead, but she didn't watch him go. She was too busy looking at the dark shape of the farmer, who had risen from his chair and was walking in his slow, stolid way towards the door.

'Well bless my soul,' he said as he opened it, and he called back to his wife, 'Here's Suki Brown come a-calling, my dear. What do 'ee think of that? Just as we were speaking of her.' He stood aside courteously to let his visitor into the house. 'Come in.'

It was a good start and better than she knew. For the sight of her, as she strode into their quiet kitchen, red-cheeked and blooming with her nice fat baby held firmly in her nice plump arms, her dark hair curled and glossy with rain, her cloak richly red in the candlelight and giving out a potent scent of warm flesh and wet wool, she roused unexpected emotions in the farmer and his wife. Until she arrived they'd been sitting quietly together, with little to say to one another, now it was as if she were lifting them up into another stronger world. The sight of her brought the taste of fresh apples into Farmer Lambton's mouth, rounded and red and luscious with juice, reminding him of the warmth and reward of harvest, yet at the same time because she was borne towards him on a gust of night air, she stirred other darker memories, of the excitement of dusk, of things sensed — half understood, half feared, primitive — of the timeless mysteries of blood and seedtime.

Annie, caught up in the daily struggle of chores and pregnancy, was suddenly aware that it was possible to carry a child to term, to deliver it healthily and look none the worse for the experience. This girl was so strong and open-faced and wholesome, like an embodiment of all things joyous and breeding, teeming fields, rich harvests, a living example that birth brought pleasure as well as pain.

'Oh, Suki,' Annie said, rising awkwardly from her chair to greet her, 'I *am* glad to see you. What you doin' here? How's your pretty babba? Sit you down. Have you had supper? We've bread and cheese aplenty an' there's beer in the flagon.'

Suki sat at the table and accepted her impromptu meal with some relief, because she was hungry after her journey and because a mouth full of food would give her the chance to think before she answered questions.

'I come to ask you a favour, ma'am,' she said, as Annie carved the bread, 'if I may be so bold.'

'If 'tis in our power to grant,' Annie told her, 'you have only to ask. Arn't that right, Mr Lambton?'

So she asked. 'The Bradburys have gone to London an' they wants the baby farmed out where 'tis healthy. I thought if I could stay here with you, ma'am, I could be here for when your baby's born, like you wanted.'

Annie was delighted and said what an excellent idea it was, just as Suki had hoped, but Farmer Lambton was cautious.

'You only got your babba with you this evening, I see,' he said. 'Where's t'other?'

'This is William Bradbury,' Suki explained, avoiding their gaze by sitting the baby upright on her knee where they could see him. The weight of the lie was so great she was afraid they would notice if she looked at them directly.

Annie was instantly full of sympathy. 'Where's — the other one?' she asked, fearfully.

Best get this over quickly. 'He died, ma'am.'

Now Annie was alarmed. 'What of? Did he take a fever?'

Suki gave the details quickly too. 'No, ma'am. Nothin' like that. He was right as rain one minute, dead the next. The doctor couldn't account for it. 'Twasn't a fever or nothing. He just died.' Annie's grey eyes were brimming with tears. She had to pause to cough and wipe them away. 'My poor gel,' she said. 'I'm so sorry.'

''Tis over now,' Suki said, trying not to eye the bread. 'Now I got to find a home for this one, bein' he can't go to London and he must stay with me to be fed. They given me ample money for 'un. I wouldn't be a burden. I got a bank note for ten pounds in my pocket this very minute an' I'd work for my keep. I could help you round the house an' with the harvest.'

'And be there when this one's born,' Annie said, looking with entreaty at her husband. Although pregnancy had rounded her belly, the rest of her body was thinner than ever and her face was gaunt, with mauve shadows under her eyes and no flesh on her cheeks. What could he do but give in to her?

But he did it guardedly. 'We will give it a try,' he said. 'For a day or two. See how we go along. Now eat up your meal.'

A try was sufficient. In three days she could be settled and indispensable if she worked well and was careful not to be a nuisance. Poor Mrs Lambton looked as though she could use some help. There was still the matter of learning how to read and write but she'd broach that later. Meantime there was Mrs Lambton's good bread and cheese to eat and the farmer's good ale to drink, and William was happy on her lap, patting the surface of the table with both plump hands and experimenting with his new noises. Mmm, mmm, dim. mmm.

'Pretty dear,' Annie said, admiring him. 'You done a good job with him, Suki.'

Suki smiled, broke off her first chunk of bread and looked round the kitchen as she ate it.

The room was as warm and wide as she remembered it, and as well stocked, with two rabbits and a side of salt bacon hanging from the rafters and vegetables piled on the workbench under the long window, but it didn't seem as well cared for. It had new glazed windows, she noticed, and the tiled floor had been resanded and polished to a sheen, but there was a slightly musty smell in the air as if too many things had only been half cleaned. This table needs a good scrub, for a start, she thought, and the pots could do with scouring. There were the same pewter plates and mugs on the dresser, the same brass candlesticks and china dishes on the mantelpiece beside the flat irons and the old stone salt pot, looking as if they'd stood there for months untouched.

They probably need a good rubbing over too. 'I'll take a look tomorrow. Then there was the workbench which would need clearing and cleaning. Oh yes, I can be uncommon useful here.

'Have you seen your family?' Farmer Lambton asked.

She pulled her attention back to answer him. 'No sir, not yet.'

'You must visit first thing tomorrow,' he instructed her, 'before they go to the fields.'

Rather belatedly, Suki thought she'd better enquire after their health.

'They're well enough,' the farmer told her. 'Your father took a nick from his scythe yesterday.' And when she frowned. 'Nothing serious. A clean cut. 'Twill heal.'

He'd interpreted the frown as concern, but in fact she was scowling because it was so typical of the man. He was always hurting himself, falling off ladders and out of trees, dropping tools and overloaded baskets on his feet, ricking his back with burdens and his brain with arithmetic that was totally beyond him, like the dear loving ineffectual man he was. 'Poor Pa,' she said. 'Did he have it bound?'

'As you'll see,' the farmer said. And turned his attention to practical matters. 'You can sleep in my brother's old room tonight. There's beds aplenty there. The babba can sleep in a drawer on a feather pillow.'

So her new status was settled. Annie worried that the mattress would be damp, but that was a small thing compared to the worries Suki had carried with her from Bath.

'I'll pick the driest one,' she promised, 'and give'un a good airing in the morning. We shall be dandy, I promise you.'

But, as it turned out, dandy wasn't the word for it, for William wouldn't settle in his drawer and insisted on sleeping beside her on a decidedly chilly mattress, and she found sleep impossible after the rush of such an eventful day. Eventually, she lay on her back among the lumpy feathers, with William in the crook of her arm and let her mind winder. It was hard to believe that less than sixteen hours ago she'd been dressing for the fair and skipping with excitement because she was so sure she was going to see the Captain again, and now Bath was left behind and there were the long hard days of harvest ahead of her and then months of winter to keep her penned in the country where she couldn't search for him, even if she knew where he was, and her life was totally changed. It was as if she'd stopped the clocks. Now there was nothing for her to do but live in the old slow country way and bide her time until things started up again in the spring, and that was anguish to her impatience. Still, the Bradburys would be back in Bath come Easter and he'd be home from the sea by then. Bound to be.

Images from the day pushed into her mind, close-packed and blurred and swiftly moving like the crowds at the fair — the African's blood spurting from those awful pink-edged wounds as he stood to endure the surgeon, Ariadne's wild face as she was fondled by the actor, the master's red one as he dragged her out of the tent, Mrs Roper's thin mouth sneering and that heavy chatelaine clunking at her waist, brooms and soot sacks in that dusty cupboard, Jessup's piddlc-stained stockings as he walked splay-footed down the stairs. What *had* he been doing there? But what did it matter? 'Twas the Captain she needed to know about, the Captain and where he was. If only she could write and send him a letter and tell him that she loved him as much as ever and that he had a fine son. He'd come and find her quick enough then. It upset her to think that she had the address of the Bradburys' house in London and not so much as the faintest idea where her own dear Jack was sleeping at that moment. Or even if he *was* sleeping. He could be anywhere: in London, at sea, galloping that great horse of his along some wild road. If only she knew.

*

He was lying in the hold of the *Bonny Beaufoy*, fast asleep on a bale of blue cotton, his discarded boots on the deck, his shirt askew and his breeches unbuttoned, one arm curved above his head and the other cradling an empty bottle of beer. He'd worked so hard that day and was so exhausted that little short of an explosion would have woken him. And as the ship was still safely moored alongside the Broad Quay there was little likelihood of that.

The cargo had started to arrive early that morning, and with it a tall man called Smith, who turned out to be the purser and a man of considerable importance because he had control of the ship's finances and according to Mr Reuben was a 'plaguey miserly old swabber' who owned a third of the ship. Whatever his wealth and status, he was a hard taskmaster and had kept the entire crew svveatingly at work from early morning until it was too dark to see in the holds. He and Jack Daventry had taken an instant dislike to one another.

He'd come on board like visiting royalty, straight of spine and sharp of eye, giving instructions right and left. 'Clear the decks, you two. Open the main hatch. Call all hands, Mr Reuben. I've cargo coming aboard in twenty minutes, and I shall need every man jack.' Then he caught sight of Jack, who was sitting at ease against the water barrel, enjoying the sunshine and smoking his first pipe of the day. 'Who's that young jackanapes? Put that pipe away, sir, I need every man jack.'

If I were a mere man jack, I would happy to oblige 'ee, sir,' Jack told him, removing his pipe from his mouth but staying where he was. 'Howsomever my name is Jack *Daventry,* and I am the slave master on this ship.' He doffed his cap in salute. 'Your sarvant, sir.'

'Slave master be damned!' the purser mocked. 'No such animal in my books, sir. Let's have no more play-acting. There's work to be done.'

'Not by me, sir, I assure you.'

The purser's temper was beginning to fray. 'By you, sir, if you mean to sail with me, sir. I'll thank you to look lively.'

'I am a man of learning, sir,' Jack said proudly. 'No jack tar.'

A flicker of interest, black eyes narrowed. 'Read and write can you, sir?'

'And a deal more than that, sir.'

'Reading will suffice,' the purser said. 'Take this note, sir. You may check the goods aboard.'

Jack took the list, feeling that he'd taken a necessary stand and won a necessary victory but the purser had been too clever for him, as he quickly discovered. As soon as he'd checked in the first batch of goods it was publicly and plainly obvious that it would take the combined efforts of every man available to manhandle the bulky packages into the hold. The purser had vanished, the master wasn't aboard and the crewmen were surly at the thought that this newcomer intended to stand idly by and let them do all the work. In the end, under pressure of their expectations and the promptings of his own conscience, he rolled up his sleeves and set to labour alongside them. He was aggrieved to have been outwitted but he couldn't see what else he could do.

Most of the cargo that day had been cloth of one kind and another — blue and white chintzes, seersuckers and heavy cambrics, striped cottons and packs of cotton breeches called Bijnta pants, woollen blankets and old sheets. It all had to be stacked amidships so as to keep the ship trim, and then re-stacked when a crate full of cooking pots arrived which was so heavy it took six men to swing it into the hold so naturally it had to be set in the exact centre and everything else shifted to accommodate it.

According to the specifications, they would be taking tobacco aboard the next day, which would be less bulky, along with brandy, rum, flintlocks, hatchets, straw hats, and beads.

Mr Reuben said that didn't surprise him. 'Uncommon fond of beads them nigger fellers. Don't ask me why.'

Jack would have liked to have asked him a great deal but that would have revealed how little he knew about the trade so he kept quiet. In any case by that time he was too tired to care. They'd been working by candlelight for nearly an hour and the air in the hold was rank with the stink of sweat and candle droppings, and so thick with floating fibres it was hard to breathe.

'Is that the lot?' Mr Reuben asked, glancing at the indecipherable hieroglyphics on Jack's paper. And when told it was, said, 'Off to the Llandoger then, me hearties.' The ship's boy had been keeping them supplied with bottles of ale all through the day but now it was time for some real drinking.

'I'll follow,' Jack promised. He still had to make a final check of the bales of blue and white cotton.

But after they'd gone, he sat down for a second against the nearest bale to finish off the last of the bottled beer, took off his boots to ease his feet, and slept where he dropped, caught out by a fatigue more intense than any he had ever known.

*

Suki was woken by cockcrow and the first fingers of light. For a few seconds she couldn't remember where she was, then William stirred too and snuffled to be fed and her day began in earnest.

True to her promise she crossed the yard to visit her family as soon as she'd finished the first chores of the day, changed William's dirty clouts, given her lumpy mattress a good shaking and hung it out of the window to air, and set the table for breakfast. Farmer Lambton was already up and out in the fields and she could hear Mrs Lambton stirring in the room overhead. There was just time to walk across and see her mother and the littl'uns before she had to cook the breakfast.

She was uncommon fond of her family, grubby and noisy though they were, but visiting them wasn't easy. She'd come back in the farmer's cart on several occasions when she was first in service, bringing presents for them all and full of excitement to tell them the latest gossip from town but, as she grew more and more accustomed to the style of life the Bradburys led, they seemed more and more dull by comparison and the cottage darker and dirtier. But the real problem was the company they kept.

Like most farm labourers, they shared their thatched cottage with two other farm families and an old lady called Mrs Havers, with one or two rooms apiece and a central kitchen to serve them all. The old lady had once been a milkmaid on a neighbouring farm and was kept on by Farmer Lambton, ostensibly to wash the bed linen and do the mending but actually because no one else was prepared to put up with her. Nowadays she virtually lived in the kitchen, sitting in her rickety chair in the chimney comer and giving a running commentary on everything that was going on, whether she understood it or not.

She'd been peculiar enough when Suki was a child but now she wasn't just odd, but messy and eccentric. The cottage was a long, narrow, single-storey stone building, heavily thatched and standing at right angles to the piggery. Mrs Havers had been given the room nearest the yard, which gradually became used as an extension of the yard itself, since the dividing wall had long since rotted away and the old lady didn't seem to mind how many creatures shared her living accommodation. The arrangement caused frequent squabbles with the three other tenants, particularly when the livestock wandered through the cottage and made havoc in the vegetable patch behind it, but nothing had ever been done about it and now they all seemed inured to it.

Only the top half of the kitchen door was closed that morning, because the bottom half was off its hinges. Through the shadowy gap, Suki could see feet and feathers and a flurry' of agitated movement. Her overactive family were in their usual state, she thought, listening to the bangs and crashes and squawks and squeals. No wronder she'd wanted to get away from it all and make a new life for herself in better company.

Sure enough, as she walked in through the door, she could see that the kitchen was crowded with animals: two pigs, blundering and snuffling, a goat nibbling rags in one comer, and a motley collection of muddy fowls, scratching up the mud floor and perching wherever they could find a foothold. Her mother was busy by the kitchen fire, removing the first of the day's loaves from the bread oven, and the smell of new bread rose appetisingly into the enclosed air. Mrs Havers was sitting in the chimney comer chewing her gums, and Molly and young Tom were under the kitchen table as far away from the sharp feet of the fowls as they could get, tattered with dirt and squabbling fiercely.

But they were delighted to see her and ran to her at once to kiss and be kissed.

'Here's our Suki come home,' Mrs Havers said as though she was telling them something they couldn't see. 'Come an' give your old aunty' a kiss. My stars, this babba of your'n gets a-handsomer by the day.'

'No,' Suki began. But it was too late. The children were crowding round the baby to kiss him and pet him and he was greeting them, holding out his arms to them in return, all bright eyes and babble as though he knew who they were.

'Comin' on lovely,' Mrs Havers approved. 'You got a lovely grandson, Mrs Brown. I never see a babba come on so well. She do you credit an' that's a fact. You got here early in the morning then, didn't you gel. Must've been up with the lark. That's why you got such bright eyes, on account of bein' up with the lark. D'you see what bright eyes she's got, this sister of your'n? 'Tis healthy living what do that. Take it from one who knows.'

If only she'd stop talking for a second I could tell them, Suki thought, but the explanation she'd been shaping in her mouth all the way across the yard seemed more and more unlikely as the old lady rambled on and on. Perhaps if I could get her to talk about something else...

'I heard about Pa,' she said to her mother. 'How is he?'

'He'll live,' her mother said, lifting another loaf from the oven. 'Your brother's gone to Bath to work with that Mr Allen. Did you know that? A-diggin' foundations so he is, for that great circus they'm a-buildin'.'

''Twill fall down as sure as Fate,' Mrs Havers observed lugubriously. 'He's got your eyes, Suki, dear little man.'

The old lady's insistence was squashing Suki into a panic. How could she explain who the baby was, or was supposed to be, if she would keep on so? Try another tack. 'Where's Meg, Ma?'

Gone into service in Queen's Square, apparently, as a scullery maid, and settling down well.

'Never see a babba so like his ma,' Mrs Havers went on. 'Same eyes, same chin, same way of looking round at you. See'un? There he go again. Never mistake'un in a month of Sundays. What d'you call'un, Suki? You'll have to be remindin' me. His name's gone clean out my head. I must be gettin' old in my old age.'

'His name's William,' Suki said, and she looked straight at the old lady daring her to disagree. 'William Bradbury. The one I'm a wet nurse to. He's been farmed out. To Mr Lambton's farm. I come here last night. I'm a-stayin' at the farm.'

She stunned them into silence, Molly and Tom looking at her round-eyed, the old lady frowning.

'Where's our babba then, Suki?, Molly asked. 'Why'aven't you brought him 'stead of this one? What you done with our babba?' It was

161

dreadful to have to tell them her lie but she had to do it. She explained, using the same words she'd used in the farmhouse, and was horribly upset when her sister burst into tears and ran away from her and her mother gave her a look of such scathing disbelief that she could feel the blood rising to her face.

'Buried?' Mrs Havers said. Oh my dear life! Dead an' buried, poor little mite. What a weary world to be dead an' buried. 'Tis uncommon hard...'

But luckily she didn't get the chance to say any more because at that moment Mr Brown came stomping into the kitchen, with his round hat in his hands, and his bandage trailing along the ground.

'Little contree Tom,' he explained, looking at Suki sheepishly. 'You keepin' well, are you? 'Tis all come adrift seemingly. They sent me back to get it fixed on account of Farmer Lambton. He reckon it's a danger to the others. I s'pose you haven't got such a thing as an old rag about'ee, have'ee, Mrs Havers?'

So Suki was able to escape, after telling her father she was sorry to see him hurt and hoped he would soon be better. But as she walked back to the farmhouse, she knew her going wouldn't be the end of the matter and that her mother would have something to say about it sooner or later. And her heart quailed at the thought of what it would be.

It was said the next afternoon, when Mrs Lambton sent her up to the fields with a basket of bread and cheese and a flagon of ale for the farmer. William had been fed to capacity and was asleep in the cradle the Lambtons had provided for him, so she was able to leave him behind. It was actually quite pleasant to be out in the open air and striding along without his weight on her back. After a few yards she began to sing — 'Heigh down derry derry ding, Life is a merry merry thing' — her skirts swishing in time to the words. She was so happily absorbed she didn't hear her mother until she was walking alongside her.

'So now we may have the truth,' Mrs Brown said, in her no-nonsense way. 'There's no one by to hear us.'

Suki swallowed.

'That baby's never a Bradbury,' her mother went on. 'Not with that face. You may fool the rest of 'em — though how you pulled the wool over Farmer Lambton's eyes I shall never understand — but you don't fool me an' you needn't think it. Did you really imagine I wouldn't know my own grandson, you foolish child?' The moment had come. Not in Bath among strangers but here, at home, among these familiar rolling fields, with the call of the reapers echoing in the distance and the smell of ripe corn filling the air around her, strong as new baked bread, here where she'd always felt secure and where the shock of being found out was doubly hard. Now she would be punished and made to tell the Bradburys and stood in front of the magistrate and publicly shamed.

'Out with it,' her mother said, watching her face. 'I needs to know.'

'Better not, Ma. I been telling lies.'

'I don't doubt it. All the more reason.'

'We could both be in trouble if I tell you.'

'I'll be the judge of that.'

A skylark rose from the corn and spiralled into the blue sky, stringing pearls of joyous sound as it rose. A year ago Sula would have listened to it with a total and innocent pleasure, now it sounded more like an avenging angel than a songbird, mocking her hopes and calling, 'caught out, found out, *seeeee*, silly silly silly'.

'You got the look of a gel with too many burdens,' her mother observed. 'Share 'em gel. Don't hold 'em to yourself. I'll not tell another living soul if that's what you want.'

The promise brought a flood of relief. 'Truly?'

Mrs Brown was forthright. 'You don't peach your children.'

So the truth was told, at first hesitantly, then, as her mother simply listened and didn't judge, at some length, for they had a mile to cover until they reached the field being harvested and they were walking more and more slowly.

'I had to do it, Ma,' Suki finished. 'You do see that, don't you?'

'No I don't,' her mother said. 'What was that husband of yourn a-doing, pray? He should've took you away an' made a home for you an' the babba.'

It was time for the worst confession. 'Me an' him never got married.'

Mrs Brown drew in her breath. 'So that's the humour of it,' she said. 'That's the sort of man he was. Love you an' leave you.' Suki rushed to deny it. Because it could so easily be true. 'Oh no. Nothing like that. He loves me.'

Her mother sighed. 'They all say that, gel.'

'No, no. He does. Truly. And I love him with all my heart.'

'Oh, Suki, Suki! I never thought I'd live to hear you talk such nonsense.'

'It ain't nonsense, Ma. I do love him. I love *him* an' he loves *me* an' we'll marry just as soon as he gets home again.'

'What you propose to do in the meantime though? Tell me that.'

'Look for him next summer and feed the babba till hem three an' then...'

Her mother looked a question at her. They were close enough to the harvest field to hear what the reapers were saying. The time for confidences was nearly over.

'An' if he don't come back, what then?'

'I don't know,' Suki admitted. 'I just got to hang on an' hope.'

'Would you like your pa to find you a husband?'

The idea was abhorrent. 'No. No. If I can't marry the Captain I shan't marry at all.'

'We'd find you a good man.'

'I wouldn't love him.'

'You don't have to love a man to many him,' her mother said. 'That arn't the way of the world. Marriage is a bargain. He gets a mother for his children and a woman to keep house for him, you get a roof over your head and bread in your mouth. Love don't come into it.'

Defiance rose in Suki's chest, making her lift her head and jut her chin. 'Then it should.'

'There's only one love of any consequence,' Mrs Brown told her, touched to pity by her boldness, 'an' that's the love you feel for your children. That never changes, as well you know, for weren't that the reason for all this?'

It was. It had to be admitted.

'Life's never easy,' Mrs Brown said, as they climbed over the stile into the field, 'an' babbas make it worse, but we wouldn't be without 'em. You'll manage I daresay. Least you'm close by an' I can keep an' eye on you.'

To be supported when she'd expected to be rebuked and punished brought Suld to tears. 'Thank'ee, Ma,' she said, leaning forward to kiss her mother's cheek.

Mrs Brown gave a wry smile. 'I'aven't been much of a help to 'ee in all conscience, you bein' in Bath an' me here.'

'I thought you'd scold.'

'Bit late for that now, gel,' her mother said, striding into the field. 'We just got to make the best of things, same as we always do. Hope an' pray. You'm a good gel at heart.'

So Suki settled to her new life on the farm and tried not to think about her problems. She scrubbed floors, scoured dirty dishes, helped pile the corn into stooks and gather the gleanings, provided the reapers with food and drink, attended church on Sundays and kept Mrs Lambton company all through the week.

It wasn't long before the two of them had established a happy routine. When the weather was warm, the farmer in the fields and the day's chores done, they took their chairs out into the garden, set the baby on his feather pillow between them, free from his swaddling bands and his tacky clouts to lack his naked legs in the sun and give his poor sore bum an airing, and sat beside him against the garden wall to gossip as they did their mending.

Suki took to telling her new mistress about the Bradburys, mimicking the young misses as they roared at one another and giving a fair imitation of Lady Bradbury and her trick of falling into a faint to get her own way. Annie thought that was very funny, although she pretended to scold.

'Oh Suki, you bad girl!' she protested, holding her thin fingers to her mouth in shocked delight. To poke such fun. She might've been ill in earnest.'

'Not her,' Suki said. 'She'm as fit as a flea. 'Tis just on account of she have to have everything her own way. Which reminds me. I'm s'posed to write to her and tell her we'm arrived.'

'You shall do it tonight. We've pen and paper.'

Suki seized her opportunity at once. 'I would if I could ma'am, but I can't on account of I can't read an' write.'

'Oh dear. Then what shall you do?'

'I been meaning to ask you if you'd learn me how, ma'am. I know some of my letters. S for Suki an' B for Bath and suchlike. I'd learn quick.'

So the bargain was struck — a daily lesson in return for more tales of the Bradburys. M shall need to write this first letter for you to copy but you can sign your own name.'

'Mr Jones shall take it to Bath for you when he goes to market,' the farmer said when he was told.

'I am to stay here then, sir?'

He smiled his nice slow smile at her. 'I think so or Mrs Lambton will never let me hear the last of it.'

So Mr Jones carried her letter on his next trip to Bath, putting it carefully into his money bag before he drove off and assuring her it would be delivered safe and sound. Suki stood in the porch and watched as the neat cart joggled through the dust towards the lane, with Mr Jones and his dog sitting bolt upright on the driving seat and swaying in harmony like two glove puppets. She would have liked to have travelled with him, just in case the Captain was in town, or to have sent *him* a letter, but she knew that neither of these things were possible.

After his second trip, he brought her back a letter from Lady Bradbury which Annie read for her, although by then she was beginning to distinguish the easy words and could have managed some of it herself. Milady was pleased to hear that William was well. Suki was to write to her every week and to keep her informed as to any requirements the child might have. Meantime she enclosed another bank note for five pounds.

So the weeks continued and William grew out of his clothes and discovered how to sit up and had the first cold of his life which puzzled him and made him grizzly. The fields were ploughed and the new seed soaked in lime and urine and left to set before being planted. And soon the first gales of autumn blew, scattering the first dead leaves and flailing the supple trees from side to side like river weed. The wind moaned down the chimney at night and set the fowls into affronted squawking by day, and Suki fretted too, alone in her white-washed bedroom, because time was passing and she hadn't found the Captain and there was nothing she could do but wait.

Fifteen

'You won't find a better horse in all Christendom,' Jack Daventry said to his companion, stroking Beau's thick mane. 'He's mettlesome, I'll grant you that, but he's a stayer.'

'Better or worse, sir,' the other man said, 'they all eat hay, an' they eats it prodigious every last animal on 'em. This here one's a regular trencher.' Beau had been stabled with him ever since Jack arrived in Bristol so he spoke with authority. 'Which as I don't need to tell 'ee sir, hay don't grow on trees.'

The two men were standing in the yard of Mr Wenham's livery stables alongside the Broad Quay, with Beau tossing his head between them, and the transaction Jack had just proposed wasn't being well received, although for the life of him he couldn't think why. Any stableman worth his salt should have been jumping for joy at the thought of accommodating such a splendid animal, not pouting and complaining.

'You'll be paid,' he promised.

Mr Wenham sucked in his cheeks. 'Aye but when, sir?'

'Forty crowns now, the rest when I return,' Jack urged. 'In full. You have my word as a gentleman.'

'Trouble is,' Mr Wenham said stolidly, 'you can't eat words, sir, as I don't need to tell 'ee. Now if you'd a mind to *sell* the animal 'twould be a different matter altogether.'

It was unthinkable, impossible. What a fool of a man he is, Jack thought, enraged by Mr Wenham's swarthy face, by his bow legs and fustian breeches, his stink of stables, his asinine inability to see what a monstrous suggestion he'd just made. The thought of being parted from this splendid creature for a whole year was misery enough. The grief of it was a physical pain, tears tightening in his throat, an anguished ache in his guts. Now he understood what the Bible meant when it wrote of the prophet yearning in his bowels'. But to be forced to sell him would break his heart.

Now that the moment of parting was upon him, he realized that he felt closer to this animal than he'd ever been to any other living creature. The series of slatternly women who'd been paid to feed and house him in his miserable childhood had been too careless and uncaring to offer him attention or affection, and although he'd professed love to many a young woman since he set out into the world alone, none of them had moved him much beyond desire, luscious though they were. There'd been a dark-eyed creature in Bath last summer who'd come closer to him than most but she was nothing compared to the bond he felt for this handsome, sensitive, noble creature, with his quick response to the merest touch of a heel, his speed over the roughest road, his sure-footedness, his wonderful intelligent obedience.

'Selling is out of the question,' he said, stiff-necked with distress.

'I wonder you don't take 'im with 'ee, sir,' Mr Wenham said, 'if that's the humour of it.'

'I would, Mr Wenham, depend on it, if there were room for him aboard ship.' Which would be sailing in less than an hour. 'So, sir, how say you? Shall you take him? 'Twould only be for a year.' And when Mr Wenham still hesitated. 'He could earn his keep, should you wish it. You could hire him out to the quality. I ain't opposed to that.'

''Tis irregular.'

'A plague o' that. Think what you stand to gain.'

'There's gains an' there's losses, sir, if you take my meaning. Twill mean a small fortune spent on hay.'

'I'll pay'ee. Forty crowns down, the rest...'

Mr Wenham sucked in his cheeks again. Thought, breathing noisily. 'Sixty.'

Jack relaxed. It was a concession. The arrangement was possible. Now it was simply a matter of haggling. 'Forty-five.'

The bargain was concluded thirty gambling seconds later. Time only to stroke Beau's nose and lay his head once more and for the last time against the graceful arch of that familiar neck — and then to run. Across the quay. Don't look back. An unnecessary leap down on to the deck. Cheerful greetings to his shipmates. Too soon, he grieved, holding a bold smile, too soon, too fast, too final. But the pilot boat was heading towards them, implacably purposeful, its long oars edged blood-red by the setting sun. His adventure was upon him ready or not.

The pilot climbed aboard, three sails were unfurled and the *Bonny Beaufoy* gave a shudder like a horse under the spur, seemed to gather herself, timbers creaking, and began to move. Jack was the only man aboard who didn't have a job to do and the lack of one left him feeling exposed, as the master boomed instructions and the crew ran to obey them, pigtails dancing, feet slapping the deck. He watched as the breeze filled the canvas with a sudden crack and the ship began to lumber after the pilot boat like a great full-breasted swan ludicrously following a duckling, stirring the stagnant water of the floating harbour as she went. Then more sails were unfurled and they were out in the great highway of the river, away from the stink and clamour of the quays and picking up speed.

Jack was exhilarated despite his grief, for the roll and dip of the ship's progress made him think of the flight of a great bird and the thought lifted him and comforted him. Was he not an eagle among men? And was this not the perfect place for him, a noble, powerful creature sailing effortlessly into the glory of the setting sun? The clouds before him massed in imperial colours, scarlet, pale gold, purple, and the water parted by the ship's black prow flowed on either side of him like arcs of melted gold.

There is nothing to keep me here, he thought, with sad satisfaction. I've no prospects and no hope of any, no family to care for me, no one to love me, not a living soul to grieve at my going except for Beau. He straightened his shoulders, lifted his chin, flexed his feet against the movement of the deck, feeling how well this new life would suit him. I shall return a rich man, he vowed. No matter what lies ahead of me, one thing is certain. I shall prevail.

'I shall be sick presently,' Mr Reuben said lugubriously, padding up to stand beside him at the rail. ''Tis allus the same, every blamed voyage.'

*

'The *Bonny Beaufoy* has sailed, me dear,' Sir George told his wife with great satisfaction two days later. 'I had a billet from my brother this morning. She caught the evening tide a' Thursday so she should be past the Scillies by now. Good news, what?'

Hermione nodded her head but, apart from that, she took no notice. She was much too busy supervising the installation of her new silk curtains. With three important dinner parties planned to start the season — one for each of her daughter's prospective suitors — she had decided to redecorate the drawing room. White was utterly passe, as she'd realized the moment she stepped into the blue and gold extravagance of Lady Fosdyke's newly decorated salon, and as she explained to her husband as soon as they were back home. 'We must be a la mode,' she'd said, 'or the Honourable Sir Humphrey will think us nothing but clod-hoppers. The dining room will pass muster, I daresay. At least for this season. Nobody sees anything very much at table, as I'm sure you will allow. They are all too fully occupied perusing at the other guests. Howsomever, *this* room will be under inspection.'

So the walls had been covered in the finest blue wallpaper she could find, every bit as expensive as that ordered by her rival, doors and shutters positively gleamed with white paint and she had invested in two perfectly splendid Venetian chandeliers, each one holding four and twenty candles and hung with four and twenty dazzling glass pendants. And now the new curtains had arrived and if only Bamaby and that stupid new boy would pay attention to what they were supposed to be doing, the transformation of the room would soon be complete.

'Have a care,' she warned, as they hauled the heavy drapery into position. 'You hold twenty pounds' worth of French cloth in your hands.'

'I've a good purser aboard,' her husband went on happily. 'Jedediah Smith. Stout feller. Good sound head on his shoulders.'

'Which is more than may be said for this oaf of yours,' Hermione scowled. 'Barnaby! How many more times must I tell you? Have a care what you do. Sir George will not look kindly upon you if you waste his good money with your clumsiness, will you my love?'

Her love hadn't looked particularly kindly at her waste of his good money and had protested long and loudly against her extravagance, but eventually he had realized that he was wasting his breath as well as his cash and now he was resigned to it. At least he could brag of his expenditure at the club and it was a visible demonstration of the healthy state of his finances. Now that the sugar crop had been sold, things were a trifle easier in that regard. But even so, he thought twenty pounds for mere curtains was a bit steep, damme if it wasn't.

'We shall be the toast of the town,' Hermione promised, slipping her hand through the crook of his arm, 'once our dear Ariadne is married into the gentry where she belongs. Think of it, my love, your daughter, the wife of the Honourable Humphrey de Thespia. Lift it, Barnaby! Don't drag it, you impossible creature.'

'She might choose one of the others,' Sir George tried to point out. 'Mr Jenkins is a fine man and uncommon wealthy.' The merchant was still his preferred choice.

'Well, we shall see,' Hermione temporized, giving him one of her rare smiles. 'I shall write the invitations for his dinner after church on Sunday and Jessup shall have them delivered on Monday morning. But first I must put my mind to the matter of Ariadne's new gowns.'

'Gowns?' Sir George protested, eyebrows raised in a new alarm. ''Od's bowels! She has a wardrobe fairly stuffed with gowns. She can't want more.'

But Ariadne shared her mother's opinion on the matter and declared that she must have no less than three new gowns, one for each dinner, lest her suitors should make comparison and feel belittled.

''Tis the least we can do. Do you not agree, Mamma?' she said. 'What man of property and estate would wish to dine with a thrice-worn gown? 'Twould be insufferable to him. Insupportable. Mamma understands such things, do you not, Mamma?'

So the gowns were ordered and the first intricate fitting undertaken and that Sunday evening, since her mother was being so agreeable about the matter, Ariadne offered to assist with the writing of the invitations by way of demonstrating her appreciation and in order to discover which of her particular friends and rivals were being invited. And found, lying on top of her mother's carefully written list, the equally carefully written, but far less elegant letter from Suki Brown.

'How now?' she drawled, picking it up and pretending not to know what it was. 'Here's a hand I don't know, Mamma.'

Hermione explained its presence. ''Tis from the wet nurse,' she said. 'She writes a poor hand I fear, but that is only to be expected. The wonder of it is that she can write at all. You may read it if you wish.'

It was read with disguised eagerness.

'Why, I do declare she's in Twerton,' Ariadne said, 'which is close to Bath, I believe. I've a mind to write to her myself, Mamma, and see if she would run a little errand for me.'

Hermione was instantly suspicious. 'What errand would that be pray?'

Ariadne recognized the need for caution, although her heart was racing with excitement. 'A trifle,' she said airily. ''Tis of no consequence. There is an excellent milliner in Bath, that is all. She had a fine stock of French ribbons. I remember one in particular of white silk embroidered with silver flowers. An exquisite article. 'Twould make the perfect trimming to my new white silk, the one I am to wear when Sir Humphrey comes to dine. I could find others here I daresay, but none so fine.'

So, since vanity and self-enhancement were perfectly acceptable to milady, the letter was written.

Its delivery put Suki into a quandary. Mrs Lambton's baby was almost due, so far as any of them could be sure. Certainly, the poor lady's belly was the shape of a ready ripe pear and her exhaustion was so extreme she could barely lift herself from her chair without being reduced to a coughing fit. In Suki's trenchant opinion she shouldn't be left alone for a minute, far less a day. But the thought of being back in Bath, of taking up her search again, of finding Quin Cutpurse or that man Charlie Moss or someone who would know where her darling was, or when he was coming back, roused her to an excitement that beat in her throat like a bird in flight.

She and Annie deciphered Ariadne's careful instructions together sitting side by side in the window seat, for although Suki's reading was coming along extremely well now that she'd mastered all her letters and was well into the complication of the sounds they made, she still needed help with unexpected words, like 'require' and 'package' and 'account'. They were both intrigued by what they read.

You are to buy two yds of the white and silver ribbon.
French, she will know what you require. We spoke of it
when I was last in Bath, amongst other things which you
may remember. Should there be any other package for me
it should be contained within the parcel of ribbon and sent
on to this address. On no account should it be the first
thing to be seen when the parcel is opened, and kindly
make sure that the parcel is addressed in your own hand.

'What *does* she mean?' Annie asked, tired eyes widened. 'What other package?'

''Tis a love affair, ma'am,' Suki told her, 'with the actor in the helmet. She'm a-waitin' for letters from him.' And she entertained her mistress with the full story of the young lady's romance and how it was being conducted — 'all in secret and right under milady's long nose'.

Annie was delighted. 'What a bad, bad gal!' she said with approval. ''Tis better than a play, so 'tis. You must go to Bath for her, Suki. We can't leave her lovelorn, poor lady. Not when she'm a-runnin' such risks.'

'But what of you, ma'am?' Suki worried.

'I shall last a day,' Annie promised. 'Depend on't. And all the better for a good tale to hear when you return.'

So the next market day, Suki wrapped herself in her red cloak against the mist, bundled William in a blanket, climbed into the cart alongside Mr Jones's dog and was rattled into the city.

It was a miserable disappointment. She'd forgotten how dull and empty the town was out of season. Last winter she'd been too hard at work and too caught up in the wonders of her pregnancy to pay much attention to what was going on out of doors. Now it was depressingly obvious that the place was deserted, the Pump Room closed and shuttered, the abbey forbiddingly dark, the great houses in the parades shut against the weather. Even the market was barely a tenth of the size it had been in the summer and Mr Jones's customers scurried to be served so as to get home again quickly to the warmth of their fires. There was no sign of Quin Cutpurse or any of his friends, although she looked in all four of the coffee shops that were open. No sign of Mrs Roper or her skivvy, although she trailed all the way to Nowhere Lane to check, no sign of life at the theatre, where the playbills were peeling from the boards and grime lay black as tar against the entrance as though it had been used to seal the place up.

I've wasted a day, she thought, trudging to the milliner's shop with William on her back. He was extremely heavy now for he was six months old and a fine fat child. I'd have done better to have stayed in Twerton and sat by the fire.

The shop was shut, which was hardly a surprise. But having come all that way and been disappointed in every other endeavour, she wasn't going to be deterred by a shuttered window. She knocked on the door as loudly as she could and kept knocking until a window opened above her head and the milliner looked out to ask her what was amiss.

'I've a sale for 'ee,' she said boldly, 'an' a message from Miss Bradbury.'

'I'll be down to attend to 'ee direct,' the milliner promised. And was.

She seemed to understand entirely that the letter she produced from a now dusty pile of hatboxes was to be hidden underneath the purchased ribbon and that the package was to be addressed by Suki. 'Caution is necessary in these matters,' she said as she rocked towards the counter with the letter in her hand.

But when the last string had been tied and the parcel sealed with red wax, it was still only midday and there were four more hours for Suki to fill before Mr Jones would make his return journey to Twerton. She was hungry and cold, her back ached, her feet were sore and William would need feeding at any minute. He'd lasted out nearly four hours and she couldn't hope for him to hold out much longer. What was to be done? Where could she go?

Sister Meg. Of course. Where did Ma say she was? Queen's Square. That was it. And that was no distance at all. Hauling the baby into a more comfortable position on her back, she set off at once. And found her sister in the third house she tried. She was wiping her hands on her apron and looked weary until she saw who was calling. Then she pulled Suki into the kitchen, sat her by the fire, found meat, bread and ale and admired her sister while the baby was fed.

'You chose a good day, our Suki,' she said. 'My ol' skinflint's out a-visitin', so I got John a-coming here this afternoon. He's still a-diggin' that old circus, but they lets him off now an' then. What larks we shall have!'

And although Suki had to tell them the old lie about William and to bear their commiserations, it was a happy afternoon, sitting on settles in front of the fire, swapping gossip, remembering old times on the farm, roasting the chestnuts that John had bought with him 'for a treat', while William sat on the hearth rug between them and played at drumming with two wooden spoons and a saucepan. She even forgot to feel guilty about leaving poor Mrs Lambton.

Sixteen

Farmer Lambton was standing at his kitchen window, smoking a pipe for comfort and watching the road. He'd been there, off and on, for most of the afternoon, and, despite the pipe, his anxiety had increased by the hour, for Annie had started her pains almost as soon as the cart disappeared round the bend in the road that morning. And although Mrs Brown and Mrs Havers had been in constant and garrulous attendance all day, the baby had refused to arrive.

His poor Annie didn't complain. When did she ever complain of anything? She simply lay in their old four-poster and endured. She was too considerate of his feelings to scream, but her smothered groans were more terrible than cries and each one tore him with an impotent pity. No matter how much they both wanted this child, it was surely wrong for her to have to bring it into the world with so much pain, and the more she suffered the more he feared that the child would be born dead or would die soon after, like all the others.

Mrs Havers had bustled in and out with potions of motherwort and dishes of raspberry leaf tea, talking endlessly, and Mrs Brown had tried every trick she knew, administering an enema and a strong infusion of senna and even binding Annie's belly with a leather belt to force the child down, but nothing seemed to help. The inexorable process continued, the farmer fretted, the afternoon blustered uselessly about the farmhouse, and still the child wasn't born.

During his enervating wait, a superstitious hope had gradually been forming in Lambton's mind. It was as foreign as a crystal in a hayrick, and so alien to his stolid nature that he would never have admitted it to anyone, and possibly not even to himself once the crisis was over. The fact was that Suki's awaited presence had become a kind of talisman. As the hours passed, he grew more and more certain that if only that sturdy girl could bring her health and vigour back into his pain-becalmed household, Annie would take strength and the child would be born — and live.

Perhaps it was just as well that Suki herself had no idea that she had been endowed with magical properties or the burden of such importance might have deterred her. As it was, she breezed into the kitchen as she usually did, cloak swirling before her, spine arched against William's weight, cheeks blown russet by the wind, dark curls damp and glossy beneath the white frill of her cap. The still air of the farmhouse rippled at her arrival, prickling with the scents of travel, the sweat of horses, rotting leaves, the trodden mud of the road. She was an interruption and a challenge, just as Lambton had hoped, and she noticed Annie's absence immediately.

'Where's Mrs Lambton?' she asked, settling the sleeping baby in his day crib in the kitchen. But she knew already. There was only one possible reason for the poor lady's absence, as her husband's anxious face revealed. She was furious with herself, torn with guilt and regret. Oh, she thought angrily, how could I have gone rushing off to Bath today of all days — and all to no purpose. I might've knowed 'twould be today. She put on a bright face to hide her feelings from the farmer and went straight upstairs to make amends.

However, as soon as she was in Annie's bedroom, her sympathy was brisk and practical. Not for her the soft-footed deference of the sickroom. 'What have you had to eat, ma'am?' she said, and when she heard that Annie had been labouring unfed, 'I could do with a good meal myself. What could you fancy?'

Annie wasn't sure she could fancy anything.

'Can't tempt her to nothing, poor soul,' Mrs Havers explained dolefully. 'She's very far gone.'

Suki ignored the old lady's happy gloom. 'Soon see about that,' she said cheerfully. 'You go on home, Mrs Havers, an' I'll cook a meal.' And she was off to the kitchen to fry bacon and coddle an egg and make flapjacks on the hob.

Within half an hour of her return she was sitting on Annie's neatened bed, gently spooning food into her mistress's exhaustion, chatting and giggling and normal. And to everyone's surprise, Annie ate nearly everything she was offered and drank a dish of tea and told Mrs Brown she was very much better. Then, even more surprisingly, she turned on her side and slept for nearly an hour.

Even so, it was a long arduous birth. By evening she had used up even the limited strength her unexpected meal had given her, and still the child hadn't emerged, although they could see the pale crown of its head advancing and retreating with every effort. Then dusk washed the room like another stealthy tide, softening the furniture to shadow and provoking yawns and weariness in all the participants. Suki and her mother set candles around the bed and made up the fire and drew the curtains against the world outside the window, and Annie took breath for one last exhausting effort.

It was a boy, pale as pearl in the candlelight with a dusting of soft down across his wrinkled skull and a cry like a kitten. Annie, huge-eyed with fatigue, smiled her great joy at him, and fingered his silk)' skin with tremulous tenderness, cradling his spine with her arm, and breathing in the erotic scent of his new extraordinary life.

'What will you call him?' Mrs Brown asked.

'Constant,' Annie said, purring the name and languid with contentment. 'That's who you are, my little lovely, arn't you? Constant, like your father.'

What an appropriate name, Suki thought, remembering the farmer's steady presence. Hasn't he always been constant, always the same, never out of humour?

Then, just as the thought was in her mind, he came into the room, his face strained as she had never seen it before and his eyes so moist, that if she hadn't known such a thing was impossible, she would have sworn he'd been crying. He was beside the bed in one easy movement of triumph and relief and open affection. Suki and her mother tiptoed out of the room at once. Instinctively they both felt that the new family should be allowed immediate privacy.

After the effort and release of the birth, Suki was very near tears herself. She was remembering William's birth and yearning, because she realized how very much she'd missed the Captain then, and how *very* much she missed him now. Oh, if only she knew where he was. Fortunately William woke before she could weep and made loud demands for his last feed of the day, so she had to hurry off to attend to him and that ensured that her sadness didn't persist. But it was there, even so, just below the surface, clouding the joy of Annie's delivery.

For the next three days, rain fell out of the sky in a never diminishing stream, to curtain across the windows and rattle on the slates and churn the courtyard to a muddy swamp. Mr Brown and the other three farmhands covered their heads and shoulders with sacks and tended the livestock as well as they could. The Christmas geese were bedraggled, the fowls took refuge with Mrs Havers, and everybody else kept within doors.

On the third morning, Mrs Havers bundled herself up in an old cloak and came scuttling through the mud, purportedly to cook a dish of groats for the new mother but actually to glean the latest news.

'Such weather!' she grumbled. 'That ol' roof of mine's a-leaking again. No better'n a sieve.'

'Ask my father,' Suki suggested, shaking the rain from Mrs Haver's cloak and hanging it on the door. 'He'll patch it for 'ee.'

'Lord love 'ee,' Mrs Havers said, filling the kettle, 'he was a-tryin' yes'day afternoon and he fell off the ladder. He can't do nothing now 'cept sit in a chair, bless him.'

Arn't that just Pa, Suki thought. 'You'll have to tell Farmer Lambton about it then,' she said. Roofs were unimportant with a new-born baby in the house and she didn't have time for the old lady's complaint nor for her father's incompetence.

On the third day the weather lifted, which cheered them all, and the farmer sent two of his other hands to mend the thatch. But by then, young Constant Lambton had found his voice and his appetite, and the house was riven with his cries. Annie fed him whenever he yelled, but he was impossible to satisfy.

'What am I to do?' she said wearily to Sula, as the small face beside her roared scarlet with impatience and hunger.

Suki was feeding her nice fat William, sitting comfortably in Annie's nursing chair with a cushion at her back. 'You'll be right as rain, once your milk comes in,' she tried to reassure. 'It's only the third day, when all's said and done.'

But Annie had dropped into an uncharacteristic misery and wouldn't be comforted. 'I been sitting here thinkin',' she said sadly. 'I'm a bad wife an' a bad mother an' that's the truth of it. He'll fade, you'll see, and die like all the others. I'm no use to him at all. A weak, useless, bad mother. Never been better'n a dead weight to my poor man, in all these twelve years.' And she wept with weakness and despair, as the child cried itself into a frenzy under her chin.

It was too much for Suki. She couldn't let this go on, she simply had to do something about it. She detached the sleepy William from her nipple and set him down gently on the bed. 'Give him here,' she said, taking the screaming infant on to her lap. 'Let's see what I can do for him.'

It was odd to be feeding such a very tiny baby, and at first the child himself was baffled by the sudden flow of milk his efforts were producing, but soon he was sucking with a will and they could hear the milk falling — glob, glob, glob, glob — down his eager throat. He fed until he slept and his stomach was as tight and round as a little drum. Only then did Suki stop to wonder whether she might have upset Annie by taking her child away from her like that. When she'd done it, it had seemed right and natural and loving. It had soothed her guilt and given her a chance to make amends. And besides, she was used to feeding two babies. But Annie might not have seen it that way.

She needn't have worried. Annie was limp with relief and finding it hard to keep awake. 'You'm so good to us, Suld Brown,' she murmured, and slept almost at once.

So they settled into their new routine. Young Constant Lambton needed what they came to call 'one good feed', at least twice every day, and, as she had plenty of milk now that William was experimenting with groats and porridge and even the occasional chunk of bread, Suki was happy to oblige, especially as Annie was so grateful to her and as it established her in the household.

At first, Farmer Lambton didn't refer to the arrangement, which was only to be expected, he simply nodded whenever he came upon Suki when she was feeding his infant. Until the last day of Annie's lying-in.

It was late at night and, both babies having been fed and settled, the farm was at peace. He and Suki had drawn the two oak settles up to the kitchen fire, and were enjoying the last of its warmth, happy to be idle at last — she to eat cob nuts, he to smoke his pipe.

'We're much beholden to you, Suki,' he said, gruffly.

She smiled at him. 'Thank 'ee, sir,' she said. 'Couldn't do nothin' else, could I? We couldn't have the poor little mite fade away for want of a mouthful of milk, an' me with plenty.'

It's not just milk, Lambton thought, admiring her. She was a source of so many good things: energy, strength, determination, life itself, overflowing with it, careless of its abundance. 'We're beholden,' he said again. 'You've made a deal of difference to us both. 'Tis a blessing to have a son.'

They sat in warm silence for a while, each privately savouring the pleasurable difference a son had made, she with uncomplicated pleasure, he anxious because he knew how vulnerable a new life could be. The gale was blowing again, pattering rain against the windows and gusting chill air through every crack in the house. But they were in a charmed circle of firelight and privacy, protected from the world by the high backs of the settle in which they sat, and the solid stones of the hearth that kept them warm. Fatigue and comfort made it possible for Suki to speak with an unrestricted directness and honesty.

'Tis no more than Mrs Lambton deserves, sir,' she said, picking a nut cleanly from its shell. ''Tis only fair, when all's said and done.'

He smiled at her sadly, but said nothing for several minutes while he turned over the implications of what she'd said and pondered them carefully.

'That is my opinion of it too,' he told her eventually, gazing at the coals. 'Howsomever, deserts don't usually signify, I'm sad to say. If they did, no innocent child would ever die, nor no wicked man ever prosper.'

'Which arn't the way of the world,' Suki agreed, watching the same coals as they shifted on their bed of ash. 'The wicked flourish like green bay trees, while the good folk go to the wall.' She warmed to her theme, thinking of all the illicit activity she'd seen while she was with the Bradburys. 'I don't know of a single servant in Bath who don't purloin at some time or another, and those as wants preferment have to lie through their teeth to get it.'

Lambton considered this for a long time, too, before he gave an answer. 'Liars may seem to prosper,' he said, 'but a lie is wrong notwithstanding and will bring its own punishment a-trailing after it. The commandment expressly forbids it.'

That begged a question and since firelight and candlelight were giving her some cover, she ventured to ask it. 'How of a white lie, sir? How of a lie told that good may come of it? That arn't so wrong, surely?'

He deliberated again, smoking slowly. 'A lie is a lie,' he said stolidly. ''Twill bring sorrow however well 'tis meant. We deceive ourselves by calling it white.'

He is so uncompromising, Suki thought, wishing he wasn't. He could have allowed her a chink of hope that her own lie wouldn't lead to trouble. She did so hope it wouldn't and did so fear it might. Oh if only she could have found the Captain. He would have known a way out of it.

'Sir George and Lady Bradbury don't tell one another the truth,' she said, turning her attention in another direction. 'If they did there'd be ructions from dawn to dusk. 'Tis bad enough when they flare into a passion. You hear things then an' no mistake. They bait each other cruelly.'

'And are saddened, doubtless.'

'No,' she said. 'It don't seem to worry 'em. By the next day they'm back pretending again. Perhaps the gentry don't have such a need of truth.'

'We all need truth,' he said sternly. 'Without truth there is no trust. And without trust, love would falter and die. And without love we are no better than brute beasts.'

She was touched and amused by his solemnity, but she still didn't agree with him. Lies were a necessary part of her existence and she wanted him to agree with her that they could be useful at the very least. 'Lovers tell lies,' she pointed out. 'They swear you have eyes like stars, an' breath like eglantine, an' such like. 'Tis a pretty fancy, no more, an' no harm in't.'

'No,' he said, more solemnly than ever, 'there is a harm, even in such a lie. If praise is fulsome, how may you recognize honest compliment? We should speak the truth, neither more nor less.'

'Then there would be an end to teasing and flattery,' she told him, 'and much pleasure gone to forfeit.' Although she was hardly aware of it, she was actually teasing him, half laughing, half daring, because his eyes were on the fire and she could mock unobserved. But he looked up at her, suddenly and unexpectedly, and caught the expression on her face and to his horror responded to it, with a desire so rapid and strong that he had communicated it to her before either of them were fully aware of what was happening. Then, of course, he couldn't look away, and neither could she, for his sudden ardour had provoked a response.

The moment held and their desire grew, although neither of them said a word to acknowledge it — he because he was ashamed to have succumbed to lustful thoughts, especially when he'd been talking about the necessity for truth, she because she was puzzled and alarmed. This was how she used to feel for the Captain, her dear Captain, whom she loved and who loved her. 'Twas unseemly to be roused by Farmer Lambton, who was old enough to be her father — and a married man, what's more, who loved his wife. She couldn't understand how her senses were in such a muddle. She wasn't forgetting the Captain, surely? No, no, no. She would *never* forget him. She loved him and would love him for ever. Then why did she feel this uncomfortable passion for the farmer? How could such a thing be happening? And even more alarming, what were they going to do next? It was unreal.

Then he abruptly turned away from her to set his pipe on the rack, and the moment was broken. She realized that she was shivering, and that the fire was giving out little heat.

He cleared his throat. 'There is work to be done in the morning,' he said, careful not to look at her again. The candles were no more than wicks among wax droppings. He handed her the larger of the two flickering stubs, and she took it, like the unmistakable signal it was. The evening and the conversation were over.

From time to time during the night she woke and wondered, feeling guilty and disturbed. But in the morning, it was as if the moment had been a dream. Lambton was his usual stolid self, going quietly about his chores, and there were babies to tend and food to prepare — with special dishes that afternoon because Mrs Lambton was to get up and come downstairs — so there was no time for foolish thoughts. By mid-afternoon, when every member of the household had been fed and Mrs Lambton had retired for an afternoon rest, she had convinced herself that she must have imagined it all.

She'd cleared the table, and scoured the dishes and had just finished feeding William when Mr Jones came strolling into the kitchen, with his dog at his heels, to tell her that the cart was waiting and to ask if she was 'ready for the off.'

'No,' she said, frowning at him. 'Course I am't. What you on about?'

He was puzzled and removed his cap to scratch better understanding into his skull. 'Farmer said you was off,' he explained. 'Moving on. I thought I was to bring the cart.'

'You got hold of the wrong end of the stick,' she told him. 'I arn't goin' nowhere. Not that I knows of. An' certainly not today.' But his words had pushed an uncomfortable wedge into her heart. Was she to be sent away? Was that it? Plainly the farmer had said something during the morning that had caused Mr Jones to think so. The old man had little wit but he was quick to respond to even the hint of an instruction. Then disquiet turned to anger as she realized what was happening. I'm to be moved on for fear of another 'moment' like last night's. That's what 'tis. An' that arn't fair, since he began it. Not that either of them had begun anything. 'Twas all in their minds and left alone 'twould stay there. A moment's folly an nothin' more. Well I won't agree to goin', an' that's all there is to that. I shall tell Mrs Lambton this minute an' see what she has to say. And, as Mr Jones went away still scratching his head, she stomped up the stairs.

Annie Lambton was resting but not asleep. 'Why, whatever is it?' she said, when Suki put her stormy face round the door.

Suki was so cross that she didn't think of the propriety of what she was saying. 'Mr Lambton wants me to leave,' she cried.

Annie was surprised and distressed but she didn't show it. 'Has he told you so?' she asked gently.

'We haven't spoke of it, no,' Suki admitted. 'But Mr Jones brought the cart for me, and said he'd been instructed, so what am I to think?'

''Tis some mistake,' Annie soothed. 'I'm sure Mr Lambton don't mean you to leave us. Not when you'm feedin' our little Constant. I will speak to him.' And being a woman of her word, she did, rising from her bed for the second time that day and searching until she found him, down in the seven-acre field checking the ditches.

He was alarmed to see her out of the house and even more alarmed when he heard what she had to say. But as he walked her back to the warmth of the farmhouse, he tried to put a reasonable point of view, although he had to admit it was as much to salve his own conscience as to comfort her.

'Twas only agreed that she should stay until the child was born,' he pointed out.

'But now she feeds him.'

'For a day or two,' he allowed. 'No more surely. Nor would you wish it. You feed him well, do you not? You arn't the kind of woman who would want to employ a wet nurse.'

'To speak truly,' Annie said wistfully, 'I cannot tell what land of woman I am. Since his birth I have been much confused and she has been an uncommon comfort to me.'

'Your confusion will pass,' he said, speaking as though he were giving her an instruction, 'once you are churched.'

His stern manner stiffened Annie's resolve. 'That may well be so,' she said. 'Howsomever, I think she should stay for as long as the child has need of her. To send her away now would be unkind and foolish. You would not wish to put our child at risk. Of that I am sure. Not when we have suffered so many losses.'

Her rebuke disarmed him. He could hardly admit to the real reason for his decision, not now, when she was low after the birth. Even if there was anything to admit. Which there wasn't. A foolish moment, grown of fatigue and the high emotions of the previous week. He was being cautious. That was all. So he hastened to assure her that Suki should stay at the farm until she was no longer needed, that of course he was grateful to her, that the baby was more important to him than any other creature on earth. 'I would not wish you to think otherwise.'

So the matter was settled. Annie went to church to give thanks for her deliverance from the dangers of childbirth and Suki sat in the pew beside her and gave thanks of her own, because she had contrived to stay where she was, with a roof over her head and food in her belly and a safe home for her son. And life in the farmhouse continued in its slow adapting pattern, day by dark November day, although, as both women noticed privately, Farmer Lambton spent more and more time in the fields as the winter deepened, even though there was less and less for him to do there.

Seventeen

'This is the life for me,' Jack Daventry said, resting his eyes on the smoke-blue curves of the distant coastline. Now that they were in calmer waters, he could persuade himself that all was well with his world, the sun strong over his head, the deck warm under his feet. He glanced around him, deliberately gathering impressions to support his sentiments, determined to be optimistic. The *Bonny Beaufoy* dipped and swung through the water, as easy as a bird in flight, the breeze continued fair, the sea was blue-green, the crest of every lapping wave flashed diamond fire in the sunlight. He was well fed and, at least for the moment, pleasantly idle. 'This is the life.' Yet his anxiety persisted, picking away at his heart with its sharp crab claws. Soon they would land and if he were not exceptionally careful — and skilful — his lack of knowledge could be exposed.

'You was singin' a different tune in the Bay a' Biscay,' Mr Reuben observed in his sour way. ''Twas all woe an' tribulation in the Bay a Biscay, as I remember.'

Jack had put that miserable episode right out of his mind. Storms were part and parcel of a life at sea and he'd soon learned that the best way to handle them was to endure them with as much 'bottom' as he could and then forget them. Live for the moment. That was the sailor's way. 'We've no storms now, Mr Reuben,' he said happily, 'and if we continue at this rate, according to Captain's estimate, we shall be in the Gambia in less than a month.' At which time he would rise to the challenge and win through.

During the trials of the voyage, the two men had struck up a lopsided friendship. They were both oddities, Jack because of his air of superiority, the bosun because of his interminable pessimism, and they'd soon discovered that they were useful to one another. Mr Reuben felt protected by Jack's high-born insouciance, while Jack was able to learn from his older companion without Mr Reuben or anyone else being aware of it. Now he could speak the language and had learnt the ropes. He could furl a sail, drop anchor, splice a rope or man the capstan as though he'd been doing such things all his life. Which was another reason for his present cheerfulness.

'You'm a rum'un,' Mr Reuben observed. 'I never knowd anyone so keen to get ashore. Well, rather you than me, my lubber. Thas all I got to say on the matter. 'Tis a mortal hard place we'm a-goin' to.'

Jack was so accustomed to the older man's dour opinions that he no longer took any notice of them. 'Courage, Mr Reuben,' he said, grinning at the bosun. 'We shall be in and out of the place in no time at all. Two shakes of a lamb's tail, I promise you. Slaves bought, ship watered and provisioned, all ship-shape an' Bristol fashion, you'll see.'

Mr Reuben stuck three blunt fingers into the pocket of his breeches, pulled out his baccy pouch, his flint and his clay pipe and began to fill it, picking out the precious tobacco very carefully so as not to waste a shred. 'Can't be quick enough fer me,' he said. 'I've no humour fer the place an' that's the truth of it. There's too many fevers thereabouts an' too many insects to bite you an' wild animals a-roaring day an' night, an' the heat's enough to melt the hat on your head. An' I ain't said nothing about the niggers which is the most treacherous cargo a' swabbers I ever come across, saving the Frenchies. I onny sailed on account of Mr Tomson.'

This time his gloom sounded rather more ominous but Jack decided to ignore it, since he couldn't prod the man to tell him more without rousing his suspicions. Luckily, at that moment, a huge shoal of silver fish appeared in the waters alongside them, scudding and tumbling, so there was a rush for nets and pipe and conversation had to be set aside.

The next day they reached the high peninsular of Cape Verde, with its two conical hills that the sailors called the Paps, and not long after that, they came to a bay fringed with palm trees and the long green island of Goree which had a harbour and a well laid out town and two massive forts built on a formidable outcrop of dark basalt. There was much grumbling from captain and crew because they couldn't land there now that the French were in control.

'Mr Pitt should send out a fleet,' Mr Tomson said, scowling as they passed the harbour, 'and send 'em packing. Good harbour like that — clean water, food aplenty, linguists, pretty girls — it should belong to all of us, so it should. We'll not find better this many a mile an' 'tis mortal hard to pass 'un by.'

As they sailed towards the mouth of the Gambia river three weeks later, Jack could see what he'd meant. For now they had reached a place so foreign and oppressive that even the sight of it was enough to provoke alarm. Even from a distance it was plain that this was an enormous, unwelcoming river. It was fringed by salt marshes and glades of the grotesque trees that he now knew as mangroves. Their twisted trunks grew so densely that they seemed to be matted together and it was so hot that they were steaming. Vapour rose from the mass to form a dripping cloud which clung about the treetops. He was quite relieved when they sailed past.

'Where do we land?' he asked Mr Reuben, as casually as he could.

'Ah now, my heart,' the bosun said, winking at him. 'As to that, 'tis mortal hard to know, on account of we got two opinions aboard, seemingly. They'm a-battlin' it out, a hammer an' tongs, this here very minute. Purser he'm all for Port James, which is the biggest port hereabouts an' built by the East Indiamen. I daresay you knows the place. Captain Tomson, he'm for headin' on to Mwamba, on account of he knows the chief there an' they done business afore. Purser says he's never heard of it an' no more has anyone else. 'Tis a right argy-bargy. I wonder you 'aven't heard 'em a-ragin'.'

Jack was instantly on the captain's side. An established port would reveal his inexperience. Better a place that no one had heard of. 'Aye,' he said. 'I have heard voices.'

''Twill be oaths presently,' the bosun said, happily grim.

But that night the ship was quiet, and the next morning they sailed past the port, which was stone built with another solid fortress, and where there were already two other slavers sitting at anchor, so apparently the captain had won his case.

They headed inshore later that afternoon, towards a very much smaller place. It was set to windward of a deep water bay at the outlet of another massive river, and, as far as Jack could see as they approached, it was little more than a collection of rough huts made of dark cracked mud and roofed with grey reeds or long grass. There was a quay of sorts and as they drew nearer he could see that it was crowded with black figures, half naked but armed with long spears and carrying shields. Some of them were squatting with their shields laid beside them, others were standing as though they were on guard, and they were all watching the *Bonny Beaufoys* arrival with a disquieting intensity.

He leaned over the rail and gazed back at them with equal concentration, glad that he had his pistols at his waist, and that he was dressed in his best — without his jacket but in tricorn hat, linen shirt, fashionable breeches — right down to his buckled shoes. It was uncomfortably hot but as he was the slave master, he had to look the style.

Now, he thought, as he climbed down into the longboat, the test is upon me. If he could outwit those hideous creatures and come away with a bargain, he would prove his worth to the ship and its owners and make a profit besides. The prospect was daunting but, as always in dangerous circumstances, exciting, for he had no real doubt that he was courageous enough to face out the worst and, given a bit of luck, to triumph in the end. But there was no more time to think or plan. They were alongside the quay.

Onshore and without the breeze of their passage, the heat was so intense that he was sweating and breathless in his fine clothes before he'd taken ten paces on to the quay, and to make matters worse he was instantly assailed by a swarm of persistent stinging flies that buzzed about his face and crawled on his hands and his clothes, no matter how often he tried to flick them away.

The stink of the place was overpowering. It was an appalling combination of all the most noisome smells that had ever clogged his nostrils — foul clothes, stale piss, stinking shit, rancid oil, rotting carcases, dried blood and Lord knows what else besides. It rose at him from every direction: from the crowd of natives who were now standing and chattering in the most peculiar grunting, clicking language as he and his companions walked past; from the baskets that were heaped at their feet, piled with odd-looking fish and fruit; from a newly killed goat that lay on the sand, leaking black blood and muzzled with flies, to the rotting mangroves that stunk and brooded at the edge of the beach. It was like stepping into a vast privy, or some huge closed stool.

'You'd forgot, my of lubber,' Mr Reuben understood, as Jack caught his breath.

'No, sir,' Jack said with feeling. 'Tain't a stink a man could ever forget.'

'In an' out in two shakes of a lamb's tail, I think 'ee said,' Mr Reuben reminded him.

'Amen to that,' Jack agreed. He was recovering his breath a little and taking stock of his surroundings, concentrating hard, it being imperative to learn as much as he could about this place — and as quickly as possible.

He noticed that the beach was short and had more pink sand than marsh, and that it didn't appear to have any shelf to speak of — so if they had to make a quick escape, it would be relatively simple once they'd negotiated the quay — that the natives were bristling with spears but had no guns, that the quay was little more than a rough stone wall and so poorly built that many stones had already come unlodged and were strewn about the sand. In fact, given the number of bodies that were presently clambering over it, it was a wonder it didn't fall down entirely. But to the east of it, facing a wide square of well-trodden pink earth, littered with piles of ash and trails of animal droppings, there was another and far more substantial building that looked like a fortress or a blockhouse. It was two storeys high and built of stone with a flat roof and deep windows and a door made of some dark heavy wood, heavily bolted. A hundred yards or so away was another rough stone building, this time single storeyed and thatched with the same long-dead, brittle, grey grasses as the huts. There were air slits set at random between the stones but no windows that he could see, although the door was made of the same solid-looking wood as the fort and was equally heavily bolted. At first sight it appeared to be empty but then he noticed that there were swarms of flies crawling over the walls and in and out of the air slits, and he wondered whether it was a meat store of some kind. Which would account for the stink.

Mr Tomson had been the first ashore, leading his crew, who were carrying gifts of cloth, cooking pots and guns for the chief. He turned to enlighten his slave master. 'That there's the slave house,' he said, 'as I daresay you know.' He was wearing a wide straw hat over his bandanna which was already dark with sweat. 'We keep 'em there 'til we'm ready to sail. Saves a deal of trouble. You must've used somethin' sim'lar, the last time you was here.'

'I ain't been in this place before,' Jack admitted, truthfully. ''Twas huts they kept 'em in at the last place, as I remember.'

The captain looked at him shrewdly. 'And where would that be then?'

Cornered, Jack thought fast. He pulled a name out of the air and offered it coolly. 'Singalee, as I remember.'

'Never heard of it.'

''Twas a deal further along the coast,' Jack said as airily as he could. Then he changed the subject quickly. 'Here's Mr Smith come ashore. Am I to attend him?'

The hot air was flurried by activity to right and left of them, for as the second longboat came rolling ashore, the door of the fortress was heaved open, screeching and sticking in the heat, and a crowd of natives emerged. These were obviously of a higher class than the loin-clothed men on the quay. They wore long blue and white gowns and their fuzzy hair was twisted into curved horns or plaited into short pigtails. A dozen of them were carrying a canvas litter between them. It was as wide as a double bed and held a wooden throne on which sat a huge, portly man dressed in a cap made of cloth-of-gold and a gown of scarlet silk heavily embroidered in gold thread. The chief without a doubt. His bearers set him down with extreme caution and then backed away from him, lowering their heads. Once they were gone, a group of about twenty beautiful black girls took their place. They too wore blue and white skirts but they were naked from the waist up — except for long strings of beads — and their oiled breasts were so delectably full and so gleamingly pretty that there was much sighing and adjustment of breeches among the crew.

The captain drew in his breath too, but for quite another reason. ''Od's teeth!' he said. ''Tis a different feller.'

The purser narrowed his eyes. 'Are you sure, sir?'

'Certain sure. Ours was a little thin lubber. An Arab.'

'You should have took my advice it seems.'

'Aye, sir,' the captain admitted, grimacing. 'Belike.'

'Do we proceed? How say you?'

Mr Tomson hesitated but before he could muster his thoughts, another group of minions arrived with the chief s furniture — a padded footstool and a long-legged table carved in the same complicated pattern as the throne, two scarlet gourds slopping with liquid, a green glass bottle also full, and what appeared to be a ceremonial whip, for its wooden handle was topped by long white silken threads. Then four men dressed in white skirts arrived with an embroidered canopy, which they held aloft to protect the chief and his harem from the sun, and four more, in canvas breeches, took up positions on either side of the throne and blew importantly on long curved horns to gather the tribesmen into the square and bring them to attention.

After that there was a pause. The chief picked up his ceremonial whip and revealed that it was a fly-whisk by deftly flicking away the swarms that were homing in upon him. Then he drank from one of the gourds, propped his sandalled feet on the footstool and waved a chubby hand to indicate that his visitors were to approach. It seemed they were about to do business.

Now that the moment of parley had arrived Jack felt exposed and uncertain. Was it the purser's job to trade with this man? Or the captain's? Or was it the slave master's? If so, how was he to go about it? So much depended on a first encounter and he was well aware that this one, here, in this hot foreign place, could be wrecked by a single mistake. Politeness came to his aid. He doffed his hat, made a leg, and gave the chief the most courteous bow he could manage, holding the tricorn delicately by one corner and sweeping it until it skimmed the ground. Following his lead the captain and the purser did likewise. The chief and the ship's crew were equally impressed.

But before Jack could think of what to say to open the proceedings, the captain stepped forward and began a speech. For a man so knowledgeable and so careful of his ship, it was a surprising offering, muddled and rambling and punctuated by coughs and splutters. But at last he made the point that they had come to trade in slaves and that they had 'cloth, pots, firearms an' so forth' to offer in exchange. 'Some of which, as you see sir, I offers to ee now, as token of our good faith, an' so forth.'

Switching the flies away automatically, like a horse flicking its tail, the chief accepted the gifts, which he obviously expected. Then he too made a speech in his own clicking grunting language.

The heat rose from the pink earth in long shimmering waves of light. The tribesmen edged closer to the action, appearing, to Jack's attentive eyes, both suspicious and belligerent.

'He don't speak English,' the purser observed, unnecessarily. 'We should've brought a linguist.'

The chief narrowed his eyes and used his whisk more irritably, the heat intensified, two great red and green birds dropped out of the trees and shrieked into the high blue vault of the sky as if they were on fire, the stink from the dead goat rose in nauseating waves, the flies increased their attacks, buzzing like saws, the tribesmen gathered about their leader ominously.

'What's to be done?' Mr Smith asked Captain Tomson, wiping the sweat from his eyes. 'Ain't there a one of 'em to speak the language?'

'Not so far as I knows, sir,' Mr Tomson said, observing the crowd. 'We only ever dealt with Mwamba. He spoke pretty well, d'you see. There was no call to try any of the others.'

'We should have used Port James,' the purser said, irritably. This is impasse and too parlous for comfort. We don't even know that this one's prepared to trade in slaves.'

'They all trade in slaves,' the captain told him, angrily. ''Tis the slave coast an' so forth.'

'He might not want to,' the purser scowled. 'I don't see no sign of any slaves hereabouts. I'm for retreat afore they breaks out.' Jack had been considering the situation too, his right hand resting on the butt of his pistol, his wits sharpened by the possibility of danger. In his opinion it was folly to have come so far and offered so many gifts only to retreat. Yet it *was* a parlous situation. The purser was right about that. The irritability around them was growing palpably. How could they make their intentions clear without words? By a mime, as they did at the theatre? Would these weird creatures understand such things? It seemed unlikely. Had there been a couple of slaves anywhere about, he could have put a rope round their necks to demonstrate that they were the sort of cattle he wanted, but the creatures that thronged about him, staring and grinning their teeth, were armed and independent and plainly not slaves, however dirty and repellant they might be. There must be *some* way to show them, he thought, some way to make our intentions known, to describe what we want, or depict it. The word rang in his mind. Depict. To make a picture. To draw. Why hadn't he thought of it at once? There was no pen and paper in such a savage place, but he had a clear expanse of pink dust and there was wood everywhere he looked. He walked across to one of the broken branches that were lying about in the square, broke off a suitable twig and, aware that he was now the centre of all eyes, returned to the chief. Then he bowed, displayed the twig to the chief and the tribesmen to indicate its importance and began to draw in the sand. First a row of human figures, standing side by side and linked by a line running from neck to neck. 'Slaves,' he said, 'for us.' Pointing at himself and his companions. Then he drew a roll of cloth, a clay pot, and a very recognisable rifle and explained them too. 'More cloth, more cooking pot, more gun, bang, bang, bang. For you.' Pointing at the chief and his attendants.

Then he waited and his companions waited with him, looking from him to his drawings and from the drawings to the chief, ill at ease and holding their breath. Despite his apparently amiable rotundity, there was an air of menace about this new chieftain, a feeling that his lolling ease could erupt at any moment into a fury and power that they wouldn't be able to control without the rifles they'd been told to leave behind in the ship. They noticed that their slave master had come armed, but one pair of pistols would do little against all those spears. Fortunately, and to their relief, the stratagem worked. After studying the drawings for a few seconds, the chief smiled, nodded to Jack and spoke briefly to his attendants.

'Well blow me down, he understands drawings,' Mr Smith said, blowing out his cheeks as if to suit the action to the wrord. 'Who'd've thought it?' He nodded to the chief and tried a question himself. 'When? Eh? When they come? W'lien slaves come? On the shell road eh? Is that where they'll come? *When slaves come?* Comprenny?'

That only provoked another outburst of incomprehensible clicking and grunting.

'Best leave it to Mr Daventry, sir,' the captain suggested, 'since he do seem to have the knack of it.'

'Very well,' the purser agreed. 'Take another tack, Mr Daventry, before we lose our advantage. You're the slave master. Ask him when they'll be ready.'

To be deferred to in such a way was the equal of being publicly acclaimed. Swollen with success and importance, and watched by the entire company, Jack drew four moon shapes, full, half, and two quarters, stopping after each one to point to the sky and say 'moon'. Then, as the chief said nothing and seemed to be brooding, leaning on the arm of his great throne and stroking his double chin and his dewlaps, he added a line from each moon ending in seven neat strokes to represent the days.

And at that the chief slapped his thigh, roared with laughter and spoke to them all loudly and in English. 'I fool you good!' he said, between guffaws. 'Make you play tomfool. Yes, yes. I speak your English. I speak good.'

For a second Jack was speechless with fury. How dare he play such a trick, he thought, great ugly, steaming, toss-pot ignoramus that he is. How dare he treat me so! He was cut to the quick to have been tricked by such a man, and tricked so easily and publicly, what's more. But he held on to his command and answered coolly. Then you may tell me when the slaves will be here,' he said, resting his hand on the butt of his pistol and narrowing his eyes with hatred at his adversary.

'Wan four,' the chief said, wiping his own eyes from the exertions of his mirth. 'Wan four.'

''Od's my life!' Mr Smith muttered to the captain as the tribe hooted with laughter and leapt with the excitement of it all. 'What a rogue the man is! Do he mean one month, or four weeks, or four months? Ask him again, Mr Daventry.'

'Twill be a deal longer than either,' Mr Tomson warned him. 'No matter what he might say. They'm wily of lubbers these nigger fellers. I never trust a one of 'em, on principle, an' I'd advise you to do the same. You may ask him if you will sir, but you'll get no other answer I'm thinking.'

He was right. Although Jack repeated his question three times, he got no answer at all, except for renewed and mocking laughter. It was a little too obvious that as far as the chief was concerned the matter was concluded. After a while, his litter was taken up again and he departed with his entourage, still laughing, and at that the tribe drifted back to whatever they'd been doing before the ship arrived, and the sailors found they'd been left to their own devices, in a heat so oppressive it crushed their skulls. Some were detailed to find fresh water, the ship's cook produced a bag of beads, walked down to where the goat lay under its crown of flies and began to barter for its meat, but the rest made a beeline for the nearest women, all except for Jack and Mr Reuben.

'Ain't you up for a piece?' the bosun asked. 'I thought you'd be the first, fine young chap like you.'

They ain't to my taste,' Jack said with perfect truth. 'I like better company. If I could have had one of the chief's women'twould have been a different matter. Besides, I'm in ill humour after such discourtesy.'

So they took the longboat back to the *Bonny Beaufoy*, where Mr Reuben found an old sail and rigged it up on deck like a rough tent to shelter them from the sun. Still brooding under the insult he'd been offered, and aggrieved that he'd had no chance to answer it, Jack checked that his pistols were still in working order and flopped himself down in the shade, suddenly aware that he was exhausted.

The sun was so bright it hurt his eyes and the dazzle of light from the water was sharp as razors. Everything about this place was extreme: the sky too high, the heat too cruel, the jokes too spiteful, the threat of danger overwhelming. It was as if it had all been created over-large and over-extravagant: rivers as wide as lakes, a sea that heaved and bubbled with fish, forests steaming, flies as thick as black rain, birds that flew like flames, and everything in strong, clear, pulsing colours, from the pink dust in the square to the brilliant reds and golds of their extraordinary sunsets. The bosun was right. 'Twas no place to dally in. The sooner they were out of it the better.

'We made a good start, I believe, Mr Daventry,' Mr Tomson said, coming up alongside them. 'Howsomever we shall need a linguist when it comes to bargaining, I'm a-thinking. That ol' Wan Four ain't a man to be trusted.'

'Amen to that, sir,' Jack said. ''Tis a foul old fraud. That's my opinion of it. He'll cheat us if we give him half a chance.'

'The men shall have a night ashore to slake their appetites, Mr Reuben,' the captain said, 'or we shall have a mutiny else. We'll take the morning tide to the Bissagos Islands. We can find provisions there.'

Which despite a contrary wind and considerable difficulty, they eventually did.

*

After the stink and tension of their encounter with Chief Wan Four, the villages of the Bissagos Islands were reassuringly civilized: the streets well swept and lined with proper wood-built houses with shaded balconies and shuttered windows, the taverns cheerfully crowded and selling rum and brandy, the bawdy houses serving a colourful clientele.

There were even carriages about, although most of them were drawn by mules, and the street traders offered their wares from stalls instead of squatting beside a basket on the ground. The inhabitants had style and were a different breed altogether from Wan Four's dusty tribe, being half-European and half-African, with features in a range of intriguing combinations and skins in every shade of brown from cafe au lait to the palest china tea. Most of them wore proper clothes if a trifle old-fashioned and most spoke a recognizable language, if not English then Portuguese or French or somesuch. In short it was a place to find allies.

Captain Tomson found one within minutes of their arrival. Her name was Mamma Poll and she was a stout cheerful woman who lived in a large white house with an impressive array of servants and retainers. She greeted the captain like an old friend.

'What I can do for you, Missa Tomson?' she asked, sliding a calculating look from him to the purser and from the purser to Jack. 'You want woman?'

'Not this time, Mamma,' the captain said, smiling at her. 'We'm after a linguist, if you got one to hand. We came to trade with Mwamba an' so forth, an' what do we find when we gets here but he's up an' gone an' so forth, an' the new feller don't speak English so good an' so forth.'

'Plenty-plenty linguiss,' Mamma said. 'Tomorrow you come. I find.'

But time was relative on these islands. It was five days before Mamma found them their interpreter, who was a pretty young woman with long, straight brown hair and a long straight English nose. But she drove a hard bargain. It took three more days before she and the captain could agree a fee. Nobody minded the delay. The food was palatable, the drink potent and the whores were obliging, providing you paid them enough. As Mr Reuben said with monotonous frequency, 'I don't mind how long we stays hereabouts. Months'ud suit me. Anything's better than old Wan Four an' his stinking savages.'

He was quite downcast when they left.

Jack tried to encourage him. 'Our slaves could be ready for us by the time we get back.'

'They could just as easy make us wait for ever an' a day, knowin' them fellers,' he grumbled. 'I don't trust a one on 'em.'

And sure enough there was no sign of any slaves when they returned and when their linguist asked how long it would be before their arrival the answer was vague. 'Two to three weeks, two to three months.'

'We could all be dead by then,' Mr Reuben said.

Eight days on the Bissagos Islands had revived Jack's spirits. 'You speak for yourself,' he grinned. 'I mean to be alive and rarin' to go.'

''Twill be a long wait an' there's narry a thing to do in a pig heap like this.'

'I shall see the sights,' Jack decided. 'I've a mind to explore the path through that forest and see where it leads.'

The bosun's eyes dilated in alarm. 'You'll do it on your own then, me hearty, if that's the size of it,' he warned. 'There's narry a man jack'll join 'ee. 'Tis a fearsome place, full a' wild beasts an' corkindiles an' such like. You'll be torn to shreds an' ate alive.'

Jack was encouraged by such forthright disapproval. Having lost face so publicly, he needed to restore his reputation. 'I shall take my pistols,' he said, And make shift to defend myself.'

'You can't shoot a swamp with a pistol,' Mr Reuben said, lugubriously, 'and none but a fool would walk alone in a forest. 'Tis the worst of follies.' But he looked at his friend with grudging admiration. Whatever else might be said about Mr Daventry, he certainly had 'bottom'.

'Watch out for the niggers,' Mr Tomson warned. 'They'm a plaguey load of swabbers and as like to stab you as spit at you.'

So, being suitably encouraged, Jack set off on his adventure, pausing just once and briefly at the edge of the trees to stand with one foot on a fallen bough to pose and wave goodbye, for if he were to run risks it was imperative that his shipmates knew of it.

Nothing could have prepared him for the height and density of the mass he entered, nor for its heat, its stink, its noise, its humidity, its obliterating darkness. Once inside he could see that the trees grew so close to one another that their upper foliage had entwined into an immense heaving canopy. It was so thick that the sunlight couldn't penetrate at all, and even before his eyes grew accustomed to darkness he knew that, although there were no savages about, which was some comfort, it was full of creatures, for it creaked and rustled and resounded with eerily unfamiliar noises. Within seconds he was ankle deep in water, and in what was left of the light, he could see that the mud he was sloshing through was the colour of blood.

But he walked on, as the darkness deepened and the trunks grew so close to one another and were so huge and dark and horribly entwined that it was impossible to tell where one tree ended and the next began. Iridescent beetles flashed points of fire as they crawled up the trunks within inches of his eyes, great flies rose in a buzzing cloud or darted straight at his head so that he had to duck to avoid them, long-tailed monkeys screamed in the branches, voiding streams of strong-smelling piddle, brightly coloured birds, with beaks like black claws, perched or hung upside-down trailing their tails or flew out of the foliage cawing and shrieking, huge snakes coiled sinister about the branches or hung suspended among the tendrils, taut and threatening, and in the matted tangle of the canopy jewelled eyes watched his progress, bright, suspicious and unblinking. Soon sweat began to bead his forehead and to run in a palpable stream down his spine.

This, he thought, wiping his eyes with his sleeve, is far enough. I have made my stand. There ain't a thing to be proved by pressing on with none to see. But as his eyes cleared he saw that the path was coming to an end and that there was light ahead and, pressing forward, he emerged on the banks of the river beside a wide expanse of muddy marsh. To his left and a mere hundred yards away was a sizeable village, its houses built of mud brick and well thatched, with a wide street between them thronged with savages. So they're a deal richer than they want us to know, he thought. They make a good living out of slaving. But he realized that to get back to the quay he would either have to run the gauntlet of their spears and suspicion or face the jungle for the second time. He sat on the nearest tussock of grass to give the matter thought, aware that thirst had dried his mouth and was cracking his lips.

The river was as wild as the jungle and there was a strong current running. It carried a deal of debris and was a most unappetising green, so he would have to look a little further to find a patch that was clear enough to drink, especially as there was a line of extraordinary creatures lying at the edge of the water blocking his way. At first he thought they were dead trees or fallen branches, for they lay perfectly still and their skins were as rough as bark and exactly the same colour, but then he noticed that they had mouths and that most of them were gaping open, as if they were waiting for prey to fall into their jaws. He could see the ranks of their sharp, pointed teeth and even the ridged roofs of their mouths, palely pink amidst all that green. What tales he would have to tell when he rejoined the ship!

A sharp sting brought him back to his present position. There was a small long-legged fly sitting on his wrist, bent forward to bite. He flicked it away, noticing that it had drawn blood. Then he saw that there were three more of the creatures on his forearm and, angry at their presumption, he slapped at them and managed to squash one into a flat sticky mess of threadlike legs and spilled blood. Time to get back, he decided, thirsty or no. There could be clear water beyond the village. Once he'd got through.

It was a nerve-wracking walk, for the savages were all intensely interested in his sudden appearance and clustered about him, pointing and laughing, their white teeth sharp and ominous. If they set upon me, I shall be lost, he thought, and he pulled his pistol from his belt and carried it before him to indicate that he would fire if he were attacked. After a few paces he found that it seemed to please them if he inclined his head to right and left as he strolled and remembered that this was how the chief had behaved as he was carried to the beach on that great litter of his. So the procession continued and lengthened and, although they clamoured about him and followed after him, laughing and calling, none touched him and presently he reached the end of the street and passed the last house, which was two storeys tall and built of stone. Since it was thronged with savages who all carried spears, he assumed it was a guardhouse of some kind, and his heart sank at the realization that this was where he could be attacked. One pistol against so many spears was a parlous odds.

But although they laughed and pointed, they waved him through and applauded when he knelt at the water's edge to slake his thirst. It had, after all, been entirely successful.

'I came to no harm you see,' he told his crew mates later that evening, when he'd described the sights he'd seen, stressing how calm he'd been — naturally — and what light hearted risks he'd taken.

'Did you see the corkindiles?' Mr Reuben asked.

'I did sir, and broke a few jaws for 'em for laughing at me.'

The boast was much enjoyed. 'Aye! Belike,' his shipmates said. And declared that they wouldn't put it past him.

'Tis a mortal hard place,' Mr Reuben said, 'an' you'm a man of *bottom* for to tackle it, my lubber.'

'Right on both counts, Mr Reuben,' Jack agreed. *'And* I ain't been ate alive, as you see.'

'Except by them pesky mosqueeters,' the bosun said. 'You'm a-covered in bumps.'

'Fleabites!' Jack told him dismissively. 'I'll take no harm from a nip or two.'

*

His fever began a fortnight later, as he was sitting on deck smoking his pipe at the end of the day, and it began abruptly with a shaking fit so acute that he had to lie down under the strength of it.

'I've t-t-took a chill,' he said, struggling to speak through chattering teeth. 'T-t-t-twill pass.'

It got rapidly worse. Soon his head ached so much it was as if it were being pounded with a hammer and his limbs were so painful he moaned at every movement despite himself. Within hours he was vomiting and delirious.

'Jungle fever,' the surgeon said, looking at the pallor of his face and noting how pinched his nose had become, 'on account of his trip to the marshes. Downright folly, which I said at the time. He shall have quinine when he reaches the third stage.'

Jack felt too ill to care what stage he'd reached or what was done to him. He was far out at sea, tossed from a heat so extreme that he was drenched in sweat and couldn't bear the slightest cloth upon his body, to a cold so terrible that he shook and shivered until he was afraid he would break his bones. He was exhausted by vomiting, torn by torments in his back and belly, crack-lipped with a thirst that couldn't be slaked. From time to time a ragged sleep dragged him mercifully away, but then his mind was racked by nightmares. He was whipped by witches and mocked by hideous old harridans, who offered him food and snatched it away before he could take it from their hands, who slapped and punched him mercilessly. Pretty women loomed into his shivering mind, their images shifting and shimmering as though they were reflections in the sea and he feared they were ghosts, but he turned to them for help even so, his hands outstretched, pleading, 'Oh love me! Love me!' and was spurned by every single one until he yearned with his old childhood anguish that he would never be loved by anyone in all his life. And he groaned as he slept. When pain pulled him back to consciousness, he was glad to see the familiar timbers of the ship beside him, anguished though he was.

Days and nights blurred and he was awash with sweat again. Then there was a hand holding a beaker and a calm voice telling him to drink.

'Is this death?' he asked, struggling to focus his eyes.

'No, sir,' the voice said stolidly. ''Tis quinine. Drink it down.' The dispassion of the voice calmed him. 'Will it cure me?'

'That's as maybe,' the surgeon said. ''Twill depend on your fighting spirit. 'Tis a mortal bad fever.'

There are others ill, Jack understood. 'Who else?'

'Ship's boy and Mr Gurney. Died on me last night.'

The news was chilling but it roused Jack's determination. 'I'll not die on you,' he promised. If he died she would be proved right and could claim that he was worthless. Whatever else he must prove her wrong, fight back as he had fought against the harridans who beat him as a little thing, outface this malady as he'd outfaced the savages, refuse to submit as he had refused in all the years of his exile, prevail against her cruelty, conquer her hatred. 'I ain't took on this job and come all this way just to die of a fever, sir. Give me the potion.'

It was so bitter it made him gasp, but he forced it down — gulp by gulp — and presently slept again.

When he woke the dreadful heat had left his body, and Mr Reuben was sitting beside him.

'Thas more like it, my lubber,' the bosun said. 'Could you fancy some grub?'

He had no appetite at all but he knew he must eat to recover. He struggled to sit up, to smile, to look alive. 'Aye, sir,' he said, speaking with an effort. 'I do believe I could.'

Even so it was a long convalescence, for the fever and the sweat returned every third day. But at least he knew they would pass and each attack was easier to endure than the last.

'Are the slaves come yet?' he asked as he roused himself from the fourth attack.

'No, sir,' the surgeon said, 'which is something to be thankful for. Time enough for slaves when the slave master is recovered. Eat well and mend, that's my advice to 'ee.'

'I will, sir. I do.'

'Aye, sir,' the surgeon said, permitting himself the first smile Jack had ever seen on his taciturn face, 'you do indeed.'

Eighteen

Far away from the sick heat of the Slave Coast, in the night time quiet of the farmhouse at Twerton, Sula lay asleep in her room under the eaves, with William snug in the crook of her arm. Outside her shuttered window the snow was falling again, white flakes drifting like feathers, softly and silently. They eddied in the warm air above the chimneys, curtained before the doors and windows, swayed gracefully away from the gusts of a harsh northeasterly, settled delicately and weightlessly on the white plains of the deserted fields, where the trees stood black and humpbacked under their new white burden.

It was no weather to be out of doors. The roads were blocked for miles around, the landmarks submerged, the winter horizon nothing but a treacherous shadow. By day, the walls of the farmhouse were damp and dark, and the garden had become a wilderness, the familiar hollows of herb bed and vegetable patch filled and forgotten. Chickens huddled together in their fetid coops, the old sow snored in the sty, the horses snorted steam in the cold air of their stables, and inside the candlelit house, Farmer Lambton and his household were barricaded in for the siege of the winter. A log fire was kept blazing in the hearth, and the warmth was carefully contained, draughts excluded by linsey woolsey curtains at the doors and windows, and every crack and cranny padded with felt. Annie declared 'twas a time for good filling meals and fed them accordingly — pies and stews, broths and pickles, warm bread and hot toddy, potatoes baked on the hearth and puddings boiled in a cloth.

The days passed slowly and, although Suki was glad she had fewer chores, she felt stultified by this winter, penned in by snow with no hope of news from anyone, even Ariadne or Lady Bradbury. Annie and the two babies took a lot of her time, for little Constant was a sickly child and didn't thrive, despite having two good feeds a day. The sight of his poor little peaky face sent Annie into a gloom, but she was loathe to hand him over completely to Suki for fear of what her husband would say. She tried to comfort herself by believing that he was one of those babies who would grow slowly, and publicly Suki agreed with her, although she was privately of a very different opinion, especially when she compared the poor little thing to her own dear fat William, who was bouncing with health and grew as you looked at him. Still at least she had the chance to practise her new skills, and she'd applied herself diligently.

By the middle of December, she could read several passages from the Bible, especially if they were familiar, and could write a fair round hand. By the time the snow brought all correspondence to an end she could compose an entire letter unaided. Better still, her enforced idleness gave her time to plan her campaign. As soon as the roads were clear she was going to persuade Ned to take her with him on his first trip to Bristol. He'd be bound to go there, as he always did, to buy tea and sugar for Mrs Lambton, and once there she would make proper enquiries at the shipping offices. She knew there were slave traders aplenty working out of Bristol but if she found out when they'd sailed she could work out which one he was likely to be on and the shipping office would know when it was expected to return. Once she knew *that*, she would be halfway to finding him. She could be in Bristol when his boat docked, or she could leave a message for him at Mrs Roper's. Oh if only the winter was over! Never 'ee mind, she comforted herself. Work hard and stay cheerful and twill soon pass.

But however cheerfully she worked by day, her nights were long and lonely and full of disturbing dreams. Half-remembered scenes shifted before her, each with its own strong emotion. Beggars plucked at her sleeves, hooves careered towards her in narrow alleys, whores shouted abuse. Sometimes Hepzie loomed towards her, sneering; sometimes it was the master, clutching his bleeding pate and roaring and making her suddenly fearful. But then the Captain was beside her, caressing her with his deft, gentle fingers, and William wriggled new-born from her body as she knelt before the ashes of her mothers kitchen fire. And warblers sang beside the river and Farmer Lambton was gazing at her with desire and she couldn't make sense of it and was so afraid and muddled by it all that she cried out in her sleep.

She woke from the confusion in a tumult of yearning to be with her own dear Jack again. The house was so quiet that she could hear the logs shifting in the grate and their tame hedgehogs down in the kitchen crunching up the cockroaches. She was aware that her nose had grown cold in the freezing air and so she burrowed into her pile of blankets to get warm again. William lay snug in the curve of her body, her hair tangled in his fists, and his spine against her belly. His warmth was a comfort to her, rescuing her from her unwanted dreams and restoring her to thoughts of the life she meant to lead once she'd found the Captain. Somewhere, she thought, he must be sleeping too, and dreaming of her, his own dear Suki. Oh if only she knew where he was! If only they could be together!

*

In London the snow was causing fewer problems, since there were skivvies to shovel it away as soon as it fell and carts and carriages to churn it into slush should it lie. For, as Lady Fosdyke observed, what were horses and servants for if not to clear the way for their owners and betters? Lady Bradbury took care to wear pattens on the rare occasions when she had to pick her way through the mire in order to reach her carriage, but otherwise she paid little attention to it, beyond ensuring that there were fires in all the main rooms and that they were well kept up. She had other matters to occupy her mind and energies.

The London season had begun most satisfactorily. For the first time since their marriage, and as a result of the interest being taken in Ariadne's imminent betrothal, she and Sir George had been invited to several of the truly grand dinners, which was highly gratifying. In addition to which, she had given two resoundingly successful dinner parties of her own for Ariadne's first two suitors and, while maintaining perfect charm and ease as their hostess, had managed to convey to Sir George that neither were suitable. Now she was making plans to entertain the Honourable Sir Humphrey de Thespia.

She was aware that she had set herself a formidable task, for the young man had a reputation for being difficult, but having accepted that he was a challenge, she had organized a dinner and a rout and had invited all her most prestigious friends and acquaintances — like the Fosdykes and the Carstairs and the great Mr Beckford and Lady Home — and had planned the occasion as though it were a military' campaign, which in many ways it was, for she meant this gentleman to be captured by one means or another.

The Honourable Sir Humphrey de Thespia, youngest son of the late Sir Percival de Thespia, and second cousin to the Duke of Errymouth, was renowned for his wit and his exceptional fragility, although his appearance was somewhat against him, for he was tall and gangly like a bolted lettuce and as pale as a lovesick maid. Despite his height, he had the face of a nine-year-old boy, round and innocent and totally smooth, devoid of any trace of hair or guile. Actually, as those who tried to know him discovered by painful degrees, his babyish expression hid a shrewd mind and an uncompromising selfishness. As the youngest in a household where love and attention were both in very short supply, he had learnt early that fragility and innocence were good cards to play in the game of love and fortune. Now at the experienced age of five-and-twenty, he had established a constitution so delicate that it was impossible for him to sleep on any mattress except his own, and every meal was a minefield of hazards, only to be negotiated by sips and starts and invariably occasioning the querulous return of at least half the dishes presented to him. Hostesses quailed at the thought of entertaining him, and felt themselves skilled indeed if they could persuade him to try more than three dishes and pronounce them palatable.

He travelled, when such exercise could not be avoided, at the head of an impressive cavalcade, with a retinue of twelve liveried servants, bearing fourteen trunks of clothes and bed linen, a tailor, a wig-maker, a French dancing master who professed to know no English, an obsequious surgeon, a suspicious apothecary, the meekest of curates, a lawyer and his own mattress. He was a challenge and a trial even to his egotistical society and he knew it was enhanced by the knowledge.

The mere thought of entertaining such an exquisite reduced Mrs Sparepenny to a state of nervous collapse. On the day of the dinner, she descended to the kitchen on three separate occasions within a single hour, to re-arrange the table decorations and re-examine Lady Bradbury's menu, and, eventually, having transmitted her agitation to every single member of the household, she retired to her room with a headache and left instructions that she was not to be disturbed, which the cook declared to be no bad thing, because it kept her out of harm's way and left the rest of them to get on with the serious business of preparing the food.

'Some a' the guests will surely bring an appetite to table, no matter what His Highness says and does,' she said trenchantly.

But even she was impressed by the gentleman's arrival, late, of course, as befitted the most important member of the party, and borne right into the hall inside his chair, like visiting royalty. It was a splendid chair, upholstered in pale blue brocade and decorated in the very latest style with an abundance of gilt carving. Conscious of its expense, the bearers set it down most delicately and waited humbly as the Honourable Sir Humphrey rose languidly from his seat, and stepped gracefully into the hall, taking his time so that the company could gather around him and savour the full impact of his first and most important appearance.

He was dressed in a coat and waistcoat of pale-pink silk, with the most refined silver buttons and the most discreet silver braid, and there were silver buckles on his white doeskin shoes. His breeches were rose red velvet, and his stockings spotless white silk, and the stock about his throat was so perfectly tied that the fold could have been pre-ordained. He took up the fashionable pose — pelvis thrust forward, upper body reclining backwards, head elegantly tilted — and held out a white hand to his hostess.

'M'dear,' he said languidly. 'I trust I do not find you *too* fatigued.'

The servants watched from the landing, as their master bowed, and their mistress dropped a deep curtsey before this extraordinary vision, and the dinner guests cooed and preened, but their astonishment grew round-eyed when he was led into the dining room, for he contrived to maintain his pose even as he walked. It was, as they told one another in the kitchen later that afternoon, one of the marvels of the age. Although Bessie said she thought 'twas a wonder the poor man didn't fall over backwards.

Despite Mrs Sparepenny's agitation, it was a successful dinner and it began well, for Hermione, skilled in the art of placating spoilt children, had the good sense to encourage her important guest to choose his place at table, stressing that she was sensitive to the importance of positioning and understood how significant it could be to a person of a 'delicate constitution'.

Not surprisingly, he chose to sit with his back to the central window, so that his immaculate wig would be silhouetted by the snow-laden white of the afternoon sky and the candlelight on either side of him would set the diamonds sparkling on his elegant fingers. The company was suitably attentive. Ariadne looked very fine in her new white silk and Lady Carstairs was at hand to provide conversation should it be needed. Not that it was, for the Honourable Sir Humphrey simply held court, dividing his attentions among all the guests and being so deliberately and suavely charming it was hard for anyone to take their eyes from his glittering presence. As an occasion, it was almost satisfactory to him, and enabled him to eat four mouthfuls of the roast and pronounce it 'not half bad' and require the cook to be complimented, which according to his own exacting standards could certainly be adjudged a success. And, as the other guests were quick to notice, the food was exceedingly good, better than they'd ever known it. Melissa ate every last crumb of every single dish that was set before her, with a stolid and greedy determination, and Ariadne dined well too, although she was careful to watch her potential fiancee — whenever he wasn't looking in her direction — since to be forewarned is to be forearmed.

But despite her cunning, her excellent cuisine and the witty conversation at her table, Hermione couldn't relax. For if there were two things she really understood they were the pressures of rank and snobbery, and both were being seriously tested by this alliance. Besides, there was a curious edge about this young man, as if he were holding something in reserve, and she sensed that it was something troubling at the very least — and possibly terrible. But the conversation continued in its urbane way and nothing untoward was said — until the dessert was carried in and set before them. She had taken particular pains to choose a spectacular dessert and the cook had followed her instructions to the letter. Every' guest was presented with a small chocolate and cream hedgehog, spined with blanched almonds and set upon a base of green jelly.

The Honourable Sir Humphrey smiled benign approval and pronounced it exquisite. Then having tasted two spoonfuls, he touched his lips with his kerchief, lay back in his chair and asked his host if he had heard the news.

Sir George laughed. 'I've heard a deal of news, sir,' he said. 'I was in the House till two this morning.'

'Then you'll have heard the news from Lisbon,' the Honourable Sir Humphrey drawled.

The sharp edge of his nature was now knife-clear to Hermione's attentive eye. There *was* something coming — and something terrible.

Sir George was intrigued. Lisbon was a great trading city and a potential rival. 'No, sir,' he said. 'I ain't heard a thing from that neck of the woods. Lisbon, you say. You're sure 'twas Lisbon?'

'Lisbon,' Sir Humphrey confirmed. He knew perfectly well that nobody at the table could have heard his news, for he'd only heard it himself a matter of minutes before his entrance, and it had come from a cousin newly arrived in the Port of London. 'A tragedy, sir.'

By now his audience was fully attentive, every bewigged head turned in his direction, agog for details. 'Tell!' they urged. 'Do tell, Sir Humphrey. 'Tis cruel to hold us in suspense when you have whetted our appetites.'

'Lisbon,' Sir Humphrey told them solemnly, 'has been razed to the ground.'

The words set off a palpable frisson all around the table. The exquisite hedgehogs were forgotten. Even Melissa stopped eating.

''Od's teeth!' Lord Fosdyke said. 'Are we at war, damme?'

'No, sir,' Sir Humphrey said, savouring the stir he was causing. ''Twas an earthquake.'

Worse and better.

'But you said 'twas razed to the ground,' Lady Carstairs protested, her tender susceptibilities fully aroused. 'That cannot be, surely. 'Tis a great city. A very great city. The equal of Paris I do believe.'

'Indeed, ma'am,' Sir Humphrey bowed to her knowledge, 'so 'twas. A city of thirty thousand souls and all of them gone to meet their maker.'

There were gasps and protestations on every side. It was impossible to accept a tragedy of such magnitude.

'How could such a dreadful thing occur?' Lady Carstairs grieved. 'How could God allow it? Are we not taught that He is the font of all goodness and the source of creation? How could He bring Himself to encompass such an evil?'

'Monstrous!' Lady Fosdyke said, as though the Almighty had been deliberately disobeying her personal instructions. 'Monstrous. 'Tis more than the human mind can encompass. Did none survive?'

'None that I heard of,' Sir Humphrey told her, gratified that the horror of his news was increasing with every word he uttered. 'Those who did not perish when the ground opened beneath them were consumed by the fires that followed, which were, I have it upon the best information, most terrible to behold. I was given a full account of it by my cousin Percy, who is newly arrived home from the Grand Tour and saw it all from a safe distance. I daresay some of you know my cousin. He is a member of the Spencer family, don'tcher know.'

What better credentials could there be for veracity? They pressed him for details, each in their own way tom with pity, fighting with incredulity, anguished with the terror that if this could happen in Lisbon, it could happen anywhere. Every heart beat in outrage, every eye was rounded with imagined horrors, every foot pressed for reassurance against the solid floor. But how delicious it was to be terrified in perfect safety!

Only Hermione kept silent, for she was aware that the guests she'd invited to attend the rout would be arriving at seven thirty. She had chosen the hour with care, knowing how absolutely essential it is for people of quality to arrive in plenty of time to be seen and acknowledged before the opening quadrille. How else could they establish their rank? To be early led to mockery, to be late could easily court ostracism — except on the part of the honoured guest, from whom it was expected. If this conversation went on too long, 'twould be a close-run thing, for she had to allow sufficient time for the ladies to prepare themselves for the evening, and for her husband and Sir Humphrey to converse, which was essential if the honourable gentleman was to open the dance with Ariadne as his partner. This was the first rout she had organized that season and she had no intention of allowing it to be marred in *any* way, not even by an earthquake. When the wreckage of the hedgehogs had been cleared, she tried to catch Sir George's eye so that he could give the signal that the ladies were to withdraw.

It took him an unconscionable time to understand her message, but at last he lumbered to his feet to throw out his customary jocular hint. She remembered, too late, how coarse his hints always were, but he was clearing his throat and the company were already looking happily in his direction.

'Time for the fairer creatures to depart,' he intoned. 'The gentlemen have need to piss and fart!'

There was the usual delighted gasp of well-feigned shock and surprise and then their guests remembered the Honourable Sir Humphrey, just as she had done. Heads turned curiously and anxiously towards him, their laughter suspended, wondering how he would take it.

He was leaning back in his chair, displaying a slight superior smile. 'Egad, Georgie,' he drawled. 'I couldn't've put it better mesself!'

Hermione was pale with relief. But at least the signal had been given and the ladies could retire to the drawing room and their expected dish of tea, and the gentlemen could be left to get down to the real business of the afternoon.

It wasn't what she imagined or hoped it would be, for what they talked about was trade.

'Can't get this business out of my head, damme,' Lord Fosdyke said, as soon as the door had closed upon the last trailing skirt. 'A tragedy sir, of uncommon proportions.'

'As I see it, gentlemen,' Sir Humphrey told them suavely, ''tis a trading opportunity the like of which ain't been seen this side of Christendom. If the city is down, 'twill have to be rebuilt, and, which is more to our purpose, materials will have to be supplied. In reputable ships, by reputable traders.'

The young man might look like a dandy but his business sense was plainly acute. 'Very true, sir,' Lord Fosdyke applauded. 'And we have the ships, as I daresay your cousin will have told you.'

'Quite so. Built for war, I believe, but serviceable to peace.'

'Mr Pitt should be with us,' Sir George declared, thumping his port glass on the table. 'For ain't this exactly his opinion. We stand for justice, morality and destiny, be gad. 'Tis the mark of our country's greatness. I heard him speak the very words not two days since.'

'A great man,' Sir Humphrey agreed, 'and sensible of the true needs of our country.'

'Which are, sir?' Lord Fosdyke asked, intrigued by the young man's confidence.

'Which are to maintain a strong fleet to defend our trade and to harry the French wherever they dare to put in an appearance. Which should have been done years since in my opinion.'

'You should join your cousin in our consortium, be gad,' Lord Fosdyke told him.

Sir Humphrey smiled. 'I would be happy to do so, sir, should you think my membership advantageous.'

He was as good as enrolled. 'How would you set about provisioning the Portuguese?' Sir Mortimer asked.

'By buying in supplies of brick, sir, and as much oak and deal as I could procure and ensuring that I had ships of sufficient tonnage to deliver 'em.'

'The *Antelope* would do it,' Sir Mortimer said. 'Don't 'ee think so, Georgie?'

The conversation continued happily, for this, as the young man had seen, was the trading opportunity of a lifetime and by now there wasn't a man in the room who didn't intend to make the most of it.

Upstairs in the bedrooms allotted to them, the ladies were completing their toilettes ready for the rout and Hermione was giving her daughter last-minute instructions. 'Should he ask you to stand up with him for the opening quadrille,' she said, 'we shall know that your father has accepted him, which would not displease you, I think.'

Ariadne was cool but she allowed that her new suitor was 'a deal better than the other two'.

'Indeed he is,' her mother agreed. 'They were men of no consequence. No consequence at all. You were wise to refuse them.' In fact they'd been decided against so quickly that Ariadne hadn't been given the chance to express so much as an opinion. 'Sir Humphrey has style and good connections and is a member of the ton besides.'

'I am mindful of it,' Ariadne murmured, admiring her reflection in the mirror and nodding her feathered headpiece at her mother.

'I am sure you are, my dear,' Hermione said, not being sure at all, 'and you will act accordingly.'

'We must go down, must we not, Mamma? Twill soon be time for the guests to arrive.'

They gentled their finery down the wide staircase side by side, and just as they reached the first floor, the drawing room doors were flung open and the gentlemen emerged in a state of high excitement, all talking at once. Was the marriage brokered, Hermione wondered, and did they all know of it? It seemed highly likely, given the smiles around her and her putative son-in-law was certainly attentive. He swayed forward, a tiptoe, to compliment her. 'A divine gown, Lady Bradbury. Delectable upon my honour,' Letting his eyes slide towards his intended, slyly enjoying the gleam of white silk against her thighs and the breathing expanse of her powdered bosom. 'We dance in an hour, I believe.'

Lady Bradbury agreed that they would, dispatched Jessup to escort her honoured guest to the rooms prepared for him and continued on her way to check that all was ready in the ballroom. She was too well pleased to be aware that her daughter was looking at the departing back of her future and mincing bridegroom with an expression of undisguised revulsion.

Oh how fine the ballroom was this season! And how wise she'd been to have it repainted. It looked so fresh and well prepared, the chandeliers scoured clean of last year's wax and dazzling with tall candles and high polish, the walls as blue as a duck's egg, the floor buffed to such a mirrored sheen that dancing pumps would slide as smooth as skates. The two coal fires had been stacked so high in the marble fireplaces at each end of the room that she could feel the heat where she stood. For once in her life, and just at the moment when it was most needed, she had achieved perfection.

The fiddlers took up their positions in the gallery, guests began to arrive, and were greeted and given hot punch to warm them. Ariadne was graciousness itself. 'Yes,' Lady Bradbury agreed with each new arrival, 'a happy occasion. Yes indeed. Sir Humphrey will be with us shortly.' The hint was enough to set the room a-buzz and the young man's tardiness served to increase the excitement.

It was more than an hour before he finally came drawling into the room to join them but his entry was spectacular, for this was the sort of occasion when he was in his element, his powdered face haughty in the flickering light, his diamonds a-shine, his demeanour cool even in the fiercest heat and the strongest and most critical scrutiny. If he had been suave in his chosen halo of white sky at Lady Bradbury's dinner table, he was elegance itself in the candlelit urbanity of her ballroom. It was nothing less than he deserved, of course, for he had dressed to impress with an attention to colour and detail that many a portrait painter might have envied. Let others choose their clothes to please themselves, he took pains to match the decor. In fact, he'd sent his man down to the house that very morning to discover what it was. Now he was dressed in a blue silk coat, most exquisitely embroidered in white and gold, and in fine embroidered breeches to match, and was the cynosure of all eyes.

Despite the low social standing of his future bride, this was a good match and, with careful handling, it would pay his current debts and increase his fortune and prestige. The new knights of sugar might look like a coarse and ignorant crew, but they certainly knew how to make money. He smiled his most benign smile at his future father-in-law and begged for the honour of partnering his daughter in the opening quadrille.

His choice caused the necessary stir and confirmed Lady Bradbury's hints. The dowagers who had clustered beside the fires to gossip were soon quite puce with heat and excitement and the dancers, as they paraded and capered behind the Honourable Humphrey and his chosen consort, were caught in gusts of speculation and such burning air that they finished the measure sweating and out of breath. In fact, by the end of the fourth dance the heat in the room was so intense that more fire screens had to be sent for and the fires dampened down. While that was being done, the more energetic of the dancers decided to take a stroll along the corridors to cool themselves. And among them were Sir Humphrey and Ariadne, who as daughter of the house and honoured guest were free to wander where they would and soon found a quiet corner for themselves beside one of the tall windows in the withdrawing room.

'They mean us to marry, I believe,' the gentleman observed, gazing out of the window at the empty paving stones below them. 'An uncommon trial but one that comes to us all, I daresay. Would you be agreeable to it?'

Ariadne gave him one of her cool regards. 'I should not be disagreeable,' she said.

'A pretty answer i'faith.'

Strictly polite, Ariadne was glad he found it so.

'I am engaged to dine with Lady Home on Thursday,' he announced, his eyes still occupied with the pavement. 'Would you care to accompany me?'

She was obliged to him.

'I will send to tell you what colour gown you are to wear for the occasion,' he said, glancing at her briefly. 'Appearances are *so* important, don't you think?'

She bowed her head to signify agreement, the feathers in her head-dress trembling above her careful curls. What if he offers to kiss? she thought, and she looked at his receding jaw, his babyish nose, his little sharp teeth and the downturned curves of that narrow discontented mouth and wondered if she could endure it.

But she needn't have worried. He leant forward, took her hand languidly, raised it and touched his lips with it, dabbing it slightly as though it were a table napkin. 'Your sarvent, ma'am,' he said.

So the matter was settled and they returned to the ballroom an affianced pair. Hermione was so delighted by the sly smile her daughter gave her on their return that she could barely restrain her impatience. 'Well?' she asked, cornering her offspring between measures.

''Tis all as you would wish, Mamma,' Ariadne said, dipping the tremble of her white feathers towards her passing guests. 'We are to dine with Lady Home on Thursday.'

Then he must have proposed and been accepted. The thrill of it!

'I shall need new gowns,' Ariadne said sweetly.

'You shall have them.'

'And a necklace.'

Of course.

'And a maid of my own.'

'You shall have Hepzibah.'

'Come now, Mamma,' Ariadne said. She was in a position of strength and meant to make the most of it. 'Hepzibah is a spy. And uncommon clumsy. She won't do at all.' She could name her price and they both knew it.

'Whom then?'

'The wet nurse.'

'But she is in Bath, dear child, caring for your brother.'

'We shall be in Bath ourselves in the summer, will we not? Very well then, she can join us there and I will train her in the way I want her to go. The wedding is not like to be until the autumn I daresay. 'Tain't a matter to be rushed if I'm to appear at my best before your family. I presume they will attend.'

'She is being eminently sensible about it,' Hennione said when she'd reported the conversation to her husband much later that night. The rout was finally over, Hepzibah had assisted her to undress and was now arranging a fine net over her mistress's complicated 'head' to keep it as tidy as possible while she slept. 'I declare I never saw a girl so changed.'

'Glad to hear it,' Sir George said, finishing his last glass of brandy and belching comfortably. 'I shall be glad to get out of these pumps, damme. My feet are pinched to oblivion.'

'A good night's work,' his wife said happily. 'I feel we may congratulate ourselves.'

'All that is required to put the cap upon it,' Sir George told her, 'is good news from the *Bonny Beaufoy*. A profitable cargo landed in the Windwards, all safe, sound and shipshape. That would suit.'

'Twill come my love, be sure of it,' Hermione smiled. 'We tread the road to success.'

Nineteen

The slaves were coming. Even in his present fever-diminished state Jack could sense it, for there was a new bristling atmosphere about the place, a sense of something sharp and cruel and excited. The tribesmen had been milling about on the quayside and running in and out of the square since daybreak and that was remarkable in itself, for he'd never seen them do anything more energetic than amble, not even when the chief made one of his appearances. As the longboat pulled in, it was obvious that they were taut with expectation, running from place to place, jumping and stamping their feet until their legs were dust-covered to the knees.

'Ask them when 'twill be,' he instructed as their linguist climbed out of the boat.

'Before noon,' the woman said. 'They no march in hot. Noon they stop.'

It was nearly midday as they spoke, the sun blazing overhead with a brazen insistence that hurt their eyes.

'If we head off to the river track,' Jack said, remembering the path he'd seen, 'we shall catch first sight of 'em.'

So they headed. It was oppressively hot. The crocodiles were airing their throats at the water's edge. Occasionally one dropped into the river and swam off with a sinuous undulation of its tail and a gentle ripple of green water and floating debris. There was the usual creaking and clicking of frogs and insects hidden in the reeds, the usual swarms of flies and midges rising to buzz about their heads, the usual throbbing heat, but apart from the crocodiles, the river was empty and so was the beaten track beside it, which meandered through the undergrowth, sometimes hidden, sometimes bright as a trickle of mercury, shuddering and shimmering in the heat haze. Steam rose from the mangrove swamps as though the earth were exhaling and the smell of rotting vegetation pulsed towards them with every movement in the branches.

'We can't stay here long,' Jack observed, wiping the sweat out of his eyes. 'Not in this heat.' But as he spoke he could hear strange noises just upriver — a thwack of blows, and then groans and women screaming — and as he peered towards the sound a line of dark figures emerged from the high grasses.

During the long wait, he'd grown accustomed to the appearance of the local natives, to their nakedness, their oiled skin and woolly hair, to teeth white against blue-black lips and feet grey with dust, to their grunting language and their habit of squatting instead of sitting. He had even grown to admire their lissom walk and the way they leapt and danced, but these were like no other natives he'd seen. These were savages — and hideous. They weren't walking but shuffling and stumbling, their faces sullen and their eyes bloodshot. The men were tied in pairs with their hands behind their backs and they wore spiked chains about their necks like performing bears. The women weren't tied, but they were all bent under burdens, with babies and small children on their backs or hips, and sacks or heavy pots on their heads. Their captors skipped nimbly beside the column, lashing out with long whips whenever anyone stopped or stumbled. Occasionally one of the slaves tried to duck away from the blows cracking down on his back, but most of them endured without expression. Their bare feet were scratched and bleeding and many had long whip weals ridging their backs, some old and pink and knotted, like ropes raised against their skin, others new and angry, red as open mouths, and still bleeding.

'We wouldn't whip our horses the way these fellers are laying into this lot,' Jack said to Mr Reuben, remembering Beau. 'We do 'em a kindness to take them from a life like this. That's my opinion of it.'

They'm savages the same as all the others,' the bosun said, without much interest. 'Kill you soon as look at you. Jest as well we've whips an' irons of our own. And that's *my* opinion of it.'

Jack was counting the number of males and females, noting that all the men had been shaved, and fairly recently judging by the nicks on their cheeks, and that some were shaven-headed too. So Wan Four is artful, he thought. He knows we're after young men and he don't mean us to see how old this lot are. Well Wan Four, there's more than one way to skin a cat. The surgeon shall examine their teeth.

'We'd best send out for Captain,' the bosun said. 'They'll be a-selling presently.'

In fact, notice of sale was already being sounded. When they got back to the square, they found that one of the chief s retainers was strutting up and down, carrying an iron bell shaped like a sugar loaf which he was hitting with a stick. As a bell, it seemed fairly useless for it only made a small clunking sound but it had already gathered a crowd and had obviously been heard — or seen - offshore, for the longboat was on its way back to the quay with Mr Tomson, the surgeon and the purser aboard.

'What have we got?' Mr Smith asked, as Jack and his shipmates walked across to greet them.

'Two dozen, thereabouts,' Jack told him. 'Twelve male and seventeen female, which ain't the best of news for I was told to take as many males as I could and young ones at that. I shall want you to check their teeth for age, Mr Dix.'

'I shall check a deal else besides teeth,' the surgeon told him. 'Have they been watered?'

'I think not.'

'Then pray tell the linguist to order it. A dry mouth don't open.'

As he spoke, the slaves were driven into the square. They brought an outburst of cruelty with them and were plainly terrified - the men taut with fear and stinking of it, blinking and chewing their mouths; the women weeping and howling every time a whip was raised; the children shaking and clinging to their mothers' legs — for from the moment their leader was whipped forward, they were surrounded by taunting tribesmen, leaping and posturing, mocking and screaming abuse. Their captors were the kings of the hour, white teeth agleam as they whipped their prize catches into line, pushing and punching indiscriminately.

Jack took charge quickly before the gathering got more unmanageable than it already was. 'Males to the right, females to the left,' he told the linguist, shouting above the din. Then give them water.' He noticed that the chief had arrived in the square too, with his harem, and was now sitting under the canopy watching the event but saying nothing, and he was glad that he, ill-used Jack Daventry, was in command and could show these leaping savages how such matters should be conducted, which was in a civilized manner and in due order.

Mr Dix was commendably thorough. Once the sexes had been divided and as many of them as could fight their way forward were allowed to gulp water from a bucket, he walked along each column, and considered each creature in turn, examining the males first naturally, since they were the better catch. He looked in their mouths, lifting their lips with a stick so that he could see their teeth at the roots, required them to stretch out their arms and to jump up and down until he was sure their lungs were sound, to turn to display their scars, and finally to splay their legs so that he could examine their privates, while the tribesmen whooped and howled their delight to see these despised, lesser creatures being publicly humiliated.

'There's a deal of pox hereabouts,' the surgeon explained to Jack, 'and one case aboard will spread like wildfire, besides infecting the crew.'

'Are they clear of it?'

Apparently so, although there was doubt about one old woman. 'Not that we'd have took her in any case with dugs like those.'

'So what's your opinion of the rest of 'em, sir?'

Two of the men and four of the women were too old, one child had a club foot and would need to be jettisoned once they were under way, and there were too many babes in arms, but they could be dealt with in the same fashion.

'Ten males ain't many,' Jack said. 'I'll not take more than eight females or 'twill set a precedent. Which are the best think 'ee?'

This time it was the sailors who bullied their merchandise into groups and once it was done and the resulting confusion had subsided, the bartering began.

For the first time since the fever struck him down, Jack felt in total possession of his powers. He knew he could outwit this chieftain, fat bully though he was, and the thought of the battle that was about to be joined between them made him feel like a warrior and one with an advantage, what's more, for his troops were well armed with crates full of tempting cargo, with shackles and branding irons at the ready, and half a dozen rifles polished and primed besides, while the chief's army was so preoccupied with the pleasures of their cruelty that they'd thrown shields and caution to the dust. Their womenfolk retreated to stand in the shade of the huts, or squat under the branches of the thickest trees, taking their mangy livestock with them, for the sun was embattled too, casting its heat straight down upon them in beams as heavy, hot and visible as great white swords. The pink earth paled under their impact and even the fortresses were crumbling, grass roofs grey and powdering, mud walls split and cracked. The sheer power of such sunlight strengthened Jack's resolve. He meant to win this fight, damme if he didn't. He'd decided on the price he would be prepared to pay and having judged that the chief would be greedy but open to flattery knew how he would start the bidding.

'Tell him,' he instructed the linguist, 'that all business will be conducted through you.'

That didn't please Wan Four. 'I speak English good,' he said, pounding his chest.

'Through you,' Jack insisted, looking at the linguist and speaking loudly and clearly. 'Tell him that we know him by repute to be a great chief and full of wisdom. Tell him that we are therefore sure that the price we decide upon today will be fair and mutually beneficial.' The last phrase caused problems and had to be given again as 'will be agreeable to us, something we desire, something we wish for.' But it was greeted with a nod of the head and a regal use of the fly-whisk. So the bargaining began.

Tell him that we are prepared to pay him ten English pounds, or its equivalent in goods, for each male to the total of ten, as he sees, and seven pounds ten shillings for each female to the total of eight, likewise.'

The offer was instantly refused. 'No good,' the chief boomed. 'You buy all slaves. You pay fifteen pounds.'

Sweat was pouring down Jack's back but he was impressively cool. 'Out of the question. Tell him we might rise to ten pounds and five shillings but no further.'

'Fourteen pounds,' the chief offered.

The bargaining continued, shilling by shilling. An old man was offered for sale because he was a 'medicine man' and rejected because there was no work in him. There was an argument about an old woman who had 'great knowledge' and 'would be of value'. 'No,' Jack said to the linguist. 'Tell him I cannot argue.'

But as both men knew, argument was not only possible but necessary — if annoyingly gradual. The two armies watched and the slaves waited, as the deal went backwards and forwards, shifting by scowls and starts towards the price both men knew they would finally accept. They reached agreement in mid-afternoon and by then everybody in the square was limp with exhaustion. Males were to be sold for twelve pounds ten shillings each, or its equivalent value in goods, females for eight pounds. The medicine man was to be thrown in for six pounds as a makeweight.

'The matter is concluded,' Jack said grandly, 'I will give you my note of hand to signify that these goods and monies will be paid as soon as the slaves have been made over to us and marked.' But apparently the goods were to be made over and the slaves branded there and then. The unwanted ones were led off to the slavehouse and the others forced to squat in the centre of the square. The fire was lit and the irons set to heat.

'Who is to do this?' Jack asked the surgeon. Bargaining against the chieftain and beating him down by quick wit and cunning had been sheer pleasure but the thought of deliberately inflicting pain on these cowering creatures was making his own flesh cringe. He'd seen enough brandings in cattle markets to know how painful it would be and, truth to tell, he would rather have walked away from it.

The surgeon enjoyed the young man's discomfiture. He'd made a good fist of the negotiations, but he was little more than an upstart when all was said and done, and needed taking down a peg or two. 'Why, you sir,' he said. 'You're the slave master.'

So Jack had to do it and found it as disturbing as he'd imagined, for even though he made sure that each slave was bound and held steady, and insisted that the arms he was to mark were thoroughly oiled beforehand, the smell and sizzle of the flesh he burned were noxious to him and the howls of his cattle a hideous irritation. One tall feller was particularly troublesome. He stood as still as a stone as he was branded and set his jaw and didn't make a sound, but when Jack lifted the iron from his flesh and stepped away from him, he turned his head and fixed him with a glare of such intense hatred that everyone nearby was aware of it. Jack jumped in alarm before he could prevent himself and had to punch the fellow violently so as not to lose face before his shipmates.

But at last the marking was done, the howling was over, and the last of his acquisitions had been led away. 'Tonight,' he said to the cook, 'we have earned a feast.'

'Roast pork!' the cook promised. 'He'm been on the spit all afternoon.'

And very succulent it was, even though it was actually roast boar, so the skin was uncommon bristly and there was only palm wine to wash it down. What did they care! By the time they reached the brandy and rum stage, the meal had degenerated into a riot of rowdy singing and drunken self-congratulation.

They were so merry that none of them noticed the approaching storm until the first distant crack of thunder. Then they looked up to realize that the sky had filled with vast banks of dark violet cloud that stretched for more miles than they could see and was massing at such speed that the sky looked as though it was boiling. Within minutes the mass was directly overhead and bearing down upon them with such weight and force that they wilted under its pressure. They only just had time to batten down the hatches and make sure all sails were safely furled before a sharp wind sprang up and the rain began.

As Jack expected, it was the fiercest storm he'd ever had to contend with. Water fell from the sky in long sharp rods, and in such torrents it was like standing under a waterfall. Their clothes were drenched in the first two seconds, Mr Reuben's makeshift tent was flattened by the sheer weight of the water that fell on it and soon they were stumbling and losing their footing on decks that were treacherous with water and suddenly rolling under the impact of the wind. And then, to add another local insult to their difficulties, the sun dropped under the horizon in its abrupt African way and left them in total darkness.

Whatever gods there are in this benighted place, Jack thought, squinting into the teeming darkness as his shipmates struggled to light the lanterns, they mean to let us know who rules here. Well, roar on, whatever gods you be. Do your worst. I ain't afeared of foreign gods nor never like to be.

He was answered by an explosion of thunder immediately over his head and a flash of blue lightning that caught the frightened faces all around him in a moment of lurid and truthful illumination. And he knew that he was as fearful as any man aboard and vowed he would never admit to it.

The next morning another coffle arrived and this time it was an extremely large one, numbering more than ninety men and women with more than thirty children. Watching their entry into the square, Jack realized that the hunters must have gathered up an entire village. This time, such was the speed at which they'd been harassed to travel, the men were unshaven so it was easier to sort out the young and fit. But with such large numbers it was almost sundown before the deal and the branding were done.

'If we continue at this rate we should have all the men we need in a matter of days,' he said to Captain Tomson.

'Never depend on nothin' in Africa,' Mr Tomson advised. 'Tis an uncommon tricksy place. We could wait another month.'

He was proved right. The next coffle didn't appear for another twenty days, and then, instead of one column, three arrived within an hour. The square was so full of slaves and their captors they could have been in the centre of Smithfield Market instead of the heart of Africa. Naturally, Wan Four chose this moment to increase his price.

The bargaining was fast and fraught, for they all knew that if it were completed quickly they could have their full cargo that night and the *Bonny Beaufoy* would be able to catch the trade winds, even, with luck and speed, to sail on the morning tide. But Jack wouldn't be hurried. He was determined not to be beaten down and argued doggedly, as the purser fidgeted and heat increased tempers and impatience all around him.

'No,' he said, over and over again. 'Tell the chief we stand by our agreement. The price is fixed.' 'No. We do not accept old slaves. There is no work in them.' 'No, that slave is diseased. She will infect the ship. The chief protects his tribe, which as men of honour we all admire. I protect my shipmates, which as a man of honour he must respect.'

Sales were agreed in batches of twenty or thirty and the new slaves were branded by two of the seamen, much to Jack's relief, while he continued negotiations. There were frequent consultations, between the chief and his entourage, the chief and the linguist, Jack and the purser, the purser and the captain. Finally the argument stuck fast over the number of females there should be in the final batch.

'He off-loads the worst of his harem,' Jack said, having recognized some of the women being urged upon them, 'the ones he's no further use for. They'll be trouble, depend on it.'

'Take four of 'em,' the purser advised. The sun was low and the last batch still to be decided upon. 'Make a concession, for pity's sake. There's no point in sticking out. Not when we're so near our number.'

'If we do, we'll have more females than we can sell,' Jack warned. 'I was given written instructions.'

'Written instructions be blowed,' the purser said. They ain't to be followed to the letter. Take that tall one. She's likely.'

'She breeds.'

'What a' that? 'Tis only a brat. We can throw it overboard. Take her and the three next to her. Twill sway Wan Four and bring all to an end.'

It was a possibility. 'What is your opinion, Mr Dix?'

'Take 'em if you must,' the surgeon said. 'They're sound and only two of 'em have young.'

One of the group had a plump three-year-old, who was lying at her feet asleep, and the statuesque female had a boy of about ten who was clinging to her long skirt. 'He might sell,' Jack said and walked across to take a closer look at him.

The woman had a strong, impassive face, broad forehead, broad nose, widely spaced eyes, full, wide, surprisingly red lips. She stood stock still and looked straight ahead of her as though Jack didn't exist. But the child looked up at his approach and with a *frisson* of surprise and disbelief he found himself looking down, not into the cowed brown eyes he expected, but into a pair as blue and bold as an English summer sky. ''Od's bowels!' he said to the purser. 'Blue eyes, damme!' And in that instant decided to buy them.

So the final sale was concluded and the final branding brutally carried out, for the sailors were tired of it and ready for their supper, and they couldn't wait for the refinements of oiling.

'We will load these now,' Captain Tomson decided. 'Put 'em in the longboats.'

It was a hideous business. The slaves were burnt and bleeding and afraid, their captors had gathered to bay at their departure, and as they were dragged along the quay towards the waiting longboat they were seized with panic. They screamed and fought, writhing away from anyone who held them, so that it took four men to heave each one off the quay and into the boat, and then only after a prolonged struggle with much pushing and shouting and whipping and hauling on shackles.

Even in the boats when it was plain that they were off to sea and there was nothing they could do to prevent it, they howled, wept and tried to throw themselves over the sides.

'Animals!' the bosun shouted as the longboat rocked towards the *Bonny Beaufoy.* 'Whip 'em, John Murphy. Lay into 'em. Stow your row, your lousy lubbers.'

There was another struggle to haul them aboard ship and a third to force them down the holds. By the time it was done, the crew were as bruised and battered as their cargo — and there were two hundred more to bring aboard. To add to their problems, another storm was bearing down upon them, still distant, but with the same dark clouds massing and boiling, blue-black and ominous, and the same sharp wind whipping the water.

Mr Tomson pulled at the ringlets of his beard and considered. 'We'll bring as many aboard as we can before it breaks,' he decided. 'What we don't ship tonight, we'll deal with first light tomorrow. Look lively, boys!'

His crew needed no urging, for now that the moment of departure was so close there was a rage to get away. It boiled in them as fiercely as the storm clouds and the pressure of it was even more intense. The slaves were dragged from the stockhouse, battered and stumbling. Bemused to the point of imbecility by the sudden impact of light, they were then beaten into the longboats whether they struggled or not, because they were shit-caked and evil-smelling.

By the time the sun made its abrupt disappearance, two-thirds of them were aboard and the hold was full of terrified howls and weeping. The noise went on all night and was renewed in even greater volume when the first of the morning batch were hauled aboard and thrown down into the darkness.

It was past ten o'clock before the entire cargo was finally loaded and by then the crew's impatience had swollen to roaring point. When they set sail for the Bissagos Islands, at last, they gave a great hoarse cheer and stamped on the deck like thunder, grinning and showing all the teeth they had, and were rewarded by a renewal of howling and screaming below deck.

'Tell all you like, you lousy lubbers,' one sailor shouted. 'We'm off to sea and there aren't a blamed thing you can do about it.' At which the cheers grew throaty and the thunder-stamping so loud that it echoed back at them from the quay as the offshore wind rolled the ship away, slowly and heavily, cheering crew, howling burden, stink, sweat, fear and all.

And Jack watched his first slave meal being cooked and went below decks with the surgeon and four protesting seamen to serve it.

It was a mess of ground meal mixed with water and boiled until it was as thick as a pudding, seasoned with palm oil, salt and a little malagutta pepper, and served in small fat tubs with ten wooden spoons to each tub to signify that it was the ration for ten persons. All of which seemed regular and reasonable in the galley. But down in the holds there was no regularity or reason, only fear and stink and bodies packed in so close to one another that they were sitting thigh to thigh, and had to turn on their sides to find space to lie in. It was extremely hot and what little air there was had grown foul with the stink of the buckets the bosun had set about the place for the relief of nature.

'Wear shoes,' the surgeon instructed before they went below. 'If you tread among 'em with bare feet, you'll get bit and turn septic, sure as fate, which none would desire on a long voyage.' And as he pushed his feet between the bodies, Jack could see how sensible the advice had been, for rough hands pulled at him wherever he went and teeth gleamed sharp and predatory in the darkness.

He kicked the jumble of legs apart and set the first tub down in the space he'd made, counted out ten spoons and thrust them into the nearest hands. Then he reached up for the next tub which was being lowered through the half open hatch. And at that moment one of the slaves struggled to his feet, dragging his shackle-companion with him, and dashed the tub from Jack's hands so suddenly and fiercely that the meal was thrown in every direction, scalding his fellows and spattering the hold from floor to bulkhead.

Jack's tension exploded into fury. He turned and wrestled the slave to the floor, pulling him viciously by the hair, the shackles, any part of him that came to hand. How dare he behave in such a dangerous way! If there was a riot in such an enclosed space with so many leg irons to turn into weapons, somebody would be injured. In seconds he had the slave under his feet and under control, with his mate moaning and torn beside him.

'Bind him,' he ordered and watched with satisfaction as the slave was gagged with a strip of cloth and had his hands and legs tied fast with ship's rope. 'He'll not bite, nor eat, till I say so. He seems to think he may waste good food, so let him starve for lack of it.' He pushed his face right down towards the burning eyes of his prisoner and glared at him.

'Let him see how well he likes *that*. Lower the next tub, if you please, Samuel.'

The lesson seemed to have been learnt. Legs were withdrawn without need of a kicking and by the time the ninth and tenth tubs were lowered, there was a sort of surly order in the business and it was safe enough for two of the seamen to descend into the stink and speed up the process. But Jack was remembering how grateful cattle were when you fed them — and how gentle — and was privately observing what ungrateful, disagreeable animals these were.

That night in the mess as he sat at supper with the captain, the surgeon and the purser, he asked how long the slaves would be kept below decks. ''Twould be a deal easier to feed them if they came on deck,' he said. 'If the holds were cleared we could get buckets emptied and decks scrubbed and sweeten the air.'

'Can't be done till we're out o' sight of land,' Mr Tomson told him, 'or they'll be over the side afore you can say jack rabbit. They'm pesky critturs. You can't trust narry a one of 'em.'

'What's your opinion of 'em, eh Mr Daventry?' the surgeon asked.

An honest answer sprang to Jack's tongue, but then he noticed the sardonic gleam in the surgeon's eye. 'I've seen worse, Mr Dix,' he said, carelessly. 'I've got their measure. Depend on it.'

Twenty

The wind continued fair for three days, although it was parlously hot, and the slaves wept and moaned below decks, clanking their chains and howling whenever the ship went about. They reached sight of the Bissagos Islands without incident and, having dropped anchor since a landing was no longer possible with so many potential escapees aboard, they lowered the longboat to row the linguist home. Captain Tomson gave her two identical letters for Mr Bradbury and instructions that she was to entrust them to the masters of the next two ships that were headed for England. The more speedy the ship, the better, if you takes my meanin'. Then, the longboat being safely returned, they raised anchor, set sail and were off again on the long haul of the middle passage.

On their third day out, the stink from the holds was so intolerable that Jack had the gratings raised above the combings with bannisters to give his cargo more air. But that made matters worse, for the narrow airspace was instantly clogged with black hands, faces pouring sweat and mouths that gaped like fishes, and soon the anguished noise behind them rose until it was as insufferable as the smell. He had to send a couple of men to whip their obstructing faces away lest their fellows died of suffocation. But even that didn't deter them, for they returned, bloody-fingered, to gasp and cry as soon as their jailers had moved on. After an hour of such foolishness he closed the gratings again, swearing at their noise and nuisance, and left them to it.

That evening the weather closed in and minutes later a violent storm blew up, whipping the waves into ten-foot peaks and hurling the *Bonny Beaufoy* from side to side as if she had no more volition than a cork. There was a rush to batten down the hatches and secure sail, which was no easy matter with the wind whipping the canvas from their grasp and the ropes rearing and flailing like live things, suddenly too strong to hold and with a sting like a snake. Soon the sky was blue-black and the waves mountainous, rolling down upon them relentlessly one after the other, roaring above the gunwales and rushing in upon the decks from every direction, one moment sucking the ship upwards in a stomach-churning swoop that threatened to capsize them, the next throwing it down into a seething trough of swirling white water.

Jack had never experienced anything so terrifying nor so relentless. We are at the mercy of the water, he thought, as the wind screamed through the rigging and his shipmates tried to yell above the noise, the next wave thundering upon them, tipping them sideways. If we turn turtle, we shall drown, every man jack of us. This time his courage was being tested until it was almost beyond his capability, for there was nowhere to hide and no one to turn to for help and nothing to do except endure, knowing that if death came it would be dark and full of horror. He tried to pray but couldn't because the words had no meaning. He wanted to scream, but couldn't for fear of losing face.

At one point he staggered down to lie in his bunk in the fo'c'sle, but it was more terrifying there than on deck, for the sounds were magnified, his imagination had horrid rein and every movement brought bile into his throat. At least on deck he could see what was happening and prepare himself for the worst, should it come. As he struggled back up the companion way, he could hear the slaves screaming in the holds and recognized that their terror was even more extreme than his own, but there was nothing he could do, so he had to ignore them. For the moment, what with the tilt and lurch of the ship, the slippery state of the decks and the unending terror of the storm, it took all his energy and effort to stay on his feet.

The tempest lasted for nearly five hours and when it was finally blown out, it was pitch dark and they were all exhausted. But by then they were well off course and all hands were piped to set the sails and get the ship under way again. After that, Jack was on watch and beginning to be aware of his bruises. So it was daylight before he could find the time and inclination to go below and inspect his cargo and by then he was stiff, aching, limb-bruised, salt-caked and wishing he were anywhere but on board.

There was worse waiting for him below decks. The filth in the holds was so noxious it made him retch before he'd kicked three steps into the bodies tangled there. The pitching of the ship had provoked vomit and reduced too many guts to flux, and, what was worse, it had spilled the contents of the buckets in every direction, so the slaves lay in their own filth, smeared and groaning and stinking. Most of them had been so battered that they could barely sit up and none could stand. Two had broken legs, one smashed so badly that the bone was sticking out of his flesh. One of the women was bruised about the head and unconscious, and there were five corpses, their eyes still held in a dead stare and an evil-smelling froth caking their lips.

When he emerged, retching, from his nightmare cargo to the cleaner air on deck, the captain was standing beside the hatch.

Jack answered his unspoken query at once. 'We must clear the holds forthwith,' he said. 'The slaves must be cleaned and the holds scrubbed with vinegar. There are five dead down there, Mr Tomson, and many injured — and the air is too foul to breathe.'

Thanks to the storm they were out of sight of land. 'Do what is needful, Mr Daventry,' the captain said, 'but have no more than forty on deck at any one time. I will send Mr Dix and order the riflemen.'

Which he did, setting six of the crew with rifles primed and at the ready to cover the first group of twenty slaves as they stumbled from their prison, blinking and gasping in the sudden light of a sea day. At first, seeing the rifles and the grim faces all around them, they were subdued, but at the sight of the sea swelling and curling in every direction, they burst into passionate weeping, clutching their heads and rolling their eyes as if they were about to take a fit. It. was many minutes before Jack could prevail upon them to wash themselves and then only after he'd had several buckets of sea water thrown over them to cool their passion.

While they were rubbing the filth from their limbs, Mr Dix arrived and went below to inspect the injuries and bring up the dead bodies, which were taken aft and thrown unceremoniously over the side so as to be rid of them as soon as possible. This caused another outburst of weeping and so much shouting that the cat-o'-nine-tails had to be used before the noise was quelled. After that, Jack thought it politic to haul the next group of twenty on deck and get them cleaned up before there was another outburst.

When he had all forty of them more or less clean, he ordered the porridge pot to be carried up from the galley to feed them, ten to each tub with a wooden spoon apiece. And once they were eating, the injured were hauled on deck and carried aft to be examined where the ship's breeze would carry their stink away.

The female was still completely unconscious and so was the male with the bone sticking through his flesh. 'They'll be dead by evening,' Mr Dix predicted.

'What of the other?' Jack asked. If they were to lose seven slaves with every storm their numbers would be parlously down by the time they arrived in Nevis, and every loss was a lessening of profit.

'He might do,' the surgeon said, stroking his chin as he considered. 'He's strong enough and young. I'll set the leg and we'll see. Send me four strong fellers to hold him down.'

'I shall need the strongest to get the slaves to work in the holds,' Jack said, 'but I'll find you four likely ones.'

As he walked back to the slaves who were squatting round their feeding tubs, he couldn't help feeling pleased with himself, despite his losses. He'd come through the storm, begun to clean his difficult cargo, maintained good order, even if it meant resorting to the whip. The cat had subdued these fellers uncommon well. They were surly but they'd learnt their first lesson in obedience. He squared his shoulders and walked with a swagger, rolling with the motion of the ship.

'Harry, Jim, Johnny, Dickon,' he said to the four toughest men he could see. 'Report to Mr Dix, if you please.' Then having chosen six more to help him with the slaves, taking care to include two of the riflemen so as to avoid trouble, he strolled across to where they were squatting and picked out ten of the biggest and strongest.

They had to be dragged to their feet before they understood that they were not to be allowed to sit on deck all day, but they took the brooms that were thrust into their hands and followed him along the deck readily enough. That's the style, he thought proudly, as they shuffled after him. Two guns and a cat-o'-ninetails and they soon fall into line.

They fell out again as soon as they realized that they were supposed to go below. Then they clung to the gratings and fought and punched against every hand that pushed them, no matter how savagely they were beaten. It took half an hour to force them down and then they crouched in that hot cramped space and shook with anger in the filth they'd left behind and refused to understand that they were detailed to sweep it away. Even after ten replacements had been allowed up on deck there were still a hundred and sixty unwashed males crammed into the holds, squatting thigh to thigh in the filth or lying one behind the other, like spoons, in the two-foot space between the long shelves and the bulkheads. He had to whip them back to make a space for cleaning and even then, when buckets of water and vinegar had been lowered and put before them, his chosen cleaners set their jaws and looked away. They wouldn't work. In the end, he seized a broom from the nearest rigid hand, threw half a bucketful of vinegar water over the furthest section of deck and set about the task himself by way of demonstration, even though the stink he stirred by his vigorous sweeping made him heave and retch until he was sick. It was a vile, hot, gut-wrenching job, made worse by the pressure of all those close-packed bodies watching and jabbering, and the terrible screams that were echoing down to them from the slave with the broken leg. But by a combination of bullying and cajoling, he managed to convince his cleaners that they had a job to do and that he wouldn't stop berating them until they got on with it, and eventually they began to work as he wanted. The last bucketful sent down contained half a dozen red-hot bullets to heighten the effect of the vinegar, which sweetened the air considerably. But they all had a long way to go until the place was clean.

Gradually, as the morning wore on, he brought up the remainder of the men, forty at a time, hauling them bodily through the hatches if they were too weak to climb, prevailed upon them to clean themselves and fed them while the space they left behind them was cleaned by their fellows. After the last group had trembled into the light, he released the women and children, keeping them aft of the men and giving them twice as much water because they had children to clean too. Then, judging that they must be very hungry by this time, he doubled their rations, despite the cook's protests. It was partly sympathy for their long wait and partly an attempt to placate them before they too went below to scrub the decks.

To his relief, they set about the work with a much better will than the males had done, seeing at once how the brooms and the vinegar water were to be used and cleaning with greater ease because they weren't shackled.

When they all climbed back on deck again, they found that the rest of the female slaves were working the corn mill and mixing the ground com with peppers, ready to make soup for supper. It was such a blessedly normal smell that Jack relaxed as soon as he got whiff of it.

'First times are allus the worst,' Mr Reuben said, coming up alongside. 'They'll know what's what tomorrow. The leg's set, Mr Dix said to tell 'ee. We can choose our women if we've a mind. Captain's just give permission.'

Choosing a woman was the last thing on Jack's mind at that moment, but he felt he should make the effort for fear of losing face if he refused. The one he picked was a tall, full-breasted creature of about twenty or so, who wore her hair in two elaborate horns that marked her out as one of Wan Four's harem. The rest were too ugly to be considered and the sweepers smelt most vilely. He resolved to wash his choice with water and vinegar before he touched her and to sluice out her mouth. Not that he would kiss her, for he never kissed whores. Meantime he ordered a bucket of vinegar water to be brought to his cabin so that he could clean himself, for by that time his smock and breeches were so stained and stinking that he smelt like a walking cesspit. Then aired and sweetened and in his best clothes, he sat on deck in the sunshine and smoked a most necessary pipe.

The females stayed on deck for the better part of the day, so that the crew could make use of them as and when they needed and their absence from the hold would give it a chance to air. At supper time the males were allowed up again, fifty at a time to eat their soup, and when the meal was done he walked four of the sweepers down to the heads, two by two, and told them in dumb show that this was where they were to relieve themselves when they were on deck, which they were quick to understand.

Up at the prow the female slaves were gossiping together, plaiting their children's hair, and strolling easily from group to group, since they had no shackles to impede them. Greatly daring, he bent to remove the sweepers' leg irons too. Without them they could walk about and spread the information to their companions.

'You have earned it,' he said to them, and mimed a sweeping action, pleased by his magnanimity.

Once the leg irons were removed, he could see what damage they had done, for the ankles that were now revealed were tom and bruised and all four men spent some time rubbing their feet before they stood to walk. But they were plainly glad of their release and hobbled off to tell their fellows what was expected of them.

That night the buckets were less well used and in the morning his unshackled slaves were quick to carry them to the hatches and more than ready to climb out of the holds to empty them over the side. The slave with the broken leg still lay where he'd been left, tightly strapped to his wooden splint and groaning, but the other two casualties were gone.

'Had 'em over the side last night,' the surgeon said. 'And that brat of a baby that would keep a-screamin' or we'd none of us have had a wink of sleep.'

Jack was surprised to hear about the baby. 'Was it sick?'

'No sir, just fractious.'

'Then 'twas alive when you threw it over.'

Mr Dix laughed, showing his white teeth. 'Not for long. Not after it hit the water.'

Jack was doubtful about the morality of such an action but he assumed that the surgeon knew what he was doing and made no further comment. There was too much work to be done without bothering about morality. The porridge pot had arrived and the cook was slopping the contents into the slaves' wooden tubs.

'Watch out for your big feller,' the surgeon warned as he walked away.

Jack turned to question. 'Which one?'

'Spilled the porridge that first morning.'

'Is he sick?'

The surgeon looked at him, straight and serious. 'No, sir. He means to starve himself. He don't eat.'

'Oh don't he?' Jack said grimly. 'I'll soon see about that.' Losing a slave to sickness or foul air was bad enough but a self-inflicted death was folly — and arrogant to boot.

The big feller was one of the second group to be fed that morning and now that his attention had been drawn to it, Jack could see that the man was refusing all sustenance except water. He sat with his arms folded across a chest grown considerably thinner, and gazed out to sea, swaying with the rhythm of the ship but otherwise unmoving and blank-faced.

'Deuce take the dog,' Jack said angrily to his three assistants. 'I do believe Mr Dix has the right of it.'

'He's uncommon determined,' Dickon said.

'He'll not determine me,' Jack said, anger rising. 'I'll warrant you that. He'll find me more than a match for him. Keep him back when the others go below and fetch me a big spoon.'

The big feller showed no concern when he and his shackle-mate were thrust back on to the deck as the others stood to shuffle to the hatches. He simply sat where he was and waited as though the world were no longer his concern. His companion, who was smaller and had fed well, was instantly and twitchingly anxious, his neck taut as a tree trunk, his eyes dilated and flickering with alarm. There were flakes of dried wheatmeal around his mouth, which he wiped with the back of his hand, nervously. But even when Jack bore down upon them with a tub of meal in one hand and a serving spoon in the other, the big feller simply sat. And when the first full spoon was jabbed at his mouth, he tightened his lips and turned his head aside at the last second so that the contents spilled over his shoulder.

'Devil take him!' Jack swore. 'I'll not be disobeyed. Pin him down, boys. We'll see about this.'

The big slave put up a terrible struggle, thrashing his arms and twisting his body violently from side to side, but between the four of them they pinned him to the deck. His terrified companion was dragged down with him, much kicked and thumped in the process, but at last he was subdued, panting but unable to move, with his fists tied hard behind his back and the vice of Dickon's scarred hands clamped on either side of his face, holding him steady.

Jack watched him with satisfaction. 'Open his mouth.'

Dickon grimaced. 'What if he bites, sir?'

Jack seized a belaying pin and flourished it in front of the big feller's face. 'If he bites, sir,' he said, speaking directly and furiously to the slave, 'We'll knock his blamed teeth out.'

He bit as soon as Dickon's fingers touched his lips, his eyes blazing hatred and defiance, and was instantly hit in the mouth with the pin. It was such a heavy blow that it split his lip and knocked his two front teeth so loose that they hung by a bloody thread.

'Quick!' Jack said, filling the spoon and thrusting it at the bloody gap. There were several seconds of confused struggle.

Blood and spittle and gobbets of meal flew before their eyes, leg irons clanked and dragged. They were all shouting, arms flailing, fists punching, and someone was screaming. But when they finally stood up, the slave's mouth was full of meal. It was a triumph.

'Swallow, damn you!' Jack roared at him. 'Swallow!' His eyes stung with fury and he was holding his spine with such tension it was beginning to ache.

It was a wasted order. The big feller turned his head to one side, spat out the meal and vomited green bile all over their shoes and the crouching spine of his companion.

Jack swore so much he made his throat sore. 'Hell's teeth! I'll not be beat by a savage. I'll make him eat, damme if I don't. Give me that spoon again! Quick! And get that blamed fool out the way.'

Dickon tried to drag the other slave to his feet and couldn't do it. 'We'll have to take his irons off.'

'Well take 'em off, dammit. I'll not be beat by a savage.'

The irons were removed and the slave dragged away by the feet, with his hands covering his eyes.

'Now!' Jack roared.

But the instant his companion was freed, the big feller had struggled to his feet and, as they turned towards him, he was running towards the side, tumbling over the gunwale, falling into the sea, straight as a plumbline. It was all over in seconds, before they could draw breath. Then all three seamen yelled, 'Man overboard!' and Mr Tomson came running to see what was amiss.

Jack was the first to recover. 'We must lower a boat.'

'Can't be done,' the captain told him, stroking his beard 'Twould mean going about and so forth.' Which was plainly true, for there was already a considerable distance between the ship and the slave, who was swimming strongly.

'We can't leave him to drown,' Jack protested. 'He's a good specimen. Worth a deal of money. Could we throw a line?'

'Not without a harpoon,' the captain said. 'Not that distance. We ain't whalers.'

'We can't just leave him,' Jack repeated. 'Something must be done.'

It was being done as he spoke. Two dark fins had appeared in the green water and were circling the swimmer. As the crew watched in fascinated horror, there was a sudden spume of white water, a chop of waves, a thrashing and bubbling as if the sea was boiling. Then a long red trail of blood threaded out from the centre and the slave's head disappeared.

'Sharks,' the captain said and went back to the bridge as if that were the end of the matter.

'They're a-tearin' him to bits,' Dickon said, unnecessarily, for they could all see the bits being tossed into the air like dark joints of meat.

'What a way to go!' Mr Reuben said, strolling up to join them. 'I wouldn't wish that on my worst enemy. Not even the Frenchies an' that's a fact.'

Jack's emotions were boiling in the same muddled and evil way as that ghastly bloodied water. He recognized that Dickon was shocked and that Mr Reuben was gloating: he knew that he'd lost face at the loss of such a prize, that he'd been defeated by this savage, and made to look a fool in front of his shipmates. He was angry and ashamed and confused, because, despite his anger, he felt a monstrous, nauseous pity for the slave — and in the midst of this turmoil of emotions he was feeling the itch so hard and strong it was too painful to be borne.

But at least now that he had chosen a female the itch could be dealt with. He turned away from the carnage in the water, strode along the deck to where his female was grinding meal and seizing her by the hand dragged her to the companion way, half walking, half running, as his shipmates cheered and cat-called after them. 'Go to it, Jack! You show her!'

He took her angrily, standing and without benefit of vinegar water, and a poor unsatisfactory congress it was, for she said nothing and did nothing but simply stood to endure what was being done to her with no expression on her face at all. The use of her body relieved the itch, that was all. But after he'd dismissed her, he was left with an intolerable sense of loss and disappointment and homesickness, remembering all the loving arms that had clung about his neck at such times, the gleaming eyes and welcoming smiles, the soft caresses and murmured endearments that had been his by right before he took ship on this accursed voyage. He was so full of misery he had to sit on his bunk to recover and it was minutes before he could think himself jaunty again and rejoin his shipmates.

That night, over their supper, the talk turned naturally to their chosen females and how unresponsive they were being.

'Tis a different breed,' Mr Reuben observed dourly. That's my opinion of it. They don't have feelings the same as our wenches back home. Can't expect it.'

'We should've brought a few whores along,' the surgeon said. 'They'd have taught 'em the ropes. They'm too sullen by half.'

'They serves,' Mr Smith told him, pulling a hunk of bread apart with his rough fingers, 'and that's all you can say of 'em. They serves an' they'm sullen an' they smells like fish.'

'Which, I might remind you,' Captain Tomson said, 'is all you'm a-likely to get till we hits land again.'

'Fish, sir?' Mr Smith asked, grinning. 'Or women what smells like fish?'

'Both, sir,' the captain told him. 'Till we hits land.'

'When is that like to be?' Jack asked, trying not to sound too eager. 'What's the quickest time a slaver's ever took? Is it known?'

'Thirty-five days from Angola to Pernambuco,' Mr Tomson said. 'Accordin' to the Portuguese. Though how 'twas done I cannot imagine. The trades must've blowed 'em mortal strong. More luck than judgement, I daresay. We reckons two months at the least to reach the Caribbean, sometimes three.'

That's ninety days, Jack thought, his heart sinking, and we've only been out nineteen. 'Tis a mortal long time,' he said.

'Could be a deal worse,' Mr Tomson said, filling his pipe. 'There's a-many don't make land at all. Ain't that right, my lubbers? Don't make land at all. As to the longest voyage — the longest I ever heard of took nine months. Twas a frigate called *Sainte-Anne*, as I recall, out of Nantes, belonged to a Frenchie, which won't surprise you none, Mr Reuben. She took nine months to sail from Wliydah to Saint Domingue, *and* lost fifty-five slaves en route.'

There was much happy talk about the poor seamanship of the French but Jack's mind wandered away from it. Three months was a parlously long time and he couldn't help wondering how many of them would survive it.

'Twill be spring in England soon,' Mr Dix observed into a pause. 'I shall be sorry to miss it.'

The word brought so many memories and so much emotion into Jack's mind that he was torn with homesickness and couldn't speak. Oh, for the smell of new leaves, and fresh grass, of warm leather and the sweat of horses, to gallop along the woodland rides on Beau's strong back, with birds singing in the hedges and butterflies among the nettles, to choose a loving woman in a new spring gown who would wind her arms round his neck and breath love at him, like that pretty girl in Clerkenwell or the dark-haired one in that inn in Kennington, or the bright-eyed one in the Spring Gardens in Bath. Oh for spring in the Spring Gardens.

But there was little to be served by wallowing in nostalgia, nor in self-pity neither, as he well knew. For better or worse he had set his feet in a new direction and now he must follow, willy-nilly, wheresomever chance might lead. There was an ocean to be crossed or to drown in, a fortune to be made or lost — and many a hazard to be faced before he was like to set foot in England again.

*

Back in Twerton Suki was feeding her baby and thinking similar thoughts. She'd come a long way since that terrifying moment when she'd swapped the babies and although a deal had happened since — a live baby for Annie, a doting love for Miss Ariadne, a safe haven at Lambton farm for herself and William — the future bobbed before her, uncertain as a cork upon the water.

Howsomever, she had proved herself the equal to a deal of trial and tribulation, which was a comfort to her, and whatever the fates might have in store for her, she was determined to triumph. 'You'll see if I don't, my handsome,' she said to her baby.

Twenty-one

The sloth of the season was a daily irritation to Suki Brown now that she'd set her heart on that vital trip to Bristol. It was nearly nineteen months since she'd last seen the Captain, and in private moments, alone at night with the household sleeping around her, she was beginning to wonder whether she would ever see him again. His ship could have been lost at sea or taken by the French. Anything could have happened. It troubled her that her memories of him had begun to blur and were now a disquieting blend of uncomfortably sharp focus and wavering unreality. She could remember the persuasive passion of his eyes — those beautiful, dark-lashed, brown eyes that could provoke love by a glance — but there were times when she couldn't picture the rest of his face at all or recall what they'd said to one another. Only their last despairing conversation remained clear in her mind and that was because it had been so fraught with loss and finality.

'I must leave you, sweetheart,' he'd said, gazing down at her from the height of that great horse of his.

'Not now!' she'd cried, breathless with the shock of hearing such an awful tiling so suddenly.

'Aye. Now. I ride to London this evening.'

'When to return?'

'Well as to that,' he'd said carelessly. 'I couldn't say. 'Tis uncommon hard to estimate such matters. There are tilings to be done. Money to be earned. You'll not say no to a trinket or two, I'll warrant, when I return.'

Trinkets meant nothing to her. 'I'll wait for 'ee,' she'd promised earnestly.

'Aye. Be sure to.'

'How shall you find me, when you return?' she'd asked. The season was nearly over and her employers would be leaving Bath at any time.

'Don't worry your pretty head on that account,' he'd said when she told him. 'If you lose one mistress another beckons. 'Tis the way of the world. Go to Lady Bradbury on South Parade, should you need employ. She will hire you.'

'But...'

He'd leant from his horse to kiss her. 'Sweetheart,' he'd said. And he'd smiled into her eyes, straightened his spine and ridden away. Out of her life for nineteen months.

At her lowest ebb, when the house creaked and the air she breathed was ice cold on the back of her throat, she would get up and tiptoe across the room to the chest of drawers where she kept his precious silk kerchief. She would take it back to her pillow to comfort herself with its softness under her cheek. Oh my dearest, she thought, my dearest darling Captain. When shall I see you again? It seemed to her in those dark night moments as if the spring would never come, as if she would never get to Bristol, never make enquiries, never find out what she wanted to know.

We must go a-marketing soon, she fretted. But however pointedly she watched the weather, the days passed and nothing was said. She tried throwing out hints, remarking on how low their stocks were getting, which was demonstrably true, for the family sugar loaf had dwindled to a sad little mound in its dish, like the blob of a burnt-out candle, and she was sure that their stock of tea was low too, for when Mrs Lambton unlocked the caddy, she had to dig deep for her careful spoonful. But Annie was unmoved, pointing out that there was still half a side of bacon hanging from the rafters, apples in the barrel and a good supply of flour, swedes, leeks and potatoes in the larder, 'Which will serve a deal longer, I think.'

She was more concerned about little Constant who was over four months old now but still spent most of his day lying listlessly in his cradle, pale and unsmiling, and showed no signs of wanting to sit up and see the world. She knew he wasn't growing as he should and that there was no strength in his little back at all. He sagged and wept when she sat him on her knee and wouldn't be comforted until he was allowed to lie down again, which was plainly wrong, even in a baby who was slow to develop.

William had been sitting up and taking notice when he and Suki arrived, as Annie remembered very well, and now he was standing and taking his first tottering steps from chair to chair or crawling about the kitchen at great speed and with the strongest determination. There were times when his healthy presence in the house felt like a rebuke to her. Oh no, she certainly couldn't leave her Precious yet awhile.

In the middle of March a post man arrived with two letters for Suki, for which he asked double the going rate, 'being the roads is a treachery hereabouts.'

The first was from Lady Bradbury, informing her that 'her dear Ariadne' was engaged to be married 'to the grandson of the Duke of Errymouth' and would consequently require her services as lady's maid on their return to Bath, and asking, almost as an afterthought, for news of 'her dear William' for whom she enclosed a bank note for five pounds, which she said was to be used to buy him new clothes, 'as I am sure he will have grown since my last billet.'

The second and longer letter was from Ariadne. It contained a scathing description of her fiance, a rambling paragraph deploring the way her mother and father were fawning upon him, 'which 'twould sicken you to see', and ended with a lengthy postscript.

I mean to follow my heart and marry the man of my choice since that is plainly the right true thing to do. No man has the right to determine my life for me. My body is my own. 'Tis not my father's nor my husband's nor any other's. I shall bestow it upon a lover who has earned it and deserves it. We shall talk further of these things since we have said nothing of consequence since we last spoke and there is much of consequence.

'She means to marry her lover then,' Annie observed, when Suki had read the letter to her. 'Twill not be easy, I fear, nor likely.'

'She has great spirit,' Suld said. 'If any are to do it, she'll be the one. I'd lay money on it.'

Annie couldn't concentrate on such an improbability. She was grappling with the fact that Suki would be leaving her in the summer and wondering whether this would be a good thing or a bad. On the one hand she would be glad to have William's rude health out of the house, on the other she knew Constant would miss Suki's 'good feed' at night time, so she hoped it wouldn't be too soon. 'When do they want 'ee to go to Bath?'

'In the summer,' Suki said. 'Twill be June, I daresay. That's when the knights of sugar come to town. Meantime, I got to buy material to make new clothes for William. 'Twill mean a trip to Bristol, don't 'ee think?' And she looked at her mistress with a hopeful question on her face.

Annie agreed that it would, but it was the first week of April before she finally decided that the cart should be prepared for them.

'This aren't a journey to be took in haste,' she explained, 'not with two babbas dependent upon us.'

Her preparations were slow and meticulous. Suki's sister Molly was summoned to look after the babies, a bowl of gruel was prepared for them and left to be warmed on the fire, a shopping list was written, bonnets and mantles brushed clean and ready, the mare groomed, the cart swept clean. It was past nine o'clock before Constant had been fed and settled and nearly half past before he and William were considered to be in a fit state to be left, even with a confident ten-year-old who said she was sure they'd be no trouble at all.

'I don't like to go without un just the same,' Annie said, looking back anxiously as the cart joggled her away from the farmhouse. 'What if he should try to sit up and tumble?'

'Don't you go a-worriting, ma'am,' Suki comforted. 'He'll be right as rain, you'll see. Our Molly's got the knack, same as me. An' we'll be back in no time. 'Twon't take more'n a minute to get our purchases. 'Tis a fine fair place, as I remember, and shops a-plenty.' And a shipping office somewhere on the quay to tell me what I want to know.

The sun was quite warm by the time they arrived and the High Street was pungent with the smell of newly ground coffee, fresh-brewed tea and newly killed meat. One butcher's shop was doing a fly-burdened trade in 'offal and suchlike delicacies', another was hung about with sausages that dangled from their hooks like long fat beads in every colour from gum pink to blood black, the baker's shops were floury with the last bread of the morning, and down by the Exchange, sugar loaves stood to attention in the grocer's shop window like a row of glistening white skittles.

By this time Suki was in such a fever of impatience to find the shipping office that she couldn't stand still. 'How if we were to go our separate ways, ma'am?' she asked, hopping from foot to foot. 'You won't need my help with the sugar on account of Mr Jones'll carry it to the cart. I could be choosing the cloth while you'm a-marketing here. 'Twould save us a deal of time, don't 'ee think.'

Annie agreed readily. Anything to enable them to get home quickly. 'Yes,' she said, her eyes on the sugar. 'That might be wise.'

Suki was gone before she could look up at her, tripping towards Broad Quay, her skirts swinging with the urgency of her walk. Now, now, now! At last!

The quay resounded with its usual important bustle. The first of the sugar ships had come in the previous day and was being unloaded under the shrewd eyes and knowledgeable comments of half the sugar merchants in town, there were cargoes of wood and sea coal and spices scenting the air, carts and drays blocking the cobbles, men bellowing, timbers knocking, dogs barking with excitement or squealing as they were kicked, and down by the coal barge two avid boys were tying a lighted candle to the tail of a scrawny black cat that was writhing to escape them and screaming in terror.

For a second, Suki was so bewildered by the rush and noise, that she had to stand still to get her bearings. She could see lines of warehouses on both sides of the quay, but nothing that looked like a shipping office. If only they'd leave that poor cat alone, she thought, I could think what to do. The noise it was making was so pitiful it was putting her in a muddle. And then, as if that weren't enough, a horse starting screaming too. She looked towards the sound to see what was happening.

It was a large bay stallion, rearing up, front legs flailing, mouth foaming, showing the whites of his eyes, as three rough men pulled at him, swearing and sweating. One was a huge fellow in his shirt sleeves, who was in a furious temper, whipping the animal with all his force and struggling to catch his flying bridle. There was something familiar about the stallion's head and neck, something she knew, and as pity rose in her, she realized what it was. This horse was Beau, Jack's precious stallion that he loved so much.

Without stopping to think, she stormed to the animal's defence, eyes blazing. 'Stop that at once,' she ordered and pushed the man aside.

He was so amazed to be attacked by a slip of a girl that for a second he didn't know how to respond, and that gave her a chance to catch the bridle and begin to gentle the horse down, speaking to him as Jack would have done, using the same words and the same tone. 'Easy now. Easy. That's my boy. Gently does it. You'm all right now. I got you.'

The fellow was impressed despite himself and that gave him the strength to attack. 'Clear off out of it,' he ordered, making a grab for the bridle. What business is it of yourn?'

She stood her ground, furiously, as Beau trembled beside her. ''Tis my husband's horse an' you've no right to whip him. Look what you've done to un. I'll have the law on you.' Now that the horse was still she could see what a bad state he was in, his mouth torn and bleeding, whip marks on his rump, hooves caked in mud, mane and tail matted, eyes staring in terror. 'You got no right to treat him so.'

The man sneered. 'Well that's where you'm wrong, my lover. 'Tis *my* horse. I paid for un fair an' square, an' I can do as I please with un.'

The news took her back a bit, but she had an answer for him. Then you'll have a bill of sale.'

He hadn't expected knowledge of the horse trade from such a young woman. 'Not about my person, no,' he blustered. 'But he'm mine, fair an' square. Depend on it.' The argument had gathered a crowd and some of them were egging him on. 'Tha's right, Johnny-Jo, you tell 'er.'

'I don't depend on nothing,' Suki told him trenchantly. 'Not when 'tis a matter of money. If he'm youm an' you've a-paid for him, you'll come with me to a notary and show the bill of sale. 'Twill have my husband's signature upon it, which I shall know, depend on it, and *then* 'twill be fair an' square.'

'Now look 'ee here,' the man said, beginning to sense that he was getting out of his depth. 'I bought un from a good stables. Reputable. Mr Wenham's Livery stables on Broad Quay. He'll tell 'ee.'

'Very well,' Suki said. 'We'll go there an' see.' And she began to lead the horse away as if she knew where she was going.

'Now look 'ee here,' the man said again, but he had to follow her whether he would or no and the crowd followed him, eager to see the end of the drama.

The stable was easy to find. She could have sniffed it out, even without Mr Wenham's brightly painted sign to point the way, and when the gentleman himself was called for and appeared, currycomb in hand, swarthy and tousle-headed, in his fustian breeches and his leather apron, she knew at once and by instinct that however hard this fight might prove to be, she was going to win it.

'Yes,' he agreed, ''tis the Captain's horse. No mistaking.'

'Which you sold to me,' Johnny-Jo said, pushing himself forward. 'Fair an' square. Six pounds ten shillin'.'

The crowd burst into a chorus of comment. 'Now we'm a — cornin' to it.'

'Tha's got her, Johnny-Jo. You tell 'er.'

Encouraged, Johnny-Jo repeated his claim. 'Which you sold to me.'

'Which I never did nothin' of the sort,' Mr Wenham said. 'I hired un out to 'ee. No more.'

Johnny-Jo was blustering too much to make sense. 'You told me... What I means for to say... 'Tain't handsome, Mr Wenham.'

Sula swept his incoherence aside and made a direct appeal to their audience. 'The one thing I do know about my husband,' she told them, 'is he never would've sold this horse. Never. 'Tweren't in his nature. He loved un too much. 'Tis a rare fine horse. Anyone can see that with half an eye. And another thing. You'd never buy an animal of this quality for six pounds. Look at him. I ask you. Six pounds? Sixty maybe. That'ud be more the mark. But six? Never in a month a' Sundays. He's making it up an' that's the truth of it.'

'I knows what I knows,' Johnny-Jo said stubbornly. 'This horse was sold to me, fair an' square. I defy Mr Wenham to say any different. Six pounds fifteen shillings. In the Seven Stars.'

'You hired un,' Mr Wenham said. 'That was all. Onny you don't recollect the manner of it on account of you was drunk.'

The blustering rose to spitting point. 'I remembers every blamed word, Mr Wenham. We shook hands on't.'

'You was drunk.'

'I was not.'

They were glowering at one another now, red in the face and panting. Suki sprang her clinching argument into the pause. 'Then where's your bill of sale?'

The chorus swayed, in both senses of the word. 'She got the right of it there.'

'Ought to be a bill of sale.'

'After all, she knows her own husband. Stands to reason.'

It was all over bar the shouting, which went on for ten more minutes and got louder and more and more ridiculous. When Johnny-Jo finally left the stables he was shouting that he'd 'have the law on Mr Wenham and that witch there. Which I means to say that witch should be set in the stocks. Flayed alive and ate she should be. I wouldn't touch her with a red hot poker. Nor the horse neither. 'Tis a vicious aminal. If you want my opinion of it, 'tis blamed injustice, that's what. I'll have the law on the whole blamed lot of you.'

The crowd booed him off the premises and were quite disappointed when he'd gone. Soon they began to drift away, there being nothing left to see and hear except horses.

'So, Mr Wenham,' Suki said, brisk and to the point. 'This horse was stabled here by Captain Jack, and you been a-hirin' him out. Is that the right of it?'

'Twas all agreed upon,' Mr Wenham told her, speaking respectfully, having learnt that she was a woman who got her own way. 'We come to an arrangement, on account of the price of hay, which he eats monstrous. He's a reg'lar trencher, you might say. Which I'aven't had no more money for his keep since your Jack set sail, which is a good long time since, as you know.'

It was time to make a decision and an offer. 'I got a bank note for five pounds in my pocket,' she said, pulling it out and displaying it, 'what say this horse is mine and his fodder well paid for? How say you to that?'

Twenty crowns was a fair and immediate profit even for a horse that had been steadily earning his keep. Not to be sniffed at certainly. 'Aye,' the stableman said. 'I'd be agreeable.'

'Then we must have a bill of sale,' Suki told him and sensing that the lack of one in Johnny-Jo's case was due to Mr Wenham's illiteracy, she offered, 'I'll write 'un for you if you wish, if you'll fetch pen and paper.'

It was fetched and a careful document written, agreeing...

The bay stallion known as Beau is henceforth the property of Suki Brown of Lambton farm in Twerton, having been stabled with Mr Wenham of Wenham's Stables Broad Quay for...

'How many months, did you say?'

'Now as to that,' Mr Wenham said, thinking so hard he had to hold his face with both hands to keep it from nodding, ''twould be around six, as I recall. He left in harvest time. October, 'twas. They were in a parlous hurry to get the ship away on account of the trade winds.'

'Which ship was that?' Suki asked, seizing her chance for more information. 'Do you recall the name?'

He was delighted to think that his knowledge was greater than hers. 'Don't 'ee know?' He tried mocking her a little. 'I'd ha' thought you'd ha' knowed your own husband's ship.'

It was a tricky moment, but she spoke through it easily. 'He sails on so many ships,' she said. 'I forgets the names of 'em. He do tell me, but I forgets.'

'I got a better memory than you then, me dear, for I remembers it clear. Every blamed detail. The *Bonny Beaufoy*. That was the ship. Belongs to Mr Smith the banker. I remembers his name too. Mr Jedediah Smith. Sailed *with* her, as I recall, which I don't see the sense of, bein' 'tis a mortal hard crossing.'

The details were being written.

...having sailed on the *Bonny Beaufoy* out of Bristol being the ship of one Mr Smith, banker. All costs of fodder ate by the stallion Beau, are now clear and paid for.

'There you are Mr Wenham, if you'll put your mark just here below where I've signed, 'twill be all correct.'

'Which I s'pose you'll want to ride un home,' Mr Wenham said, when he'd appended his cross.

She hadn't thought of riding this great beast — ambling along on Farmer Lambton's old mare had been difficult enough — but now it was being suggested she had to agree to it, even though it meant hoisting up her skirts in the most immodest way in order to sit astride Jack's high saddle. What did it matter? She had bought the horse and she would find his owner. It was just a matter of seeking out the shipping office and asking the right questions.

Pretending to horsemanship, she clicked Beau into walking, touching his flanks gently with her heels, remembering how easily Jack had ridden him, all those months ago. To her delight, he went where she led and stopped quietly when she reined him in outside the shipping office, which had been easy to find from such a splendidly high vantage point. She was charmed to notice that he came to a halt right beside the mounting block where he stood obediently, almost as though he knew she would need the use of it.

The office was so crowded she required a fierce face and considerable pushing to fight her way to the counter. But once there, her request was taken seriously.

'Yes,' the shipping clerk confirmed, consulting his ledger. 'We do have news of the vessel. The *Bonny Beaufoy*. Yes. Here 'tis. Sailed in October and left the slave coast in February. The owner had letters from the Bissagos Islands to that effect. She'm expected back in Bristol some time between May and July, depending.'

She thanked him rapturously — May! May! Next month! A matter of weeks — and rode back to the high street, singing with pure joy.

Annie was sitting in the cart waiting anxiously and crossly. 'Where you been, you bad gal?' she said. 'What you doin' on that great horse?'

Suki was still bubbling with happiness. 'I bought un.'

'What nonsense!' Annie said, and her voice was sour. 'I thought you were supposed to be buyin' cloth for your babba. You can't just go about buying horses. 'Taren't fitting.'

'Well, I've bought un,' Suki said, stroking the horse's neck. 'He's mine. Am't you, Beau?'

'Where d'you get the money from?'

'I used the bank note.'

Annie's eyes widened in astonishment and disbelief. 'All that money on a horse. You must have took leave of vour senses. You'll not have a penny piece to spend all spring and summer. And William growing so. I wonder at 'ee Suki Brown. I truly do. And what will 'ee do with it, now you've got it? Tell me that. 'Twill need stabling an' fodder an' grooming. Have 'ee thought of that?'

Suki hadn't thought of anything except rescue. 'I shall speak to Mr Lambton,' she decided. He had stable room a-plenty and would understand what a fine horse Beau was and what a bargain she'd got. Wouldn't he?

Annie was coughing with distress and annoyance. 'You've made us late,' she complained, 'an those two poor babbas awaitin', an' all you've done is buy a horse! Walk on Mr Jones, if you please. I don't know what Mr Lambton wall say.'

Mr Lambton laughed out loud, his brown face wrinkled with delight at her daring. 'What a spirit you have,' he said. 'We never know what to expect of 'ee.' He agreed that Beau was a fine strong horse and saw how badly he'd been treated. 'He'll be out of place on a farm,' he pointed out, for he'll not pull plough or cart. But I could ride him to market, I daresay. And so could you.'

So Beau was given stable room 'until you gets sent for or the Captain comes for him'. And Suki's immediate problems seemed to be resolved.

Annie wasn't pleased. She was weary after her day on the road and her conscience was troubling her for leaving her Precious all on his own for so long — even if he *did* have Molly with him. 'Have you thought of the expense, Mr Lambton?' she asked and the question was a complaint. ''Twill cost us dear, a great horse like that.'

'He shall cover our young mare, while he's here,' the farmer said. 'We could get a fine strong foal out of him. Think of that, my dear.'

Annie wasn't mollified. 'I think 'twill be a good thing when she'm sent for and goes off to join those fine Bradburys of hers,' she said. 'Horse indeed. She'm a sight too bold for the likes of us.'

'You were glad of her company when Constant was born,' the farmer pointed out, 'and pleaded for her to stay when I would have had her move on.'

But she was coughing too much to answer him, so he let the matter drop out of pity for her. A strong foal would more than make up for a few weeks' fodder and Suki herself would soon be off with the Bradburys, and might well take the animal with her, which would solve all their problems.

Suki's fine Sir George Bradbury was actually in Bristol that very afternoon. He'd travelled down with Sir Arnold Willoughby and the Honourable Sir Humphrey de Thespia in order to inspect their biggest and most impressive privateer, the three-masted frigate called *Yorick*, and to give instructions to her master for her first sailing, which was to be to Nevis to escort the Bradburys' sugar crop home and protect it from the French.

The ship had been transformed since Sir George first saw her languishing at the head of Broad Quay. Now, agleam with new black paint, her decks scrubbed white, her rigging fresh, her sails neatly furled and with the formidable addition of sixteen brass cannon, she looked every inch the man-o'-war and a most impressive vessel. It gratified them all that she was the centre of admiration and gossip the length of the quay.

'She's proved a handsome purchase, Georgie,' Sir Arnold said. 'Damme if she ain't. She'll do well for us.' Her second sailing was to be to Portugal to protect the cargo of oak beams and quality cloth that he and Sir Humphrey were currently amassing in the port of London, so his interest was keen.

Fitting her out had cost a great deal more than Sir George's original estimate, which considering the depleted state of his finances should have given him cause for concern, especially as he had a wedding to pay for in the autumn. But in fact, he was glowingly content, beaming at their fine ship and rubbing his hands with satisfaction. Taking financial risks excited him. It made him aware of his acumen and courage. And besides, he was basking in the reflected glory of his prospective son-in-law's dazzling company, having learned during the last six months that the young man was renowned and feared and admired wherever he went.

He seemed to have an influential relation in every town and city they visited. Today he had arrived with his impressive retinue to take up temporary residence with an aunt who lived in one of the prestigious new houses in Queen's Square, and had insisted that his two friends should join him there for dinner, which sent the poor old lady into a tizzy of anxiety. Now stooping delicately backwards as he ascended the gangplank of their splendid ship, he was the focus of all eyes, like the principal actor at a play.

Sir George and Sir Arnold followed at a respectful distance? Sir George looking back over his shoulder to address some happy remark to his old friends and to enjoy the stir they were causing. As he turned he caught sight of a face he thought he recognized.

'Who's that?' he said. 'Feller in a brown bob wig. Looks familiar, damme if he don't.'

Sir Arnold glanced back too. 'Not a man of my acquaintance?, me dear,' he said. 'Nor yours neither, judging by the look of him.'

There was something disquieting about the man's pointed stare, something that made Sir George think of being beaten about the head and stitched by some fool surgeon. He frowned and bit his lip, trying to remember. 'He looks this way.'

'Ignore him,' Sir Arnold advised. ''Tis an idle fellow. A poor tradesman or a bounty hunter or some such. Suchlike wretches are ten a penny hereabouts.'

They could hear Sir Humphrey drawling a greeting to the ship's master. 'Mr Swann, your sarvant, sir.' So they had to join him and leave the man in the brown wig behind. But his disturbance echoed in Sir George's mind.

The master was given orders to sail to Nevis with all speed, to wait there until the sugar ships were loaded and to escort the cargo home. He was moreover, as Sir George told him happily, 'to engage such French ships as should put in an appearance and give 'em a good trouncing.' He expressed himself mindful of the importance of his mission and promised to obey it 'to the letter, sirs, to the very letter.'

'We wish 'ee God speed,' Sir Humphrey said, bowing in his exquisite style.

'Aye, sir,' Sir George echoed. 'So we do, sir. That's the ticket, damme. Fair winds, fine weather and God speed.' And he found himself wondering what speed the *Bonny Beaufoy* was making, and how many slaves she'd lost, and what sort of price they would make in the Windwards, and how well old Jedediah was managing to ration the food stocks. I'm a man of action, he thought, mopping the sweat from his forehead, damme if I ain't.

Twenty-two

The *Bonny Beaufoy* was becalmed. She'd sat in the same flat, filthy patch of water for the last seven days, waiting for a breeze that never came and now the sea was beginning to rot around her. Strands of thick weed lay heaped and motionless on the surface of the water, brown and oily and entangled, and above her empty masts the sky burned in an endless, maddening blue, with no cloud to soften its glare.

Without movement, the heat was intense and the smell from the holds so nauseating that Jack had been allowing the slaves out on deck for most of the day, even though their sores festered in the sunlight and the smell they carried with them was as miasmic above decks as below. After three more storms and an outbreak of shaking sickness, they'd lost six of the crew and were down to a hundred and sixty-two male slaves — all unshackled save for six who were too violent — and forty-one females, which made for an impossible crush on deck. But at least the holds could be sweetened a little in their absence, and that was done every day, although their stock of vinegar was running parlously low. Lack of vinegar was the least of their worries. Their drinking water was coated with green slime, the maize barrel was full of weevils, and their diet was much reduced because all their livestock had been killed and eaten long ago. Slaves and crew alike were unshaven and unwashed for there was no wish to add to the debris floating beside them. Consequently many of them were suffering from boils and many more were too weak and lethargic to do more than sit in what little shade they could find and wait.

The dead days passed in slow hot enervating seconds. Buckets were emptied at the heads every morning but the filth lay in the weed and didn't disperse. The decks were foul for lack of a good scrub and sluice, the gunwales brown with grease. On the fourth day swarms of black flies arrived to crawl over the decks and breed in the weedstrewn water, and soon obscene grey grubs and worms like blood-threads emerged from the leathery coils to creep and wriggle as they fed upon the filth.

By day they buzzed and rustled and the noise of their pressing lives echoed through the ship as though they were consuming the very planks. At night they lit the thickened darkness of the weed with small sharp pulses of light, blood red, rheum yellow and poison green. It was as if they were laying seige to the ship and everything in it, gathering force to consume it, plank by shrinking plank, wood, brass, canvas, blood, flesh and bone, swelling bruises, running sores, rotting corpses and all. For, as if their predicament weren't bad enough, there were three dead slaves stinking in the weed a mere four hundred yards away, still lying in the spot where they had been dumped over the side on that first becalmed day when they all thought the lull was going to be temporary.

To Jack Daventry, every moment was an extension of the nightmare that had begun when the big feller was torn apart by the sharks. At the start of the voyage, when he'd been knocked breathless by the force of the first gales, he'd prayed in terror for a calm sea. Now, with the sails slack and without a breath of wind, with nausea racking him night and day, and a continual stink in his nostrils, he yearned for full sails and leaping speed and would have given all his earnings for the slap of a wave against the hull. Sometimes, as tempers frayed and sharp angry arguments broke out among the crew, and females were used so roughly that they wept, and slaves were kicked out of the way for no other reason than that they were there, he felt as though the world had been turned inside out, that reason and civilized behaviour were lost, and that they were all descending into the savagery they deplored.

Occasionally and even more pessimistically he suspected that everything would go by opposites and grow steadily worse, and that they would die stuck in this hellhole.

Nothing in this voyage had turned out as he'd expected. He'd taken the job to make an easy fortune and so far all that had happened to him was that he'd worked a deal too hard and come a deal too close to losing his life. He'd expected to be the master of these slaves and had become little more than their servant, cleaning their filth, shaving their chins, feeding them their two meals a day, even disposing of their dead bodies. He'd expected speed and adventure and success, and had found an eternity of stinking boredom. It was a daily torment, impossible and cruel, and he could have been completely cast down by it, if it hadn't have been for the baby.

On the fourth day of the lull, the blue-eyed boy climbed out of the hatch with a new-born baby in his arms. All that day, lie and his mother crouched by the fo'c's'le, sheltering the little creature with a torn piece of tarpaulin as it lay in its mother's lap and watching over it with a purity of concern that was totally at odds with the filth and stink around it. From time to time, it gave an odd mewing cry and was lifted gently until it could find its mother's nipple and feed, but apart from that the only sound from the group of women clustered around it was a flutter of hands brushing the flies away, a murmur of admiration and approval, a gentling of baby worship that was plainly sustaining them. Until that day, they'd been taut and full of alarm, afraid of their captors and scolding their children if they dared to move so much as an inch away. Now they all moved about with a peculiar ease. Even the com mill ground more gently.

By the seventh day, the infant had become a sort of talisman. Jack found himself watching for it every morning, scanning the woolly heads of the females as they emerged from the hatch and holding all his emotions in reserve until the blue-eyed boy had eased out with his little kicking burden. He was delighted when the infant grew, privately applauding as its new-born wrinkles smoothed and its little stick legs grew more rounded, and watching it suckle was comforting. It reminded him of all the peaceful beasts he'd seen in the farms and fields when he was a child: of cats suckling kittens, calves nudging their mothers' teats, lambs leaping long-tailed and stiff-legged to be fed. He couldn't help feeling that if this infant could survive, the lull would lift and they would sail again. He recognized that the idea was mere superstition but he thought it daily just the same.

Unfortunately, his crewmates didn't share his opinion. The cook complained that there was no call to give the woman extra portions. ''Twill all go to waste,' he said, slopping the stew pot down on its trivet on the deck. 'The brat will die, sure as God made little apples, an' the sooner the better to my way of thinking. I can't be doing with'em, nasty squally critturs.'

The purser had an even tougher opinion. 'We should chuck it over the side,' he said. 'Here an' now. The sooner 'tis gone, the sooner she can get back to earning her keep, which she should've been a-doin' long since. As 'tis, she'm a waste of space and fodder.' The lull had sharpened

Jack's perceptions. He saw at once that the purser wanted to use her himself and that he would kill the infant without a second thought. 'Belike,' he allowed. 'But I'd rather keep it alive until we move. Three bodies a-rottin' alongside is enough for me. Or for any man else, I dare swear.'

Mr Smith was looking at the blue-eyed slave, calculating. 'If the female's out of bounds, damme,' he said, flicking away a pair of flies that were coupling on his forearm, 'I'll have him. I've got the itch something prodigious. It must be met one way or another.'

In other days and other places, Jack would have accepted the man's decision as evidence of his human need, perverted but not open to question. Here, with his own sensibilities sharpened to snapping point, he opposed it, instinctively and with abhorrence. 'No, sir,' he said. 'I think not.'

The purser swore at him. ''Od's bowels! Am I to be allowed no pleasure at all?' And as Jack hesitated. 'Answer me that!'

There would have to be a reason and a good one, as Jack was well aware. It was in his mouth before the purser had finished roaring. 'The slave is mine.'

That was a surprise. 'How yours?'

'He is my entitlement. My choice.'

'Then you'm a bigger fool than you look,' the purser roared, delighted to be able to say so. 'He m a half-caste, damme. And a child moreover. You'll not get any sort of price for him, if you can sell him at all. I tell'ee what, sir, swap him for one of those big strong fellers an' I'll take him off your hands for you and no hard feelings.'

'No, sir,' Jack insisted stubbornly. 'He's mine and will remain so.'

'Then let me throw the brat over the side and take the female.'

Jack set his jaw. 'No, sir. You know my mind. 'Tain't to be done and there's an end on it.'

It was not. Nor could it be. The purser's authority had been challenged and, as part-owner of the ship, that couldn't be permitted. He returned to the attack at every opportunity and in every sort of company, from the surgeon to the captain.

Mr Dix was no help to him. He'd heard that there was a dispute between the purser and Mr Daventry and was disposed to take the younger man's part.

'I'd throw it overboard if 'twere fractious,' he told the purser, having cast a professional eye over the new-born. 'But 'tis quiet enough for the time bein' an' a fine healthy child, in all conscience, which'twould be a pity to waste. He could add to the price of the female.'

Mr Tomson was more direct. 'I leaves all such matters to my slave master,' he said, twiddling the ringlets in his beard, 'bein' as that's what we pays him for. Which I'd advise you to do the same, sir, and leave well alone.'

The lull continued: heat, stink and bad temper increased; the infant fed and thrived, and was beneficently quiet; and the quarrel simmered on.

Soon they were into their eleventh day of inaction. That morning they woke to a new smell and a new fear.

Mr Dix had been below making one of his regular inspections while the first fifty slaves were fed and watered on deck. When he emerged from the hold, his expression was so grave and the stink that rose with him so sour that Jack knew at once that his news would be bad. The old medicine man was blind in one eye, which had 'clouded over since yesterday' and there were four slaves in a fever with vomiting and the flux.

'Bloody?' Jack asked, having heard enough about this disease to fear it.

'Not yet,' the surgeon said grimly, 'but 'twill be proved so by nightfall, I fear.'

They went to report their findings to the captain, who said he'd feared as much too, 'being I could smell it from here. What's to be done, Mr Dix?'

'I've dosed 'em with chalk,' the surgeon said, 'but I doubt 'twill serve.'

'Will it spread, think 'ee?'

'Aye sir, I fear so. There is little we can do to prevent it in such foul air.'

Mr Tomson considered, pulling his beard, and then made one of his rapid decisions. 'Bring 'em out of the hold, Mr Daventry, if you please. Put 'em by the heads. They'll not last long and 'twill be easier to dispose of 'em from there.'

By the time two suitable pieces of canvas had been found, one to act as a ground sheet and shroud, the other to use as a sling, there was a fifth casualty groaning below deck and the bad news had spread through the ship.

Late that night, Jedediah Smith came down to the heads to join Jack and Mr Dix and to demand action. He took care to maintain a sensible distance between himself and the stink for fear of taking infection and he covered his mouth with a scented kerchief, but his order was clear despite his muffled speech.

'Twill spread like wildfire,' he said, his eyes popping with angry alarm. 'Have 'em over the side here and now Mr Dix and have done with it.'

'With respect Mr Smith, sir,' the surgeon protested, 'they ain't dead yet.'

'They soon will be,' the purser told him. 'Hell's teeth, Mr Dix. Are we to wait till they've infected us all?'

'I hopes not, sir.'

'Very well then. Over the side with 'em. You chucked the baby out quick enough and that was still living, as I recall.'

'A brat's one thing,' the surgeon said, stung by the reminder. 'Five grown slaves is another, being they'm worth good money if we can recover 'em.'

'And if we can't, they will infect us all. You can't deny it. We shall die out here in this stinking cesspit with none to help us and none to know of it. Where's the profit in that? Have 'em over the side.'

The surgeon did the only thing that was possible in the circumstances. He turned to the slave master. 'How say you, Mr Daventry?'

'Yes, sir,' the purser echoed. 'How say you?'

To be deferred to by these two men was a moment of almost pure elation to Jack Daventry. It was inopportune, there was no denying that. He would rather they'd consulted him on any other matter and at any other time, but it was rewarding nevertheless — well earned, long overdue. Remembered scenes tumbled pride and justification in his mind. The insufferable lordliness of the purser when he'd first come aboard, his odious behaviour over the female and the blue-eyed boy, his greed at table — and now he was reduced to asking advice of Jack Daventry, praise be.

'The scraggy one is dead already, if I'm any judge,' he said, bending to examine his charges. 'And t'other is far gone. He don't groan, you notice. I agree with Mr Dix. We shall have two corpses to be rid of by sundown.'

'Be rid of all five,' Mr Smith insisted, 'or we might as well sign our own death warrants here and now.'

The thought of throwing a live man over the side made Jack flinch. 'We will wait till darkness,' he decided. ''Tain't a thing to be done in daylight. The rest will be below, save for the watch, and there will be enough of a moon to see by. I will make a final decision then, sir.'

The purser actually called him a 'stout feller'.

They lowered the longboat at a little after midnight, taking a crew of six to row them and all five slaves, wrapped in their canvas sheet — two dead, one dying and two so far gone in delirium that they couldn't see, although their eyes were open. The weed was so thick that rowing was extremely difficult but the moon was as bright as a chandelier and dropped a straight silver path across the black water to guide them on their way.

Jack sat in the stern, between the surgeon and the purser, silent and brooding, with a loaded pistol in his belt and murder in his heart. To throw a live creature overboard to drown was a sin whichever way he looked at it, but did he have the right to refuse to do it when all the other lives in the ship depended upon it being done? If the worst came to the worst and the creatures struggled, he could give the coup de grace with a shot from his pistol. There was risk in it, for the sound of the shots would wake the ship. And 'twould be murder assuredly. But they would die in any event. They were as good as dead already. Not like to survive the night. And if they did 'twould only be for a day or two. And yet...

Images of the big feller tore at his mind. He saw him again, threshing and screaming in that obscene whirlpool of blood and spume, fighting for his life as his limbs were ripped from his body. He cringed again under his own dreadful powerlessness, was seared by the knowledge of his responsibility, ached to weep at the remembered terror of it.

'Well, sir?' the purser asked.

They had travelled the appointed distance. It was time. The thing had to be done. He had to decide to do it.

'Put in the ballast,' he ordered, and when that was done and none of the creatures struggled. 'Bind 'em up.'

'All of 'em, sir?' one of the seamen asked.

'Aye, sir. All of 'em. None will last till morning. They're best out of their misery.'

But for all his air of authority and calm decision, he was shaking as the heavy canvas was rolled over the side. And that night he lay wakeful in his bunk, afraid to sleep for fear of the nightmare that was pressing down upon him. He was glad when the daylight broke and he could creep up on deck and smoke a calming pipe. Like everything else on board, his stock of tobacco was running low, but that morning need was greater than prudence. He sat with his back against the main mast and his pistol reassuringly against his thigh and tried to prepare himself for whatever the day might bring.

At the change of the watch, he went below to check the slaves. There was no sound of groaning, which was encouraging, and no sign of the flux. The medicine man's eyes were oozing pus and the stink of the buckets was as foul as usual but there was nothing worse. Much relieved he walked to the galley to check stocks for the morning meal, and found that they were inadequate and that the cook was complaining, but that was usual too. So far so good. Back on deck, he opened the hatches to the female quarter and watched for the blue-eyed boy and his talisman child to emerge, which they did, both well and lively. The day took another quiet movement into normality.

By mid-morning, when he was feeding the second batch of males their limited meal, he had shaken the nightmare from his mind and was quite himself again. So he was unprepared for the sudden outburst that erupted by the fo'c'sle. The screams were so piercing that he left the porridge pot and ran to see what was happening.

Mr Jedediah Smith was standing over the tarpaulin that sheltered the infant, although it was impossible to see whether the child was still there, because the women were standing in an angry phalanx all around it, screaming at him as he tried to punch them out of the way. 'I'll take the cat to 'ee!' he yelled at them. 'Devil take it, get out of my way or you'll know the worst.'

The noise had already attracted the crew, and several of them had ambled over in hope of seeing a flogging. Jack had to push through quite a crowd before he could reach the scene.

'How now?' he said, when he was standing beside the purser. 'What's this?'

Mr Smith turned a flushed face towards him. The brat is sick,' he said, 'and must be dealt with. She'll not hand it over.'

Jack looked round for the baby and his mother. The females wrere bristling with protective anger and stood so close together that it was impossible to see beyond their bodies. The blue-eyed boy was crouched on the deck at their feet. He carried his head with the tremulous alertness of an animal that knows it is hunted, and he was looking around him, his odd blue eyes darting from side to side. He's searching for his mother and the baby, Jack thought. Checking that they're still safe. But where were they?

Then he saw the female. She was sitting calmly behind the protective wall of all those determined legs with the baby cuddled against her breast and she was murmuring to it and gazing at it with an expression of such melting tenderness that Jack felt his bowels yearn at the sight. Oh, to be cared for like that. Gentled so. Loved so. He was charged with envy and admiration, pricked by regret for the callousness of the previous night, stirred to anger at the ugly greed of the purser, spurred to a sudden, irrational determination to protect this child and his mother come what may. In one second his emotions coalesced into action.

'On whose authority, sir?' he said.

Mr Smith recognized that battle had been joined and answered powerfully. 'Mine, sir, since I own this ship and everything that sails in her. If I say the child is to be handed over, I'm to be obeyed.'

'No, sir,' Jack said, standing astride and in front of the slaves, with his fingers on the handle of the pistol. 'I think not. You don't own me, sir, nor do you have authority over these slaves, not while I am slave master.'

'Hell's teeth! Am I to be told me business by a jumped-up puppy with no breeding? I think not, sir. I think not. Damn your eyes! Now get out of my way, sir. 'Tis my slave and I mean to have her. You'll not bar me from my rights. If I say the brat is to be dealt with, I shall deal with it, and you'll not prevent it. Make way I tell'ee. Damn your eyes!'

Jack refused to move. 'The child is not sick,' he said, his face set, 'and consequently needs no attention. He is to be left with his mother.'

'Mother! Mother!' the purser mocked. 'What do they know of motherhood? They're just cattle.'

'No, sir,' Jack said hotly. 'You are wrong. They are human. As you and I are human.'

The purser roared with delighted horror to hear anything so preposterous. 'The feller's mad!' he said to his audience. 'I never heard the like. Human! The very idea!'

They agreed with him, mocking and cat-calling. Whoever heard the like? To call a savage human. The feller *was* mad. 'Took the heat, I shouldn't wonder,' the bosun said.

Much encouraged, the purser turned to bullying. 'Get out of my way, lunatic,' he shouted, looking back at his audience to enjoy the impression he was making, 'or I'll have'ee sent to Bedlam, damme.'

Jack pulled the pistol from his belt, cocked it and held it towards the purser's head. It was done so quickly and with such expertise that Mr Smith missed it altogether while he was looking for admiration, and few of the seamen realized what was happening until the gun was levelled. But none of them could miss the chill of command in his voice.

'I think not, sir,' he said quietly. 'Nor will you take this baby.'

'Hell's teeth!' the purser said and this time it was no mean oath. 'I'll have you in irons, sir.' And he turned to the nearest sailor and gave his own commands. 'Seize him!'

The sailor hesitated. Looked at Jack. And didn't move.

'Don't just stand there,' the purser roared at him. 'Seize him, you dog! Why do you wait?'

'Well, sir, 'tis like this here, sir,' the sailor explained, avoiding his master's eyes but making his point notwithstanding. 'If we puts the slave master in irons for 'ee, sir, who'll do his work? Tis mortal hard work he'm a-doing.'

The purser was spitting with anger. 'Devil take'ee! Do as I say or I'll have'ee flogged, sir.'

This time, the sailor shifted as though he was about to take a step forward but, as soon as he moved, Jack turned the pistol in his direction. 'Lay so much as a finger on me, sir,' he said, 'and I'll blow your head off.'

Flogging was to be preferred to decapitation.

''Od's bowels!' the purser roared. 'Ain't there a one of you man enough to take him?'

Apparently not. 'Not with that there pistol in his hand, sir.'

It was impasse and it froze them all into inaction, slave and master alike. They were so still that they could hear the insects buzzing and clicking in the weed, and the little lick, lick of water against the hull.

The little lick, lick of water! 'There's a breeze, me hearties!' Mr Reuben yelled. 'We've got a breeze!'

The captain was among them, giving orders. 'Clear the decks! Get those slaves below! Set the spinnaker, Mr Reuben.'

The quarrel was forgotten in instant activity, the slaves hustled below, fed or not, sails unfurled and set to catch the least movement in the air. And at last, at long, long, exhausted last they began to move, inch by tantalizing inch, timbers groaning. The lull was over.

Within an hour, they were beginning to pick up a little speed and had left their filth behind. Within two, they were under full sail. By the end of the afternoon, they were back in the bounding force of the trade winds.

The transformation aboard ship was total, as they relaxed in the triple blessing of fair weather, abundant clean water and a strong slip-stream. Nobody was flogged, the cook didn't grumble about his poor rations, the crew obeyed orders without demur. Soon the decks had been scrubbed until they were white again and the gunwales were scraped clean. Everybody on board took it in turns to wash and the barber worked all day and every day until there wasn't an unwanted beard to be seen in any part of the ship and all the male slaves were youthfully clean-shaven. Boils healed and tempers calmed. The infant lay in a cooling breeze and was fed and admired. The blue-eyed boy took to following Jack about, eager for odd jobs, which was sometimes useful and occasionally embarrassing. Best of all, nobody mentioned the stand-to. It was almost as if they'd forgotten all about it.

Except for the purser himself. He took his complaint to the captain as soon as the ship was comfortably under way.

Mr Tomson heard him out and then gave his considered judgement. 'Well now, sir, Mr Smith,' he said. 'I takes your point and so forth, but the fact of the matter is this. The man does a good job of work with our cattle, no matter what his lunatic opinion of 'em, and so forth. If we was to put un in irons, who'd look after the cattle an' feed 'em and doctor 'em and clean 'em up, an' so forth? I tell you plainly, sir, I'd not do the work for all the tea in China, and I doubt you'd volunteer for it neither.

No, sir, the way I looks at it is this. Leave him be to work on for the rest of the voyage. Then when he'm landed and the slaves are sold, you can have him back to England in as many irons as you choose and bring him afore a magistrate and so forth, to your heart's content.'

It wasn't the answer the purser wanted and he argued long and angrily against it, pointing out that the man had pulled a gun on him and wasn't to be trusted, that he was running mad and a danger to the ship. But the captain was adamant and in the end Jedediah had to accept his decision whether he would or no.

'You want to watch your back,' Mr Reuben warned, early one morning, when he and Jack were on watch together. 'You made an enemy with that there pistol of youm.'

Jack had already faced the fact that there would be consequences to his defiance, so he could afford to be casual about it. 'What of it?'

'Watch your back, that's all,' the bosun repeated. ''Tis a mean-minded old swabber and means to have 'ee in irons. Take advice from one what knows.'

'I've got his measure, Mr Reuben, don't 'ee worry. He'll not get the better of me. Have I not come through the jungle fever and outbid old Wan Four and cleaned the holds more times than I've had hot suppers? I'll not be put down by a purser, no matter how much money he's got a-jingling in his breeches.'

'What of the boy?' Mr Reuben asked, looking at the blue-eyed slave, who was sitting at Jack's feet as he usually did these days. 'He follows you about like a little pet dog. Shall you keep him?'

'Well, as to that,' Jack said, patting the child's woolly head, 'I shall see.'

'Watch you don't get bit,' the bosun warned, alarmed by such contact. 'I wouldn't touch narry a one of 'em, if I was you.'

Jack looked at his slave, who was smiling seraphically, his teeth like ivory between wide dark lips, his face moulded into placatory circles. 'Not this one,' he said. 'He'll not bite. Will you, sir?'

Then an extraordinary thing happened. The slave looked up as though he was listening, and suddenly spoke, not with the usual clicking, gonging sounds that they expected but with a single, recognizably English word. 'Bite?' he said. 'Bite?' The questioning inflection was plain.

Jack was so surprised that for a moment he couldn't answer. Did this child understand what was being said? Could he speak English? Or was he mimicking like a poll parrot? If a bird could do such a thing, could a savage?

The word was repeated, this time with more insistence. 'Bite?' There was no doubt about his understanding now.

'Bite,' Jack explained, and he put his hand to his mouth and mimed, taking his forefinger between his teeth and pretending to snap at it. 'Bite. Snap, snap.'

'Bite,' the slave said with satisfaction and smiled his broad smile. 'Bite. Snap, snap.'

He's quick, Jack thought and before he could stop to consider the propriety of what he was doing, he spoke again. 'Jack,' he said pointing to himself. 'I am Jack.'

The slave seemed to understand that too. 'Jack,' he repeated, and beating a black hand against his own rib cage, 'Oleanda.'

'Well blow me down!' Mr Reuben said. 'Here's a thing! Is that his name, d'you reckon?'

'I shall never remember it, if 'tis,' Jack laughed. 'Howsomever that's a matter can be remedied.' He turned to the slave again 'I am Jack,' he repeated. 'You are Blue. Understand. Blue. You are Blue.'

'Blue,' the slave said, smiling again. 'Oleanda Blue.'

The ship's bell was ringing the end of the watch. 'Come with me, Blue,' Jack said. 'We've work to do.' He didn't beckon, because there was no need. He knew he would be understood. 'I reckon I could teach him to speak like a linguist, Mr Reuben. What do'ee think to that? He be a trifle more than a pet then.' The boy worked all morning with the rest of the slaves, swabbing the decks with sea water and brushing vigorously. From time to time, he would look up from the streams of water at his feet, hold his arm to his mouth and say 'Bite! Bite!' laughing aloud as though the very idea was an irresistible joke. 'Bite! Bite!'

As the days passed the impromptu lessons continued and became more frequent, for as Jack soon discovered the newly named Blue had a thirst for learning and wanted every object named, touching sails, mast and spars with a query on his face, bringing lesser objects to lay at Jack's feet. 'Marlin spike', 'belaying pin', 'spoon', 'bowl', repeating the words until he could pronounce them properly. He learnt fast. By the end of that

266

first free-sailing week, he had accepted his new name and understood the use of the personal pronoun: 'I Blue, you Jack, she Umumi.' By the end of a fortnight he understood 'up' and 'down', 'here' and 'there', and had begun to use verbs. 'You thirst?' 'I thirst.' He had even ventured into the complications of the English auxiliary verb. 'You are thirsty?'

At the start of the third week, they managed their first conversation.

The evening meal was over and the tubs and spoons were being collected, when one of the male slaves walked across to the empty stew pot and began to beat a rhythm on its side with his wooden spoon as if it was a drum. It was an infectious sound and since the cook wasn't on deck to complain and Jack raised no objections, another man walked over and joined in, this time drumming the side of the pot with both hands and in a different rhythm. The sound instantly became faster and more complicated. The stew pot throbbed as both men beat with their hands and stamped with their feet. The slaves gathered, at first hesitantly, then with a happy insistence, until they'd formed a semi-circle before the drummers. A third man drifted to join them, his mouth slightly open as if he was in a trance, and for a moment on-beats and off-beats seemed to be working against each other, nudging and colliding. Then they suddenly came together in a single pounding rhythm and a woman began to dance.

The effect was electrifying for as she threw herself into the rhythm, arms raised and feet stamping, all the other women began to clap, swaying from side to side like a chorus. More and more hands joined in, and the speed of their syncopated rhythm grew faster and faster as the noise increased. Soon the woman was dancing bent double, with her body thrust forward, and her outstretched arms flailing, and her knees rising almost to her chin with every pounding step. She looked like a huge brown bird, struggling to fly.

She must stop soon, Jack thought, or she'll be exhausted. She can't go on like this for ever. But even as the thought was in his head, she let her arms drop and fell back laughing into the crowd, and another woman took her place, dancing in the same way and with the same total abandon. After that, the women threw themselves into the circle one after the other, some in twos and threes, some on their own, but all dancing in the same way, arms outstretched and feet pounding. Now and then the drummers would stop in mid-beat and pause to rest, and the dancers would be carried by the clapping of the crowd. Sweat poured down their faces, their arms fanned the air, and still the drummers beat and still they danced.

'They are like birds,' Jack said. And was instantly asked to explain the word to his slave. 'Bird,' he said, miming flight. 'Bird,' pointing up at the sky. 'They fly. Up there. Up and away.'

Blue understood him completely. 'Yes,' he said. 'She is bird. She is not here. She is bird. She fly.'

'As I thought to do once,' Jack told him. 'I thought I was an eagle.' He remembered the evening the *Bonny Beaufoy* had left Bristol and how he'd felt he was flying into the setting sun. ''Twas all folly, Blue. I was never an eagle.' The pistol was heavy against his thigh. 'A fighting cock perhaps, but not an eagle.'

Blue had listened without comprehension. 'What is eagle?' he asked.

'A great bird,' Jack told him. 'And we are but earthbound men. Human. Not birds. For we cannot fly away.' And it seemed to him that he had said something profoundly true.

Twenty-three

It was June and the city of Bath was preening itself for the start of the summer season. The King was in Windsor and the ton were entertaining at their summer retreats, but the slave-owning gentry were assembling in their customary watering place and the city stood ready to receive them. Sunshine filled the welcoming honeycomb of the Pump Room, and slanted in above the King's Bath to stripe the walls with brightness and make the gilded columns shine. It was June.

Sir George Bradbury was still in London with Sir Humphrey, supervizing the loading of their third cargo for Lisbon, which had been purchased from the profits of the first two and which they hoped would prove even more lucrative. But Lady Bradbury had arrived in South Parade the previous afternoon, and now, having taken the tinny waters for the first disagreeable time, was happily cleansing her palate with tea and Bath buns, while she regaled her dear friend Arabella with news of Ariadne's conquest.

Arabella was the most rewarding of friends. As the little orchestra produced its neat patterns of sound behind them and teacups clinked and voices rose in giggling cadences, she expressed her happiness at Ariadne's good fortune, with every indication that she meant what she said. Hermione felt she had never begun a summer so well.

'Where do you intend to hold the wedding?' Arabella asked, knowing that this was just what Hermione would want to divulge.

'At the Church of St James, in Piccadilly, at the end of September,' Hermione said with studied carelessness. She had written to her father to tell him the good news and had received an acknowledgement, which was uncommon gratifying, and the promise that the wedding 'would be attended'. He hadn't actually specified who would attend but the promise was enough and might well turn out to be the first step towards the reconciliation she desired so much. The Daventry family are usually married at St James, as you know. We could hardly break with tradition.' Arabella agreed at once and sipped her tea. I trust we shall see the bride in Bath this summer,' she said. 'And Melissa, too, of course. How happy she must be for her dear sister!'

'I left them sleeping,' Hermione said, assuming a smile of motherly concern. 'The journey down was most fatiguing. But they have promised on their honour that they will join me here within the hour.'

She would have been surprised to know that Ariadne was up, dressed, and ready to leave the house and that Hepzie, who had been given strict instructions to accompany her wherever she went, was now being given peremptory and contradicting commands.

'Melissa will be awake directly,' Ariadne said, prodding her sleeping sister in the ribs. 'You are to stay here and help her to dress. Be quick about it or she'll be late for the baths.'

Hepzie was aggrieved. 'Your mama wished me to attend upon *you*,' she said. 'How may I do that if I am to dress Miss Melissa?'

'The wet nurse shall accompany me,' Ariadne said casually. 'She is to be my personal maid. 'Tis all agreed. Were you not told? She has returned here, has she not?'

Hepzie professed not to know, although she'd watched the wretched girl walk into the kitchen not five minutes ago. Ain't that just like her, she thought angrily. Sticking her oar in. 'I'm the lady's maid. Her place is in the nursery.'

In fact, Suki was still in the kitchen and doing her best to wash her son in case milady wanted to see him. It was difficult because he was doing *his* best to wriggle away from her. He was nearly fourteen months old and a strong plump baby with a lusty voice and great determination. And as he'd beerr toddling for several weeks, he was irked by all this unnecessarily immobilizing hygiene.

'Come along, William,' Suki coaxed. 'Have your pretty face washed like a good boy, an' then you shall have some nice titty to make up for it.'

'He'll go off bang, one of these days, you keep on feedin' him the way you do,' Barnaby rebuked.

'Don't you pay that Barnaby no mind,' Cook said, pumping water vigorously. 'You give the little thing all the titty he can take. Pretty soul! Lor, what a mess this kitchen is. Don't they scour nothin' here in wintertime? That's a temptation to cockroaches, that is. Now where's that gel? Bessie! Dawdlin' again. You'll miss the pick of the market, you don't get off direct. And what milady'll say then, I do not dare to think.'

Bessie had slept badly after her journey and was drooping with fatigue. 'I does me best, mum, I'm sure,' she pleaded. 'Can't do no more.'

'We'll go to market together,' Suki promised. 'Many hands make light work.' It was the chance to slip across to the Captain's lodgings. If his ship had returned, he might even be at home. Oh she couldn't wait.

'I'm that grateful, Suki,' Bessie said, as they pushed their way into the crowds. That market fair sets my head to spinnin'. I can't get accustomed to a multitude. That I can't. Not nohow.'

They'd certainly chosen a squashed moment to set off. The streets were crowded with chairs packed against carriages, and pedestrians, passengers, horses and bearers cramped into strife and confusion because the day's beasts were being driven past them to be butchered: bewildered lambs with coats like clotted cream; sheep bleating piteously, their fleeces matted and bedraggled; frantic pigs squealing between the greasy legs of their red-faced drovers. Above the animals' frightened heads, the rich fat faces that were so soon to devour them complained loudly and arrogantly that their presence was a nuisance.

The market was noisome, too. It had been raining heavily for the past three days, so the ground was slushy with churned-up mud, and the goods were splashed and spotted. It took a long time for the two girls to find fruit and vegetables that were still wholesome enough to suit Cook's most particular palate, and by the time both baskets were full, their skirts were hemmed with mud, despite the fact that they were both wearing pattens. And William had grown uncomfortably heavy on Suki's back.

'Get you off home,' she ordered. 'I'll follow later. I've another errand to run. I shan't be long.' And as soon as Bessie was out of sight, run she did, despite William's weight on her back, as fast as she could to Mrs Roper's.

The inn at the corner of Nowhere Lane was just as she remembered it, crowded with drovers, who lounged in the doorway and waded in and out of the churned mud in the alley, clutching beer mugs and loud with greeting and argument. But the lodging house was changed. The front door had been pulled off its hinges, the windows were open and curtainless, and inside the hall, which was pungent with the sharp damp smell of new-mixed plaster, three workmen were busy at the walls, whistling as they smeared. Beyond their rhythmic arms Suki could see that the rooms were empty and the staircase ridged with mud. It was obvious that nobody had been living in the house for a considerable time and none of the workmen had heard of Mrs Roper.

'Wasn't the name of the party was it, Jess?' the foreman said, and the other two shook their heads without much interest.

'Clerk of the works is upstairs,' one said. 'You could try him if you've a mind. Not that he'd know a deal more'n us.'

He turned out to be a short stout man in a well-worn suit of stained brown fustian and an ancient bob wig made of very coarse horsehair. He was studying a crumpled plan, which he'd spread out on the trestle table before him and pinned into position with four pewter candlesticks, and he wasn't pleased to be interrupted.

'Be off with 'ee!' he ordered at once, barely giving her a glance.

'I came to enquire for lodgings, an't please you, sir,' she tried politely, bobbing a curtsey. 'My mistress sent me.'

He was partially placated. 'No lodgings here, mistress,' he said. 'Nor will be till we've made all sound.'

'I wonder Mrs Roper didn't send a billet to inform my mistress,' Suki tried, as he seemed a little more affable.

'Mrs Roper!' he laughed. 'My life, you *are* behind the times! Sold out and gone has Mrs Roper. Belongs to Chappell and Winthrop now for all the good it'll do us.'

Suki couldn't conceal her annoyance, but she did her best to fish for more information. 'What has become of her tenants?' she said.

'Prison belike,' the man said. 'Or Bedlam, I shouldn't wonder. They were a low crowd, thieves an' card sharpers an' gentlemen of the road, by all accounts. Don't you go bothering your pretty head about tenants. Tell your mistress, Mrs Roper's gone to London. Shut up shop an' gone. Christmas it was. I wonder she didn't write.'

Suki was so cross she couldn't bear to stay in the house a minute longer. She banged down the stairs and out into the street, and once there she gave the unhinged door a good kicking to relieve her feelings. What a foolish, stupid woman, she thought, as she shifted William's weight on her back and set off on the long walk back to South Parade. What folly to up sticks and go. Now how am I going to find the Captain? I can hardly ride into Bristol every five minutes to check arrivals, especially now I'm back with the Bradburys and Beau's still on the farm. But how else can I find out if he'm back? I shall need to invent a good excuse to slip away. I wonder whether Miss Ariadne would help me.

And at that moment, she came to Orchard Street and the theatre.

The stage door was firmly shut against the mud, but she could hear banging and shouting from inside the building. Of course, she thought, I'll ask the actors. I never had a chance to ask them last summer and I'm sure they'll help me if they can. He was always in the theatre and they'm uncommon friendly. Encouraged and hopeful again, she beat upon the door.

It was opened by a goblin in red boots, stockings and an ancient leather jerkin so slashed and cut about that it looked more like wickerwork than a pelt. 'Are you the eggs?' he demanded, cocking his head to one side, his eyes as bright as a bird's.

Suki told him who she was.

'A pretty demoiselle, be Our Lady,' the goblin said, peering at her face. 'But witless. Well, come in child, come in, if you're a-coming.'

'Is it the eggs?' said a voice from the stage, as Suki kicked the mud from her shoes before she stepped inside. It was all as she remembered it from the year before: dusty costumes, tattered scenery, unwashed children, the smell of greasepaint, shrieks and screams. A bower was being dismantled on stage between the pillars, and two of the players were throwing costumes into a skip. The leading lady sat on the edge of the stage in her chemise, eating a loaf of bread and looking fatter than ever.

'We shall starve to death, Charlie, I hope you realize,' she complained, 'with the eggs not come. ''Tis uncommon hard.'

The man she was addressing took off his wig and polished his bald head with a yellow handkerchief. 'Eggs!' he moaned, rolling his eyes dramatically. 'Here's Mr Clements gone a-promenading, the Lord knows where, the Lord knows why, and just when we're packing up, and the cart short by a good two feet — although how that could *possibly* have come about I cannot imagine — and the new scripts not arrived from the copier, and he'm supposed to be the *best* in Bath and promised to deliver 'em before we left, and you speak to me of *eggs*. S'blood woman, have you no wit to worry me so?' He gave his wig a good shaking, and replaced it with an air so martyred you would have thought it made of thorns. 'And what have you come here for, pray,' he said to Suki, 'if it ain't for eggs?'

'An't please you, sir, I'm looking for Captain Jack. He used to come to the play.'

'S'blood!' Charlie drawled, and he threw his head back at such a ridiculous angle that his wig immediately began to slip off his pate, and made a dramatic exit into the wings, sighing like a bellows.

'Brute!' the leading lady roared. 'Have you no heart, Charlie? Where would we be without heart? I ask myself. Why nowhere and nothing.' And she assumed her stage expression and began to rehearse her lines. 'Ah love, sweet love, that blighteth many a heart!' she intoned, clasping her fat hands to her fatter bosom. 'Queen of all passions, patroness of pride.'

'How I do agree, ma'am,' Suki said, seizing the moment. 'Without heart, we are truly nothing.'

The lady looked at her as though she was having trouble focusing her eyes. 'What is it?' she said. 'What do you want?'

'You haven't seen Captain Jack about anywhere?' Suki asked, pressing on although the odd look discouraged her.

'No, no,' the lady said vaguely, pausing in her speech to flick the words away from her like the irritation they were. 'How like th'avenging angel dost thou ride... Run along dear, there's a good creature. We open in Bristol tomorrow and there ain't a minute to spare.'

She don't care for me a bit, Suki thought, watching the performance. Where would we be without heart? indeed. They make a great palaver, blowing kisses from the stage and saying how much they love us all, but 'tis all show.

She shifted William on her back again and wandered away from the empty words and out of the theatre. The actress didn't even see her go.

It was chill in Orchard Street, for the little alley was too narrow for the sun to penetrate and the cold air made her feel lonely. She gave herself a hug for warmth and comfort, but that only made her shiver. And William was unconscionably heavy.

Down at the end of the street were the steps where Old Sheena had told fortunes and, as Suki glanced towards them, she saw that the top step was occupied by a pair of lovers. They stood together as close as statues, wrapped in each other's arms — he bending his head towards her so that their foreheads were almost touching, she gazing rapturously at the mouth so near her own. Suki had responded to them with jealous fellow feeling before she realized who they were. Then she had a moment of alarm, for the girl was Miss Ariadne and the man Mr Clements, the actor. Had she forgotten that she was being spied upon? Hepzie could come round the corner at any moment and surprise them. She must warn them, and quickly, before harm was done.

Her approach was so abrupt that they jumped apart, turning guilty faces towards her. Then Ariadne recognized her and ran to seize her by the arm.

'Say nothing!' she ordered. And when Suki answered, saying that she wouldn't breathe a word, Ariadne was eager to tell her tale. 'I have followed your teaching to the letter. This is my dear Mr Clements, who has declared his love for me. We have been writing to each other ever since I went to London, as you know, dear Suki. We are much beholden to you for all you did to bring our correspondence about. Are we not, Mr Clements?' The actor looked sheepish, but she pulled him towards her, smiling into his eyes. 'Now we are to marry,' she declared. 'Papa may think I am betrothed to his horrible Sir Humphrey but the man is an abomination and ain't fit to be considered. I cannot marry where I do not love and there's an end on't.'

'Quite right!' Suki applauded, thrilled by her courage.

'My body is my own, is't not?' Ariadne said boldly, rehearsing her new opinion and enjoying the power of what she was saying, watching for Suld's approving nod. 'Nobody has any rights upon it save me. I have chosen the man I will marry and nothing will deter me from the path I have chosen. So here we are to await our carriage. How say you to this for a wedding gown?' She smoothed the saffron silk of her bodice, blushing with pleasure.

'I wish you joy,' Suki said, 'but should you not keep better hidden till the carriage is come? Hepzibah — '

'Is taken care of,' Ariadne said, 'and the carriage will be here presently.'

It was being reined up at the bottom of the steps as she spoke, with a great clatter of wheels and much snorting and blowing from the coachman and his horses. Mr Clements was off to meet it so quickly that he could have been running a race.

Ariadne tripped gaily after him, her yellow pumps bright against the grey pavement. 'I have left Mamma a note,' she called, as the carriage step was lowered. ''Tis well hid. 'Twill not be found until the room is cleaned and we are far away.' And she climbed aboard and was gone, in a rush of dark curls, yellow silk and giggling happiness.

The note was discovered as soon as Lady Bradbury returned to the house.

She'd gone straight to her daughters' bedroom to find out why they had been so tardy. 'Fie upon you, slug-abed!' she said to Melissa, who was still sitting at her dressing table with Hepzie arranging her hair. 'You promised to join me at the baths within the hour and here you are still at your toilette. Where is your sister?'

'Gone out, I believe,' Melissa said, almost artlessly. 'She left you a billet. 'Tis behind the blue vase on the mantelpiece.' She'd watched it being written and hidden, while pretending to be asleep, and she knew from her sister's agitation that it was something scurrilous.

'Out?' Hermione said, her long face creased with suspicion. 'Out where?'

'I'm sure I couldn't say, Mamma,' Melissa told her smugly. 'Hepzibah offered to accompany her — did you not, Hepzibah? — but she'd none of it.'

''Tis the truth, ma'am,' Hepzie confirmed. 'She said she'd rather have the wet nurse for company. She said 'twas arranged.'

Hermione narrowed her eyes at their maid as she broke the seal on her daughter's letter. 'I hope she ain't contemplating a visit of any consequence,' she observed. 'We dine with Lady Fosdyke at three and her father will be here before noon with Sir Humphrey, who will be anxious to see her, I do not doubt.' Then she read the letter. And read it again, her mouth trembling. And sat down heavily in the nearest chair, her fingers pressed to lips grown suddenly pale, her face aged with distress. 'Leave what you are doing, Hepzibah,' she instructed, 'and go and fetch Mr Jessup to me directly. And the wet nurse, if you can find her.'

Melissa was delighted to have caused such disquiet. She assumed a solicitous expression as well as she could. 'Is it bad news, Mamma?' she asked when Hepzibah was gone.

The worst,' her mother said. 'Oh, my dear child, the very, very worst. I hardly know how to tell you. If I try I fear I may run distract. Oh, oh! The shame of it! The shame! I'm sure I don't know what I ever did to be so cruelly treated. How could she do such a dreadful, dreadful thing? To her own dear mamma! 'Tis beyond mortal comprehension. She has run off with an actor, and on the very day when we are to dine with Lady Fosdyke! We shall be shamed for ever. Jessup must see to it.'

They could hear his feet measuring the tread of the back stairs, his careful cough before he knocked — krmm, krmm — and behind him the babbling of a baby and a voice saying, 'Hush now, my William. Be a good boy.' And then the room was full of servants: Mr Jessup discreet in black, Hepzibah in her floral cotton, looking smug, and behind them Suki Brown, bright as sunshine in a yellow dimity gown trimmed with pink ribbons, with William toddling beside her, a blue padded cap on his curls to protect his head from tumbles, blue leather boots on his feet and his little fat legs stomping manfully beneath a froth of blue and white petticoats. 'Heavens!' Melissa said. 'Is that my brother?'

Hermione barely looked at him. After one cursory glance, she fixed her gimlet eyes on Suki. 'Ah!' she said. 'I am informed that you accompanied Miss Ariadne when she left the house this morning. Is my information reliable?'

'No, ma'am,' Suki said, looking her straight in the eye. 'I only just got here, ma'am, an't please you. I came by way of the market in Fanner Lambton's cart. I haven't seen Miss Ariadne yet. Nor Miss Melissa. Good morning, Miss Melissa.'

Lady Bradbury digested this, thinking deeply. Then she turned to her butler. 'Mr Jessup,' she said, 'when the master returns, ask him if he will be so good as to attend upon me directly. I shall be in my boudoir. Sir Humphrey wall no doubt wish to be attended *in his own room*. After his travels, he wall be fatigued.'

Jessup went off at once to obey her, but it was already too late.

Sir George was in the house and bounding up the stairs, loud with success. His wig was over one eye and his fine suit creased and crumpled from his journey but he paid no heed to any of it. He pushed Jessup out of the way and roared up stairs, two at a time, Hermione! Where are you? Weve had such a time of it. Never knew such a time. Wait till I tell you. The *Yotick's* launched at last, all shipshape and seaworthy and ready to sail!' He crashed into her boudoir, bursting through the door with such force that flakes of plaster fell from the ceiling.

Hermione was out of the bedroom and across the landing so quickly that the sack back of her day gown hissed against the floorboards. There was no time for greeting or courtesy. 'Read that,' she said, and thrust the note into her husband's hand.

Then, and too late, she realized that Sir Humphrey was making his languid progress up the stairs, pelvis tilted, white hand trailing the banister, powdered face raised towards her in concern and enquiry.

'My dear lady,' he breathed, avid for scandal, 'what is it?'

She was caught in such an acute state of embarrassment that her throat constricted. To be facing this man, at this time, when she'd courted him so assiduously and the marriage was arranged and everything was going so well... Twas more than she could bear. She wanted to faint or die or vanish into thin air. But she remembered her breeding and struggled to find breath and words to answer him. 'My dear Sir Humphrey,' she said weakly, 'I trust I see you well. Tis nothing.' Her voice was growing fainter. 'Nothing.' Fainter still. 'Of no consequence...'

She was wasting what little breath she had, for Sir George was bellowing, in a voice that would be heard all over the house, 'Od's bones and brains! You've bred a harlot, ma'am. A harlot.' 'Abate your tone, my love, I do entreat you,' Hermione whispered, glancing anxiously at the door to the backstairs, where the servants hid to eavesdrop.

Her husband saw no point in subterfuge. 'Twill be all over town by dinner time,' he roared. 'Had you no control upon her at all, ma'am? What were you thinking of to let her wander free?'

She tried to fight back. And to warn him. 'I take it hard, my love, that you should think to lay the blame at *my* door,' she said. 'As you yourself observed, 'twas a wench improved. We were deceived! That is the truth of the matter. We were deceived and *we* should make an end of it.'

He was too angry to take the hint. 'You may have been deceived, ma'am. *I* was not. She's a monstrous imp of wickedness, and should have been kept within doors at all hours. Day and night. Bad blood will out, ma'am, and there's the truth on't. We all know where it comes from.

Not *my* side of the family, as you'll allow. There ain't an ounce of bad blood on *my* side of the family. Not an ounce. 'Od's my life, not an ounce. And as to that actor fellow, devil take him, he should be horsewhipped. Let me once catch hold of him, I'll cudgel him! I'll blow his brains out, so help me!' Then he noticed Sir Humphrey's enquiring expression. 'Run off with an actor, sir, if you ever heard the like.' And to Hermione's horror, he passed Ariadne's note to her fiance. 'Read that.' Her humiliation was complete. Cheeks burning, she tried to offer an apology. 'I can scarce lift my eyes to look at you,' she whispered, 'for very shame. What must you think of us?'

The Honourable Humphrey gestured them both into her boudoir, away from listening ears, and once there, made suitably comforting noises. 'There is no need of apology,' he said smoothly. 'Tis your daughter who is at fault, not your good self.'

'You are kind to say so,' Hermione murmured, thinking what good breeding he had. And all gone to nothing. The pity of it! She cast about to find something else to say but at that point Benjy stirred from a snorting sleep on the chaise longue and lumbered to his feet to investigate the newcomer, giving a few preliminary growls by way of greeting.

Sir Humphrey lifted him deftly on the toe of one elegant shoe, deposited him outside the door, and shut it firmly. 'I think not, sir,' he said. 'We have enough to contend with, have we not, dear lady?'

The dear lady had to agree, partly because she was hardly in a position to do otherwise and partly because the awful nature of their social commitments had come pressing back into her mind. 'Od's my life!' she said, her fingers to her lips in dismay. 'We are due to dine with Lady Fosdyke at three. What is to be done? 'Tis too late to cancel, I fear.'

'Cancel? My dear lady!' Sir Humphrey said, aghast at the very idea. 'By no means cancel. Face it out, me dear. 'Tis the only possible way, We will make apologies for your daughter's absence — a chill perhaps, you will know the likeliest cause — enjoy our meal, as much as we are able, which I fear will be little given the circumstances, and return. We shall have news before nightfall, depend upon it.'

She wasn't comforted. 'I do not see how. She has fled.'

'There are two roads out of Bath,' he explained, 'and farms a-plenty all along the way. Fee'd posts, dear lady, set in position, ready to serve.

Offer the right fee and I'll lay any money, you will hear of your runaway by morning.'

Hermione deferred to her husband. 'What do you think, my love?'

He raised his shoulders and his eyebrows in despair. 'Think?' he said. 'I'm past thought. I doubt if I shall ever think again.' But he tried to be gracious, even in desperation. 'Howsomever, he may be right.'

'Never doubt it,' Sir Humphrey said warmly. 'Send two men, with good horses and full purses, and you shall see how well we fare. If they are flown 'twill be to Bristol or London, and either way we shall follow.'

Sir George sighed. 'But what then?'

'The new law will stop a hasty marriage. Unwed, the lady will return to sense. If we move swiftly, a scandal may yet be averted.'

'Would it could be so,' Sir George said, 'but you forget the player, arrant rogue, that he is.'

'All men have a price,' Sir Humphrey drawled. 'We shall find his. Send for her maid and enquire what dresses are taken. I'll lay she's worn her best, and a good bold colour with any luck. Then send your man.'

Nobody below stairs was the least bit surprised to hear of Sir Humphrey's treacherous advice and, to Suki's dismay, most of them shared his worldly opinion.

'He's onny an actor,' Cook said, 'an' gold's uncommon persuasive to the acting trade. They'll buy him off as easy as winking.'

Suki sprang to his defence before she could stop to think of the consequences. 'Not if he loves her,' she said stoutly. 'If he loves her, he'll stick to her through thick and thin. Love ain't open to bribery.'

'If 'tis love, I might agree with 'ee,' Hepzie sneered. 'But she's took her best silk gown and twenty crowns. So money is of some consequence, I should hazard.'

'If that's the case,' the newest kitchen maid said. 'He'm after her money. Poor soul. 'Tis the same the world over.'

'You know nothing of it,' Suki said angrily. 'So hold your peace.' Then, and too late, she realized that they were all looking at her, some much surprised and some a deal too knowing, and she wished she'd stayed silent.

'Hoity-toity!' Hepzie mocked. 'Are you paid to defend 'em? Is that it?'

It was a straight question and had to be answered. 'No I arn't. An' if I were 'tis none of your concern.'

'I might make it my concern,' Hepzie warned and was delighted when Suki blushed. 'Seems to me you know a deal more than you should. Seems to me you had a hand in it.'

Suki fought back hard, remembering her lie to milady. 'I only just this minute arrived,' she said. 'I'aven't had time to have a hand in nothin.'

They bristled at one another, both thinking of a retort.

''Tis my belief,' the new maid said, chopping parsley vigorously, 'there arn't no such thing as true love. 'Tis a concoction of poets. Most of us marry for money when all's said an' done. I know I would.'

'Her father got a powerful rich husband for her by all accounts,' Cook said. 'A duke or some such. She should ha' stayed home an' married *him*. She don't know when she'm well off, an' that's my opinion of it.'

'But if she loves the actor,' Bessie offered, her face anxious. 'Nobody marries for love,' Hepzie told her. 'That ain't the way of the world. You marry where your father chooses for you if you've any sense. An' if you ain't got a father to look out for you, you marry the richest man you can find to offer. That's what I mean to do. Love don't come into it.'

'Well then, you'm wrong,' Suki said. 'Love's the most important thing and nobody has the right to choose your husband for you. That's your affair. Yours an' his.'

'Oh, oh! So that's the size of it!' Hepzie mocked. 'You're still singing *that* old song. I'd ha' thought you'd've learned better by now. Well let me tell you, Suki Brown, there ain't another person in this house would say such foolish things.'

'That aren't foolish,' Suki fought on, ''tis right. Our fathers don't own us.'

'Since when? Course they own us. Our fathers own us an' our husbands own us an' our employers own us. 'Tis the way things are. If we'ave any power in anything'tis by stealth and well you know it. 'Tis the way of the world.'

'Then the world's wrong. Ask any true lover an' they'll tell you different.'

'An' you're a true lover, I suppose,' Hepzie said tartly. 'An' that husband of yours, we all hear so much about and never see, he's a true lover, too. You love him an' he loves you. We don't exactly see him rushin' homewards to his true love, do we, though? Tis my belief he don't exist.'

'He do,' Suki said, eyes flashing. 'He'll come home soon. You'll see. 'Tis a matter of time, that's all.'

'He's been gone years, to my certain knowledge.'

'He'm on a slaver. They take years.'

'Aye,' Hepzie sneered. 'So you say.'

'They'm a-ringing for you, Hepzibah,' Cook said, glancing up at the bell board, and glad of an excuse to bring the quarrel to an end. Hepzie had right on her side, but she could be uncommon sharp.

'Twas a mistake to speak out so, Suki thought, as Hepzie flounced from the room. I should have held my peace. Now she'm suspicious and will tell tales. She still felt embattled, even though her adversary was gone, for the scullery maids were looking at her most oddly. 'How hot'tis in this kitchen,' she said, fanning her cheeks. 'I shall take William out in the air for an hour or two to cool un. Milady aren't like to call for us again being they're out at the Fosdykes'.'

''Tis a-comin on to rain,' Cook warned.

But Suki already had her bonnet on. Now that she'd made up her mind, she couldn't stop in the house a minute longer. I shall visit the Spring Gardens, she said to herself. There wouldn't be anyone there to talk to, so she wouldn't say the wrong things. 'Twould be peaceful there. 'Tis a pretty place. William likes pretty flowers. Don't you, my pet lamb? I'll be back in time to help with supper.'

Twenty-four

The Spring Gardens were in full summer bloom and looked extremely fine, every flower peculiarly brightly coloured under a grape-blue sky and every bed perfectly symmetrical. There wasn't a leaf out of line, nor a shrub out of place. Arcades stretched to north and south, tree-lined walks paved with gravel, and each with its own leafy arch, led in every direction, and in the central rotunda a band played soothing music beneath a ceiling painted to resemble the sky at night. It was the hour of the afternoon promenade and the parades were crowded with new arrivals, all trimmed and titivated ready for admiration, the ladies exquisite in embroidered gowns, the gentlemen dazzling in velvet coats and silk breeches.

As Suki arrived, they were gathering beside the rotunda where three row's of gilded seats had been set to receive them. Twill be some marvel to attract 'em so, Suki thought, so she joined the crowd too, standing behind the little chairs at a respectful distance from their finery. Her entry ticket had cost more than she'd expected, so she might as well take her money's worth and an hour's idle entertainment w'as just what she needed to take her mind from her troubles.

The marvel wns an extremely fat person who dressed like a man and sang like a woman, with a high-pitched echoing voice that Suki didn't like at all. But the sugar merchants were enraptured by him and applauded his first offering most enthusiastically, so she stayed where she was at the edge of the crowd to see what would happen next. After a while, a flautist arrived in a patched coat and a moth-eaten wig, and he and the singer rearranged themselves in front of the band with a great deal of hand waving and chair scraping. Then the singer polished his forehead with a kerchief as large as a pillow case, and the introduction to the second aria began.

Suki was wondering idly whether the flautist would be better or worse than the singer when she became aware that a group of rough-looking men had taken up positions immediately behind her, and were standing a deal too close for comfort. She edged sideways through the crowd so as to avoid them, but they followed, pressing so hard against her back that she feared for William's safety. Pick-pockets, she thought, and was surprised that she felt no fear. But she'd hardly taken another step before a rough arm grabbed her round the waist and an even rougher hand was fumbling at her petticoat. Her parasol hung unopened on her left arm, and it made a splendid weapon. She stabbed it backwards against the legs of her assailant, and while he shifted round to avoid her blows, she ran, dodging through the crowd despite their displeasure. The merchants, seated in their glittering circle around the stage, took no notice whatsoever.

The walk was almost empty, so she ran like a greyhound, straight down the centre, her lungs straining and William bobbing on her back. Within seconds, her bonnet flew from her head and was lost in the bushes, but she couldn't stop to retrieve it because she could hear feet thudding after her and a rough voice yelling, 'Grab her, Johnny. She got somethin' worth the taking or she wouldn't run.'

She wondered briefly whether to turn and argue with them but it was too late, they had already caught up with her, three swarthy, sweating men, in stained coats and soiled linen, pulling at her skirts to impede her, thrusting their odious faces at her, mouthing at her with stinking breath.

'Leave me be,' she panted, struggling out of their grip.

'Why, 'tis the Captain's wench,' one said, holding her face in the vice of his fingers. 'Look 'ee here, Spider.'

Her thoughts were muddled with fear and loathing. 'Leave me be,' she said again, 'or I shall tell the Captain how you treat me. Do way your hands.'

A mouthful of broken teeth moved into her line of vision and another voice said, 'You won't tell the Captain nothing, you stupid wench. On account of he ain't here, an' he ain't the man for the likes of you. He's a gentleman of the road, is the Captain, an' may take any wench he chooses.'

He had a hand down inside her bodice fumbling her breasts — how dare he! — and William was screaming in sharp staccato cries that roused her to a surge of protective fury. How dare he do this! How dare he frighten her baby! Odious filthy creature! She turned in a storm of fear and anger and beat him about the ears with her parasol, kicking and screaming, so that a group of promenaders, who'd just turned into the walk, were stopped in their stride and began to gather about them. At that, her attackers drew back and hesitated, and that gave her the chance she needed. She ducked beneath the nearest arm and ran for the exit. Beyond the bushes she could see the ferrymen casting off. If she could only run fast enough, she could be aboard and away before they caught up with her again.

'Wait!' she yelled as she ran. 'Oh, wait for me, do!' And to her great relief, the ferryman waited, steadying his narrow skiff as the river waves slapped against its sides, and he and his passengers watched as she tumbled down the bank and scrambled aboard, panting and weeping. But safe.

They were all mightily interested in her adventure and said it was a crying shame for pockets to be picked in broad daylight, so it was, and something should be done about it. And gradually their sympathy eased her distress. Soon she was telling them the tale, and being commended for her level-headedness as they creaked their way back across the river. But when they landed in Boat Stalle Lane, she knew that the attack had exhausted her. She was compelled to sit on the bank with William on her lap for comfort and try to recover a little. It had been a disastrous outing.

'Oh, my William,' she said as she cuddled his damp face against her cheek. 'I haven't seen so bad a day as this for many a year. First Mrs Roper up and gone, and then the actors uncaring and Hepzie hateful — and now this. We got the stars against us today an' no mistake.' And as if to underscore her misery, it began to rain.

Short though it was, the walk back to South Parade stretched before her like a five-mile march. 'Come now,' she said to herself as she hoisted William on to her back again. This will never do.' And she began to sing as she trudged, to cheer them both up. 'Oh up she got, and home did trot, as fast as she could caper.' But she was still so cast down that she paid no attention to the people who jostled beside her, nor to the carts and horses in the road. Even when a voice called her name in a questioning way, she didn't bother to look up.

But it called again. And again. 'Suki Brown! Do you walk to South Parade?' And she looked up at last and saw that it was Farmer Lambton, sitting astride the Captain's beautiful horse and looking down at her with patient concern.

'Oh, Farmer Lambton,' she said and, despite herself, her eyes filled with tears. 'I've had such a day of it, you never would believe. I been set upon by pick-pockets in the Spring Gardens, of all places. You can't imagine how good it is to see you!'

He dismounted carefully and lifted her into the saddle, without a word, sitting her astride with William before her. Then, as he walked beside her through the crowded street, he questioned her gently. What had happened? Was ought stolen? Was she harmed? And satisfied that she was only shaken, he led them through the Abbey Gardens to the nearest tea house and bought a dish for them both, and a sop for William.

'A restorative,' he said as the steaming bowls were laid before them. 'Sip it slowly. 'Twill be of more benefit that way. William will sit on my knee for a minute or two.' Which William did and was as good as gold, back with a familiar face, sucking his sop and regarding the company. So Suki recovered sip by sip, and the colour washed back into her cheeks, the frown eased from her forehead and she became her pretty self again.

'Time for home,' he said as she set down her empty cup.

''Tis uncommon kind of you, sir,' she said thanking him as he lifted her on to Beau's back again. It was raining harder now and their clothes were getting damp. She opened her parasol, hoping it would give William some protection. 'I've put you out of your way, I fear.'

'No,' he said, settling William in front of her and untying the reins. 'My way is yours this afternoon. I've come to see your master.'

'Twill be on account of Beau being left on the farm, Sula thought. He wants to know when I'll be able to take him. 'I haven't had a chance to talk about the horse,' she volunteered, holding the parasol over her son's head. 'We been at sixes an' sevens today.'

'Aye,' he said, 'so I understand. That's why I'm here. I've come to see Sir George about his daughter.'

Her heart sank. 'Not Miss Ariadne?'

'She passed the farm this afternoon,' he told her. The rain was dripping from the brim of his hat but he paid no attention to it at all. 'She and her lover. Tipped into the ditch, down by Seven Acre Field, some time around noon. One wheel stuck fast. I sent your father down with Ned to haul them out. I knowed who they were the minute I clapped eyes on 'em, for I saw them both at the theatre the night I took Mrs Lambton to the play. Which I daresay you remember. So when Sir George's man come a-riding by, asking if we'd any knowledge of 'em, I knew 'twas my duty to report it.'

Suki was aghast. She had to dissuade him quickly, before they reached the house. She couldn't have them hunted down. ''Tis a love match,' she said. 'They've run away to marry.'

That didn't alter his purpose at all. 'Belike,' he said, and he spoke the word carelessly.

She looked at him earnestly through the rain. The parasol had split and was now leaking water all over William's head. 'Then you won't peach on 'em,' she said as she tried to turn it into a better position.

'It ain't a matter of peaching,' he told her seriously. 'She is engaged to many another.'

'But she don't love him.' The water was pouring over her own head now and running off the bridge of her nose.

'Marriage is too important to be left to mere liking,' he said, stolidly leading the horse. 'Her father has made a good match for her, so'tis his plain duty to bring her home to honour her commitments. Any father would do the same. My plain duty is to help in any way I can. They are runaways.'

How can he do such a thing? Suki thought mutinously. Mr Lambton of all people. Mr Lambton, the stolid, dependable, sensible... Why don't he understand? 'Oh, Mr Lambton,' she pleaded. 'Pray don't peach on 'em, I beg you. They love each other. They really do.'

'That's as maybe,' he said in his unruffled way. 'But whether they do or not, 'tis no concern of mine, nor should it be of yours. Her father wants her found and that is all we need to know. He is fearful of Mr Clements's intentions.'

'He has no cause to be. 'Tis an honest match.'

He gave her his patient look. 'If 'twere an honest match,' he said. 'Mr Clements would have spoken to Sir George and asked for her hand in the proper way. This was never done, Suki, as you must know, for Sir George's man was well aware of it and told me of it roundly. No. Marriage on the gad is rarely to the maid's advantage. Marriage on the gad to a man so far below her in rank and wealth and opinion would be the ruination of your Miss Ariadne.'

'They love each other,' Suki repeated. His righteousness was making her stubborn. She shook the rain from the parasol, feeling angry with it.

It had split in so many places it was no use to flesh or fowl. Dratted thing! Oh, she must make him understand. ''Tis a love match.'

'If *that* is the case,' he said, 'and Sir George is agreeable to it, they will wed and no harm done. If'tis not, Sir George will bring the lady home.'

'But...'

They had arrived in South Parade and there was little time left for argument. It was raining in earnest and they were all thoroughly damp. He gave her his hand to lift her down from the saddle, as Beau twitched his ears against the wet. 'Beyond the giving of information, this matter is no concern either to thee or me,' he said, and his tone was a rebuke. 'We must allow our betters to settle their own affairs.'

She made one last appeal. 'Delay for a day,' she begged as the rain ran out of her hair and down her face. ''Twould do no harm. If 'tis in the stars for 'em to be found, he'll find 'em, depend on it, sooner or later. Tell him tomorrow when you come to market. That would be time enough, surely.'

'Oh, Suki!' he said, smiling at her. 'What a spirit you have!'

Twenty-five

Frederick Bradbury had dined late that afternoon. Very late indeed. In fact, by the time the tablecloth had been removed and the port set deferentially beside his elbow, it was past five o clock. Because he was an excessively mild-mannered man and mindful of the susceptibilities of his cook, he made no comment upon the delay and asked no questions. But it upset him nevertheless and, when the meal was over, he found himself fatigued. He had the fire made up, propped his heels upon a footstool, and covering his face with a clean napkin, settled down for a late afternoon snooze.

He was considerably put out when his valet crept into the room some twenty minutes later to inform him that his brothers coach had arrived.

'Very well,' he said wearily. 'Fetch the chocks, Morgan.' And he straightened his wig and dusted his coat and went downstairs to greet his guest and all the noise and confusion he would bring with him.

It was all as he expected. Rain was spitting into the open doorway and a chill wind tossing coat-tails up into the air in the most unseemly fashion, the two greys were steaming after their exertions up the hill, Barnaby was fairly scraping the chocks into position under the wheels and Sir George was cussing and swearing as he emerged from his unsteady door on to the sloping pavement.

'Damme, Frederick,' he complained, 'why must you live on a hill?'

'A pleasure to greet 'ee, me dear,' Frederick said and tried to sound as though he meant it. 'What brings you to town at this hour? Is there news of the *Yorick*?'

Then he noticed Sir Humphrey, who was stepping delicately from the coach, wincing at the rain. 'Sir Humphrey. A pleasure, sir, I give you good evening.'

'Mr Bradbury, sir,' acknowledged Sir Humphrey. 'I wish you could, sir. Plague me if I don't.'

'Come into the powder room, brother,' Sir George said, looking at the valet's ears. He spoke so urgently and his expression was so fraught that Frederick escorted both his guests into the house at once and took them straight to the little closet beside the door, certain of bad news, and there amid spare wigs and dustsheets, face cones and bellows, Sir George told the tale of Ariadne's elopement, pacing the little chamber with furious strides and to the imminent danger of everything in it. ''Od's bowels, did you ever hear the like?'

Frederick was instantly solicitous of the Honourable Sir Humphrey, aware of what a mortal blow this must have been to his delicate constitution. 'My very dear sir,' he said earnestly, 'pray allow me to offer my most sincere apologies. My niece must have taken leave of her senses to do such a thing. I cannot tell you how grieved it makes me.'

Sir Humphrey raised his eyes to the ceiling and sighed elegantly.

'Needs a good thrashing,' Sir George said furiously, charging at the wigs. 'That's my opinion.'

'She is a female creature when all is said and done.' Frederick also sighed. 'Little more can be expected of that sex, I fear. 'Tis a different breed altogether.' And seeing that the face cones were scattered and the wigs knocked awry, 'Pray do be seated, brother. Have you cause to think she is in Bristol?'

'Her carriage overturned at Twerton,' Sir George explained, still prowling. 'Seen by a farmer. Reported to me. In a yellow silk gown, if you please. Brazen hussy!'

'They may well take ship on the morning tide,' Frederick said, 'and if that is to be the case, 'twere well to be prepared against it. There were many arrivals today but few sailings, praise be, which is one mercy, you'll allow. Tomorrow morning we will walk to the Custom House and see the controller.' He rescued the cones deftly and replaced them on the shelf behind him.

Sir George was too impatient to wait for morning. 'We must start now, damme,' he said. 'The sooner we find 'em, the less time for niggling. I've trouble enough without bastards.'

Frederick sighed again, and this time more heavily, for it was plain that his evening was to be ruined. Given his brother's anger and the distress of his illustrious guest, there was nothing for it but to take a trip down to the Backs, rain or no rain. 'We'll to the Seven Stars,' he said, 'and offer twenty crowns for information.'

'Aye, but shall we get it, think 'ee?'

'In a city devoted to trade,' Frederick said sagely, 'money buys busy tongues.'

So the valet was sent for a lantern and a woollen cloak, and presently the three men set off down the hill into the drizzling darkness. The two rivers were crowded with ships, resting in their lines, hull against hull, the forest of their bare masts black against the lights of the quay. The sight of such an immense fleet made Sir George scowl, for if his errant daughter were already embarked and aboard, how could he possibly tell where she would be hidden?

Frederick, on the other hand, gave them scant attention. He was already cold and damp, and he intended to walk to the Backs as quickly as he could, conclude his business there and return at speed.

Fortunately, the Seven Stars was crowded with likely customers, and the news that the Bradbury brothers were on the look-out for information regarding a pair of runaways brought immediate interest and scores of itching palms. Details were sought and given, of age, appearance, colour of dress, lack of wig, time of arrival, and the brothers were eagerly assured that finding such a dainty lady, even in a city of this size, would merely be a matter of time.

'I shall give this note of hand to the landlord,' Sir George declared, reading as he wrote. 'My note of hand for twenty crowns for any man who can provide me with information leading to the discovery of my daughter and a certain Mr Clements, actor.' He signed with a flourish of calligraphy and Brussels lace, and added, 'You may find me at my brother's house, which is, I believe, known to you.'

Then they returned to the house, through driving rain but in better spirits. Their capes were set to dry and a dish of tea ordered to sustain them, and they settled down to wait.

An hour passed. And then another. And nobody came. Frederick ensured that Sir Humphrey sat in the most comfortable chair before the fire with his feet propped on the fender, and did his best to make intelligent conversation, discoursing on the latest play and the latest books, the news from the Commons and even the price of sugar. But Sir George prowled the room like one of the lions in the Tower, scowling through the curtains, scuffing the edge of the carpet, flinging himself into every unoccupied chair and sofa in the room, cursing the weather, his daughter, actors, theatres, ships and Hermione, incessantly and indiscriminately.

At last, a little before midnight, Morgan came gently into the room to tell them that a seafaring gentleman was waiting in the hall, and had sent word that he had 'solid information, and required them most humble-like that they would see him below in the hall, on account of his leg didn't take too kindly to stairs.'

They went down at once.

The seafaring gentleman was an outlandish looking personage, with a gnarled wooden leg and a pair of tattered crutches. He seemed to have had a lifelong propensity for heat, for he smelt most vilely of sweat, rum and gunpowder, and his skin was burnt as brown as old leather. He wore his own hair, which was black and greasy and hung behind him in a short pigtail tied at the ends into a straight pouch of cracked black leather, and his suit was rubbed shiny with age, the right leg of his breeches tied with fraying rope just below the stump of his knee. He was totally out of place in Frederick's elegant hall, like a bug in a cradle.

'A villain, damme,' Sir George whispered as he and Frederick descended the stairs.

But Frederick thought that a good thing. 'Takes a thief to catch a thief,' he said.

The seafaring man leant on his crutches and regarded them with shrewd black eyes. 'God gi'ee good e'en,' he said. 'Which of you two gennulmen does oi 'ave the honour of sarvin'?'

'Speak to me,' Sir George said. 'Where is the lady?'

'The lady's hard by, in a manner of speakin'. Farr an' twenny crowns, oi do believe thee offered.'

'Twenty,' Sir George said stiffly. 'That was my note of hand.' 'Ar,' the man said, and lie sucked his brown lips and gave the matter ostentatious thought. ''Tis a marrtal bad night fer twenny.' 'Twenty,' Sir George repeated. 'An' you've to earn it, damme.' 'Ar,' the man said again, breathing decay upon them. 'Twenny-two'd be dandy.'

'Have us there within the quarter,' Frederick said, consulting his hunter, 'and twenty-two it shall be.'

So the bargain was struck and their disreputable guide took up his lantern and wrapped himself in his cloak, and they all set out into the rain again. He moved remarkably quickly for a man so badly crippled, lolloping downhill, past the sleeping houses of the sugar and slave merchants, past Red Lodge brooding blackly under the rain, and down Pipe Lane into the sloping terraces where the knifesmiths plied their trade. At the knifesmiths' steps, he paused to rearrange his crutches and then he was off again, swinging precipitately down into the wet unlit chasm, crutches scraping, while the brothers followed, their lanterns bobbing before them and their shoes squeaking on the wet stone of the stairs. It was indeed a mortal bad night.

As they crossed the Frome, Sir George realized that their guide was leading them into the old town, but neither he nor his brother felt any need to speak of it. They filed through the filthy archway of St John's Gate, where beggars sat against the walls snoring in their own stink, and then they were in the narrow alley called Broad Street, where ancient houses leant towards one another in the darkness, obscuring what little light there was. The seafaring man was a simian shape swinging on ahead of them over the cobbles, and now he was going at such a speed that from time to time the brothers had to run to keep up with him.

Without warning, he turned out of Broad Street into an alley smelling of piss and decay and so narrow that they had to walk it in single file, and even then they were splashed by water pouring out of gulleys on either side of them. The houses here were all built in the old style with high gabled roofs, windows dangerously out of alignment and overhanging jetties bulging down above their heads. Creaking, ancient, bug-ridden, uncivilized hovels, Sir George thought, holding his handkerchief before his nose, and just the sort of place that this foul man would use to hide his folly in.

Sure enough they stopped at the end of the alley and the seafaring man knocked at the window with his crutch, and presently a candle wavered into view behind the glass and a rough voice said, ''Oo's that?'

'Tis oi. A matter of farr crown,' the seafaring man said, with his mouth to the window, and the candle said, 'Ar!' and wavered away again. They waited in the rain and the torrent from the gulley until the front door was eased open and the candle flickered before them in the hands of a grizzled man in a brown bob wig. 'Come froo denn,' he said and, as that seemed to be permission to enter, they trailed their wetness into the house.

'Where are they?' Sir George said. The smell in that narrow hall was overpowering. It was neither the time nor the place for ceremony.

The candle led the way up a very dark staircase, illuminating a pale halo on the stained ceiling above it and leaving the brothers to stumble up in the darkness behind it as well as they could. At the top of the stairs was a candle stand with a double-headed candlestick upon it and, once this extra pair were lit and all their lights were gathered together, they could see that they were standing before a brown door, and that the man in the brown wig was pushing it open with his foot. Sir George seized the candlestick and strode into the room shedding light as he went.

The saffron gown lay abandoned across a wicker chair with Ariadne's yellow pumps beside it on a tumble of petticoats, and the high bed set against the slope of the ceiling was mounded with sleeping bodies. Without a second's hesitation Sir George seized the matted blanket in his free hand and pulled it from the bed, yelling 'Up strumpet!' at the top of his voice.

The actor slept on, with his mouth open and one knee in the air, but Ariadne woke at once and made a grab at the retreating bedclothes to try and cover herself. She was in her shift, but one breast and both legs were bare, and a garment so voluminous did little to protect her from the immodest gaze of a room suddenly and inexplicably full of men. She was afraid and bewildered, and she looked it. Then understanding cleared the fogs of sleep and she saw that she was facing her father and her fiance, and that they were both glaring at her — Sir George puce with anger, Sir Humphrey chalk white with disdain.

'Papa!' she begged, clutching at the blankets, 'I prithee don't!' 'Cease your wallowing, slut,' her father said, tossing the saffron gown at her struggling body. 'Wallowing is the sport of pigs! Rise from this foul den of corruption. 'Od's blood, it makes my brain boil, so it does! Clothe yourself for the love of God!'

Ariadne contrived to cover herself by a combination of gown and blanket, but by now she had remembered her lover and was pulling at his shoulder to rouse him. 'Mr Clements! Dearest love! Pray bestir yourself. My father and Sir Humphrey are here.'

The actor stirred in his sleep, mumbled a little, scratched his close cropped head and slept on. She persisted, 'Mr Clements! Dearest love!'

And at last he opened his eyes and looked up at the turkey-red face glowering down upon him.

''Od's my life!' he said in alarm.

'If you have harmed one hair on my daughter's head, sir,' bellowed Sir George, 'I shall have the law upon you. So help me if I don't. 'Od's blood and bones and bowels, brother Frederick, restrain me, or I shall run distract and do this villain some mischief.'

The actor stumbled from the bed and reached for his clothes. 'Your daughter, sir,' he said with as much dignity as he could muster, 'your daughter and I intend to marry, I would have you know. The banns will be called on Sunday for the first time of three. All legal and above board, you will allow, and according to the new Act. In three weeks' time, we shall be man and wife.'

'Pardon me, sir,' Sir George said fiercely. 'In three weeks' time, you will be no such thing. In three weeks' time, sir, you could be incarcerated in the nearest Bridewell. In three weeks' time, sir, you could die on a dunghill.'

'Papa! Papa!' Ariadne cried, sitting up in the bed, the straw beneath her crackling as she moved and the blanket clutched to her throat. You lacerate my feelings!' To be caught so soon and so easily and here in this filthy place was making her blush with a shame so acute that she felt as though her cheeks were afire. 'Please, Papa!'

Her father had no pity for her at all. 'Your feelings have no bearing upon the matter,' he said. His eyes never left the actor, who was pulling on his wig and making a very poor job of it.

''Od's bowels! Have you no shame?'

Ariadne drew breath to answer him but, before she could speak, Sir Humphrey stepped coolly forward and stood between them, superbly elegant in the squalor of the room. He took over, ignoring her and speaking directly to her lover.

'Mr Clements, sir,' he drawled. 'Your servant.'

The actor was surprised, impressed, suspicious — all at the same time — but he gave Sir Humphrey the expected greeting and doffed an imaginary cap out of courtesy.

'We have business to discuss, sir, I believe,' Sir Humphrey said smoothly.

Now it was Ariadne's turn to look wary and to feel afraid. What business could there be between her lover and the man she had wronged? Terrible possibilities filled her mind. A duel, a summons for damages, imprisonment, a stabbing.

Mr Clements tucked his shirt into his breeches with trembling hands. 'I think not, sir,' he said. 'What business could there be? What's done is done.'

'I think you will find we have,' Sir Humphrey told him, milky smooth, 'most profitable business. The best that has ever come *your* way, sir, or is ever likely to.'

The actor was puzzled. 'What business, sir?' he asked.

'Why theatre business, Mr Clements. Acting business. What else?' The hook was baited. The actor was intrigued. 'What would 'ee say, sir, to a part in the new play at Mr Garrick's new theatre in Drury Lane in London?'

That was so unexpected that the actor gaped. 'You jest, sir.'

'I never jest in matters of commerce,' Sir Humphrey told him sternly. *'Could* this be done?'

'Aye, sir, you have my word on't.'

Mr Clements licked his lips.

'So what say you?' Sir Humphrey went on. ''Twould be easy enough to accomplish, I daresay. Dependin' upon my word of recommendation, you understand.'

'Aye,' the actor said, understanding perfectly.

'Well then, sir, think on't. I could scarce recommend a libertine for such employ, or a runaway rake, or any other such idle fellow. That you'll allow.'

The two men looked at one another for a long moment, while the rising yellow light patterned their faces and molten wax ran down the sides of the candles like fat white tears. The room was so quiet they could hear the mice scratching in the wainscot. Sir George scowled by the bed. Frederick and the landlord stood still as stones in the doorway, their faces pale and grotesquely shadowed by the candle held between them. Ariadne sat in the shadows and trembled. Mr Clements was the first to drop his gaze.

'Five minutes for 'ee to dress,' Sir George said coldly, lifting the rest of his daughter's clothes from the chair and dumping them on the bed.

She turned away from him and held out her hands to her beloved, imploring, 'Mr Clements, I beg you!'

''Tis the chance,' the actor said, trying to hold her hands and finding the blanket a great encumbrance, 'the chance, Addy my love.'

'Have you no care for me?' she said. 'But two hours since I was your own true love, most dear to you in all the world. Have you forgot so soon?'

'Five minutes for this to be concluded,' Sir Humphrey warned, 'or peradventure I may change my mind on't.'

'Put on your gown, my dearest,' the actor urged her, touching Ariadne's anguished cheeks with placating fingers. 'I think it best. For any but Mr Garrick, I might resist, but this... Oh, my dearest Addy... I prithee put on your gown. Go with your father.'

She flung his fingers aside as though they had stung her and rose from the bed, still draped in her filthy blanket but wearing it with the dignity of a queen. 'If you betray me now,' she warned, 'I'll ne'er speak again. No, not to you, nor yet to any man. Consider it well.'

''Tis my trade,' he said and now his voice was cold and he had turned his body away from her.

She let the blanket fall and began to dress herself, without a word and without modesty, as though she were alone in the room. And at that Frederick ushered the landlord out of the room and, taking the candles from his brother, stood with his back to her so as to afford her the decency of darkness. And Sir Humphrey took a card from his pocket and handed it across to his defeated adversary, and the matter was settled.

It was blacker than ever in the alley and the walk home was pierced with rain, but Ariadne was in a trance of misery and rejection and noticed nothing. She crossed the bridge and climbed the hill without speaking and, when they were all safe within doors again, she stood quite still in the hall, gazing into space with a face so expressionless it quite chilled her uncle to see it. When he asked her if she would care to retire, she went silently to the room he indicated and, although he wished her goodnight, she made no response whatever.

'Poor soul!' he said, as the door closed behind her. 'She is much wounded, I fear.'

'And so she should be,' her father said irritably. She had shamed him before a member of the prestigious de Thespia family, and now the marriage was lost. Hermione would be angered and there were endless and embarrassing difficulties ahead of him. 'She will recover.'

Frederick was all solicitous concern. 'Should I have a room prepared for you, Sir Humphrey?' he asked.

But Sir Humphrey declined the offer, explaining that his constitution was so delicate that he could only sleep upon a mattress made to his particular design 'and then only for a matter of hours, don'tcher know.' He would prefer to sit up until daybreak, which was only an hour or two away, in all conscience. As soon as there was sufficient light to travel in safety, he would return to Bath. 'Sir George will sit up with me and keep me company,' he said. 'We have matters to discuss, have we not?'

Sir George agreed that they had, secretly wishing that he could avoid it. So the fire was made up, Frederick retired at last and the two men were left to their vigil.

'A bad business,' Sir George said apologetically 'Would t'were not so. She'll be punished for it, I promise you.'

Sir Humphrey waved his long fingers. ''Tis of no consequence,' he said, easily. 'I cannot marry her, you understand, the fault being too public, but we have avoided a scandal which is nine-tenths of the matter.'

'If the actor don't blab.'

Sir Humphrey was sanguine about it. 'Oh, I dare swear he'll hold his peace,' he said, 'with such a prize to be earned. We need have no fear of that.'

'The folly of it!' Sir George grieved. 'The wretched iniquitous folly. I thought to make you my son-in-law and now her foolishness brings all to ruination.'

'Courage, sir,' commiserated Sir Humphrey. 'You have another daughter, have you not? And one, if I am any judge, too young and sensible for foolishness. How of a match there? With a suitable dowry, naturally.'

Sir George widened his eyes. 'A capital idea!' he said. Would your father approve, think'ee?'

Knowing how much the Bradbury money meant to his family and how necessary it was for him to many into it so as to buy off his creditors, Sir Humphrey was happy to assure his prospective father-in-law that the new arrangement would almost certainly find favour. 'There is much to be gained on both sides by this alliance,' he pointed out. 'Our two families being business partners already, and in no small enterprise, as I need hardly say.'

'A capital idea!' Sir George repeated. His relief was so intense that for the moment he couldn't think of anything else to say.

Dawn was staining the lower edge of the window glass with green light, the trees and shrubs in the garden were gathering dark shape, and down below them they could see the first faint gleam of river water. Time to be on the road, I believe,' Sir Humphrey said.

So Barnaby was roared for and Morgan roused from the shelf in the kitchen where he slept. A jug of water was brought to both gentlemen to cleanse their hands, and cold beef, bread and beer provided to sustain them. Bamaby was sent to wake Ariadne.

She came into the drawing room ten minutes later, dressed and neat, quiet and withdrawn. She sat down when told to do so, took a dish of tea when ordered, but she didn't speak and she didn't look up. She might have been a statue or some life-sized mechanical toy. Neither of the men paid her any attention at all. They were far too busy discussing the excellent conversion of the *Yorick* and the fire power of her guns.

'Force, sir,' said Sir Humphrey. 'That's the only language they understand.'

Twenty-six

Suki Brown was busy dicing potatoes by the area window in the kitchen at South Parade when she was distracted by the sound of grinding wheels and looked up to see Ariadne's tattered yellow pumps stepping down from Sir George's carriage. She was instantly burning with pity' for the poor lady and furious at Farmer Lambton.'Tis all his fault, she thought angrily. They'd never have found her so soon if it hadn't been for him a-telling tales. I knew 'twould be so.

Alerted by the sound of the carriage, the rest of the servants came to join her at the window. 'Well that's put paid to that old actor feller then,' Cook said cheerfully.

The scullery maid had her nose pressed against the pane and was squinting upwards to get a better view. They'm a-coming in,' she reported. 'I wonder what's happened.'

'Perhaps they fought a duel,' Bessie suggested ghoulishly, 'and the master killed 'im. What d'you think?'

He certainly sounded fierce enough. They could hear him in the hall, bellowing like a bull, 'Hermione! Deuce take it! Hermione! Where is the woman?'

'Oh, go on then,' Cook said, as the three girls looked hopefully at her. 'There'll be no peace till you've found out what's happened.'

So they crept up the back stairs to eavesdrop.

Lady Bradbury was skimming towards the foot of the stairs, one lace-edged hand gliding over the banisters and her new sack-back gown billowing behind her like a sail, and she was scolding furiously. 'You wicked, wicked girl! How you could do such a thing to your *dear* parents who so *truly* love you? 'Tis past my comprehension. Ain't you ashamed to be so wicked?'

'You'll get no answer, ma'am, so you may as well spare your breath,' Sir George said, brusque with anger and incomprehension. 'The wench is dumb.'

'How? Dumb?' her mother demanded. 'What nonsense! She will speak to her mother.' She put out her hands to turn her daughter towards her, shaking her angrily. But Ariadne stood as still as a stone, mute and apart, looking into nothing. She might as well have been a corpse.

'Ain't spoke a word since I found her, and that's the truth of it, damme,' Sir George said, scowling at her.

Crouched behind the servants' door, Suki and Bessie looked at one another in amazement. She couldn't be dumb, surely. Something terrible must have happened. But before they could say anything, they heard Mr Jessup coughing in the passageway below them, so they had to tiptoe back to the kitchen.

'We shall know about it soon enough,' Bessie said. 'That I'm certain sure, for 'tis mortal bad to be struck dumb.'

Above their heads, Hermione was still holding Ariadne's unresponsive shoulders, peering into her empty face. Now she looked more anxious than angry. What ails her?' she said. 'Is she hurt? Is that it?'

Sir George was on his way upstairs, bellowing for Jessup.

'If she is ill,' Hermione called after him, 'we must send for a surgeon.'

'You may do as you please, ma'am,' he called back coldly, pausing briefly in his ascent. ''Tis all one to me. I've done my part. If 'twere the old days she'd ha' been whipped, which she would do well to remember. She deserves as much. I wash my hands of the whole affair. I shall change my clothes, whilst they're attending the horses, and then I'm off to the tables.' A spot of gambling would cheer him. ''Od's bowels! It makes my blood boil to look upon her!'

'My heart is palpitating!' Hermione complained to his disappearing back. 'I shall run distracted!' But he took no notice of her, even though she put her kerchief to her forehead and closed her eyes. When she opened them again, Jessup was standing politely before her, so she recovered herself and became practical. 'Pray run for Mr McKinnon,' she ordered, 'and send Hepzibah to me, and the wet nurse to attend to Miss Ariadne. You see how things are with us. We are too ill to stand.' And she sailed away towards her boudoir, with Ariadne walking stiffly and obediently behind her.

Just at that moment, Melissa returned from the baths, brick red and sweaty inside her steaming chair, and was carried into the hall, ready for Hepzie to assist her to her bed and the full sweat she needed which had now begun.

'Mamma!' she called petulantly from the damp side window. 'Pray send Hepzibah to me directly!'

'You must make shift for yourself,' her mother said, waving her kerchief weakly in the general direction of the chair. 'Your sister is returned and we are all too ill and upset for words!'

''Od's blood!' Melissa said angrily. 'It's come to something when a person may not be treated civilly in a person's own house.' She struggled out of the chair on her own, and began to puff up the stairs after her mother, very red in the face and dripping water from her bathgown as she went. 'I see I must be a runaway if I wish to be treated civilly. Those who stay at home and behave with propriety are not worth the candle in this world.'

But at that point, her father put his red face over the banisters to address her and what he had to say stilled all complaint and even startled her mother to silence. 'Ah!' he boomed. 'Melissa! You're there, are yer? You're to marry Sir Humphrey de Thespia. What d'you say to that?'

As a proposal, it lacked a certain style but Melissa was enchanted by it, thrilled, uplifted, and cattily rewarded. She had stolen her sister's fiance, which was triumph enough, in all conscience, and all without lifting a finger or batting an eyelid. And now she would be the first daughter to many, which meant that Ariadne would have to dance at her wedding while she would be the queen of the hour. And she would have a rich husband and fine clothes and a diamond necklace and the best food and a town house and a country house and a carriage with a coat of arms...

'I am honoured, Papa,' she said and dropped him a dripping curtsey to prove it.

Her father was as pleased with her answer as she'd been with his question. 'That, mark'ee, Lady Bradbury,' he said, 'is the proper way for a daughter to behave. Would you had two who knew it. 'Tis settled then, Melissa. You're engaged to dine with him at Lady Fosdyke's this afternoon.'

Hermione was thinking fast. 'Twas wondrous to know that her alliance with the great de Thespia family was still intact, but there would be all manner of problems to be solved. She would have to write to her own family, for a start, with some acceptable reason for the change of bride, or they would sense a scandal and refuse to attend. She could say 'twas a love match, perchance, that none had the heart to deny. She could stress Ariadne's generosity in standing aside for the happiness of her sister.

She was so busy with her thoughts that she forgot to applaud her younger daughter, who had to remind her. 'Mamma, am I not worth congratulation?'

'Indeed,' she said, remembering herself, 'my dearest child. 'Tis a most happy match and one that does you honour.'

'I shall need a lady's maid,' Melissa said, remembering how her sister had been treated.

'You shall have Hepzibah.'

'And new gowns?'

'As many as you wish.'

Melissa looked smugly at her sister's unresponsive back. 'And I suppose Ariadne will have to dance at my wedding?'

It was a minor detail to her mother. 'Yes,' she said, vaguely. 'Belike. But first we must cure her of this present infirmity.' And she led them both upstairs.

Below stairs, the household was in such uproar that there was barely time to pass on the gossip. The bells in the kitchen rang like church chimes, jumping and jangling until Cook declared they'd shake the board off the wall if they didn't give over. Barnaby was dispatched to fetch a barber, Jessup had gone for the surgeon, Hepzie was told to make a cold compress, Bessie was required to provide hot water, fresh towels, sal volatile, a clean chamber pot, and a complete change of linen for Sir George — in that order and with considerable difficulty, for Benjy was beside himself with so much traffic on the stairs and was soon running berserk, nipping ankles and barking himself into a froth.

Suki went straight upstairs to Miss Ariadne. She found her sitting on her bed as still as a statue and totally mute. Her eyes flickered towards her friend, but without recognition, and there was no expression on her face at all. The sight of her was so upsetting that it was all Suki could do not to cry. 'Tis my fault, she thought. I was the one what spoke of choosing your own lover. I told her 'twas the proper thing to do. She remembered Ariadne's excitement and the pretty flush on her cheeks as she'd leant towards her lover. 'I have followed your teaching to the letter.'

'Oh, Miss Ariadne,' she said. 'I'd do anything to help 'ee. Truly I would.'

'An infusion of sage tea, perchance,' Lady Bradbury said from the doorway. She was holding the cold compress delicately on to her forehead with one lace-trimmed hand but her face and her voice were distracted.

''Tis a comfortable drink, ma'am,' Suki said, still watching Ariadne, 'with no harm in it.' And no response to it either.

'I believe my daughter is bewitched,' the lady said. 'How I shall sustain this suffering I truly do not know. Oh, would Mr McKinnon were here. He is taking an unconscionable time, is he not?'

Mr McKinnon had been at the Cross Baths attending a dowager, and so he made less speed than he could have wished. It was nearly half an hour before his bearers finally brought him to South Parade. But he made up for his tardiness by elaborate manifestations of concern and the provision of three different medicaments in as many minutes; all for Lady Bradbury, naturally, since she held the purse strings. She was prescribed a restorative powder for her weakened pulse, asafoetida for her swooning fits, and a blackcurrant cordial to rouse her spirits. But Ariadne was a puzzle, as the gentleman himself confessed with much learned shaking of his fine new full-bottomed wig. 'An enigma, ma'am, I'll own it. But we will accept this case, fear not. Tis a challenge.'

'We?' Hermione queried faintly, sipping his restorative.

'Indeed so, ma'am,' the doctor said, assuming his most deeply concerned expression. 'Tis a case will require the combined wit and learning of at least... three... doctors. I have never seen the like, ma'am.' Then as he foresaw a possible loss of faith in his judgement, he continued quickly. 'A similar on one occasion, which I do assure you was treated to a most successful conclusion. Most successful. How'somever, since there are differences in this case — the lady being, shall we say, mute — I do maintain we should proceed with the utmost caution. The utmost caution. I will do myself the honour, ma'am, to call upon you again before dinner, with two of my esteemed colleagues. Did you wish me to attend upon your husband whilst I am in the house?'

Within an hour, Sir George had changed his linen, taken tea and a clyster and departed for the gaming house, leaving the foetid smell of his relief behind him.

Within an hour and a half, Mr McKinnon had come back again with his two opportunist colleagues, one short and obsequious, bearing a jar of very fat leeches from Bordeaux, the other tall and taciturn with a lancet protruding from his top pocket.

They examined their intriguing patient pompously and at length, conversing with one another throughout in hushed whispers and incomprehensible terminology. A sample of her urine was considered by daylight and candlelight; skin was scraped from her arm and hairs plucked from her head; they counted her pulse and measured her tongue and looked down her throat and took swabs from her nostrils. Finally they declared themselves of the opinion that she was suffering from one of three possible ailments, the Straight Fives, the Rising of the Lights, or Hockogrocle, and that all or any of the three could prove fatal unless professionally and expensively treated.

'We do most seriously advise, dear lady, that treatment be commenced without delay,' Mr McKinnon said.

'Oh, what calamity!' Hermione said. 'My husband and I are due to dine with Lady Forsdyke within this half hour. What is to be done?'

The doctors, being professional men, were equal to such a challenge. Without question, Lady Bradbury should honour her social commitments, they said. Her poor sick daughter could be left quite safely in their care, providing a trustworthy servant could be found to sit with her. They would commence the treatments that very afternoon. There was not a minute to lose.

So Suki was called from the nursery to be witness to Miss Ariadne's medication, and a thoroughly unpleasant, cruel business it was. On that first afternoon, they bled her until her cheeks were white and then prescribed Tartar Emetic mixed with a slimy broth made from the strained fluid of twelve boiled snails. Ariadne was heaving after the first mouthful, but they forced the whole noxious mess down her throat with a funnel, and were delighted when she was monstrously and strainingly sick. Then they gave orders that she was to be kept in bed until their return in the morning, when they were perfectly confident that speech would be restored to her, and left her, panting, exhausted and mute, to recover as well as she could.

Suki helped her into bed and covered her cold limbs with blankets. Then she went off to fill a warming pan. She was furious at their cruelty.

'Poor soul!' she said to Cook as she heaped the copper pan with hot coals. ''Tis torture no less, and more than any mortal soul deserves.'

'Aye, but do she speak?' Cook said. 'That's the aim an' purpose on't.'

'No, she doesn't,' Suki said. 'An' no more would I, if 'twere done to me. Tartar Emetic indeed.'

The next morning the torturers returned with a fresh supply of leeches, and a strong clyster. But despite all their efforts, Ariadne's silence was unbroken by speech, although this time she groaned as she was sick, and this they proclaimed to be encouraging progress.

Suki was angrier than ever at such foolishness. The poor soul can hardly swallow tea,' she said, 'an' here they are a-pourin' poison down her throat. They'll send her to her grave, that's what they'll do. I wonder they can't see it. What she'm a-suffering from is a broken heart. Poor lady.'

But the doctors continued to treat the Rising of the Lights and Hockogrocle.

On the fourth day of their administrations, since neither clysters nor emetics, nor bleeding by leech, nor even prolonged cupping had so far had the desired effect, they decided that the time had come for them to apply the very latest and most efficacious treatment of galvanization. They arrived that afternoon with so much equipment that they needed a coach and horses to haul it to the door. The first leather case contained four identical glass bowls, which were taken carefully out of their wrappings and stood upon the carpet. Jessup and Bamaby were commandeered to lift Hermione's day bed into the air and lower it inch by inch until all four legs were inside their own glass container. Then the miraculous instrument itself was unpacked and set on a table beside the bed. It was a very curious instrument, consisting of a brass cylinder with a neat wooden handle attached to it, a large rod made of golden amber and a collecting jar, coated in lead and lined, impressively and expensively, with no less an article than gold leaf.

Jessup and Bamaby were impressed by it and Lady Bradbury looked at it with suspicious interest but Ariadne ignored it as if it was of no consequence whatever, and when she was ordered to lie down upon the day bed, she did so meekly, her face still blank. Hepzie and Suki were instructed to stand one on each side of her and be prepared to hold down her arms, should she start to struggle. Then the machine was set in motion, and while Lady Bradbury watched, the amber rod was held against the cylinder while the handle was rotated vigorously by Mr McKinnon. To Suki's mistrustful eye, the whole thing looked sinister in the extreme, but even she wasn't prepared for what followed.

The rod was suddenly plunged against Ariadne's face. Blue sparks flew into the air, and there was a sizzling noise, like a snake striking its prey. Ariadne arched her back, and groaned as though she was falling into a deep swoon. Then her arms and legs began to twitch, horribly and uncontrollably, like death throes. Her eyes were open but completely without sight, and when the rod was finally taken away they remained open and her limbs went on twitching but she was deeply and terrifyingly unconscious.

'What have you done to her?' Hermione shrieked. 'My poor child! You've killed her!'

'Calm yourself, madam,' Mr McKinnon said. ''Tis all as it should be. The nature of the treatment is — '

But Hermione wrasn't listening to him. She was on her knees beside her convulsive daughter, slapping her pallid cheeks and weeping, 'Arouse yourself! Wake up! Oh, I prithee wake! Ariadne, my dear, my dear, wake I beg you!'

The taciturn doctor endeavoured to take his patient's pulse, and Suki noticed that even he was looking a little anxious, despite his professional calm. Ariadne went on twitching.

'I suggest *we* cover the patient and await the return of consciousness, which will, I can assure you, dear lady, bring the power of speech within its train,' Mr McKinnon said, ebullient as ever. And Ariadne turned her head and wras violently sick all over his breeches.

At that, and to everybody's relief, all three medical men decided to retreat. Jessup and Barnaby were dispatched to escort them to the door, and Hepzie and Suki were sent to the kitchen for cloths and warm water to clean up the mess. But it was many long minutes before Ariadne groaned her wav back to the w'orld, and then she was so weak she couldn't raise her hands from the bed, even to have them sponged clean.

'Speak to me, child,' her mother begged. 'For the love of God, have pity. A word, that's all I ask. Just one word.' But Ariadne was still dumb. Tears welled from her blank eyes and washed across her nose and on to her pillow, but there was no answer, no recognition, no sound.

'How does she fare, think 'ee?' Hermione asked, wiping her daughter's clammy forehead. 'I am mortal afeard.'

'We shall recover her, ma'am,' Hepzie said. She was on her knees and busy with the scrubbing brush, but she knew the right thing to say.

But Suki was still too overwhelmed by pity and terror to consider her words. 'They could have killed her, poor lady,' she said heatedly. 'Them an' their galvanization. 'Tis quackery to my way of thinkin' an' more like to kill than cure. Why just look at the poor creature. She's no more strength to her than a babe new born. Show 'em the door, ma'am, and let's have no more on 'em.'

Hermione looked up at the flushed furious face beside her, thinking what spirit the girl had and how honestly she spoke. 'You may be right,' she admitted. 'Howsomever, Sir George would take it ill.'

'Sir George aren't 'ere,' Suki pointed out. The gentleman was out gaming again with his good friend Sir Humphrey. 'Beggin' your pardon, ma'am.'

Hermione stood up, and smoothed her wrinkled petticoat, and made a decision. 'She shall have a day's rest,' she said. 'The surgeons need not call again. You shall sit with her and keep her company and care for her. You will report to me if there is any change, you understand. Tomorrow she shall travel to Appleton and you with her. 'Tis quiet there.'

It was a turn of events that Suki hadn't anticipated and it didn't please her at all. She'd faced the fact that it was going to be difficult to ride into Bristol now that she was in Bath but if she were sent out into the country, it would be impossible. Worse still, how would he find her if he came a-searching? Appleton was more than fifty miles away. Oh no, she didn't want to be sent out there.

'How of the baby?' she asked. 'Should I not stay here with him?'

Hermione tossed the excuse aside with a flick of her long white fingers. 'He can travel with you,' she said. ''Tis a fine strong child and will take no harm of a journey.'

And at that she swept out of the room and into the necessary organization. Within half an hour, everything had been arranged. Suki's truckle bed and William's cradle had been carried upstairs and installed in Ariadne's bedroom, and the dog cart was ordered for six o'clock the next morning.

It annoyed Suki to have been so easily overridden but, once the beds had been moved, there was nothing for it but to comply. Somebody had to look after poor Miss Ariadne and she was the best and most proper to do it. That couldn't be denied. So she made up a good fire — because the day had been chill with mist — took plenty of candles, the smallest kettle and a selection of cold meats from the kitchen, and persuaded Lady Bradbury to allow her a teapot already primed with tea in case her daughter required refreshment during the evening. Then she suckled William to settle him for the night, put him sleepily to bed, and settled down to her vigil, watching from the window as the house emptied.

First to leave were Sir George, Lady Bradbury and Melissa who were off to the masked ball at the Assembly Rooms, with Hepzie smirldngly in attendance, then the local servants went, tired but well laden and, after them, Mr Jessup, coughing like a steam engine and with his hat pulled well down over his eyes. Soon the parade was quite empty and the sky had darkened to a most oppressive grey and there was nothing to do except draw the curtains and light the candles and sit by the fire and wait. William's little silk coat had a tiny tear in the sleeve, so she took her needle and thread from her pocket and began to mend it, holding the fine work close to the candle.

There was hardly a sound in the room, except for the quiet rasp of her needle, the flicker of the coals, and William's gentle breathing, so when Ariadne began to cry the sound filled the room. Suld put down her mending at once and rushed to comfort her.

'Don't cry,' she urged her, flinging her arms round her poor

friend. ''Tis all over. I promise'ee. Plaguey doctors to hurt 'ee so! Twas more than human flesh and blood could stand. Well, there's to be no more on't. They'm all dismissed. Every plaguey one of 'em. You aren't to be tortured no more.'

'Oh!' Ariadne said, leaning her head against the comfortable warmth of Suki's bosom. 'I wish I were dead. I wish I were dead. I am shamed and ruined and sore and nobody loves me, nor is ever like to. I wish I were dead.'

It didn't surprise Suki to hear her speak, but she was shocked by her despair. No wonder the poor lady played dumb.

'He said he loved me more than all the world.' Ariadne wept. 'Twas a lie. He said we should never part. I should be his for ever. I was his one true love in all the world. 'Twas a lie, a lie! I wish I were dead!'

Suki was full of tender concern. Something must be done to comfort the poor lady. Some creature comfort maybe. 'Could'ee fancy a dish uv tea?' she suggested. 'Or are you still too sore? They pulled you about most cruel, plaguey critturs.'

'Aye,' Ariadne said, as though she was surprised to be saying it. 'I *do* thirst.'

So the tea was made and Ariadne trembled out of bed and sat by the fire to drink it, and was tempted to a little custard cup, which Suld assured her would 'slide down her poor throat, smooth as silk'. And presently she talked again, at great length and weeping freely but gradually with more sadness than passion. Soon Suki had heard the full story of courtship, proposal and betrayal.

'I shall never love again,' Ariadne mourned, gazing at the fire. 'The game ain't worth the candle. 'Tis a brave thing to vow to marry where you love, but if love ain't returned you are lost before you begin.'

'There were still some men of honour in the world,' Suki told her earnestly. They am't all rogues and vagabonds. Some has a most tender concern for their womenfolk. Captain Jack was always — '

The use of the past tense alerted Ariadne to question. 'Have you not found him?'

Suki made a grimace. 'Not yet,' she confessed. 'He'm still at sea. Due back any day, so they says at the shipping office.'

That was a surprise. How bold this girl was! 'You've been to the shipping office? All the way to Bristol?'

'Aye,' Suki said, grinning at the memory. 'And bought a horse there.'

So that story was told and much enjoyed. By the end of it, Ariadne was still sad, but had recovered enough to be philosophical. 'What is to become of us?' she said, half resigned and half teasing. 'My lover faithless, yours at sea. Could we look into the future what *should* we see?'

'There's only one I know what could do that,' Suld told her, 'and that's Old Sheena, the gypsy. She read your palm outside the theatre. Do you recall? And Miss Melissa's too.'

Ariadne remembered very well. 'Aye, she did, and saw uncommon clear.'

The idea struck them both in the same instant. 'How if we were to call her here?' Ariadne said. 'Would she come, think 'ee?'

'If we offered her silver,' Suld said knowledgeably. 'She'm uncommon fond of silver.'

'We would need care,' Ariadne said. 'None must know of it.' The thought of arranging something so deliciously illicit was cheering her visibly, bringing colour to her cheeks at last. How angry her mother would be if she knew what they were planning.

'I shan't breathe a word,' Suki promised her. ''Twould be our secret. Could you keep the door?'

'Of course. There's silver in my petticoat. Fetch me scissors and I will unpick the pocket.'

Which she did and found three silver groats and two pennies. Seconds later, Suki was on her way to the theatre.

She reached it just as the doors were being opened and the first rush of warm, stale, evocative air emitted, and a potent mixture it was, of candle wax and greasepaint, dust and orange peel, strong perfumes and stronger sweat. For a second, she stood beside the steps remembering how happy she'd been sitting in the stalls beside her darling, all those long months ago. But there was no time to stand about. Sheena must be tempted before the playgoers could dominate her.

She was in her usual place at the top of the stairs and there was already an eager crowd around her, but it was easy enough to push to the front and a simple thing to catch the gypsy's eye.

'Here's a groat says you would be welcome at a lady's house for a private consultation,' Suki said, revealing the coin tucked under her fingertips. 'And more to come when 'tis given.'

Sheena looked at her shrewdly. 'Was that one consultation or more, gel?'

'Two,' Suki said, feeling that this answer might be more acceptable.

'Palm or cry stal?'

'Both, mayhap.'

Sheena flicked the corner of her long shawl across her shoulder and removed her attention from all the other eager hands stretched out towards her. It was a bargain.

The parade was very dark and completely deserted. As the gypsy followed her down the area steps, Suki wondered whether Ariadne would have the strength to come down and open the door to them. But there she was, and with a pretty flush on her cheeks. 'Come in! Come in!' she said to Sheena. 'You are welcome here.'

They climbed the back stairs like three shadows and opened the door quietly to the warmth of Ariadne's room. She was obviously feeling a deal better, for she had placed the card table before the fire, with an armchair on one side of it for Sheena and the nursing chair on the other for herself. It was a cunning arrangement, Suki thought, worthy of her mother, for it put the gypsy on a higher level than her client, and that was both flattering and suitably deferential.

The crystal was agreed on and a second groat expended, and Sheena put her hand under her apron and produced a small globe of grey glass, clouded with what appeared to be vapour of some sort. She set it in the middle of the card table and held it between her hands as though she was warming it, the bells at her wrists whispering softly as she moved her fingers.

'I give you warning, young miss,' she said, 'my sight is uncommon clear tonight. I'ent to be trifled with.'

'I do not trifle, I assure you,' Ariadne said earnestly, leaning forward and looking up into the gypsy's dark face.

'Pain,' Sheena said. 'Sorrow. Tears. A great love lost, or missing or both. For here is money a-plenty, but not thine, aren't that right? And here's a handsome face, turned quite away. Such heaviness. Such sorrow.' The clouds in the crystal were shifting as though they were in the sky, and Sheena's face was taut with concentration. 'It changes. I can see nothing. Only heaviness. And tears are falling.'

'True. All true,' Ariadne told her. 'Would 'twere not.'

'Now here's a sea journey,' Sheena said. 'Much water. A long sea journey. Very long. To the Indies, I'll be bound, for here's a storm, and white sand, and water full of bright fishes, and here's sea under moonlight and now blue sea and weed and sails becalmed. Oh yes, a very long journey, my pretty.'

'I know of no such journey,' Ariadne said. 'But it *is* possible. My father has plantations in the Indies.'

This was no news to Old Sheena. 'Spare no tears for what is lost and gone,' she intoned, still gazing raptly at the crystal. 'An old love lost, a new one found,' and she flicked a rapid glance at her client to see how she was doing. 'Here comes the face again, young missy. And a fair fine handsome face, set between curtains of some heavy red stuff. Not a window, that I'm certain sure. A theatre, could it be?'

'Oh yes. Yes,' Ariadne wiiispered. 'What of the face? What can you see?'

'Dishonest,' the gypsy said firmly. ''Tis a fair face but a hard heart. Here's greed under that smile, and money in that hand. Woe to his black heart, I say.'

'Amen!' Ariadne agreed. 'Can you see more? I would know more if I could.' Her tone was almost humble, her face pleading.

But the gypsy seemed to have finished. 'Well, as to that,' Old Sheena said, 'I can't say. See how the clouds thicken.' And it was true. They could see swirling shapes filling the little globe. 'No. No. There is no more to see.'

Suki would have loved to have offered her palm, for she felt sure that the sea journey was the one the Captain was making at that moment, but the gypsy was already standing up and wrapping her shawls around her head and shoulders. She was looking around her in the most peculiar way, her nostrils flaring almost as though she was smelling the air. The firelight made flickering patterns on the brown skin of her forehead and the long hoops of her earrings glittered as she turned her head from side to side. 'Change!' she said suddenly. 'That's what 'tis. I 'ent felt it so strong in many a long year. There'm change a-coming.'

Her words were so unexpected and so dramatically delivered that they made the hair rise on Suki's neck. Ariadne looked as though she'd been bewitched. The room was full of pulsing shadows and redolent with the gypsy's heavy, oily scent and the strong smell of wood smoke that rose from her clothes. But she looked so fierce, they daren't question her, and presently she left the room without another word. Suki had to run after her to see her off the premises.

'What do 'ee think?' Ariadne asked the minute she returned. 'Did she speak true?'

''Twas likely,' Suki said cautiously, because she was still feeling distinctly disturbed.

'How well she described Mr Clements. A black-hearted lover. How could she know it?'

'Change is a-coming,' Suki said. 'She had that to rights and no mistake, for we'm off to Appleton in the morning.'

'Would twere change for the better,' Ariadne said sadly.

'We'll make it so,' Suki promised. 'We'm young yet and the world is wide.' There were voices in the street below. 'Milady's back,' she reported from the window. 'Shall you speak to her now?'

'No,' Ariadne said firmly. 'I shall not. She ain't worthy of speech. Besides,' and she assumed Old Sheena's tone and manner, ''twould take a powerful amount of spirit, that would.'

Twenty-seven

On the other side of the wide world, the *Bonny Beaufoy* lay at anchor just off the coast of Nevis, rocking gently on a peacock-green sea, while the island steamed and shimmered at a tantalizing distance. The last leg of their nightmare journey had been a long stinking slog. A raging fever had killed another seven slaves and four of the crew, and those who were left were too weary to clean the place properly — even with Jack to urge them on — so the smell of shit and vomit pervaded the ship. Their food stocks were so low and so badly contaminated that even the captain had been given short commons and, now, after one hundred and seventeen wretched days at sea, there wasn't a man aboard who wasn't frantic to get ashore. They ached to put fresh food in their bellies, clean air in their lungs, firm earth under their feet, an expanse of clear water between themselves and their stinking cesspit of a ship.

Like everyone else, Jack Daventry was standing at the ship's rail waiting for the local surgeon who was being rowed out from Jamestown — at an exasperatingly leisurely pace — to examine the cargo and give the ship a clean bill of health, or not as the case may be. He was uncommon well-dressed for a surgeon, in buff breeches, an embroidered waistcoat and a black silk jacket, fashionably unbuttoned but, as his boat gradually drew nearer, Jack could see that he wore his own hair and that it was shoulder length, sandy-coloured and very dishevelled, that his cravat was poorly tied and none too clean and that his tricorn hat was faded and stained, which detracted somewhat from his first appearance. Even so, he was plainly a man to be reckoned with, for he carried a gold-topped cane and an air of heavy authority.

Before he climbed aboard the *Bonny Beaufoy*, he took an old-fashioned nose cone from his medicine bag and tied it over his nose and mouth. He was instantly and ridiculously transformed, for it made him look like some huge ungainly bird with a brown beak and tufts of ginger feathers sticking out on either side of his hat.

'Can't be too careful,' he called up to Jack, his voice muffled as though he were shouting from the back of a cave. 'We can smell you on shore. D'you have no vinegar, damme?'

Jack explained that they'd been becalmed.

That didn't impress the surgeon. 'You didn't buy enough in the first place, that's the truth of it,' he said. 'Ah well, lead on. The sooner 'tis done, the sooner we can get back to civilization.'

His examination was perfunctory, which was just as well, for his extraordinary appearance struck terror into the slaves, who were already anxious at the new sounds and smells they were encountering, and had been preparing themselves for fresh horrors ever since the ship hove to. The women were so afraid of him that they cowered and shook and did their best to squirm away when he stuck his beak over the edge of the hatch and peered down into the darkness. But he had no intention of exposing himself to any infections below deck. He stayed where he was, muttering questions. 'Flux? No. Good. Good. Pox? No. Good. Good. How many did 'ee lose on the journey? Good. Good. That old feller's stone blind. Did 'ee know that? You'll not sell him.'

After half an hour, he was ready to sign the clearance paper and declare the ship fit to come into port. Then he turned his mind to business.

'Now sir,' he said. 'I need eight of your best for the Bradbury plantation. Six field hands and two for the house.'

Jack was surprised and annoyed by such a peremptory demand. 'I was told nothing of this, sir,' he protested. 'I was given written instructions from Mr Bradbury himself. I can show them to you if you wish. There was no mention of slaves being handed over for the plantation.'

That didn't concern the surgeon. 'Was there not?' he said easily. ''Tis no matter. Mr Bradbury knows of it. Mr Ferguson will sign for 'em. Those two big buck niggers in the corner would do for a start.'

Jack was in two minds. During the last days of the voyage he'd been checking the current price of slaves with Mr Tomson and Mr Reuben, who were the most knowledgeable men aboard, so he knew that his would command between two hundred and fifty and two hundred and seventy pounds each, so eight slaves translated into a deal of money to be handing over without argument. Over two thousand pounds. If he queried the arrangement, he would cause a delay and nobody would thank him for that. On the other hand, if he allowed it to go ahead, 'twould mean two thousand pounds less profit for the Bradburys and Mr Jedediah Smith, which wouldn't please *them*. The purser had been studiously polite in the last few weeks, but he knew that the animosity between them was still simmering and could be dangerous.

The surgeon took his silence as consent and went on choosing his slaves. It took him longer than his examination had done but at last he seemed to be satisfied.

'Bring 'em up on deck,' he instructed. 'Put 'em in irons. They can travel back with me. 'Tis but a short distance and I've a musket aboard to pacify 'em.'

Jack despatched two crew men to do as he required. 'Shall you see the captain, while you wait?' he asked, following protocol.

The surgeon had no desire to stay on the ship a minute longer than was necessary. 'No, no,' he said. 'We shall meet tonight at the banquet. To which you are all invited, by the bye. 'Twill be a fine occasion. A chance for you to meet your escorts.'

That was news to Jack, too.

'She arrived last week,' the surgeon said, pointing at the harbour. 'See her? The three-masted frigate. Fine ship, damme.

'The *Yorick*. Out of Bristol. First-rate fire power. You'll be safe enough with her.'

This time, Jack felt he could question. 'Safe?'

'Aye, sir,' the surgeon boomed, adjusting his nose cone. 'We're at war with France, damme. Have been since May. They took Minorca so 'tis said, on account of some pesky admiral who don't know one end of a ship from another. Left the place wide open for 'em, by all accounts. Name of Byng. Much good may it do him. Should be hung, drawn and quartered. That's my opinion of him. Howsomever, the end result is that we're at war at last. And not a minute before time. Pesky Frenchies! Now we can give 'em a dammed good trouncing, which they've long deserved. Good afternoon to 'ee, sir.' His slaves now loaded, he swung one buckled foot over the side and descended the ladder.

'He's a rum sort of cove,' Jack said to the bosun as the laden boat creaked away. 'You'd have thought he'd have seen the captain — for the sake of politeness, if nothing else.'

'There's no accountin',' Mr Reuben said, sucking in his cheeks. 'I likes the sound of that there banquet.'

In fact, the captain wouldn't have welcomed the interruption had the surgeon wished to see him because he was in the middle of an argument with Mr Jedediah Smith.

'You gave me your word of honour,' the purser was saying, 'as a gentleman, that he was to be clapped in irons the minute we arrived. The minute we arrived, sir.'

'Well now, as to that, sir,' the captain said, ''twas afore we were becalmed, as you'll allow, which have made a deal of difference to the circumstances and so forth. A deal of difference. They'm all a deal leaner than we'd intended, on account of the low state of our provisions and so forth. 'Twill take a week to fatten 'em for market, at the very least, as you'll allow, and then there's the hold to be scalded and so forth. I'd not wish my slave master in irons with such a deal of work to be done. And neither would you, I dare swear.'

The purser's face was dark with frustration. To have his wishes overridden was irritation enough, worse there were no arguments he could use to prevent it, for the captain seemed to have an answer to everything, worse still there was no higher authority that he could appeal to, so far from home. 'If I agree to this delay,' he said, 'I'd have you know 'tis against my better judgement.'

'You shall have him in irons the moment we sail,' Mr Tomson promised. 'You have my word on't. A slave master's so much waste of space on the return journey.'

Mr Smith looked at him sourly. 'He's been a waste of space, sir,' he said, 'since the day he turned his pistol on his betters.'

'Ah!' Mr Tomson said, turning his attention to the departing surgeon. 'They'm off. Now we can put into harbour. If you'll excuse me, sir.'

So the *Bonny Beaufoy* sailed into harbour at last, and Jack and the rest of the crew staggered ashore, unsteady on legs accustomed to the pitch and toss of the sea, and light-headed with euphoria at their sudden release. It was like walking into paradise, for the air was warm and clean and scented with spices and the entire island lush with trees, most of them bearing fruit. There were branches bright with oranges, lemons and limes, and others dropping huge bunches of green fruits curved like scimitars; there were trees hiding an odd-looking golden fruit that they afterwards learnt was called a pomegranate; and all along the edge of the beach, a line of tall palms waved huge feathery fronds, shushing and whispering in the cooling air of an on-shore breeze.

There was a house slave waiting on the quay, who said he'd been sent to lead them to their quarters, and two more wilting patiently beside a two-horse carriage that had been sent to carry Mr Tomson and the purser. Behind them, more than a dozen slaves were waiting in the shade with seven huge barrels from which they drew coconut shells full of water for the newcomers to drink. And uncommon welcome it was, for they were parched with heat and waiting.

Jack noticed that all their new attendants were males, that they all wore blue striped cotton breeches and that they understood what was said to them. When he asked them where the new slaves were to be housed, they rushed to point the way to the slave compound, which was sturdily built with a high stockade to prevent escape and provide shade.

But bringing the slaves ashore took him a very long time, even though he had Mr Reuben and six of the crew to help him and Blue to translate his instructions. Being in a new situation renewed their mistrust and, although Blue tried to persuade them that no harm would come to them, they struggled when they were hauled from the holds and fought with all their strength to avoid being pushed down into the longboats. Once they were safely inside the compound, thirst drove them to obedience, but they were still dirty and afraid and smelled most vilely.

'We'll get 'em washed down tomorrow,' Jack said to Mr Reuben. For the moment, he was glad to walk away from them.

Their guide was still waiting for them on the quay and having ascertained that there were 'no more English a-coming', he set off at a brisk pace following the cobbled path uphill. They arrived at the plantation house out of breath and sweating but even Mr Reuben had to agree that it was worth the climb, for it was an impressive building with a view over the entire estate — from hillside to bay. And even though it was made of wood, it had all the refinements of an English country house, being two storeys high, with elegant shuttered windows, a deal of fine carving, and an imposing flight of stairs leading up to a long veranda and a front door which was the equal of any Jack had seen in London or Bristol.

'My eye!' Dickon said. 'They live like lords hereabouts, I see. Are we to stay here, think 'ee?'

Apparently not. There was another lesser building to the right and slightly behind the main house, which their guide told them was 'de gues' house' and to which he led them. It was a long single-storey hut, blessedly cool but confusingly dark after the blaze of sunlight outside. At first sight, it seemed to be full of slaves. Their guide led them to the long room which they were to occupy, and they were brought ewers of water and cakes of soap so that they could wash. They were shown the pallets on which they would sleep and the long trestle tables at which they were to dine. 'But not tonight, massas. Tonight is de banquet.' There were even, as they discovered when they began to clean themselves, small children sitting outside the door waiting to take their soiled clothes away to be laundered.

The thought of being well dressed and clean again lifted Jack's spirits at once. He was the first to strip, the first to pour water from the ewer, the first to pick up the soap.

'This is the life!' he said, as he scrubbed away the filth of the voyage. Oh, the pleasure of stepping away from the stink of his sea clothes, the joy of seeing his hands return to their normal colour. 'If the banquet is one half as splendid as the house, we shall dine well tonight.'

It was more splendid than anything any of them had ever seen and it began with two receptions, one on the lawn for the seamen, the other — to which Jack was invited — in a small front parlour for the officers of both ships. There they were served rum punch, sherry and canary wine and felt themselves uncommon fine dogs, and were greeted by the factor of the estate, who was a roughfaced Scotsman with broad shoulders and sandy hair, not unlike the surgeon to look at, but dressed like a lord, in shoes with silver buckles, green satin breeches and a brocade coat that was the very height of London fashion.

'Your sarvent, sirs,' he said as his guests were announced and made their entrances. 'Angus Ferguson, sirs. Uncommon pleased to meet you, damme.'

It wasn't long before they'd all been introduced to one another and were well on their way to a cheerful inebriation. Jack was back in his element, talking to everyone and instantly befriending the master of the *Yorick* and his second mate, who was called Jack Jerome and had, so he said, been 'born and bred in Brissol' and consequently knew all the more shady watering holes along the quay. They were a splendid pair of swaggering rogues and reminded Jack of Quin Cutpurse and the company of the road. It was quite a disappointment to him when they moved on to make small-talk with the purser. But 'tis the way in such gatherings, he thought, as he, too, moved on. There would be other opportunities to improve on the acquaintance. Now was the time to exercise the art of conversation. Within two paces he was talking to the three surgeons about the fevers common in the tropics, within two minutes he found himself discussing slaves and sugar crops with the factor and his wife.

'You've some fine cattle aboard, I'm told,' the factor said.

'Aye sir, I believe so. Eight of our best were chosen for this estate.'

'Yes indeed,' the factor said, but his voice was vague as if the matter didn't interest him.

Jack decided to push him a little. 'You've seen 'em, I daresay, sir.'

'Not yet. sir,' Mr Ferguson admitted. 'Twill wait till morning. I can trust Mr Mackie's judgement.'

This seemed a little suspicious to Jack. If I'd spent two thousand pounds on merchandise, he thought, I'd want to see it for myself and be sure of the bargain. But there was no time to pursue the matter further for at that moment a slave in off-white breeches and a snow-white wig appeared in the doorway to beat on the floor with an ebony cane and announce that dinner was served. So, still clutching glasses, they progressed from the press and noise of the little parlour into the candlelit splendour of a large chandelier-hung dining room.

At its centre was a sumptuous table covered in a white linen cloth and set for sixteen guests with elaborate glasses and a great deal of fine blue and white china. There were three plates for every guest, a medley of glasses by every set of plates, and so many heaped platters and steaming dishes in the centre of the table that they'd been placed rim to rim in order to find room for them all. Jack tried to count them and gave up after fourteen, having established that they were all beef of some kind and very well cooked. There were several roast joints: a rump and a chine in particular, a tongue curled and flattened and set about with herbs, a beef pie, steaming most succulently, a dish of tripe, another of marrow bones, even the cheeks, baked, eyes and all, and set side by side with a mound of minced beef between them and two large leaves curved on either side of them like ears. After the paucity of food aboard the *Bonny Beaufoy*, it was positively regal and, as soon as the first toasts had been drunk — to 'William Pitt, God bless him' and 'The sugar trade, long may it prosper — they set to with a will. And uncommon good eating it made.

For the first twenty minutes, conversation was limited to grunts, but once they had taken the edge off their hunger, their host turned them to the topics of the hour, and the French took a roasting as thorough as the one that had been given to the beef. While the story of the miserable Admiral Byng was passed along the table, and breeches were unbuttoned and wind passed, the remains of the feast were cleared from the table and the second course brought on.

To their amazement, it was a second banquet and as lavish as the first had been, with just as many dishes. There were potato puddings and meat pasties, a roast leg of pork, the shoulder of a young goat and an entire kid with a pudding in its belly, a sucking pig swimming in claret wine and flavoured with sage and nutmeg, a loin of veal with a sauce made of lemons and limes, a shoulder of mutton lying on a bed of dark leaves, three boiled chickens, four ducklings, eight turtle doves and three rabbits, spread across the dishes in which they'd been cooked with their skinned legs at full stretch as if they were running away. Which is what most of the guests thought of doing, for their sea-starved bellies were uncomfortably distended by the first course and the thought of chomping through a second made most of them feel decidedly nauseous.

Except for Jack. He was looking quizzically at the factor, wondering how he could afford such a costly feast. 'Twould tax the pockets of a prince and he was a mere servant, factor or no, yet there he sat, sprawled in his chair as if he were the prince himself. Did Mr Bradbury know of his opulence? Or was it done without his knowledge? Was he billed to provide it? Or did this man have other means?

The factor caught the tail-end of Jack's calculating expression. 'You've not seen such a spread, I daresay, Mr Daventry,' he said and there was a mocking edge to his voice.

'No, sir,' Jack said coolly, pleased that he was about to contradict the man. 'Quite the reverse. I've sat at many such tables in England. Too numerous to count. My grandfather was a duke, don'tcher know, and a leading member of the ton besides, so hospitable extravagance was expected of him. De rigueur, you might say.'

The information caused the stir he intended: Mr Tomson was surprised, Mr Dix envious, and Jack Jerome winked at him across the table, raising his glass in admiration.

Mr Jedediah Smith turned his head to speak to Mr Tomson from behind his hand. 'Insolent puppy,' he said, and mocked, 'His grandfather a duke indeed. And we are to sit here and listen to such nonsense. The man should be in irons.'

'I'm surprised you undertook such a voyage,' Mr Ferguson said, 'if that's the humour of it.'

'My family deplores idleness,' Jack told him easily, 'and a man must see the world, don'tcher know.'

'You don't fear the hazards of it then, Mr Daventry?' Jack Jerome asked.

'Life is a hazard,' Jack said, easily.

Jedediah Smith scowled at him. As you will discover, he thought.

'Good appetite!' the factor said, returning their attention to the food. 'Let's have all those glasses filled, if you please, Joshua!'

So his guests settled to their second repast and, with plenty of wine to wash it all down and endless toasts to give them pause for breath, most of them did justice to it, although they ate a great deal more slowly than they'd done when their appetites were keen. By the time they reached the third course, most of them were so befuddled with drink and rich food that they no longer knew nor cared what they were putting into their mouths, and simply spooned their way through custards and creams, cheesecakes, puff pastries, guavas, plantains, pineapples and water melons without pausing. The talk grew ribald and ridiculous, the belching louder and more extravagant. When they finally staggered from the table, it was past three o'clock in the morning.

'Uncommon fine banquet,' Mr Smith told his host thickly. Thank ee mos'... mos'... squisly. Mos' esqui...surlally.' He giggled. 'You know what I mean, damme!'

Even Jack, who'd always claimed a strong head for drink, was too confused to think. He managed to remove his clothes, and to check that his pistols were still in his locker but, after that, he fell across the mattress and slept as though he'd been knocked unconscious. His messmates shuffled in and out of the hut for the rest of the night, to piddle or to ease themselves by vomiting, but he slept on, groaning, and dead to the world. The sun was at full strength and directly overhead before he woke and then it was with such a sore head and such an overloaded stomach that it took an effort to creep from the hut. Then, and with shame, he remembered the slaves and realized that they hadn't been fed or watered since the previous evening. How could he have been so unfeeling? He set off to the stockade at once to attend to them.

To his relief, they were sitting in the shade of the high fences eating the broken meats of the banquet. Most of it was already sour, and a lot was rotting and high, but they were picking it over, hungrily, their hands full and their chins dripping with sauces and gravy. After a night away from them and an evening of good food and civilized living, the sight of them appalled him. They were an affront: filthy, naked, half-starved, covered in weeping sores. Most of them were so thin, he could see their ribs and the jutting bones of their haunches, and the children were pot-bellied and snotty, with a thick crust of rheum, crawling with flies, between their nostrils and their food-smeared lips. Savages, every single one. And at that moment, Blue looked up at him from the group to his left and greeted him with his familiar wide smile. 'Good morning, Mr Jack.'

He was caught between the revulsion that was still riding strong in him and shame at what he'd been thinking. Had he not stood on the deck of the *Bonny Beaufoy*, pistol in hand, bellowing that they were human? 'You must be cleaned,' he shouted, as if the volume of his voice would make amends. 'I cannot allow this squalor. 'Tis insupportable.' And he strode off at once to arrange for it to be done.

For the rest of the day, he took his charges down to the river, twenty at a time, with six musketeers to prevent escape, and stood on the bank while they rubbed all the encrusted filth from their bodies. And that evening he made sure that a stew was cooked for them with ground maize and fresh vegetables.

'How long afore they'm a-ready for sale?' Mr Tomson asked that evening.

'Ten days at the very least,' Jack told him. 'They're parlously thin. A fortnight would be my preference.'

'Twill take a week for to scald and load,' the captain said. 'So a fortnight 'tis. I shall send instructions for notes of sale to be printed and posted for two weeks tomorrow. I daresay we can wait so long, what do 'ee think, my hearties?'

'You can take as long as you likes over it, Mr Tomson.' Mr Reuben grinned. ''Tis all one with me. Some swabber'll find me employment, I daresay. Or if that aren't the humour of it, I can alius sit in the shade and rest my bones and drink a tot of rum or two an' wait for'em. As I sez to'ee,'tis all one with me.'

That was the general happy opinion round the table.

''Tis a fortunate island to be idle in, Mr Tomson, sir,' Dickon said. 'Women a-plenty, food a-plenty, grog a-plenty. What could a man desire more?'

In Jack's case, as he discovered before the fortnight was spent, it was action. The fittest of the slaves had been set to work and the holds had been scrubbed and scoured and sweetened with vinegar. The sugar was being loaded under Mr Smith's close supervision. The slaves were fattening visibly. There was nothing left for him to do but sit in the shade with Mr Reuben and drink rum punch but, as always, enforced idleness made him restless.

'I've a mind to take a look at the plantation,' he said to the bosun.

'You'll do it alone if that's the humour of it,' Mr Reuben said. 'I've no desire to go a-clambering about in this heat.'

'Nor no facility neither,' Jack teased him. But now that he'd thought of it, the excursion was imperative. 'Come, Blue. Let us see what can be seen.'

It was a long hot climb, for the Bradbury plantation was more than halfway up the hill, separated from its neighbour by a large banana grove, and the path that led to it was overgrown and in poor repair. The afternoon sunlight columned in upon them through the banana trees, sulphur yellow, muddy and voluptuous. The air was furnace hot and oppressed their lungs. Soon they were streaming with sweat and their skin had acquired a coating of thick sticky brown dust. Sugar dust, as Jack discovered when he licked his lips.

They pushed past fields of sugar cane, where teams of slaves stooped and sweated, hauling away the tangled undergrowth and hacking at the heavy canes with vicious-looking machetes as the sugar dust rose about them in clouds of sickly sweetness. The plants were taller than they were and the smell of their sweat in that enclosed steamy field was stronger than the scent of the crushed cane. It might be an uncommon fine island for idleness, Jack thought as he and Blue struggled on, but 'twas a fearsome place to work in.

Presently they came to the factory, which had been built in a clearing and consisted of a huge mill where the cane was being crushed, a stone gulley to cariy the juice from the mill to the shed for boiling down, and the shed itself, a long wooden structure with a roof but no walls, which was full of huge cast-iron vats in which the juice was being boiled. The heat from the fires was so intense, it made the very air buckle and waver. Slaves came in from the fields, bent double under the weight of the cane they carried. Some pushed and groaned as they turned the mill stone, others, streaming sweat, stirred the boiling sugar, their feet leaving black perspiration marks on the trodden earth as they moved from vat to vat. There were scores of foremen about the place, all of them carrying whips and using them remorselessly.

'Nothing like a whip to get some work out of 'em,' one foreman explained to Jack, nodding with satisfaction at the last back he'd striped with blood. 'They're lazy beggars, d'you see, sir, every man jack of 'em. They'd be idle if they could. That's a likely looking tyke you got there, sir. I never seen a nigger with blue eyes afore.' The blue eyes were transfixed with horror at what they were seeing.

'How long do they work each day?' Jack asked.

'All day and every day,' the foreman told him. 'Sun-up to sundown, you might say. They enjoys it. 'Tis all they're fit for.'

Jack was impressed by their stamina. 'I couldn't stand such labour for an hour,' he said, 'leave alone a day.'

'Ah, well no, sir,' the foreman said, 'a'course not. You're a white man. 'Tis different for the likes of us.'

'Tis the same prejudice, Jack thought, and he ventured a sly question to prove it. 'You don't think they are human as we are?'

'Human, sir?' The man laughed. 'Lord love 'ee, sir, a' course not. They're slaves.'

It was too hot to argue with the man — and too dangerous. 'I'd like to see their quarters,' Jack said.

They were out in the fields a mere three hundred yards from the factory, four long wooden huts, thatched with grass and set at right angles to one another to contain an inner square of trodden earth. There were three women slaves simmering a stew of some kind in another cast-iron pot in the middle of the square, and gossiping to one another as they worked, but otherwise the place was deserted.

Blue went leaping off across the compound to greet them. 'We speak!' he explained, glancing backwards at Jack as he ran. 'We speak!' And was swept up into the arms of the nearest women and hugged and patted and bounced until, to Jack's watching eyes, his head was little more than a blur.

After the cruel assumptions of the foreman, Jack found himself unbearably touched by the scene and had to walk away from it before he revealed what he was feeling. He could see what looked like another compound a few hundred yards into the cut field and one that was occupied, what's more, for he could hear murmuring voices, so he decided to investigate, more by way of giving himself something to do than out of any burning curiosity.

It was a walled stockade, but there were sufficient cracks in the walls for him to peer through. As he suspected, there were several men and women inside, squatting on the earth and talking to one another as they fed from a central bowl. It seemed to contain a porridge of some kind, for the food they were moulding in their fingers was meal-coloured and fairly solid, and he noticed that they were eating in a leisurely way, as if they had no real hunger. As soon as they heard him outside the stockade, they fell silent and looked around them apprehensively, and then he recognized who they were. Six men and two women. The slaves who'd been taken off the ship on that first day for use on the plantation. So why were they here? Why weren't they working with the others? They looked as though they were being fattened up, like the rest of his cargo. But why was that? Their fellows in the field were thin and hard at work. Eager to know the answers, he went straight back to the huts to find his interpreter.

It took quite a long time before Blue could discover what was going on in the other stockade, but eventually he returned to his master with some information.

'They Mr Ferguson's slaves,' he explained. 'You leave. Then they go Jamaica night-time. He sell them.'

It was a shock but not a surprise. That accounts for his wealth, Jack thought. Two thousand pounds plucked from our cargo without the least effort on his part and no capital outlay. The thought infuriated him. We sail halfway round the world, and bargain for 'em, and feed 'em, and clean 'em, and risk death by fever and flux to boot, and in he comes at the eleventh hour, cucumber cool, to take his cut and steal our effort from us. The man's no better than a common thief. Well, Mr Ferguson, sir, your days are numbered. I shall peach on you to Mr Bradbury the minute I set foot in Bristol. 'Does he indeed,' he said grimly.

'He got sugar, too,' Blue said. 'Massa Ferguson's sugar.'

It was almost predictable. 'Can they show me where 'tis?'

They could and did, although they led him to it guardedly, watching for the foremen at every step of the way. It was a large open-sided barn stacked to the roof with cane.

'You go,' Blue translated. 'Other ship come. He sell.'

'Is't done with every crop?'

Oh yes. Every crop. They were sure of it.

'The man's an arrant knave,' Jack said to Mr Reuben when he told him the full story over breakfast the next morning.

'He's grown uncommon thick with Mr Smith,' the bosun warned. 'I'd watch my back if I was you, with them two swabbers about.'

But, as it turned out, there wasn't time to watch anything. There wasn't even time to collect his belongings and return them to the ship. For as soon as breakfast was over, Mr Dix arrived to take him to the compound to examine the slaves, and less than an hour later, having seen them, pronounced them fit for sale. He was hard at work reloading them aboard the *Bonny Beaufoy*, this time remarkably easily, for improved food and better treatment had calmed the worst of their fears.

'Capital!' Mr Tomson said, when the last one was aboard. 'We've tide and wind favourable so we should be in St Kitts by nightfall and so forth. All in good time for the sale tomorrow, eh Mr Daventry? 'Tis all a-goin' accordin' to plan. Now we shall see what price they in like to fetch for us, which I hopes will be high.' The sale was a hideous business and if Jack hadn't been hired for the sole purpose of undertaking it, he would have cried off as soon as it began. But Mr Tomson and Mr Smith had come ashore to watch the proceedings and as he was the slave master and knew he would be paid accordingly, and, moreover, as he needed the money if he were to survive back in England, he would have to go through with it, despite his deepening misgivings. So he stood alongside the slave owners — detesting their gaudy clothes and their vulgar manners — and urged the value of his bewildered slaves, stressing how strong they were and how well they would work. He stood aside as they were prodded and pulled about and had their lips lifted with the end of horse whips and canes, so that their prospective purchasers could examine their teeth. Lighted candles were held between their legs to search for signs of the pox, and they were required to bend over to check that they hadn't been plugged against the flux.

They use 'em like cattle, he thought, as the females howled and were whipped for it, and the children clung to their mother's legs, wide-eyed with terror. The most that could be said for the occasion was that he'd made a good profit on his cargo. Almost immediately, he'd sold eight slaves to a local trader who was selling them on in Jamaica — the ten strongest males had gone for £285 each, and he'd even persuaded one of the slave owner's wives to buy Blue's mother and the talisman baby 'as a pair'. But when it was all over and the purchased slaves had been taken away, he was limp with misery and the shame of what he had done.

'What's to become of the ones that remain?' he asked Mr Tomson, for the old medicine man and a young slave who'd been deemed 'too skinny by half' were still standing in the slave ring.

'Leave 'em where they are,' the captain said. 'We've no use for 'em.'

He was shocked by such a callous reply. 'They will starve with none to feed them.'

'Aye,' the captain said, carelessly. 'Belike. 'Tis what mostly happens to refused slaves. They lives on the beach or in the market place and so forth. Some of the locals feed 'em, I believe, but most of 'em die off sooner or later. 'Taint our affair, as Mr Smith here will tell 'ee.'

The ominous pressure of his words wasn't lost on Jack Daventry, but he was too caught up in concern for his last two slaves to heed it. 'We cannot leave them here,' he said hotly. ''Twould be tantamount to a death sentence and I'll not have that on my conscience. We will take them back to the plantation.'

The purser's face was dark with gathering anger. ''Od's teeth!' he said. 'What now? Are we to change our entire plan of campaign to suit two naked savages? Is that the humour of it? Have sense, Mr Daventry. They are old and sick and they stink the place out. If 'twere a farm they'd have been put down long since.'

'Howsomever this ain't a farm, Mr Smith. Nor we farmers.'

'No, sir,' the purser said angrily. 'We are traders and your foolishness is losing us time and money. Have done with it and come aboard and let's hear no more on't.'

The young slave had slumped to the ground and was sitting with his head on his knees.

'No, sir,' Jack said, his jaw set. 'We'll not leave them here to die. They return with us.'

'No, sir. I am the master here and I say they do not.'

'I take responsibility.'

'You, sir, will take a cuff of my cane,' the purser bellowed. 'Od's bowels! Am I to be dictated to by a jumped-up jackanapes with no sense and no breeding? Your grandfather a duke! D'you take us for fools?'

Jack was stung. 'Tis gospel truth, Mr Smith, and I'll thank you to mind it.'

'Tis poppycock. And we'll hear no more on't. Come, sir. Aboard, if you please. The boat waits on us.'

Jack squared his shoulders. 'I'll not move without my slaves.' The purser was furious and decisive. 'Then you must be forced, sir. Seize him, Mr Reuben, if you please. Frogmarch, if necessary.' The bosun was embarrassed to be asked to arrest his shipmate but he obeyed orders, that being his trade. 'Best do as he say,' he said in Jack's ear. ''Tis a mean old swabber an' means to have'ee in irons. We don't want that.'

There was a pause as Jack considered whether or not to resist, the captain stood aside as if it were no concern of his, and the purser watched, tapping his breeches with his cane. Whatever is done here now, Jack thought, I shall answer for it. 'Tis too public for a brawl and I've lost the argument without my pistols. They'll be the first things I look for when I get back to shore. 'Twas folly to travel without 'em. I'll know better next time and no mistake. In the end, he followed the bosun aboard, scowling and furious but powerless to do anything else.

It was dark by the time the *Bonny Beaufoy* put in to the harbour in Nevis and as nobody, except Jack, had any urge to go ashore, the gangplank wasn't lowered. But the purser seemed to be in a good humour again, regaling Mr Dix with stories of the sale, and there was such an air of happy anticipation among the crew that it made him feel easy despite the dishonours of the day. So he decided to forget about his pistols for the moment. There would be time enough to collect them in the morning.

'We'll make our adieus at first light,' Mr Tomson said, 'check the cargo, water and so forth, and then we'll be off back to old England. How say'ee to that, my lubbers?'

They lit torches and gathered on deck to sit in the cool air under a yellow moon and sing sea shanties to the accompaniment of Dickon's wheezing accordion. 'For we've received orders for to sail to old Eng-er-land. And we hopes in a short time to see thee again.'

Twenty-eight

Jack was awake, dressed and ready for the day as soon as the sun rose the next morning. Blue was lying in his usual place beneath the bunk, dressed in his new striped breeches and fast asleep, but he woke at the touch of his master's hand, and scrambled to his feet, shaking the sleep from his eyes and declaring he was 'ready'. So they swung up on deck together.

There was an encouraging swell running out at sea and, even within the harbour wall, the *Bonny Beaufoy* and the *Yorick* swayed away from the quay as if they were eager to be off. Their movement reminded Jack of something he'd heard in a theatre once, 'they strain like greyhounds at the slip', and the words sang in his head as he and Blue set off for the gangplank and the retrieval of his precious pistols. Oh, he couldn't wait to get back to England.

The quay was awake, too, and busy. The last of the water barrels was being trundled aboard with much unnecessary heaving and shouting, and Mr Tomson was ashore, patting the ringlets of his beard as he conversed with Mr Ferguson, who had come down to supervise the loading of his parting gift, which was ten crates of newly picked fruit. It was in every respect the sort of scene common to any departure and one Jack had seen on several occasions since he joined the ship. Not worth notice.

Until, that is, he stepped off the gangplank to find himself instantly surrounded by half a dozen seamen from the *Yorick*, one of whom thrust a loaded musket into his chest.

He'd been holding himself in readiness for trouble of some kind, but he wasn't prepared for anything as sudden and as violent as this and the shock of it was palpable.

'How now?' he said, pushing the musket aside, and he tried to make a joke of it. 'Do 'ee take me for a villain, sirrah?'

'Aye, sir,' the purser's voice said. 'That being exactly what you are, sir. Clap him in irons if you please, Mr Cooper.'

'I think not, sir,' Jack said, turning to face him, 'since I have done nothing wrong to warrant it.'

'I think so, sir,' Mr Smith answered, 'since you are outnumbered, sir, and have no pistols about you to threaten us with. Let's have him shackled, Mr Cooper.'

'At your peril, Mr Cooper,' Jack warned him. 'I am related to a duke of the realm, I would have you know, and my family do not take kindly to rough treatment.'

The threat stopped Mr Cooper in mid-stride. He put out a hand to stay his fellows and looked across at the purser questioningly.

The man is mad,' Mr Smith said, scathingly, 'and may be ignored. Depend on't. He thinks slaves are our equals, if you ever heard the like. "Human like us." Ain't that the way of it, Mr Daventry?'

There was a roar of happy mockery. 'Hell's teeth! What sort of folly is that!'

'Human like us! He'm sea-crazed, damn his eyes.'

'Raving mad.'

'Send 'im to Bedlam, the dog!'

'Aye, sir, so 'tis,' Jack shouting to be heard above the uproar. 'Twould be plain to see But he was wasting his breath for they were surging forward to seize and bind him. No, dammit, he thought, you'll not take me without a struggle, and he drew his strength together to fight them, although he knew it was useless, for he was outnumbered six to one and a musket is a heavy argument. He deflected blows, ducked, punched, struggled from their grasp, until they clubbed him to the ground with their muskets, and then he kicked and writhed against the hands that were trying to force his ankles into shackles. 'Hell's teeth, sir! I'll not be treated so. I am a gentleman.'

The side of his face stung from their blows and there was blood in his mouth and his ears were singing with the power of his struggle. 'I'll not be treated so.'

But in the end he was trussed and bound, with his hands roped behind his back and leg irons locked about his ankles.

They frogmarched him up the gangplank and on to the *Yorick*, opened the hatch and flung him into the hold. The last thing he heard as he fell was the purser's gloating laughter and his voice shouting, 'The equal of slaves, eh Mr Daventry? Now see how well you like their lodging.'

The ignominy of it was so extreme that for a few seconds he simply lay where he'd fallen, with his head wedged against a sack of flour and his arms and legs spreadeagled, too stunned and defeated to speak. The hatch was closed with a clang, feet stamped away, darkness and dust settled around him, musty and full of menace. Od's bowels, 'twas not to be endured.

Anger invigorated him again. He was on his feet and raging in the darkness, in a surge of fury and hatred and impotence, acutely aware of everything around him, every sound, scent and sensation magnified as if his world had suddenly been writ large. He could hear sails being set above him, the capstan protesting, the slap of bare feet on the deck, and knew from the tone of the captain's voice that he was irritable and prone to flog. He could smell every article of the cargo, although he couldn't see beyond the nearest sack, from commeal to ship's biscuit, through every variation of meat, rank, salt and freshly killed pork, bacon, beef and goat. Everything was louder, more pressing, more immediate. Rats scrabbled past his feet, their claws as loud as rakes, the timbers creaked like the crack of thunder, every slap of wave against the hull was clear as a gunshot, and his leg irons burned his bare skin with every movement he made. 'I'll not be treated so, hell's teeth! I'm a gentleman. I'll not be treated so.'

Time was an irrelevance. There was no day, no light, no freedom, no justice. Just the need to roar, shriek, protest, demand redress. 'I'll not be treated so.' It was a very long time before he realized how futile it was. He *was* being treated so. No matter how loudly he roared, nobody answered. There was nothing he could do now but endure. He slumped back on to the sack of wheat, his bound hands behind him, and abandoned himself to weeping.

Presently, there was a shuffling sound somewhere to his left and he heard a soft voice calling his name. 'Jack! Mr Jack!'

'Blue?

The outline of Blue's face moved into his limited vision, a gleam of blue eyes, the line of a cheek. 'Yes, Mr Jack?'

The shock of knowing Blue was there was almost as great as the shock of being thrown into the hold. 'How did you get here?'

'I run. I come down before.'

The trust and affection revealed by such an action moved Jack to tears all over again. But this time, they were tears of elation. 'There is more human kindness in you, Blue,' he said, 'than in the entire crew of this ship. The entire benighted crew, 'Od rot 'em. Undo these ropes, will 'ee. Ah! That's better. They fell upon me like wolves, Blue, like ravening wolves. They pulled me and kicked me and beat me with muskets as though I were a dog. 'Od rot 'em, whilst you... You treat me as one human being to another, as a friend, nay more than a friend. What friend would risk life and limb for me in this hell-pit. I was right in everything I said and you bear it out. You are human as I am human. I cannot tell you...' And he wept again.

The child didn't understand more than three words from such a babble, but he sat beside his master in the darkness, untying the ropes that bound him and occasionally patting his arm for comfort, for now they were like slaves together in this place and touch was possible. And Jack was glad of his comfort for his rage told him how low spirited he was becoming.

Time passed. They felt the ship leave harbour and hit open sea and soon they were being thrown about as the vessel dipped and swung through the swell. From time to time, Blue whimpered as a particularly heavy wave sent them both lurching.

'Take heart,' Jack said, and this time it was his turn to comfort.

'Tis only the sea, Blue, and the stronger the sea, the sooner we shall be home.'

'Home? What is home?'

'My home, Blue. England. That's where we're going. And the sooner there the better. You shall be a free man in England. I'll see to it. Providing I'm a free man myself.'

The conversation was getting incomprehensible again. 'Master?'

Best turn to something easier. 'I am glad you are here with me.'

'I am glad also.'

Hours passed. And passed. And soon, what with the stuffy air, their own inertia and the rocking motion of the ship, they both slept. When they woke, they no longer knew whether it was night or day. The heat was stifling and there was a rat gnawing at Jack's shoe. He kicked it away, viciously, before he remembered that he was shackled, and the sharp movement tore the leg iron into his skin. The pain of it brought him to full consciousness. He realized that he was in urgent need of a piddle and struggled to his feet to find an empty corner of the hold.

As he was relieving himself, he heard footsteps above his head and rough voices shouting by the hatch. 'Come out! Come out Jack Daventry! We wants to see yer.' The hatch rose to reveal a strip of blue sky and the dark outline of three sailors, who were leaning in towards him, smelling strongly of sweat and rum. Am I to be a sport to these ruffians? he thought. But he straightened his breeches and swung out of the hold as well as he could for the encumbrance of his irons, calling to Blue to follow him.

'Hello!' one of the sailors said. 'What's this? We got a nigger aboard. We'll have some sport now, my lubbers.' He had a whip in his hand and raised it to crack within inches of Blue's hunched shoulders, grinning with delight at the pain he was going to inflict.

'Send for Mr Jerome, if you please, sir,' Jack said. 'This is my servant, come aboard with me, and we'll not be flogged or I shall know the reason why.'

'He'll know the reason why, wall he, lousy swabber?' the sailor mocked and this time he aimed the whip directly at Jack's head. He was quick, but not quick enough. Jack lunged forward, ignoring the pain of his shackles, to catch his fist, whip and all, before the blow could fall. Then he was under a pile of bodies, one trying to pin his arms behind his back, another flailing punches, a third kicking and yelling and there was nothing in the world except a confused blur of fists and faces, a roar of voices, struggle, and the pain in his ankles.

A whistle was being blown, sharp and commanding. Other voices were yelling, 'Get back you dogs! Stand clear or I'll have 'ee whipped.' Mr Jerome was standing barrel-chested and splayfooted before them, bellowing that he was to be obeyed.

'Feed 'un and get'un back below,' he roared. ''Od rot it, we've no time for this sort of caper. They'm less than a league away, damme. Clear the decks.'

His voice was shaking with emotion — fear, anger, agitation, pride — and his face was red as a turkey cock. Jack was instantly alerted. He saw that they were sailing in a more southerly direction than he would have expected, that there was no sign of the *Bonny Beaufoy*, that lookouts were in the rigging, decks cleared for action, gun crews standing ready. And he realized, wdth a rush of excitement and exhilaration, that they were heading for a sea battle and that, if he made a bold enough bid for it, he could be released from his shackles to join in the fight.

'You'll need *every* man jack, Mr Jerome,' he said, 'and I'm a man jack to equal any on board. Release me of these irons, sir, and give me a pair of pistols and I'll do you good service. I'm an uncommon fine shot and cool under fire.'

Mr Jerome looked puzzled. 'You'm on deck to be fed and watered, sir. No more. What folly's this?'

'No folly, sir. Believe me. An honest offer. You'll not get a better.'

''Twill be no sawdust brawl, sir. We fight the French.'

'Aye, sir, as I see.'

'How if you were to turn your pistols on me or the captain?'

Jack made a joke of such a suggestion, laughing, 'Not an eventuality, I give you my word as an honest gentleman. For what would I do then? I'm not like to jump ship in the middle of the ocean and you've enough firearms aboard to overpower me twenty times over, which is clear to any eye. Besides, why would a man shoot his fellows when there are Frenchmen to fire upon! They will be target enough for me or any man.'

The second mate was almost won over. 'I like the cut of your jib, sir,' he said, 'damme if I don't.'

'Then let it run, sir.'Tis sound British canvas all the way from Brissol.'

'Aye dammit, so 'tis. Very well then.' He turned to give orders to his men, who'd drifted way from his conversation, irked that he should be taking the part of a madman. 'Feed un, water un, take off those irons. No more brawling, mind, which apply to all of you. If there's any flogging to be done, I shall do it, an' I'll have the skin off your backs, mark'ee. When he'm fed, send to Mr Warwick for a pistol.'

They were puzzled and annoyed by such a change of tack and one of them was bold enough to protest. 'But he'm a madman, Mr Jerome, sir. That there Mr Smith, he told Mr Cooper. I seen it all. I was one what brought un aboard. He'm lunatic.'

'No, sir,' Mr Jerome told him. 'He'm never lunatic. He'm from Brissol same as me, sir. We have a different way of goin' about things. Tha's all'tis. Aren't that the truth of it, Mr Daventry?'

So Jack and Blue were given the remains of what appeared to be the mid-morning meal, handed a mug full of grog which they shared between them, and allowed down to the heads. By that time the ships that the *Yorick* was stalking were clear on the horizon — a merchantman, heavily laden, and a frigate under limited sail.

Jack's irons were removed. The *Yorick* made good speed, visibly closing the gap between herself and the French, the wind being in her direction. The weather was warm, the sky clear. All preparations had been made, even to the production of Jack's requested pistols, balls, powder and all. It was simply a matter of sailing and waiting. Tension and irritability increased. There was much chewing of tobacco, much contemptuous spitting, much prowling and shifting of feet, more and more lurid swearing. Only Blue and Jack were calm, the boy because he had no inkling of what lay ahead, the man because he was determined to be courageous.

By three o'clock that afternoon, they were close enough to see the rims of the frigate's cannon gleaming in their portholes and to watch the French crew trimming sail so as to give the ship more manoeuvrability. The English gun crews stood to, were told to hold their fire until the signal was given, licked dry lips as the *Yorick* bore down on her prey. Their own sails were trimmed. Ropes screamed. Canvas creaked. The sea hissed from their prow. The wait was interminable, particularly as they could now see that the French frigate was going about ready to aim her cannon.

When the order came to fire it was greeted with a whistle of relief and, as the cannon recoiled from their first roaring barrage, the crew gave a cheer. It was a moment of high drama and unalloyed glory. And was followed almost instantaneously by another of sheer terror as the French guns blazed fire from every port. For a few seconds the air between the two ships was full of hurtling missiles, then the first shots landed and a French mast was split, canvas afire and men screaming, and a ball whistled past Jack's shoulder and ripped a hole in the foredeck, as they bucked through waters grown choppy with activity and received another shot amidships as they steadied in the line of fire.

It was time for Jack to take up a vantage point if he were to make best use of his pistols. As Blue watched, he loaded each in turn, opened the flashpan, sprinkled in his powder — dry as a bone — closed the cover. Then he braced himself against the rocking of the ship, climbed the rigging, a pistol in each hand, and was ready. All he needed now was a prestigious target.

The cannons were being fired again. He could hear the thunder of their ricochet and the air was full of smoke and the smell of cordite. There was a stay falling below him, fire spurting red from the quarterdeck, a line of raised muskets gleaming, and a man's hand lying in the gunnel torn off at the wrist and still clutching a ramrod. The noise was more insistent than the pounding of African drums and heat rose with an intensity that Africa had never equalled. And there immediately below him was the French captain, white gloves neat in his epaulette, gold-topped cane elegantly in hand, directing operations and too good a target to miss. He cocked the first pistol, took aim and fired. For a few seconds, the flash completely blinded him, then the red mist of it cleared and, peering through the smoke, he saw, with a sense of total disbelief and amazement, that the captain had been hit and was lying on the deck, rolling in pain and clutching at his chest. What capital sport!

A voice yelled at him to 'Look out!' and glancing down, he saw a French musket levelled in his direction and, all instinct now, he swung his body sideways away from its trajectory. After that, things happened at such speed that there was nothing but smoke and noise and action. He flung the used pistol down into Blue's outstretched hands, cocked the second, turned, aimed, fired into a muddle of half-seen figures. Missed. Plague on it! Now he must reload. But before he could move, the first pistol was handed back to him, presented by the handle what's more, and he heard Blue's voice shouting 'Tis ready, Mr Jack!' and so he turned to fire again. This time he saw a musketeer staggering backwards, screaming and falling into the smoke. Then a volley of fire peppered the sail furled below him. Oh, he was an eagle, soaring in the rigging, picking off his prey with every shot. Change hands, exchange pistols, take aim, fire, the rhythm as easy as breathing. He recognized that the *Yorick* was changing tack, and swung further aloft to take up another position, roaring with excitement and exhilaration. He was magnificent, fabulous, invincible.

Then, suddenly, it was all over. The French frigate was turning, setting all the canvas she could muster, her mainmast split and her topsail in tatters, holed at the water line and yawing heavily, admitting defeat. The merchantman was left an easy prize, without a defender and little more than half a league away. The pistol in Jack's hand was still smoking but the battle was won.

There was a flurry of doffed caps, a growling cheer, voices bellowing orders but for a while he stood above it all, unable to move because he was shaking so violently that he had to cling to the rigging for fear of falling. Blue was looking up at him, calling 'Mr Jack, Mr Jack! You want more pistol?' but he hadn't got the breath to answer. 'Od's bones and brains, he thought, what a monstrous wonder it is to go to war.

'Bully for you, Jack!' Mr Jerome called up. 'As pretty a piece of shooting as I ever saw.'

Praise gave him back his breath. 'Shall we board the merchantman?'

'Belike. Stay where you are. We may need your good aim again.'

But as they drew near to the French trader, she hove to and flagged a message admitting defeat.

'Here's a thing,' the second mate said. 'She's to be took without a shot fired.'

The captain wasn't so sure. 'We'll not trust the swabbers,' he said. 'There could be trickery afoot an' I ain't about to be caught by it, damme.'

They approached cautiously, inching towards their enemy until they could see the patches on her sails and count the members of her crew who were lined up on deck. The captain stood apart from the rest and had a distinctly piratical air about him, with a red bandanna about his neck, a black patch over one eye and a tricorn tucked under his arm. But he answered soberly when Mr Jerome took the hailer to ask if he was prepared to surrender.

'Aye, sir. We'ave Engleesh aboard.'

They were so close to one another that there was little more than a foot of water between them. 'Have you indeed?' the second mate called. 'How many?'

The Frenchman considered. 'Twenty, thirty.'

'Where are they, dammit?'

'I show.'

The boarding party swung across, muskets slung across their shoulders and bristlingly alert but there were no tricks and no opposition. Watched by his enemies, the French captain led the way to the hatches, where, after a few fumbling minutes and some altercation with two of his officers, two dozen dishevelled men emerged from the hold, blinked in the sunlight and turned to wave their thanks to their rescuers. English indeed and part of the original crew of the ship.

'She was the *Mary Elizabeth* afore she was took by this 'ere load o' plaguey swabbers,' their leader explained. 'British ship. Out of Portsmouth. They took the officers ashore in the Windwards. We was pressed to stay on an' sail her on account of they was short of crew.'

It was a common enough practice. 'What's her cargo?'

Silks apparently. Some spices, which were scenting the air now that the hatch was open. Some ivory, although they couldn't say where it was stashed. 'Might be some gold. They was cagey about it but we was give a powerful escort, which do make 'ee wonder.' 'If there's gold, we'll find un,' Mr Jerome told him happily. 'Cheer up, me lads. We'm your escort now, which I daresay you won't object to, on account of we've sent your Frenchie off wi' grapeshot in her ears an' her tail atween her legs. Now I'm a-here, to captain the ship for 'ee. Choose me a crew, sir, an' I'll send the rest aboard the *Yorick* for safekeeping. Here's our other ship a-coming, d'you see? We shall be good company.'

The *Bonny Beaufoy* was labouring towards them, low in the water with the weight of her cargo. Signals were flagged to her and she hove to and settled to wait for them. It took another hour to do all that needed to be done, and even then the wounded were still being attended to when all three ships set off in convoy to resume their journey. But the hold of the *Yorick* was full of captured Frenchmen, the crew of the *Yorick* were assured of good prize money and Jack was a free man and something of a hero.

That night, when the blood had been scrubbed from the decks and the three most badly wounded men had had their stumps sealed with hot tar and been carried below to groan until they recovered or died, Jack dined in the wardroom as though he were one of the *Yorick's* officers, with Blue behind his chair to wait on him and an admiring company to drink his health. 'You're a plaguey fine shot, sir, damme if you ain't.' By the end of the meal, since one officer had been grazed by gunshot and Mr Jerome was on other duties, he had become temporary officer of the watch, with Blue as his accepted servant. By the end of the week, he'd been accepted by the crew — grudgingly and with a deal of grumbling which was only to be expected but acknowledging that at least he was a man who'd proved his worth under fire.

Even Mr Cooper allowed that he could be gentry. 'He'm raving mad when it comes to the niggers,' he said. 'There's narry a one of us would agree with him on that score, for'tis plain folly when all's said an' done, but he's got "bottom", I'll say that for him. They'm a rum lot, the gentry, an' given to folly an' suchlike, an' he do seem to go on the way they goes on, with pistols an' all. Take that nigger boy of his'n. 'Tis the sort of thing they goes in for. They has 'em like puppy dogs. I seen 'em in London.'

So the voyage continued, more or less uneventfully except for the occasional drunken brawl, one of which ended in a flogging. The three ships kept close company in an empty ocean. The ship's carpenter repaired the deck. Two of the crippled men died and were buried at sea, the third made a slow recovery. Mr Jerome reported that there was no gold aboard the *Mary Elizabeth* but that the silk was of good quality and there was a deal of ivory. The weather wasn't always fair but what storms they weathered were less violent than others they'd known and there were no slaves aboard to plague Jack's conscience, and no sickness and no sign of the French. Best of all, as an officer, he had a chance to see the ship's charts and find out what speed they were making and how rapidly they were returning home.

'We shall be in England pretty soon,' he told Blue, one lazy afternoon, 'and then I must be taken from the ship with my hands bound, I fear.' That had been established with the captain, who said he could see no way else, or Mr Smith would want to know the reason why. 'You must take this note and hide it in your breeches and if things do not go well with me, you must go to the inn whose name I have written *there* and ask for the man, whose name I have written *there*. Do you understand?'

Blue looked worried. Although he could speak well and understand most of what was said to him, written instructions were beyond him.

'Should it come to the worst — which I doubt, but should it — find a kind person in fine clothes, and ask them to read it for 'ee.' Blue agreed, although dubiously. 'Yes, Mr Jack.'

'Cheer up, me lad,' Jack said, ruffling his woolly hair. 'It may all work out for the best yet. I'll run mad rather than be sent to prison or the hangman. I've done good service aboard this ship and when Mr

Bradbury hears of it, he'll not punish me further. He'll see 'twas folly and mischief-maldng. I've yet to tell him of the factor and his scurvy tricks, which ain't a thing to be ignored. No, no, we'll come through, the pair of us, and then we'll live like lords. What do 'ee think to that?'

Blue held the paper and didn't know what to think. 'What is lords?' he asked.

Twenty-nine

As soon as Suki Brown arrived in Appleton House, she searched out
pen, ink and paper, settled William on her lap and wrote a letter to
Farmer Lambton, explaining that she and Miss Ariadne had been
banished to the country, hoping that Mrs Lambton and the baby
continued well, and begging him please to tell Captain Jack where she
was. 'He'm bound to come to the farm, for to collect Bow, for I never
knowd a man love a horse as he do that one, which I hopes is well and no
trouble to you.' After she'd signed her name, she was tempted to rebuke
him for his part in her sudden exile, but she forbore because she was
trying to be a good Christian soul — and besides, he was still stabling the
horse, and until the Bradburys remembered to pay her, she had no money
to send him for its fodder.

She was rather put out to discover that the letter couldn't be sent until
Saturday, which was *days* away. But she couldn't complain about that
either because Mrs Norris, the housekeeper, was such a kindly soul and
explained it to her so patiently. 'Lord love 'ee, dearie, we don't get post
hereabouts. Leastways not when the master's away. 'Twill go a'
Saturday, for 'ee. I'll make sure of it.'

So Saturday it had to be and an irritating wait it was, for life at
Appleton House was slow and enervating, particularly after the bustle of
Bath. There was plenty of work going on all around her for the estate
was at the centre of a large apple orchard and had its own home farm in
the grounds, with a dairy for butter and cheese, a herd of orchard pigs to
be fed on the skimmed milk and whey, a dovecote for over six hundred
birds that had to be cleaned out most religiously every week, a sizeable
stables with its own smithy, to say nothing of all the labour in the kitchen
where bread was baked every day and ale brewed for the entire estate.
But that was no work for a lady's maid and, as her particular lady did
nothing but sit silent in her room, there was little to keep her occupied.

The house was no help to her either, for it was a dark, old-fashioned
place, with leaded windows that gave very little light and oak panelling
that was cracked and ancient and horribly oppressive in all the main

rooms. There were no modern devices at all, not even a pump in the kitchen, as she discovered on her second morning. All their water had to be drawn from a well in the courtyard, and a back-breaking job that was. As to the kitchen, that was just a low dark cave — full of grease and fumes — where the sun never penetrated and the stone flags were always chill underfoot. 'Twas no wonder Miss Ariadne was low-spirited.

Mrs Norris was most concerned about her young mistress. 'Tain't nat'ral to sit so, day after day, poor soul,' she said to Suki at the end of their first week together. 'Shall we try her with a little junket? What do 'ee think to that? If she got a sore throat 'tis no wonder she don't speak.'

But junkets didn't work and neither did apple jelly and after another week Mr Norris was called in from his work in the dairy to discuss the situation. Like his wife, he was short, stout, good tempered and hard working. But he confessed himself baffled by Miss Ariadne's silence.

'Happen a walk in the air would do it,' he said, scratching his tousled hair.

So a walk in the air was tried. That evening, when William had been fed and settled, the two girls put on their straw bonnets, wound their shawls about their waists — country style, since there were none nearby to rebuke Ariadne for vulgar behaviour — and set out for a stroll through the fields.

The moon was already out, flat and smudged as a white penny in a sky still daytime blue, the apple orchards were *heavy* with burgeoning fruit, honeysuckles breathed their languorous perfume into the evening air, and below the gentle curve of the hill, the river shimmered like shot silk.

'Tis a cruel world,' Ariadne said suddenly, 'which is sad to think upon when it can be so beautiful.' It was the first time she'd spoken since they arrived and her voice was husky with lack of use.

Suki's concern was more practical than philosophical. 'How of your silence?' she asked. 'Do 'ee mean to stay mute all summer?' Ariadne's voice was instantly firm. 'I mean to stay mute,' she said, 'until the time has come for me to speak.'

'When will that be?'

'When I have something to say, I imagine.'

'Don't 'ee fear they'll call the surgeons again?'

Ariadne grimaced. 'What worse could they do than they have done already?'

'They could kill you,' Suld told her hotly. 'I thought they had.'

'But as you see, I am still here,' Ariadne said, smiling at her briefly, 'though how I shall fare hereafter I cannot tell.'

They walked on quietly, each busy with her own thoughts.

'We will walk every evening,' Ariadne decided. ''Tis good to talk to 'ee Suki and I know I can depend upon 'ee not to tell a soul of it.'

So the pattern was set and they walked every evening.

*

The days passed slowly, for nothing was hurried on this estate. Haymaking was long over, but work in the fields still began at first light because there were cows to milk, pigs to feed, horses to groom, vegetables to tend, and it all had to be done thoroughly. After a while, Suki begged to be allowed to work in the kitchen, when looking after William allowed it, for at least kneading dough with the amiable Mrs Norris gave her something to occupy her time. William grew fatter and more handsome by the day and toddled about with her wherever she went and was admired and petted by everybody on the estate. But there were no letters from Twerton, so the Captain couldn't have come home yet, and none from London either.

'I am bored beyond belief,' Ariadne complained, when they'd been there a month. 'We might as well be dead and buried here, for all they care.'

'But we aren't.' Suki laughed, tossing William in the air and catching him, while he squealed with delight at such rough play. It had been a long hot day and he'd been too wide awake to settle, so, for once, they'd taken him along with them on their evening stroll. Now having walked as far as they could at a toddler's stumbling pace they'd stopped for a rest: Ariadne to sit in the dappled shadows of a chestnut tree; Suki to play with her child. She tossed him in the air again. 'We'm *very* much alive. Aren't we, my'andsome?'

'How you do love him!' Ariadne observed.

'Well o' course,' Suki said carelessly. 'On account of he'm my babba. Aren't you, my little duck?'

'But he ain't, is he?' Ariadne said, equally carelessly. But then she looked up and caught a glimpse of startled fear in her friend's eyes, and her own eyes widened as she suddenly saw the implication of what had just been said. 'Oh, Suki! *Is* he?'

Suki was alarmed, then ashamed for allowing herself to be caught out so easily, then relieved that it was only Ariadne who would know, because they were so used to confidence now and trusted each other. 'If I tell 'ee,' she said, 'you'll not breathe a word to a living soul.'

By then, Ariadne was agog for the details. 'You have my word on't.'

So the story was told, from Sir George's assault, which Ariadne greeted with a snort of disgust, followed by peals of delighted laughter when she heard how Suki had dealt with it, and so past the death of that poor little frail baby, whom she had to confess she could barely remember, and then to his funeral, which she remembered uncommon clearly.

'I might ha' known it,' she said, when the tale was finally told. 'You've always seemed a deal too fond of our William for a wet nurse. While as to my father... 'Tis the sort of behaviour I would expect of him, no more nor less. The man is an oaf. When you hit him 'twas richly deserved. Would I could have been there to see it. We heard him roar, as I recall, but took little heed of it, for he roars at everything.'

'He roared uncommon loud *that* morning,' Suki told her, throwing William in the air again.

Ariadne smiled with satisfaction. 'I'm glad on't,' she said. 'I hope it taught him a lesson, which he sorely needs, although I doubt he will mind it for he's uncommon settled in his opinions. He regards all women as his property. Shame upon him. We are mere cattle in his eyes, there to be bedded, or bred from, or married off to some repellant friend of his. I'm so glad you hit him.'

'And now Miss Melissa is to marry his repellant friend.'

'She'll get no joy of *him*,' his erstwhile fiancee said. 'For I never knew a man so full of himself, nor with such vile breath.'

'She'll be mistress of a fine house,' Suki said, adding with happy spite, 'which might console her.'

Ariadne was suddenly intensely serious. 'Were we wrong, think 'ee, in what we said?'

'No,' Suki said, with equal seriousness. 'We were not. If any woman marry it should be for love. Without it, we'm no better than beasts in the field, put to breed for profit.'

'How glad you will be to have your lover home,' Ariadne said enviously. For Suki had told her how soon that homecoming was to be. 'Would mine had been so true.'

'You might love again,' Suki said consolingly, 'and find a truer man.'

'I think not.' Ariadne sighed, but recovered quickly. 'One thing is most certain. I'll not stay at home to belong to my father, nor marry to belong to a husband. There must be another way and I mean to find it.'

Suki understood her completely. 'An' stay mute till you do,' she said.

Ariadne opened her mouth to agree but then turned her head, alerted by the sound of footsteps in the lane below them. 'There's someone coming,' she said. 'How if 'twere your lover?'

Suki stood up at once with William on her hip. Could it be the Captain? Could she hope for such a thing? There was such a fluttering in her throat, like a bird in a cage, throbbing and pulsing. It couldn't be him, could it? He'd have ridden Beau. Oh, let it be him, I've waited for him so long.

The footsteps drew nearer, and as the walker rounded the bend below them and emerged from the shelter of the trees, they could see that it was a stocky young man in his working clothes and that he'd walked a fair distance, for he was moving with the long-legged rhythmical stride of someone well into his journey. Suki drooped with disappointment. He wasn't the Captain. She'd have known *his* splendid stride anywhere and, besides, this man was too poorly dressed.

Then he looked up towards them and she saw that he was her brother John. 'Something's amiss,' she said and went dowm at once to find out what it was.

Her brother took off his hat at their approach and wiped his forehead with it. He looked so anxious it was hardly necessary to ask him if something was the matter. ''Tis Pa,' he explained. 'Got hurt up the quarry yesterday. Ma says can you come?'

For a second, Suki couldn't understand w'hat he was talking about. 'The quarry?'

'Yes. Ma says can you come?'

'What was he a-doin' in a quarry?' Suki said, angered by the folly of it. 'He'm a farm worker. You might ha' knowd he'd get hurt in a quarry. Hern dangerous enough with a rake.'

'He was earnin' a bit of money to buy Ma a new dress.'

'What do Fanner Lambton have to say about it?'

'I don't know. Can you come?'

'Is 'e bad?'

''Aven't seen un yet, to tell the truth,' John confessed, twisting his hat in his hands. 'That Mr Aylock's such a tartar. He don't give you time for nothing. Ma came over this morning and persuaded un to let me come here on the stagecoach to Chipping Sodbury. If we goes back the same way tomorrow morning, we can catch Mr Jones at market, an' he'll take 'ee on to Twerton. 'Tis all arranged.'

Suki wasn't interested in the stagecoach or any other travelling arrangements. Her concern was solely for her father. 'What did he hurt? His back? His legs? What part of un?'

'Fingers,' John said enlightening her. 'Fingers of his right hand. Ma says he'm bad. Can you come?'

Fingers, Suki thought. Why, fingers are nothing. He'll soon get over *that*. But she'd go and attend to him because he *was* her Pa, poor old thing — and, besides, a trip to Twerton would bring her close to Bristol and that was what she wanted more than anything. She could ride there from Twerton or tease a lift on a cart. She might even contrive to be there at the very moment when that *Bonny Beaufoy* came in. Right on the quayside, awaiting him. Oh yes, she would certainly go to Twerton.

'Come up to the house,' she instructed him. 'Mrs Norris will find 'ee some supper an' somewhere to sleep, an' we'll go back at first light.'

Given her mixed reasons for agreeing to accompany him, she was quite ashamed to see how relieved he was.

*

They set off together in the small cart with the groom to drive them, just after dawn the next morning so as to be in good time to find an inside seat on the stagecoach, but it was a long, uncomfortable, rackety journey down to Bath, even with a hamper of food and ale from Mrs Norris to sustain them on the way. The weather was sticky, the roads in poor repair, and because he was cooped up inside a coach for hours, William was fractious. He grizzled and complained and climbed all over Suki from the start of the journey to the end. She was heartily sick of him by the time they reached Bath and very glad to find Mr Jones's nice clean airy cart waiting for her in the market.

Yes, he said, he'd been expectin' her. 'Just you hop aboard, me dear. I shall be finished here in two shakes of a lamb's tail.' So she kissed her brother goodbye and settled beside the dog for the last three exhausting miles to Twerton.

It was growing dark by the time they arrived at the farm, William was sound asleep and she was bone weary. But she was encouraged by the sight of her old home. The sagging thatch was gone, replaced by a splendid piece of work, close-packed and so dry and neat that the straw ends bristled in the setting sun. The door had been mended too and the walls plastered and whitened with lime wash. This must be Pa's doing, she thought, as she carried her sleeping baby towards the door. So he can't be too bad.

But then she stepped into the kitchen and the odd combination of scents and smells in that crowded room alerted her again, for besides the ones she expected, of cabbage and boiled bacon, scrubbed table, the mustiness of Mrs Havers' unwashed clothes, the sharp ammoniac smell of chicken shit, a strong odour of pig, there was an equally strong smell of blood and another, at once cloying and rank, that she couldn't identify.

Apart from the smell, the room was exactly as she remembered it. Mrs Havers was sitting in her usual place in the chimney corner, plainly in the middle of one of her grumbles, Molly and Tom were in their usual place under the table and her mother was mending stockings by the light of a single candle, holding the work up to get as much benefit from its little beam as she could.

As soon as she saw Suki she rose to her feet with a cry of welcome. 'Oh, my dear girl. I'm *that* pleased you'm here. Thank the Lord.' And Molly and Tom scrambled out from under the table to fling their arms around her and hug and be hugged. But her father sat where he was in the shadows, cradling his bandaged right hand protectively with the fingers of his left, and Suki saw at once that he was in pain and ill. She handed her sleeping baby to Molly and crossed the room to attend to him.

'What you been a-doin' then, Pa?' she asked. Now that she was close to him, she could see that his bandages were heavily stained with blood and knew that the rank smell was pus.

'Little contree-tom,' her father said apologetically. 'I shall soon mend,' He glanced quickly and anxiously towards his wife, warning Sula in the old subtle way that she wasn't to make too much fuss for fear of upsetting her mother.

'When you last have them dressings changed?' she said, practical as ever.

'They was onny put on day afore yes'day,' he told her, still apologetic. His face was grey in the candlelight and his eyes strained.

'I'll do 'em for 'ee now.'

'No, no,' he protested weakly, but she was already bustling about the room to fetch a bowl of water and some clean linen.

'He'll let you see to un, I shouldn't wonder,' her mother whispered, producing a flat dish from under a pile of dry clouts. 'He won't let us come near un. He'm mortal bad.'

'I made un a dish of penny royal,' Mrs Havers complained. 'An' he wouldn't so much as put his lips to it. The trouble we'm in, dearie, you wouldn't believe the half of it. There's that poor little babba been so sickly you wouldn't believe, an' we all knows the outcome of *that*, an' Mrs Lambton took to her bed, poor soul, an' now your pa. 'Tis more than human flesh an' blood can stand. I said so to your poor ma onny this morning...'

Suki let her ramble on and paid no attention to her, for the smell of pus had roused the most unpleasant forebodings. She poured the last of the day's water from the ewer into the kettle, set it on the fire to warm and tore a clean clout into little strips for bandages, then dabbing and soothing, she began to ease the dirty dressings from her father's fingers. She hurt him so much that he groaned despite himself.

I must be ready for it to be nasty, she thought, as she eased the last red rags from his quivering hand. But even then, half prepared as she was by his pain and her mother's concern, she was horrified at what she saw. His two middle fingers had been hacked off at the knuckle and the stumps were swollen and black with bruises and oozing yellow pus. And I said ''twas only fingers', she thought with shame. 'Only fingers,' My poor dear brave old Pa.

'Run up the farm and see if Farmer Lambton could spare a mouthful of Hollands,' she said to her brother. But as he ran from the room, her father gave a shuddering moan and fainted away.

'Hold his hand still,' she told her mother, 'an' we'll clean it all we can while he don't feel nothin'.'

'Poor soul!' her mother mourned. 'An' never a word of complaint! 'Tis always the same with un. He don't like us to know how bad he is. Never did.'

'You'm the bravest man alive,' Suki told her father's insensible head. She was washing his wounds as quickly as she could, but even so she wasn't quick enough. He came to long before she'd finished, and had to endure several groaning minutes before Tom ran back with the gin. Then they struggled on together, in the short numbing time the spirits eventually bestowed.

But at last the wounds were clean and freshly bandaged and her father had been sick, which didn't surprise any of them, and she'd sponged his face and wrapped him in a blanket and laid him in his truckle bed.

'Don't you go a-sayin' a word, you foolish creature,' she scolded him lovingly when he tried to thank her. 'Just you get yourself warm and get yourself better. I'd do anything at all to make you better. You know that.' Then she had to turn away from him, for pity was making her cry.

'I'll clean up for 'ee,' Mrs Havers offered, gathering the dirty rags to burn them on the fire. 'I never knowd he was so bad an' that's a fact. Poor soul.'

'Shall you stay here?' her mother whispered. 'Or go up to the farmhouse?'

Suki hadn't thought so far ahead. 'I'll go to the farm, if they'll have me,' she said. 'They've a cradle there for William.'

'Then you'd best know the news,' her mother told her. 'The babba died last week. Poor little thing. She'm in a poor way over it.'

So that was what Mrs Havers was rambling on about, Suki thought. 'Poor Mrs Lambton,' she said, flooded with pity for her. What a terrible thing to happen. No wonder she'm took to her bed. They'll not want me in the house at a time like this. I shall sleep here with Molly. We can find a drawer for William, perviding 'tis long enough. I'll walk across an' see them in the morning an' say how sorry I am. What a parlous thing to happen.'

*

Such a morning it was, golden with the promise of noonday heat, lush with birdsong, heady with the scents of summer, a morning for courtship and sweet talk, for gathering flowers and stitching bridal gowns, not visiting the sick. But she coaxed her father to a breakfast of ale and bread, fed William until his belly was as tight as a drum, left him with Molly and walked across to the farmhouse notwithstanding.

She was upset to see how neglected it looked. The floor was strewn with dirty rushes, the ashes of last night's fire were still grey in the grate, and, although there was no dust visible to the eye, the bench looked smeared and the table grubby. But it was the sight of Farmer Lambton that upset her most of all, for he seemed to have aged and shrunk and was stooping in a way she'd never noticed in him before. There were more wrinkles in his cheeks, more lines in his forehead and his eyes were bloodshot and deep shadowed. But he made her welcome and urged her to come in. 'She's abed, I fear, and none too well,' he explained. 'But she'll be pleased to see *you*, Suki. I'm sure of that. Go you up.'

Annie Lambton lay propped among her pillows in a room that smelt of blood and phlegm. There was a phial full of green liquid on the table beside the bed, an unemptied chamber pot beside it, and a small white bowl, full of blood and vomit, tipping sideways on the coverlet just out of reach of her hands. The windows were shuttered, as though air and sunlight would be injurious to her, and in the half-light that seeped through the cracks in the wood, her face looked grey and heavily lined. She had made an effort to plait her long hair but the plait was tousled and straw-dry, her eyes were shut and much sunk in their sockets and she was wincing with every indrawn breath, her chest was shrivelled and sunken, too, and her hands lay against the coverlet as if they had been discarded there.

'Oh, Annie!' Suld said, forgetting the proprieties in the distress of the moment. 'I'm so sorry to see you so ill.'

'Not ill,' Annie said, with her eyes still shut, 'I'm dying, Suki. I been a-dying these seven days since my poor Connie was took.'

Suki rushed to deny it, 'No! No!' But the effort of speaking had provoked such a spasm of coughing that denial was useless. She held the bowl beneath her friend's straining mouth and caught the blood as she coughed it up and knew that death was tearing her down with every gasp.

'Could you fancy anything to eat?' she asked when the spasm was over. The poor lady was mortal thin and looked as though she hadn't eaten for days.

Annie was beyond food. 'A stoop of ale to moisten my mouth,' she whispered, and coughed again.

The ale was fetched and three sips taken painfully, the patient's face and hands were washed with a soft cloth, the bowl and the chamber pot taken down and emptied on the midden, the floor swept and sprinkled with vinegar, but no amount of loving care made any impression on Annie Lambton who had drifted into a murmuring unconsciousness as soon as she lay back on the pillows.

'She'm dying,' Suki said to her mother when she was back in the cottage.

'Yes,' Mrs Brown said. 'Poor soul. What a blessing you'm home. You'll do what's needful for her, won't you, my dear? We must pray for an easy end. Not a word of it to your pa. We'm keeping it from him, bein' he got pains enough of his own.'

And so have I, Suki thought, for I wouldn't have wished such suffering on either the one of'em, and it pains me cruelly to see it. But there was tomorrow's dough to knead and set to rise — no matter how she might be feeling — and a stew pot to fill with pot herbs and scraps of bacon, and her father to be coaxed through his supper before his wounds were cleaned and dressed again.

That night she lay awake in the narrow truckle bed beside her sister, too full of sadness to sleep. How suddenly your life can be turned about, she thought. Two days ago, I was playing with my William under the chestnut tree in Appleton without a care in the world, except for wonderin' when the Captain was like to come home and feeling cross with poor Farmer Lambton for telling tales on Miss Ariadne. And now here I am with Pa sore injured, that poor babba dead, Mrs Lambton a-dying an' the farmer like an old man. Tis a mortal sad world and we'm all a-tangled up in it, whether we will or no, on account of we loves each other. Tis only them as don't love as are free to come an' go as they choose. She knew there was no hope of a visit to Bristol now. She would have to contain her soul in patience until Jack came to Twerton of his own accord and, in the meantime, do what she could for her patients.

It was distressing work, for however hard she tried to help Mrs Lambton, the poor lady grew weaker by the hour, drifting in and out of consciousness, racked with coughing and too fatigued to lift her head from the pillows. The priest arrived to administer the last rites and sat with the farmer for two hours afterwards, doing his best to comfort him, and the farm labourers came and went, murmuring how sorry they were and hoping the mistress would take a turn for the better, but they all knew the truth of it.

'Twill not be long, I fear,' Farmer Lambton said on Suld's seventh evening in the farm.

She was wrapping herself in her shawl ready to walk back to the cottage. 'Should I stay with her overnight, think'ee?' she asked.

'No,' he said wearily. 'I'll sit up with her. Tis the least I can do and little enough in all conscience.'

It was the least and the last. The next morning when Suki came tripping back across the yard he met her at the door with the news that Annie was dead. It had been a cruel passing, with a deal of blood, and he was still stunned by it.

'I never thought to see such blood,' he said, shaking his head as if he were trying to shake the vision of it away. 'Twas the blood that killed her, Suld. She died of the blood. Such blood! Could you ask Mrs Havers to come over. She'll need laying out and there's such a deal of cleaning to be done. I never thought to see such blood.'

Suki was glad to run back to the cottage to fetch the old lady, for she was aching with such anguished sympathy for the farmer that the tears were streaming down her cheeks. How cruel to die so, after all she'd suffered. 'Twas monstrous. Monstrous.

*

It seemed even more monstrous when she and Mrs Havers arrived in the bedroom, for the bed was so badly soaked with blood that it had dripped through the feather mattress on to the floor. There were two chamber pots full of it and even the walls were scarlet spotted. 'My dear life!' Mrs Havers said. 'Tis like a shambles.' They washed their dead mistress between them, mourning at how thin her body was. They dressed her in a fresh nightgown, brushed her tangled hair, and laid her on clean sheets with a wild rose between her hands. Then they emptied the chamber pots and scrubbed the floor and washed down the walls.

'I'm beholden to 'ee,' Farmer Lambton said, when they came downstairs to tell him all was done. He had the necessary coins laid on the table ready to pay them but it took him a while to remember that they were there. 'Ah yes,' he said, when Mrs Havers looked at them and raised her eyebrows at his tardiness. 'Of course, yes. I'm beholden. Is there anything else I can do for 'ee?'

'If I could have pen, ink and paper, sir, I'd be obliged,' Suki said. 'I should write to Miss Ariadne to tell her how I fare. She'll be a-wondering.'

That night, when her father's wounds had been dressed yet again, and William had been fed and settled in his pillow-padded drawer, she wrote a long letter to her friend, describing everything that had happened, and weeping again with the anguish of it. 'How oddly things do turn out,' she ended.

When I left home for to go to work in Bath, I was mightily pleased with myself and thought I could not fail to succeed and I should return for my wedding, not for Mrs Lambton's funeral. I had a poor opinion of my family then, I fear, but tis much changed now for I see how brave Pa is and how dearly Ma loves him. I have not been to Bristol nor am I like to, there being so much here for me to do. Nothing has turned out as I expected. I confess to you that there are times when I wonder what is to become of me and my William. I wish you and I could be together again, if only for an afternoon. There is no one here for me to talk to and, if there were, there'm only sad things for to say.

Your loving friend, Suki

When she finally put down her pen and wiped the ink from her fingers, she found that the act of composition had eased her but, even so, her night was fraught with bloody dreams. When William woke her in the morning, calling 'Ma! Ma!' as he climbed out of his drawer, she was as stiff about the neck and shoulders as if she'd been carrying a pair of milk pails. But feeding him was a comfort as it always was, being patted and smiled at so lovingly with those fine brown eyes, and when she got downstairs to the kitchen, carrying him on her hip as she usually did these days, she found her father already eating breakfast and looking much better and much brighter and that cheered her even further.

'We shall soon have'ee well again,' she told him.

'Aye,' he agreed, 'once the funeral's over. Poor soul. Your ma told me of it this morning. Put your pretty babba on the stool aside me here an' he shall have some of my bread and butter, pretty dear.'

The pretty dear was a comfort to them all in the days after the funeral, for knowing nothing of the death they'd endured, he babbled and played and entertained them with his chirruping, as bright as a bird in a tree. And gradually, under Suki's gently determined ministrations, her father's raw stumps began to heal. On the fourth day after the funeral, the pus was finally gone, the bruises were changing colour and the swelling was quite definitely going down. Two days later, scabs began to form.

'You must sit out in the sunshine,' Suki said, 'and let the air heal you. See if we can't get a bit of colour back in your cheeks. Our William'll sit with 'ee, won't 'ee my 'andsome?'

That afternoon, she baked a rabbit pie for the family supper, and decorated the table with a jugful of wild flowers to celebrate her father's healing and to mark the gradual lifting of their long gloom. It made a sunny picture, for she had garnered a pretty armful, yellow celandine and mallow flowers as wide as poppies, fragile herb Robert and purple pansies, brown burnet and yellow trefoil, even six downy heads of hare's foot clover. And then, just as her mother was cutting the first slice from the pie, a postboy galloped into the yard to crown the feast with a letter for Miss Suki Brown. There was a happy scramble to find a coin to pay him, and then they all waited with cheerful anticipation for Suki to break the seal and read what it contained.

It was from Ariadne and her news was like a return to life.

We are summoned to Bath for the bride is to spend a week there to be made healthy and beauteous for her wedding, although 'tis my opinion an ocean of sulphur water could not achieve such a miracle. I believe I have found the path I must take but will tell you of it when we have leisure. I shall arrive in Bristol on the three o'clock stage on Thursday and will wait for you an hour on the Broad Quay. I trust your father is much improved and that I shall hear good news when we meet.

'I've to go to Bristol a' Thursday,' she said. At last! At last!

Thirty

'Tis a fair fine ship,' Frederick Bradbury said, pushing his telescope into the socket of his right eye with excitement. He'd been in a state of controlled elation since four o'clock the previous afternoon, when Mr Tomson's billet had been delivered. To learn that his ships had reached Eaton in Gordano and were lying at anchor waiting for the pilot was most welcome, for it meant that his cargo had come safely home, which allayed the anxiety he invariably suffered while any ship of his was at sea. To hear of the profit that had been made on the sale of his slaves was heartening, too, for he'd been anxious on that account ever since the *Bonny Beaufoy* set sail. But to be told that the *Yorick* had taken a prizeship on her very first voyage out, and with little loss of life what's more, provoked him to such raptures that he actually let out a whoop of joy, to the consternation of his valet, who had never seen his gentleman behave with such abandon. It was a triumph, a vindication of everything that he and his brother had been working for since the French attacked the *Antelope*, 'Od rot 'em. And now here was the prize herself, sailing slowly upriver between the *Bonny Beaufoy* and the *Yorick* and a fine fair ship indeed. 'I must send a billet to my brother,' he said. 'He will be cock-a-hoop.'

A strengthening sun was burning off the early morning mist, which rose from the river in long swirling swathes. There was something theatrical about it that morning, as though it was blue gauze lifted by unseen hands, something at once familiar and otherworldly, a mark that this was a special scene. The three ships sailed through it steadily, dipping with the tide and the breeze, their brass giving an occasional gleam as the sun touched it, their long masts alternately misted and golden. The oars of the pilot boat were gilded too and tipped with royal scarlet as they rose and plunged in perfect unison — and where the water was clear, its ripples sparkled as though they'd been sprinkled with gold dust. It was a sight to delight his mercantile soul.

'Fetch me my hat and gloves,' he said. 'I shall go down to the quay to welcome them home.'

He arrived to a flurry of applause from his friends, who had come down to the quay before him, for they too had seen the advance of the three ships and the news had spread like sunrise. 'A prize on your first voyage, damme!' they said approvingly, patting his shoulders as though he had captured the ship himself. That'll show the plaguey Frenchies.'

'Was there much cargo?'

'Ivory and silks,' he told them happily, gazing towards his approaching booty and swelling with the pride of the moment.

Jack Daventry was back in his cabin in the *Bonny Beaufoy*. As soon as they'd dropped anchor off Eaton in Gordano, Mr Smith had sent a boat across to the *Yorick* to fetch him and since then he'd been a virtual prisoner, with his legs shackled and his hands tied behind his back. Now, as they swayed upriver, his old shipmate, Mr Reuben, had dodged into the cabin to make a few unofficial adjustments.

'There's a reception committee awaiting us,' the bosun said, as he retied the rope, 'which you'd best be warned of, for't could cut 'ee one of two ways. If they'm in a fair mood they'll not want unpleasantness to mar un, an' you might'scape clean. Let's pray so, eh my old lubber? On t'other hand, if they'm vindictive, which jealousy do tend towards — an' there'll be a powerful amount of jealousy a-brewin' this morning — they could howl to have 'ee punished sore. You must hold fire for either eventuality, my lubber, and if you'm to run, you must jump so soon as you see a chance.'

Jack explored the slip-knot with his fingers. 'Trust me,' he said.

'I'll not be sent to the gallows, nor to prison neither, not when I've a good friend to aid me and a good horse waiting in the stables to carry me away.'

'Well, good luck to 'ee,' the bosun said, kicking Jack's discarded leg irons under the bunk. 'You'm a valiant fighter and not one to waste in a jail. What's to become of your nigger-boy?'

Blue was sitting on his heels in the comer of the cabin. 'I go with Mr Jack, massa,' he said.

'He's provided for,' Jack said, smiling at his slave. 'He knows what to do, don't 'ee Blue?' Neither of them were entirely sure that he would be able to follow his instructions but they were determinedly optimistic. 'He'll wait for me.'

The ship juddered as she began to go about. 'We'm coming alongside,' Mr Reuben said. 'I'd best be off. Good luck to 'ee, Jack.' And was gone like a shadow.

Left on his own in the stale air of the cabin, Jack sat on the edge of his bunk and tried to calm the agitated pounding of his heart. The wait seemed endless. He heard the captain shouting orders, felt the ship strain against her hawsers, saw feet scampering on the quayside, or braced against a heavy haul, but the wait went on long after the ship had been steadied to a halt. He was fevered with tension. Soon, there were congratulatory voices booming on the quay. He recognized the weaselly tones of Mr Jedediah Smith, the Bristol burrs of Mr Tomson and Jack Jerome, the precise enunciation of the ship's surgeon, the deep-throated laugh of the *Yorick's* captain, and knew that they were bragging of their successes. The wait went on. Perhaps they've forgotten me, he thought, and a little hope dampened his fever. Perhaps they'll all go swaggering off to dinner and leave the crew to disembark on their own. If that's the case, I can sneak off to the stables and be away before they know it.

There were feet tramping outside the cabin and the door was flung open to reveal the four musketeers who'd captured him in Nevis. 'Mr Cooper, sir,' he said, greeting their leader.

Mr Cooper was brusque and unfriendly. 'Stow that,' he said. 'You'm a prisoner now. On your feet! Where's your leg irons?'

Jack decided to be polite and cool. The man was an armed guard, no more, and should be handled with care. 'They were removed,' he said.

Mr Cooper looked suspicious. 'What for?'

'To allow me to walk, I daresay.'

'I s'pose they knows what they'm a-doin' of,' the musketeer said. 'Well, let's be having you.' And he jabbed Jack forward with the muzzle of his musket.

The light out on the quay was so dazzling that for a few seconds, as he walked down the gangplank, Jack could barely see. He kept his head high and his spine straight because it was necessary to show that he was a man of 'bottom', but his senses were as blurred as the faces below him. He was aware of a seething crowd: merchants in wigs and tricorns, leaning on their canes; local women waving and calling to their returning menfolk; dockers already unloading the prize ship's cargo; horses shaking their harness; dogs snarling and barking. But the reception committee was a faceless smudge of dark colour, more felt than seen, an aura of disapproval, a stab of needle voices that made his heart shrink in his chest.

'There he is!' Mr Smith shouted. 'Arrogant puppy! This is the fool that thinks he may draw pistol on his betters. Send for the constable, sir, and have him arraigned.'

Jack stepped off the gangplank, sending a quick eye message to Blue that he was to hide behind the nearest bollard. Mr Bradbury's anxious face swam into focus. 'Is this true, sir?' he was asking Mr Tomson. 'Did he draw a pistol?'

'He did, sir.'

'Was it fired?'

'Not to my knowledge, sir,' the Captain said. 'Just drawd and so forth. No harm done.'

'No harm!' Mr Smith shouted. Excitement was making him sweat. Jack could see beads of moisture forming on his upper lip and running like raindrops from underneath his wig. 'He could have blown my head off, sir, and would've done had I not been too quick for him. Have him arraigned. 'Twas an act of rank disobedience. He needs stringing up and the sooner the better. Send for the constable.'

'He is my slave master, is he not?' Mr Bradbury asked, peering at the captive's face. And kin to Lady Bradbury as he recalled. 'Twould not be politic to annoy *that* lady by arresting a kinsman. He would never hear the end of it. And yet Mr Smith was uncommon pressing and would need to be answered, one way or another. What a dilemma to be in! If only brother George were here.

There was a sudden noise to the left of them as a barrel rolled from the trolley on which it was being hauled and thundered along the quay, turning on its axis, perilously near the water's edge. It was a welcome diversion and he seized it at once.

'Have a care what you're doing, sir. You must excuse me, gentlemen.'

Mr Smith scowled and took out a kerchief to wipe his forehead, the seamen turned to watch the recovery of the barrel, and Jack was suddenly ignored and suddenly all instinct, alert to his finger ends. It was the moment. He must take it or be lost to the hangman. Quickly and now. He ripped the knot apart, tossed the rope aside, leapt into the quay, moving with such speed that it was all one action, the water closing cold over his head before his wrists lost the rope's sensation. He could hear people shouting while he was still underwater — their voices belling and bubbling — could see the hull of the *Bonny Beaufoy* encrusted with moon-white barnacles, the hawser ridged and rippling like some great sea-green water snake. Then his head was in the air again and he struck out for the opposite quayside, ears popping and lungs straining, as the sun broke on the water and the outraged roaring behind him rose to a crescendo. ''Od's bowels! Stop him, somebody!'

The water was heavy, pulling him down. He was a bird caught in its toils, struggling to fly free. He could hear the thwack and splash of his feet, feel the water parting before the force of his arms. Three strokes. Two. And there was a line dangling just beyond his grasp. He plunged at it, grabbed the air, pushed again, caught it, held on, gasping for breath. Then he was climbing hand over hand with the rope steadied between his feet and water streaming from his hair and falling in great drops from his shirt and breeches. Over the gunwale, on to warm deck, sea-brown faces in his line of vision, rough hands grabbing at him, dodging, ducking, pulling away from them, six dancing paces to the gangplank and he was free, running through the crowds on the quayside, where the merchants were too preoccupied by their own affairs to pay much attention to a running man — even a wet one.

He glanced back at his pursuers, who were charging along the opposite bank towards the head of the quay, yelling encouragement at one another. It would take some time for them to reach him and Mr Wenham's livery stables were a matter of yards away. He could already smell horse flesh, already feel Beau's supple neck under his hands, see those clever ears pricking for command. As he leapt into the yard, his mind leapt ahead of him. He was already in the saddle and galloping away.

His arrival was like an explosion. Work stopped, heads turned, mouths opened. A piebald mare being led out of her stall shied in alarm, and all the horses in the yard laid back their ears and rolled their eyes.

'Quickly!' he shouted to the nearest startled face. 'Get Mr Wenham! Jump to it!'

The stable lad jumped, but Mr Wenham was already walking out of the tack room — bandy legged and tousled, with a straw in his mouth and his cap on the back of his head — to ask what was amiss.

'I've come for my horse,' Jack said urgently. 'There's not a minute to lose.' Now that he was standing still, he realized that he was shivering and that water was running from his shoes and gathering in a puddle round his feet, but there was no time to explain his appearance. 'My horse, Beau. You remember. Bay stallion. Eighteen hands.'

'Ah, yes,' Mr Wenham said, remembering. 'You owes me money on that there hanimal, as I recall.'

Fury burned in Jack's shivering chest. To be balked now, when the matter was so pressing! Obdurate man! 'You'll be paid, sir,' he said, speaking as calmly as he could. 'You have my word on't. Where is he?'

'Well now, as to that, sir,' Mr Wenham said, 'I believe we must settle accounts afore I tells 'ee.'

'Deuce take it, man. This is a matter of life and death. You'll get your money when I get my horse.'

'Well, as to that, sir,' Mr Wenham began.

There were feet pounding the cobbles somewhere outside the yard. There was no time for politeness or sense or even thought. Frantic with fear. Jack seized the stableman by the throat and thrust him against the nearest hay bale. 'Tell me where he is, damme, or I'll put paid to 'ee. Damme if I won't.'

Mr Wenham struggled away from him, red in the face and full of fury. Customer or no, he would *not* be handled so. Not by any man. 'You can save your venom,' he said. 'He am't here.'

The news threw Jack into a panic. He could feel the fever of it, rising in his chest like a wave. He *had* to be here. He was needed. How could he get away if his horse were gone? 'You jest!' 'I never jests, sir. He arn't here.'

'Od's blood and bowels. He means it. Then where is he?'

'Your wife took un.'

'Wife?' Jack said wildly. 'What folly's this? I have no wife.'

'Said she was your wife. Anyways, she took un. Months ago.' Nightmare was closing in with the pounding feet. He was so hot it was hard to breathe. 'Where to? I *must* find him.'

Suki's carefully written note had been lost and forgotten long ago. 'How should I know, sir? She'm your wife, not mine.'

The feet were behind him and there was nowhere to run, nowhere to hide. He turned, his face wild, cast about for a weapon, saw a pitchfork

363

stuck in the straw, seized it and held it before him, daring his pursuers, 'Come on then, damn you. You'll not take me without a fight.'

It was short and vicious and drew a happy crowd. The outcome was predictable, for the young man was hopelessly outnumbered, but he was handsome and valiant and put up a splendid struggle, defending himself most courageously with his long fork, and swearing like a trouper, until he was clubbed to the ground and gagged with a bandanna. As his captors led him away, barefooted, his hands tightly trussed behind his back, with blood dripping from a split lip and a long gash across the top of his head, the spectators gave him a cheer, as though he were a prizefighter. 'Good luck to 'ee! We'll come to your hanging, boy, damme if we won't. 'Twill be a sight to see.' And most of them trailed along after him, eager for the next excitement.

Jack acknowledged them with a nod, since he couldn't speak or wave, but he was drawn with distress and fever. Heat burned out from the centre of his body, in long heartbeat pulses. Sweat ran from eveny pore. His bound hands were slippery with moisture. Even the soles of his feet were wet and sticky against the cobblestones. Worse, he was finding it hard to see. There was a film across his eyes and lights trembled and danced at the edges of his vision. He was half walked, half dragged from the yard, and jostled along the quay. Soon it took all his effort to put one foot in front of the other and he knew that the jungle fever had returned and that he was ill again. If only they would stop and let him lie down. But there was a trial to come. He had to face his accusers, to hold on, to show himself a man of valour.

Mr Frederick Bradbury was much put out to see him dragged back with a crowd in tow. To have an audience to his actions was intolerable, especially when one of the participants was related to his sister-in-law. 'We will adjourn to the manufactory,' he said, and turned on his elegant heel at once to lead the way. His office was small but at least it was hidden from the prurient gaze of hoi polloi.

They crammed into the dusty space and stood in a semi-circle before Bradbury's desk, with their backs to the neat stack of his account books: Jack, drooping at the centre of their accusations; Mr Jedediah Smith, pinched with fury and delay; Mr Tomson, twisting his hat in his hands; Mr Jerome, puffing rank tobacco smoke into the limited air; a constable, black-clad and sour-faced, wearing his chain of office; Mr Bradbury's surgeon, also in sober black and ready to assist his patron; Mr Cooper and his cohort of musketeers, smug with the success of their endeavours and the certainty of reward.

They were sealed in by the heat of the manufactory. Dust motes bounced against the window like bees. 'Well, sir,' Mr Bradbury said to Mr Smith, 'what's to be done?'

'What's to be done, sir?' Mr Smith said, spitting with fury. 'What's to be done? Why, the man is to be arraigned and took off to jail. How many more times must I tell 'ee?'

The constable wasn't sure about the practicality of such a suggestion. 'We'm full to bursting, sir,' he reported, 'saving your reverence. On account of we got all those Frenchies a youm to house and Justice Ford he been a-sendin' down villains to us prodigious the last few days. Now if you could see your way to keep un confined in your cellar, sir, for a day or two, or some such place likewise, then we could get un to court sharpish and squeeze un in afore he goes for execution.'

Mr Bradbury quailed at the very idea of having this red-faced, staring stranger under his quiet roof. 'Such a course is out of the question,' he said. 'Have you no room at all?'

'Tis my opinion, sir,' Mr Tomson said, 'begging your pardon and so forth, that the man is sick.'

He was certainly standing in a very peculiar way, leaning sideways as if he were about to fall.

'Are you so?' Mr Bradbury asked. 'Take away the gag. I'll hear him speak.'

Jack made a valiant effort to stand straight. 'No, sir.'

'He's an unprincipled villain,' Mr Smith pressed on, 'and if he's sick,'tis no more than he deserves.' And he pulled out his trump card and laid it into the argument to prove his point. 'He thinks niggers are the equal of white men.'

There was an outcry at such folly. The constable laughed out loud, but Frederick Bradbury was shocked. 'How now?' he said to Jack. 'Is this true?'

Self-preservation should have urged Jack to be cautious, to prevaricate, even to lie, but he was caught in the need to show his valour and valour drove him to honesty.

'Yes,' he said. ''Tis true as I stand here, sir. I will not pretend otherwise. They are human as we are, they bleed as we do, suffer the same pain, love as we do — sometimes better — die as we do, with the same courage. There is no difference atween us, save that we have guns and whips and are cruel enough to use 'em, and they are poor and naked. There are things done aboard ship 'twould hurt your very soul to see, Mr Bradbury, men and women branded like cattle, chained and left in their own filth below decks for days and weeks at a time, flogged until their backs are raw and they are too weak to stand, children thrown into the sea alive, even the new born threatened with death, as Mr Smith here knows very well. Ask *him* of it. They are not cattle, sir, nor property. They are human and we make 'em suffer and we'll be dammed in hell for it, every man jack of us. Only a fool or a blind man could fail to see the truth of what I'm saying. Only a fool Then he was exhausted and panting and too near tears to continue and he had to stop to draw breath and recover what composure he could. He had made his stand and he knew it would cost him his freedom if not his life, but he'd found strength and cleanliness and honour in what he'd said. Despite all the ugly emotions in that tight fly-blown room — the sick excitement that he'd seen so often when the slaves were whipped, the furious incomprehension, the hunger to hurt and punish — he'd told the truth and shamed the devil. Now let come what may.

'Why, the man's mad,' Frederick Bradbury said. 'I never heard the like. Does he often rave like this, Mr Tomson?'

Mr Tomson admitted that he had spoke so on occasions and Mr Cooper was loud in confirmation. 'Stark, starin, raving mad, sir, we allus said so.'

'He weren't too mad to know how to draw a pistol,' Mr Smith said sourly. 'He was sane enough then, in all conscience.'

The outburst, shocking though it was, had offered Frederick Bradbury an escape from his dilemma. If the man was mad, there was no need to send him to jail. He turned to his surgeon. 'What say you, sir? Is he mad, think 'ee?'

'Oh, indubitably, Mr Bradbury,' the surgeon told him. 'There's no question of it. A rising of the mother which has led to delirium extremis. A most interesting case.'

'What's to be done with him?'

366

'He should be sent to Bedlam with all speed,' the surgeon said, happily envisaging the introductory fee he would earn from the transaction. 'They are experienced in such cases and would know how to treat him.' He was already composing his offer to the surgeons there. A man who looked so wild and raved so lucidly would attract the crowds uncommon well. ''Tis beyond our competence to treat him here without the necessary restraints, leg irons and shackles and straitjackets and so forth. Bedlam is the leading asylum in the country and has the wherewithal for the most intractable cases. I could negotiate the fee and the cost of his keep, should you wish it.'

The image of his hated adversary being forced into a strait-jacket and whipped for his intransigence made Mr Smith gloat with satisfaction, but Mr Bradbury was concerned. The thought of paying for an unknown lunatic to be kept in an asylum disturbed him. What would brother George say of it? If only he wasn't so caught up in this wretched wedding and could be sent for to offer advice. Could they afford such an action? And should they? 'How long would he stay there, think'ee?' he asked.

'Ah now, sir, as to that,' the surgeon reassured, ''tis impossible to say with any accuracy but, in my experience, they rarely see out a year. Most are dead within months. Delirium is weakening.'

As if to prove him right, Jack gave a low groan and fell to the floor insensible, his head and limbs shaking uncontrollably, bound as they were, his skin grey and streaked with sweat, his eyes rolling, the very image of a madman.

Mr Bradbury leaned across his desk to look at him. 'How soon could it be arranged?'

'As soon as you wish, sir. He could be gone on the noon stage, should you require it.'

'You would accompany him?'

At a price. 'To the very gate, sir. You have my word on't.'

So it was decided. A closed carriage was hired to take the lunatic to the stagecoach, where he was dragged out, more or less unconscious and, after considerable argument with the coachman and a sizeable bribe, was pulled and pushed into an outside seat, held in position by the surgeon and joggled away to London. Such is the price for telling the truth to those who cannot bear to hear it.

Left on his own in the confusion of the quayside, Blue had sat on his heels behind the bollard, carefully hidden by shadow, and watched and waited. It was hard to make sense of what was happening around him because there were so many people about and they all moved so quickly and shouted so loudly and looked so odd with their curled white wigs and their thick canes and sparkling shoes. He realized that Mr Jack was escaping when he jumped off the quay and watched with admiration as he swam across the river and disappeared among the crowds on the opposite bank. Then he wasn't sure what he was supposed to do next, so he sat where he was and went on waiting.

He was miserably upset to see his master dragged back to the quay with blood dripping from his mouth and the top half of his body trussed with great ropes, and very alarmed when he was marched off with all those grumbling men around him and taken into one of the big houses beside the quay. But he went on waiting. What else could he do?

People came and went and presently a carriage arrived, drawn by two black horses, and Mr Jack was carried out of the house as though he were dead and pushed inside. At that he sprang to his feet, ready to follow, but the carriage was off at such speed that it had left the quay and disappeared into all the other traffic on the road before he could catch up with it. He was alone in this bewildering city, without his master and with no one who could speak his language and he would have to make his way by his own devices. But he cheered himself with the thought that there was still his precious paper. What he had to do now was to find someone who would read it to him and tell him where he was to go. Someone who looked kindly, Mr Jack had said. Someone who smiled.

It was easier thought than done, for very few people were smiling on the quayside. They scowled and argued and punched one hand against the other, and smoked pipes with such intensity and fury that they quite alarmed him and sometimes laughed in a rough barking way as though they were dogs — but few smiled.

He tried a gentleman in an odd-looking brown wig, who was writing things in a book with a little wooden stick and seemed a quiet sort of person, but he waved him away with the little stick and told him to be off. He tried a lady who was walking along the quay with a gentleman in a bright red coat, but she looked at him with such disdain that he knew she wouldn't answer even before the words were out of his mouth. He tried an old man and a young one, but the former merely frowned and the latter turned away as though he was invisible. He tried three possible ladies one after the other but they were smiling at their companions and wouldn't smile or speak to him. It was after midday, as he knew, because the sun had dropped during his search and now he was beginning to feel desperate. What if no one would help him? What would he do then? And at that point, he saw the lady. She was climbing out of a little cart which was loaded with vegetables and driven by an old man in a rough brown jacket, with a black dog sitting bold upright beside him. She had a straw hat on her head and a baby in her arms — a nice fat baby who laughed and chuckled when she settled him on her hip — and she was smiling at everybody, the man in the cart, the dog, the baby. Something in the grace of her body, as she stood swayed against the weight of the child on her hip, reminded him of his mother. He ran to her at once.

Thirty-one

Mr Jones had taken an unconscionable time to drive his cart to Bristol and Suki was sick with impatience. She'd been up before dawn to pack her bag with William's clothes and gather up her few possessions, and she'd said goodbye to her family and the farmer at first light but the old man had been so tantalizingly slow that it was past one o'clock before they finally ambled on to the Broad Quay. And he seemed to think he'd done well, foolish crittur.

'Here we are then,' he said, beaming at her as he reined the mare to a halt. 'Broad Quay as ever is. We made good speed, don' 'ee think? You haven't to meet that ol' coach till three, now have 'ee, so you got time a-plenty. Two whole hours. I'd get something to eat if I was you.'

Suki looked along the lines of ships crowded into the quay. Twould take hours simply to walk from ship to ship. But he meant well and was looking at her so hopeful of a smile that she thanked him and smiled back, despite her annoyance. After all, he didn't know she was here to search for her lover and that every minute was precious. But she *was* here. That was what mattered. She was here and in a few minutes she would know if Jack's ship was in or when 'twas like to arrive. I'll go to the shipping office straight off, she decided, and see what they knows of it. And she sat William on the seat and jumped out of the cart.

What crowds there were on the quay and how strong they smelt and what a great noise they were making, caw, caw, caw, chatter-chatter — just like a flock of crows and maggot pies. After weeks in the quiet of Twerton, she found it quite dizzying. They were fine folk, though, there was no doubt of that. She'd never seen so much gold braid or so many gold buttons, and the ladies were the equal of Lady Bradbury in their silks and satins, especially the one promenading on the arm of that tall redcoat. Her shoes must have cost a fortune. The only drab figure on the quay was a funny-looking man in a brown coat and an old-fashioned bob wig, who was sitting on the wall, busily writing in a green chapbook. There was something vaguely familiar about him, but she couldn't think what it was, not even when he lifted his head and looked across at her.

No matter. He was of no consequence. Not when she was so near to finding the Captain. She held out her arms to William and Mr Jones lowered him down to her.

'Who's a pretty boy?' she said, holding him up before her, delighting in his fine fat limbs and his fine brown eyes. 'If you'm a good babba and you lets me go a-searchin', you shall have a sugar stick, by an' by. What do 'ee think to that?' And he chuckled and babbled and reached down to catch her hair, as happy as she was. 'You'm too much of a weight to hold up for long,' she told him, pretending to scold, and she swung him about and settled him on her hip. And at that moment, a black boy ran out of the crowd and came and stood right in front of her. He was dressed in canvas breeches and a smock shirt like a sailor and he had a paper in his hand.

'An't please you,' he said. 'You read this to me?'

She really didn't want to spend any of her precious time reading to a strange boy and opened her mouth to tell him so, but he was looking at her so pleadingly and he had such an open, friendly face and such blue eyes — blue as the sky, which was uncommon odd for a black boy — that she couldn't deny him.

'Later,' she temporized. 'I can't now, but I will later.'

Mr Jones lifted the bag out of the cart and handed it down to her. 'I'll be off then,' he said. 'You'll wait hereabouts, I daresay, till your mistress arrives. There's a good chop house on the corner. Good luck to 'ee.'

Suki thanked him, for he *did* mean well despite his slowness. Then she set the bag down on the cobbles next to the black boy. 'Stay here an' make yourself useful an' look after my bag,' she commanded, as the cart rattled away. 'I got things to do. When they'm done, I'll come back to 'ee.'

He gazed at her. 'You read my paper?'

'Aye,' Suki said, scanning the quayside for the shipping office. 'Just stay there and wait for me.' She could see the door, no distance away.

Blue squatted on his heels beside the bag and settled to wait again, watching as she went swaying away, the baby's bare feet swinging at her hip. He was hungry and thirsty and the quayside was as confusing as ever, but he knew she would come back because she'd smiled as she said so.

The shipping office was in its usual state of excited activity, but this time Suki pushed to the front and made her demands in a loud voice. And was instantly rewarded with the news that the *Bonny Beaufoy* had come in 'this very morning as ever is' and was docked at the west quay, ready for unloading. 'You can see her from this windy. See? One, two, three — tenth one along. Walk down an' you'll find her.'

Walking was too tame and too slow. Even with William's weight on her hip, she ran. He was here. In just a few minutes, they would be together again and her long, long wait would be over. My dear, darling Captain.

The ship was swarming with men unloading the cargo. There was no sign of the Captain but that was of no consequence with so many there who could tell her where he was.

'Have 'ee seen the Captain?' she asked the nearest sailor.

He didn't bother to look at her. 'He'm on the quay, Missus. Conversin' with Mr Smith.'

She looked, her heart leaping, but she couldn't see him. 'Could you point un out to me?'

The sailor stood up and straightened his back. 'There!' he said and pointed. To a stranger.

She was cast down. 'That am't the Captain.'

'He's the onny one we got,' the sailor told her. 'How many captains d'you want?'

'Captain Jack,' she told him. 'He's the one I want.'

'Then you'm come to the wrong ship,' he said. 'There's no one a' that name aboard the *Bonny Beaufoy*. Our captain's Mr Tomson which is him down on the quay. There's no Captain Jack.'

'There must be,' she insisted, 'for this here's the ship he sailed on. I have it on good authority. Captain Jack.'

'Do she mean Mr Jerome?' another sailor asked, coming up to join his shipmate. 'His name's Jack. An' he were master of the prize ship on her way home, so he'rn a captain of sorts. What do'ee look like, this Captain Jack of yourn?'

She told them happily. 'Taller than either one of you, an' a deal taller than me, with broad shoulders an' long legs an' a swaggerin' way of walking. Wears his own hair, thick hair, dark brown like his eyes. White teeth, all lovely an' even. Strong hands...'

'That ain't Jack Jerome,' the second sailor said interrupting her before she could descend into further raptures. 'Except for the swaggerin'. He'm a stocky sort a' fellow with no hair to speak of, brown or otherwise, bein' his head's a-shaven.'

'He must be here,' she said, insisting because she w'as beginning to feel desperate. 'Captain Jack. You must know him.'

But they turned back to their work. 'Twas a wench in pursuit of a lost lover and not worth the waste of breath.

Suki hoisted William into a more comfortable position on her hip and thought hard. He had to be here somewhere. Those men were fools not to know of him, when this was the ship he'd sailed on. She wouldn't give up at the first hurdle. She'd ask one of the others. There were enough of them about and one of them was bound to know.

None did, although she tried more than a dozen. The answer was always the same. There'd been no Captain Jack aboard any of the three vessels, except for Mr Jerome, who turned up as she was questioning a surly fellow with a gold earring, and certainly wasn't her Jack.

'I'll not be beat,' she said to William, as she set him down on the cobbles and let him walk. 'We'll go back to the shipping office, my 'andsome, that's what we'll do, and see if they got a list of the crew.' She should have thought of that in the first place, if she'd not been so quick to get to the ship. They would know.

'No, ma'am,' the clerk told her. 'Crews are took on by the masters. They'm the onny ones what knows names and so forth. You'll have to ask the master. I can tell you who he is.'

'I know who he is,' she said drooping with disappointment. 'I seen him on the quay. Mr Tomson.'

As she trailed out of the office, carrying William on her hip again, she couldn't think what to do next. There were blank walls whichever way she turned and it was nearly time to meet Miss Ariadne. Oh what was amiss with all these foolish people? Why couldn't they tell her what she wanted to know?

The little black boy was still waiting patiently beside her baggage. Poor thing. She'd forgotten all about him and he'd waited all this time. So as she couldn't think of anything else to do, she strolled across to read his paper for him and calm her irritation by a good deed.

He jumped to his feet as soon as he saw her, smiling broadly and holding the paper out. 'You read for me now?'

'Yes,' she said, and read. 'You are to go to the Llandoger Trow and ask there for Quin Cutpurse.' The impact of the name made her heart leap. Well, here's a thing! Quin Cutpurse. The very man I should have looked for in the first place and here's this nigger-boy been a-sittin' here all this time knowin' where he is. Quin Cutpurse. She had a sudden vivid memory of him: strolling through the Spring Gardens with Jack beside him, laughing together; sprawled before her in that dreadful brothel; scolding her for daring to address him by name, with his commanding voice and his swarthy face and that black eye patch of his. What's this child doin' a-looking for *him?* 'Do you know the gentleman?'

'No, ma'am,' the boy said. 'My master, he say to find him. Where I go? You show me?'

Let anyone try to stop her.

She handed him the bag and set off at a great pace. Quin Cutpurse! What luck! Neither she nor Blue were aware that the gentleman in the brown bob wig was following at their heels.

The Llandoger Trow was crowded and there was so much tobacco smoke in the air that it was impossible to see from one end of it to the other. It gathered in dense clouds under the beams, fogged the leaded windows and ribboned about the potboys as they struggled between the tables delivering full tankards and retrieving empty ones. There was no sign of the eye patch but there were plenty of people to ask and most of them cheerful with ale. She took her question to the barman, but was careful not to ask it until she'd sweetened him with custom by ordering a pint of good ale for herself and a platter of cold meats for the boy.

'Quin,' he said, when she'd read him the note. 'You just missed him. He been in an' out these last three days. Him and his mates. Waitin' for something I shouldn't wonder.'

'This boy's got a message for him,' she explained. 'He been told to wait here.'

'Ah well,' the barman said, turning to another customer, 'that accounts. Yes, sir, what can I do for 'ee?'

She waited until the newcomer had been sewed, noticing idly that it was the gentleman in the brown bob wig she'd seen on the quay, then she pressed on. 'You don't happen to have seen Captain Jack anywhere's about?'

'I wish I had,' the barman said, frowning. 'He got two shillin' on the slate he owe me. No, I haven't seen un for months. Went to sea, so they say.'

Every road leads to a blank wall, Suki thought, and jumped as the bar clock struck three. 'Oh, my dear life,' she said to Blue. 'Look at the time. My mistress will be on the quay and I'm not there to meet her.' She led him to the corner of the room and sat him down at the end of one of the long trestle tables. 'There's your meat an' there's the rest of my ale to wash it down. You'm to sit here till Mr Cutpurse comes back. You understand? Which he'll do in a while, I'm sure of it, if he'm a-waitin' for something. I'll try an' get back to 'ee a bit later on, but don't depend on't.' And with that she left him to vitals and vigil, picked up her baggage and strode off to the quay again.

Ariadne was waiting by the shipping office, looking very grand in a blue silk travelling gown with a stomacher embroidered in pink and gold and a flat bonnet trimmed to match. 'La,' she said, as Suki came panting up to greet her. 'I thought you had missed me. Have 'ee dined? There's a chop house nearby — serves a tolerable meal, I'm told. We've an hour to spare before the coach to Bath. I've *so* much to tell 'ee.'

It was actually an intolerable meal, for the chops were burnt and the ale flat, but as they were both too excited and preoccupied to do more than pick at their food, its lack of quality went unremarked.

'We are to be in Bath for seven days,' Ariadne reported, 'which is little time for all that has to be done. Papa has taken a house in Queen Square. South Parade ain't grand enough for us now that we have a *bride* in the family. 'Tis all for the *bride*. Much good may it do her. She grows more insufferable by the hour. But to return to the matter in hand. You must go the milliner's first thing tomorrow morning, for I mean to have two gowns made up to the most particular specification, the most particular, and it must all be done in secret with none to know of it save thee and me.'

'None will, I give 'ee my word,' Suki said, gazing at her chop and wondering whether she would have time to slip back to the Llandoger Trow before the coach came. If Mr Cutpurse really was waiting for something, he could be back at any time. He could be there now, this very minute. And if anyone would know where the Captain had got to, he was the man.

''Tis a matter of outwitting 'em.' Ariadne explained. 'If I'm to be shamed before the company, then I'll be shamed in a martyr's gown and let us see how Mamma will enjoy *that*. With luck 'twill shame *her*. Which is a consummation much to be desired. It must be a plain white cambric or a calico if 'tis available, nothing too heavy for I have to move, but perfectly plain and simple, such as a nun would wear.'

'Yes,' Suki said vaguely. William was asleep on her lap and with any luck would sleep for an hour as he usually did of an afternoon. She might just have time. 'Have I got time to run a message afore we catches the coach? If I left William here with you, I could be there an' back in two shakes. He'm sound asleep and he wouldn't be a bit of bother. He could lie in my shawl on a couple of chairs. I wouldn't ask 'ee only 'tis urgent. Jack's come home. His ship put in this morning.'

'And you've found him?'

'No,' Suki said sadly. 'I asked at the quay but they all said they'd never heard of him, which is arrant nonsense. He must be somewheres about an' there's a man at the Llandoger Trow — or to speak true a man as *might* be at the Llandoger Trow — an' if he is, he might know where he is. 'Tis all unsatisfactory, I know, but he'm the only chance I got.'

She'd expected instant agreement, even assistance, but Ariadne was frowning. 'How if you miss the coach?' she said. ''Tis only a matter of minutes before 'twill arrive and they will be expecting us to travel together. I said nothing of your visit to Twerton, you understand, and 'twould be unwise to provoke 'em.'

'I'll be uncommon speedy,' Suki promised.

'But what if you ain't speedy enough?' Ariadne said. 'And what if this man of yours ain't at the inn? You said he might be, did you not? If he ain't there, 'twill be a wild goose chase and no good will come of it, no matter how speedy you are. We must use our wits and see what is best to be done. Your lover is returned, you say. You are sure on't?'

'I'm sure on't.'

'But you ain't seen him, so he must have some matter that needs his urgent attention or he'd have sought 'ee out at once. Or else he's dead at sea and none have told 'ee of it.'

'No,' Suki said stubbornly. 'He am't dead. I'd have known if he had been. I'm quite sure of *that.*'

'Then we must assume he's alive and ashore,' Ariadne went on thinking. 'Ashore and a man afoot, so he will need his horse, sooner or later. You left word he would find it at Twerton, did 'ee not?'

Suki had forgotten all about Beau. But of course, Jack would go to Twerton to find him. He might be on his way there this very afternoon. Why hadn't she thought of it? And why hadn't she thought to ask for him at the livery yard instead of trailing off to the inn? 'Have I time to run across to the yard?' she asked.

But the Bath stage was trundling to a halt before the chop house. They could see it from their seat in the window.

'You must write to your farmer,' Ariadne said, as Suki picked up her sleeping baby and gathered her belongings. 'You must give him instructions, tell him the address of our lodgings in Bath and our address in Cavendish Square, and say he is to send Captain Jack to find you wherever you are. 'Tis the sensible thing to do and, besides, you ain't got time for anything else.'

But he could be at the Llandoger Trow, Suki thought as she climbed aboard the stage. Or at the livery yard. And me a hundred yards away. 'Twas too thwarting for words. Anything could be happening and she wouldn't know of it. Quin Cutpurse could be returned and he and Jack could be together. They'd always been boon companions. A pair of rogues both. Oh, if only she could have run across to find out instead of being rushed away like this. That was the trouble with the Bradburys. They were always in a rush and Ariadne was just the same as all the others. 'Twouldn't have hurt her to let me run to the inn. I could have been there an' back in two shakes.

'Twill turn out for the best, you'll see,' Ariadne said. 'You couldn't have missed the coach. Just think of the questions there would have been. We must tickle 'em like trout if we're to succeed.'

But as Suki settled William across her knees, she was thinking of the black boy with the blue eyes. He could be talking to Quin Cutpurse at this very minute, she thought, instead of me. And the thought made her burn with impatience and frustration.

Blue was standing in a stinking alley alongside the Llandoger Trow, piddling against the wall. He'd sat in the inn for as long as he could, but

Mr Cutpurse hadn't turned up and the lady hadn't come back, and, finally, when most of the men around him had finished their ale and sloped out and there was only the man in the brown wig and a group of argumentative seamen left, his bladder was so uncomfortable that he stole out of the place to find somewhere to relieve himself.

A tall man in green breeches and a dirty black jacket positioned himself alongside. Blue shifted his feet as he refastened his breeches but the man hadn't come to piddle. 'You the young un with the message for Quin?' he said, revealing a mouth full of broken teeth. And when Blue nodded, he winked and said, 'Follow me.'

For a second, Blue thought he was going to be taken back to his seat by the bar but he was wrong. The tall man led him to a low door at the side of the building and up a narrow flight of stairs to a low-ceilinged chamber on the first floor. A man with a black eye patch was sitting by the fire with two rough-looking men beside him, all of them smoking clay pipes and deep in conversation.

'Here's your young un at last,' the tall man said, pushing Blue forward. 'Found un in the alley a-waterin' the roses.'

'You weren't seen?' Quin asked.

'No fear. I'm sly.'

Quin held out his hand for Blue's message and recognized the handwriting at once. 'Why 'tis from Jack,' he said, 'an' no news at all. 'Tis instructions to the nigger and here's us a-thinking 'twould be news of a good take.'

'Then we goes for the weddin' party,' the tall man said. 'And takes the stage tonight by way of rehearsal and for to pay the landlord. That's my opinion of it.'

Quin turned to the man on his right. 'Charlie?'

'I'm with Spider. I votes for the stage.'

'Johnny?'

'I ain't keen,' the third man said. 'Not with a thief-taker about.' ''Tis only Melluish,' Quin said, drawing on his pipe. 'An' he's a stick-in-the-mud. You've only to look at him to see that. Him and that old brown wig of his. He'd be hard put to it to catch a cold, leave alone a thief.'

'He'm a stubborn man,' Spider observed, picking his broken teeth with a broken fingernail. 'He been a-sittin' in that there corner all afternoon, awaitin' for us. He'm a-sittin' there still, I'd lay money on't.'

'Let him sit all he likes,' Quin said, laughing. 'He'd have to get up prodigious early to catch me. My vote's for the stage. He'll not trouble us.'

'What a' the nigger?' Charlie Moss wanted to know. 'What's to be done with him?'

Quin Cutpurse turned to Blue and held out the paper. 'What's your name, boy?'

'Blue, sir.'

'Well then, Blue, when did our Jack give this to 'ee?'

'Aboard ship, sir.'

'And now he'm took to London, accordin' to Spider here. Gone to Bedlam, so he has. So what's to be done with 'ee?'

'Send un packing,' Johnny said, spitting in the general direction of the spittoon and missing by inches. 'We don't want a nigger along of us. 'Twould queer our pitch.'

'We could sell him in London,' Charlie Moss said. 'There's many a nibbing cull a-lurkin' in the Seven Dials would give their lucre for a sharp lad. Pertickly one small enough ter slip in winders.'

'What's your opinion of it?' Quin asked the boy.

'An't please you, sir, I find my master.'

Johnny snorted with laughter. 'Much good may it do un if he'm in Bedlam.'

'Let him find that out for himself,' Quin said. 'He can stay here till we rides to London an' I say we takes him along. Let him sniff out the lie of the land. See how things stand, in this precious asylum of there'n. If Jack's to be sprung, he'll see how'tis to be done.'

'An' if he ain't?' Charlie asked.

Quin rubbed his thumb against his middle finger to signify the exchange of cash. 'Then we'll have us a sale, eh Blue?'

Thirty-two

By the time Ariadne and Suki arrived at their new lodgings in Queen Square, Ariadne was totally speechless and Suki totally cast down. To be caught in Bath when she knew that Jack *had* to be somewhere in Bristol was so distressing it was all she could do not to weep. But she settled Ariadne into her room, carried William down into the kitchen, inspected the room set aside for his nursery and generally tried to behave in her usual way.

The place was full of servants, but luckily she didn't know any of them, except for Mr Jessup, who was too grand to notice her, and Barnaby, who was too distracted, and Hepzibah, who was too busy lording it because she was lady's maid to the bride and felt she should be given first attention over everything and everybody in the house in consequence.

'I'd have thought you'd have been with that husband of yours,' she sneered when she saw Suki. 'Or ain't he come home to 'ee yet?'

'I got work to do here,' Suki said, huffily. 'I've a babba to feed in case you haven't noticed. Twouldn't do for all of us to be a-sitting in the kitchen stuffing our faces with sweetmeats all day.'

To her delight, Hepzie actually blushed. 'I'm tasting 'em for the bride,' she said, and carried the little dish out of the kitchen.

'If she go on a-feedin' her face the way she do,' Cook said, 'the bride'll go off bang afore she gets to the altar. I never seen a gel eat so much.' She glanced up at the bell board. 'There's your young lady a-ringing for you, Suki. You can leave the baby with Abigail.'

Ariadne was sitting at the writing desk in her room busily scratching an instruction for the milliner. She signalled to Suki that she was to shut the door and then whispered her orders.

'This is to go to my old friend the milliner,' she said. 'When 'tis done, you shall write to your farmer and then you can take your letter to the post when you deliver mine. What are the others about?'

'They'm dressing for the Assembly Rooms.'

'Good riddance to 'em,' Ariadne hissed, signing her name with a flourish. 'There!'Tis done. Now write your letter before Hepzi-bah comes to spy on us.'

So Suki set herself to composition.

I did not find Captain Jack, but I knows he is returned on account of his ship came in this morning which I have seen. Should he come to Twerton for Beau, which I will pay you for the fodder so soon as I am payed by Lady Bradbury, would you be so kind as to tell him where I am, which is at this address until Thursday morning and thereafter in Cavendish Square number 16 in London. I hopes my father continues well and he don't have no further contree-toms.

Once the letter had been handed over to the postboy, she felt cast down again, for there was so much to remind her of Bristol and her darling. There were gallants everywhere, strolling about in his easy, loose-limbed way, or sprawling in the coffee houses enjoying their tobacco, and, on her way back to Queen Square, she passed the Bristol coach as the last travellers were climbing aboard and wished with all her heart that she had the freedom to join them.

But the days passed and there was no time for anything except work. She woke every morning buoyed up by the hope that this could be the day when she would slip away and look for him, and fell into her truckle bed every night exhausted and disappointed. Ariadne kept to her room and her silence, but she rang for her every minute of the day, sending her to the milliner to bring back off-cuts of the materials she'd chosen or to make arrangements for fittings, fussing over trimmings, ordering slippers, buttons, ribbons, feathers.

'I must have perfection,' she said when Suki sighed. 'You'll not deny me that, surely. This could be the last service you will do me. 'Tis little enough when you think how Melissa is disporting herself.'

Which was true enough, for the bride had the entire household in uproar, with gowns to be fitted, a new necklace of fine pearls to be admired, special meals to be cooked to accommodate her growing appetite, wedding lists perused and the wedding breakfast chosen dish by dish in consultation with the cook and her mother, for, as she explained — entirely unnecessarily since they were both well aware of it — 'my husband has the most delicate constitution and must not be put to the least inconvenience.'

And as if all this fussing over food and clothes weren't bad enough, Lady Bradbury was determined that before she returned to London every single one of her Bath acquaintances should know of her daughter's great triumph, so the family attended every important ball, gave elaborate dinner parties every afternoon and even held a public breakfast, in the Harrison Rooms no less, as though they were gentry born. And, of course, William's presence was required in the drawing room before and after every event, so that his progress could be displayed and applauded.

'Never a minute's peace in this house,' the cook complained, thumping her mixing bowl down on the table with displeasure. 'Why she got to have a dish of coddled eggs in the middle of the afternoon I cannot imagine. I shall be glad when we all go back to London again and can have this wedding over an' done with.' Suki agreed with her wholeheartedly.

'The week's nearly up,' she whispered to Ariadne as she helped her undress on Tuesday night, 'an' I've not heard a word from Farmer Lambton, nor gone to Bristol.'

''Tis my last fitting tomorrow,' Ariadne whispered back.

She thinks of nothing save gowns and ribbons, Suki thought sadly, whilst I'm a-wondering if my lover is alive or dead, and there'm no way I can find the truth on't.

But the very next morning a letter arrived from Twerton addressed to Miss Brown. She paid the postboy with trembling hands and took William and the letter to the nursery, her heart leaping with hope. At last! Now she would know. Had he gone to Twerton for that horse of his? Oh he must've done. And if he had, he'd be coming to Queen Square to find her. Maybe that very morning. She tore the seal, bright-eyed with expectation.

It was a flat, dull, disappointing letter. Captain Jack had not arrived to collect his horse, which was in fine fettle. Her father was well. Her mother sent her fondest love to her and to William. '*There is*', Farmer Lambton wrote at the end of the first page, '*only one thing left to say.*'

Suki couldn't think of anything at all, except her misery at his lack of news, but she turned over the page to read what it was.

Since my dear wife's death, I have been giving thought to what is to become of the farm, which needs a woman's presence and a woman's care. I hope I do not trouble you too much if I say that it do seem to me that 'tis possible that your lover may not return to you, there being many hazards at sea and you having heard no word of him. Had he returned on the ship you saw, I am certain he would have met with you or come to the farm in search of his horse. That being the state of affairs at present which, believe me, I hope may change to your better satisfaction, I have a proposition to put to you which I hope will, if not meet with your approval, not displease.

I have asked your father for your hand in marriage. He is agreeable to it and said I might broach the matter when I wrote this letter. I do not expect an answer immediately for this is naturally a matter that you must consider carefully and I know you are not one to act on the gad.

Howsomever, I urge you to consider the advantages. The farm is known to you, on which account the running of it would present no difficulty. You are young and strong. The baby could be farmed here while you are still his nurse, should you and the Bradburys wish it. You would be near your father should he need your care. You have my assurance that I would be a considerate husband to you.

You would want for nothing.

Your Obedient Servant, Constant Lambton

She didn't know whether to laugh or cry and in the end did both, to William's consternation. How could she possibly answer such a letter? Oh, the foolish, foolish man! But then she remembered that odd moment in the kitchen when they'd looked at one another and been caught up in all the wrong emotions. Or had she imagined it? No. She was sure she hadn't. It *had* happened and happened to them both. And yet he'd never referred to it, either then or now. Oh, how confusing this was. And what a long time 'twould be before she could talk to Ariadne about it and hear what she had to say.

Ariadne was trenchant. 'You'll not agree to it,' she said, so annoyed by the news that she forgot to whisper.

Suki had been fluctuating all week between a determined hope that she would find her lover again, somehow or other, and that all would be well, and a growing and unhappy fear that he was lost to her, either at sea or through sickness, or maybe even through loss of love, which was the worst and deepest misery of all. 'He offers me a home,' she said, 'and if I don't find Captain jack, I shall need a home of sorts, if I'm to keep my

William.' 'Twas uncommon hard to be torn between your baby and your lover, but that seemed to be the size of it.

'But you don't love him.'

'I like un well enough.'

'Liking ain't love,' Ariadne said firmly. 'You mustn't do it.'

'I'll write an' tell un I'm considerin' it,' Suki temporised. 'Twill wait till after this wedding, when I might get a chance to visit Bristol and see Mr Wenham. There's no need to rush. He said so.'

Ariadne wondered whether she should say something comforting because it was plain that Suki was beginning to doubt whether she would see her lover again, which was an uncommon painful state to be in, as she knew only too well, but at that moment they heard the thump of footsteps on the landing and Sir George bellowing, so their conversation had to stop.

'Od's teeth!' the gentleman roared. 'Hermione! Where are you? Such news!'

Lady Bradbury was in Melissa's room helping her to decide between a pair of white satin slippers and an identical pair in cream. 'What's amiss?' she said calmly, opening the door to him.

He had a billet in his hand and waved it at her. 'Such news,' he said happily.

'Another addition to the guest list,' she said. 'I do wish people would not leave things to the last moment. Who is it this time?'

'Guest list,' he bellowed. 'There's more to life than guest lists. This is trade, ma'am. Trade. Our merchantman is back from Lisbon and we've made a splendid profit. Quite splendid. I have it first-hand from Sir Humphrey. How say you to *that?*'

'Had he no message for me?' Melissa asked petulantly.

The question puzzled her father. 'What message should he have, dammit? You're to be married a' Wednesday.'

'Which is why,' Lady Bradbury told him acidly, 'a wedding list is of some consequence.'

Sir George was too busy planning his return journey to pay attention to such a puny barb. 'We will start at first light,' he declared. 'We three will travel in the coach and four with Ariadne and the goods and household shall take the wagon. We'll harness six horses to the wagon and then we shall be well provided for.'

'I trust we shall not leave too early,' Lady Bradbury demurred. 'Arabella tells me there are highwaymen abroad. Two coaches were robbed on the new road, only last week. Would we not be wise, my love, to wait until full daylight?'

Sir George was scathing. 'Are we old women, to be frightened of a shadow? Tush wife, where's your courage?'

'We do have a bride to consider,' Hermione said. 'You would not wish her to be discommoded on her way to her wedding. 'Twould be heartless.'

His answer was immediate and dismissive. 'We will travel the old road by way of Laycock. 'Twill be safe enough there, in all conscience, even for a bride.' Then he was off down the stairs, roaring for Jessup.

'I shall be *so* glad to be married, Mamma,' Melissa said.

*

The next day dawned bold as summer and bright with sunshine. Sir George was up earlier than his servants, and seemed to be everywhere at once, supervising the packing, checking the horses, bellowing at Barnaby and chivvying his womenfolk.

'I've a mind to make you travel in the cart,' he told Ariadne, half teasing, half serious. 'You'd soon be cured of all your nonsense in that event.' But she climbed into the coach as silent as ever, and didn't look at him.

'You two had best sit facing me,' Lady Bradbury said as Melissa came yawning from the house to join her sister. There is room for my dear Benjy beside me.'

That arrangement didn't satisfy Sir George at all. ''Od's teeth!' he roared. 'I'll not have that cur upon the seat. The floor is good enough for dogs, ma'am.'

'You are to be spurned, I fear, poor dumb creature that you are,' Hermione said, lifting her corpulent animal and settling him upon the floor.

But that didn't please her loquacious daughter. 'Pray do sit the horrid creature somewhere else, Mamma. If 'twere to shit, my petticoat would bear the brunt. You know how unreliable it is. Let it sit in the comer next to Ariadne. She'll not mind, being she can't speak and she ain't the bride.'

As she climbed reluctantly into the open cart with William on her hip, Suki glanced across at Sir George, irritated by his plump face and his plump complacence. He moves us all about, she thought, whenever he feels like it, all on the gad and with no thought that we might have opinions on the matter, that there might be people we don't want to leave behind. Then it occurred to her that this was the first time she'd been near him since that awful morning when she'd hit him, and now they were to spend two and half days travelling together. What if he were to see her again at one of their overnight stops and recognize her?

But they were all settled and ready for the off and he didn't seem to be looking at her, or at anybody else if it came to that, so maybe he'd forgotten. Jessup climbed up beside the postilion, and their journey began, up the slow hill to Bath Easton, leaving the city behind. Rich men have short memories when it comes to favours asked of serving girls, she thought, and Ariadne is always saying that women are less than cattle to him. But he shouldn't be dragging me away from Bristol all the same.

After a few miles, William became fractious and began to grizzle and complain, as he always did when he travelled anywhere. And really the way the cart rocked and juddered, she couldn't blame him. By the time they reached London, they would all be covered in bruises from head to toe. Fortunately, their lead horse cast a shoe outside a village called Box, so they had to stop and wait while the limping animal was led off to the nearest smithy. 'We will take the air while we may,' Sir George decreed. So they all climbed obediently from coach and cart and stood about uncomfortably on the uneven road. This time Sir George looked straight at her and obviously didn't have the faintest idea who she was. Which was rather a relief.

Presently, Lady Bradbury and Melissa took a short promenade, dragging the unfortunate Benjy behind them like a grunting cushion, but Suki and Ariadne sat on a tussock of rough grass with their backs against a dry stone wall while William amused himself plucking the stone crop. The road was lonely and silent, save for the occasional birdsong, and now Suki could understand her mistress's fear of attack, and see that the promenade was a nervous, watchful business and entailed much craning of necks and many abrupt turns. There was some sense of security inside their vehicles, but out in the open they all felt exposed and vulnerable.

She was relieved when horse and postilion returned and the journey could continue, uncomfortable though it was.

At ten o'clock they crossed a low stone bridge over a brook and came to a little old-fashioned village called Laycock, where the houses were a higgledy-piggledy collection, small and low and much in need of repair. As they trundled through a narrow street, past the glow of the smithy and an ancient inn where two mud-spattered horses stood waiting, Sir George stuck his red face out of the window and told the coachman to stop at the Red Lion.

'We will take breakfast here,' he said. 'Rest the horses, Sam. Bowden Hill ain't a jaunt for an empty stomach.'

The Red Lion was a modern building, set right on the edge of the village. It was three stories high and made of brick, with a fine classical balance about it, seven windows to each floor, three on the central bay and two on either side, and all finely graded and neatly curtained. Behind it was a courtyard shaded by a fine horse-chestnut tree, where there was a new pump for watering the horses and very fine stables. Inside it was still old-fashioned, with low beams overhead and a great stone hearth at the far end of the room. But they served a good strong cider in the servants hall and the food was wholesome.

The postilion was too full of gloom to eat well. 'Time to take our ease when we'm atop of Bowden Hill,' he said dourly. 'Why we couldn't've took the new road, I cannot imagine. But there 'tis. You can't tell 'em nothing, not that lot. I hopes they has the good sense to walk up the hill.'

'I shall speak to Sir George about it,' Jessup promised.

At the foot of the hill, the coach and cart both stopped and Sir George and Jessup got out to discuss conditions with the coachman while the household waited. Warblers were singing shrilly in the reeds beside the river and the sky was as blue as a thrush's egg.

''Tis a fine fair day,' Sir George said when he came back to his womenfolk, 'so we will walk to help the horses.'

'My love!' Hermione protested. 'Our shoes will be worn to shreds! Have you considered the distance?'

'Shoes!' he said. ''Od's teeth. Are we to consider shoes? If you wish to be at the White Hart by nightfall, you were well to do as I say.'

'I shall be ill!' she said leaning back in her seat and clutching her kerchief to her bosom. 'Have you no care for the delicacy of my constitution?'

He snorted and scowled, but eventually gave way. 'Very well, ma'am,' he said. 'Stay where you are, ma'am, and if we are forced to travel by night in consequence, we shall know whose folly to blame.'

She protested his heartlessness, but stayed in the coach, and so did Benjy, who was snoring in an evil-smelling heap at her feet. But everybody else got out or down, and prepared to climb. And a long hard climb it was, with the coachman leading the horses, up and up and further and further away from civilization, between dense trees that creaked and whispered ominously, and over ruts and hollows hardened by sunshine and brutal to the feet. Halfway up, they passed a solitary farmhouse, settled under the rim of the road, and the farmer came to the gate to touch his cap to Sir George and wish them good day. Then they toiled on past a bend in the road and the farm was lost to view among the trees. It was very hot and they were all footsore, and William grew heavier by the minute. Sir George walked ahead of his womenfolk, with Jessup and the coachman, the postilion walked with his horses, but Ariadne and Melissa and Suki dropped further and further behind.

'How far we shall see once we'in at the top,' Suki said to encourage her panting companions. At that moment, she could see very little except the road under her feet and a few inches of foliage on either side of her.

'Tis a view I could well do without,' Melissa grumbled. 'It takes a deal too much effort.' She was watching the road as she spoke, so Ariadne was able to glance at Suki and smile.

'We shall soon be there,' Suld said, returning the smile. There was a sudden sharp noise behind her, and she turned her head to see a black shape running out of the trees towards them. Then, almost before she had time to realize how frightened she was, three more figures followed the first. Four men, in black and green, masked men brandishing pistols and shouting in loud harsh voices, dark threatening men crouching under the branches and leaping into the road. Highwaymen!

The first caught Ariadne about the neck and had his pistol pressed into her side before she could scream, the second seized Melissa with such force that she fell, squealing like a stuck pig. At that, Sir George turned and began to run down the hill.

'Stand where you are, sir!' the leader yelled. 'Stand still, damme, or the girl is dead!' And Sir George stopped as though he had been frozen to the spot, and was instantly and totally in control of himself and the situation.

'Very well, sir,' he said. 'You may take what you please. You'll not be hindered, if the ladies are not molested.'

'In that case, I'll trouble you for your purse, sir,' the leader said equally coolly. 'You will all be bound, sir, that's understood, but pervidin' you do as you'm told, you'll come to no other harm. You have my word as a gentleman of the road. Stop the cart!'

Now Suki could see that the four men were not identical black shapes at all. They were all different and they all had different jobs to do. The one tying Ariadne's hands was young and fairheaded, with awkward bony wrists like her brother John; the one pulling the carthorses to a halt was tall and skinny with long angular limbs; the one sitting astride Melissa was the shortest of the four and wore bottle-green breeches and a green cocked hat; while the leader was a stocky man, with an undeniable presence, a watchful man, his wits as quick as his movements and his voice familiar to her, although in the panic of the moment she couldn't think why. She was noticing so much, but in a disjointed way, and without effort, as if her vision were no longer capable of sustained sight, but was fragmented, so that she saw events in a series of sharp brief glimpses. They passed so quickly they were gone before she could understand them, and yet they were hard edged and indelible and in the sharpest focus.

Melissa lying on the road where she had fallen, with Fair Hair sitting astride her, the barrel of his awful pistol jammed against her throat. There was a red hand mark on her cheek, and she was struggling to cry without making a sound. Fair Hair binding her hands behind her back, tying her into a squirming bundle, rolling the bundle into a ditch as if she was of no more consequence than dirty washing.

Ariadne tied to a tree, her face totally withdrawal, and her expression as mild as the saints in the church window.

Sir George stripping off his coat and tossing it to the leader, skimming his hat after it as if he were throwing pebbles across water. Green Breeches behind him, pulling his wig from his head and hurling it into the nearest tree, where it hung, like a huge dead duck. Sir George smiling as though he found it amusing. And there, on his bald pate, the dull red scar where she'd hit him.

The coach rolling backwards, as the horses scrambled and slipped, tiying to turn sideways to recover their balance, then set free and slithering down the hill, foam-flecked and showing the whites of their eyes, with the traces trailing behind them. The coach tipping over slowly and gracefully, grinding as it came to rest in the ditch, with one wheel still spinning uselessly in the air.

Jessup and the coachman back to back against a single slender tree, bound with grey rope and trembling like leaves. Jessup coughing.

Skinny climbing the sides of the fallen coach, all straggling arms and legs, making a grab for the postilion's fowling piece.

Benjy scrambling from the upturned coach, growling. His jaws clamped about Skinny's legs. A sudden blow, the pistol descending. The dog twitching in the road, dark blood trickling from his ear.

The master handing over purse, rings, watch. Brown hands grabbing. Lace torn from a pink sleeve. White face at a window.

Black mask before her. Hard eyes. Hard familiar eyes. William burrowing into her neck, clinging to her hair with both hands, 'Mamma! Mamma!'

'Your hands! Quick! Show me your hands.' Holding up one hand, then the other, stupidly. 'Purse?'

'No. I haven't any money.' She only possessed one article of any value and that was Jack's silk kerchief. She'd taken to wearing it tucked into the top of her bodice like a fichu and it was so creased and crumpled that it no longer looked the part. With luck, he wouldn't notice it.

'Buttons?' How vilely he smelt! His sweat strong and hot and acrid, reminding her of the Spring Gardens.

'No.' And then realization, spoken at once, before she could think how dangerous it was. 'I know who you are! You'm the one they call Spider.'

Then fear, filling her throat, and making her heart leap and struggle as he pulled her to her feet, baby and all, and pushed her ahead of him, to where his leader was standing, bouncing the breath out of her body with every step. She was aware that there were black legs following them along the ruts of the road and then, breathlessly, she was in a grassy clearing and surrounded by sweaty black clothes, hard limbs and harder eyes. Four fine horses were tethered to a bush, their fat rumps like polished chestnuts and there was a black boy standing beside them, his blue eyes wide. Blue eyes!

'She knows who we are,' Spider said.

Green Breeches spat. 'Shoot her,' he said. 'She'll peach, sure as fate. Shoot her, Quin.'

'She'm Captain Jack's wench, Charlie,' Quin Cutpurse said, considering her. 'We can't shoot the Captain's wench.'

'She'll peach.'

'Bind her legs!' Quin Cutpurse ordered, and Green Breeches bound her, very roughly indeed, and sat her beside a bramble bush, with William still in her arms, still burrowing into her neck, but miraculously not crying.

She could see the wide valley below her, stretching back and back until the detail was lost in a blue vagueness of distant hills. Ploughed fields as brown as ginger, shimmering lakes of winter wheat, pasture dotted with the small humped shapes of cattle, a vast, wade reassuring landscape, patched into comfortable irregularity by dark hedges and darker copses. She gazed as though she were sitting in the Spring Gardens and had nothing to fear, and, as she gazed, an odd quiet courage grew in her breast like an opening rose, so that her heart steadied and her mind cleared.

'You need have no fear of me,' she said and her voice was calm. 'I shan't peach. You've only to tell me one thing an' you have my vow, I'll not breathe a word of this to any livin' soul.'

'Do she mean it, Quin?' Green Breeches said, wiping his nose on Sir George's fine brocade. 'What do'ee think?'

'Tell me what you want,' Quin Gutpurse said. 'There's money a-plenty. Your master keeps a fine fat purse.'

'Not money,' she said. 'Just tell me where the Captain is. That's all I want.'

'And *that* will buy silence?'

'Yes.'

'Tell her, Quin, in heaven's name,' Green Breeches urged. 'We'll not have control of 'em much longer.' He had his foot in the stirrup of his horse and wras watching Fair Hair who was covering the prisoners with his pistol, standing legs astride in the middle of the road below them.

'Mount!' Quin Cutpurse called, untying his horse.

There was a scramble of feet and hooves and all four were on horseback and the horses wane wheeling and snorting and as eager to be off as their riders. Quin swung the black boy up into the saddle before him, and then they were galloping out of the clearing and across the fields, and he was calling back to her, 'Bedlam. That's where you'll find un. Bedlam-in-Moorfields.' Then they were gone.

She realized that she was exhausted and that her legs were shaking. But she knew where to find the Captain at last! At last!

'Gorn!' William said, looking for the horses. Now that they were on their own, he was perfectly cheerful. She answered him automatically. 'All gorn! Horses all gorn!' as if they were back at Twerton and he had been watching the cows come in for milking. My hands are free, she thought, watching them as they patted the baby's back. I'd best go and untie the others. But she didn't have the energy. The Captain was alive and in London, in Bedlam-in-Moorfields. That was all that mattered. She knew where he was and now she could find him.

She set William down on the rough grass and slowly untied her legs, stopping halfway through to remove an ant that was climbing on her petticoat. After the noise and speed of the attack, everything was extremely slow and peaceful. She strolled back down the hill like a member of the ton languidly taking the air and untied the master, slowly and painstakingly, without saying a word. Then she was exhausted again and had to sit against the tree because all she really wanted to do was to crawl into bed and sleep for hours.

She was aware that the master was running about untying ropes and giving orders in a quick clipped voice that she hadn't heard him use before, but none of it was really interesting. Jessup mounted one of the recaptured horses and trotted off downhill, Barnaby was untying the cook, Melissa was crying, Lady Bradbury eased herself out of the upturned door of the coach and walked past the dead body of her pet and didn't even notice him. Her face was a terrible grey-white, her left sleeve was stained with blood and she tottered as she walked, but Suki was too tired to feel any sympathy for her.

The cart was turned round and the ladies climbed into it and sat with their feet on the dirty straw and didn't complain. Then they all went down the hill, slowly and without speaking, with the master and Jessup walking behind them, and the postilion leading the horses, down to the river and the abbey and the gentle human society of Laycock. The warblers were still singing.

Thirty-three

The landlord of the Red Lion was most concerned by their bedraggled return, and ran out into the road to assist the ladies from the cart with his own hands.

'Tis a scandal!' he said to Lady Bradbury, sympathetically, spurred on by altruism and hope of profit. 'Highwaymen in broad daylight! And on Bowden Hill! I thought we were rid of 'em. My poor dear lady, how you must be suffering. Come in! Come in! We are here to serve you!'

The lady held up her blood-stained sleeve so that everybody could see the cuts she'd sustained when the coach overturned. 'Fiends!' she said, raising her eyes to heaven as if the highwaymen were already there and being judged. 'Heartless fiends! Look 'ee here. See what they've done!'

'They will end at Tyburn on the triple tree,' the landlord promised. 'Have no fear!'

The lady turned to her husband. 'Did I not particularly warn you of this very eventuality, my love?' she asked. 'Oh, how right I am proved!'

'No more of that!' Sir George said mildly, handing Melissa out of the cart. 'The danger is past and no life lost.'

'But consider what is stolen!'

'Money. Trinkets. Nothing of consequence,' Sir George said, dismissing them. 'We can soon replace 'em. I've done it once, damme. I daresay I shall do it again.' And ignoring his deshabille, and Melissa's protest that her pearls were *not* trinkets, he herded

his ladies through the front door. Then he gave instructions, in a voice of such massive authority that smeared, bald and half-naked as he was, he was obeyed without question. He would require a private room, in the front of the house, grooms were to be dispatched to find his horses, and a boy to retrieve his wig, the coach was to be mended, a surgeon sent for, he would need warm water, mulled wine, aqua vitae, tobacco. He stood in the middle of the room radiating energy. Even Suki had to admire him.

Soon bellows were being pumped into the kitchen fire and black coals were glowing into life, all three mullers were in use and every kettle in the house had been filled with water and set to heat. The family were ushered into a side room, with Jessup, Mrs Sparepenny and Hepzibah to attend them. Lady Bradbury was provided with cushions and a footstool, and the wise woman arrived, in lieu of a surgeon, and was soon administering sage tea to her blood-stained patient, and cleaning her cuts with a distillation of hound's tongue and moonwort, binding the torn edges together with newly gathered gossamer.

'Twill do well enough, milady,' she promised as she gathered her simples ready to leave, 'do 'ee but consent to rest and keep 'ee warm. Take only soothing foods for a day or two. Honey an' arrowroot, a chicken broth. But no red moat nor wines, nor spices, vinegars, strong sauces. I give 'ee good-day.'

'We will send payment to 'ee as soon as we arrive in London,' Sir George told her. 'We are, as you will understand, a trifle discommoded at present.'

As she took curtsying leave, there was a clatter of hooves outside the window and presently a newcomer was introduced into their privacy. He headed straight for Sir George, who looked up and scowled at him to indicate that his intrusion was not welcome.

He wasn't the least abashed. 'My dear sir,' he said, holding out his hand. 'I'm uncommon sorry to hear of your misfortune. I came post haste expressly to prevent it, but I fear I am too late. John Melluish, sir, thief-taker. Pray allow me to serve you.'

'We've met before, I think,' Sir George said, squinting at the man's old-fashioned jacket and his brown bob wig.

'We have, sir,' Mr Melluish agreed as they shook hands, 'but more of that later. You were attacked nearby, I believe. Did you get a good look at the villains, sir? If they are to be caught and your goods returned to'ee, a description would be of inestimable value and, I need hardly point out, the sooner and more accurate it can be given the better.'

'They were masked, sir,' Sir George told him, 'and wore black.'

'Their usual habiliment, I fear. Did you see more, ma'am?'

'I was in the coach, sir,' Hermione said, 'and positively torn to shreds as you see. I fear I was too distressed to take cognisance of any man's appearance.'

'Quite so,' Mr Melluish said soothingly. 'What of the servants? Would any of them have had a closer look, think 'ee?' He looked round at the three in the room, all of whom shook their heads.

'You could try the wet nurse,' Sir George suggested. 'They carried her off. Spent quite a while conversing with her as I recall.'

'An't please you,' Hepzie put in, 'whatever they spoke on, 'twas to some purpose, for they forbore to tie her hands the way they did to us. She was the one what came down and untied the master when they'd ridden away.'

Her information had the desired effect. 'Did she so?' Mr Melluish said. 'Then pray let her be sent for.'

Suki was in the stable yard, holding William out over the dung heap so that he could empty his bowels without soiling his petticoats. 'They'll have to wait till he'm finished,' she said, when Hepzie came to fetch her. This arn't no job to be rushed, is it my 'andsome?' She knew from Hepzie's smug expression that, whatever they wanted her for, it wouldn't be pleasant. And when she arrived in the private room and was introduced to 'Mr Melluish, the thief-taker', she remembered him from the quayside at Bristol and knew she'd been right.

'You were taken away by the highwaymen, I believe,' the gentleman said.

She stood at the centre of the room with all eyes watching her and had to admit it.

'You spent some time conversing with 'em.'

That had to be admitted, too.

Mr Melluish gave her a shrewd look. 'Why was that?'

She had to find an explanation for him and it had to ring true, so why not tell him part of the truth? A little truth wouldn't be peaching. 'I recognized one of 'em,' she said, 'an' told un so. 'Twas a man called Spider. He tried to pick my pocket once in the Spring Gardens in Bath. I'd have knowd un anywhere. He took me up the road to where the others were on account of he wanted 'em to shoot me, but they wouldn't.'

Mr Melluish wrote it all down in his green chapbook. 'What else did they want of 'ee?'

'Little else,' Suki said. They were after money an' jewels an' such like.'

'They did not tie your hands, I believe.'

'No, sir. They couldn't on account of I was holding William, as I am now. I s'ppose they thought to leave me a fair way off from the rest, to give theirselves time to escape.'

The interrogation went on. Had she recognized any of the others? No indeed, sir. What could she remember about them? They were dressed in black and wore masks. Were any other names mentioned? Oh, no, sir. Eventually she was dismissed.

'She could be an accomplice,' Mr Melluish said as soon as she'd gone. ''Tis my opinion she should be watched and noted.' Lady Bradbury rolled her eyes to heaven. 'I cannot credit such a thing!' she said. 'She is my wet nurse.'

'What are your plans, sir?' Mr Melluish asked Sir George.

'We must travel on,' Sir George said, as soon as the coach is repaired. This afternoon if possible. We have a four-day wedding toward.'

'Then I must trouble you no further,' Mr Melluish said courteously. 'If you would be so kind as to provide me with an address to which I may write, I will report progress to you.'

The address was given with the assurance that he would be welcome there at any time and the hope that he would be successful in his endeavours.

The thief-taker bowed. 'Your sarvant, sir.'

'Send all thieves to the gallows,' Sir George told him cheerfully. 'That's my opinion on't. And accomplices too, damme.' But as soon as the man was gone he turned to his daughters with a very different expression on his face. 'Take a turn in the air, me dears,' he ordered, dismissing the servants with a wave. 'I've a word to say to your mother.'

They went obediently, Ariadne empty-faced, Melissa frowning, the servants curious. Hermione held a kerchief to her forehead and closed her eyes against whatever was to come.

'Your wet nurse, ma'am,' he said, 'is a fraud. I've found her out, damme. I thought her face looked familiar when she climbed into the cart this morning, and now I know the reason of it. 'Tis the wench that hit me with the clyster.'

Hermione sighed heavily and held up her right arm so that her injuries were towards him, but she didn't argue.

'I gave strict orders, as you will recall, ma'am, strict orders that she was to be dismissed on the spot. On the spot. And what do I find? She is still here. Still a member of our household and an accomplice to highwaymen to boot. ''Od's bowels! What is the world coming to?'

'She is a good nurse, my love,' Hermione said weakly, 'and good nurses are hard to come by. I could not find another and thought... I am sure you would not have wished to put your son at risk.'

Her husband roared at her. ''Od's teeth we're *all* at risk! She's an accomplice, damme. You heard what the man said. An accomplice. You have nurtured a tongued viper in the family bosom. A tongued viper. Well, don't blame me if we're all murdered in our beds. That's all I've got to say on the matter.'Od's blood and bowels, I never heard the like. To keep such a one in our service when I expressly forbade it. She's to be dismissed, ma'am. She should ha' been dismissed long since.'

'I give 'ee me word — ' Hermione began weakly.

'Aye and so you should!' he roared. 'Dismiss her, ma'am, and let that be an end on it.'

'I give 'ee me word,' Hermione pressed on, ''twill be done the minute the wedding is over. I can hardly spare time to find another wet nurse with Melissa's wedding to arrange. Allow me that at least.'

'Well,' he grumbled, you have the right of it in that regard, I daresay. The wedding takes precedence. But not a minute after, for I won't hear of it.'

Hermione waved her kerchief at him to signify submission.

'I'm off to attend to the coach,' he told her. 'We travel in an hour. Make up your mind to't.'

In fact, it was late afternoon before the coach had been mended to his satisfaction and their journey could be resumed. But this time they negotiated the dreaded hill without mishap and, even though storm clouds gathered over their heads as they rattled on towards Calne, nobody minded. The coach and cart were stopped briefly so that William could be carried across and settled on Ariadne's lap to keep him out of the shower but, apart from that, the journey was uneventful. They reached the Red Lion at Hungerford before dark and, although it was cramped, it was comfortable enough for one night's stay. And the Bear at Slough, where they stayed for their second night, was quite palatial, even though the food was indifferent.

As far as Suki was concerned there were only two things wrong with the journey. One was that it was too slow, but nothing could be done about *that*. 'Twas the way of travel everywhere. The other was that Ariadne had to share a room with her sister so, even though she went to her night and morning to help her undress and dress again, and to bring her water to wash with, there was no chance of any conversation. And she did so want to tell her about the Captain.

But 'twill all come right in the end, she thought, as she settled to sleep on that second night. Now I know where he is. Bedlam-in-Moorfields. Moorfields in London. And I shall be in London tomorrow. There was still William — how was she going to explain about him? But she was full of hope. I will find the Captain first, she decided, letting the thought fill her with optimism, and then we will go to the master and confess together. I will tell him how much I love my little 'andsome and how I couldn't be blamed for the death of the other poor little mite, on account of I wasn't there when he died, which he must see the truth of. Which I might even remind him of. He'll be fair about it, surely. One way or t'other. There's good in the man. He arn't all roaring an' pushing 'ee down on beds.

The last day's journey took far, far longer than it should have done. The horses were very slow and just before Cranford Bridge the coach got stuck in a ditch and it took nearly an hour to get it out again. But by early afternoon they were bowling along the London Road towards Tyburn and Suki could smell the smoke of the city. They were nearly there, praise be!

Fine coaches passed them as they progressed and the road grew more and more crowded. Soon they could hear the growling of a throng of people, and the air wafting in through the open window smelt of sweat and body heat and perfume. And not long after that, the coach ground to a halt.

Sir George filled window with his bulk and called out to the coachman to know what was amiss.

'Tis a hanging day, sir,' the coachman's voice replied. 'I doubt we shall get past.'

'Turn her sideways on,' Sir George ordered happily, and he turned himself sideways on to announce the good news to the family. 'Here's good fortune. We're to see a hanging. An' if that ain't the best medicine for a mute and the best warning for an accomplice, I don't know what is, damme.'

So the coach and the cart were turned for the entertainment, and Sir George ascended to sit with the coachman, happily if ponderously, taking Ariadne with him, and leaving Melissa and her mother to watch from the windows.

'Be sure the wet nurse has a good view,' he called across to the cart. 'I want her to see this. Mark, learn and inwardly digest. That's the style on't.'

The order sounded ominous. Tis on account of me being taken off by that wretched Spider, Suki thought. But she would have watched in any event for she'd never seen so many people gathered together in all her life. The road was packed from one side to the other, with coaches becalmed here and there within the mass. Even as she watched, their own coach was completely surrounded, and an orange seller arrived, pushing her way through the throng by dint of striking violently to right and left with her basket.

'Be good sport today, yer honour,' she called up to Sir George. 'Sweet China oranges?'

He called back cheerfully. 'Who's to go?'

'Jimmy Cade,' the woman told him. 'The highwayman. Peached by his mistress, so they say. A terrible black-hearted villain.'

'And the other?'

'I couldn't say. Any sweet China oranges, sir?'

A little ahead of them on the left-hand side of the road was a high grandstand packed with the busy wigs and fine clothes of the gentry, and immediately in front of it, the famed triple tree of the Tyburn gallows, three gaunt beams weathered black and joined at the top by three' equally forbidding cross beams set in a triangle. Nooses already hung in position on two of the beams but there was no sign of the death cart as yet so the crowd was in a state of excitement almost as high as the gallows.

Sir George bought oranges for them all, which made a wcl-come diversion, and presently while they were still moistening their dry throats with the juice, the crowd beyond the gallows began to cheer and catcall, and Suki could see the death cart rocking slowly through the mob towards its destination.

'I haven't never seen a man hung afore,' she whispered to Barnaby.

'Nor I,' he whispered back. 'Be a bit of sport, eh?'

'That's Tom Turlis, that is,' the orange seller told them, nodding her head in the direction of the hangman. Best Jack Ketch we ever 'ad. 'E'll send 'em off like ninepence, you see if 'e don't.'

The cart had reached the gallows and was being manoeuvred into position beneath the beam, and now Suki could see that the highwayman was young and handsome, like Jack. He was wearing a long white shirt of some kind and his own thick fair hair, which looked shocking somehow, among all the wigs around him, like nudity.

'Look at that 'air,' the orange seller said. 'Crowd that in jail. Make a fine wig after, that will.'

The hangman hauled the young man into position under the noose, pulling on the ropes that bound his arms, and tugging him by his fine hair, and Suki suddenly realized, with a shock that made her spine tingle, that the long white garment he was wearing wasn't a shirt at all but a shroud. Then the crowd near the gallows shushed for silence and he began to make a speech. His thin voice echoed in the vast space before him but the Bradburys were too far away to hear the words. However it appeared to be a good speech, for the crowd cheered when it was done, and cheered again when the young man bowed. Then they held their breath while he stood meekly under the noose and the hangman removed rings from his fingers and took a purse from his trouser pocket and finally fitted his white neck into the grey snake of the rope. Then they grew gradually and terribly silent.

Poor thing, Suki thought, to have to stand there waiting to be killed, and she just had time to wonder what it would feel like to be hung when the horse darted from under the gallows, taking the cart with it at some speed. The crowd gave a great guttural roar, and the young man fell, his legs kicking the air. It was so quick and horrible that she couldn't bear to look any more and buried her face in William's body while the crowd roared and cheered and threw their hats into the air. There was a lump in her throat and her heart was pounding against her ribs as though she was afraid. How fearful to be alive one minute and choking to death the next. No wonder Quin Cutpurse told her not to peach.

By the time the tumult had died down and she dared to look again, the body had gone and another cart was inching towards the gallows. This one contained a plump, solid-looking woman with a billowing bosom and a very red face. She was dressed in her best, with a fine feathered hat and a blue cape with gloves to match.

Not for her modest speech and the terrible acceptance of a shroud. She was shouting at the top of her voice, running from one side of the cart to the other to attract attention, and struggling all the time to break from the ropes that bound her hands. Her voice was so loud that Suki could hear every word she was saying. 'I never killed 'im. Never! I loved that babby! 'E could a been one of me own. I never killed im. 'Tis a lie, you nnnerstand.'

'We shall 'ave some rare old sport wiv this un,' the orange seller said, licking her lips.

The sport began before the cart reached the gallows, for the lady suddenly wriggled her hands out of the ropes, whipped her hat from her head and tossed it into the crowd, to delighted cheers. The hangman made a dive for her hands but she was too quick for him and caught him such a blow' in the stomach that he fell back against the side of the cart, momentarily winded. She had her gloves off immediately and then her cloak, and both were tossed to her friends before he could scramble to his feet and stop her. 'You ain't making money out of me, mate,' she shouted at him. 'An' don't you think it!' And the crowd applauded all round her, as her friend held up the cloak and waved it like a triumphal flag. 'You ain't stringing me up neither!' she shouted at the hangman, squaring up to him with her fists bunched like a prizefighter. Her audience was thrilled by her, and gave her another round of vociferous applause.

Could she fight him off? Suki wondered, admiring her. How proper and sensible to put up a struggle. That's what I'd do. 'Tis the natural way. And she willed the woman on.

It was a riotous fight, for the woman was a heavyweight and knew how to punch and, even though the hangman was strong, she was almost a match for him, kicking and thumping and squirming out of his grasp when he tried to tie her hands again, and on one occasion flailing him with his own rope. But at last he pinned her into a corner of the cart and tied her legs into a bundle with shreds of her own skirt. And the crowd, being an extremely sporting lot, applauded him to show how even-handed they were. Even then she went on struggling, so that he was forced to sit astride her heaving body in order to tie her hands. And that provoked much cheerfully ribald comment, and several impossible suggestions, given the present state of her legs.

It was all so good humoured and noisily cheerful that Suki found herself enjoying it, excited by the struggle and the applause. It didn't seem possible that this strong, determined woman would actually die. Even when the hangman was finally dragging her towards the noose by her hair, there was an unreality about it, like a Punch and Judy show. It was a brutal display, no more, and she half expected the two participants to stop and take a bow. But the noose was tightened about the woman's neck, the hangman stood back from his handiwork and the crowd grew silent again. And the woman suddenly flung herself forward off the edge of the cart. Her neck snapped with such a crack that they could all hear it quite clearly, and then her head jerked upwards and red blood spouted out of her mouth like a fountain, and the crowd groaned and then cheered. And Ariadne fainted away.

Suki handed William to Hepzie at once and climbed out of the cart to help her but it took a tremendous effort to struggle over to the coach and, even when she finally reached it, it was a very long while before she could get her mistress to come round, for her body was wedged against the coachman's seat and the crowd was so densely packed around them that there was no way she could be lifted down and set on the ground. Suki eased the poor girl's head between her knees and rubbed her hands and wished she had some aqua vitae about her.

Sir George pronounced it an uncommon good thing. 'She'll speak now! You'll see!'

How little you know of her, Suki thought, lifting the Ariadne's head. It made her quail to think how heartless he was being.

Below them, two women were talking about the execution, their voices clear, and their sentiments unequivocal.

'She was still a murderer, whatever you might say.'

'Such a fighter! Does yer 'eart good to see a fighter. I don't old with they meek ones!'

'She killed that babba, don' you ferget. Stole it from her ladyship an' then killed the poor little soul.'

'Tis true enough. Aye! She never 'ad no business stealing a babba. That I'll allow.'

Fear trailed icy fingers through the centre of Suki's body. Could you be hung for pretending your baby was somebody else's? Surely not. Not if you'd cared for it and loved it and kept it healthy. But then she remembered that other baby, that poor little long-forgotten baby, King on the kitchen table, pale as wax and tiny and innocent. What if Sir George accused her of killing that baby? He was heartless enough to do it, in all conscience. Please God, she prayed, don' 'ee let nothin' like that happen to me. Out there, in the bloodthirsty crowd, with Ariadne unconscious, and Sir George callous, she felt horribly vulnerable.

At last Ariadne groaned and opened her eyes. She saw Suki but, much to her father's annoyance, she didn't speak. The worst of Suki's fear receded now that her mistress had recovered, but she was still troubled, and it seemed more important to her than ever that she should find the Captain and get him to acknowledge their baby. She must go to Bedlam-in-Moorfields the very first chance she got.

But as she was soon to discover, life in London was even more frenetic than life in Bath. The house in Cavendish Square was enormous and the work there so demanding that, even though there were scores of servants, they were all hard at it from early morning until they slept at night. It was late on Sunday afternoon before Suki even discovered that her old friend Bessie was working in the kitchen. She scarcely saw Mr Jessup and Mrs Sparepenny who were distant gods in this great household, although their orders came through endlessly to each and every one of their hardworking subordinates. Every single room had to be made ready for bridesmaids or wedding guests, and the kitchen was under such pressure, feeding the household and preparing the wedding feast, that the housekeeper and the cooks barely had time to talk about anything else — and were certainly in no mood to give permission to the family wet nurse to go off on some wild goose chase to the other side of London.

'Vastly entertaining, I daresay,' Mrs Sparepenny said disparagingly, when Suki finally plucked up the courage to seek her out and ask her, 'viewing the lunatics, but 'tain't for the likes of you. Nor me neither. We've got other matters to attend to. 'Twill need to wait till this wedding's over and done.'

It was a disquieting answer. Was Bedlam a lunatic asylum then? Surely not. What would the Captain be doing in a lunatic asylum?

'Oh yes!' Barnaby said, when Monday came around and he and Bessie were helping Suki to prepare the guest rooms. 'That's what 'tis, right enough. Famous for it. They opens it up every afternoon an' people come from all over to see 'em. Very comical they are, by all accounts. I wouldn't mind going mesself.'

'I s'pose you don't know where 'tis?' Suki asked, as casually as she could.

'I do, as't happens,' Barnaby said, pleased to be the one with the information, for once. 'Me an' Dick was at an inn over there one time. 'Tis right over the other side a' London. Miles away. Took us hours to get there.'

So I'll never get there an' back while this wedding's a-going on, Suki thought. I'll have to wait till it's over. Mrs Sparepenny was right about that. But what was he doing in a lunatic asylum? Surely he hadn't taken a job looking after madmen. He was too full of life and fun. Yet Quin Cutpurse had said that would be where she'd find him. And she did so want to find him, dear, dear Jack.

*

He was lying on dirty straw, on a stone-flagged floor, struggling to focus his eyes, and wondering where on earth he was. He knew that his mouth was dry from long fever, that his hips were sore from lying on the stones, that he was achingly hungry. He could see that his arms were thin for lack of sustenance, and that he was dressed in rough canvas breeches and a filthy cotton shirt. And he realized that, wherever he was, it was a dark stinking place and full of fiercesome noises. But he'd been struggling with nightmares for so long that it was hard to tell whether he was awake or asleep.

Hideous faces swam into his line of vision, now a man with a bulbous nose and one eye lower than the other, here a mouth full of broken teeth, black with decay and green-edged, there a man with a shaven head and cheeks criss-crossed with scars, grinning and cackling. If this *was* a nightmare, it was of another kind. It wasn't like the dreams that had racked him through the long days and nights of his fever — the dreams of formidable women who'd beaten him and starved him, who'd told him he was worthless and thrown him into the holds to stink and suffer with the slaves, who'd tossed him to the sharks to be torn apart alive.

I must speak, he thought, trying to clear his throat. If he could hear the sound of his own voice, he would know that the nightmare was over. 'Where am I?' he said and was ashamed to hear how weak he sounded. 'Where am I?'

The question sent the grinning creature into hideous paroxysms of laughter and soon three more shaven heads pressed down towards him to grunt and cackle. He closed his eyes because he couldn't bear the sight of them. When he opened them again, there was a new face before him and this one was showing concern. 'Am I dead?' he asked. 'Is this Hell?'

'You got the right of it there,' the face said. ''Tis the nearest thing this side a' the Styx. But look cheerly. You ain't dead yet. You're in Bedlam among the lunatics.'

The knowledge made Jack's heart shrink. I must escape, he thought, be sprung, bribe a guard, now, this minute. I can't live with lunatics. But he barely had the energy to sit up and had to rest his back against the wall.

'That's the style,' his new friend approved, squatting beside him. 'Try some broth.' He had a bowl full of the stuff on the straw beside him. It was grey and unappetising and full of gristle, but Jack was so hungry he ate it.

'Name a' Gurney,' his new friend said, 'an' atween these four stinking walls, no more mad than you are.'

But you are unprepossessing to say the least, Jack thought, with that filthy jacket and that shaven head. And he put up a hand to his own head to comfort himself with the softness of his own thick hair, and was shocked to find that it had all been shorn to stubble. He spat a lump of gristle into the straw. Then if you ain't a madman,' he said, why are you here?'

'Had some sort of fever,' Gurney explained. 'Much like you. Raved somewhat, so I'm told. Took a knife to someone or other, so I'm told. Nothing of any consequence. But they don't take no account of what *I* say. So here I'm stuck and here I stays. 'Od rot 'em!'

The cackling man slothed towards them and made a grab for the bowl.

'Stow that!' Gurney said, swiping him round the ear. 'Unless you wants yer skull caved in.'

'Gi' us a mouthful,' the man whined. 'Tha's all I wants. A mouthful for pity's sake. You got plenty.'

'That's on account of I've worked for it,' Gurney said, slapping him again. 'If you wants food, beg for it like the rest of us, 'stead a' lying around all day.' And when the man had sloped away, he added, 'Now that one *is* mad. He reckons lie's the King a' Spain.'

'Are we let out to beg?' Jack asked. If that was the case, there was hope of escape.

It was quickly dashed. 'Out?' Gurney laughed. 'No fear'a that. They keeps us locked up night an' day. Oh no, 'tis folks they lets in that pays us. Pays handsome some of 'em, if you goes about it the right way. You wasn't ever an actor by any chance? They're the ones what does the best out of it in here.'

'I've been a good many things in my time,' Jack told him with a return of pride. 'Seaman, horseman, actor, gentleman of the road, slave master. I've seen some awful things at sea, men whipped and branded, babies thrown overboard alive, hundreds of slaves thrown into the holds to stink. 'Tis a living hell on a slave ship, I can tell 'ee.'

Gurney slapped his tattered breeches with delight. 'That's the style!' he said. 'You tell 'em *that* when they comes round a-gawping an' you could earn a pretty penny. Act up for 'em. They likes to be frighted. I tells 'em how I stabbed six men in a single night, or throttled a young female, that sort a' thing, an' threatens I shall stab 'em an' throttle 'em likewise. They screams prodigious. That's the style of it.'

'Who are these people?' Jack asked. 'Are they visitors? Or do madmen have friends and relations?'

'Relations?' Gurney said with some scorn. 'Not they. You never see relations hereabouts. Only too glad to be rid of us, relations are. No, they comes to see the sights. Weekday afternoons and twice a' Sundays. Scores of 'em. We're an entertainment for 'em.'

'And they pay us, you say?' If they paid enough, he might scrape a bribe together.

'Showers us,' Gurney told him. 'Farthings, pennies, groats. I got a gold sovereign once.'

Jack handed him back his bowl. Foul though it was to be incarcerated here, there was hope. 'I can tell 'em some prodigious fine tales,' he said, 'for I've seen more than most and much of it ugly. I shall tell 'em of fights at sea and blowing a man's brains out with a pistol, of legs smashed by cannon balls and the stumps dipped in boiling tar, red-hot brands and w'hips and cat-o'-ninetails, jungle fever and the pox and the flux, storms that could break the back of a ship in seconds. Let's see how well they like that. If there's money to be made, I'll make it, damme. I'll not stay here for the rest of my life to be made mock of.'

Thirty-four

Melissa's wedding day began with a shower of rain, but fortunately there was so much to do that hardly anybody noticed it, and those who did were far too tactful to let her know, for now that her moment of importance had arrived, she was in a state of such nervous apprehension that she was beginning to stutter.

The house was in uproar from the attic to the kitchen. There were more wedding guests than anyone could count, and each one had brought at least two servants, so every room was noisily occupied. To add to the crush, six under-cooks and more than a dozen scullery maids had been hired to help prepare the wedding breakfast, so the kitchen was full to bursting and hot with roasting spits and boiling tempers. Lady Bradbury was determined that the breakfast should be a very grand occasion, and had ordered twelve different dishes for the meat course — including roast sirloin, three mutton pies, two beef stews and a whole roast lamb — ten for poultry, ten more for fish, to say nothing of custard creams, ices, jellies and pastries. So the cooks and their assistants had arrived the previous evening arid had been hard at work all night long, under the irritating supervision of Lady Bradbury herself, who was in a state of frantic anxiety and had stayed up all night to make sure that everybody knew it and shared it. By dawn, she had infected everyone in the kitchen and as a result one of the scullery maids had burned her hand on the griddle, a dish of scallops had been dropped on the floor and, in the heat and chaos, quarrels had grown swift and sharp, even though she was present to witness them. Cook was in a towering temper.

'If I was you, ma'am,' she said at last, tight-lipped and formidable, 'I should take myself off to my chamber and have a nice lie down or you'll be in no fit state for the wedding, which you wouldn't want now, would you, saving your reverence? We can manage here.'

'Well,' Hermione dithered, scanning the food on the table for possible misdemeanours, 'I might retire for an hour or so. I am sorely fatigued. You will make sure that everything is done according to my instructions, will you not? Appearances are so important.' She put one long white hand before her mouth to conceal a yawn. 'How I shall survive this day, I truly do not know. My sensibilities are positively lacerated already. Positively lacerated. Howsomever a short rest would be within the bounds of possibility, I believe.'

'Take as long as you like,' Cook said acidly, when the lady had drifted away. There were still far too many dishes to prepare and far too little space to prepare them in. 'I've had enough of your sensibilities to last me out the week. Now let's see to that lamb or we shall have 'em all a-ringing bells for their breakfasts afore we knows where we are.'

The guests had started to arrive the previous afteroon and had spent the evening gambling at cards and wandering from table to table, gossiping and picking at the food provided to sustain them. Now, mercifully, they were sleeping off their exertions. But their servants were up and about, setting fires and brushing shoes and laying out clean clothes in the various dressing rooms, so the upper floors of the house were abuzz with whispers.

Suki was in Ariadne's bedroom and they were on their own at last, and able to talk — as well as they could with William riding his little hobbyhorse on the carpet between them.

'Are you sure 'twas Bedlam he said?' Ariadne asked. She spoke in a whisper for, even though the door was shut and William's chortles were loud enough to give them cover, she was wary of being overheard.

'Positive,' Suki whispered back. 'What do 'ee think to it? Mind the coal scuttle, William.'

Ariadne confessed that she didn't know what to think. How-somever, now that you are here, I must warn you... Mamma means to dismiss you. Papa recognized you at the inn.'

Suki was so upset it took her a second or two to absorb what she'd heard and longer to recover from it, but she wasn't surprised. She'd been expecting trouble ever since the hanging or why would he have said 'Mark, learn and inwardly digest' the way he had? 'How do 'ee know?'

'Hepzibah told the bride. They imagine I am deaf because I do not speak — poor fools — so I hear a deal of gossip. You're to leave as soon as the wedding is over, so you'd best find this lover of yours the first chance you get.'

'I shall,' Suki said earnestly. 'I've every intention. But with this wedding a-going on, I shan't get the chance till Sunday afternoon.'

'Aye.' Ariadne sighed... 'We are captive in this house till the hurly-burly's over. I shall be glad of the end of it, too. Four days is a lengthy time to have to endure.'

Suki understood how she felt. ''Twill be easier once your dance is over an' done.'

'I am quite prepared for it,' Ariadne told her, calmly. 'The gown is made to my specifications, which is a comfort, and I daresay the trough is ready. I shall do well enough. If all goes according to plan 'tis even possible I might be in a position to help you.'

Her expression was so mischievous that Suki took hope from it. 'What do 'ee plan to do?'

'Tis a secret,' Ariadne said, 'and must remain so or 'twill spoil. Keep patience until the final ball and,' she paused, 'all will be revealed.' Then, as if her words had amused her she began to giggle and had to hold a kerchief to her mouth to muffle the sound.

She am't a-going to tell me, Suki thought, watching her closely. Not with that look on her face. It irritated her to be kept out of the secret. 'I'll bring 'ee breakfast presently,' she promised. 'I dursn't stay longer or they'll come a-looking for me. Hepzie's on my back every second of the day.'

'I don't doubt it,' Ariadne said. 'Now you know why. See if you can bring me a cup of hot chocolate.'

As Suki crept down the servants' stairs with the hobbyhorse under her arm and William on her hip, her heart was constrained with misery, despite Ariadne's hint of help. She'm whistling in the dark, she thought, for she'm as powerless as I am. If ought's to be done 'twill need to be by stealth and cunning. But she couldn't think of a single trick that would help her now. Her mind was too full of the terrible certainty that if Lady Bradbury dismissed her, she would never see William again, and that was something she simply couldn't allow to happen. But she could hardly go running off to Bedlam on the very day of the wedding either, no matter how much she might want to, not when her presence could be required at any time to show her 'noble charge' to the wedding guests, and bring him in to the wedding breakfast, and the bride-bed ceremony, and all the other occasions that would fill the day. It was parlously difficult.

As she passed the dining room, she noticed that the servants' door was slightly ajar so she stopped, settled William more comfortably, and put her head cautiously round the edge to see what was going on inside. If the master was there and on his own, maybe she could catch his eye and speak to him. Beg him for help maybe. 'Twas a desperate thing to think on, but she was in a desperate position.

He was sitting at the centre of the table surrounded by half a dozen cronies — Sir Arnold Willoughby, of course, that funny little Mr Smithers, and on Sir George's left hand, a quiet man he was calling 'brother Frederick', who was keeping an anxious eye on two greedy little boys who were sitting at the end of the table stuffing their faces with cold beef and quaffing beer as though they were grown men.

'No, no,' Sir George was booming. 'You did the only thing open to 'ee in the circumstances. If a man runs distract, he has to be restrained. Stands to reason, damme. 'Twas commendably done.'

'The expense...' his brother demurred.

'Tush man,' Sir George said, whacking him between the shoulder blades. 'Expense is of no consequence. We can withstand expense. Eat up and you shall join us at Thames side and see what profits are to be made in our trade to Lisbon. We're meeting with Humphrey at ten o'clock to check the next cargo.'

'Wools and silks,' Sir Arnold said, smacking his lips as though he were tasting them. Tableware, silver, wallpapers. All uncommon fine, damme. You must see 'em, Frederick. They'll sell like hot cakes.'

They're surely not leaving the house this morning, Suki thought. Lady Bradbury will be furious. But what a diversion 'twould cause. Maybe I could slip out after all. She'd hardly notice that I was missing if he...

There was a ripple of air in the passageway behind her and Hepzie materialized at her shoulders.

'Were you sent for?' she whispered, acidly, 'or are you just playing the spy?'

Suki bristled. 'You'm a fine one to call the kettle black, the way you goes on, which I knows all about.'

'What I am is of no account,' Hepzie told her haughtily. 'You should be with your mistress, while you are still her servant. The bridesmaids are to be dressed by noon. Lady Willoughby's daughter has been ready this half-hour to my certain knowledge. I wouldn't wish to be tardy were I in *your* shoes.'

'But then you am't, are you?' Suki said crossly. And she stomped off to the kitchen to find Bessie and take a bit of breakfast, determined not to be given orders by a mere lady's maid.

The servants' table was full of breakfast dishes which had been prepared for the guests and were being served to them in their rooms, as and when they woke. So the servants were eating whatever they could find. Suki and Bessie helped themselves to a platter of cold meats, bread and ale and took them off to the nursery to breakfast in peace.

'Lady Bradbury's still abed,' Bessie reported, as she forked up a slice of cold beef. 'Lying on her back an' a-snoring fit to break the rafters.'

'Let her stay there,' Suld said with feeling. 'Then we can have a bite to eat afore they'm on to us again.'

But the hope was soon dashed. They'd barely taken the edge off their hunger before bells were being run again and they could hear people running from the kitchen, calling and giggling. Sir Humphrey's retinue had arrived with four trunks of clothes, three wig stands and his personal mattress, valet, *frisseur,* surgeon, two valets de chambre, pet squirrel and all. Soon half the household was crowded into the hall to witness the spectacle, and Mrs Sparepenny was rounding up the chambermaids so that they would be ready for the ceremony of the marriage bed the minute the mattress had been hauled into position. Suki was sent to fetch the bridesmaids and to see that Ariadne carried the bowl of rose petals that were to be sprinkled on the sheets to bring good fortune to the bride and groom. So there was no possibility of running off to Bedlam or anywhere else.

William found the whole business wonderfully entertaining and hid under the sheet as it was lowered across the mattress, and ran off with the rose petals, and romped on the bed so that the fresh sheets were crumpled — which the chambermaids said was a very good omen — and finally got tired and cross, and had to be suckled back to good humour, also on the bed, which was the best omen of all. So the job was done to everyone's satisfaction.

But it was growing late and Sir George was still out inspecting his cargo and Lady Bradbury was still asleep and the carriages were beginning to arrive to take the guests to church.

'You must wake her, I fear, Hepzibah,' Mrs Sparepenny said. 'You shall take up a cup of hot chocolate and a platter of dainties. Rouse her by degrees. She must not be agitated. Not today.'

Hepzie scowled and tried to refuse. 'What of the bride?' she said. 'I'm *her* maid now. Surely I must care for her.'

'Suki can look after her for the time being,' the housekeeper decided. 'Dress Miss Ariadne first, Suki. You've time to do both. Well look lively, the pair of you. Jump to it.'

Charlotte Willoughby was already dressed and sitting in Ariadne's bedroom. She was most distressed to find her old friend still speechless.

'Don't she speak a word?' she asked, as Suki lifted Ariadne's blue gown from the cupboard and laid it on the bed. ''Tis mortal hard to be struck dumb.'

Suki agreed that it was. 'We'm to be quick,' she explained as she laced Ariadne's stays, 'for Hepzibah is sent to look after milady and we'm to look after the bride.'

So Ariadne was arrayed in her bridesmaid's gown, with her hair au natural, and topped by the smallest of lace caps and the longest of embroidered blue ribbons, and she and Charlotte tiptoed along the corridor to see Melissa.

She was still sitting at her dressing table in her chemise and under-petticoats. Because this was a state occasion, she was wearing high-breasted stays and consequently had to sit bolt upright and keep her shoulders well down. She looked as uncomfortable as she felt, for the stays pinched her sides and made it impossible for her to breathe deeply enough to satisfy a panicking need for air. Her face had been painted with white lead powder to cover her bruises and her cheeks were reddened with two round circles of rouge. At that moment she was submitting to the attentions of the *frisseur,* who was dressing her hair in the very latest French style, the front hair being drawn up into a tall padded mound above her forehead and stuffed with an abundance of prickly black wool, the back being tortured into curls. Four separate curling irons were warming quite viciously upon the hob, and the heat they required from the fire was making the room excessively stuffy and adding to the poor girl's breathing difficulties.

'How do I look, think 'ee?' she asked anxiously when her bridesmaids came into the room, with Suki and William behind them.

Privately Suki thought she looked like a wooden doll, but Charlotte said the right thing like the kind girl she was. 'As fine as ever I've seen you, Melly.'

Melissa picked up her looking glass and eyed her extraordinary image from every angle. 'Aye,' she said doubtfully.

'You shall have the tallest head in the church,' the *frisseur* promised, wielding his curling tongs like a baton. 'When your toilette is complete, you will be *amazed*, I promise you.'

And amazed she certainly was. For what with the height of her hair, the weight of her blue brocade gown and the stiffness of her embroidered petticoat, it was impossible to move more than half a pace at a time, and as she had to carry a fan, a cane, a handkerchief and a bouquet, there was no part of her body that wasn't either tightly controlled or required for some ritual purpose. Except her eyes. And the eyes looking back at her from her looking glass that morning were far too afraid for comfort. To be the centre of attention had seemed so desirable when all this began, but now she was wondering how on earth she would ever sustain it, through all the hours and days ahead of her. To say nothing of the nights!

There was a commotion in the corridor outside her room and they could hear Lady Bradbury's voice. 'How could you *do* such a thing? I wonder at you, sir, upon my life I do. On your own daughter's wedding day. When you know what a tender constitution she has.'

Sir George was fighting back. ''Od's bowels, woman. It's come to a pretty pass when a man may not inspect his own cargo, damme.'

'A man,' Hermione told him acidly, 'may inspect his cargo on any day of the year, not on his daughter's wedding day. You have no heart, sir. I have always thought as much but now I am sure on't.'

'Heart! Tosh!' Her husband roared. 'I'm here, am I not? These are my legs, my hands.'

'Abate your tone, sir. Do you wish the household to hear us?'

'Hell's teeth! Am I to be told how to speak now? Is that the humour of it?' And he flung open the bedroom door and strode forward into the heat. 'Ready are yer?' he boomed to his daughter. 'Have a care, sir,' Hermione warned, 'lest you make her swoon.' 'She'll not swoon,' he said. 'She's marrying one of the ton.'

So Lady Bradbury left the house with the two bridesmaids, and Sir George lay on his daughter's bed and fell asleep with his mouth open, and Melissa stood by the window, stiff with fear and ceremony, and watched as her servants giggled off along the street towards the church and the coaches trundled her guests from the door one after the other.

*

The rain had stopped, at least temporarily, so the servants gathered on the pavement outside the church to watch the last arrivals. Suki and Bessie were right at the front of the crowd, with Barnaby between them, and all three were enjoying the time-honoured occupation at such nuptial gatherings of being catty about the appearance of the guests, for Suki had decided that as she had no choice but to attend this wedding she might as well get as much fun out of it as she could.

'Do ee look at those legs!' She giggled. 'That's never his calves! You can see the padding from here.'

'If I 'ad a bosom as wrinkled as that,' Barnaby observed, 'I should keep it covered so I would.'

'I'd like to see you with a bosom,' Bessie teased him. 'We could sell you to a freak show. Make a mint a' money that would.' The carriages were almost as much fun as the guests, for they too had been decked with ribbons and given a thick coat of paint, and they carried so many liveried servants that Bessie said it was a wonder the poor horses could pull them all through the streets. It was fun to try and identify the coats of arms painted so boldly on the sides of these splendid vehicles. Suki surprised herself by the number she knew, and Bessie had become an authority.

'That's Lady Home,' she said, 'An' that's Mr Beckford. He's the richest man in England, so they say. An' that's the Duke of Errymouth. I seen that one, many and many's the time.'

Jessup had been detailed to greet the arrivals at the church gate, and a pompously important job he was making of it, opening doors with a flourish of new lace cuffs and bowing and scraping as if he were welcoming royalty. Many of the guests knew him and spoke to him by name, so that he coughed and smirked with mock modesty before their faces and looked mightily pleased with himself behind their backs.

'Now who?' Bessie said, as the next coach rolled splendidly to the gate. It was drawn by four greys and had the largest and brightest coat of arms — blue stars on a field of gold, a silver helm, three red martlets, and a fierce wild boar, running.

'I know this one!' Suki said.

416

'Well course you do,' Bessie said. 'Seein' 'tis Lady Bradbury's very own family. Daventry arms, that is!'

But that wasn't the reason, Suki thought, struggling to remember where she'd seen it before. Twas nothing to do with Lady Bradbury. She was quite sure of that. But there wasn't time to think about it for the Daventrys were descending from their flamboyant coach and making an entrance. And very impressive it was.

They were dressed in the height of fashion and so highly perfumed that they scented the air all the way to the church door. Sir Francis was in blue satin, with so many gold buttons on his jacket that they were almost close enough to touch each other. His wig was a delicate shade of pink to match his velvet shoes, the fulh less of his billowing shirt sleeves and the embroidery on his waistcoat. He carried a white cane, on which he leant himself, sideways, and with the air of one almost too fatigued to stand.

But if he was a sight to stop crowds, his wife was even more splendid. She had a sharper nose than Lady Bradbury, and an expression of such supercilious disdain that she could barely focus her eyes on anything more than a few inches above her chin. She was dressed in the very latest fashion, in a cream silk mantua, embroidered all over with a delicate tracery of flowing tendrils, green leaves and the smallest rosebuds imaginable, in red and pink and saffron yellow. Her trained skirt was looped up on either side of her petticoat in curves of material that matched exactly the curved curls of her powdered hair. Above the curls was a small swathed turban, which supported a confection of pink and yellow ostrich feathers and three huge bows of embroidered ribbon. In short, she was every inch an aristocrat. When her three children stepped out of the coach behind her, she didn't even glance at them.

Jessup rushed forward to grovel and cough before her, and she squinted at him for a second and, then, to Suld's amazement, actually spoke to the man. 'Ah! Jessup, ain't it? Goin' along, are yer?'

'She knows him,' Suki said, much surprised.

''E was a Daventry servant to start with,' Bessie told her. ''E come with Lady Bradbury when she married. Cook told me.'

Which is why he runs errands for her, Suki thought. I might've known. But there wasn't time to think about *that* either, for there was Lady Bradbury herself, running down the church path to greet her distinguished guests, huge-eyed with anxiety.

'I am *so* glad you were able to attend, cousin Francis,' she gushed. 'We are all so *honoured*. Indeed we are. I was only making the observation to Sir George this morning. Such an honour! I trust I see you well.'

'Tolerable,' Sir Francis drawled. 'Ain't the weather for standin' about, though, damme.'

Hermione took the hint at once, and with increased distress. 'Pray to step inside,' she begged, bowing her entire body before them. She looked so subservient that Suki really wondered at her. Why was she so anxious to please? They were her own family, yet it was almost as though she were afraid of them. It was another puzzle in a puzzling afternoon, but there wasn't time to consider that either, for a red-faced Sir George had arrived with the whitefaced bride and the bridal procession was shuffling into position beside the church gates, their stiff petticoats swinging like bells.

And Suki suddenly remembered where she'd seen that coat of arms. It was the one embroidered on the Captain's kerchief. She wore it round her neck at that very moment, washed and pressed for the occasion. But Jack wasn't related to the Daventrys, surely.

She'd always known he came from a good family. But not the Daventrys. He'd not be living in a lunatic asylum if he were part of a family as grand as that.

'Come on!' Bessie urged, pulling at Suki's sleeve. 'If we don't get inside this minute, the service'll start without us an' we shall miss it.'

So they crammed into the back of the church behind the pews and settled to be entertained by the wedding. To Suki, used to the ornate splendour of the abbey at Bath and the sombre heaviness of the little church at Twerton, entering the church of St James in Piccadilly was like walking into light. It was so bright and modern, and full of echoing sound, from the white marble under her feet to the high white ceiling over her head. White columns with heavily gilded architraves supported the roof and the gallery was decorated with a line of complacent cherubs with golden wings; the side windows were made of clear glass, so that sunshine shone through the panes and made the gilding shine like coins; and in front of the high altar was a rich wooden screen where clusters of grapes, fruit and garlands tumbled like brown curls, and a superb mahogany eagle held up the gilded lectern. A rich man's church without a doubt.

The space between the front pews and the high altar was wide enough for a theatre and every bit as dramatic. Here the wedding party were grouping themselves, in an argumentative semi-circle facing a golden priest. On his left stood the painted statue that was the bride and, on his right, her extraordinary groom. He was dressed from head to foot in pure white satin with gold buttons on his jacket and waistcoat, and gold buckles on his white satin shoes, and a pale yellow wig on his elegant head, dusted with white powder so that it glittered like snow in the sunlight. He looked like a creature from a fairy-tale, and as unlikely a bridegroom as Suki had ever seen.

But for the moment, he was upstaged by the furious argument that was being conducted in hissing stage whispers by the Daventrys and the Errymouths, both of whom felt they should have pride of place at the centre of the group. Lady Bradbury was nearly in tears, Sir George was trying to be diplomatic, and the golden priest was wringing his hands.

Such a to-do, Suki thought, watching them bristling anger at one another. As if any of it is of any consequence. Miss Melissa will marry her ridiculous bridegroom no matter where any of them stand. And much good may it do her. I only wish they'd hurry up, for the sooner the wedding is done, the sooner we can get back for the feast. I only had a bite from that cold beef an' a bite am't sufficient on a day like this.

But if the service was slow, the wedding breakfast was taken at a snail's pace, for the carriages had to queue to discharge their occupants at the door, and then the guests had to be greeted one by one, and there was so much wine to drink and so many impressive acquaintances to meet that it was more than an hour before the party sat down to the first thirteen sizzling courses.

The bridegroom brought his squirrel to the table and fed it on tit-bits and was prevailed upon to take a sip from every single dish himself, so as to bring good fortune to the marriage. He actually ate one or two of the choicer offerings and seemed to enjoy them. His guests were most impressed and his new mother-in-law almost sick with relief. But then the toasts began and soon they were all comfortably drunk and the fish course could be served.

'I gather that your eldest is to dance in the hog trough,' Sir Francis said to his cousin.

'I fear so, sir,' Hermione murmured. 'Poor child.'

'Waste no pity upon her, ma'am,' Sir Francis advised. 'If she's too plain or too curst to catch a husband, she must take the consequences of her folly, damme. 'Twill make some sport for us.' That was the opinion below stairs where the Bradbury servants were gathered about their own table, enjoying the remains of the first course.

'Eat up!' Mr Jessup commanded happily, sitting at the head of the table, as befitted the steward of such an important household, and drinking his third glass of wine. 'And a good health to all the company — krmm, krmm — your good selves included.'

''Twill soon be time for Miss Ariadne to dance in the hog trough,' Hepzibah said. 'She'll be a-ringing for you presently, Suki Brown. I can't wait to see it. 'Twill take her down a peg or two and not afore time. All this silly nonsense of not talking. 'Tis play acting to my way of thinking. She's a deal too hoity-toity for her own good.'

Suki sprang to her defence. 'She've suffered cruelly, poor lady,' she said. 'I feel a deal of pity for her an' so should you.'

'Which is why,' Hepzie said in her superior way, 'you're still a wet nurse and maid to a total failure and I'm to travel with the bride on the Grand Tour.'

Mrs Sparepenny looked sharply at both girls, ready to forestall a quarrel but Mr Jessup was on his feet proposing another toast and the moment passed.

But Ariadne's humiliation was still to come and, although it was delayed by the wedding breakfast which went on for nearly four hours, eventually the party left the table and retired to their rooms to dress for the ball and Ariadne rang for Suki.

Her special white dress was taken out of the cupboard and lowered over her head. Her jewellery was removed and her hair brushed into careful curls. Then she sat by the bed and waited to be summoned.

'We been told we may watch from the minstrels' gallery,' Suki said, adding with feeling, 'I shall applaud when you'm done.'

Ariadne begged she would do no such thing. ''Tis a punishment,' she said, 'and must be endured.' But then there was a shuffle at the door and she had to resume her silence as Jessup came in to collect her and take her down to the ballroom.

The guests were gathered about the dance floor where the pig trough stood in smelly isolation, trailing dirty straw and still smeared and stained by the drool of its former users. There was a ripple of surprise as Ariadne appeared in her cambric gown, but as she signalled to the musicians to play and lifted her long skirts to step into the trough, surprise turned to shock, for her feet and ankles were indecorously bare.

'How lewd!' Lady Carstairs said behind her fan to her good friend Lady Fosdyke. 'Don't she know she's being indecent?'

'She has style,' Lady Fosdyke said. 'I'll give her that. To dress in the height of fashion and all in white cambric is masterly. But I should say she's a deal too cunning still.'

She was also, it had to be admitted, moving with great dignity and a total lack of emotion. She stepped into the bran as though she was stepping into the baths, and then danced so well and with such careful rhythm, that the wedding guests burst into spontaneous applause when she finished, and even the servants, who had packed into the gallery and were watching ghoulishly, had to admit that she'd taken her punishment well.

But then it was time to bring the bride and groom to bed and, that, as they all told one another as they rushed up the stairs after the groomsmen and the squealing bundle they were half carrying, half dragging, was the best part of any wedding. The chambermaids made a very thorough job of undressing Melissa, removing every single pin from her elaborate gown, and holding each one up to the company for ribald comment. 'No prick of misfortune for *our* bride,' they said. And 'here's another sharp little prick.' And 'here's the biggest prick of them all.' And the company cheered, and offered advice, 'Lie still now, me dear, for you won't get another chance till morning.' And the bride blushed and giggled and begged them to desist, and was teased and tickled and rolled about in the bed until she was stripped to her chemise and her stockings.

Then the groom arrived, carried shoulder high by his leering groomsmen, but cool and elegant even then. Not for this exquisite, the rough and tumble of a public stripping. He was disrobed, holding up an arm or a leg as required, but noticing every move his drunken friends were making and ensuring, by the severity of his glance, that his clothes were folded and hung away in the wardrobe, uncreased. When the sack posset was brought, he drank his in one draught, wiped his lips elegantly upon his handkerchief, and turned to look ardently upon his bride as she struggled to swallow hers.

'Go to it, Humphrey!' his friends encouraged him.

'You need have no fear of *that*, me dears,' he said, and pushed the bride down upon her back.

'Draw the curtains, damme,' Sir George roared in delight, 'or we shall all be shamed.'

'Patience, son-in-law,' Lady Bradbury said archly. 'You have forgot the stockings in your ardour.'

'Then you'd best be quick about it,' the gallant said, 'or breed daughter's that ain't so tempting.'

So the order was given and all young guests made a rush at the bed, the girls to attack the groom and the young men leaping amorously and noisily upon the bride. For a little while arms and legs flailed with abandon, the mattress sagged under the weight of such a tangle and there was much cheerful tickling and groping. But at last four flushed bodies detached themselves from the muddle, triumphantly waving the four discarded stockings. The cheering and laughing died down as the two girls took up their positions at the foot of the bed and, with their eyes closed, tossed the stockings over their shoulders. One caught the bridegroom across the chest, the second landed on Melissa's shoulder. Then the applause began and the chant went up, 'Who hits the mark over the shoulder, must-married be ere twelve months older.' Then it was the turn of the young men and while they were taking up their positions at the foot of the bed, Suki glanced across at her silent mistress and winked. Ariadne, looking quite impish, winked back. So the second pair of stockings were thrown and, as neither of them hit their targets, the throwers were mocked and teased. Then the bed curtains were drawn, and the guests retreated to the landing to sing the wedding song, to the accompaniment of as many members of the band as could squeeze into the crowd on the stairs, and the bridal couple were left to their own devices.

It had, they all agreed, been a splendid wedding and there were still three more days of festivities to enjoy.

*

Early the next morning a billet arrived from Bristol for Sir George. And the news it contained set the second day breakfast off with a roar. The last sugar cargo had returned to port under the safe escort of the *Yorick*, and proved to be of better quality than expected. So the groom, who had taken a share in the venture by virtue of his part ownership of the privateer, was cheered for a double triumph and the bride who had come down to breakfast in a new gown and with her face scrubbed clean, kissed her new husband, blushing almost prettily, and declared she must have brought him luck.

When the meal was over, Sir George retired to Lady Bradbury's boudoir to enlarge upon his success.

'Good news, what?' he said, hopefully. A high profit might bring him forgiveness for his misdemeanour of the previous morning. 'I shall buy you a jewel to mark the occasion.'

'A pretty thought,' she said and actually managed a smile.

The smile reminded her husband of the amorous activity that had been taking place under his roof during the past twenty-four hours, and gave him a happy idea. 'Oblige me, my love?' he suggested mildly.

'Of course,' Hermione agreed equally mildly. 'If I may just have a moment or two to prepare myself.' She had foreseen the possibility of such demands and was ready for them.

He waited beside the bed, slowly unbuttoning his breeches, while she found her library book, Mr Fielding's latest and most scurrilous offering, *Amelia*, and arranging herself comfortably upon the pillows, lifted her skirt into neat folds over her bosom. Then she opened the book and her legs, and inclined her head graciously towards him to give him permission to begin. He fell upon her at once, and soon the two of them were more or less happily occupied, he humping vigorously towards his pleasure at one end of her anatomy, she enjoying Amelia's adventures at the other. Taken all in all, weddings were really quite agreeable occasions, and this one was going well.

Thirty-five

The second day of the wedding passed without incident. Dinner was served late but that was only to be expected when half the house party had stayed in bed until noon, and those members of the gentiy who had agreed to attend didn't arrive until well past the suggested hour. But the ball began on time and was much enjoyed, for by now Sir George had forgotten his transgression and was his cheerfully rubicund self again, and his guests were all well into the spirit of the thing.

The dancing continued until three in the morning when a cold collation was served before the visiting guests departed. And once again they all slept on until midday on Friday, when they woke to dine and dance all over again.

By the morning of that third day, the huge on-going party had established a routine and a pecking order, in which Lord and Lady Fosdyke held court at one end of the social scale and Ariadne crept into the dining room to take her silent place at the other. She was so quiet and withdrawn that Suki grew concerned about her.

'Twill soon be over,' she said encouragingly as she eased her mistress out of Friday's finery. 'Sunday's a-coming.'

Ariadne's reply was enigmatic. 'And Saturday precedes it.'

Saturday was to be the grandest day of them all, since all the important guests were returning for the final ball, including Sir Francis and his wife, so preparations for the feast kept the cooks and scullery maids up all night for the second time that week. But on this occasion, as Lady Bradbury left them to it and didn't interfere, there was a deal less fuss in the kitchen, even though there were more dishes to prepare for this dinner than there'd been for the wedding breakfast.

But every minute of this last day brought Suki closer to the moment of her dismissal, and her need to find Captain Jack grew more and more urgent as the final feast and ball approached. I shall see un tomorrow, she said to herself, as she carried William into the drawing room for yet another inspection as the guests began to gather. I shall set off first thing in the morning, while they'm all busy speeding the bride and groom and standing in line for vails and so forth. And she tried to work out how many hours it would be.

'Sixteen,' Ariadne told her, as though there were no doubt of it, 'for 'tis two o'clock now and 'twill be eight in the morning when you leave the house, if all goes according to plan.'

Suki was lacing Ariadne's stomacher, but she paused to laugh, the laces dangling between her fingers. 'You speak as though 'twere ordained,' she said. 'How can you be so sure on't?'

Ariadne was wearing her teasing expression. 'I have foreknowledge, perchance.'

'Would you did.' Suki sighed. 'For if I don't find the Captain tomorrow I don't know what will become of me an' William. Even if I married Farmer Lambton I doubt if he could prevail upon 'em to keep us together.'

'Take heart,' Ariadne said, and her voice was so warm that it brought a rush of tears to Suki's eyes. 'We are both in the lap of the gods and the gods are land on some occasions.' She looked at her image in the pier glass. 'Am I subdued enough for the bride's final triumph, think 'ee?'

'You look well,' Suki told her, blinking her tears away.

Ariadne grinned. 'Appearances,' she declared, in her mother's voice, 'are *so* important.'

So the bride and groom were applauded into the dining room and Ariadne took her place at the foot of the table and the final feast began. It soon became rowdy and inebriated. So many toasts were proposed and so many bumpers drunk that the company rapidly lost count and balance, and even Frederick Bradbury began to enjoy himself; the bride ate so much that her face grew puce coloured and she had to unfasten her stomacher; the squirrel was given a long rein and ran across every plate on the top table, to the amusement of all those who were beyond its range; and Sir George told scurrilous tales to both his neighbours and was roundly chided and admired.

But Ariadne sat silent and ate little and watched everything, and when the ladies retired she went straight upstairs to her chamber when her mother wasn't looking. Which was where Suki found her, lying on the bed, stripped to her chemise and reading one of Lady Bradbury's three-volume novels.

'Yes?' she said, when Suki had knocked and entered.

'You didn't ring,' Suki said, feeling she had to explain her presence.

'No. I didn't, did I?'

'Are you ready to be dressed?'

'No. As you see.'

'Am I to come back later?'

This time Ariadne didn't even look up from her book. 'No.'

She was in such a peculiar humour that Suki couldn't think what to say next. 'Well then Ariadne turned over a page and assumed her insouciant expression. 'I have decided that I shall dress myself this evening,' she said. 'Go down and enjoy the ball. There will be much to enjoy, I promise you.'

It was unheard of for a young lady to dress herself. But she was plainly in no mood to argue about it so Suki left her. She'm a-goin' to cut it, she thought, as she went back to the kitchen, an' I can't blame her, for she'm suffered enough, what with Melissa crowing an' giving herself airs, an' Hepzie being rude to her, an' her mother an' father ignoring her. I'd do the same. 'Tis a pity she won't see the ballroom though, for 'tis uncommon fine tonight.

The household had been busy all morning preparing the place, sweeping the dance floor, clearing out spent candles, gathering up dirty glasses and smeared plates, polishing the chandeliers, setting new fires, bringing in the new decorations. Now the walls were hung with green boughs, which had been bent into curving shapes which looked uncommon pleasing against the blue wallpaper and shone in the dazzle of candlelight from Lady Bradbury's splendid chandeliers as though every leaf had been polished. To complete the picture, each green confection had been entwined with gold and white ribbons and hung with long strings of tiny golden bells that were threaded so close together and had been gathered up in such profusion that they tumbled and curled like swathes of mythical hair. Suki and Bessie were very taken with it, especially as the band were to be dressed in green and gold to match the decor and the supper tables were heavy with greenery, too.

''Tis a shame Miss Ariadne won't see it,' Bessie said, 'poor lady. But we will, won't we? We can stand in the gallery, same as last time. Mrs Sparepenny said.'

426

They managed a good position right at the front, where they had a clear view of the doors and could watch every entrance. And as they had come to expect, the entrances were spectacular.

Lady Home was in royal purple, with gold cock feathers in her hair, and Lady Fosdyke, not to be outdone by her rival, was dressed in equally regal scarlet with a bejewelled turban to set off her snow-white wig. Sir Francis wore a jacket embroidered in gold thread while his wife was caparisoned in saffron yellow with a head-dress made of peacock's feathers. Lady Bradbury, standing beside her husband to greet their guests, looked insignificant beside their splendour, for *her* new gown was pale blue, trimmed with pink embroidery, and looked decidedly out of fashion.

'She'll give that to Hepzibah presently,' Suld said, enjoying the discomfited expression on her mistress's long face.

'Here's the bride and groom,' Bessie said.

They were standing just inside the door, looking round expectantly and waiting for their applause to begin. The bride had put on weight since the start of the wedding and was waddling in a very unbecoming way, and the groom was leaning backwards at such a precarious angle that it really was a wonder he didn't topple over. But they were the cynosure of all eyes and that was what mattered.

There was the usual polite ripple of applause and those nearest to the newly weds told them how fine they were looking, and then the master of ceremonies announced that the ball was about to commence and begged that the company be upstanding for the opening quadrille. And just as Sir Humphrey was swaying his bride on to the floor, the door was pushed open and Ariadne stood in the doorway.

She had little kid slippers on her feet and wore long lad gloves to her elbows, but apart from that she was stunningly and triumphantly naked, for the dress she'd had made up for the occasion was a mere wisp of gauze and apart from a cache sexe of green leaves that was tastefully stitched to her skirt and matched the chaplet of green leaves that encircled her dark hair, it was completely transparent.

The sussuration of indrawn breath was like a gale. Then there was an outcry as her mother staggered and seemed about to faint, crying, 'Oh, the abomination! How could she do such a thing? At her own sister's wedding!' The ladies exclaimed in horror at her behaviour and the gentlemen advanced towards her, eyes gleaming and mouths moist.

Suki was so thrilled by her daring that she clapped her hands together in delight. What style she has. So this is what she meant by 'all will be revealed', she thought. And what courage! No wonder she had to keep it a secret. She tried to catch Ariadne's eye to show her how well she understood and how much she approved. But Ariadne was busy catching other eyes, as she advanced gracefully into the ballroom, smiling to right and left at the gallants who crowded around her, eager for a closer look and the chance to partner her — in one way or another. She knew she had the pick of the bunch and would choose the richest who offered, and she was happily aware that there were little dramas being played out in every corner of the room because of her — that her sister was red-faced with anger and stamping her feet, that Jessup had retired to the furthest corner, coughing fit to crack his lungs, that her mother was swaying and preparing to swoon, that her father actually had his hands over his eyes. Oh, 'twas a perfect, flesh-tingling, parent-defeating, absolute triumph.

Hermione was weeping on the shoulder of her dear friend, Arabella, there being no adequate or comfortable space into which she could swoon. 'I am shamed before my family,' she sobbed, 'and I had such hopes of this wedding. Such hopes. I shall never hold up my head again. Somebody send for Mr Jessup and tell him to deal with it.'

'Sir George will see to it,' Arabella soothed her. 'Never fear. He'll not permit a scandal.'

But Sir George was so shocked that for a few seconds he was completely speechless and could do nothing but hurrumph and splutter while his daughter continued her procession and his brother tried to reassure him.

Then he removed his hands and found his voice. 'How could she *do* such a thing?' he wailed. 'She's no better than a whore, Frederick, a common whore making a public exhibition of herself and she always had the best that money could buy. The best.'

'You mustn't blame yourself, my dear feller,' Frederick said, patting his arm. 'Indeed you must not. There ain't a thing you could have done to gainsay it. Women are a breed apart and that's the truth of it. Given to vanities and follies of all sorts. Ain't we always said so?'

'She's no daughter of mine,' her father said groaningly. 'I tell'ee that. Where's Jessup? He'll know how to deal with her. She must be moved before too many people see her. I'd, not want any of my friends — '

But his young friend, John Smithers, was already standing before the shimmering flesh of his errant offspring, mouth agape with admiration and lust. And in the second shock of the evening, the lady spoke to him.

'La, Mr Smithers!' she said, her voice high and clear and ringing like a bell. 'I thought you a theatre-goer, sir, upon me life, yet one would think you had never seen a gauze before.'

There was another intake of breath and another outburst of amazement: 'She speaks!' 'Did you ever hear the like?'

'She ain't dumb after all.'

'She does it a-purpose,' Melissa wailed, 'to spoil my wedding.'

'Ignore her,' Sir Humphrey advised, covertly watching her pretty flesh. 'Remember that you are my wife.'

'I hate her!' Melissa howled, stamping her feet with distress. 'Hate her, hate her, hate her.'

'Pray do not discommode yourself, my love,' her husband said, trying to restrain her, 'for we are to open the quadrille.' And he tried to send a signal to the band. But they took no notice of him, being fully and happily occupied watching the naked lady.

'Five pounds says my old feller is the first to squire her,' Lady Fosdyke said, offering her challenge to all the ladies grouped around her.

There were plenty of takers, there being nothing more attractive than a gamble for high stakes, especially when there were so many married fools to back.

But Lord Fosdyke was already at Ariadne's elbow and winning his wife's bet for her. 'We have seen many a gauze in our time, my dear,' he said, 'but never worn so becomingly, if I may be permitted to say so.'

'You turn a pretty compliment, sir,' she answered, smiling into his eyes. Oh, such a fine rich man! And wouldn't his wife be cross if she chose him.

'Perhaps you will honour me with the pleasure of the opening quadrille,' the noble lord suggested.

'Do you ask me to stand up with you before all these people,' she teased. 'Fie, my lord, we should cause a scandal.'

'I stand up for you already,' he said, acknowledging his wife's calculating glare with a wry half-smile. 'And as to causing a scandal, we are above such considerations.' And he offered her his arm.

So Miss Ariadne Bradbury and Lord Fosdyke opened the quadrille instead of the bride and groom. And Lady Fosdyke won her bet.

From then on the ball was one titillatingly scandalous moment after another, for the triumphant lady danced every measure, and each one with a new enraptured partner, who dared the experience even though they knew they would have a hard time of it explaining themselves to their wives when they returned to their seats.

After the third measure, Sir Francis sought out his cousin, striding down upon her with a face bright with such mischief that she looked up quailing with fear at what he was about to say.

'I congratulate'ee, ma'am,' he drawled, 'You've bred a corker, upon me life. Ain't seen such cracking entertainment in months. She'll do well with old Fosdyke. He might even get her into court.'

She was so surprised it was all she could do to summon the words to thank him.

'I'd stand up with her mesself,' he said, smiling at the temptation, 'if Virginia would permit me.'

'Which she won't,' Lady Fosdyke said, stepping up to join them. 'Leave her to my old feller. He'll see her right. 'Twon't last more than a month or two — his light a' loves rarely do — but he'll see her right. She's made a fine choice, Hermione. You should be proud of her. Won me a pretty penny, too. Whatever else, she's a sight better than that mimsy-pimsy sister of hers.'

Hermione's head was beginning to spin at such unexpected compliments. 'I'm obliged to 'ee,' she said faintly.

'So you should be,' the lady said. 'Your dance, I think, Sir Francis. I've a mind to tread the boards for once and my husband is otherwise engaged.'

Towards one o'clock, Jessup announced that supper was served and, at that, Ariadne looked up to the gallery and signalled to Suki that she was to come down.

'Bring me my travelling cloak and rny chemise and a day gown for tomorrow,' she ordered. 'The blue if you can find it. We mean to leave while they are supping.'

'I'm so — ' Suki began.

But Ariadne put a hand over her lips for Lord Fosdyke was walking towards them through the crush. 'I will send to 'ee at eight tomorrow,' she whispered. 'Pack the rest of my things tonight and bring 'em with you then. And William, too, of course, for you can travel on to Bedlam when you've delivered 'em. Did I not tell 'ee the gods could be kind? Now make haste or I shall be forced to travel as I am.'

So the few and necessary clothes were packed in Ariadne's smaller travelling bag and rushed downstairs to be handed to her as she left the house, wrapping the cloak around her as she went. There wasn't even time for Suki to wish her luck. Not that she needed it.

Thirty-six

On Sunday morning, the Bradbury household rose early, for the bride and groom intended to set off on the Grand Tour — complete with their peculiar retinue — as soon as they had taken breakfast and their mattress had been packed for transport. And although most of the guests had stayed on to pelt them from the doorstep with the traditional shoes and rice, they, too, would be taking their departure and distributing vails not long after that. But Suki Brown wasn't concerned with any of it. She was up and out of the house before Cook came yawning down to prepare breakfast, for Ariadne had been true to her promise and had sent a carriage to collect her at eight o'clock.

For once, William endured the journey without complaint, partly because he was still sleepy but mostly because it was such a short and easy ride — across the empty Oxford Street, through two sleeping squares and into a long elegant terrace where they stopped before a house with a black door and two very white doorsteps. Suki and William were admitted by a housemaid in a blue gown, who asked them kindly to step this way and led them upstairs, while the wicker skip containing Ariadne's clothes was hauled from the luggage box and carried into the hall.

Ariadne was sitting up in a very grand bed, in a very grand bedroom. She was wearing her cream chemise and, to Suki's relief, she was on her own.

'He left at daybreak,' she explained. 'I've ordered breakfast and some porridge for William. He's having bread and meats sent over and he promised 'twould be here by nine. We have plenty of time. Bedlam don't open until eleven — I've made enquiries — and the carriage will take 'ee there and bring 'ee back again. What do 'ee think to this house? 'Tis all mine, so he says.'

''Tis uncommon fine,' Suki told her and, as Ariadne was smiling, she ventured to ask, 'Are you happy here?'

'Happiness don't come into it,' Ariadne said easily. ''Tis a job, no more, no less. I've made my choice and now I will make the best of it.

432

'Tis a deal better than being forced to marry whatever popinjay my idiot father might have chosen for me. At least I don't belong to the gentleman. There's no question of obeying him or any suchlike nonsense. 'Tis a business arrangement, no more. He's a demanding lover for an old un, I'll say that, but I daresay I shall find someone younger and more handsome to pleasure me, and in the meanwhile I shall live well enough. I'm to have a carriage of my own and horses, and fine clothes and jewels — he says I've only to ask for 'em — and whatever servants I require what's more, which is why I sent for you. How would 'ee like to be my lady's maid if you don't find your lover?' And when Suki hesitated, she went on, 'You know my ways so well and I could depend upon 'ee to be discreet, could I not? 'Twould suit us both I believe, and 'twould be a deal better for you than marrying that dreadful tell-tale of a farmer of yours.'

'I must go to Bedlam first,' Suki said. 'If I can find the Captain — '

That was understood. 'Nothing need be decided yet. I have written my address on this paper — you see? — so you can write to me as soon as you know what you intend. Ah, here is our breakfast come. I trust you have an appetite.'

So they sat on two comfortable chairs beside a pretty little round table and ate the bread and meat provided and took it in turns to spoon porridge into William's mouth. Suki was too excited to eat much, but she made an effort and, although her heart wasn't in the conversation either, she talked to Ariadne like the old friends they were. When the blue-gowned maid returned to inform her new mistress that the carriage was waiting for her friend, they were still reliving the shock that Ariadne had caused the previous evening, and giggling with delight at the memory of it.

But now it was time for Bedlam and the moment of discovery. As Suki stood to leave, she was trembling so much she had to hold on to her gown to still her hands.

'You must visit again soon,' Ariadne told her, 'even if you *do* find that lover of yours, which I do truly hope for 'ee.' And in a moment of happy impulse, she seized Sula's hands and kissed her on the cheek as though they were sisters. 'I wish 'ee good fortune, Suki Brown.'

'As I do you,' Suki said, lifting William on to her hip.

Outside the house, the street was still empty, although rather more smokey than it had been when she arrived, and this time her journey was a great deal longer and more complicated.

First they travelled east along endless roads until they reached a wide street called Cheapside where there were terraces of shops on either side of them, each with its own shop sign hanging above the pavement like a stiff tin flag. Then they turned north and edged through a series of narrow lanes which were all excessively dark and dirty and smelt of piss and decay. Here the houses leant towards one another as if they no longer had the strength to stand erect and slatternly women gossiped in dark doorways, peering out at the carriage in the most alarmingly suspicious way. Suki felt decidedly uncomfortable there, especially as the overhanging houses pushed darkness into the carriage so that she could barely see where she was. And then, just as William was beginning to grizzle and climb over her lap, they were out in the light again and the coachmen called down to her that they were at the London Wall and would soon be there.

Presently he pulled his horses to a halt. 'There's your asylum,' he said, pointing to it with his whip, as Suki stuck her head out of the window. 'You've arrived.'

It was a long, stately, splendid building, like a palace, with two perfectly balanced wings on either side of a central tower. At the top of the tower was a curved tiled roof, above the roof a balcony of grey stone surmounted by a decorated clock tower, surmounted in turn by a cupola as bulbous as an onion, and topped off by the gilded statue of a flying dragon. There were rows of fine carriages waiting in the road outside, so the first visitors had obviously arrived already, and the entrance was marked with a painted placard. A flight of two stone steps led to a gate, the gate gave way to a gravelled path, which led, in turn, to a narrow door guarded by a liveried attendant in a grey tie wig. It all looked extremely fine and elegant. In fact if it hadn't been for two doleful statues brooding on either side of the gate, Suld would have had no qualms about visiting the place at all. That is until she walked up the front steps.

Then she knew she was entering a lunatic asylum because of the smell of the place. It stank of vinegar which had obviously been used by the bucketload to sweeten the air. But beneath its cleansing fumes, there were residual smells that were all too familiar — of shit and stale piss and human sweat. It reminded her of Sir George's chamber pot. Oh, she thought, how can my dear, fastidious Captain live in such a place? What on earth is he a-doing working here? The sooner she found him and persuaded him out of it, the better.

She lifted William on to her back, tying the ends of her shawl tightly at her waist to support him, and walked boldly up to the attendant.

'Penny to see the lunatics,' he said, holding out a hopeful palm.

'I haven't come to see no lunatics,' she rebuked him. 'I come to see the Captain.'

'Captain who?'

'Captain Jack,' she said. 'I don't know his other name but everyone calls him the Captain.'

'No one a' that name 'ere,' the attendant said. 'Leastways, not so far as I know.'

'There must be,' she insisted. 'I have it on the very best authority.' He must be here. He simply *must*. She'd waited so long and come so far. Her face was so fierce with distress, the attendant took pity on her.

'Stay there a tick,' he said, 'an' I'll ask Mr Todd.'

Mr Todd wore the same livery, but with rather more gold braid attached to it. He was sitting in an office beside the front door, demolishing a meat pie with total disregard for the stink around him, and with such vigour that scraps of it flew into the air as he chewed and spoke.

'The Captain?' he said. Munch, snort. 'Yes, we'ave got a Captain, Joe.' Munch munch, gobble. 'Number sixty-nine, east corridor.' Snort, crunch, smack, smack. 'That's where.'

'That'll be a penny,' the attendant said. But she was already running down the corridor, with William bouncing on her back. He was here! He was here! Just a few yards away. Her dear darling Jack. 'I'll pay on the way out!' she called.

It was a very long corridor and full of extraordinary creatures: old women, shrivelled as witches, mumbling and tottering, their eyes wild; old men, muttering and twitching, their wigs matted and their faces spiked with stubble; women in weird costumes, posturing; and men in loincloths, scratching; and creatures so deformed and smeared with filth that it was impossible to see what sex they were. In the numbered rooms they crouched on their haunches in dirty straw, rocking or spitting or lying mute as corpses. It was a terrifying place. And walking in among the wild and lunatic were groups of gentlefolk in their best clothes, scented and powdered and superior, exclaiming with mock horror at the awful sights around them, and enjoying every one of them.

Which was more than Suki could do. 'Soon be there,' she said, speaking to William but encouraging herself. 'Forty-nine, fifty. Soon be there.'

Room sixty-nine was a shattering disappointment. There was nobody in it except a half-naked lunatic with a shaven head and a scabby face, who was sitting on the floor, staring at the wall. She was so upset that the tears sprang to her eyes, and she let them fall, standing in the dirty doorway, at a loss to know what to do or where to go, or what to say.

The attendant came panting up beside her. 'Penny,' he gasped. 'Penny fer entry!'

She took a penny miserably from her pocket and put it in his palm. 'Where is the Captain?' she said. 'You told me he was in room sixty-nine. So where is he?'

And the lunatic lifted his head and looked up at her, with the Captain's eyes.

The shock was so profound that it drained all colour from her face and took the strength from her legs. She sank to the stone flags of the corridor with William clinging to her neck, and groaned, 'No, no, no! Oh, my dear Captain! What have they done to 'ee?'

'Who is it?' the Captain said, dully, peering at her. And although his voice sounded thicker than she remembered, it *was* his voice, and the sound of it made her weep again.

She leant forward into the room and took his hands, and he allowed the touch, but seemed puzzled by it. 'Who is it?' he asked again, blinking his eyes.

'Oh, my dear Captain,' she said. ''Tis Suki. Your own Suki. Come all the way from Bath to find 'ee.'

'Polly Anna, is it?' he said, peering at her again.

The name angered her. How dare he confuse her with another woman! How dare he tell her there ever *was* another woman! 'Suki,' she said firmly.

'I fear I do not know you, ma'am,' he said. 'Perhaps you mistake me for another.'

'No, sir,' she told him. 'I do not mistake you, for you fathered my child.'

He scowled slightly as if she had presented him with an enigma. 'I have no memory of it,' he said at last. 'But I confess to you, ma'am, my memory is fleeting since I came to this place, and most uncertain.'

'You said I was your one true love,' she said. 'Did you lie to me?' She was surprised by how calm she was being.

'All men lie to their wenches, one time or another,' he said sadly. ''Tis the way of the world, I fear.'

'You said you loved me.'

'Love!' He sighed. 'What is love? We seek it all our lives, but I fear 'tis only folly when all's said and done.'

She undid her shawl and lowered William very gently until he was standing in the corridor behind her. 'Your folly made a son,' she said, picking him up in her arms and turning him to face his father. 'A fine child, look 'ee. And yours. Now what do 'ee say to that?'

He glanced at the baby and scowled again. 'What can I say? I am no longer free to speak as I will. They incarcerate us here and feed us pap and laudanum until our brains are numb. If you look to find a husband and a father for your child, you must seek elsewhere. We may not woo, nor wed, nor father, and there's an end on't.'

The words burned into her brain, shattering her calm and returning her strength. She rose to her feet and roared at him in an extremity of disappointment and rage. 'Don' 'ee dare speak so. That's your child I carried, an' bore, an' fed, an' lied for. An' all for the love of you, poor fool that I was. All for the love of you! And now you say you may not wed. Where's your valour, sir? 'Od's bones it makes me sick to see 'ee.'

An attendant was behind her pulling at her arms and begging her to desist, but she was too angry to hear him and his touch was an irritant she simply shook away. She strode into the dirty straw with William in her arms and aimed a kick at her lover's scabby legs.

He scrambled to his feet in alarm and backed away from her, holding out his hands to deflect her, as she lifted her foot to take another swing at him. But at that moment, and without any warning, he looked up, staightened his spine and began to declaim in a bold unnatural voice as if he were an actor. Turning she saw that a group of ladies had gathered in the corridor to watch them and that several of them were applauding as if her anger had been part of a play.

'Shall I tell 'ee of Africa?' he called to them.

And they nodded and called out, 'Pray do.'

'Where the great chief Wan Four sells men like beads,' he said, 'and flogs 'em with a cat-o'-nine-tails until their backs are raw, and the crocodiles lie in wait at the water's edge to eat 'em as they fall. Such creatures as you would never believe. They are tall as a house and with skins like armour and they can swallow a man whole — bones, brains, blood and all, with a snap of their great jaws.' He mimed the closure of those jaws with both arms, clapping his hands together so sharply that he made several of the ladies jump with delighted terror. 'How would 'ee like to see such things as that?'

They shuddered happily and threw coins at his feet.

'Shall I tell of a sea fight when the muskets shoot like hail and cannonballs flv towards'ee, red hot, and each one capable of ripping off your arm or tearing off your leg? And what thereafter, I ask 'ee? Shall I tell 'ee? You lie on the deck in a pool of vour own blood and the pain of it too great to bear, and the surgeon takes your stump and holds it down in a tub of boiling tar, and you may scream all you please but 'twill be done though you die of it, for you will die without it, when your limb turns green and gangrenous and the poison rises to your brain.'

The shudders increased and more coins were thrown and Suki turned her head to glance at their enraptured faces while he took breath for another story. But there were no more words. Instead he gave a sudden, high-pitched, howling scream, that made them all jump with alarm. It frightened William so much that he clung to his mother's hair and began to whimper. Suki turned her head again, annoyed by such an exhibition and ready to rebuke him, but then she saw that this wasn't part of his act. It was too extreme and he was too visibly shaken, his eyes staring at some horror behind her, one finger pointing. And she turned again to see what on earth it could be to frighten him so, and found herself looking into the startled face of Lady Bradbury.

'Are you come here to taunt me, lady?' he cried. 'Or are you some ghost from my past, risen to torment me. Speak to me!'

The crowd were delighted by his appeal and turned to the lady to see how she would respond, the regulars declaring that this was the best display they'd ever witnessed.

Hermione was caught in two minds whether to swoon away or to face him out with some flippant remark. The corridor was so crowded that it would be difficult to swoon in any comfort, even with Arabella beside her to ease her to the floor, so she decided on speech. 'Tush!' she said, addressing her remarks to her companion. 'What nonsense these poor fools do talk. Do I look like a ghost, think 'ee?'

She should have chosen a fall, for he recognized her voice and was enraged by it.

'She's the one!' he screamed. 'That painted lady in her silks and her rouge. That lady is my mother, the Lady Bradbury. My mother! If you seek to see who brought me to this pass, look 'ee there. She's the one. 'Od rot her! Farmed out, kicked out, naught but a bastard, so help me, and 'tis all her doing. You may call yourself a mother, ma'am, but you have no sense of the meaning of the word! No sense at all. Reckon your ream pennies, now, you'd best, for your sins have found you out. 'Od rot her! Rot her!'

Out of the corner of her eye, Suki could see Mr Todd hurtling down the corridor towards them, and behind him a chattering crowd of lunatics and gentry. And then her eye was caught by a sudden downward movement and she saw that Lady Bradbury was falling. Suki realized that for once this was no pretence, but a genuine swoon, for Lady Bradbury was toppling sideways and extremely heavily, knocking the people behind her into awkward positions by the weight of her body and groaning in the most alarming way. The two attendants were considerably hampered by her collapse, for she took up a great deal of room in the crowded corridor and soon gathered a crowd of her own, but they pushed past as well as they could and reached out to catch the flailing arms of their half-naked captive, who was still screaming abuse at the top of his voice. It was all so sudden and violent and terrible that Suki could do nothing but cry, the tears cascading down her cheeks and dripping off the end of her nose. But it wasn't until another attendant arrived with a canvas straitjacket and a bottle of laudanum, that any kind of order was restored.

The three men worked together so quickly and brutally that everybody stepped away from them. First they flung the Captain to the ground with such violence that his head hit the wall with a crack, then they forced his arms into the stiff sleeves of the jacket while he was still stunned. Then the first bound his arms and the second chained his legs while the third poured laudanum down his throat, despite his groans. Then they gagged him with a dirty cloth, picked up the coins and pocketed them, and left. And Suki was caught up in such an overpowering rush of pity that her entire body ached with it, pity for him to be cast down so low and treated so cruelly, pity for William who would never have a father now and might lose his mother, too — how could they bear it? — and pity for herself to have come so far and tried so hard and waited so long, only to be reduced to this. 'Twas too cruel!

Now that the exhibition was over, the gentlefolk were moving on. The corridor was full of swishing skirts and happy conversation. Lady Bradbury was left propped up against the wall, looking putty pale, with Lady Willoughby kneeling beside her, rubbing her hands and murmuring to her. One of the attendants was carrying a chair towards them, and following him through the crowd was a small black boy in a sailor's smock and canvas breeches — a small black boy with blue eyes.

The sight of him was such a surprise it stopped Suki's tears. 'How now,' she said to him. What are *you* doing here?'

But he walked straight past her, and dropped to his knees beside the Captain, calling to him, 'Mr Jack! Mr Jack!'

The attendants were lifting their rich patron from the floor and easing her into the chair, profuse with apology.

'A poor sick fool,' Mr Todd said. 'You mussen pay 'im no mind, ma'am. They don't know what they're a-sayin' half the time. Laudanum you see, ma'am. Weaned on it, he was, an' now 'tis the only way to sweeten 'is foul mind.'

'This man,' the black boy said clearly, 'is my master. I tell you, he has the most sweet mind of any man. He save my mother's life. I'll not hear him spoke of so.'

'What's this? What's this?' Mr Todd said, frowning at him. 'Are we to be told our business by a blackamoor? Be off with 'ee, wretch, afore I takes a whip to 'ee.'

'He speaks true,' Suki said, standing up for him before she'd stopped to consider how dangerous it might be. 'He is not a child to lie. I met him in Bristol and know him for an honest crittur. If he says he'm Jack's slave, then so he is.'

'He may be what a' will but he'll not stay here,' Mr Todd said, 'for I've no room for him. Be off with 'ee. You heard what I said.' Blue looked at his master, then at Suki, then at Lady Bradbury who was looking down her long sharp nose at him. 'I stay with my master,' he said stubbornly. And to Suki's delight, he untied Jack's gag and removed it gently from his mouth.

'Fetch me a whip!' Mr Todd roared. But there was a gloved hand on his arm restraining him.

'We must be sorry for these creatures, sir,' Lady Bradbury said. 'I will pay you a crown for his keep if you will agree to let him stay an hour or two. I am too unwell to stay longer, as you will appreciate, but I will send my man to settle accounts with you. Suki, you will kindly assist me to my carriage. Good day to 'ee, sir.'

Suki looked back at her lover but he had his eyes closed and seemed to be asleep. The black boy was unfastening the strait-jacket and wiping the dirt from his face. There'm nothing I can do for him, she thought. I may have found him but t'was all in vain. And she lifted her mistress gently from the chair and she and Lady Willoughby led her away along the corridor. Whatever is to happen now, she thought as they stumbled forward, will happen whether I wills it or no.

Thirty-seven

It was a miserable journey back to Cavendish Square. Suki needed to cry, and to cry for a very long time, but with Lady Bradbury watchful in one corner of the carriage and Lady Willoughby looking concerned in the other, there was little she could do to relieve her feelings, except keep her head down and cuddle William. But her mind was spinning. Now that she'd got over the initial shock of seeing her lover locked up as a lunatic, she was remembering what he'd said. 'Lady Bradbury, my mother!' Could it be? Or was it mere raving? If he spoke true, 'twould explain the kerchief and Jessup's knowledge of Nowhere Lane. He'd been delivering money to someone. Why not the Captain? She looked at her mistress, wondering, and Lady Bradbury opened her brown eyes and looked back at her, hard and straight and forbidding. How much had she heard afore she fainted? Suki thought fearfully. I was yelling so loud, an' I know I said the baby was his. Over and over again. She must have heard it. I shall be punished as sure as fate. What will she say? And worse, what will she do? But Lady Bradbury's eyes were closed again and just for a moment and mercifully, she wasn't saying anything.

They were all relieved to be back in Cavendish Square which was echoingly empty and seemed a great deal larger without its guests.

'What a blessing to be returned to civilization,' Lady Bradbury said, gazing at the well-ordered balance of her hall. 'Life at this end of London is so much more polite, would you not agree, Arabella?'

You can be dismissed politely, Suld thought, as she followed the two ladies into the hall, and I daresay I *shall* be.

'Ah,' Lady Bradbury said. 'Jessup. I've an errand for you to run. Where is the master?'

Sir George was at his club, apparently, and Cook wished to know when she should serve dinner and for how many.

'Are you well enough to withstand a meal?' Arabella wondered, her face full of concern.

'Indeed yes,' Hermione said airily. 'I am *quite* recovered, as you see. 'Twould be too foolish to allow oneself to be discommoded by such a trifle. Tell Cook she will oblige me by serving dinner for two at four o'clock. I will send for you later, Suki.' It was said in such a calm way and with so little expression that Jessup didn't see the import of it. But Suki did, and it made her stomach shake with apprehension.

So Jessup went off on his errand and the ladies dined and Suki waited. The hours passed and as there was little for her to do, she sat in the nursery and darned her stockings and presently Bessie appeared with her own mending and sat down to work beside her.

'You missed a treat this morning,' she said. 'You should've seen 'em go off. What a to-do! That ol' squirrel of his got out the cage an' we was all chasin' it for hours an' hours...'

Suki let her run on but she was too worried to listen. And when the stockings had been mended and William had been settled for his afternoon nap, she was relieved when Bessie took herself off to help in the kitchen. But she'd not been gone more than a quarter of an hour before she came panting back again to say that Lady Willoughby had gone home and the mistress was in the parlour and would like to see Suki straight away.

Please God, don't let them take my William away from me, Suki prayed as she climbed the back stairs to the drawing room. Anything else, but not that. He'm all I got now the Captain's shut away. All I got, an' I love him more'n I can bear. I'll never tell another lie in the whole of my life if you only let me keep my William. I promise.

But the only answer she got was the steady ticking of the grandfather clock in the hall below, and the alarming rhythm of her own heart, which was pounding in such a frantic way she was finding it hard to breathe. She gave a timid knock on the parlour door, and while she was waiting to be told to enter, she offered up her prayer for the last time.

The room was full of afternoon sunlight, which shone through the high windows in columns solid enough to touch. There'm so much gilt and glass in this room, Suki thought, wincing away from it, and'tis all so dominating and hard. The frames glowed around respectable portraits, the mirror threw back dazzling reflections, the brass fender winked and sniggered, even the curtains were as bold as grass. How could she hope for mercy in a room like this?

Lady Bradbury sat by the fire at the far end of the room beside the marble fireplace, with the tea things on a low table at her elbow, and a mound of cushions behind her powdered head. She seemed quite herself again, and far from being angry was affable and gracious — and thoroughly terrifying.

'I sent for you,' she said as Suki hesitated into the room, 'on a literary matter. You *do* read, I trust.'

'Oh yes, ma'am.'

'A most agreeable distraction don't you find? You must give me your opinion upon a novel I have just been reading. A romance. Of great delicacy. It made the tears start to my eyes.' She gave Suki a faint smile and waved a languid hand towards a high-backed chair. 'Pray, do sit down.'

Suki perched on the edge of the appointed chair and waited. The silence in the room was painful. What will she say next? she worried. She'll dismiss me now, she'm sure to.

But Hermione went on talking about the novel, gazing into the distance, as though into memory. ''Tis a pretty history but fanciful,' she said. 'A tale of love requited. Young love, you understand, headstrong and, sad to say, unsuitable. She was the daughter of a duke, poor creature, and he the son of a gardener. But a pretty passion and uncommon sweet for all that, and all the taste of love she ever had. He told her she was all in all to him, sweeter than springtime, his own dear love, his own for ever. You know how fulsome men are when they woo.'

'Yes,' Suki agreed, breathlessly. Oh yes, how well she knew.

'She believed him, poor fond foolish child that she was. We are much deceived in matters of the heart, I fear. There was a child. A son. A pretty boy, with fine brown eyes, as I recall. But there.' She sighed. 'Her father railed at the disgrace, her mother took to her bed. The girl begged permission to marry, but 'twas out of all question and disallowed. I told'ee 'twas a dismal story. The gardener was dismissed and sent away, and his son with him, to a foreign country, as I recall. The lady never saw him again.' She paused to refill her cup and drank tea, calmly, her face perfectly controlled. 'So here you have the crux of the tale,' she went on, 'a daughter mined, a lover fled, the child in the womb. What should be done, think 'ee?'

'Were I that daughter,' Suki said. 'I would keep the child, come what may.'

'Aye, so you would. I do believe. And lie for it, if t'were needful.'

Fear tightened Suld's throat, but she told the truth. 'Yes, ma'am, I would.'

Hermione sipped her tea. Then she put down her cup and continued. 'The duke was adamant, you understand. His daughter had no choice, poor foolish lovelorn soul. The child was farmed to a labourer's wife in Ba... the — um — nearest town. And later sent to school, and lodgings found. The lady married as her father wished. A good man, to be sure, but passionless. How think you of her story? Could she do other, given the circumstance?'

'The saddest tale, poor lady,' Suki acknowledged. 'She had no choice, ma'am. I can see that plain.' Then she paused, wondering whether she dare speak further. If milady could speak in parables why not follow her example? 'Should you care to hear it, ma'am,' she offered. 'I could tell *you* a tale.'

''Tis a pleasant fancy,' Hermione said, 'and no harm in't. Pray proceed.'

'How of the child grown to a handsome man. With fine dark eyes 'an a merry way. Full of such passion. How of that?'

'It sounds most like.'

'How if he found a foolish wench of his own, who loved him true, an' bore his child. How if she then took service in the town with a fine family. The best, ma'am, if you'll allow.'

Hermione smiled to signify that she would allow it. 'What then, child?'

Suki licked her lips and hesitated for just a second. Then she spoke the truth again, but quickly before it could frighten her into silence. 'How if the mistress had a baby, too? A fine child, and very like the other. How if the lover nursed it as her own, and loved it, too, and lost it, suddenly?'

'In death?' Hermione asked, and her expression was calculating.

'In death.'

'Then she would have a choice, too, would she not? To tell the truth and lose all, or lie and keep her child in the household? Was't not so?'

'Yes, ma'am. T'was exactly so.' What else could she say? There was only the truth now.

The silence that followed was long and thoughtful. Hermione gazed at the embroidered firescreen, with her chin in her hand, brooding and scowling.

445

'The child is a fine strong boy,' Suki offered, 'worthy of any family, even the highest. If'twas a fault to keep him in the household, there are those who might not wish to see the fault undone.'

Hermione looked at her for a long fraught minute. 'I believe I would be of their number,' she allowed, 'were I to be asked. I must confess I would rather be a mother than a grandam, in all conscience, although I dare swear son-in-law Humphrey will alter that, if the deed ain't done already.' She stood up and walked to the window and stood for a while looking down into the garden.

'My advice to the girl,' she said, 'if 'twere sought in this matter, would be to say nothing but to leave matters as they are. The child will thrive, given his heritage. Tis a fine child, as you say. Why should the world and his wife be told such a tale? Some things are better left unsaid.'

Suki was finding it very hard to breathie.

'Besides,' Hermione went on, 'there is a husband in the case, is there not? A good man, as men go, and doubtless fond of the child he thinks his son. We would be churlish to harm his faith, or deprive him of an heir.'

'Tis settled, Suki thought, her head spinning with the wonder of it. I'm to keep my William, after all. She was smiling so widely she could feel the skin stretching beside her eyes.

'If I were asked for advice,' Hermione continued, 'I should say, "Find a good husband. Be known as a wife." A country husband, a farmer or smallholder for preference, where the child could stay, for rest and fresh air and suchlike, when his parents were elsewhere, where he could visit when he reached the age to be sent away and educated as a gentleman. As sent away he surely must be at the right age and the right time. That you'll allow.'

'Twill have to be, Suki thought sadly. She couldn't keep him for ever. She was lucky to keep him at all. She knew that. And eventually he would have to go to school, like all young gentlemen. That was the way of the world. 'Yes,' she agreed. She would have to give up all hope of the Captain and marry Farmer Lambton, after all.'Twas not impossible. If Ariadne could make the best of *her* situation, then so could she.

Lady Bradbury stood up, smoothed her gown and pulled the bell rope, but when Suki rose, expecting to be dismissed, she waved her back to her seat again. 'Stay where you are,' she commanded. 'I have someone I wish you to meet.'

This was so extraordinary that Suki didn't know what to make of it. She sat where she was and waited obediently and presently Jessup appeared and was sent to fetch 'the young person'. Which after a minute or two, during which time Lady Bradbury contemplated the fire and appeared to be deep in thought, he did.

The young person turned out to be a gentleman in a white bob wig. He wore black buckled shoes, a green coat and buff breeches that didn't fit him at all well and seemed ill at ease, for he was coughing nervously as he was ushered into the room. So Suki kept her eyes down, like a good servant, and didn't look at him after the first quick glance.

There was a brief silence. Then Lady Bradbury held out her hand to receive him and he bowed to kiss it, murmuring 'your sarvant, ma'am'. And Suki recognized his voice and looked at him again, this time with such wonder on her face that he smiled at her, almost as if he knew her.

'This gentleman,' Lady Bradbury said, 'is Mr Daventry, a kinsman of mine and grandson to the Duke of Daventry. He has been much abroad of late, and being returned was incarcerated in an insane asylum, through no fault of his own, where I discovered him by pure good chance this morning, and where he should never have been sent, in all conscience, not by any stretch of the imagination whatsomever. He is here to rest and recuperate and to conclude his business with Sir George.'

Suki dropped a curtsey, as that seemed to be expected, but she said nothing, there being little she could say. This is how 'tis to be, she thought. He'm here and accepted and excuses found for un. He'm to be family and we'm to be kept apart. She was powerless before the speed of so many changes — and all in one short day. Still, at least he looks more like himself, she thought, now that he'm properly dressed and he got a wig over that awful shaven head. An' that's a comfort. But she winced when she looked at his face, for his lip was split and his cheeks bruised and his eyes were empty of any love or recognition, although he was looking straight at her.

'I believe I saw you this morning,' he said. He spoke politely but there was doubt in his voice.

She answered equally politely, as a servant was bound to. 'You did, sir.'

447

'You must forgive me if I do not recall as I should,' he said courteously. 'I have been unwell, I fear, and given a deal of laudanum, which do clog the brain uncommon hard.'

He doesn't know me, Suki thought sadly. I could be any wench to him. Or any servant for that matter. But she did her best to sympathize. 'I don't doubt it, sir.'

There was a discreet tap on the door — a Jessup tap — followed by a deprecation of coughing. The master was returned, he reported.

'Ask him if he will be so good as to join me,' Lady Bradbury said. 'Tell him I have a piece of news for him, which I know he will be anxious to hear.'

For a confused second, Suki thought the butler was going to speak out of turn, for he stood where he was, hesitating and pondering and giving Jack the oddest look. But then he recovered himself and coughed away to do his errand.

'You may leave us,' milady said to Suki, 'but stay within call for we may have need of you. There is a spot just beyond the door which will serve, I daresay. It usually does if the scuffs upon the boards are anything to go by.'

So they know they'm spied upon, Suki thought, as she curtseyed and left them. I might ha' knowd it. There am't much goes on in this house that she don't know about. Still at least I got leave to listen this time. Not that it made much difference. She'd have eavesdropped anyway, with or without permission, for this was a conversation she simply couldn't miss.

Sir George made his usual weighty entrance and flung himself into a chair with such force that the castors groaned beneath him. 'How now, wife!' he said, cheerfully. 'I hear you've a piece of good news for me. Well speak on, me dear! Good news makes good appetite.'

'Your factor is proved a villain,' the lady said in her cool voice.

To be told such a thing and with so little ceremony baffled his brain with distress and disbelief. He struggled to comprehend, taking temporary refuge in teasing. 'You jest me, dear,' he hoped.

'No, sir,' she insisted. ''Tis as true as I stand here. Which this gentleman can confirm. Your slave master, sir, Mr Jack Daventry, and a kinsman of mine, as I daresay you will recall.'

Sir George flicked a limp hand towards the young man, who was standing politely waiting to be introduced, but he didn't look at him.

'Sarvent, sir!' he muttered and continued to stare at his wife. 'If 'twere true I should have known of it,' he protested. 'Frederick would have told me.'

'Frederick knows nothing of it,' Hermione told him. 'I should have known nothing of it myself had it not been for Mr Daventry. He was the one who saw all and noted it, being your slave master.' The fog of incomprehension began to clear. 'My slave master ran mad,' he said. 'Stark staring raving mad. Sent to Bedlam, damme. Frederick told me so.'

'No, sir,' Hermione said. 'Your slave master was sick of the fever and sent to Bedlam at the behest of your purser, that abominable creature, Mr Jedediah Smith, who, I might tell'ee, sir, knew of the villainy and said nothing. How you ever came to employ such a man is beyond my comprehension. Howsomever, Mr Daventry could tell you more of this than I can, should you wish to hear it.'

'Speak,' Sir George said weakly. ''Twill all be iniquity, I do not doubt.' And he sighed with the approaching misery of it.

So Jack told his tale, beginning with an account of how the surgeon chose the six strongest slaves, explaining what became of them and how they were discovered, and ending with a description of the secret hoard of cut cane that he and Blue had been shown by the slaves in the fields. 'He purloins a tenth of your crop, sir, with every harvest. Your slaves were sure of it.'

Sir George listened with increasing anger, at first drumming his fists on the arms of his chair, then on his feet prowling and scowling but heavily attentive. By the time the full story was told, he had reached roaring point. ''Od's bowels!' he yelled. 'The man's an arrant knave, 'od rot him. I never heard the like. Wants hanging, drawing and quartering, so he does. And I'm the man to see it done.' It was time for decision and action. 'I'll go to Nevis myself on the first ship, damme.' He rang the bell so furiously it was a wonder he didn't pull it from the wall. 'I'm obliged to 'ee, Mr Daventry, sir,' he said, remembering his manners. 'Uncommon grateful. There'll be a bounty in it for 'ee, you have my word on't.'

'Well, as to that,' Hermione said acidly, 'you'd best think of paying him his wages first. He ain't been given a penny piece by that rogue Smith.'

'Is this true, sir?' Sir George asked.

Jack looked him straight in the eye. 'I fear so, sir.'

'Not a penny piece?'

'Not one, sir, though the purse was agreed upon before we sailed, as your brother will tell you. Fifty-one guineas, as I recall, to be divided between Mr Tomson and myself, he to take two thirds.'

''Od's blood!' Sir George said to his wife, as Jessup materialised through the servants' door. 'I despair of human nature. We are into abomination here. All, Jessup. Pack up seven suits of clothes and so forth and lay out my travelling coat. I'm off to Nevis in the morning.' He turned to Jack, and added casually, 'You'd best come with me, young feller-me-lad, since you know the ins and outs of this affair.'

The order took everyone by surprise and, out on the landing, where she'd been standing right up against the door so as not to miss a word, Suki caught her breath so suddenly she was afraid they would have heard her and stepped back towards Ariadne's empty room in case she had to hide in a hurry. Was she to lose him again so soon?

But Lady Bradbury was the mistress of any contingency. 'Far be it from me to contradict you, my love,' she said, taking breath to contradict him soundly, 'but is this wise? I make this observation for your own good and the better accomplishment of your plans, which are too admirable to put to any hazard.'

Sir George's brain lurched with annoyance and renewed incomprehension. 'Hazard?' he said. 'I see no hazard. Mr Daventry will be invaluable, don'tcher know. Invaluable.'

'Indubitably,' Hermione agreed. 'To arrive with a witness in hand would certainly add strength to your case. Howsomever, to be seen arriving with Mr Daventry might warn your factor that his conduct is to be investigated and in that eventuality you might find — indeed, I dare swear you *will* find — that all evidence would be destroyed or hidden before you could bring it to light. 'Tis a matter you will doubtless wish to consider.'

'Aye!' Sir George admitted. ''Tis true, deuce take it. But if such is the case, what is to be done?'

'I could offer advice, my love, should you wish it,' Hermione said, adding modestly, 'such as it is.'

He waved a weak hand towards her. 'Pray do.'

The plan she outlined was neat, simple and entirely to her purpose. Mr Daventry would mark the position of the slave compound and the illicit sugar store on one of Sir George's maps. Sir George could then carry his evidence with him secretly and would be free to travel with a trusty servant, who being unknown upon the island would give no cause for alarm to its dishonest inhabitants, 'until you burst upon'em sword in hand.'

Sir George was stunned by its practicality and its self-enhancing drama. 'Capital!' he roared. 'Upon me life! Couldn't have planned it better myself.'

Jack cleared his throat discreetly and prepared to put in his own happy penn'orth. 'If I may make a suggestion, sir?' he offered. And when permission was granted with a lordly wave, 'It seems to me, sir, that the ideal companion for your adventure stands in this very room before us. I refer, of course, to Mr Jessup. I know from Lady Bradbury that he has been her most loyal servant these many years but now that all her children are — uni — settled, there will be less for him to do. Is that not so, my lady? Consequently...' And he looked at the butler with a triumphant, insolent boldness, daring him to argue or refuse.

The two men bristled at one another, Jack cool with revenge, Jessup dark-faced with suppressed anger, while Hermione watched them and Sir George roared that it was 'Capital! Capital!' and declared that Jessup was 'just the man.' Eventually the butler dropped his eyes and Jack permitted himself a smile and the matter seemed to be settled.

'You'll need to pack two trunks, what,' Sir George said jovially as Jessup frowned from the room. He beamed at Jack and Hermione. 'Now for the maps, Mr Daventry. We'll see to 'em here and now, what. No time like the present.'

Hermione held out her hand to prevent Jack from rising. 'There is still the matter of the bounty,' she said.

Sir George had lost interest in such matters. ''Twill wait till my return I daresay,' he said vaguely.

But Hermione insisted. 'I'd not wish you to travel with a bad conscience, my love,' she said, 'there being no worse companion on any journey than a pricking conscience.'

'I'll give 'ee my note of hand,' Sir George suggested.

She persisted, as Jack and Suki listened with rapt attention. 'I believe we could do better than a mere note of hand,' she said. I believe we could make this a matter of property.'

Suki caught her breath, Jack's heart was racing, Sir George looked interested. 'How so?'

'You will remember the manor farm at Appleton, my love. You have always intended it for a stud farm, have you not? Very well, then. How if you were to offer the property to Mr Daventry in lieu of capital and by way of bounty? 'Tis in bad repair, I'll grant you. The house is past rescue. But there's a deal of good land attached and with hard work and a new owner — a man of bottom and enthusiasm, a good judge of horses, and a gentleman you could trust, I need hardly add — 'twould soon be brought to profitable order. In a year or two I dare swear 'twill be a model of self-sufficiency and outshine all stud farms in the country. How say you to that?'

It seemed an admirable plan. 'Would you be agreeable, sir?' Sir George asked. 'Could 'ee take to the farming life, think 'ee?' Land of my own, Jack thought, flushed with surprise and pleasure, a home, property, a new life as a gentleman, the very thing I've always known should be my portion. He understood little of farming, but none need know it. He could learn, and quickly, as he'd learned to be a slave master. And if 'twere to be a stud farm, he would be working with horses for the most part, which would be sheer reward. He might even breed another Beau. Oh yes indeed, he would be most agreeable.

'Then the business is concluded,' Sir George said. 'Now perhaps we may proceed to our cartography.'

He reached the door so quickly that Suki only just had time to avoid him, skipping into Ariadne's room as his first broad foot splayed out on to the landing, and she'd barely reached the servants' door before Lady Bradbury was in the room and signalling to her to stand still and say nothing.

They waited until they heard the library door open and shut. Then Lady Bradbury gave rapid instructions.

'You will have heard all, I do not doubt,' she said. And when Suki nodded. 'You are to make ready to travel to Appleton with Mr Daventry and master William within the week. The tailor is ordered for tomorrow morning but I doubt if Mr Daventry's new clothes will be ready much before five days. Possibly more. Tailors are uncommon tardy. You will take one maid servant to assist you — Bessie would do well, I think — and Bamaby shall drive the carriage and look to the horses. He is a dolt when it comes to curtains, I fear, but he has some sense with horses and should do well in a stable. You will stay at Appleton until Mr Daventry's new house is ready. I will send a letter to that effect to Mr Norris. Nothing need be rushed, you understand.'

Suki dropped a curtsey and murmured, 'Yes, ma'am,' but her mind was in such a turmoil she felt as if her brain was boiling.

'Be of good cheer,' the lady advised, nodding her powdered head. 'All will be well. T'ain't the best of all possible worlds, in all conscience, but we must make what good of it we can. Ask Mrs Sparepenny to attend me directly.' And she swept from the room, straight of spine and determined.

The buzz of gossip in the kitchen was so loud that when Suki stepped through the door it was like walking into a hive. Not surprisingly, William was very much awake, but perfectly happy, sitting on Bessie's lap beside the table, chewing a sugar plum. He turned as Suki swished towards him and held out his arms to her, calling 'Mamma-Sue! Mamma-Sue!' but she barely had time to pick him up before she was surrounded by every servant in the place, all eager for the latest news.

'Is it true the masters off to Nevis?', 'Have 'ee met the young gentleman? He come here with jest a blanket round him, half in a swoon he was. Do 'ee know who he is?', 'Mr Jessup's got a face like a thunder cloud and won't tell us a thing.'

No matter what may become of me now, Suki thought, as she held her baby's lovely warm familiar body close and safe in her arms, even if Jack don't remember me, an' am't like to wed, an' is come home changed to a distant stranger I barely know, I still have you, don't I my little love, an' that's a deal to be thankful for. And your life's safe an' provided for now. You shall have fine clothes and good food an' grow to be a gentleman, with rich toys to play with an' money in your pocket an' a pony to ride an' all. She could just see him on a pony. He'd be a fine rider. Like his father. And she suddenly remembered the splendid sight Jack made astride that great horse of his. But of course, she thought: Beau. There's still Beau. He haven't been told a word about Beau. He don't know I've a-rescued un, and kept un safe. A deal of good could come of *that*. Why hadn't she thought of it before? I must write to

Farmer Lambton and tell him we shall be in Twerton as soon as may be and promise him that he'll be paid at last.

But meantime there was milady's message to deliver to Mrs Sparepenny, and after that the pressure of all those questions to answer, which she did as well as she could, prevaricating a little and ignoring those that had to be avoided. And then the chores of the day carried her along and there was no time for hope or regret or even thought. When she finally fell into bed at a little after midnight, she was so tired she slept as soon as her head touched the pillow.

Thirty-eight

Sir George left for Nevis early the next morning with a great hullabaloo and the promise to return in triumph 'as soon as I have apprehended all villainy, what!'

His wife waited for an hour in order to be quite sure he was clear of the house and then, suitably attired in a new and splendid day gown, attended by a new and superior lady's maid, and with enough clothes to sustain even the most anxious three days, she set off for a well-earned visit to her cousin, Sir Francis. Before she left, she handed Jack his earnings, paid in full and in gold coin, with the instruction that he was to take the second coach and four to Appleton when he was ready and meantime was to provide himself with clothing suitable for his new position. 'Do not stint yourself,' she instructed. 'Appearances are *so* important.'

For the next five days, Jack Daventry lived between luxury and terror. By day he was treated like a lord, with abundant food to eat, a tailor to provide obsequious service, tradesmen to offer new wigs, buckled shoes and fine linen, and Blue to wait upon him hand and foot. By night he fell into a sleep hag-ridden by nightmare, where fierce women thrashed the child he had been, and asylum keepers threw the man he had become against walls and gratings and tied him in a straitjacket so that he could barely breathe. He was tossed into the sea to be eaten by sharks and crocodiles. Muskets beat his face. Cannonballs tore off his limbs. He woke groaning, with the sweat running down his spine and falling from his eyebrows, so that he had to shake it from him like a clog, and was glad of Blue's comforting presence to call him back to the day.

In the afternoon he and Blue took a stroll in the gardens at the centre of the square and Blue told him how he had found the Llandoger Trow and travelled to London with Quin Cutpurse, and how they had held up coaches and robbed all manner of gentry and finally how the Spider had taken him to Bedlam, 'Because I ask and ask. He say, "You come back to Seven Dials after. We got gentleman for you to meet." But I find *you* so I do not go back.'

That information made Jack suspicious, knowing how Quin liked to operate. 'What sort of gentleman was that? Do 'ee know?'

'He got cats,' Blue reported. 'He is...' He struggled to remember the name. 'Cat burglar.'

'I have saved you from a life of crime,' Jack said, ruffling the boy's woolly hair. 'And not a minute too soon.'

'What is lifacrime?' Blue asked.

But he never got an answer because at that moment Suki came out of the house leading her toddling William by the hand and, at the sight of her, Jack took flight and headed off for the opposite end of the garden to avoid her. There was something about her red cheeks and those bright eyes that triggered the most uncomfortable memory, and as he couldn't determine whether it was a nightmare he was recalling or some actual and painful occasion, he simply removed himself from the pressure of it.

So when his last new jacket had been delivered and his journey was finally about to begin, he was very much put out to discover that she and the child were to travel in the carriage with him. He stood with one foot on the step, uncertain how to proceed.

'Do you go far?' he asked, wary but making an effort to be polite. But when she told him they were to travel all the way to Appleton together, he forgot his manners completely and rushed back into the house to find himself a book to occupy him on the road. The thought of sitting opposite those bold blue eyes for such a long journey was so disquieting that he had to have a barrier that could be held up between them whenever need arose.

His deliberately averted eyes made Suki ache with sadness. She felt rejected, especially after days when it had been painfully clear that he was going out of his way to avoid her. But she tried to cheer herself by observing that he looked a deal better than he'd been when she saw him in Bedlam-in-Moorfields and reminding herself that she would soon be reuniting him with his horse. He was immaculately dressed, in a brocade coat very similar to the one he'd worn on that first love-dazed summer of theirs — what an age ago that was! — the cut on his lip had almost healed, his bruises were fading, his skin was a healthier colour and his head was covered with the thick dark stubble of returning hair. It only needed his memory to return and all might yet be well. 'Twas foolish to blame him for unkindness if he could not remember her. Meantime she had taken pains to be well prepared for the journey, with one basket packed with bread, cold meats, beer and pickles to sustain them on the first leg of their journey and another full of toys to keep William amused. And she'd written to Farmer Lambton to warn him of their arrival.

It had been a difficult letter to compose, for she had to let him know that the Captain was returned without allowing him to think that they were already married or even like to be. She pondered for more than a day until she found the diplomatic words she needed, but when they were written she knew she'd done well and was pleased by her delicacy. 'Captain jack,' she'd said, 'has been uncommon ill and is still a deal too weak to plan his future or even talk of it. 'Twill cheer him to see his horse again, but we must be mindful of his feelings which are a deal too tender at the moment. I would be obliged if you would say as little to him as you may and if you would advise my parents that I hopes they will do likewise.' Now it was simply a matter of waiting and hoping.

Her letter to Ariadne, on the other hand, had been an easier task altogether. She had written to her at length and freely, recounting everything that had happened and describing her feelings in detail, from the shock of seeing her beloved as a lunatic in Bedlam, through the amazement of Lady Bradbury's story of his birth — 'which must be a secret atween us for I have given my word not to tell it to a living soul' — to the relief of knowing William's position was ensured and the embarrassment of being forgotten and unrecognized 'which do break my heart I can tell 'ee, having loved him so long and so true.'

Ariadne had sent an answer the same afternoon to say how greatly she was surprised by Suki's news and how much she sympathized. 'Do not lose heart, my dear,' she wrote.

Allow time to heal him, as it surely will. When his memory is returned I do not doubt that he will love you as truly as he ever did. I cannot wait to visit with you at Appleton, which I shall do at the first opportunity', you may be sure, for I am full of curiosity about this new brother of mine, especially as Mamma must not know that I know his circumstances, and would dearly like to meet him, particularly if he has the good sense to marry my dearest friend. Write to me at the very next opportunity for I long to hear how this matter will turn out.

But there was a deal to be lived through before that could be done and a long road to travel. Fortunately, the first part of the journey went well, for although Jack spent his time gazing moodily out of the window or pretending to read his wretched book, she managed to keep William amused with the cup and ball and the monkey on a stick and the jack-in-a-box, and fed him a sugar stick when he started to grizzle, so the time passed relatively easily.

When they stopped that evening at The Bear at Slough, Jack realized, rather belatedly, that they were on the road to Bath.

'How now?' he scowled at Suki. 'Does our coachman not know the road?'

'We are to travel by way of Lambton Farm at Twerton,' she told him. 'Milady's orders.' And her heart lifted for now she could tell him about Beau and the telling might restore his memory.

But he was already turning away from her. ''Twill be a matter of livestock, I daresay,' he said casually, and strode into the inn to make sure of a good room.

She realized that she was shivering with the cold of rejection. Oh, how easily he could cast her down. And how thoughtlessly. It hurt her that he was so unaware of her and turned away from her so quickly, for it showed how little she meant to him. And there were still two more days to journey before they would reach Lambton Farm. It was uncommon hard to have to wait so long, especially when it wasn't in her nature to be patient. But patient was what she had to be, notwithstanding. There was nothing for it but to travel on, keep her secret and feed her remaining hope as well as she could.

William was less well behaved on the second day. He grizzled and complained and climbed over the seats and smeared the windows with his sticky fingers. In the end she had to suckle him to get him to settle. But on the third day he was exhausted and slept all afternoon, sprawled across her knees and growing heavier by the mile, as the sky coloured with sunset, the horses laboured and the carriage grew dark. She was very relieved when they turned in at Lambton Farm at last, to the usual cacophony of affronted farm animals, and Barnaby drew the horses to a halt.

Jack sprang out before the step was down. 'We must make haste,' he said to Barnaby, shouting above the din of squeals and squawks, 'if we're to return to Bath and find good lodgings for the night. Who am I to see?'

'Well, as to that, sir,' Barnaby shouted as he unfolded the step, ''tis Suki you must ask. She's the one what knows.'

She was carefully carrying her sleepy baby out of the carriage, as Blue and Bessie scrambled down from their perch on the driving seat. 'If Bessie will take him,' she said, 'I'll show 'ee the way. Let un see the pigs, Bessie. He'll like that. Give him a little stick so's he can scratch their backs. 'Twill stop 'em a-squealing.' Somebody was opening the door of the cottage and she could see Mrs Havers' inquisitive face framed in the window, but fortunately Farmer Lambton was already on his own doorstep and waiting for them, so she led the Captain across to make the necessary introductions.

'Mr Daventry, this is Farmer Lambton, who been a-caring for your property since April. Mr Lambton, please to meet Mr Jack Daventry, a kinsman of milady's.'

Property? Jack thought, staring at her. 'Twas a curious word to use of livestock. But there was no time to question her, for the farmer was leading him towards the stable yard.

'He's all ready for 'ee, sir,' he said. 'You'll find him in fine fettle.'

The stable was dark with dusk but there was no mistaking the horse that stood in the first stall, pricking his ears at their approach.

''Od's teeth!' his master cried, running to fling an arm about that splendid neck. 'Tis my Beau! My Beau! How now, my beauty. I never thought to find 'ee again.' He was so close to tears he had to duck his head into Beau's mane, and the horse pawed the straw and twitched his flanks. 'Let me look at 'ee.'

He had been most carefully groomed, his bay coat brushed till it shone, not a single tangle in mane or tail, his hooves new shod.

'I had the smith look him over, so soon as I received our Suki's billet,' Farmer Lambton explained.

So she arranged this, Jack thought, glancing across to where she stood in the shadows. She's known about it all along. The more he heard about this girl the more intriguing she became. 'I'm beholden to 'ee, sir,' he said to the farmer. 'He'll have cost 'ee a deal in fodder, I fear. I trust you have kept accounts.'

He had. 'Written up week by week, sir, as is my custom.'

Jack said he was glad to hear it and promised to settle with him, 'Forthwith. You have my word on't. I'll ride him first. Aye, I must ride 'ee, must I not my beauty.' He was already hauling his saddle from its hook, impatient to be up and away. 'You cannot know what it is to find my horse, sir. I thought I should never see him again and here he is, large as life and twice as handsome and raring to go, ain't you my charmer.'

And that's the way of it, Suki thought sadly, as she watched him saddle up and ride — oh, so happily — out of the yard and off along the bridle path, easing his great stallion from trot to canter to full rippling gallop. He remembers his horse but *I'm* forgot. She felt bleak to the point of tears.

'I see I must cease my suit,' Farmer Lambton observed as they stood in the yard together, 'since your lover is returned to 'ee.'

She was confused by his directness. 'Not that I didn't take your proposal serious,' she hastened to assure him. 'Nor that I wasn't grateful to 'ee. Uncommon grateful. 'Twas just — '

'You're a good girl, Suki Brown.' he said. 'And I wish 'ee joy. Indeed I do. Now you must go and see your mother. She's been a-waiting for 'ee all this while.'

Which was plainly true, for Mrs Brown had been standing in the doorway of her cottage, with Tom and Molly owl-eyed beside her, ever since the carriage arrived.

'So he came home again,' she said, as Suki walked towards her, 'this Captain of yours. He'm a fine figure of a man, I'll grant 'ee that. Uncommon handsome, which anyone with half an eye can see even if she ain't disposed to think well on un, which I arn't. Have he put a ring on your finger?'

Such straight disapproval made Suki wince. 'Well, as to that,' she said, trying to make light of it, 'he's been ill an' aren't recovered yet. Time enough for rings and things when he'm back to health.'

'He looks healthy enough to me,' Mrs Brown said, watching as he sprang from the saddle and strode into the farmhouse. 'Got a good firm step on un, I should say. A deal too firm for an invalid.'

Suki's control was slipping. 'I tread on ice,' she said, her mouth trembling despite a mighty effort to keep it under control. 'And whether 'tis thick enough to support me or will break under the next step I cannot tell.'

'What ice?' Molly said, examining the ground at her sister's feet. 'I can't see no ice, Suki.'

And at that Mrs Brown called her youngest daughter a goose — and changed the subject, asking after the babba and the Brad-burys and so giving Suki a chance to recover. And by the time she'd told them as much of her news as she could, Jack was out of the farmhouse and back in the saddle again, calling to her and eager to be off. So she kissed her family goodbye, promising she would see them again in the spring, and returned to the carriage and her sticky baby.

'I shall ride into Bath,' Jack said, patting Beau's neck. 'Bessie and Blue can take my place in the carriage to keep you company.' But he didn't look at Suki at all. He only had eyes for his horse. 'We'll not be parted again in a hurry,' he said to the animal, 'eh, my charmer.' And was off and out of the yard before Barnaby had time to put up the step.

There was so much power about him, up on that great horse, so much pride and so much happiness. He led them into Bath as if he were at the head of a triumphant procession, looking about him like a conqueror. He'd barely walked ten yards along Stall Street before he was surrounded by old friends, calling out to him and to one another. 'Why look-ee here. The Captain's back.'

'Well damn my eyes, where have you been, you varlet?'

'Od's bones, 'tis uncommon good to see'ee, damme if it ain't. You must come and have supper with us. We won't take no for an answer, damme.'

I am home, he thought, as they trooped after him to the inn. Back where I belong. I've money in my pocket, friends at my side, fine clothes on my back, land to farm and Beau in the stable. What more could I want? The horrors are over and done.

That evening, Suki had supper with Barnaby, Blue and Bessie, who was bubbling with the excitements of the day. 'What a lovely horse Mr Daventry's got,' she said. 'He's a thoroughbred, I'd lay money, the size of him. And what a lot of captings you do know, Suki.'

Suki had been eating sleepily, worn out by travel and disappointment. 'Do I?' she asked.

'First your brother,' Bessie explained. 'He's a capting, ain't he? The one we was looking for that time. And Mr Daventry. They was all calling him Capting out there in the street. I heard 'em. And your husband. He's a capting, ain't he?'

'Yes,' Suki agreed sadly. 'He was.'

461

Bessie's kind heart was touched to see her friend so melancholy. 'He'll come home sometime,' she comforted. 'You'll see. They all comes home sometime or other.'

Suki gave her a bleak smile. 'No,' she said. 'I don't think he will now. I've a-waited too long for un. I'm afeared he'm lost to me now an' I must face up to it.'

'Tain't like you to speak so,' Bessie said, most surprised to hear such pessimism. 'Never say die.'

'You may have the right of it,' Suki admitted, although in her present dejected state she didn't believe it. 'So I won't say die. Not this evening, leastways. I'll say goodnight to 'ee and hope 'ee sleeps well. We've a long day tomorrow and a deal of travelling to do.'

But sleep came late to Suki Brown that night. The mattress was cold and lumpy and, no matter how much she turned and sighed, she couldn't find a comfortable hollow upon it. And then, when she finally drifted into a chill-footed sleep, she was plagued by a torment of dreams. She and Jack were strolling in the Spring Gardens but when they stopped to kiss, he wouldn't look at her and when she tried to put her arms about his neck, he melted into air and was suddenly on horseback and riding away from her. She ran and ran, calling his name, as he leapt from the horse into a bucking carriage and from the carriage into a fast running river. She plunged into the water after him, but he swam away from her and was lost, leaving her to struggle in a current she couldn't withstand, weeping and yearning.

When she woke it was grey daybreak and rain was pattering against the window. 'Twill be a bad day,' she said to William as she held him over the chamber pot to piddle.

In the next room, Jack was waking from a nightmare, too. This one was so fraught and complicated that he was determined to forget it as soon as he could. 'We'll make an early start,' he said to Blue, 'for the weather is against us.'

It was a sensible decision, for the next and final leg of their journey was the hardest of them all. Rain fell from the sky in sharp white rods all day, whipping the horses, penetrating coats and breeches and reducing the road — which was in a poor enough condition in dry weather — to a slime and slurry of mud. They got stuck in deep ruts on two rain-driven occasions and all five of them had to get out and put their shoulders to the wheel to heave the carriage on again. Streams of water poured from Jack's new hat and dripped from the toes of his new boots, Barnaby grumbled that he was wet to his skin, his passengers were so jolted and flung about that they were bruised beyond caring, and William did nothing but wail and wouldn't be comforted by anything, not even a sugar stick, which he bit and flung away from him until shards of it were stuck to every surface in the carriage, from the seats and windows to Bessie's skirt and Suki's hair.

They were all heartily glad when they came to Appleton at last and could get indoors to a warm fire and clean clothes. Mrs Norris bustled into the courtyard to welcome them, dispatching servants right and left to carry in their baggage and lead their horses away to the stables to be groomed, fed and watered.

'I got a good ol' rabbit stew a-boiling for 'ee,' she said. Three jack rabbits. As plump a set of fine furry fellers as you ever saw. Been over the fire since mid-morning so they have. I reckoned 'twould be today, when we got milady's billet. 'Twill give 'ee a good stomach lining, rabbit stew. What we all needs on a night like this, which am't a night to travel in and that's the truth on't. I never saw such rain, not since last Michaelmas. Come you up to the fire so soon as you'm ready.'

It was such a warm welcome and the stew smelled so enticing that Suki forgot that she had once thought the house old-fashioned, dark and draughty. Now she was simply glad to be indoors, aware of the heat of the fire, leaping and crackling in the hearth, and of the rich glow of the candles that flickered in the sconces on the wall and burned most warmly in the three triple-headed candlesticks upon the kitchen table, casting golden light on Mrs Norris's new bread and patterning the pewter platters and tankards and the two great flagons of cider with lustrous stripes of amber.

That night she slept easily in the bed she'd used during that first impatient winter and woke refreshed and restored and eager for the day. The rain had stopped, there was a pale sun lighting the courtyard and the dawn chorus was in full-throated song.

As she was stirring the porridge pot, and gossiping with Mrs Norris, and assuring William that she'd not be a minute and then he could have his breakfast with a bit of patience, Bessie came yawning into the kitchen with a message from Mr Daventry.

'He's goin' up to Home Farm, seemingly,' she said, 'for to see his property. Mr Norris is a-driving up in the cart and he says will you join him. Mr Daventry, I mean. Not Mr Norris. Though you'll be a-joining 'em both in a manner a' speaking. I'll feed the babba if you like.'

The request was so unexpected after everything that had happened on their journey that Suki was bemused by it, but she put on her bonnet and wrapped her shawl round her shoulders and went out to obey it, notwithstanding.

Mr Norris was already in the driving seat, sitting bolt upright with his old black dog bolt upright beside him but there was no sign of Beau and that was a surprise, too, for she quite expected Jack to be in the saddle. But no, he climbed into the cart and sat down beside her. And off they went, following the bridle path east without a word being passed between them.

It was Mr Norris who did all the talking. ''Tis a mile and a half or thereabouts,' he said, 'and I'd best to warn 'ee, sir, 'tain't in the best of conditions. Sir George keeps up the orchards wonderful, as you can see, sir, and the Appleton House is a model to the county, though I says it as shouldn't, but Home Farm — well now that's a different matter. Twas rented out to Mr Chomondley, you see, sir. He ran it for years, and since he passed on there's been narry a one to care for un so 'tis... Well, you'll know how 'tis, sir.'

It was a ruin. The farmhouse was built of wattle and daub and thatched in the old style, but the thatch was so old it was dust grey and full of great holes where the mice scrabbled and the small birds nested and twittered, and the house itself was so dangerously out of alignment that it looked as though it would tumble over at a sneeze. And as if that weren't bad enough, the fields were no better. Most of them were clogged by burdock and nettles, the hedgerows were knotted for lack of husbandry, the ditches clogged for lack of clearing and one field so badly waterlogged that there were pools of water shining like blue sides all over it.

Suki's heart sank at the sight of it, but Jack was determinedly cheerful.

'Twill need a deal of work,' he said, 'so 'tis as well I'm a man for a challenge. Let's see the stables, Mr Norris, since they will be my main concern.'

464

The two men walked round the house to the yards behind it, with Suki trailing after them, wondering what purpose she served by being one of the party. He'd handed her out of the cart but he hadn't spoken a word to her since they left Appleton House. In fact, he was speaking to Mr Norris again as she entered the yard and saw the stables.

'Now these are a deal better built than the house,' he was saying. Which they were, being made of stone with a firm brick floor and a tiled roof. 'What do 'ee think to 'em, Suki?'

She said she thought they would serve.

'And so they will,' he agreed. 'Uncommon well.'

'I must be on my way now, sir,' Mr Norris said, 'if I'm to be at the mill betimes. If you don't need me no more, I'll bid 'ee good-day.'

Am I to stay here, Suki wondered, or leave with Mr Norris?

She was answered at once. 'We will take a look inside the house,' Jack said, 'and walk back presently. That will suit, will it not, Suki?'

So they took a look inside the house, which was full of dust and much decayed and according to Jack 'not worth the ground it stands upon. I shall build a new house on that mound across there. In the new style, with fine windows and a good bold door, and a drawing room on the first floor where it ought to be. What say 'ee to that?'

She said it sounded handsome, since that was plainly what he wanted to hear and was true besides. But she was still puzzled and unsure of herself and wondered what they would talk about on their long walk back to Appleton House.

At first, he spoke at length about his plans for the home farm. 'I have always hoped to farm,' he said. 'I shall need a manager, I daresay, for to tell 'ee true, Suki, I know little of farming as yet, but I mean to learn. I knew little of slavery when I first set sail from Bristol but I learned that trade well enough and 'twas a deal more difficult than any farming life could be. Besides I shall be breeding horses and there's an occupation I have in my very blood. And Beau to put to stud what's more.'

As no answer seemed to be needed, Suki walked beside him and kept her eyes down and said nothing. It was a bitter-sweetness to be so near to him and yet so far from his thoughts.

They walked on in silence for several hundred yards and then he suddenly spoke again. 'I am much beholden to 'ee, I think,' he said. 'For you were the one who found my Beau, I believe, and bought him from that rogue Wenham and rode him to Lambton's farm.'

She admitted that this was so, but did not look at him.

'Then I owe you the price you paid for him.'

'No,' she said, looking at him at last and smiling because she was so pleased by what she was about to tell him. 'The money was your mother's. She sent me a note for five pounds to pay for William's new clothes. 'Twas in my pocket at the time, so I spent it. Though what she'd have said had she known I do not dare to think.'

'And what of William's clothes?'

'I made over his old ones.'

'You are a sterling creature,' he said, touched to think that she would put the care of his horse before clothes for this child she loved so much.

'I could hardly stand by an' see un beaten, poor crittur,' she said, and as his expression was encouraging, she told him the story.

'Then I truly *am* beholden to you,' he said when she'd finished.

The more he talked to her, the more strongly she was attracting him, with those fine rounded arms and that pretty bosom and her dark skin glowing in the sunshine and those blue eyes looking at him with such candour, reminding him. But of what? The curse of it was that he couldn't remember, although he sensed it to be important. Echoes rose to disturb him but faded away from him as if they were slipping into the untidy hedges. 'I must make amends to 'ee.'

'There's no need.'

'Were my mother to be believed, there is a pretty way to do't,' he said, smiling at her.

She was alerted by the smile and annoyed by the change in his tone, but he didn't notice and pressed on. 'She maintains,' he dared, 'that a farmer is twice the man with a good wife.'

Oh the misery of it. To be so near to a proposal from this man she'd loved so much — still loved so much despite his faults — and all for the very worst of reasons. 'That, sir,' she told him as coldly as she could, 'is no concern of mine.'

'But it could be, could it not, were we to marry?'

She straightened her spine, and moved two paces away from him, her face set. 'Then my answer's no,' she said. 'And you'd best know it now afore you ask. I'll not have my life arranged for me by any milady, no matter who, and no more should you. 'Tis belittling. Insulting. We should be above such things. If I marry 'twill be for love, not for an arrangement. I thought better of 'ee, sir, indeed I did.'

Her fierceness was burning away the mists in his mind. 'When you found me in Bedlam,' he reminded them both, 'you said you loved me.'

'That was then and in the heat of the moment,' she told him furiously. 'A deal has happened since. I arn't a pawn in Lady Bradbury's game nor do I ever intend to be.'

'You said that William was my child.'

'Aye, so he is,' she said. 'But they am't no reason to marry neither, since I've birthed un and cared for un on my own and now he'm to be brought up as milady's son and sent to school as a gentleman and to inherit Sir George's estate and we'm to keep our secret.'

This time, to be told that he was indeed a father filled him with an unexpected pleasure — and some hope.

'Then perhaps,' he said, 'we should keep our secret together as man and wife.'

'No, no, no!' she cried, stamping her feet. 'I won't marry for convenience. I could have took Farmer Lambton months since if I'd meant to marry so. And I won't do it. Never, never, never. 'Twill be love or nothing. Don't'ee understand?'

'What a firebrand you are,' he said admiring her. But then he saw the gleam of tears in those wild eyes and realized that her anger was caused by pain. 'I did not mean to hurt 'ee, upon my life,' he said, putting his hands on her shoulders to turn her towards him. 'I thought 'twould please you.'

The touch of his hands was more than she could bear. 'Then you thought wrong,' she said, and tried to twist away.

The movement triggered a memory that spun in his drug-tamed brain, caught, held and edged into focus. 'The Spring Gardens,' he said, staring at her. 'The Spring Gardens in Bath. You wore a pink gown and little red slippers and I stole six pinks from the border and put 'em in your hair. You are Suki from Twerton. We went to the theatre and saw the silliest play. Oh, how I do recall.'

To be remembered was such an exquisite pleasure after so much hurt and disappointment that she caught her breath and stopped struggling. 'You said I was your one true love,' she rebuked him. 'And then you forgot me. You recognized your horse and didn't know me from Adam. Your one true love.'

He was so caught up in the power of the memory that he missed her rebuke. 'And so you were,' he said. 'How I do remember. You rode before me on the saddle with your hair blown about and your bonnet on your shoulders. I loved you more than I could say.'

Her answer was bitter. 'And have forgot me since.'

'No, indeed, truly. I thought of 'ee on board ship and in the slave camp, even in Bedlam. I could not put a name to 'ee in Bedlam because of the laudanum. 'Od rot it. You were my comfort in the worst of times. I dreamt of ee in Bath not two nights since and a cruel dream it was, for I thought to hold you and lost you at every turn.'

'You said nothing of it in the morning,' she said, yearning for him. Oh if only he had spoken then.

He winced. 'Fool that I was, I did not know who you were in the morning.'

Love was stirring in them both, pulling them together by its magical cords. 'And do you know now?' she asked breathlessly.

He caught her in his arms and held her so close she could feel his breath in her hair. 'You are a sterling creature,' he said. 'A wench of pure gold. My one true love.'

She knew he was exaggerating, but it was sweet to hear the words even so and she put up her mouth for his lass as though they were still the lovers they had been all those months ago. And the lass was sweeter than any words could have been and a deal more true.

'How I remember now,' he said. And indeed he did. Those arms about his neck, those blue eyes growing languid with desire, that sweet breath playing against his lips before he kissed her again. He was restored — full of strength and hope in a world rich with colour and possibility — and confident enough to tease.

'A thousand pardons,' he said as their third lass ended. 'I had forgot. You do not wish to marry me.'

She could tease, too. Now. 'That was afore your memory returned to 'ee.'

'How say you now that it has?'

'Now that it has,' she told him with mock seriousness, 'I will give your proposal thought, sir.'

'And in the meantime I may hope?'

She knew she would marry him, although he was no longer the dashing gallant she had loved in Bath all those months ago, but a man a deal more complicated, changed by suffering, made vulnerable, needing help and support as much as she needed it herself. But, oh, a man she loved more than ever. 'In the meantime,' she said, putting her arms round his neck in her old easy way, 'we will try what a little love may do.'

Printed in Great Britain
by Amazon